WHAT YOU OWE ME

BEBE MOORE CAMPBELL

G. P. PUTNAM'S SONS   NEW YORK

G. P. Putnam's Sons
Publishers Since 1838
a member of
Penguin Putnam Inc.
375 Hudson Street
New York, NY 10014

ISBN 0-399-14784-5

Printed in the United States of America

Book design by Gretchen Achilles

WHAT YOU OWE ME

TO MAIA AND ELISHA

ACKNOWLEDGMENTS

I'd like to thank Adrienne Ingrum for her wisdom and guidance. This book wouldn't have been possible without the assistance of the Museum of Tolerance and Rabbi Alderstein, who was kind enough to help a stranger. Thank you, Cassandra Hayes and Louise Hewlitt, for sharing your expertise. Marian Wood, I couldn't have asked for a wiser, more supportive editor. Faith Sale, you are gone but not forgotten. I continue to reap rewards from your instruction. Mom, your early readings and criticism were invaluable. And as always, Ellis, you are the wind.

CHAPTER ONE

I WAS LOOKING at myself in a tarnished mirror taped to a crooked wall. I leaned my head left of the crack that split the glass and squinted my eyes to get a better view. Made me dizzy. My shift was about to start, and I was rushing to put on lipstick. The light in the room was so dim I could barely make out my mouth. The shade was too pale, but I made do and blotted on a piece of toilet paper. The door opened just as I was imagining my face with thinner lips. I turned around, and that's when I saw her, not big as a banty hen. Mr. Weinstock was right behind. "Hosanna," he said to me, "this is Gilda Rosenstein, and she'll be working with you. I want you to train her."

There were five of us women cleaning at the Braddock Hotel, all colored. I say women, but we were barely out of our teens. It was right after Labor Day, and we'd finished having our get-started cup of coffee (as compared to our keep-going cup in the afternoon and our hold-on cup toward the end of our day) in a small dark room in the basement. The manager called it the Maids' Room because we were the only ones who used it. We called it Our Room; we did everything in there: change our clothes; drink coffee; eat lunch; smoke cigarettes; steal a quick nap or a drink. Every once in a while somebody would sneak in a man. It was a gray room with peeling paint and furniture that looked as though it needed mouth-to-mouth resuscitation. Our lifeline was a little second-hand phonograph and a few old seventy-eights. Billy Eckstine, Sarah Vaughan, Ella Fitzgerald, Count Basie, and Louis Jordan resurrected us around the clock. It's been more than fifty years, and I'll bet that all of us, the living and the dead, can recall just what we were doing when we looked at Gilda dressed in that uniform. It wasn't every day we saw a white woman wearing what we wore, doing what we did. Gilda was the first, and I remember her in this life I'm living and the one I left behind.

Death isn't like I thought it would be. The Baptist church stamped me early, and I was halfway expecting pearly gates, winged angels playing on their harps, St. Peter at the door, the works. Turned out that heaven ain't nothing but a space in my mind, no more permanent than a sunshiny day; I go in and out. The background music is whatever song I'm humming. Me, I'm partial to Tina Turner. White's not the only color people wear. Heaven is a great big be-in, where everybody comes as they are. Pajamas. Wild-looking hair. Mink coats. No makeup. Blond wigs. The be-in is right inside you. I think of it as the Land of Calm, a place to reflect, without alarms going off, telling me it's time to do this or that. The only thing that moves me here is spirit.

I'm in heaven now observing my baby girl, Matriece. I say baby, but my child is thirty-eight years old. She can't see me hovering in her bathroom, watching her comb her hair and get ready to go to work. She smiles at herself in the mirror as she gives her hair a final pat. The smile is the good part. My child liking what she sees reflected back at her is the good part. I fought for that, not just for her and her big sister, Vonette, but for all the sisters with hair that didn't ride their shoulders, with flaring nostrils that welcomed air, and lips that came with a pucker. I helped convince them that they were beautiful, unchained their minds every bit as much as Malcolm X did. Now a pretty black girl can do a Mona Lisa on a billboard and sell America a beer or a lawn mower. Pick up a magazine, and there we are, smiling our cover-girl smiles. Wasn't always that way. "Because we're already beautiful"—that was my motto back in the fifties when all colored women had were Red Fox stockings and face powder so light it made us disappear. All right, maybe I shouldn't compare myself with Malcolm X, but I made a contribution. I saw a need, and I filled it. I got rewards for that while I was on earth, but somebody owes me still. I'm not talking about a debt of gratitude; I'm talking about money.

Matriece will make things right. She's the steady one. Vonette is hardheaded, always was, always will be. Fifty million hair care products for black women, and she decides not to comb hers at all. Dreadlocks. That's just to make me turn over in my grave, so to speak. Vonette and I had issues while I was alive, and we still do. But my Matriece . . . She wants what I went to my grave wanting: retribution. And she's the only one who can get it for me.

She applies her lipstick last, after her hair is right and her clothes are on. Makeup ain't nothing but a promise: Use me and I'll get you your man, your romance, your passion, whatever you want. Put me under your eyes, and I'll take away the circles, all the pain, and everything will be new. The name is more important than the purpose. That's Red Drama on her mouth.

Me watching Matriece is heaven, but I can't stop my mind from shifting. I'm not the first one to go to her grave with nothing to leave behind but a fierce yearning. Bits of my life still float by, just like when I was dying. I shine the light on all the faces, all the memories that are with me in my sojourn. This is essential: not to drift or soften, never to forgive or give up. If I find my anger waning I can always renew it just by remembering.

None of the maids at Braddock had ever worked with a white person before. Work *for* them, now that's a different story. It was soon after the war, 1948, and the five of us had put Texas, Oklahoma, and Louisiana behind us. We'd all caught that long gray dog out to Los Angeles looking for better times, plus a man. Kissing frogs and scrubbing floors—that was our lives. We traded fields for toilets, dirt under our nails for ammonia on our hands. Still had to say "yessir," "yes ma'am." Still had to live all together like lepers on roped-off acres that other people fled from as soon as they saw us coming. Watts—a sprawled-out piece of land with tiny bungalows lined up on the widest streets I'd ever seen—that's what we claimed. Come Monday, we caught the first bus. Number 86 ran from Central straight up Crenshaw; the 72 came down Wilshire. Cruising past palm trees, I took in those skinny trunks as if they were men coming to court me. My eyes traveled slowly from the ground all the way to the top and then back down again to see if I'd missed any flaws, any beauty.

When Mr. Weinstock left the room nobody said anything for a long time. Hattie, the oldest in the group, rolled her eyes. I knew how she felt. One way or another, straight through or around the bend, most of the hard times in our lives had come from white folks. The other women—Winnie, Opal, and Fern—looked at me like I was the one who should decide how we'd treat her.

All right then. I smiled, stuck out my hand, and she shook it. She was a washed-out little thing and real thin. Next to her I felt blown up and lit in neon, not that I was so big. I was average height and weight, not much up top, but I always had some hips on me. Her skin was so white I could see clear to her veins, almost to her heart. My skin was the color of pecans; nothing showed through. Frizzy brown hair touched her shoulders. I had thick rough hair that took a press and curl every two weeks. Gilda looked worn out; I had a baby face. Her teeth were brown, too, as though she hadn't brushed them in a long time. People used to always tell me I had pretty teeth, because they were big and white, so I guess that's why I noticed other people's smiles.

Gilda smelled like roses and didn't smile, but I managed to see that she needed to get to a dentist. She didn't speak much English—yes, no, please, say it again—and that caught my attention. The white folks I was used to were homegrown rattlers that damaged as they slithered. The thing that got me, got all of us I guess, was that she didn't seem to know that it was unusual for her to be working with us. She seemed unconscious with her eyes open, as though she had sleepwalked her way into Our Room. I believe if I'd poured ice-cold water on her she wouldn't have made a sound.

I could tell straight off that she wasn't used to cleaning up behind people. That's to say: She wasn't poor white trash. I came out of Inez, Texas, where PWT is a crop that doesn't need fertilizer; I knew it when I saw it. There was plenty of trash walking around Los Angeles, jug-eared, stringy-haired men and women out of Oklahoma and Dust Bowl territory, dandelions blown west during the Depression, trying to make a new start with only fourth-grade educations and their color to recommend them. Gilda was an orchid that somebody's boot had crushed.

She didn't seem to mind the job, even though that first day I had to tell her everything at least twice. When she did try to say a few things, I heard the accent, thick as sorghum, and I realized she didn't understand what I was saying. So, I slowed down.

The first month Gilda was really quiet. She did her work, drank her coffee, ate her lunch, and didn't talk to anybody other than me. "Hosanna, what is this? Hosanna, what I do?" All day long. She and I were the flip side of a record I'd been playing all my life.

We were in Our Room not long after she came, and Sarah Vaughan was crooning on the record player. Gilda sat listening, as though she were trying to memorize a bird before it flew away. When the song finished she turned to me; she was trembling, and there were tears in her eyes. "The music is so . . . It is medicine," she said.

Braddock must have seemed like the land of big white smiles to her. She hadn't been there a week when we were on the fifth floor, and I caught her staring at some guests as they were leaving their room. They were a young, good-looking couple. The wife wore a large diamond on her left hand, and she was laughing at something her husband was telling her. She had hot pink lips, thin and perfect-looking, eyes like tiny chunks of sky. Gilda looked at that woman as if she imagined pushing her hand right through her. She stared at that ring in a yearning way. Maybe she remembered it from her other life.

Whenever Gilda had a break she'd sit by herself and read from a large book. One morning she left it on the table and got up to go to the rest room. I picked it up. Hattie was sitting on the sofa smoking a cigarette. Gilda came back in, rubbing some kind of lotion on her hands, just as I was flipping through the pages. She sat down on the sofa, and I handed her back the manual. "So, you're learning English?" I was just trying to make conversation.

"I learn," she said. She had a quiet voice that stayed on one level all the time. She started pulling on the dark green sweater she always wore, then began fiddling with something in her pocket.

"You'll learn faster if you talk to people," Hattie said in a snappy tone, rolling her eyes. She had a gap between her front teeth, and sometimes she whistled when she spoke. Hattie was a big-boned Louisiana gal. Some of the tales she told, anybody would think that the devil invented white folks just to torment her. There are people in this life who believe that being the biggest victim will get them the best pork chop at the dinner table. That was Hattie. In that moment, looking at Hattie and then at

Gilda, I felt as though I were the rope each one had a grip on. I had lived in the land of blood-is-thicker-than-water for so long I didn't understand loyalty to anybody or anything other than family and skin color.

White men stole my daddy's land, more than two hundred acres of lumber and rice. They did it all nice and legal. My father got an official letter giving him forty-eight hours to vacate. Failure to pay taxes, the letter said, which was a lie. Later that day, the Hagertys showed up at our door. Big Bobby and Little Bobby, one with a shock of silver hair, the other's dark brown. I opened the door, then tried to push it closed. I don't know what made me think I could get away with that. My cheek hurt for two weeks from where the younger one slapped me. They were the power around Inez; they owned most of the land and all the politicians, including the tax assessor. When my daddy saw them standing in his house and me holding my face, he shook his head and said, "You win." Two days later he signed the papers the Hagertys put in front of him.

That was 1943. My brother came back from Europe in '45. In my family, we grew up in pairs, and Tuney was my other half. He had just made twenty and had memories of dancing with French women—a taste of freedom at a dangerous age. By that time my folks were sharecropping. Days after he got back, I heard my brother's voice coming from the back porch. "You think I'm going to stay around here and not kill those sons of bitches?"

I took Tuney's side, but Daddy wouldn't listen. He hustled all of us off the place that night. Had to raise his fist to my brother, although he didn't hit him. The rest of the family moved to Houston, but he put Tuney and me on the bus to LA. Before we boarded, he showed my brother and me the deed to his "property." "Maybe one day one of y'all can get the land back," he said quietly. "At least we got proof that it used to be ours." My daddy's face was too sad to look at, so I just turned away.

It took us a week to get there. Tuney and I stayed awake almost the entire time, two crazy spiders spinning webs of vengeance.

We calmed down somewhere in Nevada, which is to say we changed the subject. "I'm going to save my money and open up a candy store," I said.

"Don't know what I'm gonna do, but I tell you one thing: People are going to sit up and take notice. They're going to know my name," he said.

He was big and handsome, my brother, a strong man, with crinkly black hair, a neat mustache, and a mouth filled with big white teeth. He laughed a little at his own daring, and so did I. His laugh came from his belly, and he was generous with it. His dream made him happy for a little while. But then his eyes would go dark and I'd know that he was thinking about the land, and maybe about killing somebody.

Hattie had that same killing look in her eyes. I stared at her hard, and thought about my candy store. Bad times or good times, people always want something sweet to chew on. I wasn't about to let Hattie and her mess come between my goal and me. Fern, who was little and dark and liked a good scrap, at least to watch one, glanced from Hattie back to me, trying to figure out if something was going to go down. Being raised in a family of six, I learned to fight for what I wanted. I was the oldest girl, the thumb on my mama's hand. That Louisiana gal backed up because, even though I was barely twenty-one, well, I've got expressive eyes. "Jew bitch," I heard her mutter.

Gilda heard it, too. And I could tell by the way her eyes clouded over that it wasn't the first time. Maybe she didn't understand English all that well, but Hattie's tone and the looks we were exchanging weren't hard to figure out. After Hattie stomped off, Gilda came over to me and said, "What I do?"

I told her, "You have to speak to people. Say 'good morning,' when you come in. Say 'good night' when you leave. In between, ask people how they're doing. Understand?" My words were propelled by anger, and as I spoke I realized that tug-of-war was wearing me out.

Gilda backed up a little, although I have to say this, she didn't look one bit afraid. She sat in the chair and didn't say a word for a good two or three minutes. Billie Holiday was singing in the background, and I could tell that Gilda was listening real hard to the words. I was heading out the door when I heard her say, "Hosanna, very hard for me to speak."

I turned around to look at her; Gilda's eyes were the emptiest ones I'd ever seen. There didn't seem to be a life behind them. I walked over to her and said, "Well, honey, you have to try."

I'm usually one to mind my own business, but before I left that day I went to Mr. Weinstock's office. He had on thick rimless glasses, and he was sitting at his desk smoking, drinking coffee, and reading. He always seemed to be sweating; there was a shiny glaze over his face. There weren't any windows, and it felt closed up and hot. Mr. Weinstock passed a lot of gas in there.

He didn't rise when he saw me. But then, I didn't expect that. He glanced up, then turned back to what he was doing. "Yes, Hosanna?"

"Mr. Weinstock, I was just wondering about Gilda."

"What about her?" He mopped his forehead with a dingy handkerchief, then took off his glasses to reveal small dust-ball eyes, rimmed in red.

"It's not my business, sir. I'm just curious. Did her husband die in the war, something bad like that?"

He put down his paper and looked at me. "Is she doing her work?"

"Oh yes, sir, she does a good job. It's just, she always looks so sad."

"There are lots of sad people in this world. Do you like your job, Hosanna?"

I wouldn't have put it that way. "Yes, sir."

"You want to keep it?"

"Yes, sir."

"Then do your work and mind your business."

"Yes, sir."

Toward the end of the month, maybe the last day, Gilda didn't come in. We had the kind of jobs where if you didn't show up, you missed that day's wages. Most people only took off work if there was a dire emergency or almost life-and-death illness. Gilda was back at the hotel the following day, and she didn't look any the worse for wear. A week later, in mid-October, she missed another day. When she returned, I pulled her aside. "You all right?" I asked her.

"Yes," she said. "I am fine."

"Why didn't you come to work?"

"Holiday."

"What holiday?"

"Yom Kippur. Jewish," she added, then, seeing my puzzled face, "It is the day of atonement. We ask God to forgive our sins. We do not eat during the day. At night we have a feast."

The idea of dedicating one day to say you're sorry to God for everything you've done wrong and then having God wipe the slate clean appealed to me, but I had my own religion to think about. When I woke up that Sunday I was anxious to go to church. Singing always rejuvenated me, and I was a soloist in Mt. Olivet's choir. When I took off my choir robe after church, it felt good wearing a nice dress, a hat, and my only pair of high heels.

I met up with Tuney downstairs in the fellowship hall. "Hey, girl," he said. I could smell his aftershave when we hugged.

"How's it going?"

"All right. I got another interview this week." Tuney had been trying to get from behind a broom ever since we'd arrived in Los Angeles.

"Where?"

"Fountain. I'd be building airplanes."

The California Eagle had run an article the previous week on how the aerospace industry was beginning to hire back some of the Negroes who had been displaced after the war ended. I prayed that Fountain would give him a chance.

Being in the church basement was like warming our hands over a little ember of Inez. Home folks were standing around in clumps, talking and laughing, hugging and shaking hands, munching ginger cookies and sipping red fruit punch. Our pastor, Reverend Pearl, had gone to the same one-room schoolhouse with my mama and daddy.

Tuney and I spent a few minutes getting caught up with what was going on in Texas, pretending we weren't homesick. Then I mentioned Gilda. He said, "I told you that after the war things would change."

Just then I noticed some of the men smiling, and when I looked up a tall, pretty girl with wavy hair that hung past her shoulders was headed toward us. "There you are," she said, and slipped her arm through Tuney's. She smiled at him and then at me.

"Hosanna, this is my friend Thomasine."

"How do you do?" I said. My brother's motto was: New week, new woman. He'd been that way since his voice changed.

"Very nice meeting you," she said, sounding proper.

I started feeling as though someone had erased me off the blackboard. Girls who looked like Thomasine always made me feel that way. I'd never had a roomful of men smiling at me. But then I didn't have skin the color of peaches or delicate features, and my hair didn't blow in the wind. I chatted with them for a few minutes, then I made an excuse and went home.

Maybe some of the English lessons started to kick in because, as the months passed, Gilda began speaking more. When she came in she'd say good morning to Fern, Opal, Winnie, me, and even Hattie, who'd whistle something back. She asked us how we were doing and said fine when we asked about her. She wasn't having conversations, though I could tell by her expressions that she understood a lot of what people were saying. She didn't smile, not with those teeth of hers. But she was trying. Sometimes one of the women might bring in something to eat and share it with the rest of us. Gilda always refused anyone's food but her own. "I must eat special food," she told me. "It must be cooked a certain way." I learned that she was from Poland, but when I asked her how she came to be here, her eyes got that empty look, so I let that be. During those first few months, the only time I ever saw her laugh was when the children came to see her.

We had both finished our shifts, I was headed out the door and so was Gilda. All of a sudden we heard childish voices calling her name. When I turned around she was bent down and the boy and girl were hugging her. There was a stern-looking woman standing behind them, the mother, I supposed. Gilda looked up and saw me. Her eyes shifted to the woman's face, and something about her expression told me that she wouldn't introduce me, that she couldn't. Later I would remember that troubled glance, but I didn't care then. Really, I didn't notice too much other than Gilda's smile. It was the first time I knew that she still had a spark inside her, that her soul's light hadn't been completely extinguished by whatever she'd gone through. She was still able to love. Sometimes that's the only power on earth that will heal you.

CHAPTER TWO

THE BRADDOCK HOTEL was the rich old uncle of downtown Los Angeles. I'd never seen anything as grand in Inez, where the largest hotel was only three stories high and always needed a new coat of paint. Braddock was nearly fifty years old and took up half a city block; the entire front was beige marble, and the entrance was two huge glass doors. Inside there were fifteen floors and a gigantic ballroom. The lobby was grand, with two huge crystal chandeliers, exactly like the one that was in the ballroom. The walls were the color of cream and the carpet was a swirl of soft rose and green. Plush sofas, comfortable armchairs, and carved tables sitting on a soft rug—it was like a magazine picture. The guest rooms were spacious and furnished even more luxuriously than the lobby. Mostly businessmen came to Braddock, and the place got its share of conventions, too.

It was not far from the Hollywood Freeway. I was used to one-lane highways and dirt roads, but LA had the Hollywood and the Pasadena freeways, and more were being built every day, connecting different parts of the city and even the suburbs, which I'd only heard about. From the upper floors in Braddock I could look out the windows and watch cars that seemed to fly along the asphalt ribbon that was divided into three lanes. I'd never seen so many automobiles in my life, and the sight of them, the thrumming sound they made, excited me and made me imagine going places far away from brooms and mops.

By the time she'd been working at Braddock for a year, we all were used to Gilda's quiet ways. Mr. Weinstock put Gilda and me on the same shift. Some days we worked from five o'clock in the morning until two or three in the afternoon. Early morning was the time we washed the linens and towels and folded everything. We mopped the grand hotel lobby, polished all the marble and glass. Sometimes when I was giving her the ammonia our hands would touch. She had soft hands, and I wondered how long they would stay nice.

Thanksgiving rolled around again. The maids weren't looking forward to the holidays, at least not *working* them. There were always lots of parties and formal affairs at Braddock during this time. People would get plenty liquored up, and drunk people are not the most fastidious. This was the time of year we had to wipe up vomit and urine that didn't make it to the toilet bowl. And then, too, even though Los Angeles didn't have a real winter like the ones in Texas that could turn your skin the kind of gray colored folks call ashy, people still caught colds. A lot of the maids would stay out sick, and then Mr. Weinstock would put us on double shift. By Christmas we'd be too worn out to enjoy our own festivities. But what else was new?

The first weekend in December, Gilda and I both got put on midday and late shift, which meant we had to come in at one and we didn't go home until after midnight. You wouldn't think that there would be that much to do late at night but that's when Mr. Weinstock wanted us to wash windows, clean the mezzanine bathrooms, and change the big Chinese vases of flowers that were always in the lobby. It took two people to carry those vases. And he liked to have some maids on hand when there were big parties in the hotel. People would stay in bed all day and then go out at night, and when they came back they expected clean rooms.

That Saturday night around ten o'clock, Mr. Weinstock told us to go up to the sixth floor. Guests had just left, and two rooms needed to be made up. When we got there, the floor seemed deserted, except for Brewster, who did repairs. He was carrying his toolbox, standing in front of the service elevator when we got off. He smiled politely when he saw us, especially at Gilda. "How are you girls doing tonight?"

"Fine," we both said.

We chatted with him for a few minutes before we made our way down the hall.

I worked on one room and Gilda cleaned the other. They were only about three doors apart. Maybe because I trained Gilda, she and I had similar timing, and we'd end up at the carts together. That's where we were when the man came in holding the boy by the hand.

We both smelled evil at the same moment. The first thing that hit me was that the man was white and the boy, who must have been about seven or eight, was Mexican. He was a scrawny little kid, not dressed for the chilly weather. He was wearing shorts and an undershirt, and he had on sandals. His little legs and arms were dirty. The man was drunk, and the boy looked scared, the kind of scared that means he has to go along with the show because of the money that's waiting when the curtain comes down. I'd seen that fear before at Braddock, in the eyes of young hookers with old johns who stumbled down the hall beside them. I'd never seen that expression on a child's face, and to tell you the truth, I didn't want to look.

They went into the room between the ones we'd just made up. When the door closed, my eyes met Gilda's. She whispered, "He is a bad man." When she said the words her body started shaking, and she had to wipe away the moisture that started popping out on her forehead.

I knew he was a bad man but he was a bad *white* man, and he was a guest. I thought about calling Mr. Weinstock, but Ole Sweat and Farts wouldn't do anything to help a Mexican street kid if it meant offending a paying customer. I considered contacting the police, but then I'd have to give my name, take them to the room, and by that time the damage would be done. And if Mr. Weinstock found out, I could forget about my job, and my candy store.

Gilda walked right to the room. We could hear the boy crying, soft, pitiful sounds. I knocked on the door and said, "Is everything all right in there?" I tried to sound stern, like a teacher, which is what I would have been if my daddy had had money for college.

Before he could answer, Gilda had pulled out her key and opened the door. "Girrrrrrl," I said, and put my hand on her shoulder to hold her back. But she shook it off and walked in, and I followed her.

The room smelled like sour milk. The little boy was naked, lying on the bed facedown. The man was on top of him with his pants and shorts around his ankles. He jumped up. His penis was hard and red. His cheeks looked slapped. "What the hell are you doing in here?" he said. "Get out, the both of you."

"You stop hurting that boy," Gilda said.

"Get the hell outta here." He turned back to the child.

Gilda pulled something shiny out of her sweater pocket. When I saw it was a knife, I opened my mouth and couldn't close it, but not a sound came out. The next thing I knew she was stabbing the man in his ass.

He jumped up and grabbed himself, wiping off the blood and staring at Gilda as though he couldn't believe what he was seeing. Truth be told, I was looking at her the same way.

"Get out! Get out! Get out!" She was screaming, waving the knife. He started coming toward Gilda. I grabbed the table lamp and held it like I was going to bash his head in. He stopped when he saw me do that, then he started backing up toward the door, pulling up his pants. Crazy Gilda kept coming toward him, waving the knife so close to him that I was afraid he was going to take it away from her and I would have to hit him upside his head. But he kept backing up. She got right up on him and then her voice went down real low. She said, "You go tell. See what happens to you tonight. I have the key."

"Fucking bitch," he said, and with his next breath he turned to me. "Nigger." Then he fled out the door.

After he left, Gilda went over to the little boy. He was still crying and whimpering something in Spanish. We took him in the bathroom, gave him a bath and washed his hair. Gilda dried him off and took a small bottle from her sweater pocket, poured something white and creamy in her palms, and started rubbing him all over with it. Then we helped him get dressed. He didn't say anything, but he wasn't crying anymore.

We took him down the back stairwell that led to the street. Outside the air was biting. Gilda took off her sweater and put it on the child, and we each gave him a dollar. Then we watched as he walked back to wherever he came from.

"Damn, girl," I said when we were riding up on the service elevator. I kept looking at her, trying to see what I couldn't see.

We were back in Our Room when I noticed the numbers on Gilda's arm, little blue tattooed numbers, a brand. Then I figured things out, but not all of it. Even on this side of the fence, there are some things I'll never understand.

We were sitting on the broken-down sofa. There was some church music playing in the background. Gilda started talking. Gilda loved gospel music and all kinds of hymns. The first time I played the Five Blind Boys for her, she started crying. On this night, The Mighty Clouds of Joy were singing a real slow song. I can't remember the name of it but the lyrics seemed to meld into her story. She told me how the Germans rounded up her family and put them in the death camps and how everybody she loved—her mother, father, brother, aunts, uncles, grandparents—had been killed. Her father's brother had settled in America before the war. When she was liberated she came to Los Angeles, because he and his wife lived here with their children. Four people were her only remaining relatives. It was her uncle who got her the job. Mr. Weinstock's brother owned the apartment building where they lived.

Her crying started as a tiny, weak noise, like a newborn might make. Came from way down inside her somewhere and then kept rising and getting deeper. I pulled her into my chest and held her, rubbed her back a little, told her not to be afraid, that everything was all right now. I spoke the words as soon as they came to my mind. "You need to take those numbers off your arm."

She sat up, looked at me, then cried a little bit more. She said, "I have no one, no one, no one," the words an echo that kept turning on itself.

"You do have someone," I said. "You have *you*. And you have what's *in* you. That's how you survived, girl."

Gilda didn't say anything for a long time. Then she looked at me and said, "Will you take me to get it done?"

I took her to the dentist first. The way I figured, the sooner she started smiling, the better for her. I asked her if she knew of any dentists in her neighborhood but she looked troubled and told me that we couldn't go there. So, one day after work, I took her to a colored dentist over on Central Avenue. He seemed surprised to see the two of us together, but that was just in his eyes. He didn't say anything. She had to go back a couple of times but he cleaned her teeth, got all the brown off, and when she smiled that first time, she looked pretty, not like Lana Turner or Liz Taylor, or any of the movie stars or models. She had her own special kind of frizzy-haired beauty, which wasn't even American, at least not yet.

We went to a tattoo parlor not too far from the dentist and the owner examined the numbers under a magnifying glass, and then patted her arm the same kind of way my daddy used to when I fell down or was crying. He told her that whatever he could do for her would leave a scar. Gilda hesitated, then she said, "Go ahead." I guess she figured that the numbers were the worst scar. He used needles and some kind of acid. Gilda was moaning a little bit the entire time he was working on her. She grabbed my hand while he was doing it, and she liked to squeezed me to death.

Riding the bus on our way back from the tattoo place, I told her about Inez. Gilda said it was another kind of death camp, that the poison gas came out in spurts, not enough to kill the body, just the soul. She had a lot of questions for me. She wanted to know why colored people couldn't go certain places, why our hair wasn't as long as white people's, why our voices sounded different from theirs. I didn't have all the answers but I did my best.

"They are envious of you," she told me.

"Who?"

"The white people."

"Why?"

"Because you have the most beautiful skin. White people sit in the sun to try to get your color. Your features, your lips and nose, are warm. You make wonderful music. And your spirit is powerful. They try to crush your spirit, but they can't."

We never heard from the man Gilda stabbed, and she and I never mentioned him. I found myself looking whenever I saw a group of Mexicans, but I didn't see the little boy again either. Gilda and I seemed to be together a lot more after what happened. When we had lunch at the same time, we ate side by side. Sometimes at the end of our break, she'd pull out a book and start reading. She still studied from the English manual, but she read other things as well. Her books were about history and science, and she liked novels, too. Often she'd read a portion to me and get me so interested in the story that when she finished, I'd pick it up. A couple of times, Fern would ask me what I was reading, and I'd share it with her.

Gilda told me that she had been attending college when the war broke out. "I studied literature," she said, and there was sadness in her voice.

I hadn't ever had enough time to read just for the pure pleasure of it, but that's one hobby I acquired from Gilda. As I read, I became aware of mistakes that I was making when I spoke, and I began to improve, little by little. In a way, I started sounding like Thomasine, who Tuney had broken up with, thank God.

The other maids noticed the new way I was speaking. One time when I finished saying something, Winnie said, "La-di-da," and looked toward Hattie, who was muttering under her breath that I was trying to be white. She knew better than to say it to my face. But those "la-di-das" put an alley between the other women and me. Gilda and I were walking down the main boulevard together.

CHAPTER THREE

I ALWAYS DREADED the first part of April, which was when the chandeliers in the ballroom were washed. Even though Ole Sweat and Farts got a budget to hire men to do the work, he figured, why pay them when he had some mules working for him already? Nobody wanted the job, which required getting on a very high ladder and climbing onto some scaffolding that was at least twenty feet in the air. I'd already cleaned the chandelier once since I'd been at Braddock. As scared of heights as I was, I prayed that I'd be passed over for chandelier-washing duty.

Early one morning, Weinstock came to Our Room and asked for Hattie and me. "Shit, I cleaned that damn thing last year and the year before that. How come he don't make that Jew girl clean it?" she asked, the hot words whistling through her teeth. I was angry, too, not at Gilda, because it wasn't her fault, but at the situation.

We walked down to the ballroom with the spirit of women going to their own execution. When we got there, Brewster was bringing in the ladders. He was about ten years older than I was, a tall, skinny man with the biggest Adam's apple I'd ever seen and shiny brown hair that fell over his forehead. He was a decent white man, by which I mean he was polite and never tried to fool with me. When he set up the ladders, I was close enough to him to smell the whiskey that seemed to always cling to him. I wondered if the boss's sense of smell was as sharp as mine. Brewster stood watching us as we got ready to climb up, and I could tell by the expression in his eyes that he didn't think Mr. Weinstock should have had us doing that kind of work. I believe he would have done the job for us if the boss hadn't said, "All right, Brewster, I need you upstairs."

"You girls be careful," he said. He shook his head a little and added, "That's a damn shame," just loud enough for me to hear.

The next thing I knew, I was trying not to look down as I climbed up an endless ladder in the middle of the ballroom, carrying a bucket and some rags. Once I was on the scaffold I just did the work and cleaned the crystals as well and as fast as I could. The chandelier was about as tall as I was. It took me several hours to do my side. In the middle of the job, Hattie and I both had to climb down, get fresh hot water, more ammonia, and clean rags. Then up we went again.

There were pear-shaped crystals at the bottom of the chandelier that were hooked to a thin piece of wire that circled the entire fixture. I had to take off each one, the way Mr. Weinstock told us to, and dip it in the ammonia and hot water. When I say hot, I mean almost scalding. We didn't have any rubber gloves, just our bare hands. My hands were already rough, and I figured this day would just about turn them into leather.

Hattie finished before I did, and she was already on the floor when I was dipping the last crystal into the water. As much as Hattie got on my nerves, when I looked across that scaffold and didn't see anybody, I got real nervous. I reached up to latch the crystal onto the hook and for some reason I can't explain, I looked down. Everything got blurry, and I felt my knees wobbling as though I'd guzzled a quart of moonshine. I took a couple of deep breaths and the room stopped spinning. But when I tried to fasten the glass back onto the wire, the thing slipped right out of my hands and fell to the hard wood floor. It didn't hit anyone, and that was a blessing, but the crystal shattered into a million pieces. When I climbed down from the ladder, Ole Sweat and Farts was standing there glaring at me.

"I'm going to have to take that out of your pay," he said. "Go get a broom and sweep up this mess."

I didn't hear anything he said except, ". . . take that out of your pay." I felt like throwing my bucket of ammonia water in his face. But when you come off a sharecropper's farm in Inez, you think long and hard about consequences.

Sipping a cup of get-on-the-bus coffee in Our Room, I tried to keep from screaming. My daddy used to say, "Some days you eat the bear; some days the bear eats you." Right then I was feeling mighty gobbled up. I was a young woman, and everything I owned was sitting in two drawers in a tiny room in Watts. Cleaning up after prosperous people who wore nice clothes and tipped me a quarter was taking a toll. I wanted better, and right then and there it didn't look as though I'd ever have it. I looked down at my dried-up, ashy hands and I thought about my old boyfriend, Lonell. When we were kids in grammar school, he liked to walk me home and hold my hand. He sure wouldn't want to hold hands with me now. Nobody had held my hand in more than a little while.

I heard the door open, and when I looked up, Gilda was staring at me. She said, "What is the matter?" Her English was getting better every day, but she still didn't use a lot of contractions, so she always sounded a little formal.

I told her what had happened and when I was finished, I said, "Look at my hands. I look like an old woman."

She took my hands in hers, and the next thing I knew I felt something cool and creamy in my palms. She began rubbing between my fingers and thumbs. I smelled like roses.

"Lotion," she said when I gave her a questioning look. "It will make your skin nice and smooth."

I'd seen Gilda putting on lotion before. All I'd ever used on my skin was Vaseline, and that was too greasy to wear at work. She handed me a bottle that was almost empty, told me to keep it, that she'd bring me more the next day. "I probably can't pay you for a few weeks," I said.

She shook her head. "It is a gift."

"But you have to pay for it."

"No. I make it."

"You make it?"

She nodded. "Before my parents died they owned a cosmetics factory. We made soap, lotion, face powder, lipstick, pencil for the eyebrows, everything to make a woman beautiful."

"You all were rich," I said.

"Before the Nazis we had a good life." She closed her eyes, and I could hear her breathing.

"What happened to your business?" I asked.

"Nazis took it," she said. Her eyes looked dead.

"All of your money is gone?"

"No," she said, coming to life. She lowered her voice. "I will tell you something. My father sent all of our money to Switzerland. It is in a bank there."

"Why don't you go back over there and get it? Do you have the bank book?"

She nodded. "My father mailed it to my uncle, but the bank refuses to pay."

"But you have the book." I wasn't used to white folks treating each other as badly as they treated us.

Gilda made a small, scoffing noise. "One day they will pay," she said simply.

"That's what my brother says about the people who stole our land."

Gilda gave me a look, and then I told her about the Hagertys.

"I am sorry," she said when I had finished.

I shrugged. "At least you have a bank book," I said.

"What good is a bank book against liars and thieves?"

I couldn't answer that question.

Gilda brought me a big bottle of lotion the next day, just as she'd promised. After a few days of using it my skin wasn't cracked and ashy. Whenever I ran out, Gilda would bring me more. She'd never let me pay her.

I was shaking Reverend Pearl's hand one Sunday, telling him how much I enjoyed the sermon, when he looked at me and said, "Sister Hosanna, you sure have some soft hands."

One of my choir members was right behind me. When she got finished talking with our pastor, she grabbed me by my hands and rubbed them. "They *are* soft. What do you put on them?"

I told her about the lotion, and she asked me to bring her some. "I'll pay you for it," she said.

I'll pay you for it. Those words kicked up their heels and jitterbugged from one side of my mind to the other. Later that night I got to remembering how, back in Inez, when I sold fudge candy I used to love the feel of money in my hands. Even working at the hotel, when Mr. Weinstock counted out my teeny-weeny salary at the end of the week and my hand closed over those dollar bills, I felt a kind of satisfaction that I didn't get from anything else. Daddy always called me the money grubber of the family. My choir mate wanting to buy the lotion got me to thinking about my candy store. Maybe pretty was another kind of sweetness.

The next morning when I got to the hotel I found Gilda right away. I said, "Girl, I know how we can make some money."

You put a piece of meat in front of a dog, and it's going to start salivating. That's the way the thought of money works on most people. But not Gilda. She wasn't interested in pretty clothes, a car, or even a house. She didn't want to sell lotion. What she wanted was what she'd lost, and no amount of dollars could replace that.

A few days later when Ole Sweat and Farts handed me my pay envelope there were three dollars missing from my regular thirty. After I sent Mama and Daddy their allowance and paid the rest of my bills, I had four dollars left in my pocket. If I'd had a stove I would have made some fudge and sold it, but I knew my landlady wouldn't let me tie up her kitchen for as long as it would take. I considered borrowing from Tuney; he always came through for me, but I knew things were tight with him, too. Besides, he had a lot on his mind. Tuney had gotten that job on Fountain's assembly line. His boss had him and the other colored guys eating their lunch separately and using a different rest room from the whites. "Me and all the rest of the boys are walking into that rest room this week," he'd told me at church on Sunday. I didn't want to bother him with my problems. So I stared my beans-and-rice week straight in the face by myself.

A week was one thing. What I didn't want was a beans-and-rice life. I went back to Gilda and tried to convince her that we should make lotion together and sell it. All I had was a feeling but it was strong. Before the war, most Negroes moisturized their skin with Vaseline, which was a step up from the lard we used in the country. But folks were leaving their country ways behind. Colored women were sashaying into beauty parlors to get their hair done. Mammy-made stayed home on the farm. On Sunday, LA's colored women were ritzing in store-bought clothes that factory jobs provided. They wanted to look, smell, and feel better than they had in Oklahoma and Louisiana. "Don't you understand? Colored women are ready for what you've got," I told her.

Gilda only shook her head. "I do not want to sell lotion," she said.

"If we sold enough lotion we could quit our jobs," I told her one Friday afternoon when we were cleaning rooms that were next door to each other. She was standing in the hall near her cart reading a book; she always carried one with her. Whenever she had a moment she'd pull it out of her pocket and read it.

"I do not want to quit," she said, closing her book and slipping it back into her pocket.

"Girl, you want to work here for the rest of your life?" A white woman had a lot more opportunities than I did, and for her to keep saying she wasn't interested in doing better didn't make any sense. "Why?"

Gilda grabbed a bunch of little soap bars from the cart. She looked at them, and then at the scar where her numbers used to be. "Hosanna, I will never be happy." She said it the way someone might say that the sky is blue.

"Why not?" I grabbed her wrist and everything in her hands fell on the floor.

"You don't know what I did."

"All you did was stay alive."

She shook her head.

"What did you do? Kill somebody? Screw somebody? Betray somebody? Honey, people do all of that every day just to pay the rent. You were in hell, Gilda. Now is what counts."

She looked at me for a long time. "How can you be so happy?"

"What do you mean?"

"Bad things have happened to you, to your people. But you smile and laugh all the time."

I started to take offense. I knew that a lot of white folks thought that all colored people did was laugh and sing all day. I searched Gilda's face. "Girl, you can't let anybody steal your joy. Maybe if you went back to college you would feel happy again."

"It costs money to go to school."

"We could make a lot of money." When her eyes met mine it was the first time I saw a ready-for-supper look in them.

I stayed out of Gilda's way for about a week. I guess both of us used that time to mull over things.

"I would like to go to college," Gilda said after seven days had passed. We were both behind mops, going across the floor of the main ballroom.

I stopped and leaned on my mop. "That's good." I waited.

"If we are going to make lotion and sell it, there is to be a lot of work." Gilda spoke slowly, still unsure of the future tense.

"Girl, I don't mind."

"We have no machinery, no equipment. Everything must be done by hand."

I nodded. "There is nothing on this earth harder than chopping cotton under the Texas sun. Nobody can outwork me."

"We will see," Gilda said.

The next evening, before we left the hotel, Gilda and I had our first business meeting in Our Room when there was no one else around. Gilda told me that she made her little supply of lotion in her uncle's sink, mixing the ingredients by hand and stirring them together with a large spoon. "I remember the formula from when my father had the factory," Gilda said. "I would work there sometimes after school. They used lanolin, glycerin, rose water, a lot of things. I buy what I need from a store downtown. But if we are going to sell it we need to buy a lot. And we will need more bottles, labels. It will cost money to start."

"How much?"

Gilda moved her head from side to side. "It depends on how many you sell. Maybe seventy dollars."

She might as well have said one million. "Will they give credit at that place?" I asked.

"Credit?" Gilda wasn't familiar with the word.

"When you buy something and pay for it later, a little at a time."

She shook her head. "No credit."

"Do you have any money?"

Gilda shook her head again. "When I came here I had only the clothes I wore. I had to buy so much. I give my uncle money to live, and sometimes when his children need things I buy for them. He put a little in the bank for me, maybe thirty dollars, but if I ask him for it he will ask questions."

"Tell him we are going into business," I said.

Gilda shook her head. "I do not want him to know so much."

"Wouldn't he like for you to make more money?" I asked. My mama and daddy would be shouting from as high up as they could climb if I earned an extra nickel.

For a moment her eyes evaded mine. When she looked at me she appeared to be embarrassed. "He is very old-fashioned. He doesn't think that women should make money."

I was perplexed. "But it's okay for you to scrub floors."

"Only while I am single. After I get married I will not work anymore."

"If your uncle found out that you had a business, would he be angry?"

Gilda looked away.

"You can't go to your uncle and tell him that you are selling lotion?"

I heard her long sigh, saw her troubled expression. Gilda opened her mouth and then closed it. Staring at her face, I remembered the day her aunt had come to Braddock and she didn't introduce us. I knew I didn't want to hear what she was going to say. "Not with you," she said very softly.

Me. Colored me. Was I so busy breathing in fantasy that I'd forgotten about reality? Here she was, my coworker, cleaning toilets and scrubbing floors, not even a citizen yet but way ahead of me. She didn't have to climb up a twenty-foot ladder like some jungle monkey. When Gilda didn't have on her uniform, strangers in the hotel called her "Miss." I only heard that word on Sundays. She hadn't been in this country two minutes but already she'd learned that she was better than I was.

"I see." I left without saying good-bye.

Hattie noticed right away that Gilda and I weren't speaking. One morning in Our Room, when Gilda and I were keeping out of each other's way, I heard her muttering, "Somebody must have gotten tired of being white." She and Opal started laughing.

I got right up in Hattie's face. "I know you're not talking to me."

Hattie had punk written all over her. She backed up but instead of shutting her mouth, the fool whirled around to Gilda. "Hey, Miss Pollock. You come to America to scrub out toilets like us?"

Gilda didn't say anything. She grabbed the book she was reading and tried to walk out the door, but Hattie's big hips blocked her way. "I'm talking to you, Miss Pollock."

"Why do you call me names? Huh? I do not call you bad names." Gilda spoke in a quiet voice, but there was no fear in it. I don't believe she was capable of being afraid during those first years after the war. Hattie had to be stupid or blind if she didn't see that.

"Ain't you a Pollock?" Hattie inched closer to Gilda, and I could hear her breathing. Fern was working on the third floor, but Winnie and Opal were in the room. They didn't say anything. The enthusiasm in their eyes was loud enough.

"I do not want to fight with you," Gilda said. She looked around the room. "We all have to clean the toilets. Do we have to hate each other, too?"

Hattie stepped back to let her pass, but Gilda didn't leave. She stood there facing all of us. "Do you want to hate me because I'm not like you? Go ahead. Go ahead."

Nobody said anything.

"I know what hate can do. You do not want that in Our Room."

Gilda cornered me in the hallway of the fourth floor later that day. "He isn't a kind man, my uncle, but he and his children are my only family." I waited for her to elaborate but all she said was, "Be my friend again. Please."

I didn't say anything, but when she put her hand in mine I let it stay there.

Gilda and I never again discussed what her uncle felt about Negroes, nor did we apologize to each other. Without discussions or even a plan we began to move forward. The two of us were a soft breeze gathering velocity. What began to grow between us was a new understanding, an intrinsic part of who we were and what we were about to become: business partners.

CHAPTER FOUR

THE NEXT DAY, right before our shift began, Gilda and I had another business meeting in Our Room. Right off Gilda wanted to know who would buy the lotion.

"The women at my church," I said.

She tilted her head. "How many women?"

We were sitting on the sofa with our feet tucked under our bodies. I said, "Well, there are about a hundred and fifty women in my church." I took a deep breath. "They all want a bottle."

"All of them?" Her eyes opened wide.

I nodded, as I picked lint off my uniform.

"How do they know about the lotion?" she asked. Was that suspicion or curiosity in her voice?

"I let everybody have a little sample from the last bottle you gave me. They really liked it."

Gilda started nodding, more to herself than to me. "Because it is the best lotion, the very best," she said. I could hear pride in her voice that I hadn't heard before. "You must take the, the . . . How do you say what you have when someone promises to buy something from you?"

I thought. "The order."

"Yes. You must take orders. Then you deliver the lotion to them, and they pay you."

"How much? A dollar?"

"In the store they sell a big bottle of lotion for fifty-nine cents. It is not as good as the one I make. And we are delivering."

We agreed on seventy-five cents.

That Sunday I turned one of my lies into the truth. As folks were leaving the church I stood outside the door in the vestibule, just a little beyond two ushers. As each of the sisters passed me by, I said the same thing. "Good morning. Hold out your hand and I'm going to put something nice in it."

I don't know what they were expecting but they squealed like happy kids when I rubbed lotion into their palms. They were make-do women. I felt their calluses and all the rough spots as I massaged them with that cream. My soft touch was as good to them as rose-scented lotion. Standing so close to the women of my church, I got a better look at them. They were mostly brown-skinned, plain-featured, nothing like Marilyn Monroe or Thomasine either. But they looked all right, maybe better than all right. I remembered what Gilda had told me. The thought landed inside me, worked its way up from my heart to my mind. *Our kind of beauty hasn't been discovered yet.*

"This will keep your skin soft and nice," I told them. I was surrounded by white gloves and pocketbooks. "You won't be ashy. I'm going to be selling this soon," I said, taking out my order tablet. "How many of you want to buy a bottle?"

"How much it cost?" somebody asked.

"Seventy-five cents," I said. Soon as the numbers left my mouth, I was standing in the middle of my moment of truth. Lots of people will have their hands out if you're giving something away, but those same fingers will flip you the bird when they see a price tag. Several of the older women disappeared before I could say another word. I figured they'd pledged allegiance to Vaseline for so long that they couldn't make a break. The younger women stayed, and I left church with orders for sixty-three bottles of lotion. I knew that those numbers would grow.

Tuney helped me that day, chatting with the women who were waiting while I massaged their hands and wrote down their orders. I'd been telling him about the lotion and my idea for selling it, but seeing me in action made the idea real to him. When he saw all the orders he got excited for me. "Maybe you could be a third partner," I said.

"Nah. You always been the money grubber in the family. Besides, things are going better at work." That's when he told me that he and the other Negroes at Fountain had begun using the same bathrooms as everybody else. "They haven't said a word," Tuney said. "It's almost like they've been expecting the revolution. Know what I mean?"

I nodded, glad that the California Klan hadn't rigged up a flaming cross for my brother and his colored coworkers.

Tuney lowered his voice. "The Hagertys are drilling on our land."

Max Schmeling's fist crashed through my chest. "Who told you that?"

"Travis Carter wrote me."

Travis was the older brother of my old boyfriend, Lonell. They both still lived in Inez. I felt nauseous, and I couldn't breathe. I couldn't turn off the hate inside me.

Tuney put his arm around me. "Don't give up," he said.

I had a headache that lasted for almost two weeks. The only thing that made me feel better was the fantasy that one day I'd be rich from selling lotion, rich enough to bring the Hagertys to their knees. It was a pipe dream, but it sustained me and kept me from going crazy. Every Sunday I returned to Mt. Olivet Baptist, gave away free samples, and collected more names on my tablet. On my day off I went around to different beauty parlors, massaging hands and writing down more orders; by the end of the month I had nearly two hundred. That was one hundred and fifty dollars, and don't think I wasn't counting my money.

While I was busy selling, Gilda was occupied with other aspects of the business, things I hadn't even thought about. We had to buy bottles and labels for the lotion, and our product had to have a name. We sat up in Our Room for hours trying to come up with something sophisticated but catchy, too. We ended up calling it Satin Skin Lotion. We decided on pale pink labels with rose-colored print. The printer charged $16.43 for one thousand labels. Plastic bottles were cheaper than glass but they didn't look quite as nice. Still, neither one of us wanted to risk breakage so we chose the plastic. The bottles, Gilda told me, would be another $37.84. What we owed was a big yellow jacket buzzing around us; we ducked and dodged it for as long as we could.

The day arrived when the yellow jacket lighted right on us. Everything was done. We had the name. We had the orders. We knew exactly what we had to buy and where. Feeling optimistic, I'd told my customers that they would have their lotion in a week, and the delivery day was approaching fast.

Five days before the lotion was supposed to be delivered, Gilda and I were too busy hustling to actually have a conversation. An automobile dealers convention was taking place at the hotel, and most of the guests had asked for early check-in; Gilda and I were moving like speedboat motors, zooming through the halls, racing from room to room. They were a pretty demanding bunch, especially the wives, who were bored all day while the men were thinking up new ways to make money. They reminded me of the white girls in movies who stood back and screamed while somebody was beating up their man. The ones who'd brought their children were just about out of their minds. Kids were racing up and down the halls, yelling so loudly the walls seemed to rattle. Every few minutes housekeeping would get calls to send facecloths to this room, towels to that room; everything had to be done in a hurry. Gilda and I passed Brewster several times during the day. The hotel had recently installed televisions and some of them weren't working properly, so he was making repairs, listening to the auto dealers' wives as they whined and complained, and trying not to step on stray children.

By the end of the day, everybody who was working at Braddock had become a zombie. Our ears were ringing from all the noise those damn kids had made. Our knees were aching from scrubbing out so many tubs. Stomachs were growling because we hadn't even had a chance to eat. As I made my way down the back staircase my mind was traveling toward green grass and a blanket. I surprised myself when I almost stumbled over something. I looked down and there was Brewster in a heap at my feet.

He didn't seem to be moving or even breathing. I thought he'd had a heart attack, even though he couldn't have been more than thirty. "Brewster!" I whispered. He didn't move. "Brewster!" I said again, a little louder but not loud enough to call attention to myself. Lord, don't let him be dead. When he still didn't answer I bent down to shake him. That's when I smelled the whiskey. I shook him hard then. Just as he began blinking at me, I heard somebody open the door on the landing right above us and then came steady footsteps descending to our level. Brewster stirred on the floor and raised his head. He seemed to be in a confused fog, but he wasn't so drunk that he didn't hear the noise on the stairs. He had the good sense to appear alarmed. He stood up but he was so wobbly that I yanked him by the back of his belt and held him upright as we both waited to see who was coming.

"What are you doing?" It was Gilda.

"He's drunk," I said.

"He must leave. I just saw Weinstock, and he was looking for him."

She'd no sooner uttered the words than we heard Weinstock, the heavy thud of the thick-soled shoes he always wore. We both grabbed Brewster by his belt and dragged him to Our Room. Fern was the only one there. She had just arrived and was rushing off to work her floor. She looked surprised when she saw Brewster, but she didn't ask any questions.

Gilda fixed two cups of get-on-the-bus coffee for us and one cup of get-out-the-door coffee for Brewster, who kept setting his container on the small rickety table next to the broken-down sofa and trying to lie down. Gilda and I made him walk around and sip from his cup. We heard Weinstock's hard steps in the hallway outside. Gilda pushed Brewster into the bathroom, and I opened the door. Sure enough, there was Weinstock, his face sweaty, his glasses sliding halfway down his nose. "You seen Brewster, Gilda?"

"No, sir."

I watched him as he disappeared down the hall.

After about fifteen minutes, Brewster started perking up, figuring out who he was and where he was and how he'd gotten there. He kept saying, "Gee, I want to thank you girls."

"Don't worry about it," I said.

Gilda made us some more coffee. Sitting there, the three of us so friendly with our hot drinks and thank-yous and don't worry about its going back and forth I found myself wondering if an opportunity wasn't staring right at me.

"There is a way you could thank me," I told Brewster.

"You name it, hon," he said.

"My mother is very ill, and I need some money to pay her doctor."

Gilda nearly choked. Brewster looked startled. "How much money?"

"Seventy dollars. I'd pay you back in a couple of weeks. I'm expecting a check." I looked at Brewster imploringly.

"Gee, Hosanna, I don't have it."

"That's okay." I knew it was a long shot.

"Would forty-five help you any? I'd have to have it back in a month. I'm getting married, and it's for my honeymoon."

Forty-five wasn't seventy, but it was better than nothing. I figured that the rest was up to Gilda or our business had ended before it began. She'd put on a little weight, there was color in her cheeks now, and she wore her frizzy hair in a nice style. After Brewster left I told her, "Honey, you better use what you got."

Gilda looked pained when I said that. I put my arm around her shoulder. "Girl, stop going back there. You know what I mean. You're a pretty woman, Gilda. Just smile and look kind of pitiful at the same time and get us some credit."

She still looked disturbed, so I took her hands in mine and started doing a little jitterbug. Louis Jordan was howling some old song. Gilda let me move her, and after a moment or two she was dancing on her own, a little bit off the beat, but dancing just the same.

Gilda did just fine. She gave the printer, the bottle manufacturer, and the chemist half of what we owed, promising them their money in a week. I went to all the places with her but, of course, I didn't go in. I waited outside on the street, feeling anxious and angry all at once. I wanted to be inside sitting with Gilda but if wishes were soap we'd all smell sweet. When the gentlemen held the doors for Gilda as she left each place, I imagined it was me. Keep your eyes on the prize, I reminded myself.

We decided that the best place to mix up the lotion was the hotel. Three days before I was supposed to make my deliveries, Gilda and I met at Braddock around four o'clock in the morning. We checked the records and found an empty room at the end of the corridor on the sixth floor. Gilda put the bolt on the door, and then we went to work.

Mixing the lotion was easy. We poured the ingredients into the tub and stirred for at least an hour, then added the fragrance. The room smelled like a garden. Gilda put in about thirty drops of something that she said would keep everything from separating. When we tested the cream on our hands we broke out in grins.

Bottling our concoction was a challenge. We'd brought funnels, but the lotion was so thick and heavy, and the mouths of the bottles so small, that pouring it took a lot longer than we expected. We filled the containers steadily until it was time for us to punch Braddock's time clock. There were still about one hundred empty bottles. Gilda and I looked at each other.

If we were late to work, we'd lose money. If we stayed in the room too long somebody might find us. If we didn't put the lotion in the bottles, where the hell could we put it? "We'll go to the kitchen and get two great big pots. We can pour the rest of the lotion in the pots, hide them in Our Room, and finish later tonight," I said.

So we locked the door, went down the back staircase, sneaked into the kitchen, borrowed two huge pots while nobody was looking, and trudged up the back stairs. When we got to the room, the door was halfway open and the scent of roses was wafting in the air.

I tapped on the door and said, "Maid service." It wouldn't do to barge in on a guest, and if Mr. Weinstock had stumbled upon our moonlighting, well, we'd simply deny everything. Just when I was about to knock on the door again, a familiar voice said, "Come in." Gilda and I gave each other a look, and we both went inside. Crouched down on the bathroom floor, trying to figure out what was in the tub, was Hattie.

When we came in she spun around and stood up, her face suspicious. "What are y'all doing?" she asked.

Some days you eat the bear; some days the bear takes a chunk out of your behind. After all the mess I'd been through I wasn't about to become a snack for some grizzly. I wouldn't trust Hattie with my man, my money, or my business, and right now she was a threat to two out of three. Before I could think, Gilda spoke up. "Hattie, we were just looking for you. How would you like to make some money?" she said.

A look of intense interest flickered in Hattie's eyes, and I knew she was about to ask some questions. "Hattie, Gilda and I are doing a little moonlighting for a company that manufactures lotion. There's too much

work for two people, and we'd be happy to cut you in if you're interested."

Gilda didn't say anything as I was speaking but her eyes widened.
Working with Gilda was like dancing with a partner who understood my
next step even before it was executed.

"How much money?" Hattie asked, and I knew we'd hired our first
employee.

Gilda and I went downstairs to punch in. When we returned to the
room Hattie was busy pouring lotion into bottles. The three of us worked
for nearly two hours, each of us taking turns as lookout. When we finished we washed out the tub, returned the clean pots to the kitchen, carried the bottles down the back stairs to Our Room and hid them there.
Later that night, Bill, one of Tuney's friends, picked me up in his car. We
put the bottles into the trunk to keep until Sunday.

Sunday morning Bill took me to church early. He parked the car
about twenty yards from the entrance. I had barely slept the night before,
thinking about all the money I was going to collect. There was a hat I'd
seen in a department store window. When I got paid, the first thing I was
going to do was buy it. Sitting through Sunday service, Tuney had to
nudge me when it was time to stand up and pray. Next to him was his
new girlfriend, some Louisiana gal with long legs, slim hips, and hair that
trailed her shoulders. Her skin reminded me of half-done roux, the kind
that makes weak gumbo. Eulalie told me she was Catholic, and she acted
afraid to be sitting in a Baptist church. When the lady in front of us
jumped up and got happy, I thought Miss Bayou was going to bolt out the
door. She was the same kind of high yellow pretty as Thomasine—I guess
that was Tuney's type. Only, for some reason I didn't feel unattractive
standing next to her. I guess I realized that I was the treasure the world
hadn't discovered yet. Besides, my mind was on my wallet, the past and
the future of it. I bowed my head for the benediction, but I was out the
door before the preacher finished dismissing the congregation, running
so fast I could hear the quarters I'd gotten from the bank to make change
clinking in my pocketbook.

I positioned myself at the curb in front of the car. Bill stood next to
me. By the time he opened the trunk, Tuney and Eulalie arrived. I saw

several of the women who'd placed orders with me, and I waved them over, holding a bottle of lotion in each hand. My grin was giving me lockjaw. Three women approached me. But only one handed me a dollar. The other two were giving out excuses. "Well, girl, I sure thought I'd be able to get that lotion today but this has been a rough week. How about next Sunday?"

In all my thoughts of a loaded wallet and a new hat it hadn't occurred to me that my customers might not pay me. I was too stunned to speak. All I could think of was the money Gilda and I owed the supplier, not to mention Hattie. Suppose I brought the lotion to church next week and they still didn't buy? People used to ask me how I learned to sell, and I never could explain it other than to say that one day I was standing on the ledge overlooking the abyss, and I grew wings. "I tell you what," I said to the women who were paying with IOUs. "It's probably a good thing that you don't have the money because I believe I oversold. Everybody wants to buy a bottle. Why don't you give me twenty-five cents today, and when you finish paying me I'll bring you some freshly made lotion? How's that?"

The two women fished around in their purses and came up with their quarters. I wrote twenty-five cents next to their names. I gave the other woman a bottle of lotion and wrote *paid in full* next to her name and gave her a quarter change.

When my last customer was walking away I had the feeling of a diner who'd eaten some food but not enough to satisfy her hunger. Eulalie turned to me and said, loud enough for my brother to hear, "Girl, you're doing things the hard way. You need to put that same energy into finding a good man who'll take care of you." She slipped her arm through my brother's and tossed her hair.

As Tuney and the Praline Queen were about to leave, I pulled Tuney aside. "You hear that? She's telling you she ain't going to hit a lick once she gets married," I hissed.

Tuney just laughed, then sauntered away with Eulalie practically falling all over him.

I didn't know why I felt so angry and betrayed and scared. There was something about Eulalie that made me feel as though she were trying to steal the only good dress I owned. All of my good feelings about me evaporated; I forgot everything Gilda had told me. I wanted to scratch Eulalie's pretty face, and pull her hair out. None of the women I'd known had ever been taken care of. My mother had six children and she worked every day the Lord sent. Maybe women like Eulalie got to sit down, but there weren't any easy chairs in my life.

But I didn't have time to brood about Miss Jambalaya. Money was on my mind. When I surveyed my list about half the people had paid the full amount. Most of the others had left quarters, although some put down a promise for a deposit. Sitting in the trunk of the car were two boxes that I'd expected to be empty. Only one was. My customers had turned my cash cow into the layaway plan. I had one hundred bottles of lotion left. Who knew how long it would take the women to pay me?

I ruminated a little bit as I stood by the car. It was Sunday afternoon. Back then most employed colored women were working either in private service or in factories. Sunday was their day off, a time to go to church, write letters home, maybe even court a little bit. I wasn't too proud to take my goods door-to-door, but that might turn out to be a lot of work for pretty thin results. I needed to go where there were a lot of women with dry skin.

I looked at my watch. My church was small. There were several larger ones in the area. Tuney's friend drove me to the nearest one; the people were still spilling out. He parked the car a few feet from the front door, and as the women walked by me I called out to them. "That sure is a beautiful hat you have on. Come on over here and see what I have for you today."

Of course they came. I was dressed up in my Sunday best, and they could hear Down Home dripping out of me like bacon grease. I looked them in the eye and never stopped smiling when I asked them to hold out their hands. They closed their eyes when I massaged their fingers with the lotion because how many soft touches does a colored woman get? There was nothing in my mind except one word that kept repeating: Sell. It mesmerized me, that word; it wouldn't turn me loose. I sold twenty-three bottles and took seventeen orders.

Bill's car rattled and shook as we drove to a few more churches. By the time we left I had more orders, and there were only forty-five bottles in the trunk. But I was running out of churches. Of course, I could always come back in the evening and make the rounds to the various Baptist Young People's Unions, but I didn't know how long I'd have access to a car.

"You done good," Bill said, and I knew he was hinting.

Not good enough, I thought. I asked him to take me one more place.

When southerners and Texans wanted a taste of home without doing their own cooking, they went to Mooney's for the best southern cooking in the city. It was located at Twelfth and Central, the heartbeat of the Negro Community. Everything seemed to radiate from that spot. The avenue paralleled the Southern Pacific tracks, the train most of the people in the neighborhood had ridden to Los Angeles when they left the south. Sometimes I liked to look down that block of Central just so I could feel proud. There was a newspaper publisher, two dentists, doctors, and two insurance companies in the same block, and in the next one there were a host of nightclubs, the Jungle Room, Club Alabam, the Parisian Room, and a little farther was the Dunbar Hotel. Mooney's was walking distance to many businesses that clustered in the area. Tuney and I had visited several of the nightclubs and sampled some of Mooney's ribs during the first weeks of moving to Los Angeles. Now I'd come to Central Avenue on a different kind of mission.

The hungry weren't going to give me their supper money, and I couldn't massage fingers that were dripping with fried chicken grease, so I caught folks as they were coming out the door. "Did you enjoy your dinner?" I said with my saleswoman's smile. Before they said yes, I was rubbing their hands. In less than an hour I took fifteen orders and sold eleven bottles. Things were looking pretty good until the police came.

There were two of them, big, ruddy men with unsmiling faces. The first one said, "You got a license?"

Bill was sitting in his car. I heard the click of his lock. When the LAPD came around was no time for a colored man to play hero. Black folks and Mexicans weren't safe around cops. I said, "A license?" trying to think faster than ants can scurry.

"To sell on the street you need a license."

I tried to figure out if they wanted money or just a chance to harass me. The answer wasn't in their faces. Had they just happened upon me? Had someone called? "I wasn't really selling, officer. I was delivering."

The taller one gave me a skeptical glance. I was a roach that had crawled onto his path, and he couldn't decide whether to squash me, toss me, or let me go free.

He turned to his partner. "She's just delivering," he said, his voice laced with sarcasm.

I appraised the officers, then grinned my saleswoman's grin. "Yes, I was delivering some lotion to some of my church ladies I missed at today's services. Say, I bet you have nice wives, maybe girlfriends. Come over here. Let me show you something. I'm not trying to sell you anything, because I don't want to break the law."

I dug inside the trunk and pulled out my sample bottle. "Hold out your hands," I said to the short one, who seemed more receptive. He did. I rubbed the lotion on him. "Smell it. Nice, isn't it?" The officer nodded.

Long Tall stood back, looking stern. "No. That's okay," he said when I moved toward him.

I held the bottle out to him. "Try it yourself. I sell it for this man named Mr. Jenkins. He owns the company. He lives in a great big house over in Beverly Hills. He's made a fortune. His other brand is really expensive. Jane Russell doesn't go out the door without putting some on. But he mixed this up so that the average person can afford it. Go on and try it."

He came closer, holding out one hand. I squirted a few drops and watched him as he rubbed a little, sniffed a little.

"Now if you took a bottle of this home, you'd be a big hit. Of course, I can't sell you any on the street. That's illegal."

I charged them a dollar apiece. They slid the money in my palm as we pretended to shake hands.

I sold the rest during the week. On the following Saturday, I went into several barbershops and talked the fathers into buying a bottle for their wives. Then I visited about a dozen beauty parlors and sold directly to the women who were getting their hair done. When Sunday rolled around the entire process started up again. That Monday Gilda and

I paid off our suppliers and ordered twice as much as we had the first time.

Throughout the next year things went well for Gilda and me. There were plenty of challenges. For one thing, the lotion was so thick and con-centrated that it lasted a good long while. If I sold one bottle I didn't get a reorder for three months. We ended up using round bottles that looked as large as the original ones, but held less lotion. Some of the ministers were opposed to commercial transactions on Sunday, so I had to figure out a new way to get to their congregations. What I came up with was to let other women sell for me. I gave them fifteen cents for every bottle they sold. I was afraid those commissions would cut into our profits, but the first month we paid them, we made more money than ever before. I began to realize that Negroes were more spread out than I had thought; in fact, all kinds of people were moving here, trying to work in the aero-space industry and even become movie stars. So taking on commission saleswomen widened our market. Come to find out, some of the women were even selling the lotion to their madams and other white women liv-ing in the neighborhoods where they worked! It got so that six months into the business we had to pay somebody to drive us around to make the deliveries. After a while we added Opal, Fern, and Winnie to the payroll to help make the lotion. We were so busy that everybody was on shifts, with all the maids taking turns coming in early and staying late. We sur-vived a price increase by our suppliers, the time an entire batch of lotion had to be sent back because it smelled like rotten eggs, and slow-paying customers—and still we made money.

We had divided our labor right down the middle. Gilda was the pro-duction person: She made sure the lotion was made according to her family's formula and that we received it in a timely manner. She met with the suppliers and paid them. I was in charge of sales. It was my idea to give people a nickel rebate if they returned their old bottles. Even after we paid workers to wash out the bottles and handed out nickels, we still saved money.

One day during the week we both arranged with Weinstock to leave Braddock for an hour; Gilda and I walked three blocks and went inside a bank that was located right across the street from Gilda's bus stop. I was the only colored person in the place. To tell the truth, it was the first time I'd ever even been in a bank. Mostly, I put my money under my mattress, same as most of the colored people I knew. Gilda didn't pick up on my hesitancy. She marched straight past the short line and sat down in front of a big walnut-tinted desk where an older gentleman with bulldog cheeks was peering at some papers. She nodded her head at me to join her. I did, but it was clear I might as well not have been there. When he stood up, he looked past me straight into Gilda's eyes and asked her what she needed.

"We would like to open up a savings account," she said. She didn't seem to notice that he wasn't talking to me at all.

"I see. Under what name?"

"Gilda Rosenstein and Hosanna Clark."

He nodded and his loose jowls shook a bit. For the first time he glanced my way, but only briefly. "How many signatures will be required to withdraw money?" he asked.

Gilda and I looked at each other.

"One," we both said in unison.

"Either/or," the man said, as he rose. "Please wait here." When he came back twenty minutes later, he handed each of us a bank book that had both our names in it. "Thank you for banking with Los Angeles National," he said to Gilda.

I put mine in my purse and stared straight ahead.

Gilda and I saved most of our profits and, at my request, she did most of the banking. Going into that place took away the good feeling that earning my money brought me. When I needed money, I asked her to get it for me. From time to time, we'd pay ourselves, not a real salary but a little bonus for all our hard work. Gilda would buy books and go to the movies or a play. I sent Mama and Daddy extra money, paid for driving lessons, and started looking at used cars. I bought clothes, too: a slim red skirt that clung to my hips, a blouse that revealed just a bit of cleavage, high heels that showed off my nice legs. I bought a full-length mirror, propped it against the wall in my room, and stopped looking at the one at work.

Gilda still had her mind set on going to college and becoming a teacher, but my candy store dream had been replaced with a sweeter one: to quit my job and open a real cosmetics company.

"Why should we just sell lotion?" I asked Gilda. "Didn't you say that your parents used to make all kinds of cosmetics?"

"Yes, but I don't remember the formulas."

"We can find some kind of pharmacist or chemist to mix up something for us. Powder and lipstick are probably easy. We could start with those and expand to eye makeup later."

"But there are companies selling these things already," Gilda said.

"Not for colored women," I told her.

I didn't nag her. I was learning that I could sell whatever I believed in; sooner or later I knew that I'd sell Gilda on the idea of quitting our jobs and going into business together full-time. Maybe she didn't notice, but I began to realize that as we sold more and more lotion, Gilda had fewer depressions. In the two years that I'd known Gilda, she'd turned from a scrawny see-through rag doll into a pretty young woman, with life in her eyes. Her eyes and teeth sparkled, and it wasn't a rare thing for her to laugh real hard, just like Sarah when the Lord told her, "Have I got a surprise for you."

CHAPTER FIVE

A FEW WEEKS later, on a Monday morning, Gilda came to work humming. She'd learned a lot of the words to Ella and Sarah's songs, and sometimes she'd sing along when a record was playing. But the song she was singing that day sounded more like old, familiar church music. At the same time Gilda was perked up like a country girl who'd just seen the big city but from a distance; she was breathing out excitement and wonder, too. I kept asking her what she'd done that weekend, where she'd been, and she just kept humming her little song. When I got near her I smelled lavender.

Finally, at lunchtime she told me that she'd met a man named David Abramowitz. "He is the son of my uncle's friend. His family came to the house on Sunday, and we had dinner. All right? Now you know."

A hungry dog wants more than just a smell of bone. "What's he look like?"

Gilda shrugged. "He looks regular."

"Tall? Short? Fat? Skinny? Handsome? Ugly? Hairy? Bald?"

"Not too tall. Not short. Medium. Not handsome. Not ugly. Medium. With lots of hair. All right? Okay?"

"What did you all talk about?"

"Nothing." She slapped her hands against her thighs. Once. Twice. Looked up with eyes full of longing. "He wants to take me to the movies."

"When are you going?"

She hesitated. "I cannot go."

"Why not?" I asked.

She gave me a look of astonishment. "I do not want to go out."

"What's wrong with him?"

Gilda looked pained, confused. She glanced down where her numbers had been, staring at that bit of scarred flesh as if she expected it to speak.

"Have some fun, Gilda. Go to the movies. What's wrong with that?"

She opened her mouth, about to make some excuse, but I cut her off. "There's nothing wrong with it. Do you think you are supposed to be lonely for the rest of your life?"

Our eyes met. "It is time to go back to work," Gilda said. She got up and left me sitting alone.

Later that day, when Gilda and I were cleaning on the same floor, without saying a word we went into an empty room and locked the door behind us, then stretched out on the bed.

"Before I went into the camps I was supposed to get married," Gilda began. "Tibor was my sweetheart from when I was a little girl. Our mothers were great friends. They would tell us that Tibor and I were talking to each other in their bellies. We were born a week apart. I do not remember a time when he wasn't my boyfriend. He is the only man I ever kissed"—she looked at me and then at the ceiling—"until I went into the camp.

"The soldiers took my family first. They ordered us on one train. So many people, all crammed together like sand in a bowl. Tibor's family was to go on another train but he didn't want us to be separated. He asked to accompany me, and when they said no he ran toward my train. They shot him. The last time I saw him he was lying in the street and blood was pouring from his body. I heard later that his parents were killed in the camp."

"Do you think that he would want you to be alone for the rest of your life?"

Gilda put her hand on mine. "You do not understand."

"What don't I understand?"

We wore uniforms that zipped from the neck to the hem of the dress. Gilda unzipped hers past her bra, past her waist. She lifted up her slip. A jagged purplish scar ran from the center of her cleavage line to below her navel. I gasped when I saw it. "What happened?" I asked.

"I had been at the camp three months when one of the female guards asked for all the young women to line up. Anyone under thirty years old. She told us we were going to be given special jobs in the kitchen. We

were then working in a laundry, and it was hard because there was so little food. So, we all rushed to the line.

"She took five of us, but not to the kitchen. We went to the infirmary.
It was a small building where the German doctors did their experiments
and operations. The guard told us to take our clothes off and then we
took showers in very hot water. After we were dry the guard led us to different rooms. In mine there was a table and above it was a huge light.
There were men, doctors, standing around. One of them stuck me with
a needle, and I became unconscious. When I woke up I felt woozy and
then very sore. As the anesthesia wore off the pain became unbearable.
They told all five of us the same thing—that they had removed our ap-
pendixes. Days later one of the women whispered to me that it wasn't
true. They had opened us up to experiment on us," she whispered.

I pulled her close and put my arm around her.

"I do not know what they did. I do not know what they took."

"You haven't been to the doctor?"

"I am afraid to go. No man will want to look at this body," she said.
After a while she started humming that same song again.

I released her. Funny how one person's bad memory can lead you to
the one hiding in the back of your mind under the rock you pressed on
top of it. "Back in Texas I used to make fudge candy, and I'd sell it on Sat-
urdays. I was on my way home and I was counting my money, walking
up the road that led to our house. I remember that there was a grove of
pecan trees up ahead of me. All of a sudden two men came out from behind them. They were running. I couldn't see their faces but something
about the way they moved put a chill on my heart. They didn't have any
business being on our land. I stood still until they were gone, and then
I ran toward the trees. First thing I saw was blood in the dirt, and I heard
my baby sister crying. Lucille was on the ground. Blood was running
down her thigh and somebody had spit on her. They'd raped her, passed
her back and forth like she was a bottle of whiskey for them to share. It
was terrible. Terrible. She told me that one of them had said to her, 'You
go tell your daddy he don't give up that land, your mama will be next.'
She wasn't but fourteen years old.

"For almost three generations our family owned land right outside of Inez, Texas. My mama said my great-granddaddy saved the money from barbering. My daddy said he gambled and loan-sharked for it. One thing is for sure: nobody gave it to him. Because we had that land my mama and daddy were able to make their own living without having to hold out their hand to anybody. We weren't rich but we weren't starving. That was the problem. Where I came from white folks liked to see colored folks starving.

"The Hagertys had been after our land for years. After what happened to Lucille, my mama, my sister, and I were never allowed to be alone. But it wasn't any use. The Hagertys were the power in our county. Owned everything and wanted more. Nobody would give Daddy a decent price for his crops. Burned down his lumber. In the end they got him on taxes. Came up with some trumped-up papers that said he hadn't paid. Goddamn them! I wish I could kill them all."

Gilda and I held hands for a moment. She looked at me once or twice, but she didn't say anything. After a while we got up and went back to work.

Gilda went to the movies with her David, and he invited her out again. The Monday after her first date, she came to work smiling. "He is very smart," she said when I caught up with her in the hall. "He knows a lot. He has graduated from college, and he reads books all the time."

"Oh, Gilda, that's good." I was glad my friend had something in common with the nice man who wanted to take her to the movies.

"His father owns a men's clothing store, and David and his brother work for him. He has a sister and she is married. His father is very stern, and his mother is quiet and sad-looking."

"Were they . . ."

"They were in America during the war, although some of their relatives died."

"Did you have a good time?"

"Yes."

Gilda and David started going out every Sunday afternoon, and every Monday she gave me a report. I learned secondhand what music and books David liked, his favorite foods and movie stars, his opinions, his temper. "He gets very angry sometimes," Gilda told me once, "mostly when he has to do something for his father that he doesn't want to do." In the next breath she said, "Look what he bought me." She held out her wrist to show me a charm bracelet.

From time to time I would suggest that Gilda go to a doctor but she refused. I knew she was afraid of discovering that she couldn't have children. As long as she didn't know, it wasn't true. That was like playing cards in the dark. Me, I wanted to see the hand I'd been dealt.

These were hopeful days for Tuney. There was talk in LA about hiring colored firemen. "Yeah, girl," Tuney said, "I wouldn't mind being the first one to do that."

"But it's dangerous."

"Not as dangerous as being in a war. Being the first, well, it's harder but once the hard part is over, I'd be more protected, and other opportunities will follow. Look at Jackie Robinson. You think when his baseball days are over they're just going to let him disappear?" Tuney shook his head. "They're going to take care of him. Give him a showboat job because that makes them feel better about themselves. Yeah, I want to be the first fireman."

Los Angeles was a boomtown throbbing and swelling with people and so many cars that traffic jams were the rule. We all claimed a section that we drenched with our food, our fun, our blues, our dreams: Negroes ate barbeque and held rent parties in South Central; Mexicans hawked tamales and celebrated Cinco de Mayo on the east side. The Japanese who'd been locked up during the war came home to Torrance and Gardena, their spirits shattered, their property and jobs long gone. All of us were immigrants together.

Of course there was the air, heavy as bad feelings some days, and so grimy it made eyes water and burn. That day Gilda came dragging through the door of Our Room wearing trouble for a collar I thought something had blown into her eyes. Then I saw Mr. Weinstock just two steps behind her. Fern, Hattie, and I were getting ready to go home, but we stopped moving when we saw him. Weinstock cleared his throat and pressed his glasses into place. "Girls, starting Monday, Gilda will be your supervisor. You'll take your assignments from her, and she'll report to me. Hosanna, you let the others know."

I barely managed to nod before he was gone. Nobody said a word. We were all shocked, including Gilda, who looked as though someone had smacked her just hard enough to wake her up. What was in the air was the kind of feeling that comes when sisters are standing around in homemade dresses and a strange woman twirls in wearing fancy store-bought. The first sound came from Hattie, and it was a grunt, long, low, and filled with the kind of ugly that's mostly sorrow. "So, now you gone be the overseer." Hattie sucked her teeth.

The rest of the women just looked at her, including me. I knew that Gilda hadn't asked for the job. The offer had given her a new kind of misery. But seeing Gilda's pained expression didn't take the lumps out of the mess of grits I was trying to swallow.

After everyone cleared out Gilda said to me, "He picked me because I am white, yes?" she asked.

I was too angry to sugarcoat it for her. "That's right," I said.

"Now everybody will hate me."

"Just Hattie," I said.

"You, everyone has been here longer. You know the job better. Why does he pick me just because I am white?"

"That's the way things are," I said, my voice tight.

"But this is not Texas, Louisiana. This is California."

"It's America."

In the days that followed I tried not to resent her. Winnie, Fern, and Opal were grumbling, and Hattie had her lip out so far I was surprised she didn't kick it. Gilda let their attitudes get to her. Sometimes she almost seemed to be apologizing when she told them what to do. Winnie, Fern, and Opal had a conscience, and they did their jobs; Hattie got positively trifling. She worked like the field hand she used to be for Mr. Weinstock but for Gilda, she left beds half-made, bathroom floors dirty, and she didn't vacuum.

I found out that Hattie was messing up when I saw Gilda cleaning behind her a few times. I sat her down and said, "Listen, you can't let Hattie get away with not doing her work. If you do, the rest of them are going to slack off. I don't want that."

Gilda sighed. She looked at me. "It was getting to be nice, everybody working together. I'm going to tell him that I don't want this job."

"He'll just hire somebody else white. At least we like you."

"Still?"

"You can't help being white. In time even Hattie will accept you if you start acting like the boss. You have to tell her what to do. You have to let her know you'll go to Mr. Weinstock if she doesn't work." It made me feel uneasy telling a white woman how to boss colored women.

"I cannot do that."

"You won't have to if she thinks you're serious." She looked forlorn, like a lost child in a windstorm. "What's the matter?"

"I hate that."

"You hate what?"

"To run and tell. There is always someone who runs and tells, who gets people in trouble, gets people killed just for an extra piece of bread, to live one more day. I do not want to be that person."

"You can also do us some good, Gilda." She looked surprised. "Maybe you can talk Weinstock into getting us a better sofa for Our Room. You can ask him if we can get free breakfasts, or at least some doughnuts. Maybe you can get us a raise."

Gilda smiled. "I never thought of this."

"You know, as long as somebody else is paying you, you have to do what they say. You ought to work for yourself and set your own rules."

When she looked at me I saw the first smile I'd seen since she became my boss. "You are becoming a little monster. Yes? You sell the lotion, now you try to sell everything, all the time."

"Girl, you better think about what I'm saying."

"Umph," she said, sounding just like Hattie.

Gilda continued to clean up after Hattie, whose attitude didn't show any signs of improving. I'd said my piece. Besides, my goal was to get us both out of Braddock, and I figured that Gilda would leave an unpleasant situation a lot faster than she'd leave a pleasant one.

I concentrated on the business, which was going great. I was selling lotion all over the city. Our bank account had swelled to nearly seven hundred dollars—more money than I'd ever seen in one place in my life. When Mama wrote me that Lucille sometimes wouldn't leave the house, I mailed my sister two cases, hoping that selling would ease her mind. A month later, when Lucille sent me the money she'd made, I told Tuney I would treat him to a trip home. Neither one of us had had a vacation in all the time we'd been in Los Angeles; we hadn't seen our family in four years. My brother went with me one Saturday and helped me pick out a used Ford; I paid cash. It was summer, which is not the time to go to Texas, but I took off two weeks anyway. We loaded up my car with clothes, gifts for my folks, and two boxes of lotion, and then my brother and I headed down Route 66.

CHAPTER SIX

IT TOOK NEARLY four days to get to Houston. Tuney did most of the driving and practically all of the talking. He and Eulalie had broken up, and he was courting again. Some Mississippi gal had a ring in his nose. All the way to Houston it was Rosalee this and Rosalee that. He was singing love songs clear across the desert.

My brother insisted on driving through Inez. I knew seeing our old land would make both of us angry, but anger is like gas to Tuney; it keeps his motor running. The sun was setting when we came up on the outskirts of our property. There had been a lot of old pecan trees growing there once, but they'd been cut down. Instead of seeing rice plants, which should have been high that time of year, the land was fallow. We saw the oil riggings.

"Son of a bitch," Tuney said. His eyes got real tight and dark, and his mouth bunched up. He didn't have to say another word. The Hagertys were going to be rich off the sweat of my ancestors.

"Don't say nothing to Mama and Daddy," I said.

Tuney nodded. They probably already knew what was going on, and talking about it would just make it worse.

I'd left Texas riding that gray dog so it was a big deal to everybody that I was coming back in my own automobile. Colored people who went away to places like New York, Philadelphia, Chicago, or Los Angeles carried the hopes of an entire family. Everybody knew that the big city could kick an ass faster than it could grow one. Maybe I was scrubbing out toilets and cleaning up after folks but my hair was done and my clothes were new. I might not be driving a Cadillac or an Oldsmobile but I had a five-year-old Ford so shiny people could see their faces in it. That car was a rainbow, coloring my path to better days.

Mama and Daddy liked to eat Tuney and me up with a spoon. They put four years' worth of missing and loving into their hugs and kisses. My three younger brothers jumped all over us after our parents stepped back. Lucille, who was the oldest of the four kids still at home, gave Tuney and me a kiss on our cheeks, but she didn't say much. Lucille was like a porcelain vase that somebody had shattered; she was glued back together, but I could still see the cracks.

Before we were in the house five minutes Mama was crying and Daddy had gone to the back porch to be alone. When he came back in, Mama was putting food on the table, talking about how skinny I was and how big Tuney had gotten. "Tuney has a bunch of women feeding him," I said. Mama and Daddy shook their heads.

After we ate I had a chance to look around. There wasn't much to see. The house was a hot tiny box that needed paint. I had to bunk in with Lucille, and Tuney slept with the boys. Still, it was better than what we'd left behind in Inez. Daddy was working for an oil company, basically sweeping up, but it beat sharecropping. Mama had a lady she cleaned for across town. The kids were doing all right in school, and thanks to what Tuney and I sent them, they had decent clothes. But I wanted them to have more. At Braddock I watched rich people coming and going all day long, and just seeing them had triggered in me the notion that there must be enough for everybody.

"How did you get started selling this here lotion?" my daddy asked me after supper. My mama and the rest of the family eyed me curiously as I told them all about Gilda.

I could tell by their expressions that the notion of a colored woman and a white woman working together was a song in a foreign language. Daddy's foot kept tapping. Mama rubbed her hands together. My brothers gave one another strange looks. Finally Daddy said, "A Jew, huh."

Later that night, my mother sat down on the bed that held my sister and me. "Hosanna," she whispered, and I sat up, leaning against the headboard. Lucille lay beside me, whimpering in her sleep. For a moment Mama and I both stared at her sleeping body. There were wrinkles across my mother's forehead that I'd never noticed before.

"Ma'am?"

"You gotta be careful, girl. You're doing real good for a woman. Better than most. Don't you dream too big. Hear me?"

"Yes, Mama."

She didn't get up. Just sat there with her hand on my shoulder sending warmth down to my bone. "I ever tell you that time I seen Madam C. J. Walker?"

"No, ma'am."

"You know who she is?"

"The straightening comb lady."

"That's right. She was at a church in Houston, the first time I came up here. Oh, she was fine, all right. Dressed up like a rich white woman. And her hat, Lordy me. Ain't never seen anything so beautiful in all my life."

No colored mother in her right mind would encourage her daughter to quit her job and start a business. Moonlighting was one thing. But thinking you could make a living without a weekly check signed by a white man, that was lunacy. Still, when Mama told me about Madam C. J. Walker, I knew that was her way of letting me know that somebody who looked like me had succeeded in life.

After Mama left I lay back down and put my arm around my sister. Lucille was lying on her side. She was really thin; I could feel her ribs. I thought she was asleep, but she turned toward me and stared. "What?" I said.

"I miss you."

She kept staring. "What?" I asked again.

"How can you trust a white woman?"

"Lucille," I began but I didn't finish. There was nothing I could say that my sister would understand. "Go back to sleep."

The next few days I went out and sold lotion. I sold door-to-door, at beauty parlors and barber shops, outside grocery stores, too. Even lowering the price a little—because people didn't make as much money in Houston as in LA—I still did okay.

By Sunday I was as tired as if I'd been scrubbing tubs at Braddock. We got up early that morning and dressed for breakfast. I could smell the food before Mama put it on the table: sausage, scrambled eggs, grits, corn bread, fried fish. I hadn't had eating this good since I'd left home. After we ate we all said prayers together and then we went to church. Mt. Zion was only two blocks away, but I drove Mama and Daddy and Lucille while the younger kids walked with Tuney.

The church was new to me, and I wasn't expecting to see anybody I knew since all my home folks were in Inez. But when I slid into the pew the very first person I bumped up against was Lonell Carter, my old boyfriend. We both did a double take and then grinned so hard we could see each other in our teeth.

About four years had passed since I'd seen Lonell. We kept whispering and passing notes during the service. As soon as church was over we ran outside and hugged each other as though we'd never been apart.

Lonell looked good. His peach-colored skin had a glow. He'd picked up just enough weight to fill out his arms and chest, and he'd grown a couple of inches, because the last time we were together I hadn't been looking up to him. He was at least six feet now. His hair was full of stocking cap waves. He was still living in Inez and had come to Houston to visit his brother. "But I'm thinking about moving here, or at least going somewhere," he said. "How are you liking Los Angeles?"

"I like it fine," I said, and then I told him about the weather, how it never really got cold. "I have an orange tree in my backyard," I said. It sounded so silly we both laughed at the same time. I described Central Avenue and how on Friday and Saturday nights, blues and jazz music settled over the area like a low-flying cloud, spraying rhythm and laughter instead of rain. "Tuney's working at an airplane factory. And the city's fittin' to hire colored firemen."

"Colored firemen? That's something," he said, and whistled real low. "Whatcha been doing?"

"I'm working in a big hotel." I didn't have to elaborate. "I also sell lotion on the side but I'm hoping to make it a full-time business."

We were standing outside the church, just beyond the steps, and Lonell kind of reared back a little. "Full-time business?" he said, and in his voice there was laughter the size of a flower bud. "You done gone out to Los Angeles, and now you trying to be white. You even talk different."

"I'm not trying to be white," I said.

"Aww, I'm just playing with you, girl. You sure are looking fine. How long you gone be in town?"

"Until Thursday."

"I'd like to spend some time with you. There's a baseball game this afternoon. You want to go?"

After supper I picked him up. Tuney came along, too, and he brought a pretty little string bean he'd met at church. "What about Rosalee?" I whispered.

"Rosalee ain't here," he said with a grin.

Lonell's brother didn't live too far from my folks, which wasn't surprising since most Negroes formed a black sash across the city called fifth ward, a run-down neighborhood of clapboard houses, no sidewalks, and an occasional pecan tree. It was a noisy, crowded community filled with new arrivals from Inez, Crockett, and other little Texas towns. The only other sizable colored population was located in third ward, where the people lived careful lives: careful not to get dirty, not to talk too loudly, very careful not to be mistaken for somebody from fifth ward.

Jackie Robinson had been playing with the Brooklyn Dodgers for only a few years at that time. Major League baseball was still white baseball. The game we went to see that day was played between two teams from the Negro Leagues, the Pittsburgh Crawfords and the Kansas City Monarchs.

In the last inning the Pittsburgh batter struck out and the Monarchs scored a home run. Houston favored the Monarchs, because Kansas City was closer to us than Pittsburgh, and because two homeboys were on the team. When the game was over maybe a couple of hundred people, rushed onto the field, so excited and happy they were just hugging each other and dancing. Everybody was feeling really good, and as folks began heading toward their cars I saw a prime opportunity. Scrambling down off the bleachers, I rushed to my car. "Girl, where you going?" Lonell asked.

"To sell lotion," Tuney said, as I raced toward my Ford. "I told you Hosanna's train runs down a one-way track."

I opened the trunk. I went over to the largest group of women I could see and threw my net out as wide as I could. By the time Lonell, Tuney, and his friend got there, I had already sold seven bottles. Those Texas gals bought up all the lotion I had left.

I was about to ask Lonell if he was ready to go but when I looked at him his face was sort of crumpled like paper that had mistakes written on it. "What's the matter?" I asked. I thought he was feeling bad, that he'd gotten some kind of ache.

"Oh, nothing," he said, and then he grinned at me, his smile so dazzling it erased whatever problems there had been.

Later that night, after I'd dropped off Tuney and the girl, Lonell and I were sitting outside his brother's house in my car. He pulled a flask out of his hip pocket, unscrewed the cap, took a swig, and then offered some to me. Whatever was in that bottle burned like hell going down. I wasn't much of a drinker. Lonell laughed as he swatted me across the back. I passed the bottle back to him, and he took a couple more swallows. He told me that he had plans, big plans. "Gonna build houses," he said. His words came together slowly, like slippery beads that keep falling off the string and won't make a necklace. "Since the war ended people have money to spend. They want to live good, even colored."

Lonell's father had been a carpenter in Inez and had built many of the small homes that the town's more prosperous colored folks lived in. His sons had always helped him. Lonell's goal excited me as much as my own. I hadn't thought much about getting married and raising a family, but listening to Lonell, it occurred to me that the kind of man I wanted for my husband was somebody who would do just what I was doing: seize whatever opportunities came his way.

"There's more to learn about than what Daddy taught me. Plumbing. Electricity. Masonry. I'm planning on starting school in the fall at Texas Normal, or maybe I'll go somewhere else. Out in California."

Can somebody smile and kiss at the same time? I felt Lonell's lips turning upward and opening as he pulled me into him. When his lips parted I could swear I tasted his grin, or maybe it was just the moonshine.

In the next few days I sampled Lonell's smiling kiss again and again. I felt his fingers through and under my clothes, and we both wanted more. On our last night, as I dropped him off at his brother's house, he turned and called out, "Don't be surprised if I show up in Los Angeles."

The night before Tuney and I left, Mama was up late frying chicken and baking corn bread and biscuits. We'd have to drive a whole lot of seg-regated miles before we reached Los Angeles, and my mother wanted to make sure that her children ate. At daybreak she handed me a greasy bag and some wisdom. My mama had seen Lonell hanging around. She pulled me out onto the back porch, then spoke in a low whisper. "Lotta these young gals getting themselves in trouble around here. You gotta be careful, honey."

"I'm not doing anything, Mama."

"I know, baby. Mama just doesn't want you led astray." She stood over me with her head bowed, her lips moving. When she finished I kissed her good-bye.

CHAPTER SEVEN

TUNEY AND I arrived in LA early in the morning. From a distance the city looked like a song, full of high notes and complicated chords. When I saw that big old orange glow glittering from the highway, I could hear a melody of ocean roars and the drone of Santa Anas, of whispering palms blowing in the desert winds. I couldn't drive fast enough to get to it, to be filled with it. LA was my song.

I was bleary-eyed and bedraggled when I arrived at Braddock hours later. I'd come in a little early and nobody was in Our Room when I walked in. To my surprise, the sofa was gone and the three chairs were stacked in one corner. The air was stale. I looked around for the coffeepot, but it wasn't on the rickety table, and the hot plate was gone, too. For the last four years, the first thing I'd done at the start of every work shift was to have a cup of coffee, and the last thing I did before I left was to have another. How was I supposed to do my job without my morning wake-up jolt? What was going on?

I changed into my uniform and went around to the service elevator so I could go up to the housekeeping supply room to get my cart. When the elevator doors opened, there was Brewster. The door closed, and the elevator ascended to the next floor.

"Well, hello there, Hosanna. Heard you were away." His Adam's apple bobbed up and down in his throat as he spoke.

When Brewster wasn't in his cups, he always had a kind of genteel charm. He'd gotten married a few months before, and I hadn't seen him drunk since that time in the stairwell.

"I went home to Texas. Houston. Sure am glad to be back."

"It's hot in Houston."

"I don't know how I stood it when I was living there."

Brewster laughed. "Oh, you've just gotten soft since you've been in LA."

"I guess so."

Brewster's face got kind of strange suddenly, and he said in a whisper, "You hear what happened?"

"No. I just got in."

"Hattie got fired."

No more whistling. Before I could ask why, when, how, the elevator door opened again, and Mr. Weinstock was standing in front of me. Brewster gave me a quick look, and I read a warning in it.

"Hosanna, I'd like to speak with you," Mr. Weinstock said, and the way the words came out of his stony-looking face kind of shook me.

"Yessir," I said, thinking about Brewster's expression.

We walked to his office in complete silence. When we got inside, he sat down at his desk while I stood in front of him. "Hosanna, how long have you worked here?"

"Four years, sir."

"And do you like your job?"

Did he really think anybody enjoyed scrubbing out toilets? "It's fine," I said.

He swiveled around in his leather chair. There were holes in both armrests, and I could see the stuffing coming out. His shirt had a tear in the right breast pocket. His glasses kept slipping and he pushed them up every time they fell down. Then he took them off and stared at me with his tiny granite eyes. "Hosanna, I know you were in on it. I want the truth. Don't lie to me."

I wasn't thrown at all. When Brewster told me that Hattie had been fired, I went on alert. A woman like Hattie lives by the misery-loves-company code. I did what any colored woman in her right mind would do when confronted by a white man trying to make her life more miserable than it already is: I played dumb. "What do you mean?"

"You know damn well what I mean, girl." He wiped his sweaty forehead with the back of his hand.

"No, I don't."

He was angry because I hadn't fallen into his trap. Now he had to tell me what he'd wanted me to tell him. "You and the rest of them have been mixing up stuff in hotel rooms and then selling it. You're running a little business out of here, aren't you?"

"Running a business? Mr. Weinstock, sometimes I'm so tired I can barely get on the bus when I leave here. How would I have the energy for a business? What kind of business?"

He gave me a sharp look, and I gazed at that man, exuding Mammy, Butterfly McQueen, and Stepin Fetchit all rolled into one getting-over-woman.

"Well," he said, and I could see the doubts crowding his mind. I'd never caused him trouble before. He was sitting on his fence, trying to decide which way to jump.

I attempted to force out a couple of tears, but one was all I could manage. "I try to do my best here, sir, and I just don't think it's right of you to make fun of me." Sniffle. Sniffle.

His head jerked up. "Make fun of you?"

"I only finished the tenth grade. Maybe if I had an education I could be in some sort of a business. Mostly, I wanted to be a teacher growing up, but my mama and daddy were too poor to send me to school. But we're hardworking, God-fearing people. We don't steal. We don't lie. And my folks always told us it's wrong to make fun of people, especially—"

"Now, see here, Hosanna . . ."

Sniffle. Sniffle. "Each and every time you see me, I'm busy cleaning. And I don't believe anybody has ever complained about me, have they? Didn't I return that twenty-dollar bill to you that those people left last year?"

"Hosanna, I never said—"

"And it just makes me feel so bad inside to think that you—"

"All right. All right. That's enough. I accept your explanation. I see that a mistake has been made. You can go."

Sniffle. Sniffle.

"I said you can go, Hosanna."

"You have upset me, Mr. Weinstock. I'm so upset I can't even move."

"Well, I'm, I'm . . . Now look here, Hosanna. I want you to leave my office and get to work right now."

"I don't know how I'm going to do that, upset as I am. If I could have a cup of coffee, maybe I could get myself in order. But when I went to the maid's room everything was in disarray, and the coffeepot was gone. None of us can get started, not to mention keep going, without our coffee, and our room."

Our eyes met and I managed to get in one last shoulder-shuddering snort, which I hoped was a mask for what I knew was shining from my eyes: the knowledge that Mr. Weinstock had taken away the room as a punishment.

Every shade of red was on that man's face. "Hosanna," he said, his voice growing louder with each word, "you can ask somebody in the kitchen to give you some coffee for now."

"But what about later?" Sniffle.

Mr. Weinstock sighed. "We'll see about later."

That afternoon I saw Fern, who told me that Hattie had started in on Gilda from the day I left. I could see the excitement in her eyes as she replayed the battle scene for me. "You know Hattie can get trifling, Hosanna," Fern said. "Got so she wouldn't hit a lick. This went on for about a week. We were all in Our Room when finally Gilda told her she'd have to do better. Soon as she said that, Hattie hauled off and slapped her in her face.

"But you know what, Hosanna? That little Gilda fought that big ox. She sure did. And she was more or less holding her own. I guess Brewster heard the commotion; he came in and broke them up. Told Gilda to go on home, and she was heading out the door when that fool came after her again. Sure did. That's when Weinstock came by. Uh-huh. And didn't even ask what happened. All he needed to know was that a colored woman was fighting with a white one, and just like that Hattie was gone.

"As soon as he said the word 'fired,' Hattie started yelling and screaming about how you and Gilda were running a business out of the hotel. And Gilda, child, that girl didn't skip a beat, you hear me. Talking about, 'Hattie is lying. I don't know why she's making up such stories.' Didn't bat an eye.

"But then Hattie ran to where she thought you and Gilda had put the empty bottles. She was going to show them to Mr. Weinstock, but they weren't there, except for about five of them. And Hattie says, 'If you all aren't mixing up lotion, what are these doing here, huh?'

"Gilda just laughed. She told ole Weinstock that she kept water in those bottles because she got dehydrated easily. Instead of filling up one at a time, she'd fill them all up in the morning and would try to drink them during the day. I don't know if Weinstock believed her or not. The next day after the fight, he told us that Our Room was off-limits because the hotel needed it. She gave her a black eye."

I drew in a breath. "Who?"

"Gilda."

"Hattie gave Gilda a black eye?"

"No, girl. It was the other way around."

I had to sit with the news about Hattie being fired. Hattie was wrong, and I didn't have a lot of love for her. But I knew what had made her wrong. I walked in those same worn-out shoes that she walked in. They rubbed my heels and pinched my toes just like they did hers. Maybe my feet were stronger. I don't know. As much as I cared about Gilda, as much as Hattie got on my nerves, I didn't want anyone to ask me if one of them had to go, which one I would choose.

By the end of the day the sofa was back in Our Room and the coffeepot was bubbling. I was sipping a cup when Gilda came in. What she told me with her eyes was that she understood that my loyalties were divided and she didn't hold it against me. It wasn't until I was right up on her that I saw that the left side of her face was bruised. I touched it lightly with my finger. "I heard about what happened."

Gilda shrugged.

"Fern said she looks a lot worse than you do."

She didn't smile. "She told him everything," Gilda whispered.

"I know."

Without saying anything we both sat down on the sofa. "She is very angry inside. I understand. She looks at me, and she remembers the evil that has been done to her. If I see Germans I will feel the same way."

She cleared her throat. "We cannot prepare the lotion here anymore. It is not safe. Weinstock isn't a fool. He is still suspicious. If he finds out he will fire all of us," Gilda said. "We should find another place to do it. We have money to pay a little rent, to pay for help. We could mix it on our days off. And then, maybe in some months, when we have enough money saved, we can leave Braddock and just sell our lotion and other things."

Our eyes met. "What about college?"

"I will get there," she said. "I cannot stay here any longer."

Once Gilda decided to leave Braddock and go into business with me, she took charge. The two of us had been running a bootleg operation, selling lotion without benefit of a license, without having our product approved by the government. We hadn't paid one dollar in taxes, which was fine with me, but Gilda said that if we were going to grow we had to be legitimate. She hired a lawyer and started the process of getting our affairs in order.

I wanted to leave this part of the business to Gilda, but she wouldn't hear of it. "You must learn everything that needs to be done," she said one day when I was cleaning rooms on the fourth floor.

There was no arguing with her. She made me memorize all the laws regarding cosmetics, and I learned all about the Food and Drug Administration. Every two weeks Gilda would go over the books with me. Gilda had a real book, not just scratch paper, and she wrote down names, dates, amounts, the price of the products, when this bill was due, when that bill was paid, everything. She knew every penny that came in and what went out.

Not long after the fight, Gilda discovered a place where we could buy cheaper bottles. On the day of Gilda's appointment with the supplier I drove to work. Afterward, I took her to the plastics company and waited in the car while she was inside making a deal. Within thirty minutes she came outside, a big smile on her face. "Four cents cheaper a bottle," she said, after she got in.

We decided to celebrate by going out to a little diner at the edge of downtown. It was a tiny little place that served good home cooking and plenty of it. I was surprised that Gilda would eat at a regular restaurant. "Just once won't hurt," she said. "Besides, when David and I go out to eat, it isn't always kosher."

"I thought he was the same kind of Jew as you."

Gilda shrugged. "In this country it is different. Besides, keeping kosher doesn't make me a good Jew. I know bad people who keep kosher."

I detected bitterness in her tone, but I didn't ask any questions. She started humming that hymn, the one I thought I knew.

After we finished eating, I drove Gilda about a block away from her home and parked. I never dropped her off in front of her house. There was still her uncle to consider. It was early evening, and inside the car Gilda kept tapping her feet to the radio music and making clicking noises with her tongue. Neither one of us wanted to let go of the good feeling we were sharing. "You know so much about business, Gilda," I said. "You must have picked up more than you thought from watching your daddy."

She stopped rocking but didn't answer for a minute. Then she said, "I had to sneak around to learn the family business. My father wanted my brother to take over. My parents expected me to get married, have babies, and stay at home."

I was used to hearing sadness in Gilda's voice whenever she spoke about her family and the past but this time I heard resentment. There was anger in her bright eyes. "I had to beg and beg and beg my father to let me go to the university. For my brother it was assumed. Of course he would be educated. Of course he would run the company. But for Gilda, who was smarter than her stupid brother, my father had no dreams, only of grand babies.

"When my brother and I were children, we used to go with my father to his factory. Jakob always played. He liked sports. He wanted to run outside. Sometimes he would cry when my father made him come in to learn what was going on. For me there was no pleasure greater than watching the machines and the workers. I asked my father a thousand questions, and when he tired of answering them I would be very quiet, afraid that he would send me home. I would ask the workers all the questions my father wouldn't answer.

"I wanted to know everything: how the lipsticks could be so many colors; what made the powder so fluffy; why eyebrow pencil was different from regular pencil. I was a very curious little girl. Why? Why? Why? I drove my father crazy," Gilda said with a laugh. "He wanted my brother to work with him during the school holidays but Jakob was interested only in throwing a ball. 'Let me work, Papa,' I'd say, but he'd shake his head and tell me that it was not for a girl to do."

"What would he think about you now?" I asked.

"He would not be happy. But maybe, in time, he would become used to the idea that I am a businesswoman." She squeezed my hand quickly. "I want to ask you something, Hosanna."

"Go ahead."

"Should I tell David about my scar?"

"Are you thinking about showing it to him?"

"I think he might like to marry me one day."

"Do you want to marry him?"

"I don't know." Gilda sighed, and I sensed that there was something she wasn't revealing to me.

"Have you ever talked with him about what happened to you during the war?"

"We talked about it a little. He knows that my family died."

"If you get serious with him, then, yes, I would tell him. But wait a little while. You may meet someone you like better."

Gilda shook her head. "My uncle likes David. He wants me to marry him."

"Your uncle can't pick a husband for you," I said, feeling indignant.

Gilda smiled, then patted my hand. "Good-bye," she said, getting out of the car. She closed my door and without looking back began walking down the street.

I watched her for a moment. She passed an old woman who was lugging a grocery bag, and several boys, all wearing little beanies on their heads. Yarmulkes, Gilda called them. Gilda nodded to the boys as she passed them. She carried herself erectly. The boys turned and watched her after she'd gone. Of course they admire her, I thought. Gilda looked like one of those billboard women with the pretty faces and happy smiles, like one of those white girls from Inez or Houston, the ones I used to call ma'am. Her accent was so faint these days. Who could tell the difference between her and a regular white girl?

The following week I went out searching for a site in my area, since it would be easier for Gilda to be in a black neighborhood than for me to come and go in hers. There actually were a fair number of white folks in South Central, not to mention Mexicans, Japanese, and some of everybody else. The area had been all white before southern Negroes thronged there when the factories that began churning during the war beckoned them to the assembly lines. When I was a child in Inez, white people would give their maids hand-me-down clothes; here in Los Angeles they passed down their neighborhoods. Watts fit me just fine.

Gilda and I were still thinking small; our plan was to continue to mix the formula ourselves, using Fern, Winnie, and Opal to help us. What we needed most of all was a work space big enough for a long table and a big tub, where we could stir the lotion and pour it into bottles. There were several factories in the area; I passed them going back and forth to Braddock and some of the men in my church worked there. I thought about approaching the supervisors to see if they'd be willing to rent out some space on the weekends and in the evenings. The thing was, the neighborhood was mostly black but the factory owners were all white men. Gilda ended up talking to them but they turned us down.

A few months passed before we actually found something. We were still selling lotion during that time. I paid my landlady extra money, and she let us use the hall bathroom on Thursday, which was my day off, and on Saturday, which was Gilda's. But it was rough mixing and pouring alone.

What put sugar in those lonely weeks was the letters I got from Lonell. He couldn't write as sweetly as he talked and he sure couldn't spell, but every few days it was nice to go to the mailbox and read how much he missed me. I got the feeling that he wasn't doing much in Inez. He'd helped his daddy build one small house, a job he described as "pretty easy" but he didn't elaborate on it. My letters ran on and on about the business. Lonell's letters were filled with how much he missed me, how he couldn't get enough of my sweet kisses; he longed for us to be together. Reading them, I'd start missing my romantic boyfriend.

I marched all over Watts looking for space, but I kept running into dead ends. The funny thing was, the lotion was selling better than ever. We couldn't keep up with the demand because we didn't have a facility. I took tons of orders and then hedged on when I'd deliver, which isn't good business. People don't like to wait forever for what they've already paid for.

Sunday had gotten to be my biggest sales day because of my church sisters. I know my mama and daddy wouldn't have been too happy about me working on the Sabbath, but in the interest of commerce some sacrifices had to be made. I'd long since quit the choir, and if I could sit through an entire service once a month I was ahead of the game. Of course, I still said my prayers. But I guess I began to think about the Lord in a different way, to thank him more and beg him less.

Mooney's usually had emptied out a bit by the time I got there. One Sunday in early October I seated myself at a vacant table and was giving the waitress my order, already tasting that succulent pork barbecue I was craving, the sauce and juices, when I heard the sound of water.

"What's that noise?" I asked the girl, who was writing down my order.

"What noise?" She paused and listened for a second. "That's just Mooney in the kitchen hosing down the tubs."

"Tubs?" I said, and already I was standing, moving toward the sound.

"Where he washes off the meat. Hey, where you going? You still want your barbeque?"

I called over my shoulder. "I sure do."

If Jebediah P. Mooney was eating any of his own cooking, it didn't show. My mama would have said that he had more hair than butt, and she'd have been right. In fact there wasn't anything plentiful about Mooney, except what was bulging in his hip pocket, a fat wallet that was visibly outlined because he was so thin. A lot of people said that Jebediah

P. Mooney, world-class southern foods chef, was one of the richest colored men in Los Angeles. He owned two restaurants in South Central. As lucrative as his restaurants were, he was said to make even more money catering parties for the rich whites who lived in Beverly Hills and Hancock Park. Mooney could cook practically anything, a skill he'd inherited from his mother, who'd catered their way out of Mississippi, or so the story went. The word was that Mooney's mother had financed his first business, and now the old lady didn't do a thing but wipe barbeque sauce off her lips and belch.

But if Mooney was made of money, as people said, it sure wasn't showing anywhere other than in his billfold. His hair didn't appear to be combed. He was dressed like a stevedore, in dirty gray pants that hung low on his waist, and big brogan shoes that were run down at the heels. He resembled the hired help instead of the proprietor of a thriving business. Mooney was crouched down on the floor just outside the kitchen door. There were five big tubs of corrugated metal, the kind southerners use for washing clothes and kids. He was scrubbing one with a scouring pad, then hosing it out. There was a drain in the middle of the floor. Next to him was a small boy, no more than six, who was wiping another tub with a towel. Mooney glanced at the boy, smiled a little, and said, "You sure are doing a good job, son." He didn't realize I was there until I was standing right next to him.

"Honey, you're in the wrong place. Food's outside," he said. His voice matched the pad he was using, and he barely gave me a look. The boy, who favored his daddy, stopped drying and stared at me.

"Junior, you keep doing your job," Mooney said, and the boy started in rubbing again.

"Mr. Mooney, my name is Hosanna Clark and I've been wanting to meet you for the longest time, sir." He turned his head, picked up another tub, and began scrubbing. I wasn't sure he was listening. "I want to say that I admire you so much, all that you've accomplished. Your barbeque is the best I have ever eaten, and your sweet potato pies are out of this world. And sir . . ."

"You couldna ate all that much. You ain't that big."

Junior giggled, and his daddy smiled. A lot of times people thought I was younger than I really was. Mooney appeared to have a good ten or fifteen years on me.

"Oh, no, Mr. Mooney, I'll be—"

"What exactly is it you want? I done bought enough Girl Scout cookies to feed Africa. I contributed to 'bout fifty 'leven women's days. I bought the uniforms for the football team over at the high school. Now what is it?"

"Oh, I don't want money, Mr. Mooney. In fact, I want to give you some . . . money."

He put down his soapy pad, and I suddenly had his full attention. His sharp eyes lit up in a way that reminded me so much of me when money touched my palm. Suddenly I felt right at home. "You want to give me some money?"

"Yes. I do. I want to give you some rent."

"Oh, you want one of the apartments over on Imperial. You need to talk with—"

"No, I don't want to rent an apartment. I want to rent your kitchen space when you're not using it."

He quickly scanned me from my feet to the top of my head. "Little lady, I'm in the business of selling food. If I rent you my spot to sell your cooking I'd be a fool, now wouldn't I?"

"I wouldn't be cooking. I'd be manufacturing lotion." Mr. Mooney set his washtub down and stood up. He was only a few inches taller than I was. I spoke fast and used my hands to make my point, resting my fingers against his forearm. By the time I was finished, he knew Gilda's and my plans.

He appeared to be ruminating over my words for a few moments. Then he said, "I've heard about you. Couple of my waitresses have bought some lotion off you. Sounds like a good little business."

"Oh, it is, Mr. Mooney," I said quickly, "and it could be even better if we had our own place. We wouldn't get in your way. We'd work when you're closed."

"Monday is the only day I'm closed."

One day! One day wasn't enough to do what we had to do. Besides, neither Gilda nor I had Monday off. "What hours are you open?"

"Tuesday through Friday, we're open from eleven to nine o'clock. Saturday, from noon to nine. Sunday, from noon to six."

"You never take a break," I said, thinking aloud.

"Colored people don't get no breaks," the boy said. He looked up at his father.

"Colored people don't get no breaks," Mooney repeated. "You might as well learn that lesson early. Ain't nobody giving away nothing on this earth, especially to us. Everything I got I sweat to get it, and you can see me sweating to keep it." He peered at me. "You know anything about sweating, little girl?"

My words shot out like bicycles speeding toward the finish line. "Maybe we could work out a shift for us. Some weekdays we could come in from six to ten, or come evenings after you're through."

Mooney eyed me silently, studying the places on me that he'd overlooked. What he was thinking I couldn't tell. Maybe he was trying to figure out if I was serious, if he could trust me to do what I said. I wondered what he'd think if I told him that my partner was a white woman, but I decided to keep the rest of the story to myself.

"Now, we'd pay you rent in advance, and you'd find the place just like you left it."

Mooney began shaking his head. I opened my mouth to counter any argument he could muster, but he put his hand up to shush me. "Don't you ever keep quiet?" When I started to answer he shushed me again. "I got the health department to worry about, Miss Clark. You come in here with lotion. That's got chemicals in it. Any of those chemicals slosh up against a side of pork ribs and I've got big problems."

"But the food would be put away. We wouldn't be working anywhere near it."

"But anything could happen. Y'all could slip and fall in here, and then you'd want to sue me. Or suppose I come in one day, and my potato pies are missing. Who'd be answering for that? Miss Clark, I don't mean no harm, but really, I don't know you, now do I?"

"No sir, you don't."

Mooney stood up and extended his hand. His palms were hard leather. "I wish you well, one businessman to another."

"I understand," I said. Then I reached in my purse and pulled out a bottle of lotion. "Here's a little something for your mama."

He took the bottle and grinned. "Now, that's good," he said. "Gotta prime the pump. Thank you." He gave me a nod. The little boy didn't even look up.

I was surprised that when I got back to my seat my meal wasn't waiting. But not long after I sat down the waitress appeared with a plate piled high with succulent ribs, potato salad, collard greens, candied yams, macaroni and cheese, corn bread, and a huge slice of potato pie—much more food than I'd ordered. I stared at the steam rising from the ribs until the meat cooled and the fragrant vapor began ebbing away, like a future I couldn't quite grab onto. Feeling more disappointed than hungry, I signaled the waitress over and told her I'd take my dinner with me. When she took away my plate, I leaned back in my seat and contemplated my next move. I'd gone to churches, barbershops, beauty shops, restaurants—every business there was in the neighborhood that might offer Gilda and me the kind of room we needed. I'd even tried renting rooms, but the ones that were affordable didn't have private bathrooms or kitchen use.

Sitting at the table, I stared at my hands, softer now, thanks to Satin Skin Lotion. But my heart was getting harder and rougher the longer I stayed at Braddock. If I didn't get out of there soon, no cream in the world would be able to help me. The waitress appeared with my bag just at that moment and handed me a piece of paper. I figured it was the check and started digging around in my pocketbook for my wallet. Then I heard her say, "Everything is on the house." When I looked up she was giving me this "I know something" look. I read the note in my hand. It said, "I close up in a little while. Wait for me." There wasn't any signature but I knew who it was from, and that's when I opened up my paper bag, grabbed a rib, and started eating. I ordered a cup of coffee, loosened my belt, and had my own private picnic at the table.

By the time I was finished I was the only one in the place, except for the waitress, who was clearing the tables around me. I could hear glasses tinkling and silverware rattling. After a while, she disappeared in the back, and then I saw her passing by the window on the street, wearing a dress instead of a uniform. Only when she disappeared did I allow myself the excitement of believing that Mr. Mooney had changed his mind.

The waitress had turned off some of the lights. The restaurant was dim and empty. Without the people it seemed smaller, somehow, as though all the noise and talking, the laughter and lip smacking, expanded the place. Mooney was supposed to be one of the richest black men in Los Angeles, and this was his empire. White folks had buildings and factories; they had cities and governments. And what did we have? Barbeque. It was like my daddy always said: A rich colored man is a white man just getting by.

Mooney chose the chair next to mine, then pulled it around so that he was facing me. He had on a clean white shirt and dark pants. His hair was combed. He smelled like ribs and greens and barbecue sauce mixed with a musky, sweaty scent. His face wasn't handsome, but it was strong. His broad nose and full lips, his high forehead made him interesting-looking. Manly.

"Thank you for my dinner," I said. I could hear my heart.

"Glad to do it." Mooney looked at me and smiled before he spoke, smiled like he was trying to get to know me better in a hurry. He said, "I've been thinking about your offer, Miss Clark."

I said, "You have?" and hoped that my words didn't sound nervous. I'd been at ease with him in the kitchen. Now that he had nothing in his hands he made me feel tense.

He patted my hand and said, "I sure have."

"Well, did you change your mind?"

"Maybe. That depends on you, Miss Clark. What did you say your first name is?"

"Hosanna."

"Hosanna. That's what you say when you're real happy, ain't it? You a happy woman?"

"I try to be." I wasn't a fool. I thought about Lonell for a moment, and then I put him in another compartment in my mind.

I stared at Mooney. He was starting to look a lot younger to me.

Glancing down at his wedding band hand I didn't see a ring, but I knew that he was married. In the quiet of the room I could hear the boy's thin, childish voice talking to himself in the kitchen. It occurred to me that a lot of women had sat right where I was sitting, making the decision that I was mulling over. What did they do it for? I wondered. A dress? A couple of free dinners? Cash? I'd been to bed with a man before, well, two men, but I'd done it because I wanted to, not because I wanted something. If I was selling me—and I wasn't certain that I was—I damn sure wasn't selling cheap, and not fast either. Mr. Mooney may not have believed it, but he was dealing with a businesswoman. I wasn't striking some slam, bam, thank you ma'am deal. If he wanted me, Mooney was going to have to woo and pursue. And that would take time.

"I sure would like for somebody to make me happy. You're a good-looking woman, Hosanna."

I leaned closer to him and felt his stiff, scratchy shirt against the back of my hand. "I guess everybody is looking for that, Mr. Mooney. What would make me happy is to have a space for my business."

"And if I make you happy?"

I smiled, trying to act a little more sophisticated than I was feeling, trying not to think about Mooney's wife or hear his son's quiet movements. "Well, then maybe we can talk about me making you happy."

CHAPTER EIGHT

THE FOLLOWING THURSDAY morning at seven o'clock, Gilda and I met Mooney at his second restaurant, which was located on Central Avenue, about a mile from the main one. It was on the ground floor of a four-story building that stood between a small hotel and a nightclub called Brown Eyes. He'd had it for less than a year, and it was much smaller than the first place, with only ten tables in a room not large enough to do a split in. "This is mostly takeout," he explained, after he'd unlocked the front door.

I could tell that he was surprised to see Gilda with me, and that he was trying to figure out if she was a white woman or the lightest-skinned Creole he'd ever seen. But when Mooney heard Gilda speak he knew her accent didn't come from Louisiana. Seeing a white woman and a colored woman together in any capacity other than madam and maid was like looking at a dog walking a parakeet. Mooney had been in Los Angeles a lot longer than I had, but when I introduced him to Gilda, he hesitated for a moment before he cautiously shook her hand.

Gilda, of course, just smiled sweetly and said, "How do you do." What she thought of Mooney, I had no idea. She was her usual polite self. She stood back until we got inside the facility, then she strode around the restaurant before wandering into the kitchen. Mooney and I followed her and watched silently as she surveyed a big, old-fashioned sink, deep and wide enough for a whole pig to fit inside. She looked at the long wooden table in the middle of the room. Hanging on the walls were five pots, the same type I'd seen Mooney washing out the first time we met. There was an old cabinet large enough for us to store several hundred bottles of lotion. He had a large stove with a huge grill and hood. Across from it stood a large refrigerator and next to it a freezer. Gilda turned to me and said, "This will work very nicely." Then she looked at Mooney and asked, "What kind of food do you cook?"

"Southern food, ma'am. Fried chicken, collard greens, candied yams, barbecue—stuff like that."

I could see in her face that she wasn't familiar with the word "barbecue." "Pork," I said, "in a hot tomato sauce."

"You ain't never had barbeque?" Mooney said.

Gilda shook her head. "I do not eat the pork."

Mooney gave her a strange look, and then he said, "We got some beef barbecue, chicken, too. I'll just have to fix you some."

"How much do we have to pay him?" Gilda whispered when Mooney went around to the back of the restaurant. I looked out the window and saw a large truck with a variety of meats painted on the side. The driver began unloading sides of pork. With his helper he brought them into the kitchen and put them in the industrial refrigerator.

"We're still working that out," I said.

"How do you know we can afford it?"

"It won't be that much."

Gilda raised her eyebrows but didn't say anything. "Is he a friend of your family?"

"No."

"He wants to go to bed with you." It was a flat statement.

I didn't respond, and Gilda's eyes narrowed. She touched my hand. "We will keep looking."

"I've been everywhere. We've got orders that we can't even fill. If we don't get the lotion to the customers we'll lose them." I hadn't realized that my voice was getting louder until Gilda put her finger to her mouth. "Don't worry about Mooney. I'm not stupid."

Gilda's smile was faint. "You are a foolish baby," she said. "You do not know that the things you trade, you cannot get back."

I opened my mouth to answer her, to say something fast and flip. I heard Mooney coming back, so I just closed it. Gilda was extending a twenty-dollar bill toward him by the time he appeared. "It is enough?" she asked.

Mooney stared at the money for maybe half a second, then he glanced at me. "Don't worry about the money. Me and Hosanna have us an arrangement."

Hearing him speak, I felt somewhat less committed than I had previously, more like a child who's changed her mind about keeping a promise. I put my hands on my belly and pressed down hard, trying to rid myself of the feeling that worms were crawling around inside me.

"You are mistaken," Gilda said, in a voice that was louder than usual. "I handle all the money. I am the older one. She is the baby, not yet a woman." She stuck the bill out farther and didn't take her eyes off Mooney's.

"What you mean, she ain't a woman? How old are you, girl?"

"I'm . . ."

"Soon she will be eighteen," Gilda said, cutting me off.

"You ain't eighteen?" Mooney seemed to sink into himself. "I be damned." Then he peered first at Gilda, and then at me. He started chuckling to himself.

"She is the baby. I am the legal woman," Gilda said.

"And I'm the fool," Mooney said, still laughing.

"It is enough?"

Mooney took the money out of her hand. "That all depends on when you plan on giving me another one of these," he said.

"Every two weeks. We will use only a little water. The lights will stay off. When we are finished we will clean up. It is enough?"

"It's enough for now," Mooney said, folding the money inside his already bulging wallet. He looked at me. "I can tell that you gonna be a success. You already ruthless."

The plan was simple: Gilda and I would come to the restaurant four days a week at seven in the morning and leave at eleven, an hour before our noon shift at the hotel began. We'd store the lotion at Mooney's until it was time for us to deliver it. We were going to double, maybe even triple our business, save our money, and be out of Braddock in six months.

After church on Sundays, I still went to Mooney's first restaurant to sell. A few weeks after we started working out of his number-two spot I saw him through the window of his bigger place; he motioned me to come around the back. "How's it going?" he asked when I appeared.

"I'm doing fine, Mr. Mooney. How about you?"

"Working hard, that's about it." He gave me a long, hard gaze. "Say, you ain't really seventeen, are you?"

"I used to be."

Mooney grunted. "Look here, what's that woman's hold on you?"

I was confused for a minute, and then I understood, or at least I thought I did. "Gilda and I work together. We clean rooms at the Braddock Hotel."

"Uh-huh," he said, pondering my answer. "She ain't trying to put anything over on you, is she? She making you work for her?"

"No. We're in the business together. It was my idea."

"Your idea?" He gave me a long sideways look. "You gotta be careful out here. This ain't like back home. They got all kinds of strange people in Los Angeles. Try to use you, know what I mean?"

I shook my head, unsure of where he was heading.

"That woman ever try anything funny with you? You know what I'm talking about? Anything unnatural."

For a moment, I couldn't breathe. "We're businesswomen," I said.

Mooney's eyes got tight and small. "Uh-huh," he said. "Say, what kinda white woman is she?"

"She's Polish."

"She a Jew?"

I nodded.

"You gotta watch them out both your eyes. They love money more than life."

"She doesn't love it any more than I do," I said. "Or you either, from what I've heard."

Mooney's eyebrows shot up. "I'm not telling you something I heard. I'm telling you what I know. You be careful, little lady."

In the weeks and months that followed, Mooney kept sniffing around. Sometimes he'd be at the restaurant when we came in, and he'd make some excuse to get me alone. The boy was often with him, and Mooney always spoke to his kid in a nice, friendly voice, even when he did something wrong. Usually, he gave Junior a job to do that would keep him too busy to notice the interest his daddy had in me. Mooney gave me presents: a bottle of perfume one time, a bracelet another. He kept asking me when I was going to let him take me out, and I kept making excuses. One time I said, "But Mr. Mooney, you're married."

He said, "That ain't your problem."

I used to wonder why he allowed us to stay at all. For the first few weeks I'd walk into his place always expecting him to put Gilda and me out. But he never did. Sometimes I'd catch him watching the two of us, staring as though he couldn't quite figure out what he was seeing.

When we were setting up the legal framework of the business, Gilda and I went to meet with a lawyer, a man from her neighborhood named Mr. Wahlberg. She must have told him about me because he didn't look shocked when I walked in and sat down next to Gilda.

I paid attention. There was so much I didn't understand. The man handed me contracts with words in them I'd never seen before. Even though English was new to Gilda, she was way ahead of me. Gilda had been to college; she spoke Polish, German, French, and English. I'd gotten to tenth grade in a segregated country school in Texas. Scrubbing floors didn't reveal my shortcomings but trying to read a contract did. Sitting in that office, listening to big, important words that affected my future, I longed to be able to ask questions, but found myself letting Gilda do all the talking.

The day after the meeting, we were sitting in Our Room. "You must go back to school, Hosanna," Gilda said.

I just stared at her, and Gilda acted as though she didn't read the surprise on my face.

"You are a very bright woman. Very smart. You must learn to read and write better. Improve your mathematics. Otherwise, we cannot be partners."

My mouth fell wide open. How was I supposed to work two jobs and go to school?

Gilda waved her hand. "You say that we will be rich, yes? Do you want to be rich and ignorant? You will have a new house, new car, and not be able to read all the words in the newspaper. Is this the life for you?

"And what if something happens to me? Will you be able to meet with lawyers and accountants, get the taxes paid, follow all the laws? Maybe you will lose the business because of what you don't know. After all our hard work, is this what you want?"

"No."

"You need to learn about cosmetics. You say you want to make lipsticks, powders. Do you know the ingredients? You must learn chemistry. You must learn about the laws, taxes, unions."

"Unions?"

"For our hundreds of workers. You want to grow?"

"Yes." I nodded. "All right," I said. I would go to school, better myself. I liked the idea.

"Colored people need more education. David says that's their problem."

Their problem. Her tone was ice water tossed in my face. But she had her arm around my shoulder as she spoke, and when I looked into her eyes she was my friend who had my best interest at heart.

The night school was located about two miles from where I was living. It was a great big three-story brick building that took up the entire block. I had to go three nights a week from seven until nine o'clock. At first I was tired but it was a *good* tired. I loved school. Every time I strolled through those high, wide oak doors I could feel myself traveling toward a new place. There was no boulder I had to push out of my way. My path was lit by books. Guided by teachers of English, California history, and advanced arithmetic, I sometimes stumbled but I always managed to get back on course. The classes weren't large, not as many students as in one classroom in Inez. During my last year in high school there were sixty kids in a class that combined ninth and tenth grades. Back home when it rained, the teacher had to set out buckets and pans to catch the water that leaked through the roof. In warm weather we baked; when it was cold we froze. During cotton-picking season hardly anybody showed up, including the teacher. But even though it was too cold or too hot, not enough books, and too many kids, I always liked learning.

At my new school I enjoyed raising my hand and answering the teachers. Sometimes I'd get so excited that I'd holler out when they didn't call on me. Sitting in bed late at night, doing my problems and having them come out right was a new kind of joy. Writing essays made me salivate for more. It got so if I didn't have a scrub brush or a bottle of lotion in my hand, I was carrying a book. Gilda had already gotten me started reading but after a while I didn't have to keep running back and forth to the dictionary. Of course, I sold lotion to all the teachers and students in the school. But the sales were actually the gravy this time. My pork chop was knowledge, and the power that it gave me. Later, when I got my high school diploma in my hand and I was still hungry for more education, I had Gilda to thank. Because of her I wanted to send both my girls to college.

The first Sunday after I started classes I told Tuney that he should go back to school. "You have the GI Bill; you might as well use it," I said.

"High school diploma isn't going to help me," Tuney said, speaking like a man who can't see farther than his outstretched palm. "What I need to do is get some money to find a smart lawyer so we can get our land back."

As always when our stolen land was mentioned I felt a surge of anger making my body hot and tight inside. I thought of the lines on my parents' faces, the emptiness in my sister's eyes. But this time, instead of allowing my passions to become inflamed I sought a way to extinguish them. Maybe one day we'd recover what was stolen but there was no sense not making the best of the opportunities that were in front of us right now. Anger wasn't going to put one nickel in our pockets. Going to school would.

"You're always talking about how things are going to change. You have to be ready for change, Tuney," I said. "The more you know, the readier you are. You think you can just walk into the fire department? Boy, you're going to have to pass a test if you want to be a fireman. And it's going to be a hard test, because they don't want you there in the first place. I'm telling you, school is the answer."

I nagged my brother for weeks, and it paid off. When the new school term began, Tuney enrolled.

I got behind in my letters to Lonell after I started school. There were only so many hours in a day, and I had to prioritize. I didn't mean for him to come last, but that's the way it worked out. After a while I didn't think about him so much. The less I wrote to Lonell, the more letters he sent me. It got so I dreaded going to the mailbox. My mind just wasn't on romance, and that's all Lonell seemed to think about. I still had fond feelings for him, maybe I even loved him a little, but by the time he wrote that he wanted me to marry him, I'd already figured out that Lonell needed something to do with his life. He was trying to use me to fill up a big empty space.

I'd talked with Gilda about expanding our product lines to include other cosmetics, but she was cautious. She kept telling me that we should wait until we were more established, but I couldn't sit still. There was a Negro pharmacist who went to my church. One Sunday after services we got to talking, and I ended up paying him some money to create a face powder for colored women. Mr. Epps owned a little drugstore in Watts; he told me it would take him a few weeks to come up with something that worked. Every Friday I went to see him to get a progress report. It was on one of these visits that he told me how to make lipstick.

Mr. Mooney looked at me strangely the morning I asked him if I could have the discarded fat from his ribs, but he gave me two bucketsful. The next day I arrived at his second restaurant before the sun came out. I lit two of the pilots on his stove and put a heavy iron skillet on each. Then I melted the fat in each pan, cooled it, then dumped it first through a sieve, then through cheesecloth. I pressed out all the lumps. I used one food color, a vivid red, and I poured it into the fat and stirred until my arm got tired. I spooned the mixture into some little molds and let them set in the refrigerator. When the concoction had hardened, I removed it from the molds and stuck each on a circular base, slightly smaller than a dime, that had a thin plastic prong jutting up in the middle. A white plastic top covered each one. They weren't exactly lipsticks, because they didn't swivel up and down. But they did the same job. I took one into the bathroom, stood in front of the mirror, and applied that greasy, porky lipstick to my own lips.

I don't know how long I stood there smiling at myself. I was wearing my hair rolled under. Raking my fingers through the tight pageboy, I loosened the curl. When I took another look, my whole face seemed softer. *I'm pretty.* I didn't say the words aloud, but I felt them.

Gilda asked me what ingredients I'd used when I showed her our new product later that day. She put some on her lips and shook her head. "I can taste the meat," she said. "I can smell it, too."

"That's okay," I said.

She looked at me as though I'd lost my mind. "Who wants lips that smell like food?"

"Girl, you'd be surprised."

"You put in nothing to preserve it. They can become moldy."

"How long will they last?"

"Maybe three days."

"How about if they're in the refrigerator?"

Gilda pondered this. "A week. Maybe two."

"Two weeks," I repeated. "I'll only sell it to people with refrigerators, and I'll tell them it only lasts for two weeks."

"You cannot sell this," Gilda said.

"I've been working all night. Now, the next time we can put in the missing ingredient but I'm selling all of this."

The ladies of the evening who hung around Central near the clubs were some of my biggest lotion customers. They bought the lipstick for a quarter apiece, even with my warning. They stored them in the refrigerator at the hotel where they took their clients. And they came back for more, too.

Gilda and I sat down one day in mid-February and decided that Braddock wouldn't have us for another spring. She was still going out with David every Sunday. Mostly they went to the movies or to museums. He bought her lots of presents—books, candy, scarves, and costume jewelry—and I know these things made her happy. But sometimes I wondered if *he* did. She told me once that they had argued when she didn't agree with something he said, and that by the end of the evening he wasn't speaking to her. Sometimes she would talk about Tibor, but when I asked her if she still liked David, she said, "Of course I do."

Even after I'd bought my car I continued to use the bus to get back and forth to work. From the bus stop to the house where I rented a room was a two-block walk. My steps were high and light that late winter day when I passed the familiar small bungalows with neat lawns and bougainvillea. I'd never seen bougainvillea before I moved to Los Angeles, and the colors captivated me. I stopped to gaze at the blossoms covering a high stucco wall that served as a barrier between the house and street. It was almost March, but no matter what the season, I could depend on seeing the deep violet, pink, gold, and white blooms as they climbed higher and higher.

I had just passed the wall when I smelled something burning, heard shouting and screaming. Down the street dark smoke was billowing out of the roof of a white house. As I got closer I could see flames exploding from the front window. Standing along the sidewalk, an old woman was waving her hands in the air and screaming. A large man grasped her by her upper arms. Several people were trying to calm her. "My grandbabies is in there," she said over and over again, trying to break loose.

A man suddenly staggered out the front door. He was holding two children under his arms. His face and hairline were singed, and the skin on his hand was bubbling. I wasn't the only one who gasped. He gently placed the boy and girl on the sidewalk. Neither child appeared burned. The little boy was coughing and crying. His sister wasn't moving much and didn't make a sound.

The grandmother pulled away from the man's grip and rushed to the children, hugging the boy to her, then shaking the girl. "Speak to Grandma, baby!" she said. She turned around. "Where's the firemen?" A low grumbling traveled from one end of the growing crowd to the other, getting louder and louder as it moved, until finally it was a shout. I heard someone say that a neighbor had called the fire department and an ambulance nearly twenty minutes earlier. Nobody heard sirens for another fifteen minutes. The entire building was a flaming torch by the time the five white firemen climbed down from their truck.

"These children were inside. Might have smoke inhalation," one of the men said to the one who seemed to be in charge. "The boy seems okay. The little girl may be in shock."

The fireman glanced at the colored man as though he was thinking about swatting him away. "You a doctor?" he asked. He didn't wait for an answer. "We'll do our jobs, okay, buddy?" Then he turned to the crowd and said, "Everybody stand back."

The man's shoulders moved up and down really fast, and his face appeared to have darkened. When he spoke again his voice was like a gunshot. "If you were doing your jobs it wouldn't have taken you thirty goddamn minutes to get here."

Somebody in the crowd said, "Yeah, that's right." And then other people began voicing their agreement. The fireman looked around him. There were a lot of men on the street.

"Would you just help my grandbabies and put out the fire," the old woman cried.

"Yes, ma'am," he said, his voice softer, more humble. He called over two others, and they carried the children to their truck.

The entire community was upset. Firemen had been late arriving to the scene of burning buildings in our neighborhood before. Too often. "This ain't down south," people said.

"We need some colored firemen."

"I carried a gun for Uncle Sam. You mean to say I can't carry a fire hose?"

The clamor spread throughout South Central, and the chant was taken up at Urban League and NAACP meetings. "We want some Negro firemen!" *The California Eagle* did an editorial about Los Angeles's segregated fire department. Sometimes, after I'd finished my homework and I was pleased with my row of correct numbers, the way my words came together in my essays, I would lie in bed and think about my beautiful, intelligent brother. His vocabulary had grown since he'd been going to school, and the way he spoke had changed. He, too, sounded "proper." Why shouldn't he be able to put out fires and get paid the same money as white men? How long were we supposed to wait for what we deserved?

CHAPTER NINE

IN ORDER NOT to call attention to ourselves, Gilda and I had designated two separate days one week apart as our individual "Giving Notice Day." We decided that she should go first. Right before the appointed hour Gilda and I met in Our Room. "I am ready," she said. I watched as she marched down the hall to Mr. Weinstock's office.

In ten minutes she came back smiling. I was waiting for her at the door. "How'd it go?"

"He is very sad to see me leave," she said solemnly, and then we both burst out laughing. "I said that I had found another job, at a dress factory, that paid more and that a week from today would be my last day. He said that would be a wonderful opportunity for me." We laughed. "I also told him that my uncle was very upset that I had to travel far, so please not to mention the new job to him."

The following week, in the middle of March, I knocked on Mr. Weinstock's door. When he saw me he said, "I'm very busy, Hosanna. What do you want?"

"This won't take long," I said. Inside I was gloating. "I wanted to let you know that next Wednesday is my last day."

Ole Sweat and Farts gave a start. "You too? Today's Gilda's last day."

"It is? Oh, yes, I believe she did mention that to me," I said, with as much innocence as I could muster.

"Good luck to you, Hosanna." He nodded quickly and then looked away.

Something told me that Mr. Weinstock was so sure that I was leaving one mop for another, so sure that my life was just going to be a series of floors to scrub and windows to wash that he didn't even need to ask me where I was going.

"I'm going to have my own business," I said, my voice sounding loud and high in the silence of Mr. Weinstock's office.

He looked at me then. "What's that you say?"

"I'm going to be rich."

There was amusement in his eyes. "Rich? You?"

"Yes, me." I spoke so viciously that Mr. Weinstock reared back in his seat. "We're going to be rich."

I wanted to put my hands around his throat and shake him until he believed me. I wanted to strangle him just as much as I wanted to kill the Hagertys.

Weinstock leaned forward, and now there was interest in his eyes. "What 'we'?" he asked.

I opened my mouth, then closed it, tasting my own stupidity.

Mr. Weinstock waited; his eyes were sharpened razor blades. "How about you just make today your last day? How about that?"

On the way back to Our Room I passed Brewster. "How ya doin', Hosanna?" Then he must have read my face. "What's wrong?"

"I just got fired."

He turned bright red. "Why, that miserable old . . ."

I waved my hand. "Don't worry about it. I was going to quit anyway. So long, Brewster."

"Well, gee. So long, Hosanna." He stood there looking uncomfortable. I thought about how he'd loaned me the money I needed to get started in business. He'd been surprised when I paid it back so quickly. Brewster was all right with me. He grabbed me in a quick good-bye hug. "You take care of yourself, hear?"

I nodded.

Back in the room, Gilda was waiting for me. I just looked at her, not speaking. She knew that something was wrong. "Tell me what happened," she said.

"He fired me," I said.

Gilda stared at me without blinking. "How can he fire you? You quit."

For the first time in a long time I held back from Gilda. I didn't want to let her know how foolish I had been to brag about my glorious future.

So I just said, "I don't know. When I told him that I was leaving in a week he told me to go today."

Gilda looked at me and saw how devastated I was. She was quiet for a while, then she walked over to me and put her arm around my shoulder. "When I was in the camps I would say poems and tell myself pieces of great books. This kept me sane. I would also say this: 'One day they will be sorry. I will be rich and beautiful and they will be sorry.' " She looked at me.

"He'll be sorry," I said. "One day I'll be rich and beautiful and he'll be sorry."

"Yes?"

I smiled. "Yes."

CHAPTER TEN

ONCE I RECOVERED from the shock of being forced to leave Braddock earlier than I'd planned, I saw it as the blessing that it was. I now had an extra week to help Gilda get things in order. There was more time to study for the finals that were coming up, and to figure out how to discourage Lonell without hurting his feelings.

My brother said, "You better tell that boy something."

Tuney was used to breaking up with people. He had married Rosalee, and in no time they'd split up and he was back to courting. I knew that I should officially quit Lonell, but I didn't want to do something so final. Suppose I was just going through a fickle period? Why couldn't Lonell just figure out that I needed some breathing room? "Some people just ain't that bright," Tuney said.

Since I couldn't resolve the issue of my lopsided romance, I put it out of my mind. That was easy enough to do since there was so much else crowded in there. At long last Mr. Epps had come up with a winning face powder dark enough to sell to medium-brown-skinned women like me. As soon as I picked up the first batch from him I went into Mr. Epps's bathroom and dusted some on my face. Then I applied Hot Sauce Red lipstick. When I stepped back into his office Mr. Epps let out a long wolf whistle. "Well, look at you," he said.

I got him started working on both a darker and a lighter shade. While he was creating new colors, I wanted to mass-produce the first powder and begin selling it immediately. Of course, I needed new containers, which called for a design. I thought that Gilda and I could come up with one if we had a spare moment.

Because my bootleg lipstick had been such a big seller, Gilda had been researching ways that we could produce a similar product, only minus the pork and with FDA approval. It was easy enough to find out the ingredients for lipstick. Where and how to manufacture it was a bigger problem. The kitchen in Mooney's restaurant wouldn't work. Gilda was looking into paying a jobber, a firm that manufactured products for established cosmetics companies, to produce a low-cost brand for us that we would sell. We didn't have the money to lease space and equipment to do it ourselves. But one day soon, money wouldn't be a problem.

Three days after we left Braddock I was sitting in the reception area of the lawyer's office waiting for Gilda to arrive. Two weeks earlier she and I had met at Mr. Wahlberg's office and gone over everything we wanted included in our partnership contract. The week before we'd signed the papers. Today we were picking up the notarized copies, which Mr. Wahlberg had had bound.

Lawyers and legal documents were all new territory for me. In Inez, colored folks met their lawyers in jail. Where I came from, when marriages fell apart, men walked out without so much as saying good-bye, let alone signing anything. When your daddy died, there wasn't anything to inherit, except maybe his endurance.

Mr. Wahlberg didn't appear to be very prosperous. The room I sat in was dreary and dimly lit, the air heavy and stale, and the blinds were covered with a thick coat of dust. Mr. Weinstock would have had somebody's head if he'd seen anything like it on the windows at Braddock. I glanced at the clock on the wall and felt a trembling in my belly knowing that in a few minutes Gilda and I were going to receive the completed documents that would validate our company. We'd already come up with a new schedule for working at Mooney's, and a plan for getting our own space within six months. And when Gilda arrived from the bank she'd be carrying enough money to pay for our first batch of lipsticks. I'd already sold most of that order.

From time to time I'd catch Wahlberg's secretary staring at me. Her eyes were the color of dingy snow and just as cold. When I returned her gaze she glanced away quickly, as though she'd been caught going through the pages of *Ripley's Believe It or Not!* and enjoying the freaks too much. Get used to us, I thought smugly. Outside her door there was an entire world of colored oddities: big-boned black girls, fresh from Mississippi, intent not on being a maid but on portraying one in the movies. There was a new Mooney being born every minute, men who'd put their days of "yas-suh, boss," behind them and who were going after a piece of the good life. Not five miles from where I lived, colored people had their own insurance company, housed in a building that was shiny and new. All of us had come to Los Angeles looking for more than lemon trees and sunshine. Tuney had put in an application to the fire department, and when he was turned down, he put in another one. When that one came back he went down to the headquarters and demanded a meeting with the head of personnel. They wouldn't see him, of course, but he took off a day of work and just sat in the office. He said he wasn't going to stop trying, that sooner or later he'd be the first. And I told him he was right.

Our appointment had been for two o'clock. I waited until five o'-clock, when the office closed. On his way out, Mr. Wahlberg handed me my copy of the documents. He told me he would mail one to Gilda and keep another copy for his files. We'd already paid him for his work. "I don't know what happened to Gilda," I said.

"Perhaps she will contact you at your home."

I nodded.

The lawyer's office was located in the Fairfax district, not too far from where I'd dropped Gilda off several times before. As I walked back to my car I passed a group of men. Bearded and wearing yarmulkes, they had long shawls draped across their shoulders, and were talking in a language I'd never heard before. These were Gilda's people; if she'd been here she might have been able to tell me what they were saying. Without her, they felt foreign to me, strange.

Sitting in the car, I tried to imagine what type of emergency would keep her away. Sickness? Accident? Death in the family? I even drove one block past where I used to drop her off, hoping I might see her. But I didn't, and after a while it didn't make sense to be waiting for someone who wasn't there. There was no use in getting upset. I'd see Gilda tomorrow, and she would explain everything.

I had a hard time sleeping that night and woke up hours before I usually did. As soon as I got to Mooney's, I took down the tubs and started mixing. I had half my mind on what I was doing and the other half on the clock. I listened for buses as they passed, hoping that Gilda would soon be walking in the door. But she didn't come. And she didn't come the next day or the next. Each day that passed I tried to stave off the panic that coated my throat by making excuses for her: she had to go out of town suddenly; she was sick. Each day I grew a little crazier and more afraid. Was she in a hospital somewhere? Was she dead? Tuney told me not to worry but I was very frightened. We'd always glossed over the fact that I had to remain a secret in her life. She could traverse my borders but I wasn't allowed to cross hers.

It came to me after a week that her uncle must have found out about the business. I refused to believe that she was sick or dead. Gilda was waiting until the coast was clear. I convinced myself that it would be only a matter of days before she appeared, and once she did, life would resume the way we'd planned. We. I wasn't ready to be an I, to be alone with the business. It was our company, Gilda's and mine. But I was afraid.

I kept to the schedule Gilda and I had set for ourselves. Fern, Winnie, and Opal helped. They asked about Gilda, of course, and I said she'd gone on a trip. Two weeks of pouring, stirring, lifting, labeling went by in a blur. If anyone had asked me how I spent each day, I would have said, "Waiting." I wasn't conscious of the work, of the cycle of days that began and ended with the same question: Where is Gilda? At night I sat in a tub of hot water, glad for aching muscles, glad to feel something other than numb.

It was at the end of the second week, when early one Friday morning Mooney came looking for his twenty dollars, and I allowed myself to face my deepest apprehensions. Where was the money Gilda had been bringing from the bank?

"Mighty funny, Gilda going off for so long right when you're supposed to be getting started," Mooney said after I told him I didn't have his rent.

He was standing too close to me, as he always did whenever we were alone. Only when Gilda was around did he keep his distance. His fear of her was understandable. He'd come from a place where a white woman's word—lie or truth—could result in a colored man's nightmare.

I could feel the heat of him. "If you would be a little nice to me, girl, maybe you wouldn't have to be paying no twenty dollars."

I stepped away from him. "Mr. Mooney, I'll get you your money."

I went to the bank that afternoon. Standing in the line, I was distracted and tense. I didn't want to think about Mooney, but I couldn't ignore what might turn into a big problem. Without Gilda's "protection," I'd have to deal with him. If things turned ugly, where could I go to make the lotion? For that matter, how would I make it without Gilda running interference? She'd always dealt with the suppliers. What would they say when they saw me?

When I finally got to the teller's window, I handed the woman my withdrawal slip and my passbook. She disappeared for a few minutes, and when she came back I could see that she had no money in her hand. She passed everything back to me. "The account is closed," she said. She had on heavy perfume that smelled like overripe gardenias. My head began aching, and I felt myself getting dizzy.

An old woman behind me said, "You all right, dearie?"

I had just enough breath in me to say to the teller, "There must be some mistake, miss."

"There's no mistake. Next."

The manager seemed surprised when he discovered me waiting for him in his cubicle. I hadn't seen him since the day Gilda and I opened the account. He still wouldn't look me in my eyes when I spoke to him, even though he was polite and professional.

"Where is the other lady?" he asked, his loose jowls shaking.

"I'm the one in front of you. Speak to me," I said, and his eyes popped wide open.

At last, he showed me the records and signature.

When I left Los Angeles National there were two facts I plucked from the wreckage: there was no money in my account; and I no longer had a partner.

I don't remember getting in the car after I left the bank. The streets blended into each other. How I managed to get home is a mystery. I guess I made the right turns and stops because the next thing I knew I was in front of my rooming house. I turned off the motor and sat in the car, my head pounding. I felt as though I'd been tossed like garbage. I had helped her, trusted her. We were friends. How could she have done this to me?

The betrayal was unbearable. And I was suddenly overcome with loneliness. Gilda was my only girlfriend. Whenever I learned something interesting at school, I always told Gilda. If I read a good book, I shared it with her. The lonelier I felt, the angrier I became with Gilda and with myself. I should have known better than to trust a cracker. And that's all Gilda was: a cracker with an accent. A goddamn Jew.

I examined the word that had exploded out of my mind: Jew. What my mind had spit out had been all around me for so long. Didn't everybody get "jewed" out of money at some time? Wasn't every storekeeper a cheap Jew? Now I had my very own no-good dirty Jew story about the woman who stole from me.

As the days passed, my anger fueled me. I imagined what I'd do if I ever saw Gilda again. I wanted to kill her. Rage was like a virus that worked its way into my system. I couldn't sleep. I couldn't eat. I had to work but I felt tired all the time. It was the same sick feeling I'd had when Lucille was raped and our land stolen. Everything in my body felt shut down. As I stirred the lotion and washed the tub out all alone, I thought about the old stories; Daniel in the lion's den; David in the valley.

One day I went to Mr. Wahlberg's office. He looked surprised to see me. "Miss Clark, what can I do for you?"

I was seated in the reception area, and he had just emerged from his office. I stood up in order to follow him back. As soon as I did, he walked over to me.

"I still haven't heard from Gilda. I misplaced her address. Would you give it to me?" I was barely breathing.

Mr. Wahlberg looked surprised. "It's on the contract."

I felt very foolish. I'd never even noticed it. Mr. Walhberg wrote down the address on a slip of paper and handed it to me. "Good luck," he said.

I drove to Gilda's street and parked in front of her house. After I turned off the ignition I sat still, trying to collect my thoughts. I told myself to get out, walk up the steps, find her apartment, and get my money. But when I got out of the car the people on the street stared at me. I was very conscious of being the only black person around. Two older women were walking toward me. They seemed almost angry to see me, as though I'd wronged them in some way.

"Who are you working for?" one asked in a loud voice.

I shook my head, which had begun to throb. Suddenly a man appeared. He didn't take his eyes off me. I felt very frightened and very alone. I was only a few feet from Gilda's building, but I turned around, got back into my car, and drove away.

I was working early one morning toward the end of April when I heard a tapping on the door. I'd been expecting Mooney, because his payday had rolled around again. But Mooney had a key; he never knocked. I went to the window and looked out, then I opened the door. "Brewster! What are you doing here?"

"Hi ya doin', Hosanna," he said, looking to his right and left and behind him in a way that let me know he was nervous being in my part of the city.

He stepped inside, and I closed the door, leading him into the kitchen. We sat on the counter. Brewster smelled like the early morning beer he'd already drunk. "How did you know where I was?"

"Gilda told me."

My whole body jerked. "Where is she?" My thoughts were coming so fast I could barely get them out.

"Two days ago she came to the hotel and told me to give you this." He reached in his pocket and handed me an envelope. He looked around. "Is this where you work now?"

I nodded. "Did she say anything to you?" I asked.

"No. She seemed to be in a hurry. Her husband was with her. Did you know that she got married?"

"No."

"I sure miss you girls," he said with so much sincerity that I was touched. I gave his arm a quick pat. "I have to go," he said, "or Weinstock will be screaming. Take care of yourself, Hosanna."

"You do the same."

By the time Brewster had closed the door I had the letter out.

My Dear Hosanna,

*I am so sorry we must part in this way. The night before I was
to meet you at Mr. Wahlberg's office, my uncle came to me. He had
the bank book in his hand and demanded to know where the money
had come from. Hosanna, I lied to my uncle and told him that the
guests at the hotel had given me tips. He knew better, because Mr.
Weinstock had spoken with him. I know now what you told Mr. Weinstock to make him fire you. When you said you were going into
business he recalled Hattie's words and figured out everything. He
went to my uncle and told him what he thought. You remember that
my uncle rents the apartment from Mr. Weinstock's brother?
Hosanna, my uncle said if I continue with you he will not speak to
me, nor will he allow his children to have anything to do with me.
He and his wife haven't been kind to me but he is my father's brother,
and without him and his children, I am alone in this world. I cannot
face that, my friend. I am not as strong as you.*

*I have married David. My uncle says I will be happy. He speaks
of happiness as if it is a bus that will stop at the corner where I am
waiting and pick me up. You have given me happiness, Hosanna, and
I am sorry to cause you this pain.*

*I have never met anyone like you, and I pray that you won't
think unkindly of me. I hope that we will meet again. I have enclosed
a check for $1500.00 for you, also, the names, addresses, and phone
numbers of the suppliers, and the formula for the lotion. You can still
do the business and make it a big success. It was your idea from the
start. God bless you, my dear friend.*

Gilda

I held up the check for fifteen hundred dollars. It was drawn against
our joint account. How could she write me a check if the account was
closed? What I held in my hand was a worthless piece of paper. Standing in the kitchen alone with the early morning rays of sun filtering
through the window, I felt stripped down and mud-caked, as my daddy
used to say. What kind of game was Gilda playing? God, I hated her, and
I hated myself for ever having been dependent upon her. I wanted to be

strong, but I couldn't stop the feeling of panic that suddenly overtook me. I felt as though half my power was gone. Sure, I could sell anything I put my hands on, but there were lawyers, taxes, suppliers—how was I supposed to do everything and pay rent, too? I already owed Mooney forty dollars that I didn't have.

Confusion and fear pelted down on me like hail, chilling my body, stinging my heart. I tried to think rationally but my tears wouldn't wait for me to collect my thoughts. I hadn't had a good honest cry since the first night I spent in Los Angeles when homesickness wrapped itself around me like a snake in a bad dream.

My head was bowed down, my eyes running over with tears when I heard Mooney's voice. "What's the matter, sugar? Somebody bothering you?" He was standing in the doorway. He reminded me of my daddy, the way he stood, so stiff-legged and strong. My daddy didn't like to see his "womenfolk" sad, and he'd let you know in a minute that whatever the problem was, he would take care of it. Mooney even sounded like my father, not his voice exactly, more like the tone he used.

I shook my head.

Took Mooney only seconds before he was by my side. "Then what you cryin' for?"

I hunched my shoulders, which didn't stop the tears from flowing and didn't stop Mooney.

"Girl, you ain't got nothing to boo-hoo about. You a smart, ruthless businesswoman, ain't you?"

My sudden wails must have startled the man. He grabbed my shoulders and pulled me into his chest. I held onto him until his shirt was as wet as my face. When I stopped sobbing and shaking, he pulled me away from him, held me by my wrists, and said, "Now, lookahere. What happened?"

"Gilda left, and she took all the money," I said, my voice loud and strident. "We were supposed to meet at the lawyer's office to pick up our partnership papers but she never came. I haven't seen her in . . ." I couldn't even remember how long it had been, whether days or weeks. "I don't understand. I don't understand. I went to the bank yesterday and the account was closed. Today a man we used to work with brought me a letter and a check from her. My share. Only it's worthless. Why would she do this? Why would she steal from me? I've been nothing but good to her. I was her friend. Why would she do this? Why? Why? Why?" I began to get hysterical, my sobs were loud and I couldn't tone them down.

When I finally got quiet Mooney said, "So, what you gone do now, Hosanna, find you another job cleaning up somewhere?" His question was a surprise snowball smacked in my face.

My rage cut right through the last sob I had in me. "I'm never cleaning up for anybody ever."

"You sure don't talk like no crybaby." There was nothing in Mooney's expression to indicate that he cared one way or the other about my answer. Then he squeezed my wrists. "Listen, when you're in business, you got to ride the waves, especially if you're colored. Especially if you're a colored woman. Ain't but one person you can count on in this life, and that's you. You sure can't count on nobody white. You shoulda known better. All right, so Miss Gilda pulled out. Good. More money for you."

I stared at him.

"Yeah, that's the way you gotta look at it. More work, and more profit for you."

"But the money, my money, is gone."

Mooney tilted his head, pursed his lips, and sucked on his teeth. "Yeah, that's a hard row. But you gone hafta hoe it anyway. Ain't no way you can get that money back. Did the account require two signatures?"

"Either/or."

Mooney whistled. "Girl, kiss it good-bye and make you some more. Ain't no judge gone give you that money. Gilda worked you over, sugar. And you're just going to have to start again. Won't be the first time it happened. Won't be the last. You're young. You say you all had a contract?"

I went to my purse, pulled out the copy, and gave it to Mooney, who scanned it quickly before handing it back. "Looks legal all right. Put this somewhere safe," he said.

"Why?"

"Because you never know. Another thing: Take the check to the bank. Get them to mark 'insufficient funds' on the back of it. Keep that check

with the contract. You still got a friend," Mooney said. He moved his
hands up my arm until he was holding my shoulder and we were standing close.

I can't say he made me. We moved into each other. Next thing I
knew we were kissing, his lips softer than I thought they'd be, and spicy
hot. That first kiss was a blindfolded dive into waters that were deeper
than I'd expected. His lips pulled me into the current, and when I floated
free I was gasping for air.

"Ain't gone force nothing on you," he whispered in my ear. "Not
that type of man. What I want, I want to want me back, see?"

I nodded. My mind was treading water, trying to think and stay above
the surface at the same time. Salvation was a rock, surrounded by waves,
and I was leaning against it. Old folks say your life flashes before you
when you're about to die. My mama's face broke through choppy waters;
her hands reached out to pull me to shore. I pushed Mooney away. "No.
I can't do this."

He let me go. I felt saved but not safe. Maybe it was because Mooney's
lips were softer and hotter than I'd expected, or maybe it was the way he
held me. Even as he released me I felt the pull of the current.

"Don't worry about the money you owe me. I can wait," he said.
"Ask for help if you need it."

My brain started clicking, lining up all the things I had to do. I
looked at Mooney. If he wanted to help me, I'd give him a chance. "I need
money for a suit," I said. "Can you loan me some? I have to meet with
people, all the people Gilda used to see."

He nodded. "What do you think a nice suit will cost?"

I'd never bought one before. I shrugged. Mooney reached in his back
pocket and pulled out his wallet. He handed me thirty dollars. "This
ought to do it. Buy something navy. Navy blue is a business color."

I nodded.

"Hosanna, you ain't got time to be mad at that woman or yourself,
otherwise you're gonna find yourself pushing another broom. You were
breathing and moving across this earth before you met Gilda, and you're
still living now that's she gone. A grudge ain't nothing but a brake; it'll
stop you every time."

The next day I went to the bank. When I left I had a check marked "insufficient funds" and a letter telling me that the account had been closed. Later that day I went shopping for a navy blue suit, a white blouse, a pair of navy shoes, and a bag to match. I tried on suit after suit. The jackets always looked great, but the skirts didn't fit properly. I had the same problem with all my slim skirts and dresses: they cut too tight across the butt, even when the waist and every other part fit. Finally I went to a store and found a suit that had a skirt that fit a little better, although it was still snug. I wanted my clothes to caress my body the way they did the ladies I saw in magazines, or the mannequins in the department store windows. All the skirts I bought seemed made for flat behinds, not a round, high bottom like mine—most colored women's. But I bought the suit. At least it had a long jacket.

But I couldn't find any Red Fox stockings. That was cause for panic. Red Fox was the only color a brown-skinned colored woman could find that was even close to her skin. The next shade down was a pale pinkish brown they called nude that made my legs look ashy. The next shade up was black. I bought black.

Later that afternoon, with my hair in a French twist and wearing my businesswoman's outfit, I went to see Mr. Reed, who sold the ingredients for the lotion. He was a plump, rosy man with a worried air. His secretary brought me into his office, and when he saw me come in, he stood up. But I could tell that his rising was an involuntary act, because when I was in front of him he was so nervous and flustered he didn't know what to do. "Have a seat," I finally said, and he sat down.

"Mr. Reed, Gilda got married and she's not in the business anymore. You'll be dealing with me from now on," I said.

At my next stop, I said the same thing to the man who ran the place that manufactured our lipsticks. His eyes nearly popped out of his head, too, when he saw me, but I didn't pay that any mind. Both he and Reed listened to what I had to say. They smiled and shook my hand and stood up when I left.

Two days later I got letters from both of them withdrawing the credit they'd extended to Gilda. Without a white partner, the business would be on a cash-only basis.

"But I don't have any cash," I lamented to Mooney. "Do you think the bank would loan me some money?"

Mooney laughed out loud. "Which bank? Los Angeles National? Listen, you see how packed my place is. I went to them for a loan. My credit was clean as the Board of Health. They turned me down flat. And the colored bank don't do business loans." He shook his head.

"So what am I supposed to do? I've got orders but I have to have the supplies to fill them. I don't have money, and the suppliers won't give me credit."

"Better ask your mama."

"I send my mother money."

"Girl, you need a sponsor," Mooney said.

There was that same current pulling me back into deep water. "Mooney," I said with a sigh, "don't take advantage of me when I'm down."

"That's the only time to take advantage," he said. "How you think I got started in business, huh?"

"I don't know."

"I took advantage." He chuckled. "My mama started off cooking for one family in Mississippi, the Hurds. They owned a lot of land in the Delta. Cotton-rich crackers, that's what they were. Jackson Hurd was a real son of a bitch, pardon my language, and his boy was worse. They were political, and they'd done so many dirty deals between them that they had all kinds of friends and twice as many enemies. More than one man in the county would have paid money to see Jackson Hurd dead and buried. And I knew that, see, because all the time I was helping Mama cook, I kept my ears open, and I looked when they didn't think I was paying attention. A colored man's always got to pay attention if he wants to get ahead, and sometimes if he wants to stay alive. And that goes double for a colored woman.

"Anyway, the Hurds were backing Lemuel Stewart for governor; this was about ten years ago. The Augustines were another big property family down there. There was bad blood between them and the Hurds. They were for Harry Dubonnet. Didn't make me no difference which one became governor 'cause wasn't neither one of them gonna do a colored man any good. I was listening to Jackson and his boy talking one night while I was cleaning up after Mama, and I found out that whoever backed the winning man stood to make a lot of money off some roads that were going to be built. If Dubonnet got in, the state would buy land from the Augustines. If Stewart won, the state would buy Hurd land. All that would have been useless information if I hadn't had a photograph of Lemuel Stewart doing something he didn't have any business doing. You ever hear of cocaine, Hosanna?"

I nodded.

"You'd be surprised what goes on in these little southern towns. Anyway, Lemuel Stewart had him a cocaine habit. I was twenty-two years old, and I told Mama to pack up everything, because we were moving to California with a lot of money in our pockets. See, whenever I put out trash for white folks I always went through it. I learned a long time ago that rich white folks throw away a lot of things that are still useful. The most useful thing I'd ever found in the Hurd trash can was a picture of Lemuel Stewart bent over a tray of cocaine.

"I went to the Augustines, and I told them I had some information to sell to them for twenty-five hundred dollars. I couldn't hardly get my mouth around those numbers. Mr. Augustine laughed his head off, say, 'Boy, what the hell you talking about?' I told him I knew where he could get a photograph of Lemuel Stewart snorting cocaine powder up his nose. That cracker set straight up. He didn't want to pay me until after he had the picture, and I knew if I stayed around that long I might be dead. So he ended up paying me half up front in cash, and then I hid outside of town. I figured I'd be ahead of the game if that's all I got. But after he had the picture, he gave my mama the rest of the money. We left that night. When we got to Los Angeles me and Mama went into business."

Mooney must have seen the look of astonishment on my face because he leaned into me and said, "Tell you what I'm going to do. I'll loan you some money. How's that? You pay me back as soon as you can. And don't think I ain't charging you interest, girl, 'cause I am."

Mooney National became my bank. I soon learned that he was the credit union for a lot of people. Los Angeles may not have been Mississippi, Louisiana, or Texas, but working capital was still out of our reach. In the south, wealthy colored men made extra money loan-sharking; Mooney did the same thing in LA. He charged most people ten percent; I paid a lot more.

CHAPTER ELEVEN

THERE WERE ROUGH times after Gilda disappeared. Winnie, Fern, and Opal still helped me at first, but when my money got thin I had to cut back. Mostly I ended up doing everything myself. The funny thing is, I didn't care. I stirred. I poured. I labeled. I kept moving fast so that the blues couldn't catch me.

"I was the one who came up with the idea to sell lotion in the first place," I told Mooney the night I repaid his first loan to me. It was August, and a dry heat had settled over the city. "Gilda wanted to work at Braddock for the rest of her life."

"Some people like to stay in one place," Mooney said. He was wearing a suit and tie that evening, and his hair had just been cut. Mooney smelled good from some kind of aftershave. He said he was coming from a business meeting. "The NBA," he said, then added, "The Negro Business Association." He could tell that I'd never heard of them. "We're a small group. We've only been together about five years."

"What do you do?"

"We try to help each other build up our businesses. Most of us can't get bank loans. Sometimes we help each other with money, sometimes information. We try to keep up with the new trends in each industry. It's slow-going," he said with a sigh. "What I'd really like to do is get the men to pool some money so we can put a new business together. That's what rich white folks do. They put all the money in a pot. Colored folks ain't used to trusting each other. You find two colored men with two quarters apiece, and they're too busy trying to outdo one another to think about putting the money together to make more." He sighed. "We been thinking like that since slavery, and it's gonna take a while for us to change."

"You look nice," I said, and I meant it. I liked listening to Mooney talking about colored people and business. There was a lot of patience in his voice, even when he discussed our faults. He made me think that maybe we could have some better days, even if it did take a long time. Standing in front of me, he didn't remind me of my father at all. "I couldn't have made it without you, Mooney," I said, and I meant that, too. "You've been a good friend."

"I'd like to be a better one." He held out his hand, and I don't know why but I took it. When he kissed my fingers I could feel his heat.

"Mooney," I said, but I didn't pull back. And when he stepped forward I didn't move away.

"Awww girl, you know I'm your friend."

Years later I'd ask myself why. Maybe it was the same force that brings the tides that pulled me into Mooney's arms that first night, and maybe I was just lonesome. I didn't know there was a room in the back of the kitchen, a room with a bed and a table and a radio. I don't know how we got to it, whether Mooney carried me or led me. Our clothes were a puddle on the floor. His hands on my body felt nice. Mama's face floated all around me. It disappeared when he pulled himself into me and became the ship that rocked me soft, then harder, harder, harder, until my moans got drowned in the waves.

He got up an hour later, bent down and kissed me on each breast, then licked both nipples like they belonged to him. "You sure are beautiful. I believe you have the prettiest lips I've ever seen." He stared at me as though he meant every word he said, and then he kissed me again.

"My lips are too big," I said. It was the first thing that came to my mind. Mooney blinked. "Who told you that?"

I shrugged my shoulders. "The mirror," I said, trying to make a joke.

"Then you're looking in the wrong mirror, baby."

I must have dropped my eyes because then I felt his finger lifting my chin. He was looking straight at me. "Don't you let these white folks mess with your mind with their Miss Americas and movie stars. You're beautiful all over. I mean what I'm saying, Hosanna."

He did. I could tell. But I didn't believe him, and he knew it.

"How are you supposed to be selling beauty products to colored women if you don't believe in your own beauty? I believe in my food."

When I didn't answer him, he got up and went into the kitchen. He brought back a mirror. "Look at yourself, Hosanna."

He held the mirror so we both could see. "Now, aren't those some pretty eyes? Isn't that a pretty nose? Aren't those some beautiful lips?"

He went over my entire body like that, telling me that everything on it was pretty, over and over, until I started to believe him.

"Me and you gone have some fun, baby," he said.

And we did. Being Mooney's "woman on the side" had benefits. There was the money, of course, gifts instead of loans. And he took me places, too: out-of-the-way restaurants, movies, jazz clubs, and parties. Early in the morning, and sometimes at night, there was our little room, our narrow bed, the taste of hot and spicy. I didn't stop thinking about Gilda or feeling the pain that came from that, but the headaches went away; I was able to sleep at night. There was more going on in that bed than body heat. Mostly, we talked. That is, I asked questions and Mooney answered them. I wanted to know about business, and he taught me everything he knew. We discussed our plans and took each other seriously. Mooney was the first person I told when Mr. Epps finished the light and dark shades of powder. When I announced that my cosmetics firm was one day going to manufacture everything from eye shadow to foundation, he didn't laugh. When he told me that he wanted a chain of restaurants throughout California, I said, "If anybody can do it, you can." Lying on crumpled sheets, Mooney and I rooted for each other. And over and over again he repeated that plain colored me was beautiful. His telling me that made me look at what I was trying to do in a whole new way. When I went out to sell my products I told my customers that they were beautiful because I knew they were as hungry for those words as I was. Mooney and I became friends in that bed, and we talked about everything on those sheets, everything except his wife and son.

But the thing is, I thought about them. Mooney and I were together for almost a year, and I never stopped thinking about them, ruminating over the Ten Commandments, or visualizing my mama's mouth turning downward. The first time I caught myself wondering what he was doing when he wasn't with me was scary. I already liked him a whole lot. It wouldn't take much for me to love him. I wanted to move far beyond temptation.

I begged my hairdresser to let me work temporarily in her beauty salon after hours. I'd asked her before but this time she needed the extra income, and so she agreed. I gave her twenty-five dollars for the first month. Late one night in June, I piled my car full of the equipment I kept at Mooney's. I locked the door behind me and mailed him the key and a letter with a good-bye enclosed.

I took forty-seven dollars, the cost of a one-way train trip from Inez to Los Angeles, went to Western Union, and addressed the wire to Mr. Lonell Carter. I wanted to be respectable as soon as possible. Maybe his life was emptier than mine but I could help him fill it. I still had some feelings left for him, enough for a new start.

I'd never told my brother about Mooney, but he knew that my decision to marry Lonell had come out of the blue. Tuney told me that I needed to spend time getting to know Lonell. He'd already married wife number two, Bertha. He was wearing a fireman's uniform, and he looked good in it. Tuney got his picture in the paper for being the first. Later, when the journalists went home and the flashbulbs stopped popping, the old guard let him have it. For almost eight years he slept in a kind of shed behind the barracks. The other firemen wouldn't eat with him. They urinated in his food and stole his uniform. They left him for dead in a world-record inferno that took out a city block on the east side. There were nights in that firehouse that he slept with a knife in his hand. But if they thought he was going to quit, they didn't know my brother. Giving up just wasn't in Tuney.

It was his idea to hire a lawyer to work on getting back the land. Took him one whole year to save up enough money for the retainer. I went with him to Graham, Windsor and Chapman, one of the biggest law firms in the city. The building was right around the corner from Braddock, but it was newer. The law offices were paneled in dark shiny wood, and there was thick carpeting on the floor. The only other Negro we saw was the man who took us up on the elevator; he stared at us as though we were two purple rhinoceroses. We rode up to the fifth floor, where we had an appointment with an associate of Mr. Graham's, somebody named Billingsley. His secretary looked as though she were seeing purple, too. "Just one moment, please," she said, and disappeared into a room. When she came back moments later she was smiling too hard to have good news. "I'm very sorry but Mr. Billingsley has informed me that an emergency has come up. He won't be able to see you today." She immediately sat down at her desk and started fumbling around, pretending she was looking for something that was missing.

I could tell by the set of Tuney's mouth that he was getting ready to say something. I grabbed his arm. "Let's go," I said.

Mr. Billingsley's secretary never did look up.

It took three months for Tuney to find somebody else. He went over to Central Avenue. The two colored lawyers laughed at him and declared that he'd never get the land back, that he might as well forget all about trying. He was more disgusted with them than he was with Mr. Billingsley.

Finally, early one Monday evening I picked Tuney up, and he directed me to a street not far from where Gilda lived. It felt strange going back to that side of town but I didn't mention it to Tuney. We parked in front of a small two-story brick building. There was a sign on the door that read WEISS AND WEISS. One of Tuney's fellow firefighters had told him about the lawyers.

Mr. Herbert Weiss looked surprised to see us but he didn't seem at all displeased. He was a serious-looking man, small but sturdy. He appeared to be in his early thirties. "What can I do to help you?" he asked, after he ushered us into his office.

He listened attentively while Tuney told him the story. When my brother had finished he asked a few questions about the Hagertys, the tax bill. "Do you have your tax records? Do you have the original deed? Do you have any correspondence between you and the people you say took your property?"

Tuney answered yes to all the questions. My daddy had given Tuney all the paperwork. In a way I had let go of my parents' land. I was still angry about the loss; I always would be. But I had a new grief to bear. I couldn't carry both loads all at once.

"I'm not promising anything, but I'd like to see what I can do," Mr. Weiss said. He shook hands with my brother and me.

"Mr. Weiss is going to get us our land," Tuney said jubilantly after we left the office.

I didn't say anything but I thought about those oil riggings, that and my baby sister with spit on her body. *Dream your dream, brother, but I know this: When evil has a grip, you have to cut off fingers.*

Sometimes I think about how my life would have been if I'd sat behind a counter selling Baby Ruths and chocolate Kisses. I didn't listen to Tuney. Lonell and I got married right away, and stopped smiling at each other just as quick. Lonell turned out to be puffed up with air, not ambition. Everything he touched turned to dust. Soon, I had two children to feed, Vonette and Matriece, so I hustled my wares, first door-to-door, then store-to-store, trying to convince my sisters of what I was just beginning to believe: We were already beautiful. All we needed was a little enhancement. I dragged my girls with me, trying to pass on my dream. Matriece grabbed hold of it; Vonette threw it right back in my face.

Lonell seemed to resent my little bit of success and anybody else's. All around us, colored people were trading backseats for those up front, exchanging segregation for integration. Los Angeles now had not only Negro firemen but policemen as well. Our men began driving buses and our girls started working in department stores. Turned on the television one day and there was Nat King Cole with his own show, not to mention a house in Hancock Park. Dorothy Dandridge was nominated for best actress, with her pretty self. The next thing I knew, a king ascended to his throne, Negroes were marching their way to dignity, and even Congress said that the time had come for change. Maybe there was too much progress for Lonell when none of it was his. Maybe he saw the desire in my eyes whenever anybody mentioned Mooney's name. We hung on until right after Kennedy got killed. I guess the gunshots woke us up. We split up Inez-style: Lonell just walked out without signing the paper first.

Through all those years, the Hagertys' theft and Gilda's betrayal were machetes whacking away at my mind. As the weeks turned into months, the years stacked up like a brick wall around my heart, and I began to fill that void with bitterness, the rage finding no bottom.

Never did get a chance to show Ole Sweat and Farts how successful I became. All during that time when I was mixing up lotion and going door-to-door, borrowing money and selling, selling, selling, I told myself that one day I'd go back to Braddock and show Weinstock just how well I'd done. Times were good when I finally walked into the hotel; I wasn't rich but I had my products in beauty salons all across the country and was hoping to get them into department stores. I was looking extra fine, wearing a new suit, my hair freshly done and makeup just right. I marched in the front door, and right off, somebody asked me, "May I help you, ma'am," and that sure felt good. Standing in the middle of the lobby, I thought the place looked smaller, like the old decrepit body of a prize-fighter whose bones have shrunk. I searched around for somebody I knew, but it seemed as though everybody working there was a stranger. I'd never seen any of the people at the reservations desk, none of the bell-hops either. I took the service elevator and rode up to the housekeeping floor, but all the maids were Mexicans, not one single black. I was on my way back down when who should I run into but old Brewster. He was gray with a little paunch, but other than that he hadn't changed. We grabbed each other at the same time and hugged real tight, then he led me into the employees' lounge, where we each had a cup of coffee. He caught me up as fast as he could.

I congratulated Brewster when he told me that he'd been promoted to be superintendent of the entire facility. Winnie, Opal, and Fern were long gone, and he hadn't seen Hattie since she was fired. The last he'd heard from Gilda was the day she gave him the check, but he knew that she'd had a baby and that her husband and uncle were in the cosmetics business, because Weinstock had told him so. I already knew about Gilda Cosmetics because I started seeing the products in drugstores about a year after I left the hotel. Looking at those lipsticks and lotions the first time, I had to hold myself back to keep from knocking everything off the shelves. But none of them were being marketed to Negro women. After a while I didn't see them anymore. A few years passed; then one day when I was browsing in Broadman's, a really nice department store, I saw an entire line of Gilda Cosmetics in a display case, and I thought I'd just go up in smoke right there. The buyers at Broadman's had refused to meet with me. I felt an echo of that rage listening to Brewster, but by that time I was used to the feeling.

Brewster did give me one shock. When he said that Weinstock had died in a car accident, I got mad. I'd wanted Weinstock to know I hadn't mopped anybody's floor but my own since I'd left Braddock. But then, I got cheated a lot in that other life.

Over the years, Tuney went back and forth to Mr. Weiss's office so often it seemed as if going there was his second job. I stopped accompanying him after a while. Just took too much out of me, especially after Mama and Daddy passed, and Lucille started acting so crazy, locking herself up in her room for days at a time. I had to go to Texas to see about her. Wound up having to pay somebody to take care of her. Mr. Weiss hung in there with us until he retired, and then his son William took over. The son had an earring, a ponytail, and more energy than two trains. He told Tuney, "Let's approach this another way," and started making trips to Inez, talking to as many old black folks as he could find.

But the Hagertys still owned everything in Inez, and most black folks were scared of them. "Be patient," Tuney told me.

As for Mooney, he never could get the colored businessmen to do anything but showboat and run their mouths, according to him. For as long as I knew him, he was going to one meeting after the next. He'd get disgusted with one group, quit them, and start another. I could tell that he was frustrated. But that was one man who couldn't be stopped. His business just kept growing. But then he worked a lot, especially after Junior died from spinal meningitis. Child wasn't sixteen years old. Part of Mooney shriveled up after that happened, but he kept going. He had my shoulder during those hard times and my love. He always will.

It took me a long time to realize that how Gilda hurt me wasn't just about money. I could have forgiven her that. She shifted shapes on me, like some magician's prop that went from being a dove to a weasel right in front of my eyes. There was a reason she studied that English book so hard. Payday came at the last page. No, she didn't look like those blond, blue-eyed beauties in the movies with their thin, turned-up noses, but she didn't look like me.

America loved her better. All she had to do was spread her wings and fly. She got more out of being here than I did, and she hadn't been here as long or worked as hard. When I was dragging my girls around to beauty salons in a car that was louder than Vonette's grumbling, sometimes I'd think about her sitting pretty someplace, having everything. I forgot about her struggles, the pain we had in common. She became as much my enemy as the Hagertys.

Many years after Brewster gave me the envelope, I went to where Gilda Cosmetics headquarters was located. I drove downtown, parked my car, and stared at the building. In the mid-seventies, after the company had expanded and moved to its current Beverly Hills location, I used to stand outside that splendid office with my mouth twisted and my fists balled up at my sides, thinking about everything I never got. I was long dead before I figured out why I never went in. Once I thought I saw her entering the building. Oh, she looked fine and important, her hair glossy and straight. The place on her arm where the numbers used to be was covered with expensive fabric. She carried herself erect. I had to look twice to make sure it was Gilda. I wonder if she even recognized herself. I sure didn't recognize me with my brows creased in vindictive contemplation, me muttering "bitch" under my breath, me all broke down with diabetes and high blood pressure, carrying more weight than I ever thought I would, me lashing out at the ones I loved and not being the mother my mama had been. It was all her fault.

I passed them on: the debts, the hatred, my rage, and all my fervent desires. As I lay writhing on my bed that last night, I could see Vonette crying as she stood by the door. But my baby girl's hand was the one I clasped. Matriece is the responsible one. I pressed her flesh, tried to whisper, but I couldn't speak. It is hard work to cross over. But it didn't matter. She knew.

Sometimes it takes more than one generation to complete a story. The rest of the tale is for my girls to tell. I hum my song, and if I don't know all the words, at least I can feel the meaning. Closure is what I'm seeking. Death ain't nothing but another opportunity.

CHAPTER TWELVE

THE AIR IN the third-floor conference room of Gilda Cosmetics, Inc., vibrated with fragrance and colors that Wednesday morning in September. After years of working in the beauty industry, Matriece Carter's senses went on alert as she surveyed and smelled the dozen women gathered around the oval oak table where she was seated. Ordinarily, Matriece would have been behind the two-way mirror that formed the back wall of the room, studying these focus group participants with her staff. But Matriece wanted to put her personal touch on this gathering. The women seated before her were there to help shape the advertising campaign for next fall's launch of Brown Sugar, GC's new line of cosmetics for African-American women. The ad campaign, including hiring an agency and finding that all-important spokesmodel, had to be completed by March.

The women were the representatives of that most coveted of markets: the eighteen- to thirty-four-year-old professional. Among them was a manager, engineer, teacher, lawyer, physician, singer, actress, several wannabe actresses, and an assistant pastor. They had incomes ranging from twenty-two thousand dollars a year to six figures. Matriece was surrounded by an array of sizes: petite, shapely, plump, and jumbo queen. They wore their hair natural, pressed, locked, braided, twisted, curled, twirled, and done up in a swirl. The women were single, married, shacking, divorced, looking, and looking high and low. But they all wanted to be more beautiful.

A mélange of scents from perfumes, colognes, eaux de toilette, and lotions rose up from their bosoms, wrists, and behind their ears. The aroma of warm pastries and fresh coffee couldn't mask the arresting blend of spice, flowers, and musk that clung to the women. Foundation, loose powder, blush, eye shadow, and lipsticks highlighted and camouflaged the features each woman loved or wished Mother Nature hadn't given her, respectively. Their fingernails were polished with vibrant shades ranging from red to gold.

The scents blazed a trail through Matriece's olfactory center to the financial portion of her brain; she estimated that the women seated before her were wearing between four hundred fifty and seven hundred dollars' worth of fragrances. Matriece recognized the old scents—Chanel No. 5, Shalimar, White Shoulders, Chloe. The woman at the far end of the table with a half carat in each ear was wearing Joy. The young girl with the silver dagger nails was doused in Charlie. To her left was L'Air du Temps. The youngest women were wearing the newest perfumes: Azzura, Mania, Green Tea. Someone was drenched in Angel. Matriece even smelled Radiance, the eponymous signature scent of the largest African-American-owned cosmetics company in the world. It was a perfume Matriece was more familiar with than any of the others. She'd helped launch the marketing campaign for it when she was Radiance's youngest vice president.

The makeup was harder to price or even identify. There were so many small cosmetics boutiques springing up all over that it was becoming increasingly difficult to tell one brand from another. Most of the women seated at the table were into a natural look; the subtlety of their collective touches made brand recognition even more difficult. Of the four who were wearing foundation—which ranged from maximum to sheerest coverage—Matriece didn't recognize one, except for GC's Ultra Sheer. Ultra Sheer gave skin a telltale glow; it was Gilda's biggest seller, last year earning the company nearly one fourth of its five-hundred-million-dollar revenues. She discerned which eyebrows were filled in with powder and which with pencil treatment and immediately detected that the woman with the large hoop earrings had permanently arched her eyebrows with a tattoo. Matriece spotted three pairs of lips that were lined by Mac and filled in with Clinique. Very Berry. Amber Glass. Deep Lacquer. Miss Joy was wearing Platinum, Lancôme's pale silvery shade, which managed to be both matte and moist at the same time, and, of course, there were lots of Revlon lips. Charlie's just-above-minimum-wage angel was sporting a combination of Mary's Beauty Supply store no-name and enough Vaseline to make it last beyond the one hour for which it was guaranteed. Only one woman had on Radiance lipstick—Plum

Passion. A good serviceable shade, capable of taking a woman from her day job into the wee hours. She'd instructed her staff to require all focus group participants to be women who wore makeup frequently, as in every day, and they had done a good job finding them. Matriece estimated the women had spent well over three hundred dollars on their faces. Her goal for the morning was to figure out the best way to claim some of those dollars for Brown Sugar.

The women helped themselves to the continental breakfast. One of Matriece's assistants made sure the food didn't run out, while the other helped the videographer. Above the table that held Danish, muffins, croissants, fruit, orange juice, and coffee was a large silk banner that proclaimed, "Brown Sugar . . . Because you're already beautiful." Below the heading in smaller letters were the words "Coming Next Fall." There was a low buzz throughout the room as the group, strangers for the most part, began chatting. At exactly nine o'clock, Matriece rose from her seat at the head of the table. The participants sat down, and the room grew quiet. "I'd like to welcome you. I'm Matriece Carter, president of Brown Sugar Cosmetics, a division of Gilda Cosmetics. I know that you're all familiar with our parent company. Gilda Cosmetics is one of the forces in beauty, the tenth largest in the industry. We're not the biggest but we think we're the best. GC's experience and clout are helping to produce what will become the premiere cosmetics for today's black women. We'd like your help."

Matriece sensed a bit of nervous tension in the room as the camaraderie that had developed over breakfast began to evaporate. Icebreaker time.

Matriece held up her purse, opened it, and retrieved her makeup bag. "We asked you all to bring your makeup kits. Would you take them out, please." She waited a few moments until every woman had placed a bag on the place mat in front of her.

"Would each of you take out your oldest lipstick and hold it up. No gloss, just lipsticks."

She heard zippers and snaps popping. The women, each waving a lipstick, eyed her curiously. "Now, I'd like you to take off the tops and swivel your lipsticks up."

Matriece pushed back her chair and began walking around the room. "Did you know that how you apply your lipstick provides a psychological profile of you?" She stopped in front of one woman whose lipstick tip was pointed. "Everybody, this is an aggressive woman."

The participants laughed, and Matriece continued around the table, making comments and jokes about the shapes of the lipsticks she saw, returning to her chair when she sensed that most of the women were in a congenial mood.

"Okay. This isn't an ordinary focus group. We're here to discuss makeup: foundation, powder, lipsticks, eye shadows, mascara, and feelings," she said, her tone warm and intimate. "What you like, what you don't like. Gilda Cosmetics wants you to help us earn the right to call you our loyal customers. Brown Sugar debuts next fall, and here at GC we're excited about this new line of cosmetics, designed with the black woman in mind. And let me tell you, we plan to have us looking super fine. Halle and Vanessa better step aside."

She bent down, picked up a small wastepaper basket, and held it up. "Okay, let's dig in those makeup bags again. Take out the biggest mistake you bought in the last year. Tell me what went wrong and why you'd never buy that item again. I'll start."

She held up a small tube. "If I don't get enough sleep you can tell it under my eyes. I let a saleslady talk me into buying this concealer. Big mistake. It is very, very drying. This stuff makes every line stand out, and the result is that"—she put her hand to her brow, a gesture of mock humiliation—"I look older. Gotta go." Matriece pitched the small container into the basket. Several women laughed and a few applauded.

Miss Joy raised her hand and held up a mascara wand. "I bought this three weeks ago. It's supposed to separate, thicken, and lengthen your eyelashes. All it does is clump. And it takes forever to wash it off." She passed the mascara around the table until the woman next to Matriece tossed it into the basket. The women clapped again. One by one, they identified the duds in their makeup kits.

After the last of the rejects hit the basket and the applause had died down, Matriece leaned forward. "I'm going to tell on myself. As a teenager, whenever I looked in the mirror, all I saw was lips. I thought I had the biggest lips in the universe. So, when I started wearing lipstick I used to color inside my lip line to make them seem smaller. Yes, ladies, I was perpetrating a beauty fraud."

Several women laughed, others smiled and whispered. "At sixteen I was saving up for lip surgery, one baby-sitting job at a time, when I fell in love with Kevin—Kevin the Kisser."

Laughter exploded in the room and when the women quieted down, Matriece said, "But here's the thing: Kevin told me that I had the most beautiful big juicy lips he had ever seen."

The women chuckled and so did Matriece.

"Do I need to tell you that my big-lips complex ended at the age of sixteen?"

Matriece had the attention of every woman in the room. She smiled and made eye contact with all of them. "I've told my story. I want to know yours. At what point in your life did your so-called flawed features become okay with you? Come on, it's confession time."

Matriece was about to offer more encouragement when Miss Chloe raised her hand. Matriece nodded to her. "I used to hate my skinny legs. I thought they looked like baseball bats; I'd never wear dresses. But when I was fourteen my uncle moved in with us. He was the kind of man who made everybody feel good. He zeroed in on my not liking my legs, and one day he said, 'Sugar, your legs are small but they're shapely.' I kept telling myself that until I believed it."

Gradually, most of the women took a turn, discussing everything from facial scars and mustaches to how they felt the first time they wore lipstick. They mentioned the aunts and neighbor ladies, the uncles and fathers who'd made them feel beautiful.

"I guess you didn't think this would be a therapy session," Matriece said when the last woman spoke. She smiled. "Makeup is therapy, probably the cheapest you can buy. No lipstick can give me what Kevin did, but maybe when I apply it I can relive Kevin's words. Brown Sugar's philosophy is: 'Because you're already beautiful.' We think that's a pretty good way to reconnect you with the experience in your life that turned your so-called flaw into a plus. By sharing your stories with me today, you help me refine our philosophy and our products, so that they help you feel good about you. That's our mission."

Matriece looked at the clock on the wall. "Ladies, it is ten-thirty. I want to thank you for your time, your energy, and your spirit. As you leave, please pick up a gift bag from the table near the door. When Brown Sugar debuts next fall, we will be mailing you another gift. Thank you so much."

After the women left, and her assistants had cleaned up, Matriece sat down in front of the television next to the now empty table. She inserted the morning's tape into the VCR. Pulling a legal-size tablet from her briefcase, she began taking notes.

Matriece was about to replay the tape when she glanced at the corner of the room. She inhaled sharply as she saw the luminous glow. Right before her was a pale, almost transparent Hosanna. Whether ghost or dream, her mother appeared as though death and time had no power. Hosanna's eyes settled on her. Matriece wasn't afraid. In the sixteen years since her mother died, Hosanna had appeared often. Matriece loved seeing her. She just wished that Hosanna looked happier.

What do you want me to do? Matriece placed her fingers on her temples, massaged them lightly, and then closed her eyes for a second. She could sense her mother's exasperation, her impatience and brooding. She's fussing at me, just like when I was a kid and I didn't put the lipsticks in the box quickly enough to suit her, she thought, lowering her head. *I can't make it happen any faster.* Maybe her mother heard her. When she turned back to the corner, Hosanna was gone. Matriece sat staring at the spot where she had been, powerless against the intense loneliness that began to fill her like the words of an unbidden song. She was used to the melody.

"You go, Uncle Mooney," Matriece said to herself, feeling a surge of pride as she pushed open the door to Mooney's early that afternoon. From inside the entryway she scanned the large packed room. Most of his lunch customers had migrated eastward from office buildings and shops in Beverly Hills where they worked. His eatery was only five minutes from

Rodeo Drive. If the wind was right, the aroma of barbecue mingled with the scent of high-priced steak from Lowry's. "Baby Girl," Mooney had told her, "white folks love our cooking. They just don't want to come to our neighborhood to eat it."

This theory of his, what he called the "proximity factor of marketing black to white," had proved to be absolutely unassailable. More than three-quarters of his restaurants were located in or close to white areas. The Beverly Hills–adjacent restaurant was Mooney's twenty-fifth in southern California, one of one hundred restaurants in a chain of prosperity that extended from California to Arizona and Nevada and included a line of frozen pies and barbecue sauce sold in grocery stores across the country.

Although he had told her that he'd be sitting in a booth up front, Matriece knew that Mooney couldn't help going into the kitchen of any restaurant he owned. She found him there, walking briskly around the slabs of beef, pork, and chicken parts on an assembly line that dipped them into the secret spice mixture that had made Mooney's reputation and his fortune. There were at least a dozen workers, mostly Latinos, clad in barbecue-spattered white uniforms, who were chopping, cooking, or preparing food in some way. Mooney stood in the middle of the chaos barking orders in Spanish, then segueing easily into English as his predominantly black staff of waiters deposited and picked up orders. Matriece knew that he saw her but he didn't stop his work. Work always came first with Mooney.

Ten minutes later, the old man turned to her. "Hey, Baby Girl," he said, then took her firmly by her arm and led her back outside to a booth near the front.

"How come you can't stay out of the kitchen, Uncle Mooney?" Matriece said. "Relax. Let your managers earn their money. You should be hitting the golf ball."

"Let Tiger do what he does best, and let me do my thing. How's the job?"

Matriece smiled. "It's fine. We had a focus group come in today. Part of the marketing effort."

"Last time we had a focus group was when we were thinking about adding Lite Ribs to the menu," Mooney said.

"When was that?"

"Oh, about twelve years ago."

"So what happened?"

Mooney chuckled. "Turned out that people who eat ribs don't count calories. That's what I get listening to college-educated Negroes."

"Like me, huh?"

The old man winked at her. Mooney had paid for both her undergraduate and her graduate degrees. While they were still laughing, a waitress appeared with two plates piled high with ribs, greens, and potato salad. She placed the meals on the table and returned moments later with sodas.

"What you learn from your group today? You on the right track?"

"I think so."

Mooney snorted. "Just give 'em a good gift with purchase. They'll come. You know what my gift with purchase is?" Mooney asked, his old face solemn. "The food they paid for."

Matriece laughed, then shook her head.

"The group that came, they were your eighteen- to thirty-four-year-olds?"

Matriece nodded.

"If I recall, that's the age that you wanted Meeks to pay more attention to."

Matriece sighed at the mention of her former employer and tried to fight off a wave of guilt. To Calvin Meeks, founder and CEO of Radiance Cosmetics, GC and all white-owned companies with black makeup lines were the enemy, and she was a traitor. "He told you?" Matriece said.

"We still have our little group, you know. Not that we're doing anything, but that's another story. Baby Girl, either he'll get over it or he won't. You gotta see your own big picture."

"Oh, God, Uncle Mooney. I never thought this would be the picture, me actually working for Gilda."

"Gilda was looking for the best and she heard about what you'd done over at Radiance. That party-in-the-mall idea of yours was a stone-cold winner. You made Meeks a whole lotta money, so don't feel guilty about nothing. Rich white business folks buy what they need—your service, your silence, whatever. Simple as that."

"It's so strange. We have meetings together. I talk and act just as though everything is normal between us. Half the time I feel like screaming at her, 'You stole from my mother.' "

"It ain't screaming time. Listen, if nothing else, you're getting a hell of an education. But I have a feeling something will come out of your working for her. Otherwise, I wouldn't have told you to take the job."

"That last year when Mommy was alive, all she talked about was how Gilda had done her wrong. Not to Vonette, just to me. I thought that if I started Brown Sugar over from scratch and made it successful, she'd, I don't know, rest in peace. I mean, I'd sue Gilda if I had proof. But I don't. Mommy talked about some papers and a bank book but she never could find them. I didn't want to be like my Uncle Tuney, a lifetime of litigation, with nothing to show for his trouble."

"There were papers. I saw them."

"Well, where are they?"

Mooney shrugged. "Why you looking so glum?"

"Because I feel like I'm letting her down."

"You know, your mother was what they call a visionary. When she was coming along, there wasn't anything to make a black woman look good other than a straightening comb, some grease in a can, and maybe a red dress. She was way, way ahead. You're president of a subsidiary of Gilda Cosmetics. Your momma would be proud. You need to relax. Eat your food, Baby Girl."

"Mommy, I'm hungry!"

The youthful voice was unexpected, out of place in a room filled with hungry adults. Matriece glanced briefly at the young black boy before turning back to Mooney. But her godfather was still looking at the boy, his old eyes soft and sad. He made a noise in his throat, a faint groan that hovered in the air even after he began eating.

Matriece speared a rib with her fork. The meat was succulent and juicy. Before she could begin chewing, barbecue sauce squirted out and spattered onto her silk blouse. Matriece groaned as she glanced down at the spreading stain. Mooney never even looked up from his plate until she asked the waitress to bring her some club soda and a rib dinner to go. He was too busy eating his own food.

Later that evening back at the office, Matriece opened the latest issue of *The Rose Sheet,* the organ for the toiletries, fragrances, and skin care industry. Under the heading "The News This Week" was the announcement of the sale of Corsin's Lookin' Good and High Gloss brands to Darden Products for seventeen million dollars. "And another one bites the dust," she said, setting aside the paper. Corsin was a black family-owned company; Darden Products was white. In recent years, a number of African-Americans in the beauty industry had bailed out. *Pretty soon there won't be any of us left.* The word *us* stuck in her mind. Technically, she wasn't part of *us* anymore. Matriece leaned across her desk, staring at the array of lipsticks, shadows, nail polishes, and foundations assembled there. She didn't want to think about the decline of the black beauty industry. She smiled when she saw the woman standing in her doorway with an unlit cigarette in her hand. "Hey, girl," Matriece said.

"'Shappenin'?" Blair Priestley plopped down in the chair next to Matriece's desk, then stepped out of her shoes and placed her feet on the rug. Her feet matched the rest of her. They were long and narrow. She put the cigarette in her mouth and sucked in so hard that her cheeks became concave, then she blew out the imaginary smoke with a languid sigh.

"Get the patch," Matriece said.

"Soon."

"We got some very good information this morning," Matriece said.

Blair nodded. "Good. Did you all discuss packaging?"

"Indirectly. You know, I'd like a signature scent. Not immediately, but maybe a year from now."

"Unisex?"

"Absolutely."

"In a clear box. Clear bottle."

"We can call it—"

"Clear. No real fragrance to speak of."

Matriece chuckled. "Right. Kind of like—"

"Air."

"Hundred bucks a quarter ounce."

"That would be the toilet water, sistergirl."

"Right. Perfume, at least five hundred, for an eighth."

Matriece felt her shoulders going down as she giggled. From the large picture window across from her desk, she could see the Los Angeles sky, still light in mid-September. The windows of the high-rise buildings sparkled as the sun's rays hit them. It was as though someone had un-furled a carpet to reveal a cache of glittering jewels, some real, some fake, but all dazzling. That was LA: a combination of the real and unreal. The city had the power to blind those who gazed too long at her brightness.

Blair rose from her chair and walked around the office, uncon-sciously sucking and blowing out pretend smoke, her toes sinking into the thick pile of the carpet. She stopped in front of a radio placed on the middle shelf of a bookcase. Within seconds the air around them vibrated with the wails of a hip-hop diva. Rhythm and blues rocked the room. Blair started dancing toward Matriece, pushing her auburn curls out of her face.

"Come on," Blair said. "You won't have to do the treadmill tonight. Get up."

Their movements were similar: smooth, spare motions with their arms and shoulders, a lot of rotating action with their hips, feet holding steady, occasionally sliding back and forth. They held hands, then let them go, circled each other, twirled and dipped. They'd been friends for nearly ten years and were used to dancing together. When they caught sight of their reflection in the picture window they saw two slim women, one white, one black, gyrating fluidly, their smiles familiar, their steps in sync.

"We have color presentation next Thursday," Matriece said when the song ended.

Blair nodded. "They're right this time. You'll approve. Hell, the Old Broad Herself will approve."

"If the color's not right, nothing's right," Matriece said sharply.

"Got it."

"I talked to Asia Pace's manager about the spokesmodel thing. He acted sort of lukewarm about the whole idea."

Blair twisted her lips a bit, then relaxed them. "He's supposed to act blasé. That way he can make you pay grand theft dough to associate his little Grammy winner with your brand. Plus, she's nominated for about three Diamond Disc awards. Her star is still rising. Anyway, didn't you say you know her?"

"Knew her—a long time ago." Matriece got quiet for a moment and then began collecting her belongings.

Blair retrieved her cell phone from her purse. "Hello, Judd," she said. "How's it going?"

Matriece said, "Tell him I said hello."

"Matriece says hello, honey." Blair covered the telephone with her hand. "Judd says hi." She paused for a moment and then spoke into the receiver again. "Did you and Dad eat dinner?" She frowned. "I told you I'd be working late tonight." Her frown deepened. "What do you mean he's not there?"

Matriece could hear Blair's sudden inhalation, watched as she flicked imaginary ashes from the cigarette. "All right. Okay. Have you gotten started on your homework?" She paused again. Her tone changed. "Get started now. I'm on my way. Do you hear me? Judd? Judd?" She made a noise full of frustration and irritation, clicked the end button, pushed down the aerial, thrust the phone into her bag, and turned to Matriece. "They must share a brain," she said. "I told both of them that I was working late. Do you think Porter might have, I don't know, bought some McDonald's, ordered pizza? Something. Of course not. He's not home, and my kid hasn't eaten."

"Judd's not going to starve because of one missed meal."

"That kid is always starving. Honestly, Porter is so . . ."

"Porterly," Matriece said dryly. She snapped her fingers, then opened a door that revealed a walk-in closet where she kept office supplies. Pressed against the wall was a miniature refrigerator. "I brought you something." She retrieved a large bag that had Mooney's name and logo on it, then handed it to Blair. "Some barbeque, greens, and macaroni and cheese."

"My sister," Blair said. Her grin was instant and genuine. "A little touch of home. You didn't forget the pot liquor, did you?"

Matriece chuckled. "It's in there."

In the elevator, Blair opened the bag and smelled it. "You tell your uncle that his ribs are as good as Southside Junior's." Blair chuckled to herself, and Matriece sensed a story. "I told you about this rib joint around the corner from where I grew up?"

"Is this about the drunk guy whose face was stuck to the ice?"

"Oh, yeah, I did tell you. People would come from all over Chicago for Junior's ribs. It must have been, like, five thousand degrees below zero one night. My mom sent me out to buy some ribs. There was this drunk black guy lying on the sidewalk in front of Junior's, and his face was stuck to the ice. People just stepped right over him to go inside and get those ribs. Nobody paid him any attention. I was just staring at him, and he opened his eyes and said, 'Is you an angel?' "

Matriece let out a perfunctory chuckle.

"After a while the paramedics came and got him loose, and he staggered on down the street. But, I mean, nothing stopped commerce at Southside Junior's."

The two women were parked next to each other in the garage below the building. "So, don't murder anyone at your house," Matriece said lightly.

"Oh, yeah. I still have the Uzi from that Crip I used to date."

Matriece shook her head. "Don't talk about my people."

"Oh, sorry. He was a Blood." They both chuckled. Blair lit her cigarette. "Get some rest. That is, unless Montgomery's coming over."

"We're going out Friday night."

"You guys have been hanging in there. I thought you were operating a turnstile a while back. Next!"

Matriece gave a short laugh. "Frogs, all frogs."

"That dentist was a nice guy."

"Rivet!" Matriece said, her version of frog-speak.

"And Tony. God, what a bright man."

"Rivet! Rivet!"

Blair shook her head as Matriece giggled. "Girl, don't dump Montgomery."

"What are you talking about? I told you we're going out Friday night. I may even let him spend the night."

"You know how you are."

Matriece fanned the air as though chasing invisible cobwebs. "I really like him but . . ."

"What's wrong with the brother?"

"Not him. His mother."

"What's the matter? You didn't do Jack and Jill? Are you in the wrong sorority? Too dark for the family?"

"How do you know all this stuff?" Matriece asked, shaking her head.

"Survival. You try being a white girl coming of age on the south side of Chicago after all the other white people have split."

"In answer to your question, it's all about control."

Blair's eyes widened. "You should get pregnant. Are you fertile? You can do it Friday night. Listen. Listen. Upper-class family. He will marry you. Moms will be reconciled because of the kid. Perfect."

"Go home, Blair. You have lost your mind."

By the time Matriece reached the twenty-four-hour Ralph's where her sister worked, it was almost eight o'clock. Vonette's shift didn't end until eleven-thirty, and there were three people lined up at her station. She got behind the last person, a young pregnant woman with long braids and swollen feet that were stuffed into a pair of sandals. Standing there she could hear her sister's exuberant laughter filling the aisles.

"Girl, you're crazy," Vonette said as she chuckled. Her laughter seemed to spread through her entire body; she was lit up, a one-woman party.

"How you doing, baby?" she asked as the next customer, an older woman, took her turn. Matriece could hear her murmuring sympathetically as the old lady talked about her sore knees and stiff fingers. "Honey, take your little self home and get in the bed," Vonette advised after she'd bagged her groceries.

"That's just what I'm going to do. You have a good night, sweetie."

"You too."

By the time the pregnant woman had left there were several other people behind Matriece. Even so, Vonette leaned across the counter and hugged her sister for a few tight seconds before releasing her. Standing close together the two women were a study in contrasts. Neither one was pretty, but of the two Vonette came closer because of the softness of her round face. She resembled Hosanna, although her pale, peachy complexion was like her father's. Vonette was carrying at least forty pounds more than she should have been, and when she moved everything shook: her large breasts, her belly, the shawl of blond dreadlocks that trailed down her back.

Matriece's skin was lighter than Hosanna's deep syrupy color and darker than her father's. Her body was athletic with long, muscular legs and arms, a high behind, and small breasts. Everyone in her family said that she looked like her aunt Lucille.

"This is my sister, and we need to talk for half a second, okay?" Vonette said to the two men waiting to be helped.

"What's going on?" Matriece asked.

Vonette lowered her voice to a whisper. "Okay, listen to me and don't say nothing. I went to see Daddy last night."

"Vonette . . ." Matriece felt her body tightening, her mind locking into position, her smile disappearing.

"Just listen. He's in bad shape, Triecy. I'd like to get him in a better place. I was wondering if you could loan me—"

"I'm not giving you any money . . . to . . . help . . . him. I don't give a damn where he's living, Vonette."

Her sister stared at her for a moment. "Don't get upset. I didn't want to get you all upset, Triecy." Vonette put her face close to her sister's. "I'm sorry I asked. All right?" She grabbed Matriece around her shoulders and squeezed her. Just as she was about to pull away, Vonette said, "Oh, I may need you to take Tavares to choir practice on Friday. Boot's working in the valley. Chazz will be at a game. Is that okay?"

Matriece felt her sister's arms around her. "Okay."

"Thanks."

As Matriece was walking away, the words "I don't give a damn" reverberated in her mind. Behind her she heard her sister. "How you doing, baby?"

CHAPTER THIRTEEN

THE FOLLOWING FRIDAY evening, Montgomery Briggs III was drumming his fingers on table number one in the main ballroom of the Century Plaza Hotel, the site of the Morehouse College Scholarship Dinner. The cocktail hour had ended moments before, and most people were still moving to their seats from the mezzanine area outside the door where the bar was located. Every few minutes or so he looked toward one of the entrances, hoping to see Matriece among the crowd.

"What time did you tell that girl to be here?" Montgomery's mother asked, then smiled at him cheerfully. At nearly sixty, Nadine Briggs looked a decade younger. Her sharp pale features were contoured and powdered artfully to conceal whatever lines and puffiness her last cosmetic surgery hadn't erased, and her clothes were tailored to minimize her thickening waist and hips.

"Her name is Matriece, Mom," Montgomery's sister, Juliette, said easily. Nadine was seated between her children. Juliette turned her head slightly away from her in order to give Montgomery a conspiratorial wink.

"Matriece told me that she'd be late, Mom. She had a meeting," Montgomery said.

Nadine sighed. "I don't know," she said, patting his hand. She smiled, tightened her fingers around his, and then turned to her friends who were seated at their table and said, "Isn't this lovely?"

Montgomery pulled his hand away after a moment and resumed his drumming as he glanced around him. The ballroom was festively and expensively decorated. Each of the sixty tables was covered with a beige linen cloth with a metallic gold overlay, and in the center was a large glass vase filled with a bouquet of long-stemmed pale orange roses, calla lilies, and birds of paradise. Every seat was filled by someone who had paid anywhere from one hundred to ten thousand dollars a ticket. The souvenir book on each seat was bursting with full-page ads from the city's well-heeled professionals and businesspeople, all of them here to praise his father and to wish him well.

This year's honoree, Montgomery Briggs, Jr., was seated at the dais on the stage directly in front of his son, along with many of Los Angeles's black elected officials and members of its business community. He could hear his father's booming voice as he shouted out greetings to those at the table of honor, as well as to friends and associates he saw on the floor below him. Studying the crowd, Montgomery saw some of the city's and even the nation's wealthiest African-Americans. There were those who owned fast-food franchises, shopping centers, and medical buildings. He was surrounded by the possessors of both city homes and Laguna or Vineyard retreats, by people who'd long ago ascended beyond the black middle-class prosperity of Baldwin Hills and View Park and were now ensconced in the lofty heights of Beverly Hills, Hancock Park, and Pacific Palisades. His father was a prime representative of this select group: Montgomery Briggs, Jr., had amassed a small fortune with a collection of twenty-eight radio stations all across the country that had begun with a small AM station in Los Angeles. Seated across from Montgomery was J. P. Mooney. At another nearby table was Calvin Meeks, the CEO and founder of Radiance. They were like unharnessed electricity, he thought, capable of giving off a huge amount of light, if only they knew what to do with their collective energy.

"Hello, everyone, sorry I'm late. Hello, Mrs. Briggs. You look fantastic. Hello, Juliette."

Montgomery felt soft hands squeeze his shoulder. The touch calmed and excited him all at once. He was grinning as he rose and pulled out Matriece's chair for her, taking his seat again after she was settled. Beneath the table he reached for her hand. "How are you doing? You look great," she whispered to him.

"Thanks. I'm fine. Glad you're here."

"I had to take my nephew to choir practice. My sister and her husband were working late. He has a solo this Sunday. You know he sounds just like Marvin Gaye. Seriously. The boy can sing."

Montgomery smiled. "I should have known that Tavares was involved. How's he doing?"

"Great. Don't forget you promised to take him on a tour of your offices."

"I didn't forget. Are you going to push me as hard as you do Tavares?"

She tilted her head a little and gazed at him for a moment. "Do you need a push?"

He laughed. "Are we still on for tonight?" he asked. "I'm wearing my purple silk drawers." It was both a joke and an invitation.

"Ooooh, goody," Matriece said, and they both giggled. "Yeah, we're still on." He didn't know what to read in her eyes.

"Well, Matriece, we were beginning to worry about you," Nadine said. "Montgomery honey, introduce Matriece to everybody?"

"Oh, I've met everyone before, Mrs. Briggs," Matriece said in an even tone. Montgomery gave Matriece's hand another squeeze. God, she felt good.

At exactly seven-thirty the program began. The master of ceremonies was the weatherman from Channel Seven, a palm tree of a man with a lively wit and ready humor, who entertained the audience with jokes and mimicry as he introduced the speakers. Montgomery, watching Matriece, saw her eyes light up as she waved to an elderly man sitting at the table directly across from theirs.

"How do you know J. P. Mooney?" he asked.

"He's my godfather."

"You never told me that."

Matriece smiled. "You never asked. Do you know him?"

Montgomery nodded. "He helped finance the first radio station my dad ever bought. Charged a lot of interest, so the story goes."

Matriece laughed. "That's my uncle Mooney, loan shark for the 'hood."

After the minister from one of the city's oldest black congregations blessed the food, Montgomery and Matriece stood up.

"Where are you two going?" Nadine asked, her voice sounding a note of alarm.

Matriece smiled sweetly. "I'm kidnapping your son, Mrs. Briggs."

She let a few moments pass before she added, "We're just going to say hello to my godfather."

"And who might that be, dear?"

"It's Mooney, Mom."

Nadine rose majestically. "I'll go with you."

Montgomery detected a slight tightening of Matriece's jaw, a motion she covered with a smile. The three of them trooped over to Mooney's table, and Matriece bent down and kissed the old man on his cheek. "Hello, Uncle Mooney."

Before he could respond, Nadine kissed him and said, loud enough for the entire table to hear, "Mooney, it's been too long. I've been telling Monty we have got to get together, and not for business. I know that you men have your meetings. How have you been?"

"I'm doing fine, Nadine. Good seeing you."

"You remember Montgomery," Nadine said, and Montgomery could feel her arm around his waist.

"Sure I do. It's been a little while. Your daddy talks about you all the time, young man. How are you?"

"I'm fine."

"Mooney, I just had no idea that you were Matriece's godfather. She's such a wonderful young woman," Nadine said, patting Matriece's arm.

Mooney nodded. "That's my heart," he said, looking straight at Montgomery. "Come talk to me before you leave," he told Matriece, who nodded and then gave him another kiss.

The salads were on the table when they returned. Four more courses followed, and by the time the brigade of Latino waiters cleared away the dessert plates, the weatherman reappeared to introduce a local singer. After her rendition of "Lift Every Voice and Sing," the councilman for the Crenshaw district, Thomas J. Ford, walked over to the podium. As he began to rattle off Big Monty's accomplishments, Montgomery could almost feel himself shrinking. He thought of his father's study at the family home, every inch of wall space covered with plaques, citations, letters from mayors and governors, one from Jimmy Carter and another from Bill Clinton. He recalled how once when he was a small boy he had stood in the middle of that room and spun around and around. When he stopped, he'd thrown up all over himself.

Big Monty strode to the stage. He was nearly six foot five, with highway-size shoulders, a massive neck, and an imposing head. In his football days, his belly had been as hard as his skull; he was still hard-headed, but time had both softened and expanded his middle. Despite his receding hairline and the slight stiffness of his gait, there was an aura of the gladiator that still clung to him. Montgomery didn't laugh with the rest of the audience when his father grabbed the councilman in a bear hug, lifted him from the floor, and then set him down. He, too, had been caught up in his father's exuberant arms at times, hoisted to heights that he couldn't reach on his own. He didn't crack a smile when the official leaned into the microphone mounted on the lectern and said to the six hundred people who filled the room, "Big Monty is as tall as I am, he's just standing on his wallet. And I ought to know because I've been dipping in it for a long time." Everyone knew that for the last thirty years, Big Monty had contributed financially to nearly every black Democratic officeholder in the state. My dad the power broker, the black kingmaker, he thought to himself, his face unsmiling, almost grim. He'd been told often enough that he resembled his father. His own mirror confirmed the similarity of their smooth dark brown skin, large eyes, strong chins. But there were always those inches that separated them. At not quite six feet, sometimes Montgomery felt the strain of looking up.

Beneath the table he could feel Matriece's hand squeezing his knee. She leaned over and whispered in his ear, "Dang, are you some kin to Big Monty?"

He laughed in spite of himself. It was their little joke. He and Matriece had met at an art gallery when he overheard her negotiating with the owner for a painting. He was impressed with her bargaining skills, and even more so when she turned to him, winked, and said, "Ain't too proud to beg." After he'd stopped laughing, she said, "Are you buying something?" When he showed her the painting he was about to purchase, she proposed that he bargain for both hers and his, as though they were together, in order to get a better deal. "I'll pay for them, and then you give me a check, a good check."

"That'll work," he said.

At the end of the evening, she agreed to have a drink with him. When he handed the waiter his credit card, the young black man exclaimed, "Dang, are you some kin to Big Monty?"

Matriece talked a lot that night, and he liked listening to her. She was so full of exuberance and she'd set big goals for herself. "I want to own a cosmetics company," she told him, "an international company."

"You know," he said, when she finally paused, "I don't have big dreams. What I've got has been handed to me, and it's enough."

She stared at him for a long time. And then she said, "Maybe you just haven't discovered what you're good at yet."

The audience was still chuckling as the councilman handed a plaque to his friend and supporter. The noise died down, and the two men put their arms around each other, smiling for the photographer from *The Los Angeles Sentinel,* the largest black newspaper west of the Mississippi. When the photographer had taken the requisite number of shots, the councilman left the stage, and Big Monty took his place at the microphone.

"Friends, you know you can always tell a Morehouse man but you can't tell him much." Big Monty's voice was a lion's roar.

The familiar aphorism went over well with the crowd, which was composed of many alumni of the fabled alma mater of so many black luminaries. Montgomery could feel Matriece's gaze. "You're not laughing," she whispered.

"It's the ten millionth time I've heard it," he whispered back.

As he looked around the packed room he saw the familiar face of the school provost. When the older man's eyes met his, Montgomery nodded his head. Staring at the official who'd labeled him a firebrand after he was elected president of the student body, Montgomery ruminated over his exploits, while his father regaled the audience with recycled humor. It seemed so long ago when he was the young man who'd assembled a committee of his fellow students and created a plan to buy the dilapidated inner-city property that surrounded the college. He was so far away from the person who dreamed of transforming that bleak landscape into the kind of thriving commercial center that bordered most white universities. Of course, his father had intervened. "I've made a life for you," his father told him after he flew to Atlanta. The longer his father railed, the more Montgomery's renegade spirit seemed to shrink. Later, when he returned home and began working for his father, it disappeared altogether.

". . . without the support and love of a good woman, my wife, Nadine."

Montgomery felt the rustling of his mother's long gown as she rose from the chair next to his. Montgomery knew, even without looking, that his mother was in her element. She made the most of these fleeting moments when all eyes were on her. A quick glance confirmed that Nadine was smiling, as she waved to everyone in the room.

His mother liked to say she'd been married to Big Monty her entire life and that her only job had been being his wife and the mother of his children. But Montgomery knew what the public didn't: Forty years earlier, Nadine had persuaded her then fiancé to leave his native Washington, D.C., and move to her hometown of Los Angeles. Once they married, she urged her husband to invest the money they'd earned on a shrewd real estate deal that she'd brokered in a radio station, instead of the apartment building he was going to buy. She had done both the paperwork and the legwork to get them through the FCC's arduous licensing process, and while her husband was figuring out everything he needed to know about programming a radio station, Nadine was managing the tiny staff, her husband, and her children. Her reward was financial success beyond anything she'd ever imagined. But Montgomery knew what she'd lost.

The applause tapered off, and his mother took her seat. He felt her hand on his knee, her fingers pinching him just slightly. Your turn next, the touch said. "Smile," his mother whispered.

". . . and my beloved children, Montgomery the Third and Juliette."

Montgomery's sister, Juliette, stood up immediately and her smile was full-wattage. Eight years younger than her brother, she had recently shed forty-five pounds and was happy to display herself at any given opportunity. Montgomery rose more slowly, conscious of the appraisal he was getting from everyone in the room.

The honoree spoke off the cuff for ten or so minutes. His remarks were humorous, full of homespun wisdom, self-deprecation, and sincere inspiration as he exhorted the audience to try harder, work smarter to achieve the American dream. How does he do it? Montgomery asked himself, watching his father hold six hundred people under his spell. He'd probed that question for most of his life, as he witnessed his father succeed at complex feats of prestidigitation that always resulted in finding money in the most unexpected places.

"Finally, I just want to say a word about something I know is on a lot of minds. Last week there was an article in the *Times* that said some of our Mexican-American brothers who have a pile of money are trying to buy your two favorite radio stations."

Boos and hisses erupted at various tables throughout the room. Big Monty held up his hand, and there was instant silence.

"Some of you are wondering how long KBOM and KRPP are going to be around giving you the best in black music and talk. With all due respect to my Spanish-speaking brothers and sisters, I want to let you know that even though I may be collecting my social security check, I'm still working hard for the people in my community to make sure that when you drive to and from work, you can hear something that's all about you. I thank you for this tribute, and I thank you for your continued support."

The standing ovation lasted until the waiters began clearing away the coffee cups. Montgomery was ready to flee, but his mother took his hand and his sister's, holding them both firmly in her own iron grip. Montgomery whispered to Matriece, "We'll leave in a minute, okay?"

She nodded. Her eyes told him that she was anxious to be alone with him. He thought he saw a promise in her glance.

Hordes of people clustered around their table to congratulate Big Monty, who'd come down from the stage to stand by his family. Nadine was good at prying away those who would cling too long, cutting in at just the right moment so that the others who were waiting could greet Big Monty.

The photographer from *The Sentinel* came over to the table. "Big

Monty, I'd like to get one more quick shot of you with Mr. Meeks and Mr. Mooney," he said. As Montgomery watched, his father walked over to where the other two men were standing, positioned himself in the middle, and smiled as the photographer took the picture. Mooney, Meeks, and Big Monty: the Triumvirate.

"Excuse me," Matriece said as soon as the men were assembled. As Montgomery watched, she moved away so quickly she appeared to be fleeing. When she returned, the photographer was gone and so were Meeks and Mooney. He suspected she didn't want to see her former boss.

"Congratulations, Mr. Briggs," Matriece said to Big Monty.

"Hello, dear," Big Monty said in his loud "campaign" voice. "Good to see you again. Your old man is tired," he said, turning to Montgomery. "Nadine," he said sharply, "what did I tell you to remind me of?"

"Honey, didn't you say you had something to talk over with Montgomery? Why don't you ride with him."

"Yeah, that's right." He turned his back to his wife.

"Dad . . ." Montgomery said, looking at Matriece, who was staring at him.

"Yes, you boys can talk in the car, and that way Monty can sleep a little later in the morning. You all have a big day ahead. Aren't the people from Arbitron coming? And then you have the meeting with Cortez and his folks."

"Hey," Big Monty exclaimed, taking in his son's disapproving glance, "I need you in pretty early."

"Might be a good idea for you to spend the night, Montgomery," Nadine said easily. She smiled at Matriece, who said nothing, then added, "Matriece is a big girl. She can drive herself home. Can't you, dear?"

"Not a problem," Matriece said.

Montgomery felt his father's free hand across his back. "I'm sending you to Houston next week. There's a station down there I want you to check out. May be a distress sale."

"Excuse me for a minute," Montgomery said, steering Matriece to an empty table in the ballroom.

"Don't be too long, honey," Nadine called out. "Good night, Matriece. Wonderful seeing you again."

"Good night," Matriece said. She turned to Montgomery before he could speak. "Don't worry about it," she said. "I understand." Her voice sounded even and calm, but Montgomery could see disappointment in her eyes.

"Listen, I'll take my dad home, and then I'll—"

"No, Montgomery. We'll get together some other time."

"I didn't know that . . ."

She put her hands against his chest. "I understand. Listen, I'm going to try to catch up with my godfather before he leaves."

"I'll call you," he said.

Matriece waved.

CHAPTER FOURTEEN

"DAMN THAT WOMAN," Matriece muttered under her breath as she glanced around the ballroom looking for Mooney. The anger and disappointment that rose in her were unexpected and unwelcome.

She found her godfather in the parking lot, just as he was getting into his new Lincoln. "Uncle Mooney," she called.

The old man leaned out the door. She heard him speak a few words to his driver.

"I thought you forgot about me," he said when she appeared at the car. "Get in."

From inside the car, Matriece could see the crowd flowing out of the hotel. She peered into the throng, hoping to catch a glimpse of Montgomery, even though she was still angry with him. When she didn't see him, the sudden sadness felt like an unwanted parcel someone had suddenly thrust into her hands.

"How long you been going around with Big Monty's boy?" Mooney asked, his eyes on her face.

"Six months."

Mooney gave her a sideways glance. "How old are you now?"

"Thirty-eight."

"You want him?"

She looked at Mooney, then smiled sheepishly. "I don't know."

"Either you do or you don't, Baby Girl. If you make up your mind, maybe he'll make up his. The mama's not helping, I can tell you that right now. What do the kids say? 'Get a life.'" He patted her knee. "The problem with people who've had everything given to them all their lives is they don't know how to work for anything. But sometimes working for something is exactly what they need to do." He peered into her eyes. "You scared of that boy? I don't mean—"

"I know what you mean."

"Well, are you?"

"I don't know."

Matriece could see that the outside light was off at her house when she drove into her garage. In the darkness her disappointment was a cold draft that made her shiver. She might as well admit that she was lonely for Montgomery. Hosanna had warned her and her sister about becoming too dependent on a man. If Montgomery disappeared and never called again, she had to be able to keep on stepping the way her mother had when her father left. And yet, for the first time that she could remember, Matriece felt like standing still.

She slipped off her shoes in the kitchen and turned on the light. The clock on the kitchen wall said ten-thirty, not too late for a phone call. Blair answered on the second ring, her voice still crisp in a way that let Matriece know she hadn't gone to bed yet. "Hey, girl," she said.

"What are you doing calling me? I thought—"

"He didn't quite make it."

"Don't tell me: Mommy Dearest."

"Precisely. She announced that he and his dad had an early meeting and shouldn't sonny boy drive Daddy home and spend the night."

"I think it's time to hire a hit man. Hit woman. I'll do it. The Uzi is loaded. On the other hand, men who treat their mothers well treat their wives well. Listen, I told you what to do."

"I'm not getting pregnant, Blair. I want him to be more independent. I want him to come home with me when . . ."

". . . you're horny. Some dick when you want it is not too much to ask. That was always my bare minimum, so to speak: Can I have the dick when I want it?"

"I'm not sure I was going to sleep with him tonight."

Blair hooted. "Do you have batteries in your house?"

This time it was Matriece's turn to laugh. "This conversation is deteriorating. I'm getting off the phone."

"I'd send Porter over but to tell you the truth, I think you'd be better off looking for batteries."

"Good night, Blair."

"C, as I recall. Or maybe A, depending on what size you're used to."

"Good night, Blair."

Matriece couldn't fall asleep right away. I do not need him, she told herself over and over. After a while she felt herself drifting off. Then she saw the light.

Hosanna was wearing yellow, and she wasn't old. There was a pale glow shimmering through her hair, the same brilliance that always accompanied her. It seemed alive, that light.

"Mom," Matriece called softly. But her mother didn't answer. "Mom," she repeated.

The older woman stared straight into Matriece's eyes. She came toward her then, stretching out her hands, and Matriece reached out for them. She felt her mother's arms around her, her kisses on her face, and then her fingers rubbing lotion into her hand, her thumb kneading her palm, circling it. When she awoke later that morning the image of the woman in yellow was as vivid as if she were still in the room. She began smiling. Her mother dressed in yellow always presaged a blessing.

Matriece forced herself to get started, to rise, make her bed, shower, and put on her clothes. Somewhere in the day's secret chest there must be a gift for her. Standing in front of her bathroom mirror, Matriece sensed her mother's spirit flowing through her mind, clearing it of worry and doubt. She's giving me peace of mind, Matriece thought, and as soon as the idea came to her she was compelled to turn around.

Her backyard was full of butterflies. Looking down from her bathroom window she counted one, two, three, four, five monarchs flitting across the wide expanse of blue-green grass that ran from her patio to the iron fence that bordered her property. The wavy line of yellow and black entranced her. She stared at the winged quintuplets as they looped themselves around her rosebushes and then chased one another across her pansies and calla lilies. They gathered in a tight circle above one of her rosebushes, hovering in midair like a winged security force working the early shift.

CHAPTER FIFTEEN

THE LONG WHITE limousine parked outside the Brentwood townhouse belonging to Asia Pace, newly anointed Empress of Hip-Hop, had been sitting for forty-five minutes, and the diva still wasn't ready. As Asia was perched on a tall cushioned stool in front of a vanity table, her manager, Claude Renfro, poked his head into her dressing room and caught his client's eye. With a custom-made belt containing the tools of her trade, the makeup artist was busily coloring in Asia's full lips. Claude held up his hand, pulled his tuxedo sleeve back, and tapped at his watch. Asia made a face. It seemed to the singer that her whole life was about limousines waiting for her, whisking her to brightly lit places where doors magically opened and crowds burst into applause as though her every appearance was a performance. The crowds had grown larger and the clapping louder since her smash hit *Truth Be Told* had gone double platinum and she'd won two Grammys.

"After the Diamond Discs are handed out tonight, you won't be able to go to a *7-Eleven* without a bodyguard," her manager said gleefully. He stepped just inside her bathroom door, watching Toni contour the singer's cheeks. "You look beautiful, just gorgeous. Even without the makeup."

Asia's hair, which would soon be a frothy confection of braids, curls, pearls, and ribbons, was covered by a do rag, similar to the ones her mother had wrapped around her head when she was a child. That much, at least, hadn't changed, although the "rag" that she currently wore was of the finest silk. Klieg lights framed the mirror in front of her. On the table itself was an array of foundations, powders, lipsticks, concealers, blushes, eye shadows, lipsticks, eye liners, lip liners, and mascara, in shades that differed from the ones in Toni's all-purpose belt. The young woman stood in front of her, deftly arching her brows with a thin brush that she dipped in dark brown powder. Her hairstylist was inches away.

Toni handed Asia a mirror, and she frowned as she peered at herself. "Make that a little darker," she said, pointing to the tips of her eyebrows.

"I'm trying to go subtle," Toni said.

"Darker," Asia repeated. The makeup artist pressed the brush across the brown powder and applied a bit more. "That's it," Asia said, still frowning.

Claude cleared his throat. His main goal was to get his client out the door and into the limousine in fifteen minutes. "You have eight minutes," he said. He motioned to the makeup artist. "Help her get her gown on and then, Phyllis," he said, nodding to the hairstylist, "comb her out."

The dress was a Vera Wang, blue and form-fitting; there were sequins across the bodice. Asia stepped into it, and the makeup artist zipped it up. The back was low, and the front revealed just a hint of cleavage. Above the swell of her breast was a small tattoo, a star. "You look elegant," Toni said, and indeed she resembled a debutante. This was not the dress she would have worn three albums ago when she was one of a trio of hootchies with harmony who never sang a note unless their navels were showing. Three albums ago she couldn't even spell Grammy, but even before the high-price gowns and limousines, she had the feeling that other people's boundaries didn't apply to her. Where that belief came from she didn't know. She'd tried to get the other group members to share her vision of the future, to see the great possibilities she saw for them, but they couldn't get past buying houses for their mamas, and flossing on Crenshaw in a slick ride. She knew early on that they wouldn't stay together. Later she discovered the price for leaving them behind.

Phyllis, whose gum was popping explosively, draped a cover around her and untied her scarf. "The men are gonna be foaming at the mouth," she said good-naturedly. "Why? Because Miss Phyllis is about to lay your hair out like a dead body, honey. Oh yes."

Gently combing Asia's hair, which was a combination of what grew from her head and what had been donated by unknown Korean women, the stylist skillfully arranged a combination of braids into a bouffant French twist, letting a few curly tendrils flow down her back. The effect was breathtaking. But when Asia looked in the mirror her frown deepened.

"Oh, no. I don't see a frown. I know I don't see those lips going down."

"You look fabulous, honey. Doesn't she look fabulous?" Claude asked.

"Claude, how the hell do you know what looks fabulous?" Asia snapped. "Just chill for a minute." Claude wasn't going to be the one people were checking out for what was wrong. He wouldn't be the one on the worst-dressed page in the *Star*.

She pulled on one of the curls, rearranged another of the braids, and stared at herself in the mirror with a dejected look on her face. "I don't know. I don't know," she said softly.

Claude's voice rose a decibel. "You don't know? Honey, you look beautiful. You could put on a sack and look better than most of the women who'll be there tonight. What is not to like?"

Asia sighed. "I don't know."

She couldn't explain how she was feeling, only that looking in the mirror as she was about to go to the Diamond Disc awards, knowing that she'd already won Grammys, was supposed to feel better somehow. She'd been called beautiful, sexy, talented, and yet, sitting in front of her own mirror in a townhouse that cost more than her mother had made in her lifetime, all she could see was a brown-skinned girl with cheekbones that took up most of her face and a nose that was too flat. She remembered when the children in her neighborhood used to tease her about her features, and now *Vogue* proclaimed her this season's exotic beauty.

"Asia, we have to leave in five minutes. Trust me, darling, you look stunning. Beautiful. When you go up on that stage to accept your awards, mouths are going to drop open all over America. Am I lying?" he asked, looking at the two stylists.

"You look gorgeous, sweetie," Phyllis said, still poufing and styling. "But if you want me to whip it some more, or some other way, you know I will. But I'm telling you, you can take this hair to the cemetery because it is The End. And I'm not trying to suck up, 'cause I'll take my ass back to Compton and do hair for the gangstas' babymamas. Shit, they spend more money than you do."

Asia started laughing.

"Just look at that face," Toni cooed.

Their voices sounded so sincere, but Asia didn't know whether she could trust any of them. "Well, change the lipstick," she commanded. "I want something brighter."

Toni picked up three tubes and held them up for Asia to see. "Which one?"

Three brownish shades. Natural. She chose the one in the middle, and as soon as she felt her lips being wiped, relined, filled in, Asia was unsure once again.

"Time to go," Claude said, and he took her by the hand. Leading her past the huge floor-to-ceiling mirrors he whispered forcefully, "Don't look." And because he had that tone, that fatherly, brotherly, man tone, Asia cast her eyes downward and kept walking.

The limousine cruised along Wilshire Boulevard, and when they arrived at the Shrine they were greeted by hordes of screaming fans shouting out her name as she and Claude strode along the red carpet into the auditorium. Inside, the famous and near-famous grazed one another. Asia ducked into the ladies' room twice before the show started. Each time she looked in the mirror and flicked a curl, pressed her lips together, stared. Around her other women, some of them stars, were doing the same thing. She rushed to her seat at the last minute.

Then the program began. Music filled the room. Star presenters drifted to the stage and read their magic words from the cue cards. Pop. Country. Rhythm and blues: her category. Her name was called out with several others. Snippets of songs rang through the air. She heard the announcer. "Best female single, rhythm and blues. 'My Heart Is Yours,' Asia Pace." She was floating, floating to the podium, thanking her manager, her agent, her producer, her recording company executives, her mama. And then again. "Best new female artist, rhythm and blues, Asia Pace." More floating. Thank you, thank you, thank you.

The evening was a swirl of colors, noise, applause. Backstage, Asia blinked as the photographers snapped picture after picture and journalists called out questions. Claude ushered her outside, and two bodyguards flanked her as Asia ambled down the walkway back to the limousine, the two statues in her hands. Two. She felt light-headed. She had won two Diamond Discs! All around her, people were waving, calling out her name. She saw three girls who'd gone to her high school. Renee. Tisa. LaQuanda. She felt their cool appraisals, then turned to smile and wave at strangers.

The man appeared suddenly. Just a face in the crowd but instantly familiar. He stared at her quietly, almost sadly, the way he always did. He was a big man, an older guy, maybe forty. She remembered the first time she saw him at the Soul Train Awards. It was a late spring evening in Pasadena, the air chilly. Claude was seeing about the limo and she was shivering a little, wishing she had brought a coat instead of trying to floss in a strapless. All of a sudden the man took off his jacket and handed it to her across the rope that separated the stars from the regular people. She put it on, and she could feel the warmth of his body. He stood back then, the way he was standing now, not waving or calling out her name, just looking. When Claude reappeared to take her to the car, she passed the jacket back to him and their hands touched.

She began seeing him at other events. There were plenty of guys like him who appeared regularly. Harmless fans. But there was something different about this man, the way he looked at her. The first time he gave her a card was the night she lost the Lady of Soul award. Just wasn't her time, that's what Claude told her. That was the year that Charity Hall cleaned up and took home everything. She remembered the way the bodyguard said, "Hey," in a menacing way when the man leaned over the railing and handed her the envelope but really, there was no need for alarm. Asia felt that instinctively. He didn't try to get all up in her face or anything. He put the envelope in her hand, and then he backed away. She told him thank you, and his eyes held hers for the longest time.

She gasped when she opened the card that night and saw a one-hundred-dollar bill inside. She'd seen large bills before. Her dates, hulking basketball players and intense rappers, seemed to keep a supply on hand for when they went out clubbing. And then there were the one or two guys who expected her to have a cash crop growing, the Can-You-Loan-Me Boys, she called them. "See ya!" That's how she handled gigolo scrubs trying to get in her wallet, the fiends who offered her ecstasy and cocaine.

She'd stared at the bill the man had given her; it was bright green, brand-new, clean-looking. The card had a rose on the outside and inside he'd written, "Your turn is coming soon. Buy yourself something pretty. May God bless you." He signed it "Your Biggest Fan."

No fan had ever given her money before. She'd received flowers, of course. She couldn't count the bottles of Moët that had arrived backstage. She went easy on that, too. Champagne was just alcohol, and that could take her off the stage just as fast as drugs. A couple of old heads, record executives and one producer, had given her jewelry, some golden bangles, rings. But nobody had ever given her money.

Was he trying to buy her for one hundred dollars? Was he trying to impress her? He was way too old and regular to be trying to date her. The money didn't feel insulting; the bill she held was a sweet gift. Buy yourself something pretty. That was a nice thing to say. She liked the way that sounded. The next day she bought flowers with the money, bunches of roses and carnations, baby's breath and Shasta daisies.

Outside the Shrine, her biggest fan was smiling his same sad smile. And then he lifted up both his hands and began clapping. Asia nodded and mouthed the words "Thank you." He pulled the envelope out of his pocket and handed it to her. The bodyguard made a growling noise. "It's okay. I know him," Asia said. She didn't know why she didn't refuse the money; she just couldn't. She turned to say good-bye but the man had disappeared.

Claude's hand was firm on her arm, guiding her through the crowd. "*People* magazine on your right," he whispered in her ear, and she smiled brightly as the paparazzi descended.

Inside the limousine Claude sipped Moët, and Asia drank water. They stopped in at three after-parties. Asia was tired and wanted to go home, but Claude insisted that she be seen. The evening didn't end until after two o'clock; by then she wasn't sleepy anymore. When she closed the door to her townhouse and came inside, she let out a little yell. She placed the two statues on the bureau in her bedroom, staring at them as she lay down on the bed. She rewound the VCR tape she'd left running and watched the part where she went to the podium over and over until she fell asleep.

"Didn't I tell you you looked gorgeous," Claude said to her on the telephone several days later. "You made the cover of *People*. I'll have it sent over."

When it arrived, the first thing Asia saw was that her lips were too dark. She put the magazine facedown on the bottom of a heap of publications on her coffee table. It was then that she remembered the card. This time there was a little bunny rabbit on the front. Inside were the words "God bless you. Your Biggest Fan," and, of course, the money.

Asia put her fingertips against the words, and put the card on top of the marble counter in the bathroom next to her lipstick.

Her trainer arrived the next morning at eleven. He was a small Russian man named Sergei who hadn't been in the country for more than five years. Claude had hired him for her. For two hours every day he put her through rigorous paces. When she let him in he said, "Do you have water to drink?" It was what he always said right before they began.

"Yes," she said, holding up the bottle.

They went into her gym, which originally had been a third bedroom, and Sergei began stretching her out. "I understand you win another prize," he said.

"Yes."

"Congratulations."

"Thank you."

"In America, anybody can win prize." The words sounded hard and sharp, as though he were spitting out tiny stones. "Not like stinking Russia where everybody lose. Here you can start out with no money and become rich. Begin in ghetto and end up in Beverly Hills. Little girl sing in church choir, next stop Carnegie Hall." He paused, glanced around the room at its state-of-the-art equipment. He knew that just outside in the hallway were fresh-cut flowers in crystal vases sitting on fine wooden stands. His voice became low, his tone sly. "You start out black, become white." He laughed uproariously. "Leg higher, hold it, hold it," he commanded. "Do not let go yet. Not yet. No. No. No. Why you let go?"

Asia stood up. "I'm tired," she said, and she walked out of the room. As soon as Sergei left, she lay across her bed. She picked up the telephone, called Claude, and told him to find her another trainer. "Somebody black," she said. What difference does it make? she asked herself as soon as she hung up. She was still for a moment, looking up at the ceiling, then she called her mother.

"Hey," she said, when her mother answered. She always enjoyed that first moment of hearing her mother's voice.

"Hey, Miss Diamond Disc. Whatchu doing? Girl, I walked into the shop yesterday, and you could just hear the women buzzing. I could barely get a shampoo before they started coming up to me, bringing me CDs for you to sign. So I have about six of them over here for the next time you come by."

"You can sign them."

Her mother giggled. "Me." She giggled again. "You want me to sign your name?"

"Yeah. Nobody will know."

"All right. So, what are you doing? Oh, I've been meaning to tell you that I had to take back the DVD player and exchange it. Something was wrong with it. So, when I went to take it back, they didn't have any of the kind you bought me, so I had to get another kind. It was a little more expensive, not much."

"That's okay."

"I told Monroe that you wouldn't care."

Monroe was Ruth's current boyfriend. He was living with her at the house in Inglewood that Asia had bought for her mother. Neither Ruth nor Monroe worked, unless unpaid public relations counted as employment. Ruth was only forty, and she could have been productive but whenever Asia suggested that she get some training for something she might enjoy, her mother changed the subject. For a while, Asia put Ruth on her payroll as a kind of companion, dresser, cook, housekeeper person. But Ruth was a slob, a terrible cook, she couldn't keep her clothes straight, and she got on her nerves. It was better just to send her mother a monthly check. She resented supporting Monroe. But at least he didn't beat up her mother. And Asia was grateful that he'd never tried anything funny with her. But then, she'd gotten past that particular danger point.

Any man who came into her mother's life now would be too in awe of Asia, too fearful that she'd pull the plug on the money to try putting his hands on her. Those men were behind her.

"I talked to your brother last night," Ruth said, changing the subject.

"How's he doing?"

"He's doing," Ruth said. Her voice brightened. "He's still going to school, reading a lot of books. Donny always was smart. He said the parole hearing is coming up soon. Think he'll do better this time?"

Asia sighed. "I hope so, Mom."

"Yeah. So do I. I mean, he's got too much sense to have it be a revolving door. Kier and the baby went up there to see him last month. I guess I'll go next week. You want to come with me?"

"Mom . . ."

"Yeah, I know. I know you can't do that. He's so proud of you, that you made it."

"Has he been singing? Does he still have that group?"

"He didn't mention it the last couple of visits."

She felt a shadow crossing her soul as she remembered how she and her brother used to sing together in church and at talent showcases. He'd organized their first group and found a manager. Without him, she'd have nothing. "He's the one who can sing. Listen, Mom, I hafta go."

"Well, all right then. Oh, have you had your talk with Triecy?"

"Not yet."

"Yeah, her and me been going to the same salon, same stylist and didn't even know it. Ain't that something? Usually she goes on another day, that's what she told me. So it was just a coincidence, us meeting. I didn't even recognize her, it's been so long. But she knew me right off. So that's how we hooked it up, you know, you being the spokesmodel for her company, or whatever. Gilda Cosmetics. That's a big company. Everybody's heard about them."

"Uh-huh."

"So, that's a good thing I did, getting y'all hooked up and everything."

"Yeah, Mom."

"She said I owed her for all the times I didn't pay her for baby-sitting you." Ruth laughed. "Those were the lean days."

"I'll talk to you later, Mom. I love you."

"Me too."

After she hung up the telephone she turned on the television set, using the remote on her nightstand. She selected BET's afternoon music videos, and as she watched, she critiqued the performances. After the awards, everyone in the world wanted to interview her but today she had no appointments at all. Asia slipped off her sneakers and stared at her toes, wondering if she should call her manicurist. Some weeks she saw the woman four times. But not today. She wanted company but she didn't feel like going out alone. She picked up the telephone and dialed Phyllis's number. She got the answering service. "I just wanted to . . ." She stopped to think. "Just to talk. Call me," she said.

Later that afternoon the telephone rang. It was Claude, telling her that the negotiations with the record company were close to being settled. "Don't forget that tomorrow you have the appointment with the woman from the cosmetics company."

"I know. Bye."

Thinking about her upcoming meeting with Matriece Carter made Asia happy. She hardly ever encountered anyone from the world she'd inhabited before triple platinum became her domain. But tomorrow she would see Matriece, and for once she'd meet the old neighborhood halfway.

CHAPTER SIXTEEN

HIS MANTRA WAS a whisper in his mind. Sam heard the word inside him and let it push out all other thoughts. At his sides, his arms went limp and then his legs. He could feel his head falling forward. Bright light rose up like a new dawn and claimed him. That light was hands caressing him, arms holding him, warmth and serenity. The face of God in him, that's what it was.

When Sam finished his morning meditation, he sat still for a moment, allowing the sensations and tranquil energy to ebb away slowly. On his knees he said a quick prayer before he got up. He stood in front of the television in his bedroom for a few seconds, then glanced at his watch. Even though his time was short, he decided to look at the video once more. It was already in the VCR, turned to the only part he liked. He was a big man but he crouched down on the floor, his face almost touching his television set as he pressed the power button and then hit play. He liked to see her close up, so close he could imagine holding her in his arms. Here was the part. Luther Vandross made the announcement. Ole Luffer. "And the winner is . . . Asia Pace." Sam watched as the young woman walked across the stage. She was proud-looking, an elegant young lady. And so beautiful. "I'd like to thank . . ." She rattled off a list of names he didn't recognize, people from the record industry, from her world. He listened. Sam knew the list by heart now. He'd been looking at the same video for the last few weeks. When she was finished, when she walked off the stage, he rewound the tape again and then played it one more time. One day he would put his arms around her. He'd hold her and tell her how much he loved her, how long he'd been loving her. *My good is here right now.* It was his own special prayer.

Sam made his bed and rushed through his small two-bedroom home. He'd purchased the Inglewood bungalow a year before; it was the first piece of property he'd ever owned, and he was proud of it. He put last night's dinner dishes in the dishwasher, placed the old newspapers in the bin in the garage, fluffed the pillows on the couch he'd fallen asleep on in his den. As soon as he finished, he took a quick shower and got dressed in faded khaki shorts, a white T-shirt, and thick boots with rubber soles. He had purchased some new shorts but he was saving them for tomorrow. Friday was the only day he wore cologne, the day he saw the customer he wanted to look good and smell good for.

Back in the kitchen, he set out a bowl of cereal and milk, poured juice, and ate quickly, then ran out of the house. His big white van was parked in the driveway. Sam surveyed it to make sure it was absolutely sparkling. With a barely damp cloth, he buffed the side that had a likeness of his dark face and shiny bald head. He polished the words that read: "Big Sam Your Detail Man." Below them was his motto: "Your Ride Should Look As Good As You Do." In Los Angeles, people, dogs, lawns, and cars were groomed weekly; Sam had found his niche in a society that was obsessed with appearances. Once he was satisfied that not a particle of dirt was to be found on his van, he got in, turned on the ignition, pressed on the CD player, and when the vehicle was filled with the sound of Asia Pace's voice, he took off.

Kent Bridgeport's house was always his first stop on Thursday mornings. It was a huge mansion, the kind of home most people dream about. Sam figured that Kent was somebody as soon as he met him when he was working at a car wash on Sunset Boulevard. When he handed Sam his tip, the man's fingernails were clean and buffed. His clothes were expensive and his voice was strong but not loud; he looked like money.

Sam envied Kent nothing. He didn't have "living large" fantasies anymore. Wanting more than he was willing to work for had earned him fourteen years for armed robbery in the state penitentiary. The years had taken away more than time. There were some things he could never get back.

It was seven o'clock when he rolled into Kent's driveway. The house looming before him was mammoth, a two-story white palace that went on and on like a long-legged woman. Kent's dark Mercedes was parked outside, but his wife's car wasn't there. Sam hadn't seen the silver Jag in months.

Sam saw that Kent was at the door, the paper in his hand, a cigarette in his mouth. He was already dressed, although his clothes appeared wrinkled, as though he'd slept in them. He'd always thought that Kent was in his early fifties, but today he looked like an old man. His face, usually rosy and clean-shaven, appeared puffy and shadowed. There were deep circles underneath his blue eyes.

"Good morning, Kent," Sam said. From the beginning the two men had been on a first-name basis, another reason Sam liked him.

Kent leaned against his door and sort of doubled up, as though he were in pain. The cigarette fell from his lips.

"You all right," Sam said, rushing to the man's side and grabbing him as he slumped forward. Was he having a heart attack? What should he do?

"I'm all right, just tired," Kent said after Sam had helped him inside. The house smelled like stale cigarettes. Sam had never been beyond the front door. The inside of Kent's house was as lavish as the outside. Nothing was out of place. It looked as though it was more for display than for living in. The furniture was plush, the colors rich. Nothing really matched, but everything seemed to go together perfectly. The older man led him into the kitchen, then sat down at the table. He motioned for Sam to have a seat. "I didn't sleep too well last night." He took out a cigarette from a pack on the counter, lit it, and inhaled deeply.

"You get nights like that," Sam said. He didn't like the tone the conversation was taking. As far as he could tell, Kent was straight, but his years in the joint had taught him to be wary. Even before he went away he knew guys who lived their out-front lives as heterosexuals but jumped out of the closet every chance they got. If Kent was fixing to go freaky on him, he'd lose one of his best customers. He glanced at Kent's hands and was relieved to see that they were folded on the table in front of him. There was no desire in the older man's eyes, just sadness.

Sam heard the dull thud of footsteps. When he looked up he saw Kent's wife. He breathed in sharply. The last time he'd seen her was nearly six months ago. Then she was a well-preserved older woman, and not bad-looking, with a head full of frosted hair and a fondness for orange lipstick. He'd been wondering where she was and thinking about asking

Kent, but now he knew. The woman who stood in front of him looked half her size. She walked slowly, and when she got closer he could see that the left side of her face was slightly lower than the right. "Keh," she said, and Sam realized that she was calling her husband's name. A stroke, Sam thought.

Kent stood up immediately. "What are you doing out of bed, honey?" He walked over and put his arm around her shoulders. "I'll be right back," he told Sam.

As soon as they left the kitchen, Sam could hear their voices. His wife did most of the talking, or what might pass for talking, slow guttural noises that sounded like gibberish. Poor lady, Sam thought. Poor Kent.

"She'll be okay," Kent said, when he returned.

"Sure she will," Sam said. He didn't know what was wrong with Kent's wife, but she looked a long way from okay.

"Peggy had a slight stroke a few months ago. Well, maybe not so slight. It's taking her a while to bounce back."

"That's too bad," Sam said. "She's a nice lady. Hey, man, she'll get better," he added when he noticed how dejected Kent seemed.

"She's never been sick before. Never," Kent said, his words sounding flat and hollow in the large kitchen.

"Sometimes you have to ride out the bad times," Sam said. "Take it from me, Kent, there's always a new beginning."

"I'm sixty-four years old, Sam. Peggy's sixty. I wonder if we have any new beginnings left."

"It ain't as bad as you think, man. You have to trust God. No, seriously," he said when Kent just shook his head. "You know my story. I told you before. I spent fourteen years locked up. If anybody was down for the count, it was me, right. But here I am, five years later. I own a home. I have a business. I still can't get a woman to go out with me," he said, and both men laughed. "I'm serious. Six months ago I met a nice woman, and I took her to the movies. We got to talking about our lives, and see, I try to be up front, so I let her know about my incarceration. I told her I'd had a room at the State Home for Adventurous Men. She changed her phone number on me." He chuckled. "That's all right. Everything's going in the right direction. I've got my eye on somebody else. She's way above me—

education-wise, money-wise, too—but you never know. When I work up the nerve I'm going to ask her out. Sometimes you just have to trust God."

Kent couldn't stop himself. "Sam, you ever gamble?"

Sam shook his head.

"You're smart," Kent said. "I took out a second on this house, close to two million dollars. I bought some stocks on a tip, one of those dot coms. They went right into the toilet, and they've been there for six months. Now I hear the company might be declaring bankruptcy. And that's not even the half of it. Man, I've got so much debt. I owe everybody. The owner of the company I work for told me she was thinking about retiring, and if she does, her son will probably take over. I know he'll come in with a whole new regime, and I'll be out. Just like that. More than forty years down the drain. I could lose everything I've got."

Sam tried to conceal the fact that he wasn't surprised. When he was working at the car wash where he'd first met Kent, he'd overheard his cell phone conversations. He'd known for a long time that Kent risked his good life regularly, foolishly, and with a vengeance. Sam glanced at Kent, who was looking at him with apprehension. "Hey, man," Sam said quickly, "don't worry. I'll keep this just between the two of us."

Kent reached over and patted Sam's hand. "You're a good guy, Sam."

"Hey, man, so are you. It's going to be all right. Trust in God. When I was incarcerated, everybody I counted on let me down. My mother died. My wife left me. My brothers and sisters stopped coming to see me. All I had was God. It turned out God was all I needed. Prayer works, Kent. I'm a witness."

Sam stayed seated until he saw Kent get up and walk over to an electric coffeemaker. "You want a cup?" Kent asked.

"No, man. If you're okay, I'm going to go outside and do your car. Are you okay?"

Kent was still for a moment and then he nodded. "Yeah, I'm fine."

"Is your wife's car in the garage? Do you want me to get it out?"

Kent hesitated, and just that moment when his eyelids flickered sadly told Sam more than he wanted to know. "It's uh . . ."

"You had to put it in the shop?"

Kent looked relieved. "Yeah. It's in the shop."

"I'll just do yours then. Are you sure you're all right, Kent?"

"I'm fine."

No he wasn't, Sam thought as he began washing the sleek black Mercedes. That silver Jag had been repossessed. The truth was written all over Kent's face. Sam knew that kind of truth, the way it etched itself into all the sad crevices of a man's mouth. Kent thought that he was okay, but he was putting his faith in the wrong place. He was sitting inside his kitchen, sipping expensive coffee, wondering and worrying about his wife and his money, not knowing that God was the only one who could make things right, not knowing the moneymaking, healing power that was no further away than a thought. All anybody had to do was lean on that power and he'd be all right.

CHAPTER SEVENTEEN

BY THE TIME Kent had showered and changed his clothes, his head had begun to unclog, and the world around him didn't look quite so bleak. Sipping a second cup of coffee, lighting another cigarette, Kent forced himself to contemplate his current dilemma, something he'd been assiduously avoiding for weeks. He walked over to the marble island in the center of his kitchen and stared at the stack of bills that his accountant had sent over. They had arrived at his office via Federal Express. When he had opened the box, he saw that Craig had hand-printed in red ink: "These must be paid. We have to talk." Red ink! Jesus, was that supposed to be symbolic or something?

Well, he didn't want to talk with Craig, not until he'd thought of a way to extricate himself from his current financial difficulties. He was behind, a little behind but there was no need to panic. He picked up one of the bills. Eighteen thousand dollars for a live-in nurse. Illness cost, that was for sure. But Peggy had to have round-the-clock care, and he certainly couldn't give it to her. Poor Peggy. She'd always been such a trooper. Never made any demands, the perfect hostess. Stayed with him when any other woman would have left. He certainly had thought about leaving her. If she had had any inkling of that, she'd never let on.

He picked up the American Express bill. The total for the month was thirty thousand dollars and some change. His eyes scrolled down the right side of the bill. They were mostly cash advances he'd gotten. There was nothing to show for the cash except the memory of hours spent at the blackjack table or his time playing poker. He'd always had a penchant for gambling, but since Peggy had become ill, he'd gone overboard. Those were the debts his accountant knew nothing about.

He flung the American Express bill on the counter and picked up the electric bill. For forty-five days the power company was charging them nine hundred dollars. Jesus! The house was eating him alive.

He closed his eyes for a moment. There it was, the tiny third-floor walk-up they'd lived in during their first year of marriage. He remembered everything: the dingy walls, the stains that couldn't be scrubbed out of the bathtub, the exquisite happiness he felt every time he opened the door and found Peggy waiting for him. He expected to feel that way about her forever, but it didn't last. Nothing good in his life ever had. Oh, God, he thought, opening his eyes. But even with his eyes open, he couldn't stop that other memory from pushing through.

It was a snowy afternoon, the flakes coming down fast and hard, and already there were a few inches on the ground of his small Kansas town. Miss Grady, his fifth-grade teacher, had dismissed everyone early. The rush of students turned the dismissal into a melee of sorts. Children ran into the school yard and began pelting each other with quickly formed snowballs. He didn't feel like playing. Instead of joining in with Buster and Larry, he waved at them and began walking home alone. He thought there might be a letter from his father, who was away fighting in Japan. It was Tuesday, the day his father's letters usually arrived. He remembered running through the snow, hearing the soft crunch of his shoes against the tamped-down ice. He and his mother would sit together on the sofa in the parlor. She would put her arms around him as she read the words that kept him connected to the most wonderful man on earth.

The house was dark when he got there. Usually the shades were up, but at one o'clock in the afternoon they were still down. The door was unlocked, as usual—nobody in their small town locked their doors—so Kent walked in, dropping his book bag by the chair in the parlor. He could hear his mother laughing in her bedroom. Maybe his father had put a joke in his letter. He walked toward the sound of his mother's happiness, wanting to be a part of it. Kent opened her bedroom door without knocking. And then the laughter stopped.

He had never seen his mother naked. For a moment all he could do was stare at her body, the way her breasts and hips swung from side to side. There was a naked man who almost seemed to be riding her as if she were pretending to be his pony. Kent had opened the door so quietly that at first they didn't realize he was standing there, mesmerized and confused by what he saw. His mother saw him first. She was screaming softly—he thought for a moment that the man was hurting her—and then she turned her head, and when her eyes met his she began really screaming.

"You can never tell anyone," she told him, after the man had hurriedly put on his clothes and fled out the back door.

He knew that, even without her saying the words. He knew it was a secret that he'd be forced to harbor within him forever.

Only it wasn't a secret. Neighbors had seen the man and other men coming and leaving his house. At school, the children began to whisper, just loud enough for him to hear. One by one, he found the boys when they were alone and vulnerable. He beat them quickly, silently, always warning them not to tell. He began to steal. At first he took things from the youths who talked about his mother, pencils, erasers, small things. Later, he began to pilfer from the grocery store on the main street in his small town. He took gumballs and penny candies, comic books. The thrill of taking such a risk took his mind off his mother's sin, but the shame stayed with him. When his father returned from the war they moved to Los Angeles within a year. A new start, he heard his mother say.

Kent opened his eyes and lifted out another bill from the stack. There it was. He was behind three months in his child support to his former mistress for their eight-year-old daughter. Like mother, like son, only his philandering had caught up with him. What a bummer that had been. Peggy had called him an asshole when he'd confessed. His wife had suffered three miscarriages. They had never had children together. But she'd stood by him when things got ugly and Vanessa hired a lawyer. Now every month he had to send that gold digger five thousand dollars. And that was only the beginning. Vanessa usually came up with something extra. Jolie needed braces. Jolie needed piano lessons. Jolie's private school wasn't good enough. It didn't hurt that Vanessa would still occasionally come across with a blow job, or maybe go all the way, although he'd only succumbed in a few weak moments, because the last thing he needed was another kid. He wouldn't put it past Vanessa to try to get another meal ticket out of him. He loved his child, but she was still her mother's only way of making a living. At least Vanessa was good about letting him visit with her, and she hadn't poisoned the kid's mind. Peggy knocked herself out for the little girl and had taught Jolie how to cook and knit. She actually spent more time with his child than he did. Kent sighed. Now that Peggy was sick, Jolie didn't seem to want to come around as much. Kent slammed down the bill and pushed it into a pile with the others, then shoved them all away from him. He was grateful when the doorbell rang and he went to let in the nurse. He'd deal with his finances later, when his mind was clearer.

When he got outside, his Mercedes was gleaming. That Sam was a real pro. He hated the fact that his car washer had to witness his poor wife's misery, but at least Sam had voiced some concern. Some of his so-called friends hadn't even come to see Peggy. Too busy with their little child brides to care about a really decent woman. Of course, the people at work had been great, especially Gilda. She'd been truly wonderful, calling and sending flowers. His employer for almost forty years, Gilda seemed more like a friend. He got in the car, then slumped back against the seat and breathed in the scent of citrus. Sam always left the car smelling so good.

Heading toward the 405 freeway, Kent stopped off in front of Los Angeles National Bank. He had eight dollars and change in his pocket. He went to the ATM machine and put in his card, pressed in his code, then requested two hundred dollars, enough money to get him through the next day or two. But the sign across the screen kept telling him to ask for a lesser amount. When it denied him twenty dollars, he shoved the card back in his wallet, took out his Visa card, and punched in the numbers for a cash advance. The word "denied" flashed across the screen. What the hell was he paying Craig for? He reached in his wallet and tried his other Visa. Denied. He had four Visas, one American Express, three MasterCards, and the ATM denied them all.

He felt himself hyperventilating. Standing in front of the heartless machine, he reached in his suit pocket and pulled out a tiny envelope. Inside were flat coral-colored pills. Xanax. He swallowed two. Thank God

Raymond, his physician, was a friend. Thank God the pills were so small that he didn't need water.

It would be wonderful if he could sit down to a poker game right now. He could hear the slapping of the cards, the rough jokes of the men. His poker gang was very different from his business associates. The hotel room was always filled with cigar smoke and the odor of scotch. Sometimes they had girls come over to entertain them, just like at an elite men's club. Kent sighed. His favorite game was closed to him until he paid back the $125,000 he owed the house. And he would pay it. He had to pay it soon. Thank God he'd get his salary at the end of the week. Of course, that one was pretty much spent. He'd have to hand over the next six months' worth of checks to the guy holding his debt. In three months he had a balloon payment due to the tune of two million dollars. He didn't want to think about where that money was coming from. He couldn't go to his brother again. And Peggy's sister was out of the question. For a fleeting moment he thought about asking Gilda to give him an advance. No sooner had the idea formed in his mind than he began worrying in earnest, as he made himself confront what was as fearsome as his debt: the prospect that his employer, his friend Gilda, was leaving the company.

"I'm getting older, Kent," she'd said to him several weeks before. "Daniel is anxious to take over. Perhaps it's time for me to retire."

As Kent shoved yet another card into the ATM he tried to imagine Gilda Cosmetics without its founder. Her leaving couldn't come at a worse time for him. Jesus, how in the world had everything gotten so out of control? How could the stocks have tanked? Everybody was making money off the market. He didn't mean to gamble so much, to bet so high on cards and football games. Well, he'd pay off his current debts somehow, and then that was it. He wasn't going to gamble again. If only Gilda would stay a little longer. There was no telling what would happen if her son took over. Daniel wasn't a bad guy, but he was impulsive and headstrong. Kent thought about the time he insisted that the entire spring line of lipsticks be lightened just because he was dating some bimbo who told him that pale shades were in. The look that fall was dark, and GC lost a lot of money. Daniel wasn't mean like his father, but he was a hotshot, anxious to prove that he was in charge, just like his old man, David, the first of Gilda's four husbands. Now, there was a real asshole. Kent had to give himself a pat on the back every time he thought about that time. It was almost prescient how he had known instinctively to side with Gilda when the couple split up. It was he who helped her recover the power her spouse had usurped during their marriage, after Gilda had been relegated to the sidelines of her own company. He took Gilda by the hand, helped her find the right lawyers, and showed her everything that was in the books that David had hidden from her. Oh, they were a team all right.

Tiny spritzes of tranquilizer magic began to pulsate inside his brain. Hail to the chill, familiar, lifesaving. He breathed deeply and felt as if tender, loving fingers had just massaged his mind. One thing at a time. Back to the matter at hand. Of course. There was still his savings account. He'd been trying to get money from his checking account. He slipped his ATM card back into the narrow slot, pressing his secret code, and then touched the savings account button. He punched in the amount of $200 and waited. A sign flashed across the screen. Request a lesser amount. All right then, $180. The same grim words appeared. His requests descended by twenty until he requested $40. In seconds two slick twenty-dollar bills appeared. He gratefully snatched the money out of the machine, took his card and receipt, and then hurried back to his car. Once inside he glanced at his clock. He'd spent twenty minutes fighting with the ATM machine. Now he'd have to speed to get to his meeting for Brown Sugar. Such a whimsical name. Brown Sugar. He'd have to hold himself together until the end of the day when he was scheduled to meet with Gilda. He'd find out soon enough whether his future included a declaration of bankruptcy. *Don't leave now, Gilda.* Kent pressed his foot hard against the gas pedal and the car surged ahead. Onward!

CHAPTER EIGHTEEN

MATRIECE SCANNED THE chart of lipstick shades on the table in front of her, then took the sample tubes and swiped multicolored stripes across her wrist. She studied the lines against her brown skin, first holding her hand three inches from her eyes, then six inches away, then a foot. Close up or from a distance, the colors had to be right in this world and probably the next one. She'd learned that rule at her mother's knee. Blair had finally gotten the message to the colorists after not one, not two, but three attempts. The too-vivid reds had been eliminated. Gone were the pale golds. There was not one shade that screamed last season; no burnt oranges, no warmed-over browns from yesteryear.

Matriece rose from her seat, walked over to the large picture window in the conference room, held her hand up toward the sun, and studied the colors again. Red on a piece of paper was one thing, but how color and light transformed skin, that was the true test. In the final analysis, sales would be based on the shades, the glimmer of bronze that seeped through the softest mauve and lightest beige. Next fall was going to be a subtle season, everything underplayed almost, but of course, not to the point of being natural. The beauty game was all about nuance and silent promises, and the perception of difference—meaning, not the same as last year's. That all translated into an ever renewable need from women: the need to look as good as Every Other Woman. That ubiquitous Every Other Woman peered from magazine pictures, smiled with Chiclets teeth from billboards, wiggled one-hundred-pound bodies on music videos, and radiated dewiness at the Oscars. Physical perfection was the new religion, and every woman wanted to be saved. Matriece was going to make sure that black women were baptized in Brown Sugar's holy waters.

Matriece's staff was seated at a long table in the center of the room, along with Kent Bridgeport, GC's chief financial officer, Daniel

Abramowitz, who had hired Matriece, and Rachel Fine, his half-sister, whose job description as her brother's assistant was as vague as her flexible hours. Ordinarily, Matriece's decision about the colors wouldn't have called for so many upper-management cooks, but because this was the third time colors had been presented, Daniel had insisted on coming with backup. Their presence didn't alarm Matriece. He can bring anybody in here he wants, she thought; the colors get approved when I say so.

Matriece looked around the table. Fontaine Blount, the youngest in the group, leaned forward in his chair as though he were ready to spring into action as soon as she gave the word. Blair kept jiggling her foot, and Matriece realized that she wanted a cigarette even more than she wanted her affirmative decision. Kent's fingers were tapping lightly on the table. Another nicotine junkie. Daniel's jaw was tight. As for Rachel, she seemed to be daydreaming as she slowly rubbed the diamond-crusted gold Star of David that hung around her neck. Matriece stared at the rainbow on her own hand again, then she smiled. "This is excellent," she said, finally willing to make a commitment. "Perfect," she said. "What do you all think?"

"The colors are awesome. Pastels are it for next fall. We'll be way ahead of whatever else is out there," Fontaine said. "We're going to be a hit."

With those words everyone at the table broke into applause.

"Great colors! Fabulous!" Daniel said as people were getting up from the table. His voice was like a sudden, unexpected blast from a rock station with the volume turned all the way up.

"Thank you, Daniel," Matriece said.

"You were right to hold out," Rachel said to her as everyone in the group was dispersing. "I've never seen anything like these shades."

"Thank you," Matriece said. With her long wispy hair and sad gray eyes, Rachel seemed like a little lost girl. Watching her leave with her brother, Matriece had the feeling that she needed a hug.

Kent and Blair rushed out of the room together, their cigarette packs and lighters in their hands. Matriece knew they were both on their way to the courtyard behind the building where they would fire up. Codependents. As long as they had each other, neither one would quit.

Twenty minutes later Blair knocked on her door, giving off the odor of tobacco as she sat down in a chair in front of Matriece's desk. "You and Kent finished shooting up?"

"Oh, that's cold, sisterwoman. We snort." She grinned. "He's excited, Matriece. He called you a 'brilliant, decisive leader.' "

"He did?" Matriece couldn't help feeling pleased.

"He admires you for sticking to your guns and getting the colors you felt were best, even if Daniel was getting impatient."

"Daniel wants everything now." Matriece shrugged.

"Daniel wants everything yesterday. Between the two of us, Kent smoothed it over for you with him. He made him understand that you were being deliberate, not cavalier."

"What is it with Daniel? We're under deadline." Matriece shook her head. "Well, he ought to be happy now," she muttered.

Matriece poured them each a glass of diet cola, which shimmered and bubbled in the sunlight streaming through the large picture window in her office. Below them, Los Angeles, with all her commerce and traffic, her babble of tongues and multifarious accents, seemed as contained and remote as a smile on a billboard. Matriece held out her tumbler and when Blair's glass clinked against it, she said, "To moving on."

"Damn, I'm glad that's behind us," Blair said. "Girl, the shades are hot. The sisters are going to love this stuff."

Matriece felt a slight twinge of annoyance that she couldn't explain.

"Black women set the style for this country."

"You think so?" Matriece asked.

"Definitely. When I was in eighth grade, this big girl named Denise Wooten and some of her friends were going to kick my butt after school. When I got outside they all had on the same pleated skirts, and they had their socks rolled down in the same way. Their haircuts were identical, real poufy on top with spit curls around the ears. It was like Diana Ross and the Supremes came to beat my behind."

"What happened?" She was used to Blair's "adventures in the 'hood" tales.

"I ran, honey. After that I went to stay with my mother's sister. She and her husband had money. I spent a semester living with them—all-white neighborhood, all-white school. Talk about culture shock. No Supremes there. Anyway, the reason I'm remembering is that I was thinking about the inner-city woman's style, you know, how we could use that in marketing the product. Maybe we show a young woman putting on our lipstick on Sunday morning. She zooms up to Ebenezer Baptist on a motorcycle or in a convertible and here comes Grandma strutting down the street, wearing this baaad hat, you know, feathers and beads, everything."

"And then some sort of catch phrase—"

"Yeah," Blair said, growing excited. "Like . . . I don't know. Let the ad people figure it out."

"My mother was always too busy working to go to church," Matriece said.

"She was in sales, right?"

"Yes."

"What did she sell? I forgot."

"Things for women. Grooming items."

Blair nodded. "Are you going to call Gilda about the colors?"

"In a few minutes."

"Anyway, the Old Broad Herself won't be able to stop grinning, as soon as she gets her stitches out." Blair whispered this last, and giggled softly.

The fact that the founder and CEO of Gilda Cosmetics was only a few miles away recuperating from cosmetic surgery was a secret that couldn't be kept. The company-based rumors described as "the works" the lifting and tucking of the makeup maven's face, neck, thighs, and belly. Matriece put her finger to her lips and gave her friend a glance that was tinged with a warning. She hadn't divulged any information about Gilda's condition to her colleagues, and as close as she was to Blair, she felt vaguely uncomfortable gossiping about her boss. Matriece didn't want anyone ever to think that she had anything but the highest regard for Gilda.

"We be stylin'," Blair said.

"What?"

"The catch phrase. Think about it."

"We be stylin'," Matriece repeated silently after Blair had gone. She scratched her arm and then the back of her neck, feeling as though she'd discovered someone wearing her clothes without her permission. Then she sat down at her desk and began dialing a number that hadn't so much been given to her as bestowed upon her. Moments later she heard the voice that always made her think of both her past and her future.

Gilda's accent was faint but still perceptible. "Ah, Matriece. My dear, I hope that you have some good news for me."

CHAPTER NINETEEN

BLAIR'S HEELS CLICKED against the marble floor of the restaurant as she made her way toward the back where Rachel was seated. She'd read about Ambience in an article in last month's *Los Angeles Magazine,* a publication she perused faithfully in search of the new and the hip, particularly in the San Fernando Valley, where she lived. The walls were a muted swirl of earth tones, and the tables were dressed in pale golden taffeta. Gorgeous. Peeking at the plates of the diners she passed, Blair smiled in anticipation. Wonderful presentation! Head up, shoulders back, she told herself as she passed the tables filled with twenty- and thirtysomething trendsetters. God, I can't believe I'll be forty in a couple of years, she thought. The women around her had glowing skin, thick glossy hair that they tossed easily as they ate and chatted. Blair sucked in her stomach and tossed her chin-length hair. She'd dressed in her very best for this chic lunch. I have arrived, she told herself, if only for my lunch hour.

Rachel stood up and kissed her on both cheeks. She self-consciously returned the gesture, recalling how she and Matriece used to laugh about double cheek kisses from people they barely knew and how phony they felt. Blair still felt somewhat awkward around Gilda's daughter. They weren't exactly coworkers, and yet it was too soon to think of themselves as friends. But she was getting to like Rachel. And she certainly liked the fact that the younger woman had a penchant for picking up the checks for expensive lunches.

"You look great," Rachel said as they both sat down.

"Thanks. You too."

Rachel had been to the restaurant before and made recommendations after the waiter brought the menu and the wine she'd ordered. She took a sip, then set down her glass. "So, what was the problem with the colors?" she asked.

"Matriece was looking for lipstick shades that will complement most African-American skin tones, so that a light-skinned woman and a dark-skinned woman can wear the same pink or orange and still look good. That's tricky. But I don't blame her for holding out. In the long run, a line like that will be much more profitable."

"She's very bright, isn't she?"

"Matriece? Off the charts. She knows the business, and she knows her customers."

Rachel took another sip of wine. "My mother thinks highly of her; my brother, too." She made a face, as though the wine was bitter or had gone down the wrong way. "Where's she from?"

"Matriece grew up here in South Central."

"Was she poor?"

Blair found Rachel's steady gaze a bit unsettling. "I don't think so. Her mom was in sales. I think they did okay."

"Where was her dad?"

"You know, she never talks about him. I don't really know. How are things going for you?" Blair asked, wanting to change the subject.

"The usual."

The younger woman always spoke vaguely about the work she did. Blair got the impression, not only from her descriptions but from what she'd gleaned from other people, that Rachel was a glorified gofer for her brilliant older brother.

Rachel leaned across the table. "I saw that film last night, the Australian one."

"How was it?"

"Fabulous." Rachel immediately launched into a descriptive critique of the film's flaws and virtues, going over the movie scene by scene. Her memory for detail was amazing.

After she finished, Blair said, "Well, there's no reason for me to see it now."

Rachel laughed. "I didn't tell everything."

"You didn't?"

"No. You have to see it."

"I'll try."

"One of the reasons I'm so enthusiastic is because that movie really captured some of what I'd like to say in my film. Of course, mine would be a documentary."

Oh, God, not "My Film," Blair thought. She felt her back pressing against the chair's plush cushion. She knew what was ahead. "My Film" had been a staple of Rachel's conversations with Blair since the two began having lunch together.

Blair looked around the room. Whoever owned the place had spent a fortune decorating. Above her, three huge inverted domes made of a milky colored glass housed the lighting. The tables were of dark glossy wood and the chairs were covered in a thick tufted silk. On the far side of the room, a floor-to-ceiling plate-glass window looked out upon a beautiful garden, with a fountain in the center. It's so lovely, Blair thought as she settled back into her chair. These were the kinds of places she'd dreamed about as a child. And regardless of how she'd gotten here, she was here. She smiled sweetly and said to Rachel, "So, tell me what's happening with your project?"

"I guess I'm in what you'd call the conceptualization stage. I've given myself until the end of the year to gather my thoughts, and then I'll begin the actual writing."

"Great," Blair said, trying to sound enthusiastic and peruse the menu at the same time. She wanted an appetizer: lobster ravioli. And for the entree. Her eyes scanned the right side of the page. More lobster? Or jumbo prawns? Ooooh, Chilean sea bass. "Do you have an agent yet?"

"That won't be a problem. I've got contacts in the business. You know, Blair"—she pronounced her words in such a way that Blair was forced to put down her menu and look at Rachel—"I don't know why I ever wasted my time with acting." She laughed. "I guess it was a young girl's fantasy. But really, there's no power in being an actress, unless you're really big. And that takes so long. Writing is an easier way to the top of the profession."

"I don't know, Rachel," Blair said thoughtfully. "I've heard of scripts languishing for years before they're turned into films."

"Really?" Rachel asked, her gray eyes filled with wonder. "But I've got connections. My father is . . . was . . . Anyway, I plan on independent financing." Her voice was baby soft.

Well, of course, you little trust-fund kid, Blair thought to herself, hoping her face didn't reveal what was on her mind. "It's such a great story," she said. "I can't wait to see it on the screen." She paused and smiled at Rachel. "I'm so hungry. What are you having?"

The lobster ravioli was even more delicious than Blair had imagined. As she ate, Rachel bantered about her film about the Holocaust; Blair only half listened, more attentive to the people around her than she was to her friend. The women were all so pulled together, so elegant; they looked as though their fingernail polish never chipped. They wore large diamond rings and smaller stones sparkled in their ears. Their hair was shiny and blond, and their bodies were lithe and tan. They had perfect smiles and laughed a lot about everything. At the tables near her she heard famous names clattering like silverware, and Blair wondered what it must be like to say such important names so casually. She tossed her hair.

After they shared a crème brûlée and each drank a cup of coffee, the waiter placed the bill on the table. Rachel handed him a platinum American Express card.

"Thank you, Rachel," Blair said. As head of the design team she was earning a very good salary, but she was grateful for the treat and conscious that she wasn't expected to return the favor.

"How's your little boy?" Rachel asked.

"You mean my big boy. Judd is sixteen. He's fine," Blair said. Blair took a fleeting look at the plush decor, the elegant faces of the diners, and breathed in the richly perfumed air. She didn't want to think about Judd right now, not while she was in the midst of such splendor.

Both women had walked over from the office and as they made their way back they crossed Rodeo Drive. "Can you stop in this store with me for a second?" Rachel asked.

"Sure."

Belle Epoque was as plush as the restaurant. While Rachel spoke with the saleslady, Blair browsed through the racks of designer clothing. Look but do not touch, she told herself, remembering that working in

Beverly Hills was an occupational hazard. She was congratulating herself for her willpower when she made the mistake of pulling out a dark green silk Armani pantsuit. She'd never seen anything so gorgeous in her life. The fabric felt so soft. Hell, for thirty-four hundred dollars it ought to walk and talk and pour my coffee, she thought. She was chuckling to herself, about to return the suit to the rack when she heard Rachel's voice behind her.

"That's fabulous. Try it on."

"Oh, no. I was just looking."

"Try it on."

Moments later she emerged from the fitting room.

"Blair, you look fantastic," Rachel said.

Then the saleslady chimed in. "You really do look great. It's perfect. That is a wonderful color on you."

Standing in front of the full-length mirror, Blair could see that her admirers were right. The green matched her eyes, and was a gorgeous contrast to her dark auburn hair and pale white skin. She did look good. It was the kind of classy style her Aunt Tess would wear. Just looking at it reminded her of her mother's sister. Blair's sigh was full of longing. "It is beautiful."

"This kind of suit never goes out of style." The saleslady's voice was soft, persuasive.

Blair took a long look in the mirror. The lines of the outfit were elegant, classic. She could wear this ten years from now. Let's see, ten goes into thirty-four hundred . . . She felt Rachel's eyes on her.

"Think of it as an investment," the saleslady murmured.

An investment. Like their house. The mortgage payment was due. She fingered the fabric one last time. "It's not a good time," she said sorrowfully, and walked behind the curtain.

Rachel had a bag in her hand and was putting away her credit card when Blair came out. "What did you decide?" the young woman asked, nodding toward the suit.

"Not today," Blair said.

Walking back toward the office, the spicy taste of lobster and grilled fish still on her tongue, the bright colors of nouveau design still swirling in her brain, Blair tried to hold on to the intoxicating memory of an all-too-brief moment in a world she couldn't afford.

By the time she was back at work, Blair was transported to another land entirely. She met with several of the members of her design team and together they discussed the rough sketches and computerized mock-ups of the makeup containers that would eventually hold Brown Sugar's products. She worked steadily through the afternoon, refining her designs, pausing occasionally to take a sip of coffee, to duck outside and smoke a cigarette. She was pleased with the results she was getting, and she felt certain that Matriece would like what she was doing.

She hadn't quite detached from work but now her mind was beginning to crowd with thoughts of dinner. Glancing at her watch, she saw that it was nearly five. Was there anything to eat in the house? She called home. On the fourth ring the answering service came on. She felt the anger seeping through her. Judd knew damn well he was supposed to come straight home and stay put, his punishment for his latest school ditching. Now where was he? She called Porter at work and then on his cell phone, but both times the answering service picked up. "Goddamnit! Where are you?" It was the same old question, and the same old answer came to her, the one she didn't want to hear.

Blair was hanging up the phone when her assistant knocked on her door and handed her a package. She had ordered some design books but the weight felt too light. When she opened the box she had to sit down. Inside was the green suit from the boutique, and she knew it was from Rachel. Nothing she owned except her house and her car, certainly nothing she wore, had ever cost so much money. She was so stunned that for a moment she could scarcely breathe. She thought about returning the suit, and envisioned the scene. "Oh, no, I couldn't possibly accept."

But then she tried on the jacket again; felt the silk, the fit. She buttoned it, then walked around. Is she gay? Blair wondered, trying to glimpse herself in her office windows. She'd stumbled down that road before. God knows, at her large state school, for a reason that she couldn't decipher, she had been the lesbian magnet. "Why do they always like me?" she'd asked her roommate.

But something told her that Rachel wasn't gay. Maybe she was after something. "But what could she want from me?" she wondered. "Hell, she's not trying to use me to get to the top." She had to laugh at the thought. There was nothing she could do for Rachel.

Does she feel sorry for me? The thought caught Blair by surprise. So many years had passed since she even considered that question. *Do I still look like poor white trash?*

She peered into the window again, and there she was: stringy-haired, wearing a hand-me-down dress, coming out of a house that smelled like pee and whiskey. *Is that smell still on me, that smell of potato famines and Chicago walk-ups?* She saw her father in the glass. He was reaching for her, trying to hug her. She could feel herself squirming, trying to get away from the stench of sweat, beer, and defeat that was clinging to him, that touched all of them. Even after her daddy died it was still there. The black kids on her block taunted her about it. "Get outta here, smelling like poor white trash. Tell yo' momma to wash you in pot likker."

Blair turned away from the window. She looked at the box on her desk. The old clothes and Christmas dinners from the black Baptist church always came in boxes. She was the child who was sent to the door to smile, to say, *We appreciate your kindness very much.* She picked up her purse, her cigarettes, and headed upstairs to Rachel's office.

Rachel was coming out the door when Blair reached her office. "Rachel, I just got the pantsuit. I don't know what to say."

The younger woman seemed suddenly shy. She ran her fingers nervously through her short curly hair. "I knew that you liked it."

"But you didn't have to . . ."

"I know. I wanted to do it. I hope that you enjoy wearing it."

"Are you sure that—"

"Yes," Rachel said firmly. She clasped Blair's hand. "I have to go now. I'm supposed to meet my mother and brother. I don't want to be late."

"Of course. Rachel, thank you so much." Her words echoed back to her as she watched the boss's daughter rush down the hall. Rachel is lonely, she thought. It's as simple as that. And if she wants to be friends, why not? It wouldn't hurt to be friends with the boss's daughter. Maybe Gilda would make her a president.

CHAPTER TWENTY

GILDA EYED THE small gray laptop on the desk in the far corner, then shifted her body under the warm covers and sighed indolently as she looked around her. Within the leased walls, feng shui reigned. The spacious bedroom was a paean to sybaritic delights reserved for the entitled few. Gilda had long grown accustomed to suites like the one she was presently enjoying. At the moment, she didn't feel like lifting one well-manicured finger to get up and retrieve the computer. In a life filled with industry and achievement, she'd had few chances to be absolutely, decadently lazy, so that when the opportunity arose she liked to indulge herself. She knew that she could press the small buttons on either side of her bed and a nurse would come in immediately to do her bidding. But she didn't feel like being intruded upon. Besides, in a little while, she reminded herself, like it or not, the peace she was enjoying would be shattered, so she'd better hold on to it for as long as she could.

Gilda grabbed the television remote from the night table. After pressing the power button, she hit the channel for the evening stock reports, then settled into the plumped-up pillows that supported her back. She studied the numbers, conscious of changes, the improvements and casualties that eight hours had wrought. Her holdings were considerable, but her personal accounts didn't concern her at present. She scanned the listings until her eyes came upon the G's. When she came to her company, she stopped. The numbers were unchanged from the morning and the day before that, which meant that they were still stuck in the morass of moderate success. The numbers hadn't increased or decreased more than half a point in more than five years. Gilda flicked away a bit of invisible lint from the bedcover. She was glad the firm had been holding its own against the hot new crop of Internet buzzards that hawked their wares over AOL and CompuServe, the myriad cable television malls with their call-in sales, but she yearned for higher revenues, not for her but for her children. The company was her legacy to them.

Gilda forced herself to relax her features as she zoomed through classic movies, local news, game shows, and cable networks before finally clicking the power button off again. Frowns and creases were what had brought twenty-one days of virtual solitude in this Shangri-la of a recovery suite. It was costing her four thousand dollars a day. She needed a retreat far from public view so she could heal from her fourth cosmetic surgery in twenty-five years, performed two weeks earlier at the renowned Beverly Hills hospital located just three blocks away. She would be leaving in another week and by then the swelling and bruising would have vanished, so that even those suspicious Beverly Hills matrons who knew when crow's-feet, laugh lines, jowls and throats, bellies, and thighs had been youthenized with a skillful slit here and a deft stitch there, would pause to wonder. Good. The face of Gilda, aesthetician for women of five continents, had to be the embodiment of youthful beauty. Skin care was her business, and she had to be its best advertisement.

Gilda smiled carefully as she thought about her new boyfriend. At the age of seventy, with four marriages behind her, she never intended to be a wife again. But she was committed to experiencing the pleasures of being a girlfriend for as long as possible. And if she had to pay for the privilege, well, she didn't mind. Everything had a price. Why not fun? The man in question made her laugh, was a sweet and tender lover, and treated her as though she were his treasure. She wasn't a fool. But pretending for a little while, there was no danger in playing that game.

Gilda pressed her fingers against her temples. She'd spent all day trying to decide whether she would retire or continue to serve at full capacity as the CEO of her company. Tonight she'd announce her decision. Her declaration would not be made to the public, which included her employees, stockholders, and the business press, because they were unaware that such a move was even being formally considered. There certainly had been a number of rumors, even a spate of newspaper and magazine articles written several years ago; all posed the question: When will the cosmetics queen relinquish her throne to the prince, a not so thinly veiled reference to her son, Daniel, her chief operating officer.

There was so much to consider. Daniel was brilliant, knowledgeable in all aspects of the firm's business. As COO, Daniel had helped the wheels of Gilda Cosmetics continue turning smoothly, but now he wanted to do bigger things. Then there was her daughter. In theory, Rachel assisted Daniel, but she'd never shown any real interest in GC, other than reaping and spending the rewards from it as foolishly as Gilda permitted. But if she allowed Daniel to take over, she'd have to do something comparable for Rachel.

As she sipped a cup of tea she thought of Kent Bridgeport, who'd been with the company for nearly forty years. The chief financial officer was plodding and methodical, a man who paid attention to detail, exactly the kind of man her son would get rid of as soon as he took over. The company was Kent's life, as it was hers. Without his job, what on earth would he do, particularly now that his home life was so depressing? At the thought of Peggy Bridgeport dragging her damaged body around her large house, unable to speak, Gilda felt a wave of pity pass through her. She didn't have any close women friends, she was too different from most women her age, but she'd always liked Peggy. Gilda shook her head sadly. The poor thing didn't deserve such a harsh fate, but then, who knew better than she how unfair life could be?

Gilda grimaced as she turned on her side and then let out a little groan. Even as she involuntarily acknowledged her current discomfort, she had only to glance at the tiny scar on her forearm and the faded stitching that ran the length of her swollen torso to recall so much worse. If only there was an operation that would erase her memory, a procedure that would dissolve the pain and misery that was stored there. She'd once thought that the years would free her, but the horrors of her past were still vivid. There were times when she looked in the mirror expecting to see the shaven-headed starving woman she'd once been. German soldiers plagued her dreams. After years of therapy and support groups, sometimes all she could do was hold herself tightly and rock back and forth. Her memories came unbidden. There was no door she could close to shut them out. Even now, surrounded by a luxurious suite filled with a round bed, silken upholstery, thick carpeting, a bathroom replete with costly marble, beveled mirrors, a sunken Jacuzzi, two sinks large enough to swim in, music playing all around her, golden trays filled with fruit and pastries on the tables, even in the midst of such sumptuous plenty, the Ghost of Degradation and Wretchedness still haunted her. His companion, Guilt, was never far behind.

Gilda sighed as she took stock of herself in the full-length mirror on the closet door. Her face, her thighs, and belly were slightly tender to the touch, although the swelling had almost disappeared; the bruising was fading. The healing process wasn't fast enough for her. Gilda was still in a rush, counting the days until she could return to work. She had never been able to bear being idle for too long. When she was moving, it was easier to outrun phantoms.

They stared back at her from the looking glass: her mother, father, brother, boyfriend, grandmothers, grandfathers, one aunt, all the ones who'd perished in the camps. They looked just as they'd appeared before their internment. Through the years since the war, they'd become her companions. They never spoke, only stared, as if they were searching for more than she could give them.

As she peered at them she wanted to apologize for having lived, for being stronger, for being blessed. Survivor's guilt, the therapists and support groups called it. During the years right after the war, she walked with her head down and didn't smile. She refused joy as if it were a bowl of food not to her liking. She wanted only numbness in those years when she was coming back to life. She feared that feeling would be too painful, like having a scab ripped off too soon.

Her healing had begun with a touch from skin that was different from hers. The black woman had removed the scab slowly, gently. Every day she thought of Hosanna, every day she mourned their friendship and rebuked herself for not having had the courage to fight for whom she wanted in her life. If she had been stronger, things would have turned out differently. She would still have a friend. Hosanna taught her how to move forward; she gave her back her life. Gilda knew that now. "And how did I repay you, my friend?" she spoke aloud. If she knew where to find Hosanna, she would make amends, not only for the money that her uncle and bastard of a first husband had taken from their account, but for a greater perfidy that even fifty years later she couldn't yet acknowledge.

Her thighs were throbbing but Gilda didn't want to call for any painkillers. Instead, she checked her watch. At that moment the buzzer rang and the on-duty nurse's soft voice announced that her son, Daniel, was on his way up.

Gilda began smiling as soon as she heard her son's light tap on the door. "Hi, Mom," he said when her attendant came from the sitting room to let him in. He bent down to kiss Gilda's cheek. "Hey, sexy."

She giggled and her son hugged her again. "Hello, darling. You look wonderful, too."

"Not as good as you. You think if I get a few tucks I can shave twenty years off my driver's license?"

Gilda laughed again. "And how is Dana?" she asked, referring to his ex-girlfriend.

"Mom, Dana is history. You know that. I haven't dated her in months."

"She's a lovely girl, Daniel. Just because your marriage didn't work doesn't mean that you can't try again."

He gave her a droll look, a silent comic reference to her own four marriages.

"Look at me!" they both said together, laughing before they could get the words out.

"You are a very bad son to make fun of your mother," Gilda said, feigning indignation. "If you choose Dana I am sure that you will stop at two. Besides, I'd like grandchildren before I die."

"Okay, Mom, I'll work on that part."

Gilda swatted his arm as they walked into the living room and sat down on a sofa. "Would you like anything, dear?"

"No thanks."

Gilda frowned. "You should eat a little something. I have wonderful cheese. Let me get you some."

"All right."

Gilda went into the small kitchen and in a few moments came back with a plate filled with Brie and fancy crackers. She and Daniel munched and chatted until Gilda looked at her watch. "Where's that sister of yours? Didn't you tell her what time to get here?"

"Of course."

Gilda sighed.

Nearly half an hour later Rachel appeared. When Daniel led her into the living room, Gilda tried to look at her daughter quickly, to glance and not focus on any one part of her body. At thirty-two, her daughter was lean and muscular. An adolescent boy came to mind, although Rachel's face was soft and feminine, a pretty face. Gilda didn't want to appear to be observing her, to show too much pride in her beauty or too much concern about her slimness, lest she be accused of judging. How could she explain to her daughter, who'd grown up in a world where fleshy women were looked down upon, what curves and plumpness meant to her? She reminded herself that her daughter was fashionably thin from working out and counting calories, not from starvation. One quick appraisal left Gilda with the impression that Rachel was no thinner than the last time she'd seen her. "Hello, sweetheart," Gilda said softly.

"Hi, Mom," Rachel said.

"Have some cheese and crackers, dear."

Rachel frowned. "I don't want anything."

"Daniel, Rachel, my dearest darlings, thank you for coming. As you know, for the last year we've been talking about the possibility of my retirement. The business has grown tremendously in the last few years, and to tell you the truth, I've been too busy to give any thought to stepping down. But I've had time recently."

Daniel leaned forward just slightly, and Gilda could see that he was breathing rapidly. He looked so much like his father at that moment. *How quickly he can change from my son to the businessman, as though they are two separate people.* He was a smart, ambitious man, anxious to get her out of his way so he could take charge. She wanted him to have his chance. "I've come to a point in my life where I want to slow down and pursue other interests. I'd like to revisit Israel. My charity work is becoming more important to me."

She could see the anxiety on Daniel's face. *Just tell him I'm leaving,* she thought. She opened her mouth but just as she was about to speak she saw them. The phantoms. They were waiting for her. How could she outrun them if she slowed down?

"Mom, what is it?" Daniel asked.

There they were: her mother, father, brother, her grandparents, aunts and uncles, all waiting to claim her. Gilda closed her eyes and saw long days that couldn't be filled with charities or even trips. *Keep going.*

Her voice was a whisper. "I want to work a few more years, no more than five. Please, be patient with me."

Daniel slumped backward, and Gilda could hear him exhaling; the air sounded as though it was coming out of a punctured tire.

"Daniel," she said quietly, "you're young. You'll have your chance soon enough."

He nodded somewhat feebly.

"Mother, you're seventy years old!" Rachel said loudly, breaking through the heavy silence that had suddenly descended upon them.

"Rachel, I know how old I am," Gilda said somewhat peevishly. "But I'm in fantastic health. I'm not ready to stop working yet."

"Mother, do you think you're just going to work until you drop?" Rachel asked.

"If that's what I choose to do," Gilda said briskly. "But who said anything about dropping? I told you that I will continue for no more than five years."

"Mom," Daniel said. "Rachel and I are concerned about you. Whether you feel your age doesn't mean that you aren't your age. You can't ignore the years. We thought that at this time in your life you'd like to take it easy, to travel a little, maybe take up golf. You've got nothing to prove to anyone."

"Why are you in such a hurry?" Gilda asked.

"Mom, we're in a whole new era. Gilda Cosmetics is falling behind."

"We sell in the finest department stores," Gilda shouted.

"Those stores are losing business to the Internet," Daniel said quietly.

"We're on the Internet!" Gilda retorted.

"But not in the way we need to be," Daniel shot back.

"I'm looking into expansion. We've added a new line."

Daniel sighed. "Mom, you just can't handle the business the way you used to when you were younger. Why not come in one or two days a week? Why are you pushing yourself?"

Rachel suddenly rose from her chair. "Oh, let her. Let her work herself to death," she said. "The company is the most important thing in the world to her. Why shouldn't she die working. That's what she loves to do."

"Rachel," Daniel said in a warning tone.

"Rachel, what? She's never been happy doing anything else. She certainly wasn't happy being a wife or a mother. Unless you call someone who lets a nanny raise her children a good mother. She didn't stay married to your father, and she kicked mine out."

"Knock it off, Rachel," Daniel said quietly.

"Listen," Rachel said, and she seemed to be spitting out every word, "she did kick my father out! And she wouldn't even let me see him."

"Rachel," Gilda said, trying to speak in a gentle voice, "he wasn't in the best shape to be a father."

"My father wasn't a drug addict!"

Gilda sighed.

Rachel turned toward her brother. "She's never going to retire. She doesn't want to give up being the great businesswoman."

"Rachel, Mom has every right to run the company for as long as she wants." He turned to his mother and put his hand on her shoulder. "We just want you to be happy. If working a little longer makes you happy, then we support you, don't we, Rachel?"

"That's all I've ever done is support her. When has she ever supported me?" She left the room so quickly she appeared to hurl herself out the door.

"Rachel!" Gilda called.

"Let her go, Mom," Daniel said. "She wants to be angry."

"What does she mean, I don't support her. She dropped out of three colleges, and each time I was there to get her into the next one. I paid for everything while she was in drama school and going on all the auditions that never did pan out. When she wanted to make jewelry, I supported her. Why is she so angry?"

"I don't know, Mom."

But she's been angry for so long, Gilda thought. Her sweet little girl had turned into a ball of rage almost the moment she developed breasts.

The darling child who used to clunk around the house in her high heels, the sweetie pie who cuddled with her and told her, "Mommy, I love you," had metamorphosed into her most hateful adversary.

She patted her son's hand. "Be patient. Your turn will come. I'll be gone soon enough."

"Don't say that, Mom," Daniel said. He was facing Gilda, but his eyes were trained on something that seemed far in the distance.

She sat on the sofa for a while after Daniel left. When Gilda finally rose, she saw that something was caught between the cushions. She retrieved the movie ticket stub. Rachel was the movie buff. What's she seeing now? Gilda wondered. She peered at the small print: *The Diary of Anne Frank.* As soon she read the words she crushed the paper and threw it away. "Those days are over," she said.

CHAPTER TWENTY-ONE

SAVED, THAT'S WHAT he was! The hand of God had parted the clouds, reached down to earth, and handed him a reprieve. Hallelujah! Kent tried to look pleased but not too grateful. He didn't want Gilda to know how desperate he had been.

"Daniel is disappointed," Gilda was saying. "He's in a hurry to be in charge. Of course, Rachel is furious with me, but what else is new. She's like her father, too sensitive. I suppose in some ways, they're both like their fathers." Gilda sighed, and Kent reached out and patted her hand.

"If anyone had told me that I'd have been divorced four times I wouldn't have believed it. When I was growing up in Poland I thought that I would marry my sweetheart and that would be the end of it. But then, things turned out differently."

She fell silent, and Kent knew she was thinking about the men she'd married. David wasn't the worst. He recalled Barry, Gilda's handsome second husband and Rachel's father. When they married, he was a film producer. He paid all the bills and told Gilda that whatever money she earned was hers. But then Barry got snared by cocaine. His addiction ended his career and came close to ending Gilda's when he began forging her signature on checks against the company's account. He took them to the brink of bankruptcy. After that divorce, Kent had to work feverishly to get GC back on solid footing. Her third husband, Harry, claimed to be a businessman, but it turned out that his only business was spending her money. John, her fourth, was the only one who helped her make money. A real estate developer, he doubled her fortune but cheated constantly and nearly drank himself to death.

Gilda looked sad for a moment, and Kent was sure she was thinking about her difficult daughter. He believed that the girl was really angry with her father but took it out on Gilda. The last he'd heard, Barry was off drugs, living in Arizona, and running a bed-and-breakfast with his latest wife, a former stripper. And he hadn't seen his daughter in years.

It didn't feel odd conducting a meeting with a pajama-clad Gilda, whose face was still puffy and slightly bluish as she lay in the bed. Over the years Kent had been called to his employer's bedside more than once. "I'm glad you're staying on, Gilda," Kent said. "You're still too vibrant not to be actively involved in the business. I know you could have a full life just doing your We Mean Business work and the other charities, but the company is your heart. Quite frankly, nobody can run it the way you do."

"You don't think that Daniel is ready?"

Kent shook his head. "He's smart and quite dynamic. And let's face it: He has the energy of youth. But I don't think he's quite seasoned enough. A few more years as the prince won't hurt him."

"I hope he sees it your way," she said softly. Suddenly, her mood shifted. "Now," she said, "tell me everything that's going on."

Kent opened his briefcase and drew out a sheaf of papers he hadn't bothered to put in a folder. Something fell on the floor, and when Kent looked down he saw that it was a check. He froze as Gilda leaned over and picked it up. "Taper Industries," she said, reading the name of the payee. "Who is that?"

"New supplier," Kent said. He didn't breathe again until Gilda handed him the check. He placed it facedown on top of the folders inside the briefcase, then closed the top.

He lined up the papers he needed to refer to, and then, slowly, methodically, he went through each of the sheets, pausing to answer any questions Gilda posed. She didn't ask very many, and Kent would have been surprised if she had. She knew that when it came to the company, he was accurate and thorough.

After the business matters were concluded, Gilda leaned forward eagerly. "I spoke with Matriece. I understand that the colors are fantastic."

"It took her a long time to choose them. She's very particular."

"We're paying for her opinion," Gilda said sharply.

"Yes, of course. It's just that we've got a deadline to consider if we want to get this line out by next fall. The ads have to be completed by March."

"I'm sure she's aware of that." Gilda settled back. "She's the kind of person who always makes her deadlines," she said.

"You're quite invested in her success, aren't you?"

"It's not just her success; it's the company's as well."

"I realize that. I'm just saying you seem to be taking a personal interest in Matriece."

Gilda didn't respond.

"I find it intriguing that you finally decided to manufacture products for African-Americans after talking about doing it for so long. I mean, a lot of the other major firms included a black line years ago. I would have thought you'd have introduced something in the seventies."

"I wasn't ready then," Gilda said sharply.

He remembered sensing that she was almost afraid to do it, that her reticence didn't stem from a fear of losing money. There was something else operating deep within Gilda. Something he couldn't understand.

"How is Fontaine coming along?" Gilda asked suddenly.

Gilda had asked him to have Matriece find a place in Brown Sugar for the grandson of one of her old cronies. Kent suspected that the grandmother was a Holocaust survivor, since Gilda had so few friends, and her support group was her only social outlet, other than her charities. The young man had spent several years in the fashion business and Matriece, after looking over his résumé, felt sure that he could be a nice linkage between the two industries. Kent thought Fontaine was a personable young man, although a bit too laid-back. He did his job well enough but at most of the meetings Kent had attended, Fontaine was content to let others do the talking. He wasn't who Kent would have chosen, but because Gilda had made the request, he kept his criticism to himself.

"He seems to be contributing. He rounds out the team."

Gilda smiled, then cleared her throat, and Kent could tell that she wanted to be alone. He gathered his papers and then stood up. "You look great," he said. "Get some rest, and I'll call you in a day or two."

Gilda gave a slight wave of her hand. "Thanks for stopping by."

It wasn't until Kent was seated in his car that he allowed himself the luxury of trembling. "How could I have been so stupid?" he said. He opened the briefcase, took out the check, and looked at it. He couldn't believe that Gilda had actually held it in her hands. He felt shame rising up inside him, and then he put the check away.

CHAPTER TWENTY-TWO

OUTSIDE IN MATRIECE'S driveway, Big Sam Your Detail Man was loading his cleaning supplies back into his ever gleaming white van. When Matriece stepped into her hallway, she could hear the doors of the vehicle opening and closing. She peeked out her living room window, hiding behind the curtains. From there she could gaze at her Detail Man's splendid legs, which were thick and heavily muscled. In his shorts, he reminded her of a gladiator. Several times when it was hot, Sam had taken off his shirt and his chest was every bit as appealing as his legs. "You're a bad, bad girl," Matriece told herself with a giggle.

Five minutes later, Big Sam was facing her, a smile on his face, a bill in his hand. "Looking good, Miss Carter," he said, his glance both admiring and businesslike.

It was Kent Bridgeport, of all people, who had turned her on to Sam. "Best car wash you'll ever get," was how the chief of finance put it. He hadn't lied. And he hadn't even told her about how punctual and efficient the man was. Unless it was raining, if it was Friday morning Sam was at her house, and usually he wore shorts.

She got a whiff of his spicy cologne. Even though he was a little sweaty he still smelled good. "Almost as good as my car," she quipped, and she began to feel lighter. Sam always put her in a good mood. Her shining BMW was parked in front of her garage. The day was bright and warm. She took in a deep breath and let it out slowly.

"Nah, you couldn't look any better if I detailed you myself. You must be going somewhere important."

Matriece could feel his appreciation of her tan suit and silk blouse. There was interest flickering in his eyes. "A meeting. I told you I've been working with my staff to get the colors together for Brown Sugar."

Sam nodded.

"Well, now I'm moving ahead to find a spokesmodel for the company. You've seen the ads for makeup where an actress or a singer is used to represent the product?"

Sam nodded again. "Thanks," he said as Matriece handed him a ten and a five.

"Today I'm going to meet with Asia Pace to see if she'll represent Brown Sugar."

Sam's hand opened, and the two bills fluttered to the ground. Matriece bent down to retrieve the money. When she handed it back to him, he appeared flustered and upset. "Asia Pace?" he said.

"Yes."

"She's my favorite singer. She's beautiful."

"I think so. I used to baby-sit her when she was little. We lived right next door."

Sam moved closer to Matriece.

"She was a sweet little kid." She stepped back away from Sam, who appeared a little dazed.

"I've gotta go," Matriece said, looking at her watch.

"Yeah, me too. So, when are you gonna get with Asia Pace?" He seemed reluctant to leave.

"We're supposed to have breakfast in a little while, which is why I'm in a hurry."

"Yeah. Sure. Well, God bless you."

The phone rang after Matriece closed the door. The voice on the other end was early morning husky. "Good morning, Matriece," Montgomery said, and as soon as he did she thought about Big Monty's awards dinner. She hadn't seen him since the week before, although he'd called her several times, once from Houston.

"Hi. How are you?"

"I'm fine. How about you?"

"I'm fine, Montgomery."

"I wanted to wish you luck with Asia Pace."

"Thanks."

"Are you going to the Four Seasons?"

"Yes. How did you know?"

"Just a guess. How much time are you going to spend with her?"

"I don't know, maybe an hour. Why?"

"I'll be in the area. I was wondering if you'd have a cup of coffee with me after the meeting. Call me on my cell if it works out for you. If not, don't worry about it."

"Okay."

"Matriece, I've really missed you."

She hesitated. "Well, maybe we'll do something about that."

As she drove down the wide curving street she lived on, Matriece considered the job at hand. Years ago she had cuddled a sweet little girl and rocked her to dreamland. If the world was fair that would guarantee her everything. But the little girl had grown up to become a young woman wielding the kind of power that makes forgetting old friends not only easy but recommended. In a town renowned for make-believe, reinvention was a virtue and betrayal as ordinary as changing one's mind. Nothing was guaranteed. Since the last time she'd seen her, Asia had become a star and was on the verge of becoming a superstar. She wasn't quite sure about how to approach the Grammy winner she'd once babysat. Should she hug her when they met and start talking about old times? Or should she ignore the past, extend her hand, and give her her props? Call her Miss Pace or Asia? Kiss her ass or be for real? Relax, she told herself. This was supposed to be a friendly little breakfast, a chance to get reacquainted. Anyway, she told herself, everything will work out fine.

There was a limousine sitting outside the grand hotel where the restaurant was located; the chauffeur was slumped in the driver's seat. So she's traveling diva-style, Matriece thought to herself, as a uniformed attendant took her car keys and another held the door for her. Maybe she should extend her hand instead of hugging her. Once inside the restaurant she searched for Asia, half expecting to be blinded by klieg lights surrounding her table, but to her surprise the singer wasn't there. Looking toward a corner table she did see the celebrated star of a slew of hit action flicks, bordered by men in suits. He'd been a star for at least twenty-five years but his face was as smooth and tight as a young man's, which gave credence to his lady-killer rep. He didn't smile at all.

Matriece ordered herbal peppermint tea, sipped her first cup, and then beckoned to her waitress to bring her a second. Is this child going to stand me up? she wondered. And then she saw her, posed in the doorway and searching the crowd. Tall. Slim. Ginger-colored skin. High cheekbones. Large eyes. The lips of a goddess. Just what they were looking for: a face made for makeup. Matriece stood up and waved, then waited as Asia started coming toward her.

The younger woman ignored her outstretched hand. Instead, she grabbed her former baby-sitter and hugged her exuberantly. "Triecy! My girl."

Close up, Matriece could see how truly extraordinary-looking Asia was. Hers was a face that epitomized black beauty, but wasn't "too" black, a face that had "mainstream" appeal but wasn't "too" light. Asia Pace was perfect. She had skin the color of a white girl's dream tan, a skin tone that the masses of black women looking for beauty could identify with, that hip Latinas could relate to, a complexion that would lure those young girls who believed that love could be found using a tube of lipstick as a searchlight. Asia's lips were full and sexy, with a soft sheen that lipstick would only enhance. She had the cheekbones, the cleft in her chin, the oval face and long neck, the big eyes and seductive smile—she had it all. Not only was she gorgeous, but at the same time she possessed just the right kind of interesting flaws. There was the tiny scar above her left eye, the dark fish-shaped birthmark on her cheek, and then there was the hair, a thick, glossy sash that hung between her shoulder blades. Perfect. Asia's lips, eyes, skin, and cheekbones would frame the color, underscore the tint, promote the powders, lipsticks, shadows, and foundations, and ignite the desire in the psyches of the feverish twentysomethings, the panic-stricken thirty-pluses, the desperate over-forties. Matriece would turn her beauty into sales.

Their meal was extended by the laughter attached to the reminiscences that seemed to overflow from a deep well of memory that Asia had stored inside her. The time Matriece took Asia swimming. How Matriece combed her hair. The stories she used to tell her.

"You remember all that?" Matriece asked in an incredulous tone. "You couldn't have been more than five or six."

"I guess you stood out for me. When my father left I was really small but it just seemed as though my mom couldn't get it together. She never really got a good job; she didn't go back to school. Her whole life was about struggling and not having enough money and dealing with some dude who wasn't about nothing and just . . ." She waved her hand. "I mean, she's still the same way, only I pay for everything. But what kind of life is that? Your father left, but your mother had it together. You had pretty things in your house. And books. I used to pretend I lived with you." Asia shook her head softly from side to side. "She used to give my mother lipsticks."

"My mother didn't give lipsticks away."

"That's right. Fifty percent discount."

"There you go."

"So, what's all this about, Triecy?" Asia put down the glass of orange juice she'd been drinking and sat back in her chair. She glanced around the room, spotted the actor and his entourage, then slowly angled her body so that they could see her. The movement seemed more automatic than heartfelt, a kind of reflex that Asia had no power to control. As she watched the young singer sitting in the chair arching her back, Matriece thought of an exquisite jewel in a display case. Asia let out a peal of charming laughter, then smiled when the men looked her way. That's right, honey, do yourself some good, Matriece thought to herself.

Asia turned back to Matriece and reduced the wattage of her smile. "My mom said that you work for Gilda Cosmetics, and you're looking for a spokesmodel. I told her that I'm sure I'm a little too dark for the job."

"Actually, you're just the right color," Matriece said. "Gilda is introducing a new black line. The products are wonderful, and I think you're the person who can tell black America all about Brown Sugar."

"Brown Sugar. That's nice."

"It's a quality line, one you'd be proud to have associated with your name. As the spokesmodel, your picture will be everywhere. And, of course, we'll make it well worth your while."

"What would I have to do?"

"Yours will be the face of the product. Your image will appear in all our advertising: print, television, in-store, Internet, the works. You'd have to make appearances at promotional functions, and you'd be in all the commercials."

"What do you do for Gilda Cosmetics?"

"I'm the president of Brown Sugar."

Asia gave her a long, admiring look. "My mom always said that you were like your mother. Your sister . . ." Asia looked at her questioningly.

"Vonette."

"Yeah. Vonette was the laid-back one. She got married young and had a bunch of kids, right?"

"Just three."

"Okay. Yeah. How come you're working for another cosmetics company? Whatever happened to your mother's business?"

"Well, she was sick for a long time before she died. I was away at school a lot, and when I got back here the company was in shambles. It folded. But Gilda's a good company. And Brown Sugar is my baby. I can't go into any details, but believe me when I tell you that we're doing something that's going to revolutionize the industry."

"Triecy, you ever see anybody from around the way?"

The intensity of the question surprised Matriece. "My sister still lives in the neighborhood. Sometimes when I visit her I'll see people."

"But you don't really hang with any of the neighborhood people anymore, do you?"

Matriece smiled, unsure of where Asia's questions were leading. "I'm so busy these days. To tell the truth, I hardly see anybody."

"Yeah, me either. Sometimes I go for weeks and the only people I see are the ones who are interviewing me, plus my agent and my manager. Do you think that maybe you and I can hang out sometime? Maybe have dinner or go to a movie?"

When Matriece looked at Asia, there were tears puddling in the younger woman's eyes.

"Oh, honey, what's the matter?"

"I just get lonely, Triecy." She dabbed at her eyes with a napkin.

"Well, you can call me. I'd love to go out." She pulled a business card from her wallet, wrote her home number on the back, and handed it to

Asia, who promptly exchanged her own card. "Listen, you've accomplished a great deal. You deserve to enjoy your life. Whatever you decide about Brown Sugar, we can still be friends. Okay?"

Asia nodded. "I get down sometimes. I don't know why. Listen, I'd like to be the spokesmodel for your company. Just call my manager and tell him I said so."

Matriece held out her right hand across the table. Asia stuck hers out as well. Their fingers met, then Asia turned her head. Across the room the actor and his companions stood up. He was shorter than he appeared on-screen. Withdrawing her hand, Asia swiveled her torso around. She slipped her fingertips inside the opening of her V-necked blouse and languidly rubbed the skin just below her neck. It was a pose that was at once casual and frankly suggestive. Great shot for the ad campaign, Matriece thought.

Asia stood up hastily. "I've got to go, girl. It's been great. My manager will take care of everything."

Before Matriece could respond, Asia was gone. From her table, she saw her through the window of the restaurant talking with the actor. Standing in the sun Asia glittered and sparkled like a gem determined to be bought.

Matriece refilled her teacup, pulled out her cell phone, and dialed Montgomery's number. He picked up on the first ring. "I'll be there in ten minutes," he told her.

Matriece saw the flowers before she saw Montgomery. He was carrying a huge bouquet of roses and calla lilies that almost obscured his face. "I brought you something," he said, handing the flowers to her.

She could tell he was feeling a little unsure of himself, that the flowers were both an apology and a token of affection. Matriece hated seeing that look on his face. She'd noticed the same expression before at times when he was talking with his father. She stood up and kissed him, and was glad to see him relax.

"Thank you. They're beautiful," she said, taking her seat.

"Roses for a rose. So, how did it go?" he asked, sitting down.

"She wants to do it," Matriece said, allowing herself to exult as she felt the full impact of what had transpired between Asia and her. The hottest singer in the business had promised to represent them. "When we come out in the fall, our products are going to fly off the shelves. Hey, now," she said, snapping her fingers and shaking her head.

Montgomery held out his hand. "You the man." He leaned back against the chair and grinned at her.

He's happy for me, Matriece thought. The idea both warmed and alarmed her.

"Let's go out tomorrow. We'll celebrate. Is that okay?" he asked.

She nodded.

CHAPTER TWENTY-THREE

AS THE SALESLADY at the Robinsons-May department store in the Crenshaw Mall rang up her stockings, Matriece, despite her better judgment, peeked into the cosmetics department. From her vantage point she had a view of the swarm of diverse humanity on parade in the adjacent aisles as black, brown, yellow, and a few white women shoppers strode through the walkways, stopping to try this and test that, to sniff this and compare that, as they milled around from counter to counter. Inside the store the air vibrated with activity and that peculiarly female energy that is the adrenaline rush of those who are truly born to shop. Getting pretty was on their minds.

The Radiance counter, in particular, was packed. The third Saturday in September was when that company introduced its fall line of new lip and nail colors. Hordes of shoppers had come to try the autumn shades, to have free makeovers, and to participate in the annual gala that was part of the company's national kickoff. Matriece turned her head and peered into the corridor of the mall where a crowd had gathered around a stage set up just outside Robinsons-May. A party was in progress. Radiance kickoffs were always the talk of the mall and today was no exception. Not ten feet from the store's entrance was a long table filled with cookies and lemonade. Several pretty young models, who smiled with huge pouty lips glowing with coppery wetness, served the people. Behind them were large posters of the Radiance spokesmodel, star of a canceled Fox sitcom, a lovely young woman whose bronze skin and sculpted cheekbones were the embodiment of the beauty Radiance wanted to project. To the left of the table, seated majestically on a high-back wicker chair reminiscent of Huey Newton's famed portrait, minus the leather and guns, was the star herself, in all her ethereal loveliness. People were lined up waiting patiently for her autograph. While she signed, the crowd swayed to the beat of Tiara as they belted out their hit record "If You Can Stand the Heat" from a nearby stage. The crowd of mostly black young people and their parents was singing along, and some were dancing in the space in front of the stage. All across the country in urban shopping centers the scene was being repeated. Get people partying and they will open their wallets. A simple concept. And it worked, just as Matriece had told Calvin Meeks it would when she conceived the idea. Inside the store, Matriece watched women swipe so many lipstick samples against the back of their hands that their skin was a cross between the rose family rainbow and third-degree burns. They blended so many different shades of foundation on the underside of their wrists that they appeared to be in the initial stages of vitiligo. The air was heavy with a mixture of fragrances, the result of quick spritzes from testers. Women sniffed the air and smiled, then sniffed the air and frowned. They squeezed three drops of miracle cream that looked and smelled suspiciously like perfumed mayonnaise into aging palms and dreamed they rubbed the years away. They waved plastic, checks, and cash and bought and bought and bought, which made Matriece feel jubilant, even if she no longer worked for Radiance.

Matriece had not come to the mall to participate in the beauty circus that Radiance put on each year. In fact, her plan was to avoid the event entirely. Her trip to Robinsons-May was an emergency of the highest order: Saturday night date, no stockings. In her frenzy to complete her outfit she'd actually forgotten that today Radiance premiered its fall line. She made her purchase, took one last look at the Radiance counter, and turned to go.

It was at that moment that Matriece heard the sound of gunshots, muffled but distinct, and then screams and shouts. The shots had come from outside the building, the report echoing from somewhere on Crenshaw Boulevard. It wasn't every day that gunfire exploded on that resilient avenue.

Crenshaw was where Korean shopkeepers sold doughnuts and all the wigs a sister could want, where delicate Vietnamese fingers held sturdier black ones and applied polish, hot-mama nails, and good-time fantasies. The street was where Jews, who'd long ago defected to Beverly Hills to live, still sold carpet and furniture and cars. And Crenshaw was home to

black barbershops and beauty parlors, where African-American shopkeepers traded everything from clothes to liquor.

Anything could happen on Crenshaw but violence rarely did. The
years since '92 had brought a modicum of revitalization and prosperity,
which made the shots ringing out above the din and hustle-bustle of the
mall all the more unexpected. The report rose above the noisy cars ca-
reering down the street, and momentarily stilled the voices of the black
and Latino shoppers, the handful of Japanese who came from only blocks
away where they resided in their own little enclave in the 'hood, and the
emboldened young whites, who'd bought into the surrounding area after
the memory of the fires of '92 had grown dimmer than the harsh reality
of housing prices on the west side. For a moment they all paused in
wonder.

But nobody moved. The customers, Matriece among them, seemed
riveted to the floor.

"Somebody was shooting up at South Central High, and now the
cops have him on Crenshaw!" The voice came from the entrance to
the department store. A skinny old woman, her wiry gray hair cut close
to her head, her clothing long and flowing, was making her way through
the crowd. The people in front of the counter remained still, although the
questions on their faces were almost audible. They looked at the woman,
and then at one another.

Matriece began trembling. Tavares had choir practice at South Central that Saturday morning. Pushing her way through the crowd, she
reached the parking lot, got in her car, and drove two blocks on a back
street to the school. Police were all over the campus, and from where she
parked, Matriece could see way back to the mall entrance, which was
clogged with police cars. The entire football team was standing in front
of the school, along with several men Matriece assumed were coaches.
"My nephew's inside. He's in the choir," she explained to a police officer
who stood at a barrier.

"Sorry, lady. Nobody can go in."

"Was anyone hurt? Has anybody been shot? What happened?" She
hadn't meant to raise her voice, but Matriece couldn't control herself.

"Nobody was hurt. Far as we could see it was gang-related. I don't think anybody in the choir was involved. They were all dismissed about thirty minutes ago."

Matriece began dialing as she walked away. "Vonette," she said, when she heard her sister's voice.

"He's here, Triecy. Tavares is okay." Her sister yelled in her ear, "Boot, didn't I tell you it was Triecy calling up about this knucklehead boy." Matriece heard her brother-in-law's low voice in the background. "Is it on the news?"

"No. I heard it at the mall. Anyway, I'm on my way over."

"Oh, you just want to see him for yourself," Vonette said, then her voice became lower. "Listen, before you come, I just want you to know—"

"I'm on my way."

CHAPTER TWENTY-FOUR

MARIECE DROVE SOUTH on Crenshaw and then east on Imperial. After several blocks she turned left onto a narrow street and began searching for a parking space as she passed a row of tidy stucco houses with small, neat front yards. Here and there were one or two dilapidated houses badly in need of painting and with lawns that were mostly uncut weeds. But in general, the neighborhood she grew up in exuded respectability and decorum, a sense that the denizens within each dwelling lived orderly lives, filled with eight-hour weekday shifts, regular paychecks, diminishing benefits, union dues, stacks of bills, Friday night movies, church on Sunday, high school graduations, and even a few commencement exercises for college seniors.

Vonette and Boot's house was the same style as the rest of the small three-bedroom, one-story homes that lined the block, except that they had added a second story several years earlier. It was freshly painted in a soothing combination of white with gray trim, and the front porch was filled with potted ferns and impatiens in hanging baskets. The windows were newly washed—they sparkled from the street. The yard, however, made the windows seem dull. The tiny plot of grass in front of the house was the greenest and hardiest in the neighborhood, rivaling in beauty any lawn in Beverly Hills. Matriece smiled when she saw the freshly mowed grass, recognizing the handiwork of her nephew, Tavares. The lawn was his weekly job and seeing the grass, she visualized her nephew's sweet face as he set about his task. Bordering the dazzling display of emerald was a helter-skelter bouquet that, if gathered, would have lent grandeur to the wedding or funeral of the city's most elite citizen. Scattered about the yard in no particular pattern were rosebushes with blossoms the size of grapefruit, pink, orange, white, and blazing red. There were delphiniums, dahlias, and thick bunches of multicolored impatiens bordering the thin walkway. At first glance there seemed to be no particular plan or pattern to the profusion of blossoms, and yet every plant was in the position that best enhanced its beauty and helped reflect the subtle symmetry of the entire garden. In the center of the lawn was a lemon tree, its branches weighted down with fruit that barely fit in the closed palms of adults. Huge asters were grouped near the doorway, and nestled at their feet was a strawberry ground cover. In the small backyard, a multitude of wildflowers bordered a white fence that encased peach, plum, avocado, and orange trees. Matriece could have found her way to her sister's house blindfolded, with only the perfume of her glorious blooms to lead her to the dwelling. The garden was Vonette's handiwork. Her sister was happiest when tending to living things, even though at times she appeared to let them go wild.

Matriece could hear music coming from the house. Tavares was playing the piano and singing, his rich tenor wafting through the open window onto the street. Pausing to listen, Matriece could only marvel at her nephew's gift. There was no telling where his voice could take him. But first he had to have an education, and she was going to see to that.

She could hear Boot and Vonette fussing. Matriece chuckled at the thought of her sister and brother-in-law. At times their house was like a twenty-four-hour "Def Comedy Jam" special. Her mother had always called Matriece and Vonette the ant and the grasshopper respectively, and her sister had married a man with a summer soul to match her own breezy, careless ways. Matriece could already hear their screams of laughter as she made her way up the crooked walk that led to their house. There was nothing wrong with their kind of happiness, but Tavares was going to have more options. He was going to be somebody.

Just as Matriece reached the top step of her sister's porch, Boot opened the front door and then shut it behind him; she knew he'd been watching for her. Her brother-in-law put his hand on her shoulder. "Uh, Triecy, your dad's inside."

She moved away from him so fast that when she looked back his hand was still where her shoulder had been. The liquid hatred she felt pushed out every other emotion. She tossed the words as she marched down the steps. "Tell Vonette to call me when he leaves."

She heard Boot running behind her and then his hand grabbed her forearm. "Triecy girl, he's still your father."

"Don't have one." She kept walking.

"Look, I know the story," Boot said.

She stopped then and turned to face him. "You just think you do. Tell Vonette to call me on my cell."

By the time she was sitting in her car Matriece couldn't remember walking to it. She wanted to yell; she wanted to cry but not a sound came out. When she looked down at her hands they were shaking. She turned on the ignition, then cut it off, leaned against the steering wheel and let her head drop forward so she couldn't see what was ahead of her. But what was behind her was as clear as ever.

"Goddamn him!" Matriece heard her words as if they were traveling through yards and yards of gauze. As she thought about the man who'd walked out of her life so long ago she was reminded of how bereft she'd felt when her father left, how that initial yearning for him had threatened to swallow her like a deep grave. But gradually her childish tears had given way to a hardened heart, and now she couldn't soften it. "Why can't I stop hating him?" Her spoken words seemed to surround her in the car. The answer remained buried but not so deeply that she didn't realize that the enmity she felt was part loyalty. Hosanna's bitterness toward Lonell was infectious, and had informed her entire childhood. She was young when she struck a silent bargain with herself: If her mother despised her father, so would she.

Vonette called her while she was circling the area, and within an hour, Matriece was standing on her sister's porch for the second time that day.

"Hey, Aunt Triecy," Chazz said as Matriece was about to open the front door. Her sister's oldest child's angular frame was crunched down on the newest acquisition for the porch, an old-fashioned aluminum glider that Vonette had rescued from a yard sale. Last week Matriece had seen what appeared to her to be a heap of rusting junk when Boot unloaded it from his trunk. But she knew that her sister's hands were magic. Vonette had painted blue and orange stars and moons on the furniture that she first colored a pale silver. Huddled among the moon and stars and the silvery sky was Chazz, who had his arm around a girl who in no way resembled the one he'd been hugging last week or the one the week before that. Matriece didn't even try to keep up with her player nephew. She bent down and kissed his cheek and received his in return. "Hi, Chazz." She nodded toward the young lady. "How are you, honey." Why bother with an introduction?

As soon as Matriece opened the front door, which was kept unlocked during the day, she felt herself being sucked into the powerful vortex of Vonette's world, which was so different from her own that sometimes Matriece had to remind herself they really were sisters. There were people at Vonette and Boot's house, which isn't to say that the couple had visitors. Nobody ever visited Vonette and Boot. Rather, folks came to be in the midst of their easiness. The Ramirezes from next door, the mother and two of her four daughters, sat at the kitchen table drinking sodas, their glorious black manes trailing down their backs. The oldest girl and her mother chatted amiably while the younger child sat in sullen silence. Vonette was talking to someone on the telephone; she waved and blew a kiss when she saw Matriece. Boot was watching television and drinking sodas with one of the guys who worked for him in his small painting company. Matriece knew that people would stay all day, held in place not by scintillating conversation or tasty snacks or even the supply of sodas and tea, which was endless. They remained because Vonette and Boot welcomed them so sincerely and effortlessly that their guests forgot they were not at home, as did their hosts, who chose their friends based on some uncanny instinct that never failed them. Those they let inside their home gained admittance to their hearts as well.

"Triecy, tell this Guadalajara fool that black people had their own colleges since after the Civil War," Vonette said, hanging up the telephone. She walked over to Matriece and pulled her into a quick embrace before she could reply.

"What happened at the school?" Matriece asked.

"Some fool came up there with a gun. He had some beef with one of the football players," Vonette said.

"One of the cops told me it was gang-related."

"Them cops think everything south of Wilshire is gang-related," Boot said.

"Where was he shooting?" Matriece asked.

"On the field at first. Then the guy with the gun started chasing the football player down Crenshaw," said Boot. "I wish I could have that little asshole for a week. He wouldn't be chasing nobody else with no gun."

"Some lady said that he was in front of the mall," Matriece said.

"I think that's where the cops caught him," Vonette said.

"So, where was Tavares while all this was going on?"

"Oh, he was inside the whole time. None of the choir members knew what was happening until the cops evacuated the building. One of his boys brought him home. I was so scared when Tavares told me."

"Her knees were shaking," Boot said.

"Mine too," Matriece said.

"She was talking about, 'I want him outta that school,' weren't you, baby?"

Vonette nodded.

"Well, you know I always wanted him to go to a better school," Matriece said.

"We can't afford private school, Triecy, and you're not paying for it."

"Okay. What if I can find a really good, safe public school for him? Would you consider that? I mean, suppose somebody had been shooting up there during the school week? Tavares could have gotten hurt."

Vonette looked at Boot. "I know." She sighed. "Uncle Tuney said to tell you hello. I was talking to him when you came in."

"Oh, what's going on with him?" Matriece knew enough to recognize that the subject had been changed.

"Our land, of course. He's talking about getting rid of Weiss and hiring Jimmy Durden."

Matriece shook her head. "If Jimmy Durden knows what's good for him, he'll stay the hell out of Inez. Those crackers don't play."

"I don't think Uncle Tuney's going to switch lawyers. Weiss probably pissed him off. He and the father used to argue; now he and the son get into it. Whenever they start fussing and cussing each other out, then

Uncle Tuney says he's firing William and he's going to hire Jimmy Durden. I sure would like to see this thing settled."

"Yeah."

"Remember how Uncle Tuney used to take us down to Texas to see Granddad and Grandma and them? He had that big old trailer, and he used to drive straight through, and you and I would be sleeping in the back," Vonette said.

Matriece found herself grinning as she recalled those trips. "He used to stop off in Inez to visit the ancestral land. 'Now, you kids listen up,' " she said, imitating her uncle. " 'All this land belongs to our family. Uncle Tuney's going to get it back. If anything happens to me, you find my lawyer, Herbert Weiss. He'll know what to do.' "

"Yeah," Vonette said, chuckling, "and you were like, 'What's a lawyer, Uncle Tuney?' "

Both women were laughing now.

"It is a pretty place, at least the part that doesn't have the oil wells on it. I sure wouldn't mind being a multimillionaire," Vonette said.

"Right."

"Uncle Tuney thinks they're getting close." She looked at her sister, who rolled her eyes. "Anyway, he was running, as usual. Had some new lady waiting for him, and oh, she's just the sweetest, prettiest thing, and I never ever felt this way about anybody before, and oh, baby doll, Uncle has to bring her by so you can meet her," Vonette said in a perfect imitation of their mother's brother.

Matriece chuckled, stifling her hurt feelings. Neither her aunt Lucille nor her only living uncle bothered to call her. She recognized that the few times her uncle had telephoned she was always rushed, working on some project that she'd brought home from the office. Matriece knew that her uncle and aunt preferred Vonette, who kept in touch with everyone she loved. She took care of people as she'd once taken care of Matriece when she was little and their mother was busy working. "So how old is this one, twenty-five?"

"No. He says she's forty-four."

"That's ancient for him."

Vonette shrugged. "Hey, she's over twenty-one."

"How old is Uncle Tuney?" Matriece asked.

"Mom would have been seventy-one. He's seventy-three."

"Leave the man alone," Boot bellowed. "When I get seventy-three you can believe I'm going to have me a chippy, too. I'ma have me three or four."

"Chippies cost money, Boot," Vonette said. "You won't have a big fat fire chief's pension and a home in Ladera Heights to woo nobody with."

"Hey, I'm a good-looking guy."

"Now that's true," Vonette said with a grin. "That's why I'm not letting no chippy get you."

"You better treat me right then, woman. Else I'm out the door."

"Oh, *cariño,* don't leave me," Vonette said in a pretend baby voice.

Raphael Valdez, Vonette's Mexican-American husband, stood in the center of their tiny living room trying to scowl. His placid face with its heavy jowls was more suited to his usual expression of contentment. His slick black hair was pulled back into a black ponytail. He had been very handsome once, and there was still the shadow of beauty on his face; his eyes were arresting, large, deep, and very clear, and Matriece had always found his mouth sensual, perhaps because when Vonette was younger she used to describe in great detail the pleasure Boot's dark lips gave her. But Vonette's good cooking had stretched her husband's belly beyond the confines of the puny leather belt charged with holding it in place. Matriece remembered when he swaggered into their lives with no more to recommend him than an ability to live in the moment with a force that matched Vonette's so precisely that Matriece sensed immediately that fate was the architect of a head-on collision. And yet, although Vonette and Boot hadn't prospered financially, the marriage had not been a disaster. The two had sped around corners on two wheels but they'd never really crashed. Their years together had steadied them, and if they occasionally swerved they were always headed in the same direction.

"Triecy, what I marry this black woman for?"

It was Boot's favorite question, one he posed whenever Vonette rightfully challenged him on any issue. He walked over to Matriece and gave her a quick hug, and she returned his embrace.

"Needed a green card . . . Burrito Head!" Vonette said and laughed.

It was her favorite joke. At the kitchen table the Ramirezes smiled. They were used to The Vonette and Boot Show.

"Burrito Head!" He turned to the mother and daughter. "You hear that? Our people were here when your people were still picking cotton. We used to own this whole thing. So, you better back up, Aunt Jemima."

"Yeah, yeah, okay. But you never had your own colleges."

" 'Cause we were smart enough to get into the white ones!" Boot screamed with laughter, and Vonette broke out in a broad chuckle. Matriece laughed, too. Boot and Vonette eased her mind without even trying.

"Where's Tavares?" she asked.

"That boy!" Vonette said, trying to sound exasperated but failing because there was too much adoration in her tone. "Tavares!" she called. "Auntie Mommy's here to see you?"

Tavares's smile entered the room before he did. He went straight to Matriece and embraced her. "Hey, brotherman," Matriece said, kissing his forehead. He smelled like apples. "Are my shoes ready?"

"They're shinier than Michael Jordan's head!" Tavares quipped.

Vonette shook her head. "Boy, go get your auntie's shoes."

Tavares loped up the stairs and when he returned he presented Matriece with three pairs of heels, all polished to a high gloss.

"These look new," Matriece said. She gave her nephew another kiss.

"Ta ching! Ta ching!" Tavares sang out.

"Who said anything about money?" Matriece teased.

"Now, Auntie, I know you gonna treat me right."

Matriece reached in her wallet, pulled out a twenty-dollar bill, and handed it to Tavares.

"Don't give him all that," Vonette said.

"Mom, why you all up in the Kool-Aid? Your beautiful sister happens to be more generous than you are." He turned to his aunt. "I worked so hard to make your shoes look as lovely as you are, my dear Auntie. I hope that you are wearing one of these pairs out tonight."

"As a matter of fact, I am," Matriece said, smiling.

"Who you going out with?" he asked, trying to sound older than his years.

"Montgomery, that's who she's going out with," Vonette volunteered.

"Dag, this is getting serious. You been going out with him a loooong time, 'cause, Auntie Triecy, you be putting brothers in the wind before they mess up. Auntie Triecy don't play."

Vonette plucked his head. "Mind your business."

Matriece plucked his head. "Mind your business."

Before Vonette or Matriece could remove their fingers Tavares covered them with his own hands and patted them, then he disappeared into the kitchen.

Matriece sighed and looked around. The Ramirez women were staring at her, their faces expressionless. Boot's coworker said nothing. Vonette and Boot didn't mind their lives being an open book but she did. "Where's Shalimar?"

"She's upstairs on the computer."

"I see Chazz has another mystery woman," Matriece said. Chazz had discovered girls at the tender age of four, and had been fascinated ever since.

"Ah, yes. He is majoring in the ladies. Getting straight A's." Vonette smiled. "Chazz," she said, smiling warmly, "draws people to him. That's his gift."

Vonette went to the stairs and called, "Shalimar! Come down here and say hello to Auntie Triecy." She waited in silence for several minutes and then climbed two stairs and called again. Silence. The third time her voice grew louder, sterner, and her command was followed by a warning that if her daughter didn't show herself, she and Auntie Triecy would come to her. As they waited, the younger Ramirez sister frowned as she rolled her eyes at her mother.

"Carla, you need to cut that out," Vonette said. "You're not sleeping here tonight, so you better learn to get along with your mother."

"Your mom loves you, girl," Boot said. "Quit giving her a hard time."

Before Carla could respond, Shalimar slouched her way down the stairs with a pained expression on her face. "Hello, Auntie Triecy," she said, as though each word was agony. The child is seventeen going on nine, Matriece thought.

Shalimar allowed herself to be kissed but she didn't return her aunt's embrace and, once she was released, gave her mother a pleading look. "You can go back upstairs," Vonette said.

"She's coming around," Vonette whispered as her daughter climbed the stairs. "Her grades are going back up. She started reading again. That girl loves learning. She's just going through something. She's coming around, though."

"I just want her to be able to pull her grades up enough so she can get into a good college," Matriece said with a worried look on her face.

Vonette snorted. "If she doesn't, she'll go to a bad one, Triecy. Or maybe she won't go at all. Maybe she'll do minimum wage for a while before she figures out that she's brilliant. I don't believe a report card can hold my baby down."

Matriece watched her niece retreat to her room. She'd been away at college when Chazz and Shalimar were born. But when Vonette had Tavares she and Boot had been separated, and Matriece was between college and graduate school. The moment she saw the baby Matriece could feel her heart journeying toward him. She moved in with her sister for a year, baby-sitting her infant nephew while Vonette worked. In time Matriece began to feel that her sister's youngest son belonged to her. She still felt that way.

Matriece sat down on the sofa and declined the soda that Boot offered her. "I want to talk with you both," she said, and Boot and Vonette sat down beside her. Matriece had whispered this, but Mrs. Ramirez still leaned forward. Boot's coworker kept watching television. Carla sucked her teeth.

Turning toward her brother-in-law, Matriece said, "Boot, I can get Tavares into a great public school in the suburbs where the kids don't carry guns. It's a wonderful opportunity for him. Shalimar is in a good magnet school. Chazz is in college. The term has barely started. There's no reason why Tavares can't take advantage of this."

Vonette spoke quickly, looking away from her husband. "What are you talking about?"

"I'm talking about taking Tavares out of South Central and putting him into a suburban high school. We can use Blair's address."

"Where does she live?"

"Sherman Oaks."

"That's too far, Triecy. If anything was to happen, if he got sick, I couldn't get to him."

"Vonette, how many times has Tavares gotten sick at school? I'd rather he get sick than shot at. He'll get a better education."

"Just because it's white doesn't mean it's better. I mean, Tavares isn't some great athlete. His grades are just average. Why are those white folks going to care about him? At least his teachers at South Central like him. And what about band and chorus? They may be closed to him at Castle Heights."

"You're the parents. You go up there and get him in."

Boot sighed; he looked at his sister-in-law and then at his wife. "Triecy got a point, Vonette. Let the boy have his opportunity. I think he should go," Boot said.

Vonette looked from her sister to her husband. Behind her the Ramirezes stirred. "Have you talked to Blair?"

"Not yet, but it won't be a problem."

"I don't know. Tavares isn't going to want to leave South Central," Vonette said.

"It ain't about what he wants," Boot said. "I want him to go, and he's going."

"It's going to take him two hours to get there and back," Vonette said.

"He's young. He can study on the bus," Boot said.

"All right," Vonette said.

Matriece hadn't been aware that she'd been holding her breath until she suddenly felt the exhalation moving through her. "I'll talk to Blair."

Vonette's mouth went slack for a moment and Matriece could tell that she was still mulling over the decision. Her eyes seemed a bit cloudy for several moments before her face brightened. "Come upstairs. I want to show you something," she said.

Taking her sister by the hand, Vonette led her into the small jumbled bedroom that she shared with Boot. On her dresser were countless pictures of her children and husband, and several of Matriece. On the floor beside her bed was an unwrapped box the size of a telephone book. The top of the box said "Brown Sugar" in raised bronze letters, and there was a pair of full red lips, the company's logo, just below the name. Matriece gasped when she saw it. Vonette bent down, picked up the box, and handed it to her sister, who opened the lid. Her mother's life was inside that box. Neatly arranged on top of the red satin lining were the beauty products her mother had manufactured and sold, as well as written material that explained the concept of Brown Sugar, the cosmetics company that Hosanna had founded.

"This was Uncle Mooney's idea," Matriece said, holding the box.

"It was?" Vonette seemed surprised.

"Yeah. You remember how he started coming around after Daddy left? One night I heard them talking about what Mom could do to get in the department stores, and Uncle Mooney suggested she have sample boxes made up to leave with the store executives. Only it didn't work."

"She did okay with the beauty salons."

"Wasn't the same thing."

"Hell, Brown Sugar was all over the country."

"Not all over the country. Just California, Texas, the south, a couple of Midwestern cities, and a few in the northeast. And only for a little while. When Radiance got in the department stores in the seventies, Brown Sugar began to die. She should have been the first."

"So how many black women do you know who got as far as Mom, huh?"

"She wanted more, Vonette. She should have had more. Mom was cheated."

"You mean by Gilda."

"After Gilda disappeared, Mommy used to look for her. She ever tell you that?"

Vonette shook her head.

"She told you. You just weren't listening. About six months after Gilda split, Mom went to a drugstore. They were selling the same lotion that she and Gilda used to make, only it was in a different bottle and it had a new name. But the name of the company was on the bottle: Gilda Cosmetics. After that she started searching for her; Mom wanted her money. You don't remember this story?"

Vonette shook her head wearily.

"She'd go to where the Jews lived, the Fairfax District, and just walk around, looking for Gilda. And then one day she saw her. She was with her husband and she was pregnant. Mom said it was the happiest she'd ever seen her, and she couldn't bring herself to talk to her. She didn't want to ask her about the money. So she just walked away without saying a word."

"Why'd she do that?"

"She never told me, and I couldn't figure it out. But later, when Gilda got so big and Brown Sugar was dying, I think she regretted not speaking to her." Matriece sighed. "I wish Mom had married Uncle Mooney."

"He was already married, plus he was too old."

"He wasn't too old. He was nice to her, and they loved each other."

Vonette shook her head. "If he loved Mom so much, why did she have to work so hard, huh?"

"Mom loved him. She never asked him for money when the business was going under, because she didn't want to depend on him. He paid my way through school, and he would have paid for you, too."

"I didn't want his money," Vonette said.

Clutching the box to her chest, Matriece sat down on the bed. "Where did you get this?"

"Daddy gave it to me."

Matriece wanted to throw down the box, as if she'd suddenly discovered that it was contaminated. But she fingered the containers of powder, the plastic cases with blushes and eye shadows, the bottles of liquid foundation, the lipsticks. When she pulled out a bottle of foundation the color was mottled and separated. No matter how hard she shook the bottle, the color refused to blend.

"He wants to see you," Vonette said softly, interrupting Matriece's reverie.

Matriece frowned.

"He's sick, Triecy."

"I don't care."

"Why do you think everything was his fault? Mommy had faults, too."

"Mom fed us. He didn't."

"I . . ."

"What?"

Vonette put her hand on her sister's shoulder. "Look, don't get upset. I'm thinking about having him come here to live," Vonette said.

Rage and disgust began rising within her. "I can't believe you'd do that."

"I said I'm thinking about it," Vonette said.

"He never did one thing for us, and then when she died, he shows up at the lawyer's office looking for money. What kind of man is that?"

"You keep living in the past, Triecy. Just because he has problems doesn't mean I can't love him. At least he was kind to me. He played with me. He made me feel important, which is more than Mommy did."

"Maybe she would have had more time for games if Daddy had been able to keep a job."

"That's not why she worked. I mean, yeah, she had to feed us, but she wanted to be a big success. Her business was first. We came second."

"That's not true."

"Then why couldn't she ever pick us up from school on time? She was always late. Remember the time the dog almost bit us? We were the only kids left at the school. When she finally drove up the vice-principal told her she had to be more punctual."

"You make it sound like she was late every day."

"She was. Mommy didn't even have any friends. She never even talked to any of the women in the neighborhood. All she did was work."

"Those women respected her. She was the only black woman around there who had a business, except for some hairdressers. She's the reason there is a Gilda Cosmetics. It was her concept, her energy, her faith."

"Stop trying to live her life. Whatever she didn't accomplish here on earth, it's not yours to do for her."

"Vonette."

"What?"

"I see her sometimes."

"Who?"

"Mom."

"You mean you dream about her. I dream about her, too."

Matriece shook her head. "They're not always dreams. Sometimes I'm awake."

"I dream about her, too, Triecy," Vonette repeated.

"It wasn't a dream. I don't know. Sometimes I feel as though she's watching me. And other times I feel as though she wants something from me, Vonette."

"Well, it's too late. You can't give it to her."

"I want my own," Matriece whispered softly.

"You mean you want what Mommy wanted."

"What's wrong with that? Why can't I make my mother's dream come true? Why can't I own a cosmetics company that will be right up there with the big boys. I'm talking international, baby."

"Like Gilda's."

"Yeah, like Gilda's."

"Don't forget to live life," Vonette said softly. She had a troubled expression on her face.

Matriece fingered the outside of the box, then closed her hand into a fist and let her knuckles graze the tops of the small containers of powder, blush, shadows. She turned the tubes of lipstick upside down and read off the names of the shades to Vonette. "Aretha Red, Diana Rose." The two women started giggling and by the time Matriece was finished, they were sprawled in a heap on the bed howling at the memory of the day they'd made their mother laugh by naming her lipsticks after black entertainers.

"She wanted the business to be so great," Matriece said wistfully, as they walked down the stairs.

Mrs. Ramirez and her oldest daughter had left. Carla sat alone at the kitchen table. Boot and his coworker were still watching the game.

"Carla, you need to go home now," Vonette said.

"Lemme stay here. I can't stand them."

"You go home, and do what I told you to do," Vonette said.

Carla got up reluctantly. "Bye," she said.

Vonette sighed as she watched the girl leave.

"She'll be back," Boot said.

Vonette sighed again.

Matriece called out her good-byes. At the door, Vonette said, "Tell Montgomery I said that Tiffany's is having a diamond sale."

"You want to hook Montgomery, you gotta throw down in bed, like your sister here. Ain't that right, baby," Boot said, his laughter filling the room.

"Thank you, Boot," Matriece said, "That's quite enlightening. Who said I wanted to hook Montgomery? Both of you are moving way too fast."

"Girl, you need to be with somebody," Boot said. "You can't date for the rest of your life."

"Leave Triecy alone, Boot. She's just being careful, that's all."

"Don't be too careful, girl. End up by your damnself. Need to take a chance."

"Right," Matriece said, and she wasn't smiling.

As Matriece walked toward her car she didn't even want to think of Brown Sugar and all the work she had to do. She had shiny shoes and new stockings and tonight she was going on a date. *Need to take a chance.* Matriece glanced in the rearview mirror and saw a face filled with indecision and fear. And the eyes she saw staring back at her belonged to Lonell Carter.

CHAPTER TWENTY-FIVE

THE BOOMING VOICES of KBOM's Saturday morning wake-up team made sleep impossible. Montgomery lay in bed listening to the three disc jockeys bantering back and forth, their exuberance energizing him, coaxing him into full consciousness. Under the soft covers he stretched, flexed his toes, and scanned the to-do list that was forming in his mind. He had to meet his father for breakfast and then accompany him to a funeral. In the evening he'd go out with Matriece.

After a few minutes, Montgomery got out of bed, put on a T-shirt, shorts, and sneakers and began easing into his exercise routine, starting out with a slow warm-up. He'd been a sprinter in college, and he could call forth quick bursts of energy effortlessly, but he wanted to increase his endurance. His kick-off stretching unclogged his mind. Once he felt his blood flowing, Montgomery climbed onto the treadmill, pressed the steep incline button, and trudged along for nearly thirty minutes. He let his mind wander as his legs struggled to keep up the pace.

Thoughts of his date brought a smile and a stirring in his groin. He was relieved he and Matriece were going out. Montgomery had detected coolness from her since the awards dinner. When he'd called, she seemed reluctant to share her day with him and didn't ask him about what he was doing. Since his teenage years, Montgomery had been escaping women intent on pinning him down, boxing him in, taking from him what he didn't have enough of for himself. He wasn't used to women running in the other direction. The possibility that Matriece's affection had shifted filled him with unexpected panic. He felt something being snatched from him, something that he wanted: a smart, determined woman with legs long enough to wrap around him, arms strong enough to thrust him forward.

By the time Montgomery turned off the treadmill he was sweating.

He paused for a few minutes before he grabbed two forty-pound weights from a rack and began a strenuous series of lifts that lasted twenty minutes. Toward the end, his arms were shaking with pain and he was gasping with exhaustion, but he continued to push himself until he'd completed the number he'd set out to do.

It was nine o'clock when Montgomery, freshly shaved, showered, and neatly dressed in a dark suit and tie, pulled up in front of Avenue Café. The restaurant was his father's secret indulgence. Ever since what Big Monty termed "his little false alarm," Nadine had refused to allow pork in their house: no bacon, no sausage, no chops. His father appeared to cooperate with his wife but nearly every Saturday he fell off the dietary restriction wagon with a vengeance.

As soon as he walked in, Montgomery saw his father seated at his usual large table in the center of the room. Big Monty was laughing and holding a biscuit in one hand. He was surrounded by people who, seeing him in full reach of their adulation, had let their own breakfasts grow cold as they hurried over to greet the man who set their drive time to music.

Montgomery had long grown accustomed to the hordes of well-wishers and followers his father attracted. At times women had thrust their children toward him, especially their young boys, almost as though they believed his father capable of blessing them, transferring his Midas touch. "Black people think success is something that can rub off, like luck," Big Monty once said. Usually he was generous with his time. It's good business, he told his son. "Did you order for me, Dad?" Montgomery asked pointedly, after he'd shaken hands and sat down. "You know we don't have a lot of time." The people stared at him. Montgomery smiled back and then looked at his watch. Taking the hint, the fans retreated to their own breakfasts.

"Good thinking," Big Monty whispered. When the area around them was clear, he said, "I think we're going to go with the Houston station. Might have to send you back there this week to work out some of the details. It looks solid though."

Montgomery could feel a dim shadow falling over him, a sudden tiredness. His father's voice droned on, exploring every tiny facet of the proposed deal, turning it this way and that, as though searching for coins under a sofa cushion. Montgomery tried to pay attention but the prospect of buying yet another station didn't excite him in the least. The thought of spending weeks and perhaps months overseeing the sale and then assessing the management situation depressed him. "Maybe you should rethink this whole thing, Dad."

Big Monty was about to shove another biscuit into his mouth. He put the bread back on his plate. "Huh?"

"I'm just saying, maybe something better, more interesting, will come along."

"Montgomery, what the hell are you talking about? I've gone over the numbers and the numbers make sense."

Montgomery sighed, suddenly feeling very unsure of what he was trying to say.

"What?" Big Monty leaned across the table. He stared at his son for a few moments, his eyes gleaming with expectancy. He put both his elbows on the table and cupped his chin in his palms. When Montgomery retreated into silence, his father slumped back in his chair as though he were suddenly overcome with exhaustion.

The food came. Waffles and scrambled eggs for Montgomery, the same for his father, with the addition of three links of pure pork sausage. The men ate in silence. When they were finished, Big Monty paid the check, left a healthy tip, and waved to everyone as they headed out the door.

"There's another level," Montgomery said, as they walked to their cars.

"Another level?"

"I can't explain it. I just think that we could be doing something a lot bigger."

"What are you saying? What is it you want to do?"

Montgomery took a deep breath. "I don't know."

Big Monty's shoulders slumped; he looked tired, like an old man. "Well, until you do, I'm still in charge, and it's my decision that we proceed with the deal in Houston. That all right with you?"

There were cars lined up three deep on the street outside St. Paul's

Episcopal Church. Montgomery followed his father into the parking lot to the area marked RESERVED, and found a space close to his. By the time he got out of his car, Big Monty was already in conversation with two men who'd just arrived. Montgomery walked behind them into the church, catching pieces of their sentences as they floated backward over their shoulders.

The sanctuary was cool, despite the fact that it was almost full. Sunlight streamed through the stained glass faces of Christ and his disciples. The air above the pews was thick with the cacophony of greetings from the bereaved who'd come to mourn the passing of Calvin Meeks's older brother. Although Calvin had founded Radiance and was more closely associated with the cosmetics empire, it was Lawrence who had been responsible for the day-to-day operations of the company. Only weeks earlier the dead man's son had assumed his father's duties and already rumors were highlighting the younger man's deficiencies; some of the whispering that filled St. Paul's on this late September day was filled with dire predictions for the firm. Other conversations were more mundane.

"Didn't see you on the Vineyard this summer."

"Did you get your ticket for the Links luncheon? Girl, you'd better hurry."

"Which chapter of Jack and Jill do you belong to?"

"It's a small company and nobody's heard of it yet, but that's why I'm telling you to buy now. In three months the stock will be through the roof."

As they crowded into the mahogany pews, men and women scanned the crowd for those who counted in the world of commerce and society. Before the priest had led the mourners in prayer the most ambitious and cunning were mapping out their exit routes through the maze of rows and aisles to reach the people who could do them the most good.

Looking beyond many of the faces he'd seen at the awards dinner, Montgomery spied his mother, and guided his father toward the third row, where she was seated. Juliette was notably absent. Montgomery's sister had long ago mastered the art of wiggling out of "family obligations," and he wondered just how bad her "cramps" were today. There was no pain that Montgomery could invent that would excuse him from showing up at St. Paul's. Although he had met the deceased only once or twice, his father had commanded that he be present.

He felt his mother's elbow. "There's Calvin," she whispered. "His jacket isn't hiding that big belly, is it?"

Montgomery chuckled, as he watched his father and Calvin Meeks greet each other. Within seconds, he heard his father talking about the new station in Houston he was about to acquire. Meeks immediately launched into his plans for expanding his operations in Bermuda.

Montgomery shook Calvin Meeks's hand. "Good to see you, sir."

St. Paul's was known for brief, emotion-free services, and the funeral of Lawrence Meeks was no exception. Less than forty minutes after he sat down, Montgomery was rising for the benediction. Nadine's hand was soft but insistent as she guided him toward the family of the deceased; they lined up behind others who stopped by to murmur words of sympathy and encouragement. Montgomery heard his father say, ". . . such a terrible thing," as he patted the widow's shoulder. Montgomery went down the line, repeating the exact same thing to each person until he heard his mother say, "Here's Gretel," in a bright, chirpy voice. Eudora Meeks, Calvin's wife, smiled fondly and desperately in his direction.

Montgomery kissed his friend's cheek. "I'm sorry to hear about your uncle," Montgomery said to Calvin and Eudora Meeks's only child.

"Thanks." When Nadine looked away, Gretel winked at Montgomery. He winked back. They had long ago joined forces in laughing at their mothers' attempts to match them, an exercise that had begun when they entered third grade. He thought of her as a sister, and he knew he didn't appeal to her as a lover at all.

"She's a beautiful girl," his mother whispered as they walked down the aisle. He could hear his father behind them, greeting people and stopping to chat.

"Who?" he asked, just to tease his mother.

"Gretel Meeks," Nadine said easily.

"Mom, I have a girlfriend."

His mother appeared unperturbed. "I'm just saying that Gretel is from a wonderful family and that she's a lovely young woman."

"I agree," he said smoothly. His mother didn't respond. Seconds later he heard her greeting a friend. Montgomery caught her eye and mouthed his good-bye. His father was surrounded by people.

Montgomery was about to get into his car and drive off when he noticed Mooney sitting in a black Lincoln that was parked beside him. Montgomery walked over and tapped on the back window, which rolled down swiftly. Mooney peered at him for a moment before recognition began filling the old man's eyes. "Hello, Mr. Mooney."

"How are you doing, Montgomery? Did you know Lawrence well?"

"I met him a few times."

"What I liked about Lawrence was that he had more sense than ego. He was forward-thinking. I speak my mind," he said, giving Montgomery a penetrating look.

"Yes sir, nothing wrong with that."

"There was a lot of money sitting in that church today. Lawrence and I used to get together and talk about what we could do with a lot of money. He was the brother with the vision." He appraised Montgomery coolly. "Get Matriece to bring you by sometime. Or better yet, come on your own."

"I'd enjoy that, Mr. Mooney."

Montgomery turned his car onto Crenshaw and drove toward the freeway. Traffic was backed up for blocks; when he finally passed the mall, he could see the crowd gathered outside and the police cars surrounding it. Six, he counted. Even with his windows rolled up Montgomery could hear the angry voices, one louder than the others. He kept driving but his progress was slow and he couldn't stop looking behind him. As soon as the traffic cleared he felt something, a kind of electricity, sparking up and down his spine. It wasn't painful, but it got his attention. He felt almost as though he wasn't steering his own car. For no reason that Montgomery could think of he turned onto a side street, parked, and walked back to where the people had gathered. Across the street from the mall Montgomery could see that cops had one boy spread-eagled against a wall. He stood on the fringes of the crowd for a few minutes, asking questions of those around him, who told him about the shooting at the school two blocks away. He recalled that South Central was the high school that Matriece's beloved nephew attended.

"They need to put that fool under the jail," one old woman said. "Try to give your children an education and here he comes shooting up the place."

Around him there was loud agreement.

Montgomery watched the boy. Even from across the street he could see the fear and panic in his face. No alternatives, he thought. But, of course that wasn't true. He could have chosen a different path. What would it have taken for him not to end up where he was? As the bystanders began wandering away, Montgomery looked around Crenshaw and saw the small businesses that crowded the block. McDonald's. Burger King. Krispy Kreme. Mama's Soul Food. House of Wigs. Hollywood Video. That young man couldn't make a living anywhere on this street. *Transform the street, and you transform the lives.* The words sounded familiar, like a poem he'd memorized in the third grade for Parents Night and hadn't recited since. He still knew the verses; he still felt them.

CHAPTER TWENTY-SIX

THE FIRST THING Matriece noticed when she opened her door was that Montgomery appeared bigger, as if he had grown or spread out in a way that couldn't be measured in inches. When he moved around her living room he seemed to take up more space than his body actually required. As he sat down on her sofa she could hear the cushions collapsing beneath his weight. Glancing at Montgomery's face, Matriece found him more serious than he'd ever been. He's met someone, she thought. He doesn't want to see me anymore. As the words surfaced her stomach tightened as if around a fist, and she braced herself for another blow. It had been a long time since a man left her. She'd forgotten how they ended things, the words they said or didn't. What Matriece remembered was the pain.

"Why are you staring at me like that?" Montgomery asked.

She shook her head, rousing herself from a daze. "Sorry. Do you want a glass of wine?" she asked.

"Sit down next to me," he said. When she was beside him he took her hand in his, and she thought, Here it comes. "I had an experience today, and I don't know where to put it," he said. "I went to Lawrence Meeks's funeral this morning."

Matriece nodded. "I heard that he died. I didn't get a notice. I'm persona non grata at Radiance."

He nodded. "On my way back I took Crenshaw, and when I passed the mall there was a crowd outside and a bunch of police cars."

"Yeah, I was there, too. Some kid was shooting at my nephew's school. I got so scared when I heard about it."

"I figured something must have happened, and my intention was to keep going. Then, I don't know why, but I stopped. I ended up parking on a side street, walking back to the crowd, and just standing there with them. I don't know why but it felt so good doing that." Montgomery paused for a moment. "You look pretty," he said, as though he was just noticing her.

"Thank you." She didn't know what else to say. The conversation wasn't going in the direction she initially feared it would, and now that she realized her mistake her relief was palpable.

He gave her hand a squeeze. "They had a young brother up against one of the stores, and he looked so scared. He was in the wrong—it wasn't a case of 'Free Huey'—but why was he in the wrong? I guess the thing for me is that I haven't even thought about that kind of brother in a long time, and when I had to confront his plight, if you want to call it that, it felt good to think about him. I've always gone along with things. I take orders; I don't give them."

She knew he was referring to his father. It was the first time he'd spoken about their relationship, the first time he said aloud what she'd sensed when father and son were together: Big Monty had Montgomery on a leash that was choking the life out of him. Matriece was quiet but she moved closer to him. Her thigh grazed his.

He spoke more slowly when he continued, as though each word were being weighed and measured. "That's not really true. There was a time when I was the leader. When I was at Morehouse I was elected president of the student body. You know how it is on most black campuses; you step one foot off school grounds, and you're right in the ghetto. There's no restaurants, let alone clothing stores or any kind of entertainment. When I was a sophomore, a student was killed off campus. Wrong place, wrong time. Bottom line: the neighborhood wasn't safe. Still isn't. I got this group together and we came up with a plan to buy up the property."

"The entire neighborhood?"

"Just about. It was a really complex idea that involved selling stock and raising municipal bonds, a university investment . . . It was something."

"How old were you guys?"

"Nineteen or twenty."

"Young geniuses."

"It was the kind of plan that would turn a place like Crenshaw, which isn't bad at all compared to a lot of other black urban strips, into—"

"What an average white business area looks like."

"Exactly. You've had the fantasy?"

"The why-doesn't-Crenshaw-Boulevard-look-like-Rodeo-Drive fantasy? Oh, yes. I've had it."

"When I was standing in that crowd outside the mall I felt like who I was in college."

"What happened to your idea?"

"We presented it to the president in good faith, and he called our parents. My father flew out and told me that he had another plan for my life. And that was the end of that."

"Obviously not."

He gave her a grateful look. "It felt so good standing there, letting my mind go where it wanted to go. Even if I didn't do anything, just thinking about the possibilities made me feel alive."

"So, you're a nationalist revolutionary Black Panther, Malcolm X type of brother," she said in a teasing voice. She poked him in his chest with her finger.

"The revolutions in my mind are made of money. No guns. No blood. Just money."

"A financial revolutionary. I like that. And I thought you were just a mama's boy," she teased.

"Matriece," he said, and he looked at her for a long time.

I've offended him, she thought. "Montgomery, I'm—"

"Don't apologize. My mother . . ." He began, then he looked at her. "My mother has taken a whole lot of shit from my dad. I try to humor my mom because I know how much she's been through. I keep waiting for her to rise again."

"I didn't mean . . ."

His eyes met hers.

"Yeah, I did. Sometimes it seems as though she has you wrapped around her finger, and I know she doesn't like me. I guess I was . . ." She could feel her heart quickening as she spoke. Matriece was suddenly aware of how close she was sitting, and she moved away. "Anyway."

"I think, in time, you'll like each other."

"I don't dislike her. I thought she didn't like me."

He looked at her, opened his mouth, shut it, and they both laughed.

"She's probably got somebody picked out for you."

Montgomery stared at her again. She could see the incredulity in his eyes as he tried to compose his face. There was somebody else. For the second time that night she felt fearful but she tried not to show it. "Oh, yeah," she said, "some rich, willowy, Creole-looking heifer with a trust fund and long straight hair." She gasped. "Gretel Meeks." Montgomery's face confirmed her guess. "Damn, I'm good."

He moved closer to her, pulled her to him, and kissed her. "I pick the woman I want, okay?"

I like him, she thought, looking into his eyes. He's sweet and he's smart; he's open and he's decent, and I like him so much. Don't be afraid, she thought; he's not leaving. The thought made her tremble. She wanted to be by herself so she could examine her feelings, pick them apart. Get rid of them before they overwhelmed her.

When Matriece started to pull away Montgomery gripped her shoulders. "Where are you going?" When she settled against him he said, "At least you've met my family. Are you ashamed of me?"

Matriece sat up. So sincere, she thought, studying his expression. "I . . . I . . . ." she began. "My mother's dead. My sister and her family and an uncle here are all I really have here. I mean, there's an aunt and some cousins in Texas, but I don't keep up with them. Vonette does. My uncle was the first black firefighter in Los Angeles, and he was the first black fire chief. And he's a player. He's old and he's been with a million women and he's still going strong."

"I think I heard about your uncle. Tunis Clark, right?"

"Yes."

"What about your father?"

She should have expected the question, but it caught her off guard. "What about him?"

"You didn't mention him."

"I don't really. . ." She sighed, thinking about the possibility of Vonette letting Lonell live with her family. "We don't speak. Same old sad story."

"He walked out?"

Matriece nodded, and in the middle of that gesture she felt her eyes welling up. "Let me get us some wine," she mumbled, standing up, but Montgomery caught her by the wrist.

"Hey," he said.

Standing there with her knees brushing his, Matriece took three hard breaths. The tear rolled down with the third exhalation.

"What's the matter, baby?"

"I went to see my sister this afternoon, and she told me that she might let him live with them. I can't stand the thought of that. He did nothing for us. Vonette can forgive him, but I can't. That's my little personal tragedy." She tried to laugh, but she made a gagging sound. She felt his hands playing with her fingers. "I can still remember when he left. He used to sing this silly song. It was something he made up for me. He had another one that he sang to Vonette. After he left we'd sit in the bathtub and sing our songs. Then one day I forgot the words."

Matriece wiped her eyes, then smiled at Montgomery. "My sister and her family are kind of rowdy."

"Rowdy's okay."

"Vonette works at Ralph's. She's a master gardener. She's very artsy-craftsy, and she's a fabulous cook, wife, and mother. Her husband is Boot. He's Mexican-American, and he owns a small painting company; he does a great job. Boot's a funny guy. Chazz is twenty; he's a ladies' man. Shalimar is seventeen, the moody teenager. And Tavares is fifteen, and he's my perfect child."

"When do I get to meet them?"

"Whenever." She was trembling again. She sat down beside him. "What are you going to do with your rediscovered revolutionary soul?"

"I don't know." He put his arm around her shoulder.

"We don't have to go out," Matriece blurted out at the exact same moment that Montgomery was saying, "Let's stay here."

They both tried to laugh but instead they sat up and reached for each other. Montgomery's hands left a trail of warmth across her back. She kissed him, and didn't stop until she had to take a breath. She was falling, plunging into a space that didn't have a bottom. "Come upstairs," she said.

In the bedroom they began kissing and undressing at the same time, tossing their clothes on the floor. Montgomery sat down on the edge of the bed, opened his legs, pulled Matriece between them, wrapped his arms around her, and kissed her until she was dizzy. Matriece placed her hands on Montgomery's shoulders to steady herself; he lifted her up and put her on the bed, staring down at her. There was a moment as his face got closer to hers when she feared what was coming more than she desired it. Then she felt herself letting go, succumbing, receiving, and the fight went out of her.

When Matriece awoke in the morning Montgomery's heavy arm was flung across her breasts. Her leg was beneath his. She moved closer to him, wanting more of his weight and heat. Her head grazed his chest; she could hear his heart beating. Lying next to him, she was lulled momentarily. I could be this close to him all day, she thought. I could just lie here and touch him until night comes. The thought was a kind of meditation that made everything else in her mind recede. She was in the center of her own perfect reverie when she saw a flash of blue.

Hosanna stood in the doorway, wearing a shirtwaist dress dipped in sky. She looked as she did just before she died, her face creased and sad. "Mom," Matriece whispered.

Hosanna stared right at her daughter. She shook her head from side to side, kept shaking it until she faded away.

She doesn't want me with him. "Mom," Matriece whispered. But Hosanna was gone. You're wrong, she wanted to tell her. But what if she wasn't?

Montgomery moaned in his sleep. She was suddenly aware of the weight of his body. He was too heavy for her. Carefully she extricated her limbs from his. She got up, walked over to a chair in the corner of her room, picked up her robe and put it on, then sat down. Her arms were coiled around her middle as she watched the steady rising and falling of Montgomery's abdomen. His belly was hard and warm to the touch but Matriece didn't dare touch him now. Her own fingertips were her enemy, and she stood guard. She wouldn't try to hold him even though the chill of the early morning breeze caused her to shiver. It hurt to look at him.

Matriece didn't realize that she was moving fast until she felt air on her face. *Don't run away.* Taking the stairs two by two, she was panting a little when she reached the landing. *Don't do this.* It was then she heard the car in her driveway. She opened the door just a crack and was surprised to see Sam standing in front of her. He was dressed in a dark blue suit with a pale blue shirt and paisley tie. "You came Friday," she said, feeling as though she'd just emerged from a deep meditation.

"Yeah, I know, Miss Carter. Matriece. I'm on my way to church now. I was just wondering if you'd like to . . ." He stopped and stared at her. There was a wildness in his eyes that she hadn't seen before. His intent was nestled inside that wildness and she knew it, knew every word he was about to say before he opened his mouth. ". . . go to brunch with me after."

She could still feel Montgomery's leg on top of hers, his arm against her breasts, his hot limbs trapping hers. Her breathing was rapid. She was staring at a way out, an escape. *Don't do this.* "What time?"

"Church gets out at one o'clock."

"I'll be ready."

Sam was still standing there as Matriece closed the door softly. She leaned her back against it and could feel his presence coming through the door. Or maybe it was just heat.

Montgomery was still in bed when she returned to her room but his eyes were wide open. He was smiling. "Where'd you go, baby? I was missing you. Come over here."

She stood by the door and didn't move.

"Hey," he said playfully. Then his smile disappeared, and he was by her side, his arm heavy on her shoulder. "What's the matter?"

She put her hand on his arm for a moment, almost as though she were steadying herself. "I have to go out," she said softly.

Montgomery looked surprised. "Is something wrong? Do you want me to drive you somewhere?"

She shook her head.

"What is it?" he asked.

Matriece felt the full weight of his arm. She tried to pull away from him but he caught her wrist. "What's going on?"

"I . . . I can't. I'm not ready." She was conscious of how she was sputtering. Why couldn't he just go?

"Not ready for what?"

"For you. For a relationship. It's not going to work out, Montgomery."

He looked as though she'd slapped him, and it was then she realized that she was shouting.

"What did I do?"

"You didn't do anything. It's me, okay? Would you just go, please."

"Can't we talk about this?"

She shook her head. "No."

He reached for her. "Baby . . ."

"No!"

He didn't slam the door, as some of the others had. He didn't mutter, "Crazy bitch." She'd heard that before, too. There were no tears, and yes, she'd been through that, too. The noise of his car starting drew her to the window. Watching him drive away, she could feel herself starting to cry. No! The shout was internal, reverberating inside her body. It bounced against the loneliness inside her.

Matriece was on her way into the bathroom for a shower when the telephone rang. When she answered, Blair's voice reached into her reverie. "You just popped into my mind. Did you and Montgomery have a nice time last night?"

"Yeah."

"Did he spend the night?"

"He just left."

"Oooh, that sounds like progress. How did everything go? Bottom shelf? Top shelf?"

"Listen, I can't really talk now. I'm on my way out."

"You sound strange. Are you okay?"

"Yeah. I'm fine. I need a favor, though."

"Sure."

"There was a shooting at my nephew's school. Can my sister use your address to get him into Judd's school?"

"Of course. I'll ask Porter but I'm sure it's not a problem. Matriece, did something happen?"

Matriece was silent.

"Oh, my God. You broke up with him."

"Blair . . ."

"All right. All right. I'll shut up. You call me later, you hear?"

"Yeah."

Matriece had finished showering and dressing when the doorbell rang. She knows me so well, she thought as she picked up the intercom and buzzed in Sam. Blair the mind reader, she thought as she walked down the stairs. She felt strangely composed as she extended her hand to Sam. He turned his head toward her, and she looked into his sad, kind eyes. No danger there, she thought. None at all.

CHAPTER TWENTY-SEVEN

SATURDAY NIGHT SAM dreamed his prison dream. The same four Mexicans surrounded him in the yard. He was alone, and they had shivs, which they brandished as they cursed him in Spanish. Weaving and bobbing away from them, he tried to get back to the other black prisoners, but the knives stopped him. The men had no faces, just hanks of dark, straight hair. He kicked dirt toward where their eyes should have been, but they kept coming. As soon as he saw an opening he ran toward it.

He was still running when he woke up Sunday morning. He wiped his eyes as he dropped to his knees. "Mother Father God . . ." he began. He felt clearer as he prayed, and his fear slowly vanished. After he finished, he began humming the first song that came into his mind. He couldn't even remember the words or the title, but the hymn soothed him.

Sam had pressed his clothes the night before; after he made up his bed, he laid out his outfit, the dark blue suit, pale blue shirt, and paisley tie. "Looking good," he told the image in the mirror after he was dressed.

The volume of the CD player in his van was turned up high while he drove to church. When he stopped at the red light, Sam was mouthing the lyrics to one of Asia's slow songs, filling up with the happy, sad, scared, and lonely feelings her singing always gave him. The words she sang seemed so personal, like pieces of her soul set to music. He glanced out his passenger's window as he waited. A woman in the car next to his was peering at him. Their eyes locked for an instant. He saw the surprise in hers and then rage. Before the light had changed to green, her car streaked ahead of his. Without a moment's thought, Sam followed her.

They raced for several blocks until she finally parked. Sam pulled in behind her and got out. She was sitting in her car smoking a cigarette with the window rolled up. He tapped on the glass. She ignored him. "Ruth," he said, "please open the window."

The window came down. "My baby isn't giving you a damn cent. You hear me?"

"What are you talking about?"

"Don't try to act like you don't know Asia has blown up. Everybody in America knows that. I guess you figure you'll try and get a little bit of her gravy."

"Ruth—"

"Well, let me tell you something: You ain't done nothing for her since you made her. I raised that child, not you. I put food on the table, not you. She hates you. She's not going to give you any money. So, you might as well stay away from her."

"Ruth, did it ever occur to you that I don't want anything from her? Maybe I'd like to give her something. I'm a different man, Ruth. I've got my own business. I'm trying to make something of my life."

"Everything she wants she can get for herself. Asia don't need a father anymore, Sam. She's grown. It's too late for you to be the daddy. You had the chance, and you blew it." Ruth turned on her ignition.

"I'm sorry," Sam said quietly.

"What?"

"I'm sorry you went through hard times, you and Asia and Donny. I'm sorry I wasn't there for the three of you. It must have been hard. I'd like to try to—"

"Yeah, Sam. It was damn hard. You try raising two kids on minimum wage. Try feeding them on a dollar and your last food stamp. You try dealing with a dude you can't stand just because he'll cover the rent. You wanna hear some more about how hard it was?"

"How is she?"

Ruth gave him an incredulous look. "She's on top. That's how she is."

"No," he said quietly, "that's where she is. How is she feeling inside?"

"Niggah, please. She's feeling fine, okay. She's happy."

"I'm glad to hear that. Listen, I've been out for five years. If I wanted something from Asia, don't you think I'd have come around before now?"

Ruth lifted her hands from the wheel for a moment. Her face registered confusion, doubt, and suspicion.

"I've stayed away on purpose because I wanted to . . . What I want is to be able to pay her back. I want to see my daughter, Ruth."

Pure fire shot through Ruth's eyes, and her fingers closed in around the steering wheel and gripped it tightly. "You got a son, Sam. Why ain't you anxious to run up to the joint, huh?"

"Ruth—"

"Leave her alone, Sam. She don't need you anymore."

Sam stepped back just as Ruth's car motor roared, and she took off down the street.

Sam got back into his car, then looked at his watch. He was going to be late for church. In a few moments meditation would begin. It was the part of the service he enjoyed most. When the sanctuary lights were dimmed and the room was silent, the congregation was connected by breath and a collective search for inner peace. His mind had once been his enemy, but now it was his refuge. He closed his eyes and silently repeated the mantra that always led him into his deepest consciousness. After a few moments he could no longer hear the traffic sounds that he knew were all around him. His mind whispered his mantra again; the sound pushed aside the nagging worries about Asia that threatened to become invading thoughts. Like a surprise sun, the bright white light that was his friend slowly emerged. Sam concentrated on that light, dazzled by it as it turned into colors, then shapes and pictures. He could no longer feel his body, only the images that filled his eyes. Sam knew he was breathing but he couldn't identify his breath. Everything was wonderful. Everything was possible.

Sam was still somewhat dazed, not completely free from the meditative state when he saw her face. "Matriece Carter," he said. He opened his eyes.

The waitress led Sam and Matriece to a table next to a window where they could gaze out on the blue water of the Marina and see all the boats anchored near the pier, then handed them menus. "I used to dream about owning boats, big houses, and cars, but now it's good enough to simply enjoy looking at them," Sam said.

She smiled, and he could tell she felt unsure of herself, a little uncomfortable. Sam, too, was surprised at how quickly she'd agreed to go out with him, almost as though she'd been sitting in her house waiting for him to come along and take her away.

"Sam," he heard her say.

"Yes."

"Do you want some champagne?"

The waitress was staring at him.

"Oh. No. I'll have orange juice. How about you?"

"I'll take a glass of champagne," Matriece said. When the waitress retreated she turned to Sam, and he noticed how warm her eyes were for the first time. "This is a nice place."

"I like to be by the water."

"You swim?"

"Yes, but mostly I like to look at the water. Sometimes I go to the beach near the Santa Monica pier, and I'll take a book and spend the day on a blanket reading."

"What are you reading now?" she asked.

He laughed a little nervously. "The title just went out of my head."

"What's it about?"

"First Ladies."

Matriece looked surprised. "The wives of the presidents?"

Sam nodded. "It's a book about their lives, how they integrated who they were with being the power behind the throne, so to speak. History tells us all about the men, but we don't know what kind of impact being married to a particular kind of person has on the job the president does, what he accomplishes."

"Like Franklin and Eleanor Roosevelt."

"Exactly. She was one of my favorites because of the role she played in advancing civil rights issues. But you know who I really admire?"

"Who?"

"Betty Ford."

"I can see that."

"Here was a woman who gets breast cancer in an age when it's hush-

hush, and she talks about it. She's an alcoholic in a time when people are just coming to grips with thinking that alcoholism is a disease, and she not only goes public, she starts a hospital."

"Gets a face-lift and doesn't try to hide it."

"Just an all-around out-there woman. I'm impressed with her. I like the fact that her husband didn't try to hold her back. He had his moment to shine, and then he let her have hers. To me that's saying that he knew he was with a great woman."

"A lot of guys can't admit that."

"No, they can't."

There was silence between them for a moment, and then the waitress brought their drinks. Sam took several sips of orange juice, then put down his glass. "I'm also reading a book about playing the stock market. I just got into that a couple of years ago."

"Made any money?"

"Yeah, I did. That's how I got my house."

Matriece grinned. "Maybe you can give me a few tips."

"You just study the company you're interested in. Read their annual reports. Use their products if possible. Ask other people what they think. When in doubt, hire a broker. And pray. But that's good for everything."

"I knew you were a reader, Sam. You always had books in the van."

"I thought you were too busy checking out my legs to be worried about my books."

Matriece choked a little on her champagne, and quickly drank some water. When she started laughing, Sam joined in. "Well, they are nice, Sam," she said. "Your chest is, too."

"Thank you. I used to work out a lot when I was in prison."

As he watched, Matriece set down her glass carefully. "Oh, really," she said. "How long were you there?"

"Fourteen years."

"That's a long time."

"Armed robbery."

"I see. Did . . ."

"Nobody got hurt. Listen, if you ever want to hear about what happened, we can talk about it. My thoughts weren't right during that time. That's how I wound up in prison: bad thinking."

"You're honest."

"Back then I didn't realize who I could become, what I was capable of doing in this world. I didn't think I could work and play the stock market, buy a house, own a business, expand it. I'm getting ready to buy another van in a few months. I'll be hiring somebody to work for me. After a while, I'll buy another van. And I won't stop there. But you know about that kind of vision. That's how you got to where you are in life. I've admired you for a long time, Matriece. Took me a while to work up the nerve to ask you out. I know it sounded sudden. I just had to move with the spirit. It was nice of you to come out with me on such short notice. I didn't think you'd be available."

"I have been seeing somebody."

"I haven't been seeing anyone."

"I don't know where I am with this other guy."

"That's okay. Maybe I can help you figure that out if you're willing to hang out with an ex-con with a GED, who's not into pressure or stalking."

Matriece chuckled. "That's good to know. Oh, I have something for you," she said, reaching into her purse. She pulled out a CD and handed it to Sam. When he saw Asia Pace's face on the cover he smiled.

"Her manager sent me a couple. Some variations on her new single. I thought you might like to hear it since you're her biggest fan."

"Thank you," he said. "You couldn't have given me a nicer present. Did you guys ever hook up?"

"Yeah, we did. And she wants to be our spokesmodel."

"That's good," Sam said. "How is she?"

"Beautiful."

"What kind of person is she?"

"You know, Sam, to tell you the truth, she seems a little sad to me. I think she's lonely. She asked me if we could hang out together sometime. I told her we could."

"Yeah," he said. "Are you going to go out with me again?"

Matriece paused for a moment, and he could tell what was going through her mind. A woman like her would think more than twice about dating an ex-con.

"Sure."

"Just one thing: I'm not washing your car for free. So, don't ask."

CHAPTER TWENTY-EIGHT

THERE WAS AN American flag behind the vice-principal's desk, just to the right of the man. As Blair studied the Stars and Stripes on Tuesday morning, she assiduously avoided looking at Dr. Sable, which wasn't difficult to do since he was just as assiduously avoiding looking in her direction. Dr. Sable was peering at Judd, who stared back at him with exactly the same passive expression that he had while watching MTV. Blair didn't want to be where she was: sitting in a hard-back chair in front of the unsmiling and all-too-familiar face of Dr. Sable, dean of discipline for Castle Heights High School. Castle Heights. Such an improbable name for a school located in the Valley. She especially didn't want to be there without her husband. She felt defenseless and puny without Porter beside her. "Your stupid movie can wait!" she had screamed at her husband that morning. But, of course, show business waited for no one. It was the deity they all genuflected before. Sitting in Dr. Sable's office, Blair was fighting back tears. I will not break down, she told herself. I will not! She looked across at Judd, who sat very straight in the chair next to her. His head was completely shaved, and he was wearing pants that were at least three sizes too big. She sighed and counted the stars on the flag again. Her fingers twitched as she listened to Dr. Sable rattle off Judd's crimes against humanity: cutting classes; ditching; smoking on school property; and now the latest, being caught with a joint in his possession. She wanted to reach out with her twitching fingers and snatch her son by his collar and shake him; she also wanted to hold him the way she did when he was a child, rock him in her arms and tell him that everything was going to be all right, that whatever was wrong Mommy could fix it.

Dr. Sable's eyes met Blair's. "Mrs. Priestly, by all rights, Judd should be expelled." He leaned over so that she could see his fillings, smell his breath when he opened his mouth. "Having any kind of illegal substance is—"

"That wasn't mine, Dr. Sable," Judd said. "Somebody put it in my bag."

Blair looked at her son. She could tell that he wanted to laugh. No, he couldn't possibly think that this situation was the least bit funny. "Judd," she said, feeling angry and weary at the same time. But when he smiled at her, she didn't know how to finish the sentence.

"Young man," Dr. Sable said sternly, "don't interrupt me." He wiped his forehead, pressed back into place a lock of hair that was the color of a bathtub ring. "Your track record for this year nullifies everything you have to say on your own behalf."

Hearing the principal, Judd sat up even straighter, as though he were trying to stretch himself as far away from that airless room as possible. And yet he didn't seem unhappy being there under the gaze of Dr. Sable or facing Blair's own wondering countenance. He didn't seem unhappy at all.

This is starting to feel normal, Blair thought. Twice since September she'd sat in this very chair.

"Judd, you're a very intelligent young man, and you obviously come from a good home. There is no reason why we should ever have to meet again under these circumstances. Don't you agree?" Dr. Sable waited.

"Yes, Dr. Sable," Judd said, shifting in his seat. "Dr. Sable, I don't know how that bud got in my bag, but I can tell you that it won't happen again." His expression was one of sincere contrition.

"It had better not, Judd. I can't continue to go out on a limb for you." He stood up. He was a large man with a belly that his suit coat only partially hid. "Go back to class."

After Judd left, the room fell silent. Dr. Sable picked up a pencil and began ruffling through the papers that were on his desk. Nitty-gritty time. Blair could feel the tears again, a strong flood waiting behind her eyelids. She reached inside her purse and pulled out the sealed envelope, which she placed in front of the principal, who put it into his pocket without looking at her. "Thank you, Dr. Sable," she said, and then she left.

Blair was lighting a cigarette by the time she reached the parking lot. She inhaled deeply. *I just gave a man five hundred dollars so he wouldn't kick my kid out of school.* When she was seated behind the wheel she began sobbing. "Oh, God. Oh, God," she said. Blair tried to recount the steps it had taken to get to the point where she was sliding an envelope filled with money to a man who held her son's future in his hand. She recalled the way Dr. Sable had suggested she make a contribution to the football team. At first she hadn't comprehended. And then she did. It was just business. An underpaid school administrator trying to make a buck. It was the way things worked. *What wouldn't I have done?* she wondered. Goddamn Porter, ducking out on her, leaving it all to her to handle while he had fun all day with his latest tits-and-ass queen. She couldn't let Judd be expelled, not with his grades. Getting into college was going to be hard enough without having an expulsion on his record. Blair took a long drag and held in the smoke until she could feel it pushing against her throat. She didn't want to think anymore; she had to go to work.

It was a little before ten by the time Blair got to the office. For the last few months she'd been meeting with in-house artists and designers, trying to motivate them to come up with new, innovative concepts for lipstick containers. Blair had started out as a fine artist, and she brought to her commercial work a love of balance and symmetry. When she told her staff that she wanted each lipstick container to be a work of art, she meant it. Now she had the samples, and as she examined them, she breathed a sigh of relief. They were good. One was a miniature clear plastic jar for lip gloss, along with a small brush with a retractable tip. In another version the gloss was held in a small steel pot that snapped shut. The other samples were different but each variation was a clever, modernistic design. Blair picked up one of several small boxes meant to hold the gloss pots. It was made of heavy, corrugated cardboard, which gave it a funky, Bohemian flavor, a good melding of hip-hop flavor and sophistication. The lettering was going to be equally eye-catching. Her idea was to reproduce on the package the actual handwriting of the spokesmodel, whoever that turned out to be. On the box would be written the color of the gloss or lipstick, the celebrity's signature, and of course, the words "Brown Sugar" and the company logo, which was a pair of very full, dark lips. "Chaka Khan lips" was the way Matriece described them.

Fontaine waved her in when Blair knocked on his door. He was seated at a long table on which he'd spread out pieces of fabrics and photos of various fashions, all slated for next fall. He was talking on the telephone as he peered over the pictures and swatches.

"Come to my office," she mouthed when she caught his eye. He nodded.

A few minutes later he appeared at her door, smiling. "How's it going?" he asked cheerfully.

She pointed to the mock-ups that she'd placed on the table in the corner.

"What have we here?" Fontaine said as he walked over. He picked up each of the sample containers and examined it. "These are very creative," he said. "Will Kent be pleased?"

"I'm on budget. Why? Do they look expensive?"

Fontaine nodded. "I wouldn't have been surprised if they'd taken you over."

"Do you like them? Do you see a fashion connection?"

"I like the steel pots. That utilitarian thing is hip. The teenies will love it." He palmed the small container in his hand. "It's nice and light. Bags are smaller next year. This cardboard is nice. What about the colors?"

"Bright red."

"Really?" He laughed. "That would be wild." He paused. "Can't say there's a fashion tie-in. Are we doing bags?"

"I was going to propose that, but I don't think Kent will go for it. Why?"

"I like a finished look, you know? A complete outfit. Red, huh. Next fall is totally understated. But, hey, we'll get noticed. Maybe you could mute it in some way, take out some of the intensity."

"Don't they call that pink?"

Fontaine chuckled. "I guess you've made up your mind."

"Will you support me?"

"I'm not going to argue against your decision. But I do have to point out that red is going against next year's fashion trends. I'm still on your side."

As soon as he left, Blair felt the urge for a cigarette. She hated the fact that she was a smoker. She would quit soon. But not today.

The courtyard was a small parklike area behind the building. In the center was a miniature rectangular lawn bordered by multicolored flower beds. Around it was a cement walk and several wooden benches. Kent was sitting in the courtyard alone. Plumes of smoke surrounded his head like fog and then drifted away. Blair took at least twelve cigarette breaks a day. She suspected that Kent took more.

"We have to stop meeting like this," she said, sitting down next to him on the bench. He leaned over and pressed the tip of his lit, unfiltered cigarette to the one that Blair was extending toward him. "Thanks," she said, exhaling, then looking closer. "Are you all right?"

"I'm just tired," Kent said.

"Yes, well, you've been doing double duty for a while."

"My work here has never been a problem. It's exhilarating. I've helped Gilda build an institution."

"Oh, I didn't mean . . ."

Kent waved his hand. "You don't have to explain." He was silent for a moment, staring at the smoke that wafted around him. "My wife's nurse usually stays with her until she goes to bed, but for the last few weeks she's been ill. I haven't been able to find a replacement yet. It's funny, Peggy always waited on me hand and foot, and now the roles are reversed."

"That's got to be hard," Blair said. She had heard about his wife's stroke, but he'd never spoken about it.

Kent nodded wearily. "She's a very strong woman." He paused. "I guess in addition to everything else about the stroke, it's just so damn surprising. I mean, here is this active, vital woman and all of a sudden, she's drooling, confused, and the worst thing of all is that she knows it. She knows that she's failing." He looked haggard and sad. Blair reached over and patted his hand, and to her surprise Kent held hers for a moment, squeezing as though he were attempting to wrest some strength from it.

During their shared silence she began to relive the full dark weight of that morning's encounter. "I had to go to my son's high school this morning. He almost got suspended for having a joint in his pocket."

Blair laughed uneasily. She hadn't meant to tell anyone at work about Judd. And she didn't mean to equate her troubles with a wayward son with Kent's wife's illness. "Please keep that confidential."

"Of course."

"He's not a bad kid. Judd has always been mischievous. He's had behavior problems ever since he was little. I guess most teenagers these days experiment with marijuana. I'm glad it wasn't anything stronger. Judd will be a senior next year. Based on his test scores, he could go anywhere he wanted to college. He's got nearly perfect PSATs, and his state tests are always in the highest percentiles. He's a brilliant kid. But his grades are another story. He's never been much for studying."

"Sometimes boys get a little crazy during their teens," Kent said gently. "God knows I was a handful when I was young, and during my junior high school years I was a terrible student. My mother was weak," he added, his voice edged with contempt. "If my father hadn't been really strong, there is no telling where I might have ended up. He was the kind of guy who wouldn't give up on me. Every mistake I made, he was right there. He'd give me a good kick in the pants when I needed it, but he'd always talk with me. Sometimes he'd even read the Bible. Oh, he was a wonderful guy."

"My father was always working. His being away didn't affect me so much. We lived in a pretty bad neighborhood. I spent a lot of time at my aunt's house. She exposed me to a better life. I think my brother really needed my dad. He never went with me to Aunt Tess's. He's an alcoholic who lives off my mother. I know that if my husband were participating the way he ought to, Judd would be fine. My husband leaves everything to me."

Blair could feel her voice quavering and hot tears gathering in her eyes. Oh, God, please don't let me cry in front of Kent, she prayed. But she couldn't help herself. A tear slid down her cheek. She brushed it away quickly.

She felt the pressure of Kent's hand as he squeezed hers harder. "Have you spoken to your husband about your concerns, Blair?"

"He's always too busy," she said bitterly. "Working. Supposedly." Blair wanted to bite off her own tongue as soon as the words were out.

But Kent's expression was both sympathetic and alert. "Do you think that your husband is having an affair?"

Blair was so surprised by his bluntness she could only nod.

"I would caution you to be very sure about that. Men stay out late and travel for all different reasons that have nothing to do with other women."

"I don't have any real proof, just a feeling," Blair said. As she heard her own words she was surprised to feel more relieved than ashamed. Looking into Kent's eyes she saw something she hadn't expected: understanding, and perhaps some help.

"Blair, men have affairs mostly because of their own fantasies. Don't think of it as your failure. Perhaps you can reel him in before tragedy strikes."

"Tragedy is already striking on a regular basis."

Kent gave her a wry smile. "Depends on your definition of tragedy."

"What's yours?"

Kent paused for a long time. "Let's just put it this way: I've been where your husband is, and it sounds to me as if he's standing on the precipice. You've got to pull him back."

"So it's up to me to come to the door in Saran Wrap."

"Listen to me, Blair. As long as he is your husband, you have the upper hand. If you're ready to throw in the towel, then you can end your marriage. But, of course, if your son is acting out in order to get his father's attention, he'll have even less of it if your husband leaves. Isn't that right?"

Blair nodded glumly.

"If Saran Wrap will get the job done, then use it. I'll tell you this: You know what it takes. You live with him."

Blair was surprised that she felt so comfortable. She'd always kept her feelings inside. Still, she was concerned. Perhaps she'd revealed too much.

"Kent," she said, "I really appreciate your listening to my woes. I hope you didn't get the wrong impression. None of my problems affect my job in any way. In fact, I think I'm more productive than I ever have been because I can come here and just lose myself in the work."

"Don't be paranoid," Kent said easily. "I know that your work is good. I also know that Matriece runs a pretty tight team. She's not the type to let anyone sit around being nonproductive."

"Yeah, too true. Let me put it this way: She'd fire herself." Blair chuckled.

"That tough, huh?"

"She's a perfectionist. We worked together at Radiance for five years. They brought Matriece in because the sales had started going down. White firms had invaded the market. Matriece was head of marketing, youngest in the history of the company. Do you know Calvin Meeks, the president of Radiance?"

"I've heard of him."

"Very cheap guy. *Guiness Book of World Records* cheap. Anyway, he was screaming about the sales drop, but he didn't want to cough up any money to do a better marketing job. So Matriece had the entire team come to her house and we stayed up, literally, for a whole weekend. By the time we were finished, we had a brand-new concept: the party in the mall. Came in under the budget Calvin Meeks had allocated, and sales went through the roof. Oh, she was the golden girl after that."

"They must have hated to lose her."

" 'Hate' is too mild a word. They were outraged that she'd leave them and go to a 'majority-owned' firm. Her last days there were horrible. Nobody would speak to her."

"Why did she come here?"

Blair leaned her head closer to Kent's. "Well, I told you that Meeks was cheap. Matriece likes to live well. Who doesn't? As soon as she got this job she went right out and bought herself a big house. But then, Matriece is very driven. I've never met anyone as ambitious as she is."

"President of a company before she's forty. I'd say she's succeeded."

Blair shook her head. "Those are normal standards."

"What's she after then?"

What was Matriece after? Blair wondered. From time to time they'd talked about their goals. She knew, of course, that Matriece wanted Brown Sugar to be a big success, but she'd never told Blair what more she wanted. And yet she knew that Brown Sugar wouldn't be the end of Matriece's career, that there was something out there that she was still striving for. Blair stubbed out her cigarette in the sand-filled receptacle, then stood up. "More. I guess I'd better get back upstairs."

"See you later."

The real world was waiting for Blair. Her first call was to the gas company: she changed her account to Matriece's sister's name. The clerk faxed over the paperwork and Blair placed it on top of the pile on her desk. In between subsequent telephone calls and meetings, thoughts of the slick one-hundred-dollar bills plagued her. Her son's face, revealing not one iota of contrition, was everywhere she looked. Is my kid falling through the cracks? she wondered. *Well, five hundred bucks says he makes it.*

There was a car ahead of Blair's as she stopped at the guard's station in front of her housing complex. She didn't recognize the Saab or the person whose face was reflected in the rearview mirror, but that didn't stop either of them from waving at each other. A fleeting thought assailed her: if she and Porter attended more of the homeowners' meetings, they would probably get to at least recognize their neighbors.

Linwood, the security guard, opened the gate for both cars. Blair smiled at the tall, dark man as she passed him. Driving inside the complex, Blair felt transported to her own personal Shangri-la. She'd never thought of herself as a person who would reside behind a gate, but somehow the iron fence was reassuring. If she didn't know most of her neighbors after six years, she could rest assured that the bond they shared was that their lives were important enough to be guarded.

Judd's car was parked outside the garage. Blair was convinced that her son's managing to block her entrance was a feat of stupendous premeditation. She didn't feel like getting out of her car to confront him. She pressed her horn. The blare was startling. Two or three minutes passed. She hit the horn again with more force this time. Still, Judd didn't come out. "Shit," Blair muttered, reaching for her cell phone. She dialed the number to her house; after five rings the answering service picked up. "Shit," she said again. She dialed Judd's cell phone and a recording came on. As a last resort, she paged him but then clicked off before inserting her number. If he wasn't answering his phone, he certainly wouldn't answer his page. Blair slammed her car door behind her.

The house was cool, quiet. The kitchen looked undisturbed. No crumbs on the counters, no smell of popcorn lingered in the air, no dirty dishes on the breakfast-room table. It was clear that Judd hadn't even entered the house. This, after she'd told him to come straight home from school. Five hundred dollars could buy a reprieve; it could not, however, buy obedience. Blair looked past her gleaming stove and cabinets, through the window to her backyard where daisies, impatiens, calla lilies, azaleas, and roses called to her.

She left her clothes on her closet floor, put on her sweats and sneakers, bounded down the stairs and out the back door. Her gardening equipment was in a cabinet in the garage. She employed a gardener only to take care of the grass. Blair did everything else herself.

Dandelions that had sprung up in a bed of pansies caught Blair's eye right away. It seemed that only a few days earlier she'd cleared the same area, but in a garden whatever was most unwanted was the most relentless. Blair sank down to the soft dirt on her knees and began pulling out the weeds. She welcomed the work. She was used to retreating to her yard, crouching down in the dirt, yanking out intruders, pruning rosebushes and fruit trees. When she was in the garden she didn't have to think about Judd, where he was, what he was doing, what rules he was breaking. For the time that Blair worked among her calla lilies and roses, life was made of petals and sweet smells. She set aside her anger and her jokes and didn't think of Judd as she breathed gardenia-scented air.

It was not quite dark when she put away the trowels, what was left of the fertilizer, dumped the weeds into an outdoor trash can, took off her soiled gloves and slapped them together twice very hard. As she looked back at the house she could see that the kitchen was lit and the refrigerator door was open.

Judd had his back to her when she came in. "Hey, Mom," he said, his words sounding garbled because of the food in his mouth. He was holding a half gallon of one-percent milk in his hands. Blair knew that he'd probably already drunk some straight out of the bottle, or he was about to even though she'd asked him time and time again to pour his milk into a glass.

Blair suddenly felt a familiar panic overtaking her. Jesus! Why had she never in her entire married life been able to get a meal on the table before eight o'clock? No wonder the kid didn't want to come home. No wonder he chugalugged milk straight out of the bottle. "Here, honey," she said, handing him a glass. His response was a grunt that may have contained a thank-you. He poured the milk, drank it, then put the container back in the refrigerator, the glass on the counter, and brushed past her on his way up the back staircase.

What is that odor? Cigarettes? Reefer? She tried to look in his eyes but his head was turned away. The smell was faint, so faint she immediately began to wonder whether she'd imagined it. Maybe he had been sitting in a room with people or a person smoking. Maybe somebody had stood over him with a cigarette. Or, okay, maybe one of the other kids had been smoking dope and the odor got into his clothes, and that's what she smelled.

"Dinner will be ready in a little while," she called up the stairs.

The ground lights that automatically came on at dusk were flickering in her backyard. Blair could barely see the flowers, the lemon, orange, and plum trees. She remembered how very much she had yearned for all this when she was growing up on the south side. And now she had it.

Blair looked in the refrigerator, closed it, then opened the freezer. Nothing. Nothing. Nothing. Not one microwavable thing that could be surrounded by lettuce and couscous and pass as a meal. Nothing but chicken breasts, which would take at least an hour if she baked them and she couldn't think of anything else to do with them. Of course she could cut them into pieces and sauté them with some kind of a sauce, maybe add some pasta. She looked in the cabinet. No pasta. No couscous. No nothing.

Fast! Blair needed fast food, another no-frills dinner. When was the last time they'd had pizza? Not yesterday. Yesterday they ate out. Did they have pizza on Saturday? She couldn't remember. She picked up the phone and called Pizza Guy. Blair knew the number by heart. "Delivery," she said when a young man answered the phone.

Blair and Judd ate in silence. She attempted to start several conversations or at least to ask Judd some questions but his answers were monosyllabic. She wanted to know where he'd been, but she wasn't ready to mete out punishment for breaking the rules. Blair felt the need to conserve her energy. She had to get on the computer later, pay bills, make some calls. If she started arguing with Judd, she wouldn't be able to do anything but go to bed. Where was Porter? And then she remembered. He had a meeting. Of course.

Judd wolfed down four slices of pizza, and when Blair reminded him that his father had to eat, he downed another one. Now there were only two slices left. Porter never ate less than three, and Blair was still hungry. She thought about her options. If she ate another piece of pizza there would be just one remaining slice, and she'd have to cook something for Porter. But one tiny slice wasn't enough to fill her. All of a sudden she felt as though she could eat an extra large pizza all by herself. She should have ordered another pizza, a medium one. If she did it now it would take at least forty-five minutes for it to arrive, probably an hour. She had only the crust of one slice left on her plate. She went to the refrigerator, opened the door, and took out the soft spread that looked like butter and tasted like butter but wasn't. She slathered some on her crust and took a big bite. Another bite and it was gone. Blair eyed the remaining pizza hungrily. There was a little bit of prewashed salad in the refrigerator. She could add some croutons, a little cheese. That ought to fill up Porter. And then she could give him some ice cream. If he wasn't full after all that, well, shame on him. She wasn't full. Was the slice of pizza talking to her? "Eat me eat me eat me eat me."

"Are you finished?" Blair asked irritably.

Judd looked surprised. "Yeah."

She snatched his plate away from him. As she took it over to the sink, she saw the one intact pizza crust on her son's plate. Blair picked it up and put it in her mouth. Delicious. As she was chewing, out of the corner of her eye, she saw Judd going toward the remaining pizza. "Don't you dare," she said, and the partially dissolved pizza dropped from her mouth onto the floor.

"Damn!" she muttered. Scooping up the mess, she said to Judd, "That pizza is for your father. If you want something else to eat, get some ice cream."

"You don't have to be such a bitch," he said, his tone casual, as he headed for the stairs.

Blair rushed over to Judd and grabbed his arm. "Don't you ever call me that," she screamed so vehemently he stopped. "You don't know how fortunate you are, young man. Your father and I work hard to give you things that I know I never had, and you don't appreciate anything."

"Let go," Judd said, pulling away from her. He climbed the stairs without looking back.

She stood watching him, almost expecting him to come back and apologize. When he didn't, Blair sat down at the table, put her face in her hands, and began crying. What good is anything if he's not going to be okay? she thought. What can I do that I haven't done?

Her brain seemed clogged, and after a few minutes Blair got up, went to the refrigerator, took out the quart of butter pecan ice cream, and opened the top. It was empty except for a tiny piece of pecan at the bottom. There was only one person in the world who would devour an entire quart of ice cream and then put the empty container back in the freezer. Blair threw the box away. She fixed herself a bowl of cereal and milk and, leaning against the refrigerator, ate the food as fast as she could without really tasting it. By the time she'd finished and she could feel the first bubbles of gas being created in her belly, she remembered Porter saying it was a dinner meeting. "Damn!"

The telephone rang just as Blair was about to run water for her bath. She felt irritated as she said hello, but the woman on the other end had a warm, hearty voice. She felt calmed by it. "Blair, this is Vonette, Matriece's sister. How you doing?"

"I'm fine, Vonette. How are you?"

"We're all doing great. Listen, I want to thank you for letting Tavares use your address. I really do appreciate your kindness."

"Well, I'm just glad to be able to help you out. Is Tavares excited about starting a new school?"

Vonette laughed. "Honey, you know kids. Anything we say is good for them they don't want. Let me put it this way: He's not excited yet."

Both women laughed.

"Why is that?" Blair asked. "Why can't they just do what we tell them to and know that it's for their best."

"Oh, some of them do. I mean, Tavares is the kind of kid who'll go along with the program. He's easygoing. But you hafta remember: They're all wired differently. You have to respect that."

"Yes," Blair said. But why did I have to pay five hundred dollars to keep my child in school? She wanted to ask Vonette that question, wanted to hear her answer. She found the cadence of Vonette's voice soothing. There was no judgment. But she couldn't speak the words aloud. How could she tell anyone what had transpired between Dr. Sable and her? And besides, she didn't want to remind herself.

"Lord have mercy. Hold on a second, Blair."

Blair heard Vonette's loud voice in the background. "Carla, what did I tell you? You are not spending the night. Go home right now. And you be nice to your mother. Hear me? And you'd better get at least a B on your test if you want to come over tomorrow. Good-bye, Carla."

When Vonette got back on the telephone her voice was tinged with exasperation.

"That was my next-door neighbor. She gives her mama a fit, then she tries to get me to let her spend the night here. Sometimes I think I have another child. Anyway, I'm not going to keep you. I just wanted to let you know that we'll be bringing Tavares to the school on Thursday."

"You'll drive him the first day?"

"Me and my husband."

"Oh. That's nice. I'll tell my son to look out for him. His name is Judd. He's in eleventh grade."

"Thank you for everything, honey," Vonette said. "And listen, you don't have to be a stranger. Get Matriece to bring you by the house some-time. It's been too long since I've seen you."

Blair had a sudden memory, at least seven or eight years old, of sit-ting in Vonette's backyard, eating barbeque and admiring her plants, of the two of them talking about compost and soil, roses and bougainvillea. She remembered how her family circled around her like a halo to her moon. "I'll do that. You still have your garden?"

"Oh, sure. How about you?"

"I work in it every chance I get."

"Kind of relaxes you, doesn't it, honey?"

"Yeah. It does."

"Honey, flowers and plants are spiritual, just like people, except they're more peaceful than people. Flowers don't start any mess. You know what I mean?"

Blair laughed. "And they don't talk back."

After she hung up the telephone Blair went upstairs to Judd's room. She knocked on the door three times before she heard her son's voice.

"Yeah."

"Judd, open the door. I need to talk with you."

"What?"

"Open the door."

When he finally let her in Blair waded through the junk on his floor, cleared a space on her son's bed, and sat down.

"What, are you moving in?"

"Judd, I just finished talking with Matriece's sister, Vonette. Her son Tavares is going to be using our address so that he can go to your school. Do you remember Tavares?"

"No."

"We went to a couple of barbecues at his house when you were younger. And you and I and Matriece and Tavares went to the zoo, the children's museum, stuff like that. You don't remember him?"

"No."

"Anyway, his name is Tavares Valdez."

"I thought he was black."

"His father is Mexican. I want you to show him around, introduce him to people."

"What grade is he in?"

"Tenth."

"Black and white don't hang together at our school, Mom."

She could feel herself turning red. "What is that supposed to mean? I can't believe—"

"If you wanted me to hang with black kids, why are we living in Castle Heights?"

She wanted to slap his smug little face. "Let me tell you something.

Where we live has nothing to do with not wanting to live near black people. I grew up around—"

"Yeah, yeah, yeah. I know all about the good ole days in the 'hood, Mom. Except, you never go back there. None of your good ole friends ever call. We don't even go see your family."

Blair took a deep breath. "I'm just asking you to say hello to Tavares, help him out if he needs something. Can't you do that?"

"If I see him, I'll speak to him. Okay?"

"Fine. Thank you."

Blair took some Maalox before she got into bed. She tried to read but grew bored and turned on the television. The news was on. Between the rumblings in her stomach and the ones in her mind, she couldn't focus.

Blair woke to the smell, pressure, and warmth of Porter next to her. "Honey?"

"Hi," he said. "How did it go today?"

"Porter," she said, and then she swallowed.

"What happened at the school?"

"They didn't expel him. I had to—"

"I knew they wouldn't. Smoking a joint isn't a big deal. What kid hasn't done that?"

"We have this great house, and we make so much money. God, we make a lot of money. But something is wrong, Porter. Judd is—"

"Judd's going to be all right. He's just a teenager."

"Porter, I had to pay the vice-principal five hundred dollars."

"What are you talking about?" He sat up and looked at her.

"I bribed the man, Porter. Otherwise, he was going to expel Judd."

"You're kidding me," he said. He repeated the words several times, and then he slumped down until his head was on the pillow. "I can't deal with this right now."

In seconds he was snoring softly. Blair reached out for his arm and put it around her. For a moment she felt warm and safe, but then he took his arm away and turned over on his side, leaving a space between them.

CHAPTER TWENTY-NINE

EVEN IN THE dim bedroom that morning, Vonette could see that Hosanna's face was stern. Her mother stood over her and looked down as she lay in the bed. She was screaming at her. But that was nothing new. Hosanna was always yelling at her about something.

"Mommy, stop hollering."

"I think you're making a mistake," Hosanna said.

"Leave me alone, Mommy. This is my life and I want Boot in it."

"A mistake, girl."

"I don't want to hear anything you have to say. You sent my daddy away. Don't try to tell me what to do."

"Listen, baby. Listen to me."

"I won't. I won't. I don't want to hear anything you have to say."

It was barely light outside when Vonette awoke that Thursday, perspiring and breathing hard, as though she'd been running. In her hand was a fistful of sheet. Sweat rolled down her neck, settling in the hollow at the base of her throat. Vonette glanced around the room. Whenever she dreamed of Hosanna she always woke up feeling as though she had actually been with her. She couldn't even remember what the dream had been about, except that they were arguing, which was all they'd ever done in real life.

Vonette groaned a little as she sat up, not because she was actually hurting but because getting up at the crack of dawn was the closest thing to pain she knew. In an hour she would have to brave three freeways and nearly forty miles to deposit Tavares at Castle Heights High School. She said her prayers sitting on the bed, apologizing to God for not getting on her knees as she usually did. Beside her Boot lay snoring, his thick body alternately inflating and deflating. He smelled like paint and appeared completely unconscious, but when Vonette got out of the bed her husband gave a quick shudder, lifted his head, and then opened his eyes. His wide fingers encircled her wrist. "Hey! ¿A dónde vas, Vonette?" he said.

She gave him a warm glance filled with hidden shrewdness and then bent down closer to him. He put his hand on her hip and pulled her nearer. "I hafta take Tavares to the school," she said.

Perplexity creased his features for a moment, and Vonette knew that Boot had been dreaming in Spanish and was having difficulty translating her extra-early morning English. "Go back to sleep, Burrito," she said softly.

"Watch it. Watch it," he said, and then he let go of her and his head slumped against the pillow. But she knew that he was still awake.

In the small bathroom Vonette showered, dried off, then lotioned her body. She dabbed her face with a little powder, put on lipstick, and untied the scarf that held back her bountiful hair. She shook out her locks, and they tumbled around her bare shoulders. Staring at herself in the small mirror above the sink, Vonette smiled as she heard shuffling feet moving across the carpet. She inserted large golden hoops into her ears, then stepped back so Boot could see her better.

"Hey, Mommy, you look good." Boot's English was clear and deliberate. Vonette felt her husband's hands cupping her behind.

"Boot, stop," she said playfully.

"Come on, Vonette. Give me a little bit," he whispered.

"Boot, I got to go."

He pressed against her. "This ain't gonna take long."

Vonette laughed. "What's that supposed to mean? Only one of us is going to be happy at the end?"

Boot chuckled. "You gonna be happy, too, baby. Just give me a chance to show you."

Vonette turned around and faced him so that her breasts were touching his chest. "If I give you a chance, what will I get?" She smiled.

"I'ma do you right, girl. Come here."

"What will I get?" she repeated, her hand against his thigh.

"What do you want?"

"A sister likes a little cash, you know." She giggled.

"What! I got to pay for some? Vonette, you crazy." He laughed.

Vonette leaned into Boot. "Well, you gotta give me something."

"What?"

"I want you to drive me out to the school."

"Aww, girl, that's a long way. I got a job in Hollywood. S'pozed to be there at nine."

"We'll be back." She put her hands between his legs.

He laughed. "Okay, if I go with you out to the school, you gonna do what Monica did?"

"What?" she whispered. "Write a book? Go on 'Saturday Night Live'? What did Monica do?"

"You play too much, girl."

She pulled the string on his pajamas and they dropped to the floor. She crouched down. Peering up at him, she said, "If Monica could throw down like I can, she'd be laying up in Lincoln's bed right now."

Fifteen minutes later, Vonette and Boot were both smiling. Vonette dressed quickly, and when she heard Boot coming out of the shower she roused Tavares, who seemed to sleepwalk into the bathroom. She stood outside the door until she heard water running.

In the cramped kitchen, Vonette put the English muffins in the toaster, poured orange juice into three glasses, and boiled water for one-minute oatmeal. She drank a cup of instant coffee, black and sugary, while she waited for her son and husband to come to the kitchen. When they both appeared, all three sat at the small kitchen table. Vonette said grace and then they ate quickly without any conversation.

Just before they were about to leave, Vonette went into the room where Chazz was still sleeping. She checked his alarm clock to make sure it was set early enough for him to make it to his first class on time. As she moved away, she stepped on the shirt and pants that he'd dropped on the floor. Muttering under her breath, Vonette stooped down to pick up the clothing. When she lifted the pants, something small and white fell from the back pocket. It was a joint.

"Ow!" Chazz said, as he woke up. He grabbed the shoulder his mother had just punched. As soon as he sat up the joint was in his face.

"What the hell is this doing in your pocket, Chazz? You better talk to me and you better talk truth."

"Mom, I . . ."

She balled up her fist and gave him a solid pound in his chest, then began swatting at him with her hands dead upside his head.

"Mom, stop. Stop!"

"You think I'm spending my time raising a junkie? Huh?"

When he didn't answer, Vonette hit him again, and Chazz yelled louder. Boot and Tavares rushed into the room.

"What's going on? Chazz, what did you do?"

"Nothing, Papi."

"You're lying, Chazz. Tell your father what you did." Before he could answer, Vonette held up the joint. "This fell out of his pocket, Boot."

Boot pushed his wife out of the way and lunged toward his son, grabbing the hapless Chazz by his pajama top, lifting him out of his bed. "I'm not raising no fucking junkie. You wanna smoke that shit, pack up and go get in the streets with your boys."

"I'm sorry, Papi. I'm sorry, Mom."

"Sorry don't mean shit to me. You better tell me something better than some old 'sorry.' "

Vonette looked toward the door and saw Shalimar.

"I'm sorry, and I won't ever smoke dope again. Never."

"You know what? You wanna get high? I can take you higher than you ever been. That ain't no problem. You wanna get high?"

When Chazz didn't answer, Boot looked at Tavares and Shalimar, whose eyes were as round as dinner plates. "I'ma tell you kids something, and I'm serious as double pneumonia. If I catch you smoking, snorting, sticking anything in your body, I'ma hurt you. And your mom's going to help me. You saw what this shit did to my brothers. Didn't you?"

They all nodded.

"All right then." He turned back to Chazz, whose arms were wrapped tightly around his body. "Boy," he said, and he sat down on the bed, "you supposed to be setting the example. Now listen, you go to school, you come home. Sunday, you go to church. That's it. That's your life until I tell you different. All them little girls, your boys, you ain't hanging with them no more. And if you such a man you don't want to hear that . . . there's the door. You understand me?"

"Yes, Papi. I'm sorry." He looked at his father and then at his mother, his face forlorn.

Vonette stared hard at her oldest son, disgust filling her eyes. She shook her head and then faced Shalimar. "Listen, we're getting ready to take Tavares out to his new school." She paused. "You go back to bed and make sure your clock is set. You don't have to get up for another hour. Be good," she added. "We love you."

Boot was still grim-faced when he drove out of the driveway that morning. Tavares was slumped down in the rear, his backpack beside him. Looking over her shoulder, Vonette felt a little sorry for him. "You still sleepy, honey?" she asked.

"Yeah, I'm sleepy. Mom, if I don't like this school, can I go back to South Central?"

"You'll like it," Boot said. "Tavares, did you know your brother was smoking weed?"

"Me, no."

"You telling me the truth? You didn't know?"

"I didn't know nothing. I don't think he ever did it before, Papi. Like, maybe this was the first time."

"Better be the last," Vonette said.

"Mom, I'm not going to know anybody at this school. It's gonna be a bunch of white people up at that school."

"Boy, please. First of all, it's not all white. Second, you've never been lonely in your entire life, and you're not going to start now. Besides, all your boys are still in the neighborhood. And you have friends at church." Vonette tried to make her voice sound reassuring.

"But it's not like having friends at school, Mom. That's where I spend most of my day. By the time I get home it's going to be too late to hook up with anybody. How come Triecy wants me to go to this school, anyway?"

"I don't want you in a school where kids are shooting at each other."

"Mom, kids shoot at each other everywhere, not just at South Central. That was the first time it ever happened there that I can remember. Anyway, there's always some crazy white kid going off in a suburban school."

"They got better teachers. Better courses. Your Auntie, she knows about this stuff. So you just make up your mind that you're going to like it. Okay?" Boot said.

Tavares slumped farther into the seat. Vonette gave her husband a look that told him he had been harsh. His return glance conveyed to her that she had entered the realm of macho, and to make a silent retreat.

Vonette sighed. "You're going to like it," she said to Tavares, who didn't respond.

Even though it was barely seven o'clock, the 405 Freeway was crowded, not quite bumper to bumper but stop-and-go enough to make Boot say, "*¡Mierda!*" over and over again. He pulled into the car-pool lane, which was traveling only slightly more quickly than the fast lane. The line of cars ahead of him slowed down as soon as he moved over, and the lane that he'd just exited from sped up, relatively speaking. Boot immediately put his right-turn signal on and looked for an opening. No one would let him in. After a few more attempts, he caught the eye of the driver in the car directly across from him. Boot motioned that he wanted to get over; the man nodded. But just as Boot was about to make his move, the car in front of him veered right into the spot that he had been eyeing. "*¡Hijo de tu puta madre!*" He turned to Vonette. "You see that? Fucking idiot!"

"See, Mom. Driving way out to the 'burbs is giving Papi road rage. We don't get back to the 'hood, he's going to explode."

"You better get nothing but A's up at this school," Boot said to his son.

The traffic cleared a bit after they passed the Getty Museum. Behind the sound wall that bordered the freeway, trees loomed, and below them the tic-tac-toe assembly line of western Levittowns seemed endless. The houses were nondescript, the trees young and sparse. Every few miles they came to a mall, sleeping like an unresurrected body waiting for the call.

A sign announced Sherman Oaks several miles before the Ventura Boulevard exit. They followed Blair's directions and turned right off the highway and drove for two miles. The street was wide and clean. There was an island down the center where magnolia trees and rosebushes grew. Vonette looked from one side of the block to the other. The houses were large and new. They were grand. She hadn't realized that the neighborhood would be so fine. Not one piece of paper marred the pristine perfection of the sidewalks. There were no liquor bottles in the gutter, no billboards announcing HIV clinics. This was a place that pestilence passed over. *This was what Mom always wanted.* The words inserted themselves inside her mind, uninvited. And so did Hosanna's face, her eyes, tired and remote. Vonette willed away the image.

"When Uncle Tuney gets us our money, maybe we can buy us a big ole house, Boot," Vonette said.

"I thought you didn't care about having a big house," Boot said.

"It might be nice for you and the kids. I wouldn't mind going down to Texas and living on the property."

"Texas!"

"There's plenty Mexicans in Texas. You won't be lonely."

Her husband laughed.

"It's not that I'm against having money, Boot. We're going to need some to get Tavares and Shalimar through college. And like you said, you do need a new truck. There's a lot of things I want."

As Boot drove down the wide, pristine street, the few people Vonette saw—young professionals hurrying off to work, mothers escorting little children to school—were all white. She wondered whether Tavares wasn't right.

Castle Heights High School seemed to float above them, somewhere between heaven and earth. At least it seemed that way to Vonette, as Boot drove up a steep driveway that led to the school. Before them, like a small kingdom, was the huge main building; surrounding it were smaller structures. "Whoa," Tavares said, sitting up.

The campus was at least seven acres. "You'll need roller skates to get around this place," Vonette quipped. It reminded her of a college. Students were streaming into several of the buildings. They were mostly white but she saw some Asians and Latinos and even a few blacks. The sight of the latter reassured her. The young people seemed agreeable. There was some jostling and high-spirited running, but no one was fighting. The lawn was newly cut and the buildings were all bordered by rose- and hydrangea bushes. "It's beautiful," she said finally and for the first time she felt glad. Tavares would do well in this fabulous school. He'd learn a lot. She took Boot's hand and squeezed.

"Don't get all excited, girl. Just a school," Boot said. "It's nice, though. Hey, Tavares, you act right, hear me? I want to see some good grades. Wish I'd gone to a school like this."

"Yeah," Tavares said.

Vonette thought he sounded a little nervous.

"You'll make a lot of friends," she said. "Just make sure you memorize the new address. Don't slip up."

The three of them climbed the winding stairs that led to the main building and followed the signs to the administration office. Boot was fidgety, still perturbed about being aced out by another driver; he let Vonette do the talking. The process was fairly simple. She gave the clerk Tavares's school records, the phone bill, and the receipt from the gas company that Matriece had given her, and within a few moments she and Boot were telling Tavares good-bye as a student walked him to his first class. Boot and Vonette followed him into the hallway and watched as he trudged away. His head was down. Vonette wanted to call out to him to raise his head, but she didn't. Boot was fussing that they had to leave, that he was going to be late, so she didn't tell her son to keep his head up.

CHAPTER THIRTY

WHEN THE ALARM went off at five-thirty on Thursday morning, the October sky outside Tavares's window was barely light. The boy rose slowly, as though he were sleepwalking. The week before, his mother had awakened him, fixed his breakfast, and chatted with him while he ate, but this second week at his new school he was on his own.

Sitting on the edge of his bed, Tavares fought the urge to get back under the covers. If he'd still been going to South Central, he would be sleeping for another hour and a half. At least he didn't have to line up for the shower at this time of the morning. That was the only good thing about going to this new school.

Tavares felt sad walking through the quiet house. He passed through the kitchen without getting anything to eat, even though his mother had set a place for him the night before. He took a banana and shoved it into his backpack. Trudging up the street, he felt dejected. He was used to bustling mornings, shouting at his brother or sister to get out of the bathroom, his parents' loud voices as they argued and joked with each other, the smell of coffee and toast coming from the kitchen. As he stood at the bus stop shifting his backpack, far heavier than when he was at South Central, he tried to remember a time when he went to school without his mother's good-bye kiss, but he couldn't.

The bus was filled with Latinos, some men in clean work clothes, but mostly women on their way to their housekeeping jobs, chatting noisily with one another in Spanish. Tavares felt warmed by their conversations. He was fairly fluent, if not grammatically correct, in Spanish, because of his father and his relatives. When he laughed as two of the women teased each other, one of the women sitting closest to him nudged him. "Do you speak Spanish?" she asked.

"Yes," he said.

"Are you from El Salvador?"

"No. I was born here."

"Where are your parents from?"

"They were both born here."

"Ah," the women said, almost in unison, and he could feel their eyes turning to his hair, which was a combination of African and Mexican. When he spoke Spanish around Latinos, they always wanted to know about his hair.

"My dad is Mexican; my mother is black," he said.

The women nodded, then turned away from him and lowered their voices. Tavares felt the slight but didn't take it to heart. He was too sleepy. He was almost nodding when the bus stopped. The sound of stomping feet aroused him. Opening his eyes he saw three boys around his age peering at him. He'd seen them once or twice the previous week. They wore athletic shoes and baggy pants, and glared at him in a way that made his stomach lurch. There were gangbangers at his old school, but he knew who they were, their affiliations, and how to stay out of their way. Watching the trio, Tavares tried to see himself through their eyes. His clothes were nice but not too flashy. He'd purposefully worn old sneakers for his ride to and from Castle Heights. He didn't want to tempt anybody.

What he needed to do was reach into his backpack and pull out his algebra book and start studying, but he wasn't about to open up a book while the boys were checking him out. He slumped in his seat and scowled, not *at* his adversaries, but in no particular direction. By the time they got off five stops later, his face was sore from grimacing, and his neck felt stiff. Watching them without seeming to look in their direction, Tavares felt exhausted as the bus pulled away. The bus rolled down the street and he began dozing, his head falling forward and then snapping back with each sudden stop. He was in a nod when he heard the driver calling out, "Hey, kid."

Tavares scrambled down the steps and stood in front of the courthouse, trying to collect his bearings. Before he changed schools he rarely came downtown. The streets still confused him. He turned left and walked one block and waited at the corner until his second bus came.

Some of the same Latinas who'd accompanied him on the first leg of his journey were with him on the second. Their Spanish was slower and softer, as though they were trying to conserve their energy as they got closer to their jobs. Tavares took a seat in the back, immediately opened his algebra book, and immersed himself in its pages until it was his stop.

The bus drove past the Sherman Oaks Galleria, a sprawling mass of stores, eateries, and a twenty-five-screen movie house. Although sometimes his mother and father would drive out to one of the suburban malls when they were buying something special, usually they patronized the shopping center on Crenshaw. That place looked like a swap meet compared to where his new schoolmates shopped.

He got off several miles after he passed the mall. Even after a week, as he walked the three blocks to his new school eating his banana, Tavares still felt like an accidental tourist. Everything seemed new and spotless. He was surrounded by five different styles of Spanish stucco mini-mansions, and all of them seemed beautiful to him, although he knew instinctively that his mother wouldn't like them. His mother liked old things best. And his mother wouldn't appreciate any of the gardens that he was passing. They were too neat, too organized. Nothing grew outside its borders. There was no tumble of blossoms where a person least expected them to be. But as Tavares walked to school he admitted to himself that when he got older he wouldn't mind living in a house like the ones he saw, and that neat yards appealed to him.

Tavares took a last bite from his banana and looked for a place to throw away the peel. He ambled across a driveway and then stared down it. He saw an open can and tossed what was left of the banana in it. He didn't notice the car backing up until he felt it grazing him and heard the brakes squealing. A woman sitting in the passenger's seat let out a scream, and seconds later both she and the driver, obviously her husband, got out of the car.

"Are you all right?" the man asked. He was tall and white with sandy hair. "Lisa, calm down," he told the woman, who was making tiny gulping noises. "Are you all right?" he repeated, walking toward Tavares.

"My bad, man," Tavares said. "I mean, my mistake. I wasn't looking where I was going. The car barely touched me. You weren't driving that fast."

"Thank God," the woman said.

"All right? We're cool. I'm not going to call my lawyer or nothing like that." Tavares grinned.

The man and woman looked at each other and then stared at Tavares uneasily.

"I'm just playing."

"You need to watch where you're going," the man said sternly. "What are you doing around here anyway? Do you live in this neighborhood?"

"No. I mean, yeah." Tavares looked around him. Across the street, a man was standing in his driveway watching him. Two houses down he heard elementary school children calling out good-bye, their voices light and high and unafraid. He looked at the woman and her husband, who returned his glance with hard, focused eyes. "Listen, I hafta go to school. I'll be late."

Tavares began running. At the end of the block he turned around, and the couple was still standing in their driveway staring at him.

The bell began ringing just as Tavares slid into his homeroom seat. He felt a tap on his shoulder, and when he looked behind him, a small girl with shoulder-length blond hair smiled and said, "Hi, Tavares."

"What's up," he said and turned back around.

A few other people greeted him. Across the aisle, another white girl was checking him out.

Mrs. Taylor, his homeroom teacher, stood in front of the class calling out the roll. Tavares tried to focus on her face for a few minutes, but looking at her made him nervous, even when she smiled at him. Around him some students chatted with one another, while others did homework or read books. There were twenty-two students in the class. There were more kids in his old homeroom, and they were always crazy loud until fat ole Mrs. Morgan would shout for everybody to sit down and get quiet; even then the noise level just got lower, it never disappeared. In his new homeroom Tavares could hear himself think. He'd have to get used to that.

"Whazzup, Tavares?" Brian, a white boy who sat across from him, smiled when he looked his way.

"Hey," Tavares said, giving him a nod. Brian had been speaking to him since the first day he'd arrived the week before. Brian and his friends were who Tavares had in mind when he told his mother and father that there were some white boys at school who dressed like hard-core bangers from the 'hood. "They know the words to every gangsta rap that's out," he told Chazz.

His mother told him not to even fix his lips to ask if he could wear his pants low, and his father agreed. "You can't come like they come, boy," he told him.

Mrs. Taylor walked around as she called off the names, making a comment to each student or just smiling. She gave Tavares a pat on his shoulder. "How are things going?" she whispered to him in a voice that said she knew him better than she really did. He suddenly wondered what fat ole Mrs. Morgan was doing.

"Fine," he answered.

"That's good," she said, as though she was personally tickled that he was making out okay. Tavares opened his algebra book and studied until the bell rang.

California history was his first class, followed by computer studies and then English, each one located in a different part of the campus. During Tavares's initial week at school, he'd been late twice as he hustled across the campus from one building to the next, not quite sure of where he was going. Now he felt more confident, although he was still a little lonely, not to mention tired from carrying so many books. He was surprised that some of the students in his classes were Mexicans and blacks. It almost felt as though he were back at South Central, except for the fact that there were white kids in the room. The only white people at South Central were teachers, and a handful of kids in the highly gifted magnet.

At the beginning of his English class, the teacher reviewed grammar and went over the vocabulary. He liked the sound of the words she gave them. "Segue," he repeated in his mind, and then he made up a sentence for it. He'd throw that one on his auntie the next time he saw her. Toward the end of class the teacher read aloud to them from a book called *The*

Grapes of Wrath. She walked around the classroom from row to row as she read. Tavares closed his eyes, and when she stopped in front of him and said, "Tavares, are you with us?" he opened them.

"I'm just imagining everything," he said. She nodded toward him.

As they discussed the migration of the dust-bowl farmers to California, he recalled his history teacher telling them about that same era. It dawned on him that it wasn't a coincidence, that his classes were purposely coordinated so that what he learned from one teacher was supported by information from another.

The lunchroom was a huge sea, parted if not by unseen hands, at least separated by them to reveal a multitude of islands. Each ethnic group clung to its own piece of ground. There were tables filled with Mexicans, others with Armenians. White tables dominated, and occasionally there were Asians, and people of color at others. Tavares walked straight to the back where he saw two tables filled with black people.

"SC, SC, SC," the boys at the table began chanting when Tavares sat down. He had earned a new nickname as soon as he told his new friends that he'd attended South Central High.

Tavares held his mouth in a way that he knew was cool and impressive and nodded slightly toward the boys.

"Whazzup?" he said.

Several of the boys returned the pounds he gave with his balled-up fist.

"Sit next to me, SC." Her name was Kara, and she smelled like strawberries when Tavares got close enough to tell. She said something to one of the other girls at the table, and both of them laughed and looked at him.

To Tavares's ears she sounded like a white girl doing a television commercial. He liked how her ponytail swung back and forth when she talked. He followed her hair with his eyes.

"So where do you live, Tavares?" one of the boys asked him.

He told him the street without looking at him, and hoped his voice didn't give him away.

There were several conversations going on at the same time, but Tavares kept trying to hear what Kara was saying. One time she caught him looking at her and she stared right back, neither one of them looking away, even though she kept right on talking to her friend. One of the boys at the table called out, "Uh-oh, dog, your eyes are locking," and everyone laughed. Kara laughed, too, and so did Tavares, but he didn't show any teeth. It was his cool laugh.

As he was leaving the lunchroom, Kara came up to him. "I'll walk with you," she said. "Where do you live on Hunter Drive?" she asked. "Which house?"

"10238," he said quickly.

He could tell by her expression that she knew.

"I live on that block," she said, "right across from Judd." Their eyes met. "I won't tell anybody," she said.

He stared at her.

"So you still live in South Central?"

"Yeah."

"And you come all the way out here. Must be true."

"What?"

"A mind is a terrible thing to waste."

This time he showed his teeth.

"How did you get to use Judd's address?" Kara asked him.

"My auntie works with his mother."

"His mom is cool. She's all friendly and everything. She acts kinda black, in a weird way. None of the black kids at this school really hang with any of the white kids. That's just the way it is. And Judd's kind of a stoner, if you know what I mean."

"I'm not trying to hang with him. I'm just using his address."

"That boy is always high. Do you smoke bud?"

"Nah."

"Me neither. I tried it once, well, I tried it a couple of times, but I didn't like the feeling. What's it like at the school you came from? It's fun, isn't it?"

"It's cool."

"You guys have good teams, don't you?"

"Yeah."

"Did you play anything?"

"Me? Nah. I'm a singer."

"Oh, yeah? Sing something."

He kept walking and began crooning a popular new song, one he knew she'd heard before. Tavares knew that he sounded better than the man who'd recorded it.

Kara stopped. "You can really sing," she said. "Do you have a contract?"

"Not yet."

"You'll get one. Plus, you look good, too. Grammys, here you come."

"That's my plan."

"I'm a cheerleader for the football team."

"Oh, yeah?"

"It's supposed to be a big deal, but believe me, it's not. They had to let in somebody black, so they picked me because I'm black, but not too black, you know what I mean? They weren't about to let in anybody really dark. There's one Mexican girl, one Korean girl, one Armenian, and the rest are bleached blonde. And the football team is pitiful. I wish I could go to South Central."

"It can get kind of rough."

"You have a lot of gangbangers and stuff, right?"

"You have to learn when to stay out of their way."

She looked at him for a moment without speaking. "Are you mixed, or something?"

"What do you mean? Mixed up? Am I confused?"

"You know what I'm talking about. What race are you?"

"My dad's Mexican and my mom is black," Tavares said.

"That's a combination you won't see out here. Mexican and black don't hook up. I don't know why. And the Armenians and the Mexicans can't stand each other. They fight all the time. Armenians start something, and then the Mexicans get suspended. Black people kind of keep to ourselves. Every once in a while maybe somebody will try some ghetto mess. Sometimes the black guys who grow up out here try to act like they're all hard-core. And as soon as they do, they get kicked out of school fast. Then, you have the jungle-fever brothers. They only date white girls. You like white girls?"

"For a girlfriend?" He shook his head.

"What kinda girls do you like?"

"All kinds. Except white girls."

"You have pretty eyes. And your hair is pretty, too. You like my type?"

He felt good all of a sudden. Kara was small; she had to look up at him. "What type are you?"

"Friendly. Affectionate. I like to kiss. Are you a good kisser? You got nice lips. I bet they fit mine perfectly. What do you think?"

Tavares started laughing. Kara laughed, too.

"I go to cheerleading practice after school. It's out on the field. You want to come watch? Maybe afterward you can show me how you kiss. If you can kiss I might let you feel me, too. How about that? I mean, I'm not gonna let you do it to me or anything like that. I'm still a virgin. But I don't know how long I'm gonna stay one. Are you a virgin?"

Tavares chuckled. "Girl, you ask a lot of questions."

"I like to know things."

"I guess."

"So, you gonna come to my practice today?"

"I can't stay too long. I hafta catch a bus."

"Then we can kiss for a little while. Hey," she said, as though she'd just thought of something. "I'm not trying to, like, blackmail you or nothing. I mean, if you come or if you don't, I'm not telling anybody about your address, okay?"

He nodded, only half listening. Kara chattered on about the kind of test they could expect. Tavares looked across the hall and saw a boy staring at him. He'd only seen Judd a few times, years before, but Tavares recognized him, even though he was older and looked kind of high and goofy with his wannabeabrother pants and shaved head. He nodded, and at the same moment Judd nodded in his direction, and Tavares felt as though they both determined simultaneously that a nod was about as far as they would ever go with each other. Stoner, Tavares thought, looking at Judd, listening to Kara, getting his head ready to take his test.

CHAPTER THIRTY-ONE

JUDD HAD SMOKED a joint on his way to school, and the bud always made him acutely aware of other people; he thought he could see the newness in the boy's face. That's how he recognized Tavares. Castle Heights had so many kids it was hard to find anybody, let alone some black dude he'd met maybe three times in his life when he was, what, nine years old. But the boy passing by, laughing with the only black cheerleader—what was her name?—was familiar to him. Seeing him Judd recalled that day at Tavares's house when they raced around the yard and stuffed themselves with hot dogs. He wondered how the black boy was fitting in. He'd been going to school with a lot of the same people since junior high, and they still seemed so distant to him, so cold and impenetrable.

Tavares was watching him. He nodded when Judd did. The cheerleader didn't notice. Judd could tell that she was talking a mile a minute. She's a cute girl, Judd thought. Hell, Tavares doesn't even need my help. He's only been here for a week and he's already got a girlfriend. He's doing better than I am.

The bell rang, and Judd watched as Tavares and Kara disappeared into the classroom. The hordes that packed the hallway scattered, trailing through different doors. The din quieted. Judd stood in the hallway, watching the doors of the classrooms close. He wanted to go to physics, but this moment when the hall was nearly empty pressed down on him like a heavy hand over his heart. As he walked toward his classroom, he could see Dr. Sable in the distance going into his office. In a few seconds the patrols would come on duty. Judd was three doors away from his destination. Between him and it was a short hall that led to a side door that exited to an area near the parking lot. He looked all around him. There were only a few stragglers with their backs to him. Dr. Sable was gone, and there were no patrols in sight. There was only the side door, the quiet, the lure of quick freedom.

Outside the air was hot and still. The lawn that stretched across the campus was dotted with brown patches, which was usual for southern California in October. Not too many miles away the autumnal fires were raging in the Angeles National Forest. Judd breathed in the burning scent as he made his way to his car. He passed throngs of students milling around the campus, most either going to or returning from work/study programs. There were also a few teachers, but he walked with a confident air and managed to slip past them unnoticed.

By the time he reached the parking lot, Judd had a plan: he would sit in his car, smoke a joint, and then go to the nurse's office and feign sickness. That way he'd have an excuse note to give to his physics teacher. If it weren't for his last visit to the vice-principal's office, he'd just leave, but he didn't want his mother to get another call from Dr. Sable.

Judd reached under the driver's seat and retrieved a small plastic bag filled with marijuana. He shook it slightly, and the seeds fell to the bottom. The papers were in the back pocket of his jeans. He rolled quickly.

There was a tap on his window just as he was preparing to light up. Quickly he dropped the joint and the bag of dope on the floor. Pretending he was looking for something, he shoved them under the seat.

"Share and share alike, dude."

"Motherfucker, quit sneaking up on people," Judd said, and then he laughed as his friend slid into the seat next to his. Judd pushed the power button for the CD player, turned the volume down low, and lit the joint. Rap music filled the car. He took a long toke and then passed it to Vacuum, who'd earned his nickname because of his powerful suction capabilities. He pulled a pint of Jim Beam from his backpack, took a swig, and passed the bottle to Judd.

"Some nasty shit," Judd said after he'd taken a big gulp. They finished the joint and both lit cigarettes.

"My sister got into Stanford," Vacuum said. "They're having fireworks over at my house. My father was like, 'If you had put half the effort into your work that your sister has, we'd have another success to celebrate.'" He laughed. "My old man can be so fucking dramatic. He is the king of the guilt trip. Hell, I didn't shuffle the genes. My sister got all the high-caliber smarts."

"So where are you going to school, young man?" Judd asked in a voice that mimicked Vacuum's father.

"Fuck you. Where the hell are you going?"

"I got SAT scores, bro. One-five-eight-oh. Those digits will get me into a lot of schools, even with my grades."

"Yeah, but first you have to graduate from high school."

"True that. My mom had to take a little trip to see Sable about a week ago. They were threatening to expel my ass, so she was all upset and shit."

"What'd your dad say?"

"Same thing he always says: nothing."

"Shit. I'll trade."

"No, you wouldn't. I think he's fucking around on my mom. He's like, never home, and when he does show up it's late."

"Sounds suspicious, bro."

"My mom is so naive, I wonder if she even realizes what's going down. She's so busy trying to lead a respectable life and shit, she can't even see what's right in front of her. My dad's folks are, you know, college-educated, middle class. My mother grew up in a fucking black neighborhood. Her brother's an alcoholic. I think her dad was, too. She doesn't even want to associate with them."

"Your dad is her trophy?"

"Exactly."

"That's some deep shit. So, did your mom have to pay Sable?"

"She'd never tell me if she did. My mom would be too ashamed. It's like, she'd never want me to know that she didn't do the right thing."

"Yeah, right. Getting expelled builds character."

"Whatever. She'd never tell. What do you think he'd charge?"

"I hear it's five hundred. You know Bufurd?"

Judd nodded.

"Dude paid him out of his own pocket, and Sable never even called his parents. That's a slick motherfucker right there."

"He's an asshole." Judd spat out the word.

"What's the matter with you? You're all red and shit."

"Nothing." He grabbed the bottle of Jim Beam and took several big swallows, paused, and then gulped down more. "Listen, let's get outta here."

Vacuum looked startled at first, then he composed himself. "Word."

Judd drove out the back way. He had no idea where he was headed. "You hungry?" he asked Vacuum.

"I can always eat."

"Got any money?"

"Sure."

Judd grew excited as he drove. He turned the volume on the CD player all the way up. He and Vacuum shouted the words, "SO MOTH-ERFUCK YOU, NIGGER, 'CAUSE I TOOK YOUR BITCH!" and then laughed uproariously. Judd's mind was spinning. There wasn't a lot of traffic to worry about. The speedometer kept getting higher. Sixty. Seventy. Eighty. Ninety. Vacuum was making loud noises and laughing as the car went faster and faster. Judd didn't even know where they were going. He passed McDonald's. Sped by Burger King and Domino's. They could go to the mall, just hang out. They had Mrs. Fields at the mall. Brownies. Chocolate chip. Oatmeal. He wanted all the cookies in the world in his mouth.

The siren was nothing but background music. It blended in with the shouts and screams coming from the CD player. "MOTHERFUCK YOU NIGGER, 'CAUSE I TOOK YOUR BITCH!" The siren and the rappers were far away, so far away they couldn't be seen or touched. Where did music come from? Judd wondered. How did the notes and lyrics coexist so perfectly? He could taste the music, feel its power. Judd wanted his car to roll on and on and on, for the rapping never to stop. The rapping was exploding inside him, and it felt so good being filled up with words and anger and curses, so that he didn't have to say anything, just breathe, because it was all being said for him. Except now the sirens were so loud they were overpowering the words, and he could hear Vacuum's frantic voice. "Dude. Dude. Open the windows. Open the fucking windows. Put the shit under the seat."

Then everything slowed down. The sirens stopped. The rapping stopped. He felt hands frisking his body, then cold steel around his wrists. He heard the officer talking on the radio, and then he felt fingers pressing down his head under the car door. The voice was very, very harsh. "You're under arrest for driving under the influence."

Judd didn't say anything. Not to Vacuum. Not to the cop. He sat in the back of the car and watched hamburgers and Mrs. Fields cookies floating out of his reach. Even the music had disappeared. When the car stopped he saw the sandstone building, new like everything else in the area. Inside, a woman in a uniform took his thumbprint and led him to his cell. As he sat there, Judd thought, *I wonder if he'll show up now.*

CHAPTER THIRTY-TWO

GILDA AROSE AT six o'clock that Thursday morning. She changed into her workout clothes and exercised for thirty minutes with her trainer. She'd been out of the hospital for nearly two weeks, and it felt good to stretch and reach. The tug on her stomach muscles as she did sit-ups, the pull of the three-pound weights made her feel vibrant.

When her workout was complete, Gilda took a quick shower. Drying herself off, she observed her recently rejuvenated face and body in the full-length mirrors in her bathroom and couldn't help smiling. The swelling had vanished; the bruising had disappeared. Gone were the bags beneath her eyes; the drooping eyelids had become taut again. The lines that ran between the corners of her mouth and her nostrils were softened. Best of all, her face was smooth and tight again. She touched her belly and thighs and felt the hard ridges of flesh where the cuts had been made. It would take months for that skin to become normal but the visual improvement was dramatic. Her sagging bottom was higher; her thighs were tight again, and the protruding pouch that had been her stomach was firm and almost flat. She'd been plump as a girl, but in the camps she'd willed herself not to think about eating or hunger; afterward she was no longer interested in food. Gilda ran her fingers over the part of her forearm that used to be decorated with blue numbers and then touched herself where the jagged scar once bifurcated her body. Everything had faded.

Gilda smoothed perfumed lotion into her skin and then deftly applied her makeup. In her large dressing room, she put on the clothes her maid had pressed for her the night before. On her way downstairs she passed through her bedroom. Gilda leaned over the still form in her bed. Even after three months, sometimes she still got emotional just by looking at his face. She resisted the urge to give him a kiss. As she straightened up, she felt his fingers encircling her wrist. "Come here, Before and After," he said, lifting his head and grinning at her.

"Fontaine, don't be naughty. I have to go to work."

"I want to feel your new body. I'm lonely," he said as he cheerfully snuggled under the covers.

"Well, darling, if you hurry and get up I know a place you can go to where there are lots of lovely people around. Actually, they are waiting for you to arrive." They both laughed.

"I don't want to go to work. I want to stay home and play with you," Fontaine said.

"Now people will think I look like your mother instead of your grandmother," she said.

"Youth isn't always about flesh and blood, Gilda. Sometimes it's an attitude. You've always had a young attitude. I liked you when you were Before, remember?"

"Yes, my darling, I do remember."

He pulled on her wrist. "Stay and play."

"Ahh. I shouldn't have let you come over during the week. From now on, back to weekends for you. I must go to the office, and so must you." She kissed him on his forehead, waving to him as she left the room.

"Are you getting ready to dump me?"

It was their little joke, and Gilda laughed, even though Fontaine's eyes were serious.

"Not yet, but soon," she said. "You know my rule."

"What if you're desperately in love with me after nine months?"

Gilda smiled. "It always takes me a year to fall desperately in love."

"What if I'm desperately in love?"

"You're very young. You'll get over it."

"So what am I, just a piece of eye candy?" he yelled as she left.

Kent was waiting for Gilda when she got to her office. He was sitting at a small conference table across from her desk, sipping a cup of coffee that she knew was probably his third of the morning. He looks so weary, she thought to herself. It pained her to see him going through such hard times. She knew Kent hadn't been a faithful husband, but she realized that he loved his wife; her suffering was ravaging him.

"Good morning, Kent," she said, setting her briefcase down on her desk. She walked over to the table and sat in the chair beside his.

"Good morning, Gilda."

Her assistant came in with another cup of coffee, which she placed on the table beside Gilda as Kent handed her the latest financial reports on the company. Gilda sipped her coffee and read the papers.

"We're up a quarter," Kent said.

She shrugged her shoulders.

"You don't seem very happy."

"When I started the business, every dollar was cause for celebration. I guess I've grown used to prosperity." She was quiet for a moment. "If my father had lived to see my success, that would have been something. Now, for me the excitement is in giving away the money."

"I think you probably would have retired years ago if you weren't still trying to fund your charities."

"You're right. But, proceed. I'm listening."

As Kent rattled off the figures that should have been near and dear to her heart, Gilda felt distracted. Nevertheless, as she listened to him droning on about the sales and profits, the cash flow and balances, she zeroed in on the important items and had Kent clarify whatever she didn't fully understand. Kent drained his cup of coffee and began putting his papers back into his briefcase.

"You look fabulous, Gilda. We could put your picture on the package."

"Thank you, Kent. I feel wonderful. It's nice to be young again." She laughed lightly. "Youth is so ephemeral and yet so important in this society. I don't think any people on the face of the earth worship it the way Americans do. A woman can't just look good; she must look like a girl: no lines, no gray hairs, no sagging body, nothing to tell anyone that she has ever really lived at all. But who am I to complain? I've made a wonderful success selling the promise of youth. Haven't I?"

"Yes, you have."

"It's so strange that I sell beauty. For so many years in my life there was no beauty. Like a blackout. Beauty isn't durable, you know. It falls apart so easily. Heartbreaking. During the war when I was in the camp I saw so many lovely women, so many handsome men, Jews, Germans, too. They are a handsome people, the Germans. I can admit that. But my people, oh, there were some gorgeous ones. They would come into the camps with their dark eyes and dark curly hair, their full lips, and even though they'd already been through some hard times the beauty was still intact. And then, bit by bit, it all fell away. It is shocking what a shaved head does to beauty. Brown teeth, rotten teeth, missing teeth, they take away good looks. Skin turned coarse and wrinkled because there was no lotion, no creams to rub on at night. With Germans the meanness seeped into their skin. The cruelty began to work like acid on their faces. Oh, my dear, I saw so many people lose their beauty." Gilda uttered a moan, a cross between sadness and rage. Her own words had startled her as much as they had Kent, who looked pained. "I'm sorry," she murmured. "I don't know where . . . I don't know . . ."

"It's all right. I'm just surprised. It's been so long since you've spoken of that time."

"Yes, I keep it here," she said, pointing to her head. "There were numbers once, to remind me, but they're gone. My first cosmetic surgery." She smiled. "I had a friend, a wonderful woman."

"Hosanna, the woman I tried to find."

She had a flash of the time after her first divorce when she enlisted Kent to search for Hosanna. "She took me to a tattoo parlor, and the man removed the numbers. They'd been on my arm for maybe five years or so. I don't remember even thinking about them after I left Europe. It is wonderful when a friend sees what you need, even when you can't see it for yourself. I wish you had found her."

"I tried. Are you all right?"

"I'm fine. A little outburst every fifty years or so is good for the soul, yes?"

Kent took her hand and patted it. "Gilda, I know I have no concept of what you had to endure over there, but if you ever need to talk about it, I am a good listener."

Gilda nodded and whispered, "Thank you. I'll see you in about an hour."

After Kent was gone Gilda remained at the table. Closing her eyes, she leaned back in her seat and stretched. In a few minutes she would begin a frenzied round of meetings with company executives that would take up the bulk of her morning. But for now she wanted to be still. As the quiet filled the room Gilda's mind formed pictures, images from long ago. The brown face hadn't aged one bit in her mind. She wondered if her friend's ambitions were ever realized. Common sense told her that she couldn't have gotten very far without the money David had stolen, or even with it, but Hosanna wasn't an ordinary woman. *I would have given up,* she thought, *but not her.* Perhaps the black woman's success hadn't been as great as her own, but Gilda never doubted for an instant that a portion of Hosanna's dream had come true. At least she liked to think so.

A few minutes later Gilda ended her reverie. It was time to get back to work. For the next hour she reviewed Gilda Cosmetics's last five ad campaigns. She had to decide whether to retain the advertising agency the company had been using. She studied the photos and prints that were on the computer, making quick notes to herself. Then she pulled up recent ads for three of her competitors. Just as she was finishing, her assistant buzzed her, announcing that Kent, Daniel, and Matriece were waiting for her in the meeting room.

Rachel arrived just as she was introducing the third of three advertising executives vying for Gilda Cosmetics's spring line. She frowned at her daughter. *Why must she always be late?*

Mr. Fremont exuded energy as he narrated the video presentation. "The concept is very simple," he told the group, as they watched a plain-Jane model go into her bathroom in the first scene. In the second, another woman, a young pop star, emerged, looking ravishing, and descended stairs where a handsome date was waiting. "The message is sexually charged but not overtly so. We'll use an up-and-coming pop star, so the cost will be reasonable. Bottom line: we think we can sell a lot of your products."

As Kent asked a few questions and jotted down some notes, Gilda looked at Daniel to see his reaction. Since her return to active duty, she'd been deliberately letting her son take the lead in meetings of this sort. Despite her unwillingness to step down, she wanted Daniel to begin to assume more and more of the running of Gilda Cosmetics. As Daniel asked questions she began smiling in his direction. *He's so bright. When I retire he will take this business to another level, something I cannot even imagine.* Out of the corner of her eye she saw Rachel staring at her, a wistful, almost forlorn expression on her face. She turned around to smile at her daughter, but when she did Rachel was looking the other way.

"Mr. Fremont, that's a fabulous piece of work. Since GC is going to be running the television ads for such a short period of time, I was wondering if you've given any thought to a magazine and billboard tie-in for the same campaign?" Matriece asked.

This meeting was the third that Matriece had attended with the CEO, and was part of Gilda's efforts to get to know her newest president better. If only her own daughter had one iota of Matriece's drive and knowledge of the industry, Gilda thought, as Mr. Fremont answered the younger woman's questions. Gilda stole another look at Matriece, who was reminding the ad executive of something he'd said earlier. How self-assured she is, Gilda thought. So intelligent. There was something so familiar about her, so comfortable.

After Fremont had left and the meeting was ending, everyone from GC began talking. Daniel was standing next to his mother and he put his hand on her shoulder. How handsome my son is, she thought. "We should go with this one, Mom. Hands down, it's the best."

Kent was noncommittal. "Let me crunch the numbers," he said.

"It's a great concept," Matriece said.

Only Rachel was silent. She looked uncomfortable, like someone squeezed into a garment that is too tight.

"Let's talk more this evening," Gilda said. "Kent, will that give you enough time?"

Kent nodded.

Rachel left without saying good-bye. As she watched her departing, Gilda couldn't help thinking that she'd never know her daughter.

"Gilda, I'll see you later," Matriece said.

Looking at the black woman's face, Gilda felt a rush of energy, like a strong wind pushing her forward. What she loved lay ahead. Gilda took Matriece's hand. "I'd like you to clear your schedule for the next two hours and meet me back in my office in ten minutes. I'm taking you to the We Mean Business luncheon."

CHAPTER THIRTY-THREE

MATRIECE LEFT BLAIR a message canceling their lunch date, then rushed down to Gilda's office where the Old Broad Herself was waiting for her. "I'm so glad you can accompany me," she said, as they stepped onto the elevator.

Later, in the car Matriece tried not to stare at Gilda but she couldn't help examining her skin. Sitting only inches away from her, she could tell that the changes were dramatic. Twenty years had disappeared from Gilda's face, and even with her clothes on Matriece could see that her body looked thinner and tighter. Matriece wondered what the operation had cost. Whatever the price, the results were spectacular. How wonderful to be able to turn back the clock just by writing a check.

Ensconced in the luxurious Lincoln, Matriece couldn't help thinking that her own mother had had no such power. "Black don't crack," Hosanna used to quip, and it certainly was true in her case. Whether melanin would have proven to be the greater adversary against time was never put to the ultimate test. Hosanna wasn't even sixty when she died. If those years had spared her face, they had taken a toll on her spirit. She never got a chance to ride around in a limo, Matriece thought. Stealing another look at Gilda, she felt the ancient inherited anger rising up within her. She was sitting next to the thief who'd stolen her mother's life.

"I suppose you can tell that I have improved myself?" Gilda asked with a quick, light chuckle.

Gilda was smiling, her cool fingers giving Matriece's arm a little squeeze, as though they were two old friends. Gilda's raised eyebrows, the look of amusement in her eyes, her laughter was an invitation to closeness that Matriece didn't want. "You've always looked great."

"I have had lots of work done," Gilda said quietly. "For myself alone, I would be content to grow old gracefully, even with wrinkles. But a woman who looks her age is no good for the company. That dame with the cotton candy hair who gives out the pink Cadillacs had the right idea. Cosmetics must exude the image of youth and vitality, otherwise why will anyone buy our products?"

"You didn't look old before, Gilda, and you definitely don't now."

"I am pleased with Brown Sugar thus far," Gilda said, abruptly changing the subject. "The colors for the lipsticks and nail polishes are exceptional. How are the foundations and powders coming along?"

"We're working on them now. What will set them apart from everything else that's out there, of course, is our concept of the customer blending her own foundation. No oxide."

"Ahh. Good. We don't want the ashy look."

Matriece chuckled. "Right. In the next month or so we'll begin to do the sample mailings."

"Next September there will be two very important events: the debut of Brown Sugar, and the tenth anniversary of We Mean Business. I am the founder of WMB, and Gilda Cosmetics, along with several other companies, is its sponsor. I thought it would be a good idea for you to see some of the women who are part of this wonderful organization. I am hoping that once Brown Sugar has been launched, you may wish to play a larger role with WMB."

Matriece nodded, not sure of what to say. She had known about WMB even before she joined the company. In fact, she knew several entrepreneurs who'd been assisted by the program, which paired a seasoned business owner in a mentoring relationship with a young minority entrepreneur. From what she'd heard, the program had been successful.

"My cosmetic surgery may have taken years off my face and body but not my life. I want to be sure that when I'm gone what is important to me continues. WMB is very important to me, and I think you might be the right person to help the organization continue to grow. Anyway, today you will get acquainted."

Gilda opened her purse and peered inside. She pulled out a bottle that said "Gilda Gold," then squirted out a few drops in her palm. "Would you like some?" Before Matriece could answer, Gilda reached for her hand and began to rub in the lotion, her thumb kneading her palm. The sensation was comforting and familiar.

Gilda and Matriece were the first to arrive at the hotel. Participants began gathering in the area outside the Grand Ballroom. A bar had been set up and women formed a line, ordering white wine and soft drinks as the social hour began. There was a pleasant hum as greetings and conversation were exchanged. Gilda took Matriece by the hand and introduced her to the luncheon speaker, the three key WMB administrators, and some of the business owners. Several of the entrepreneurs hugged Gilda, who seemed to welcome their embraces. After Matriece met the director of the California program, she discovered the woman had a sister who'd gone to graduate school with her. As the two went down the list of people they both knew, Gilda stood back and listened intently. Later, as Gilda and Matriece were walking away, the older woman said, "The school you mentioned?"

"Howard?"

"Yes. Where is that?"

"In Washington, D.C."

"Right. One year WMB had an awards banquet on the campus. We have several successes who graduated from that school. Did either of your parents attend Howard?"

"No," Matriece said quickly. Her shoulders stiffened.

"What did they do, your parents?"

Matriece's stomach gave a lurch. She put her palm across her belly. "My . . . my father would, uh, fix up old houses and sell them. My mother was a, uh, homemaker. I have an older sister and my mother took care of the two of us."

"You had the childhood every American kid wants. I wasn't so fortunate to be able to remain at home." A troubled look clouded her face.

"I think children adjust, either way," Matriece said quickly. "I have a good friend and his mother stayed at home. She's a very aggressive, smart woman, and he feels that she made a big sacrifice in giving up her career. She sort of lost her place in the world, and now that her children are grown up, she can't get it back. If a woman is frustrated being at home with her children, I don't think it's pleasant for the kids or the mother. I couldn't stay at home full-time with my children. I'd go nuts."

"But then if you don't, the children feel cheated and they blame the mother, of course. And sometimes we are at fault. We mothers never intend to harm our children. We think we are on the right track and then, poof, we get lost somehow."

For an instant there was such palpable distress on Gilda's face and such obvious regret that Matriece thought the older woman might cry. She knew Gilda was referring to her own daughter; it was obvious that she and Rachel weren't close, that she preferred Daniel. Her father's weathered face streaked through Matriece's mind like skywriting, but she pushed away the image.

"Are you close to your mother, Matriece?"

"I was," Matriece said slowly. "She died."

"Oh, I'm sorry. And your father . . ."

Matriece folded her arms across her chest. "He's . . . dead, too."

"Were you young when they died?"

"In my twenties."

"I lost my parents when I was a teenager. I still needed them very much. Their deaths drove me a little crazy. I could barely function. It took many years before I finally adjusted."

Hosanna had told her the story about Gilda's parents years before she died, but somehow the white woman's loss had been minimized so that it paled beside her betrayal. But listening to her boss, scrutinizing her stoic face, Matriece realized that her mother wasn't the only survivor.

"Some of these women who are here today have had traumas in their lives. I admire them because they don't feel sorry for themselves. They are simply looking for a little help. I can give that to them," Gilda said.

It was nearly twelve-thirty by the time the social hour of the WMB quarterly luncheon ended and the last woman had taken her seat. In all, nearly one hundred African-American women and a few Latinas were assembled in a partitioned ballroom in the Beverly Hotel. As they dined on Waldorf salad and grilled salmon and vegetables, the speaker of the hour, a black woman who owned a five-million-dollar employment agency, came to the podium and talked about her path to business success. Matriece was engrossed by the speaker's tale of starts and stops, and the difficulty she experienced in getting a bank loan. Very little had changed since her mother was scrounging around trying to save her company so many years before. "I went to thirteen banks, and they all turned me down," the woman said, as others in the audience nodded their heads.

Matriece glanced around the room as she sipped her coffee and listened to the question-and-answer session. If she hadn't been working for Gilda, she might have been among them at some point. If she'd been born at a different time, so might Hosanna. It struck her that the women gathered in the room were just like her mother in spirit. She could see the fervent striving in their faces. They wanted to be somebody, to get somewhere in life. And Gilda—was she noble, or just self-serving? She feels guilty, Matriece told herself. Besides, for every woman she helped, Gilda was gaining a hundred customers. Hadn't she placed a giveaway bag of sample cosmetics on every seat? It was advertising, plain and simple. Every cent she'd spent could be written off.

"The luncheon was lovely, Gilda," Matriece said when they were on their way back to the office. She would say what was expected. There was no danger there, no lure that would pull her in farther than she wanted to go.

"I'm glad you enjoyed it," Gilda said. "You get to a certain age and you want to give back." She patted Matriece's hand. "You will get to that point, my dear."

"But I'm sure that other groups would love for you to join them. Why these women?" She didn't mean to ask such a probing question.

"When I came to this country, I had nothing. My first job was as a maid in a hotel. It was very difficult. My father had owned a cosmetics factory in Poland before the war. World War Two," she added. "I remembered the formula for some body lotion that he used to make. It was one of the few things from my old life that I kept in my head. I had a friend, a woman who worked with me at the hotel, and she suggested that we could make the lotion and sell it to people. On my own I never would have thought such a thing. In my country, business was for men. And even here, it was very difficult for women. It still is. And more difficult if the woman is black or brown. If my friend hadn't urged me to manufacture the lotion, I might still be scrubbing floors somewhere. She was a black woman. We lost contact with each other over the years," Gilda said sadly, "but I still think of her. She was a very courageous woman. Intelligent. Strong. And she could make me laugh. She was a good friend to me. I was not so . . . The times were bad for such a partnership. Working with these women is my way of honoring her. Matriece, what's wrong?"

The tears had surfaced before she could stop them. As Matriece dabbed at her eyes with a hastily retrieved tissue, she tried to clear her mind, to think of a coherent response. She could feel something within her shifting, a block of ice breaking free, floating into warmer waters. She couldn't stop the melting.

"I have a friend like that," she murmured.

Gilda patted her hand. "You are very fortunate."

Back at her office, Matriece spent the rest of the day returning phone calls and trying to track down Asia. The firm's lawyers had hammered out a deal memo and sent it to the singer's manager several days after they'd had breakfast, but her people hadn't responded yet. She and Claude had been leaving messages for each other for more than a week, and Matriece was beginning to worry. It was one thing for Asia to *say* she was going to get on board, but the deal wouldn't be finalized until the ink was on the paper. She thought about calling her hairstylist and finding out when Ruth came in. Maybe if she talked with Asia's mother again she could get something going. When they'd met for breakfast, Asia had been such an "around the way girl" that Matriece had momentarily forgotten that she was a platinum-record-selling megadiva, fully capable of giving her the Hollywood runaround. Now, as she hung up the phone after leaving yet another voice mail, she wondered if that was exactly what she was getting.

At the end of the day she stopped by Blair's office.

"What happened to you?" her friend asked as soon as she saw her.

"You didn't get my message?"

"I got the message; it didn't say where you were."

Matriece closed the door and sat down in the chair in front of the table where a number of mock-ups for the packaging were displayed. She didn't answer Blair's question.

"Check out the container for the mascara. It's on the far right. You like that?"

Matriece held up a small plastic object shaped like a kidney. "How does it open?" Before Blair could respond, she pressed a small indentation and the top lifted off. Inside were three compartments, all of equal size.

"Remember, it's going to have three shades of one color. I like it because it's so light but it's very durable. This top will not crack. No angry e-mails."

The both laughed at the reference to a batch of lipstick tops that Radiance had discontinued because of customer complaints.

"Let's cut some corners around here," Blair said, using her generic older-southern-black-man accent. Mr. Meeks's memorable command had led to the ordering of the substandard lipstick tops.

Matriece laughed in spite of Blair's grating imitation.

"So, I hope there was no emergency," Blair said very deliberately.

"Gilda called me at the last minute and asked me to go with her to the We Mean Business luncheon."

"Oh," Blair said, and she grew quiet. "Who else went?"

"Just the two of us."

"Oh." There was another pause. "How was it?"

"Very nice. Maybe a hundred people attended. It was at the Beverly Hotel in one of the ballrooms. There was a speaker, some woman who owns an employment agency, and afterward she took questions from the audience."

"All women?"

"Yes."

"All black?"

"A few Latinas."

"So does Gilda—I mean the company—just give them grants or something?"

"My understanding is that the company, along with some other corporations, fund the WMB Institute. The organization provides education, loan referrals, a host of supports for aspiring entrepreneurs who are minority females. I don't think they fund the businesses directly. I'll tell you one thing: Gilda cares a lot about it. I was really impressed. She took me around and introduced me to everybody, chatted with people. Those women love her. They think Gilda is the man."

"She's grooming you," Blair said.

"Why do you say that?"

"Isn't it obvious? She gives you the number to her recuperation palace. She takes you to her pet charity meeting."

"Grooming me for what? Her kids are going to take over the business."

"Daniel, definitely. Rachel, I don't know. We go to lunch sometimes, and I'll tell you: the kid is not interested in next season's lipsticks."

"So, she's going to X out Rachel's name in the will and put mine in? I don't think she loves me that much."

"I'm not saying all that. She's very impressed with you, Matriece, and I think she has a larger role for you with the company in mind."

"Maybe." Matriece hesitated.

"What?"

"She did say that she was interested in my becoming active with WMB, after Brown Sugar has been launched. But that's not the company."

"No, that's her life." She gave Matriece a wry smile. "Don't fight it, honey. You're going to be large and in charge. How does she look? I've only seen her from a distance since she's been back."

"Amazing. Gives a whole new meaning to the term 'older woman.' She said she only did it because of the company. Otherwise she'd be content to grow old gracefully."

"I'm surprised she told you that. Do you believe her?"

"Yes. She doesn't strike me as being all that vain. You know how some of those rich white women just let their age show? I'm not talking about the Zsa Zsas. I mean the busy ones who do important work. The Kennedy women. Gilda strikes me as one of those. Somebody who's really about the interior, but who just happens to make her money on the exterior."

"When did you start liking her?"

"What do you mean? I don't—"

"You like her," Blair said firmly. "When we first started working here it felt to me as though you were trying to keep your distance from Gilda, your emotional distance. And that's not like you. At Radiance you were very political. As soon as we got here you zeroed in on everything that had to be done for Brown Sugar, but you didn't seem to reach out."

"I didn't know the game," Matriece said. "I was trying to figure things out." Matriece wanted to change the subject. Gilda probably never noticed anything out of the ordinary about her attitude, but leave it to Blair to figure things out.

"So anyway, at the same time Brown Sugar debuts, WMB will celebrate its tenth anniversary. Gilda wants us to plan a tie-in. I think the WMB celebration will come first, and it will garner a lot of national press. Then here we come maybe a week later, after our CEO has been in papers across the country smiling with a lot of sisters. Very slick."

"So there's a reason she likes black women."

Matriece arched her eyebrows.

"You're amazing, you know that? You go from not liking the Old Broad Herself to defending her."

"I'm just telling you what I think. And I never really disliked Gilda."

"Oh, please."

The silence between them was not entirely comfortable, but not uncomfortable either. They gave each other half smiles at the same time.

"So, you never did tell me what happened with Montgomery."

"Oh, Blair," Matriece said. It wasn't that she begrudged her the details; she just didn't feel like being introspective, or blamed. She didn't want to talk about Montgomery because then she'd have to talk about Sam. And Sam didn't make any sense. She didn't need Blair to ask her what the hell she was doing going out with the man who washed her car. She was already asking herself that question. But sooner or later she'd confess, because that's what usually happened. Or Blair would figure out everything anyway, goddamn her, because that was her power. Matriece looked at Blair and bit down on her lower lip. Why was it so hard to keep secrets from her? What was the point of not telling her? She might as well confess now and get it over with. "All right," she began, and then the telephone rang.

Something was wrong. Matriece could see the outlines of unspoken catastrophe etched in the turn of Blair's lips, the rapid pulsing in her neck, the way she automatically reached in her purse for a cigarette and held it. "Blair, what is it?" she asked.

Blair turned her back to her, cupped the receiver with her hand. She heard her say, "I'll be right there."

When Blair faced her, her eyes were wild birds straining against the cage. "Judd's been in a car accident," she said.

"Oh, God," Matriece said. "I'll go with you."

"No," Blair said so sharply that Matriece felt slapped. "He's all right. Nobody is hurt. Porter's on his way. I'll go."

"Oh, sweetie. I'm so sorry," Matriece said. "Call me tonight."

Blair hurried out without responding. She looked both terrified and weary. Her expression was familiar to Matriece. The tense mouth, the sucked-in jaws, the downcast eyes were always the same whenever she spoke of Judd. Something is very wrong, she thought.

Crenshaw had worked hard all day, and now it was worn out. All along the street owners were closing their businesses for the night. Tired pedestrians, dragging their shopping bags behind them, trudged toward their bus stops. There were lines at all the fast food restaurants as commuters bought their dinners before heading in for the night. When Matriece passed the Third World Record Shop on her way home, the sound of Nigerian high life drenched the street like water from a renegade fire hydrant. Matriece was suddenly glad for the red light, happy to be stationary and awash with music. The song was entirely appropriate. Crenshaw, even this slowed-down, heading-home version of it, was like one huge African marketplace thrumming to its own multifarious rhythms. Tribes from Mexico, Korea, Japan, Europe, and the African diaspora soaked up the song and added their own lyrics. The results were sometimes melodic and sometimes just a mess.

Matriece saw the car in her rearview mirror. Inside, the driver and his companion were laughing. The teeth were perfect, both sets. Expensive smiles. She couldn't hear the laughter, but something was hilarious, the way they were carrying on. The light turned green and then she heard the horn. Right behind her. Not an impatient blare, more of a "hello" kind of honk. She saw Montgomery. His eyes widened, and the woman beside him kept laughing, but he stopped. He gave a little wave, and she waved back. Then she waved at the woman, because, after all, it wasn't as if she didn't know Gretel Meeks.

Well, I guess ole Nadine is finally happy, Matriece thought as she turned off Crenshaw up toward the hills. Blair was right: Montgomery could be prodded toward the altar. Gretel Meeks and her mother would know just how to do that. It sure hadn't taken Montgomery much time to get over her. He probably hadn't been into her in the first place. What commitment had he given her? For all she knew Montgomery had been seeing the two of them the entire time.

As she pulled up to her driveway, Matriece pressed the remote above her rearview mirror, and the garage door started going up. She didn't wave at Jose, her gardener, who was mowing the grass. She drove into the garage and sat in her car until the light went out. In the dark she fought with images of Montgomery and Gretel kissing. Matriece reached for the door handle and held it. She knew the pictures in her mind would follow her into the house. She didn't want to be alone with them. What she wanted was a welcome, heartfelt and genuine. What she needed was a hand as strong as a chain to pull her out of misery's mud. She suddenly yearned to feel like somebody's baby girl. Matriece pressed the button above her and began backing out as the door started rising.

Mooney was sitting in a big comfortable chair in his family room. He was wearing a red jogging suit and drinking a Dr. Pepper. A tray table had been set aside with a plate that held the remnants of a T-bone, a half-eaten baked potato, and a few string beans. The television was turned to CNBC, some financial show. Two men, their voices loud and fervent, were offering stock tips. Mooney was holding a notepad and a pencil. He patted her cheek when she kissed his forehead. "Listen up, Baby Girl," he said. They watched the program in silence until it ended five minutes later. He turned off the television.

"You making money, Uncle Mooney?"

"I invented money. Taught the white folks everything they know. You want something to eat, sugar? Mrs. Wilson fixed a couple of steaks. They're still warm."

"No, thanks. Looks like you enjoyed yours, though."

"I enjoy every meal I eat. Lemme tell you something: you are looking at a man who's glad to have his teeth. Yessirbuddy," he said, deadpan, as Matriece cracked up. "Maybe teeth don't mean that much to you, Miss Missy, but when I was coming up, I'm telling you, a lotta Negroes was looking like jack-o'-lanterns by the time they turned fifty. And that's a fact. I seen more black folks gumming barbeque than you can shake a stick at. First real money I made I bought my momma a set of choppers. Back when I was a boy, black folks couldn't even spell dentist, let alone go see one. First of all there wasn't no black dentist, and second of all, the white one wouldn't work on us. Scared to put his hand in our mouths, you understand." He stopped talking when Matriece started laughing. "That may sound funny, but as soon as I got to Los Angeles, I started going to the dentist, getting my teeth cleaned, having my cavities filled. And look at me," he said, opening his mouth and then closing it. "I got all my teeth." He smiled proudly. "You take care of your teeth, Matriece?"

"I've got all of mine, too," she said.

"That's good. Now, what's on your mind, sugar? Your face is looking mighty long. What's got you down? Is ya PMSing?" He cracked up as soon as the words left his mouth and Matriece joined in.

"How do you know about that?"

"Women tell me things."

"I'm not PMSing. I just feel mixed up."

"Hormones will do that to you." He let out a little chuckle.

"It's not hormones. It's my job, my relationship, me. Everything." She looked at him, and he leaned forward a bit in his chair, his face serious. "Montgomery and I broke up two weeks ago, and it was my fault. I just saw him in a car with another girl, and I've started going out with somebody else. He's a nice guy, my new friend, but, I mean, I felt bad when I saw him today. Montgomery," she added, looking at Mooney's face, which was creased and questioning.

"Matriece, if you start to feel bad enough, you'll do something about it. You have to decide what you want."

"I know. I know," she said, her words gushing out. "Maybe I shouldn't have taken this job. You said it would be an opportunity, and it has been but . . ."

"But what?"

"I never expected to like her, Uncle Mooney."

"Like who?"

"Gilda. I mean, she stole from my mother. She took her money, her ideas. I've known about it for practically my entire life. But, Uncle Mooney, she's so gentle and nice, and she cares about people. I can't believe she'd steal from my mother. And I know, people change, and maybe she's not the same person she was fifty years ago but . . . Is there any way that my mom could have been wrong?"

Mooney had his hands in his lap and he stared into them as if they were printed pages filled with words he couldn't understand. "Ain't this a brand-new day," he said finally, whispering almost. "You like her." He shook his head. "We're such an emotional people, and it trips us up every time. We forgive everydamnbody. George Wallace say he's sorry, and we fall all over ourselves voting for him. Thomas Jefferson kept his black woman on a chain, and we break our necks trying to get buried in his cemetery, trying to claim his name. White man does everything he can do to keep us down, and we want to live next door to him. You think Jews forgave Hitler? You think they go to Germany for vacation and spend their money there? You confused? Let me unconfuse you. It ain't about you liking her, Matriece. It's about the money. If Hosanna didn't know that coming in, she sure 'nuff knew it going out. Doesn't matter whether she was right or wrong. That was then, this here is now. The opportunity isn't going to come from you liking Gilda. Get her to like you."

"You're right. I know you're right. Everything you said, I've been telling myself. She does like me. Maybe I should just tell her who I am."

Mooney shook his head. "Now, why would you want to do that?"

"It never bothered me before. Today I started feeling as though I'm living a lie."

"Let me tell you something: Most people live lies all day long. Matriece, sometimes truth is worth money. Don't play your trump until you know what Gilda's holding."

"You say that as if there's going to be a big payoff for me down the road."

"Don't nobody know what's down the road until you get there."

CHAPTER THIRTY-FOUR

PORTER WASN'T ON his way, and Blair knew it. As she drove toward Sherman Oaks, she attempted to reach him on her cell phone but his answering service picked up. She called his office number but his assistant said he'd been on the shoot all day. When she tried the phone at the site it rang and rang until finally someone answered. She recognized the voice of one of the young actors. He sounded tired and irritable. The star had seen Porter moments before, but now he didn't know where he was. "Look," Blair said with more patience than she felt, "can you find him for me? This is his wife, and it's an emergency concerning our child."

"I'll see what I can do," the actor said.

Porter didn't pick up the phone for ten minutes, and when he did he sounded as fractious as his young star. "Blair, what is it?"

"Porter, Judd has been arrested for speeding and driving under the influence. I'm on my way to the jail now. I want you to meet me there.

"Porter," she said, when she heard the catch in his throat, the soft, muffled sobs. "Oh, baby," she said. She knew that the phone on his set was in the back, next to where the stars were touched up by the makeup lady. It was after six. She hoped that nobody was around. Porter couldn't stand being embarrassed.

"What the hell can we do with him?" Porter shouted, his voice loud enough to warn Blair that he wasn't concerned about who heard him, that he was, in fact, out of control, or on his way to being out of control. "I mean, the kid has had every fucking thing in the world. We got him a shrink. Nothing fucking works. What the hell are we supposed to do now? You tell me."

"Porter, calm down," Blair said, and as soon as she said it Porter began crying again, sobbing loudly.

"They're going to fire me," he said, his voice a sudden whisper.

"What?"

"We're way over budget; we're late. The star acts like he has a stick up his ass. My career is going to be in the toilet after this."

Flames shot through Blair's stomach and ascended into her throat. "Porter," she said, "Judd is in jail. I want you to meet me there. I want you to come right now."

"We've got a meeting in ten minutes." He was whining now, like a baby.

"Go to your fucking meeting, Porter."

Blair had no trouble finding the place, and no trouble locating her son, who was brought out after she posted his bail and signed the release papers. The clerk told her about the court date. "What about his car?" she asked.

"You can pick it up in the morning," the clerk said.

Once they were driving home she could smell the alcohol, the garbagelike odor of vomit. When she looked at Judd he didn't look as remorseful as he did sad. *It's always going to be like this. He's never going to get any better.* Blair turned on the radio. She didn't want to hear her own thoughts.

"So, where's Dad?" Judd said when they got in the house. They were standing in the kitchen. Judd opened the refrigerator, took out a bottle of milk, and began drinking. What's the use? she thought, looking at him.

"I couldn't reach him." The lie slipped off her tongue easily. "Judd . . ."

He held up his hand. "You don't have to say anything, Mom. I know I fucked up again. I know I'm your little loser." He put the milk on the counter, the top beside the bottle.

She watched him as he disappeared up the stairs. Seconds later his bedroom door slammed shut. Blair sat down at the table and stared out into her garden. She wanted to prune her roses. There were five flats of chrysanthemums that she needed to plant but she couldn't get up. She felt immobile, as though she'd just been run over by some big heavy piece of machinery and it still had her pinned down and flattened out to nothing. The telephone was in her hand before she realized that she'd picked it up.

"Mom," she said, when she heard her mother's voice.

"Oh, Blair. How are you, honey?" Her mother always sounded so worn out, as if she were dragging around a weight she couldn't let go of. Most times she didn't burden her, but today was different. Blair felt so alone. So hopeless. She didn't feel comfortable talking to Matriece about Judd. Matriece didn't have children of her own, but she made Tavares sound so angelic that Blair couldn't bring herself to tell her about Judd's troubles. Her friend's life seemed so calm and perfect compared to hers, even the way she discarded men. She wished she could let go of Porter, just walk away and never look back. But she couldn't do that, and she didn't have Matriece's life. Today she wanted her mommy.

"Not so good, Mom."

She could hear the evening news in the background, the calm, rational voice of Peter Jennings as he described one calamity after another. Then she heard cursing, loud and deliberate, and she knew that her brother was there.

"How can you stand it, Mom? Why don't you just put him out?"

"Ah, Blair, let's not get into it. I got a headache as it is. You said things weren't going so good. What's the problem?"

"Never mind," she said. Her brother stopped cursing, and Peter Jennings's voice suddenly seemed louder.

"There. He's gone upstairs to sleep it off. Now what is going on with you?" There was a bit of excitement in her mother's raspy voice; she sounded almost eager to hear new troubles, different troubles.

"When's the last time you were out, Mom?" Blair asked.

"What do you mean? I go out all the time. I was out earlier today. I went to the grocery store."

"Did you talk to anybody?"

"Did I talk to anybody? What kind of question . . . Of course I did."

"You been to any good movies lately?"

"Ahh, they're all full of naked people who curse. Who needs it? I can stay right here and watch that trash on cable."

"I'm going to fly out and see you soon, Mom."

"That would be lovely. Only you know your brother's here, and I don't want you two getting into it. When do you think you'll come?"

"I'm not sure."

"Well, winter will be here before you know it, and you can't take the Chicago cold anymore. Your California blood is all thinned out." She chuckled, as though she'd put one over on her.

"I've still got a winter coat, Mom."

"Listen to her. I'm telling you, you couldn't make it through one January day here. You've gotten soft from having it so easy, weather-wise."

"So, you doing okay?"

"There's nothing wrong with me. How about you? What was it you wanted to tell me?"

Blair hesitated. The last thing she wanted to do was burden her mother. "Did you ever feel as though you ended up with the wrong children? Like it was a mismatch?"

Her mother laughed. "What's Judd gone and done?"

"Nothing," Blair said. "It's just that I don't understand my own child."

"You kids with your little troubles. I tell you: you don't know how to spell trouble. You try raising kids with no husband and the neighborhood going colored on you. God knows I couldn't have made it without some of them. But I wish you could see the place where you grew up now. Like a sewer. And the drugs. Jesus. We got out of there just in time."

"Remember when you sent me to live with Aunt Tess?"

"When those girls were trying to beat you up? Sure. Tess was a godsend."

"It was nice at her house."

"I wish I could have sent the lot of you to her. Your brother might have benefited from the peace and quiet." She sighed. "Judd will be fine, Blair. You and Porter are doing a good job. How is Porter?"

"Porter's having some problems on his job, Mom."

"But he still has a job, right?"

"Oh. Sure. It's not a big deal. The movie he's working on is a little over budget, and so he's freaking out."

"When it costs more like that, what does that mean?"

"It puts more pressure on them to recoup the money at the box office, which I'm sure they will."

"Of course. Porter's movies do well, don't they?"

"Oh, yeah."

"So, it's really not such a big deal, is it?"

"I told you. Nothing to worry about."

"That's good."

"So, okay, Mom, I'm going to go. I love you."

"I love you, too, Blair. Kisses to the boys."

Blair leaned against her chair after she hung up. She couldn't hear any noise from upstairs. She remembered then that she had promised to call Matriece. Her hand covered the phone but she didn't pick up the receiver. She didn't feel like talking to anybody else. "I am a potential freeway killer," she said aloud, and then giggled because her delivery was funny and because she envisioned Matriece laughing with her. It seemed as though she'd been making black women laugh her entire life. She felt tired all of a sudden.

Looking through the sliding glass doors, she could see the flats of chrysanthemums sitting near the fence out in the yard. If she'd been a drinker, she'd be craving a taste of something right along now. But instead her fingers itched for dirt. She went upstairs and changed her clothes quickly, then rushed back down and out the door to the yard. Daylight was fading. She sank to the ground in front of the first flat. Blair's shoulders went limp as she pushed the trowel into the earth. The hole grew wider and wider, then she tapped the bottom of the flat until each plant was loose. She gently pulled a plant out of the plastic container and set it down in the hole. As she spread the dirt all around the roots and tamped it down, she could feel her breath coming evenly, barely audible. She began thinking that she could get through the rest of the evening, put dinner on the table, go to bed and sleep even, when she looked up toward the back window, which was Judd's room. It was open. Wafting from it was a thin, steady plume of smoke, the kind that travels on light breezes and causes eyes to tear.

CHAPTER THIRTY-FIVE

WHIRLWIND, ASIA THOUGHT, as she sat in the office of the president of Talmadge Records. He was seated beside her at a glass table with a gathering of smiling executives, the head of her division, her publicist, and people she'd never seen before. Her producer, Shark, an overweight nineteen-year-old from D.C., a genius with lyrics, arrangements, and beats, who had never met a drive-through he didn't like, was there, too. Check out my man, she thought, rocking a mustard-yellow jumpsuit, with matching yellow boots and sunglasses. Asia wanted to crack up, the way Shark was nodding his head to the silent music he alone could hear. Claude was sitting right next to Asia, on her other side, looking sharp in his navy blue Armani suit and Ferragamo shoes. Claude was a short guy and not good-looking; the clothes helped him a lot. His head was still but his eyes were lightbulb bright, and a tow truck couldn't have removed the grin from his face. Counting his money, Asia thought, smiling the seductive smile that she'd mastered. She could smile for hours at a stretch, even if her head was aching, even if she wanted to go home. It was harder keeping a sincere "glow of happiness" emanating steadily from her eyes. That was the tricky part, she learned one day when a photographer shouted at her, "Where's that glow of happiness in your eyes?" and the entire shoot was stalled for hours while she tried to understand what he wanted.

Her current smile was for the more than half a dozen photographers from various newspapers, tabloids, and magazines, not to mention television crews, who were surrounding her. In front of her were the papers she'd just signed. The contract had been inked: three albums in five years, in exchange for a sum with lots of zeroes, although not an unprecedented number. Whitney, Mariah, and Janet made more. Celine, Jewel, and Britney definitely made more. But Claude said that this was only the beginning, that she would surpass this one and that one, all of them. The way he said it made her think of a line of racers, a shot in the air, the gun trained on runners who elbowed one another and stuck out their feet to trip the unsuspecting. Sitting at the table, she could still hear the two girls she used to sing with accusing her of leaving them behind. "Same old bullshit," Claude told her when, two years before, she came to him crying about the unkind things Bellice and Nikki had said to her. "Same thing Mary and Florence told Diana. Same thing Nona and Sarah told Patti. Don't even think about those bitches."

Asia closed her eyes for just a moment and visualized the two girls she used to sing with sitting here with her now. We'd all be grinning, she thought. *We'd have gotten our nails and hair done together. We would be rocking some coordinated outfits. And then later we'd get in the limo and scream our heads off.* They would have had big fun. No doubt. Her former group members had babies now, and no record deal. She hadn't seen the kids, of course, but sometimes she imagined herself holding them, their little fat legs kicking softly against her chest.

Two men in white jackets came in carrying trays of champagne-filled glasses. The men smelled just like the president of Talmadge Records. Asia wondered about that: how poor people could smell like rich people. Had the two waiters stumbled into a sale? Were they wearing knockoff scents? Or could it be that the president's cologne wasn't as expensive as it smelled? Maybe the company bought the cologne in bulk and gave it out to everyone. They passed out the drinks quickly. When everyone had a glass of champagne, the president rose and looked down at her. His cologne mixed in with the scent of the waiters who'd just come by and the combined odor was almost intoxicating, so overpowering that Asia felt light-headed for a moment. The president was a short, round, pale man with hip, youthful glasses and a way of looking at her and not looking at her that at times made him seem cockeyed. "To our golden nightingale," the president said. People around her laughed at the witty play on words. The "golden" referred, of course, to the money the company expected to earn and to her voice, but also to the clothes she was wearing, a tight gold minidress with a high collar and boots in deeper tones of the same color. Everyone stood; the glasses clinked and the smiles wouldn't quit.

Claude leaned over and whispered in her ear, "That cheap Jew bastard is happy now."

Asia couldn't wait to leave.

It took a while before Asia finished shaking hands. The executives lined up to hug and kiss her. "You're just fabulous."

"Asia, all the best. You're beautiful."

"You may be wearing gold, but we're going for nothing but platinum. Heh heh heh."

"We're privileged to have you."

As the president and the A&R were leaving, Shark waddled over to her and whispered, "Yo, listen up, girlie. Don't take nona dis shit to heart. Don't believe nuffin' these motherfuckers say, 'cause I'ma tell you: ain't none of them got your back. And don't be giving your money away to no pimpass motherfucker wita six-pack. Yo, you should marry me. You know you ain't nothin' but a 'hood rat. We could be down. Have a couple of fat baby girls. Ice them out with some little-bitty diamond earrings and shit, little-bitty tennis bracelets. Hey, why you laughing. I'm serious."

That was the only real smile of the day for Asia, and she was still laughing when Shark left. Then back to work. She grinned for the photographers, then turned and showed more teeth, until Claude grabbed her arm and said, "That's all, folks," to the photographers.

Claude took her to an upscale soul-food restaurant in Beverly Hills that was owned by a famous black football player. There were several huge black guys standing outside, the same kind of roughneck black boys she'd grown up with, only these were wearing suits and ties and being polite instead of calling after women in the street the way they did in her old neighborhood. She figured they were part of the football player's family, or maybe just his buddies. She recognized one of them. "Hi, Bunky," she said.

"Asia girl, you doing it."

She laughed. "How you been?"

"Not as good as you."

She laughed again.

"How's my boy Donny doing?"

Her smile froze. "He's doing."

"Yeah. Yeah. Hey, I hope he's still singing." He turned to his friends. "Her brother can sing. Shit. Luffer Vandross wish he could sing like Donny. Damn, I hope he's still singing."

Claude cleared his throat.

"Aw'ight. Y'all enjoy yourselves. Nice seeing you, Asia."

"He knows my brother, Donny," she explained to Claude as they walked inside. "He's the real singer in the family."

"Oh, yeah. Let me hear him. Maybe I can get him a deal, too."

"I'll talk to him."

There were no windows in the restaurant, which was filled with huge vases of exotic flowers. The artificial light was soft, soothing, everyone looked good under its hazy glow. As they followed the maître d', the other diners stopped eating and talking and just gawked.

They slid into the booth in the back. A few moments later two little girls appeared at their table. "Excuse me, Asia Pace," the older one said in an unexpectedly formal voice. They squealed with delight when she gave them her autograph.

When the girls left, Asia thought more people would follow. She braced herself, but nobody came. "Is this dress okay?" she asked Claude, who assured her that the dress and everything else about her was more than okay. But she knew better than to believe Claude.

Asia ordered fried chicken, candied yams, and collard greens. Corn bread and biscuits arrived and she took one bite of each. No butter. She hadn't worked out in more than two weeks, and she didn't want to gain weight. When her order came she picked at the food, even though the yams were really good and she was hungry. Size two. That's the size she needed to stay.

Claude ate as though he didn't know where his next meal was coming from. "How does it feel to be rich? Didn't I tell you I would make it happen?" He made a noise that was part laughter and part crowing, and then wolfed down another biscuit. "How are rehearsals going?" he asked between mouthfuls. Asia was scheduled to appear on "The Tonight Show" around Thanksgiving and had been preparing two songs.

"I sound good," she said.

"What are you wearing?"

"I don't know yet."

"Wear something short but not scandalous. I want the people to see that Tina Turner isn't the only one. We want Hanes to come calling someday, Asia. Let me tell you . . ."

She'd learned how to tune out Claude, to appear to be listening by simply watching his lips. Her manager had a million ideas, some he forgot as soon as he said them. Asia started paying attention only when he started saying the same thing for the twentieth time. Then he was serious. "The MTV thing is going to take a little more time. I'm . . ." Claude said, and then stopped, realizing his mistake. He had other clients, other superstars in the making, and she knew that he had confused her with someone else. "Oh, how's that chicken? Mind if I have a bite?" He picked up an untouched chicken wing and began eating it.

"You can have it all," she said. Asia knew that his sudden interest in her food was Claude's way of changing the subject. He never wanted her to know what he was doing for his other clients.

"I know Bellice and Nikki are eating their hearts out today," Claude said.

"They have babies," she said softly. "I heard they were trying to start a new group."

Claude grunted. "They didn't sound that great when you brought them in to do background vocals. They didn't even show up half the time."

Asia didn't say anything. How could she tell Claude that she felt sorry for Bellice and Nikki, that she missed them?

The waiter brought the check, and Claude paid for the meal with a platinum American Express card. Claude took care of everything for her. All she had to do was show up and sing. She didn't even have to desire anything. Claude did that for her, too.

". . . and that brings me to the movie," Claude said. He took a sip of coffee. Asia angled her head toward Claude. He had been talking about the movie for months. "The producers want to see you the week after Leno. Soon as I have the exact time, I'll let you know."

"What's the movie about?"

"Some kind of updated *Mahogany*. You know, the picture Diana Ross did years ago. I'll get the sides tomorrow and have a messenger bring them over to you."

"Did you talk with somebody named Matriece Carter? She's with Gilda Cosmetics and she wants me to be their spokesmodel. I told her I'd do it."

Claude set down his coffee cup. "Asia honey, you need to run things by me."

"Claude, I grew up with Matriece. She used to baby-sit me."

"Well, see, that's why you have to run things by me. Just because somebody used to baby-sit you isn't any reason to cut a deal with them. We have to see what kind of money they're talking about." He picked up his coffee cup and stared into it. "Maybe we can play them against somebody else. Get the money up."

"Claude, I don't want to do Matriece like that," Asia said.

"Honey, this isn't personal. Believe me, if they find somebody they like better they'll drop you like a hot turd. They'll drop you if their product doesn't sell. They'll dump you if you hang out with the wrong rapper. Big business ain't loyal to nobody but itself. Remember what happened to DJ de la Soul—all she did was say the mayor of New York needed his ass kicked, and boom, no more soda contract. You have to be loyal to you. Let me handle your business, okay?"

Asia nodded.

After the limousine driver dropped off Claude, Asia thought about the movie, about being a movie star. That was what she had been after from the start: the world looking at her on a big screen, applauding her downcast eyes, her upturned mouth, her bare back, watching her kiss and cry and rage, loving everything she displayed.

Asia was still hungry. There was Perrier in the car, and when she finished two bottles she felt as though she were going to burst. That feeling would leave her too quickly, she knew. She remembered *Mahogany*. She'd seen the video when she was a kid and had been impressed by the thin, elegant character Diana played, all big eyes and cheekbones, who learned the hard way that being a superstar model doesn't take the place of being loved. The story probably made more sense now than it did in the day when there was maybe one black supermodel. Now there were at least three.

She could pretend that she was a chain-smoking, cocaine-snorting, don't-care-about-nothing-but-getting-to-the-top model. And she'd make everybody believe her, too. Being a model was just a different kind of show business. Same highs, same lows. Same no looking over your shoulder. *I'll wear a red beaded gown to the Oscars.*

Her house was quiet and dim when she went inside, and it smelled like the perfume she'd put on that morning, a house full of her smell and nobody else's. The rest of the afternoon and evening lay in front of her like a beach with no footprints. She knew that she should exercise, but she didn't feel like it. She wanted company.

Who? She thought for a moment. Her last boyfriend had been banished months before, a result of his acting just a little too starstruck when he went with her to a movie premiere. Gawking at people, poking her in her ribs to look, look, look—nah. She couldn't be having all that. She was fresh out of cool guys. Claude said some director he was representing, real up-and-coming, had asked about her, but he was white. Claude thought she should date white guys with money. "When the marriage ends you want them owing you, baby girl, not the other way around." Like she knew what to say to a rich white man, or a poor one either, for that matter. She told Claude she'd find her own men, but her boyfriends never lasted very long. They always seemed to make her angry. They would say something stupid or do something stupid, and the next thing she knew she'd be showing them the door. Then they'd leave, and she'd wonder where all her anger had come from. Her hairdresser told her that she had to learn patience. Phyllis had been married for nearly twelve years, and she said that patience was the glue in her marriage. " 'Cause men, they just like kids," Phyllis said.

Asia figured that she needed a girlfriend right about now. Maybe they could go to the movies or something. Go shopping. Maybe get their nails done, although she'd just had hers done yesterday, and she generally had a girl come over because she didn't like sitting in a shop around a bunch of people, all trying to look at her to see if she had corns on her toes, which she didn't.

Maybe I should go see Bellice and Nikki. They lived in the same building, on the same floor in apartments right across from each other, somewhere in Inglewood, not too far from her mother. If times got rough, Asia knew they would move in together. *I could just show up with presents for the babies. Phat little Baby Guess outfits. Or maybe a thick gift certificate, so they can have a little shopping spree. I can buy my way back in.* She turned that last thought over in her mind, then she lay down on her bed and fell asleep.

Asia woke up to a ringing telephone. When she saw that just under an hour had passed, she was disappointed. She wanted it to be nighttime.

"Hey, baby."

"Hi, Mom."

"I just saw you on television. You looked good. Beautiful. So, everything went all right. You signed the contract?"

"Yeah. Everything went fine."

"They said on the show that you were getting almost twelve million dollars." Her voice was full of awe. Her words were tripping over themselves. It was a stranger's voice.

Asia hesitated. "I can buy a better weave," she said, and then she giggled. She wished she could shout, "I'm a millionaire, Mom. I can buy a big, big house in Beverly Hills. I can buy a Rolls or a Bentley, or take a trip around the world." She didn't say anything. She didn't like talking about money with her mother.

"You're going to have to be careful now, Asia. You may not want to talk about money, but a lot of people watched that show. Folks are gonna start coming out of the woodwork. You thought it was bad before with Pooky and them asking to borrow money off you. People are going to be turning up who were nowhere around when I was struggling with you back in the day. People who didn't do a damn thing for you are going to be lining up with their hands out, looking all pitiful and trying to talk you out of your money, and I'm telling you, girl, you have to think about the people who knew you when the going wasn't so easy."

"What are you talking about, Mom?"

"Nothing. I'm not talking about nothing. Just saying that you have to be careful, that's all. People will try to guilt-trip you and make you think they're entitled to something when he ain't entitled to a damn thing. Keep on stepping, that's what you have to say, otherwise—"

"Who's 'he,' Mom?"

"He?" Ruth sounded as if she were startled. There was the same kind of apprehension in her voice that had been there when Asia was a child and she woke up her mother after she had passed out from whatever she was drinking or snorting or smoking. "I just mean people in general."

"I'll be careful," Asia said in the same quiet voice she'd always used to calm down her mother. After all these years, that was still her job.

He, she thought after she'd hung up. The pronoun lingered in her mind like an old boyfriend who refused to go home. Asia couldn't explain why the word alerted her. He.

She slid back down on her bed and stared at the ceiling. Then she got up and walked over to the coffee table in the sitting area of her bedroom. There was a very beautiful card on the table. She picked it up, fingering the flowers on the front and then the signature inside. *Your biggest fan.* She sat down on the big love seat, holding the card against her chest. Asia began singing one of the old songs she'd recorded with her group. She opened her mouth wide when she got to the high note, the money note, Claude called it, the one that had made her a star. She held that note for a long, long time, thinking about how the group had loved that song in the beginning, how proud of her they were, and then how everything changed when the photographers began seeking her out, when the microphone was always thrust in her face. *Now they have babies, and I can't even hold them.* She felt the first tear dripping down her cheek just as she ran out of breath.

Asia pressed the automatic dial for Phyllis's number, and wiped her eyes as she waited while the telephone rang. She could hear laughter in the background when Phyllis answered.

"What are you doing?" she asked.

"My cousin and her husband just got in from Houston with their three bad kids," Phyllis said, her voice becoming amplified as she spoke. It was apparent that she was really not directing her words to Asia at all.

"Oh."

"Yeah, they're over here trying to eat me out of house and home and tear up everything, too." She laughed again, and Asia heard her chuckles echo. Then the music grew louder. "Where are you, honey? You home? Oooh! I just got a hold of some Brazilian hair. It's the real deal, baby. I'm going to take that Korean stuff out the next time I see you and put this in. Fierce, baby. You doing okay?"

"Uh-huh."

"Asia, lemme call you back in a little while."

"I'll be here," Asia said. She sat still on the bed, then glanced at the clock. It wasn't even four o'clock yet. Too early to eat again. She stared at her fingernails, and then she inspected her toes and ran her fingers across the smooth part of her heels. Asia picked up the telephone and called the nail salon. She asked them to send out May. May wasn't the best manicurist, but she always talked so much, always had a little joke.

CHAPTER THIRTY-SIX

WHEN KENT SHOOK Matriece's hand at the beginning of the meeting, his trembling fingers were so wet and slippery they almost slid between hers. God, he looks bad, she thought, staring into his sunken, averted eyes. He eased his body very slowly into one of the chairs at the round oak table in the center of Daniel's office. Matriece was alarmed. Kent's hair seemed grayer and thinner, his face creased in a way that made him appear harried. Poor guy, she said to herself as she sat down across from him.

Daniel got up from his desk. His ruddy face, well-proportioned body, and thick head of hair were the antithesis of the tired figure Kent presented. As he joined Matriece and Kent at the table he bantered and joked, managing to make even Kent laugh. At the same time, his eyes searched both Kent's and her face, as if they were different pieces of an intricate puzzle he was trying to put together.

Rachel was the last one to arrive. Dressed entirely in black, her skin seemed even paler than usual. She flounced into her seat as though she were a recalcitrant ninth-grader who'd been given another chance after returning from the vice-principal's office. Matriece didn't really understand why she came to the meetings at all. She contributed nothing, asked no questions, and appeared deeply and chronically bored. She could feel her eyes on her, and she knew that Rachel was staring at her again.

Matriece dispensed with the weekly update of Brown Sugar as quickly as possible. "Blair has just about completed the choice for the packaging. . . . We are going to be naming the lipstick shades this week. . . . There has been a slight glitch with the foundation, but the chemists are rectifying . . ." She took a deep breath. "Asia Pace has not yet signed the contract but I'm anticipating that I'll have her signature imminently." Matriece imparted this last information with a straight face, despite the fact that her stomach was spurting out just a bit of acid as she spoke. *Asia is going to come through. She's my homegirl.*

"She's really the key, isn't she?" Daniel spoke pleasantly enough, but beneath his well-modulated tone was a polite warning: Get the contract signed immediately.

Matriece spoke carefully. "Asia Pace is having a very hectic, successful year. Grammys, Diamond Discs, and now there is a new recording contract, talk of a film. The more publicity she garners for herself, the more valuable she'll be for us."

Kent leaned forward. He smiled for a moment, opened his mouth, closed it, then smiled again.

What the hell is wrong with him? Matriece wondered.

"And the more money she'll want," Kent said finally, his tongue appearing thick. "Maybe we'd better latch onto her before she gets too overpriced."

"Do you know her?" Rachel's voice was unexpected.

"I knew her when she was a little girl, but we hadn't been in touch until I asked her to be our spokesmodel. I hope the fact that I know her will work in our favor," she added smoothly.

Rachel never took her eyes off Matriece's face while she was talking. When she'd finished, the younger woman was still staring at her intently. She seemed awestruck. If I didn't know better I would swear that the child admires me, Matriece thought.

"Well," Daniel said, rising, "I'm sure you'll get a signed contract sooner as opposed to later." He smiled at her but his eyes were two security doors locked up for the night.

At the close of the meeting, Daniel caught up with her on her way out. He put his hand on her shoulder. "I understand you accompanied my mother to her We Mean Business luncheon. That's a project that's near and dear to her heart. You should feel honored."

Rachel was right behind her and when Matriece glanced at her she could see pain in her eyes. *Poor thing. She feels left out.*

"I do," Matriece said.

"And I'm sure she's told you of the plans for overlapping WMB's tenth anniversary with the launch of Brown Sugar," Daniel said.

"That's going to be fabulous," Matriece said.

The phone rang, and Daniel walked over to his desk to answer it. "Hi, Mom." He mouthed a good-bye to Matriece, Kent, and Rachel, whose mouth was twitching just slightly.

Kent shook her hand at the door. "Let's talk numbers for Asia on Monday. I've been scouting around for the going rate for spokesmodels. It can be pretty steep. I was thinking of making our deal a bit more creative, with less of a cash outlay."

"Companies are going to be vying for her, Kent," Matriece said quickly. "I think we should be as generous as makes sense. Her face will make us money. I guarantee it."

"We'll see," Kent said.

When Matriece returned to her office she stood behind her desk to face the large picture window. The Los Angeles sky was dull and hazy. Below the smog, the buildings appeared gray and cheerless. Call me, Asia, Matriece thought. She stared at the skyline, wishing she could harness all the power that flowed in and out of those buildings. LA was a relationship town, a city of connections. She had one with Asia, but if it was going to do her any good, things were going to have to move faster. Matriece didn't want to think about what would happen if Asia didn't come through for her. She'd be back at ground zero with not a lot of time to start over.

Matriece sat down at her desk, then turned away from the view. She didn't want to worry about Asia. It was Friday night, time to go home, work out, drink a glass of wine, and chill. Maybe she'd get a massage. Matriece felt buoyed by the thought of supple fingers kneading her sore muscles. But she had one more chore to dispense with before she could even think about leaving.

"Hosanna" was the password to get into the Brown Sugar financial accounts file. Matriece punched in the letters of her mother's name, and in a few seconds the most recent expenditures for the fledgling subsidiary appeared on the screen. Matriece checked the numbers every month, even though Kent had told her it wasn't necessary, that he'd take care of the money. Budgets weren't her strong suit, but Matriece liked to

see the numbers for herself. At this point, of course, there were only expenditures for Brown Sugar. No money was coming in.

She scanned the line of figures carefully. There was only a slight dent
in her four-million-dollar budget. The design phase of Brown Sugar was
mostly an in-house operation. It wouldn't be until manufacturing got
started that real dollars would be spent. Of course, there had been con-
sultation fees, as well as the cost of mock-ups and colorists. Most of the
payees had remained pretty constant for the entire year that Matriece had
been president of the division. Then she saw it: Taper Industries. One
hundred seventy-five thousand dollars. The company name wasn't unknown to her. She checked the account code: 134-0029-66. Brown Sugar
was 134-0029-67. Sixty-six was the hair-care division. The last time
Taper Industries had shown up on her financial status sheet she'd asked
Kent to take care of it, and he'd told her that hair care had made a mistake. She thought about calling Kent now, but then she visualized his
haggard face. Matriece knew that his assistant had been out ill for a week
or two. She might as well save him the trouble.

Matriece picked up her telephone, dialed the company operator, and
asked to be connected to Leonard Smiley's office. Leonard was the person in charge of accounting for hair care. She'd met him when she first
arrived at Gilda's.

"Matriece," he said jovially, once she told him who she was. "Good
to hear from you. How are things going? We understand you're going to
be the big earner over there. We're going to have to struggle to keep up."
He let out a big guffaw, and Matriece joined in.

"Well, we won't be able to make any money at all if we have to pay
your debts."

"What's that?"

"The reason I'm calling is that I was going over Brown Sugar's financials for the month, and I think we got one of your bills by mistake."

"Really? Which one?"

"Taper Industries. One hundred and seventy-five thousand. I figure
the same thing happened as the last time."

"What last time? We don't use any Taper Industries. I've never heard of them."

"You all are sixty-six, aren't you?"

"Yeah, that's our code. But we don't buy from any Taper Industries. I know all of our suppliers."

"That's funny."

"Check with Kent, dear. Good talking with you."

"I will. Nice talking with you."

Matriece was perplexed when she hung up the telephone. If hair care's code was sixty-six, how could the bill not be theirs? Besides, Kent had told her that Leonard had sent his apologies for the previous error. What the hell is going on? For a moment she considered calling Kent again, but then she looked at her watch. It was six o'clock on a Friday evening. Let the poor man go home and get some rest. Besides, she was tired, too, and she had to go to her sister's.

By the time she reached Vonette's house, Matriece felt lighter. Her sister met her at the door. Before she could cross the threshold, Vonette said, "I don't know about Tavares going to this school, Triecy."

Matriece tried to control the alarm she felt rising inside her. Leave it to Vonette to want to rock the boat after she finally got Tavares where he should have been all along. "What do you mean?"

"He's always tired," Vonette said. "Some evenings he can barely get in the door before he conks out. I have to wake him up to eat. And then he has to do his homework. That takes half the night. He's up at, like, five-thirty in the morning, and it starts all over again. I feel sorry for him."

"Vonette, let the boy grow up a little," Boot called from inside.

Matriece peeked in the house and saw her brother-in-law sprawled out on the couch.

"He started something; let him finish it." He muttered in Spanish, then winked at Mrs. Ramirez, who was seated in a chair near the sofa.

"I know what you said," Vonette yelled. "And don't be trying to get Marguerita on your side, either." Vonette stepped onto the porch next to Triecy. "I am not trying to make Tavares a mama's boy. I'm just thinking about his health."

"Vonette, he's young," Matriece said. "His body is adjusting. What's wrong with his taking a nap when he comes home? He can catch up on his sleep on the weekends."

"Exactly what I told her, Triecy," Boot yelled from inside. "Come on in the house." The two women went into the living room. "Tavares likes the school."

"He doesn't like it," Vonette snapped. "He said it was okay."

"Girl, it's only been a few weeks. He has some friends. His grades is good. You ask me, he's doing fine. Leave him right where he is," Boot said.

"Hello, Mrs. Ramirez," Matriece said, nodding to her sister's neighbor. "Give it a year, Vonette," Matriece said softly, afraid that if she was too vociferous in her objections, her sister would become more insistent that Tavares go back to South Central. In a year, her nephew would begin seeing the big picture, all the opportunities he could have. By then, he'd want to stay.

Vonette scowled but she didn't say anything. Her face looked troubled. Poor thing, Matriece thought, this is so hard for her. Think of his future, she wanted to tell her sister.

"Tavares, come on downstairs. It's time to go. Triecy's here." Vonette looked at her sister. "All right, I'm going to go along with you. But I want you to know something: It ain't all about grades and the best schools, Triecy. It ain't all about being the biggest success in the world, either." Her eyes flooded with tears. "Me and Tavares used to have more time to talk and be together. You'll find out. They grow up fast, Triecy, real fast. You blink and they're grown. I don't want to lose him before I have to. And I don't want him lost to the rest of us. If Tavares gets so high and mighty, where does that leave our family? How do we fit into his life when he's making tons of money and married to some white girl, huh? My children love each other. They didn't get sixteen hundreds on their SATs, but they love each other. I don't want them to wind up not connected, like you and me."

"What do you mean?"

"We got nothing in common, Triecy. We don't even hang out."

"Vonette, you're my sister and I love you. I love your family."

"Triecy, I know you do. It's just that I don't want to wind up worshiping Tavares. I just want to love him."

"Ain't nobody gonna be worshiping nobody around here. Tavares ain't never gonna get so much money that I can't beat his ass if he needs it," Boot said with a growl. "And if he gets big time and marries a white girl, we'll just have to party with her, too. Shit. Your mama didn't want you to marry me, and you know my mama didn't want me to get with you. Now she loves you to death. See, you need to chill. What I marry this black woman for, Triecy?"

Vonette didn't say anything.

Matriece didn't talk as she drove with Tavares. Usually they joked and chatted, but she felt somber as she mulled over the things her sister had said. Stealing a quick look at her nephew, she wondered if he felt the same way his mother did. So many black kids missed the boat because they didn't have anybody in their corner, and she was just trying to support Tavares. Boot saw that. Why couldn't Vonette?

"How's school?" she finally asked Tavares. She was almost afraid to hear his answer.

"It's okay."

She took a deep breath. "Do you like it?"

"Um, kinda."

"You kinda like it, Tavares?" She couldn't help smiling.

"Yeah, I mean it takes forever to get there and come back. I don't like the travel. But the school is tight. The work is harder, but I enjoy it. And I like the girls, Auntie Triecy. The girls are phat."

Matriece rolled her eyes at her nephew.

"Come on now. If I didn't notice the girls, there'd be something really wrong with me, Auntie."

She laughed. "Do you have a girlfriend?"

"Oh yeah."

"Is she white?"

"Nah. She's a sister. Not that the white girls don't love me."

"Do me a favor. Tell your mother your girlfriend is black."

Matriece pulled into the parking lot behind the building that housed KBOM and KRPP radio stations, turned off the car, and sat for a moment.

She hadn't spoken to Montgomery since the night they'd broken up, and she didn't know how she'd feel seeing him again. When he'd called to remind her that he still wanted to show Tavares the station, she was surprised. Maybe she should have backed out then. She felt awkward.

"Let's go, Triecy. I'ma be a deejay," Tavares said.

Matriece laughed and got out of the car.

Montgomery met them at the front desk. He was wearing jeans and a sweater; he looked good. He gave Matriece a quick hug and shook Tavares's hand when she introduced them. "Heard a lot about you," Montgomery said.

"Heard about you, too," Tavares said, grinning.

Montgomery walked Matriece back to the elevator, but neither of them pressed the button. Finally, Matriece said, "I can come back and get him." She glanced at his face, then turned away. She felt nervous and excited at the same time.

"Listen, it's no trouble. I'll take him home."

"You sure?"

Montgomery nodded. He gave her a long stare. "I've missed you," he said. "I've missed you a lot. I don't know, it just seems to me that we were just getting started, and then all of a sudden we ended. I can't figure it out."

"Montgomery . . ."

He placed his fingertip under her chin and lifted it so that she had to look at him. "Look, Matriece, I don't want to put you on the spot, but can't we talk about this, about us? How about I come over later tonight?"

There were so many reasons she didn't want to look at him. God, I miss him, she thought. Even as she admitted the truth to herself, she could feel the fear coursing through her body. She could manage this pain but not more. "I can't tonight, Montgomery." She pressed the button for the elevator.

"I'll call you," he said, as she got on.

"Thanks for looking out for Tavares."

"Your prince is my prince," he said.

Matriece could hear her phone ringing as she punched in the numbers of her security system.

Asia's voice was sultry, a little breathy, with too much 'hood in it to be sophisticated. Matriece was both surprised and a little angry when she heard her. She had been calling Asia and Claude for weeks and was beginning to worry. Matriece was about to say, "Girl, where have you been?" but she swallowed that admonishment. Diva, she thought. "Oh, Asia, I was wondering when I'd hear from you."

"Oh," she said quickly. "I've been running around so much I guess I haven't been in touch. And Claude's had a lot to do. He'll be calling you soon. I'm going on 'The Tonight Show' in a few weeks, so I've been practicing for that. I guess you know I signed my record contract."

"I saw the news. Congratulations. You have a good financial person, Asia?"

"Yeah."

"You know, it might not hurt to take an accounting course. You can do it over the Internet. Always get a second opinion if your financial manager tells you anything you're not comfortable with, any wild investment schemes. You want your money to last, Asia. You meet with him regularly?"

"Every month."

"Do you understand everything he says?"

"Pretty much. I ask questions."

"Keep copies of everything, all the statements."

"Okay, Mom."

"Oh, did I go there?" Matriece asked with a laugh.

"That's okay. I like that. Anyway, I called to ask you what you were doing tonight. I thought we might hang out or something."

"Oh, sweetie, I wish you'd called sooner. I have a date."

"Oh."

Matriece could hear the disappointment in her voice. "But what are you doing tomorrow? Want to go to brunch?"

"Yeah, that would be nice. About eleven?"

"I'm going to church tomorrow. My nephew is singing a solo. So let's make it about one-thirty. Is that too late?"

"No. Where's he singing?"

"Faithful Tabernacle. You know, you should come hear him. If you ever need backup, Tavares is your man. Do you want to come?" Matriece heard Asia's throat catch.

"Well, maybe. But if I don't make it just come to Café Luna in the Marina at one-thirty. Do you know where that is?"

"Sure." Poor kid, she can't even go to church, Matriece thought as she hung up.

At exactly eight o'clock the doorbell rang. Matriece gave her hair a final pat and appraised herself one last time in the full-length mirror in her hallway. She was wearing a black dress that had a slit in the front and revealed a bit of thigh. *Montgomery loves this dress.* She could hear her heart as she walked to the door. I'm going to be with Sam tonight, not Montgomery. *What the hell am I doing?* She didn't know. She didn't want to know.

Sam stood in the doorway for a second, not moving, not speaking. Then he said, "Wow," and handed her a bouquet. It felt okay, him standing there, looking at her, smiling. It felt all right, him saying nice things about the dress, about her hair, the way she smelled. His words sounded familiar. It was all new-date talk; she'd heard it before, many times.

Sam turned into the parking lot of a strip mall on Hollywood Boulevard that Matriece recognized, and drove to the far end, where he found a space. After he parked he walked around to her side and opened the door for her, then took her hand. Matriece could hear the music as soon as they got out of the car. Loud Latin rhythms blared out into the parking lot from a Cuban dance club, one of her favorites. How did Sam know she liked to salsa?

"Do you salsa?" Sam asked her.

"A little bit," she said, trying not to sound smug.

Inside a big band, full of horns and percussion instruments, was assembled in front. Three guys in ruffled shirts were singing, and the floor was crowded with dancers, all ages, all sizes. The music was so loud it was impossible to talk, so Matriece followed the waiter who led them to a table. They ordered wine and dinner, and when the waiter disappeared, the band began another song. Sam extended his hand to her. "Let's dance," he said.

Matriece knew that he was a good dancer the moment he stepped out onto the floor. He held her firmly, his hand on her back, his palm pressed close to hers. He pulled her to him, and she could tell that he was breathing in time to the music. So was she. He led her effortlessly and she followed every step, every turn. Every move he made she was right there with him. She stole a look at him while he was dancing, and she could tell that he was completely relaxed, completely self-confident. She liked the way she felt in his arms.

They danced for four songs in a row, and then they returned to their seats. The wine was waiting for them. They both took sips.

"Where did you learn to salsa?" Sam asked her.

"In D.C. I went to Howard, and on the weekends I used to party in this neighborhood called Adams Morgan. A lot of Puerto Ricans, Salvadorians, all kinds of Latinos lived there, and they used to salsa in some of the clubs. So I picked it up. Sometimes I'd go to New York on the weekends and I'd go to the Latin clubs and dance. How about you?"

He looked at her for a long time, then he shook his head, as though he was about to tell her something and changed his mind. "I really can't remember where I learned. Seems like I've always been doing it."

"Salsa music is so passionate."

"Yeah," Sam said, and he was smiling.

"What?"

"I knew we had something in common other than your car." They laughed.

"Yeah, I wanted to mention the car."

Sam raised his eyebrows.

Matriece kept a straight face. "Terrible job on Friday. Smudgy as I don't know what. I really shouldn't have to pay."

"There you go. I told you, no freebies."

"That's cool. Next dance will cost you five dollars."

They finished their wine and danced several more fast numbers. The more they danced, the more intricate Sam's moves became. He twirled her around until she felt dizzy. He bent her backward, and just when she thought she was going to fall he pulled her back up. With her heels on she was almost as tall as he was. Sometimes she knew what he was going

to do before he did it just by looking in his eyes. She was always ready
for him. When the music slowed down, his hand on the small of her back
pressed her into him. She draped her arm over his shoulder, and they
rocked from side to side, their feet barely moving.

They ate fried plaintains, black beans and rice, and chicken steeped
in garlic and lime juice as they watched the other dancers. An older couple, small, plump people, their worn faces exuberant and happy, danced
merrily across the floor. From time to time younger men and women cut
in, and the older man cavorted with women who could have been his
granddaughters while his wife dipped and twirled with boys. "They are
the king and queen of the club," Sam said. "You can salsa until you get
old. That's what I like about it."

"So, you plan to be a dancing old dude."

They were sitting next to each other but she still had to shout to be
heard. Sam moved his head closer to hers and his hair brushed against
her cheek. His forehead was damp and a little shiny. He was smiling and
looking in her eyes. "Yeah, that's part of my plan."

"What's the other part?"

"To have a good woman, children, money, God's grace."

"All of that?"

"Why not? I didn't get as much education as I needed, so I'm making my way through life by the sweat of my brow. Washing cars isn't
what I want to be doing when I'm old, so I have to have a plan. Everybody needs one, though. Take Kent, for—" Sam stopped. "I'm talking too
much."

Matriece knew he had started to tell her something about Kent
Bridgeport but had stopped himself. When she looked at Sam's face she
realized that he'd never tell her anything he didn't want her to know.

They were both sweaty when they left El Coyote. Sam held her hand
as he walked her to the car. It felt natural. He'd been holding her hand
all evening. When he kissed her in the car, that felt natural, too. It was a
soft, sweet kiss, just his lips brushing against hers but it had rhythm, just
like his dancing. She recalled Montgomery's kisses, how confident they
were. He assumed that her lips were his. Sam was more laid-back, as

though he wasn't sure where their lips would lead. But he kept kissing her, at red lights and stop signs, and by the time he drove up to her driveway his lips were bolder, more insistent, and so were hers.

They sat in her family room, and she poured them both another glass of wine. She played some more salsa, and they danced again. He showed her a new step, and they practiced until their bodies flowed together like some unguent pouring from a bottle.

"Did Asia become your spokesmodel?" he asked when she sat down beside him. The lights were dim, but she could still see how eager his eyes looked.

"She hasn't signed the contract yet, but we have a verbal agreement. She might come to church with me tomorrow, and then we're supposed to have brunch."

Sam sat up. "What church? What time?" he asked.

Matriece laughed. "Faithful Tabernacle, ten forty-five. Are you coming just to get her autograph? Should I be jealous?"

"No, you shouldn't be jealous. I like women my own age; Asia's just a child. It's not lust, just admiration," he said, and Matriece believed him. "She had a hard time coming up, that's what I heard. I look at her the same way I do some of the rappers, not the ones with the nasty mouths, but the ones who evolve. And for the record, I go to church every Sunday. I'm not looking for autographs, just serenity.

"I admire people who make it through, you know. So many people give up. A lot of people can sing and dance and act and do all kinds of things, but so many of us don't emerge. Like Eleanor Roosevelt. She could have remained a homely white woman with a big heart who never did anything about it. Know what I mean? When someone gets through, I have to take my hat off."

"I see. So I'm in the presence of a serious fan."

"Yeah, serious." He added quickly, "I'm a Matriece fan, too."

"Me? I can't sing."

"I don't imagine you had it easy, getting to where you are. And you're going higher, I can tell. If I can help by keeping your car shiny, well, Miss Lady, it's my honor." He lowered his head in a mock bow.

Matriece poked him in his side. "You need to quit."

"Girl, I just wanna shine your car."

He leaned over and kissed her. Matriece kissed him back and then they were dancing again, finding the rhythm, keeping the beat, their arms around each other. She felt his fingers rubbing her neck, her shoulders. She pulled away first, and Sam released her. He looked a little dazed.

"You dance good; you kiss good. The job is yours."

Matriece laughed. He must have read the confusion and uncertainty in her eyes. "I'd better go," he said.

She walked him to the door. When she reached for the knob, he took her hands in his. "Listen, I had a great time, best time I've had in a while," he said. "I'm not going to push up on you. It's all your call. There's miles between us, Matriece. I know that. I understand roadblocks. If you just want to go salsa with me every once in a while, that will be okay by me. If you wanna bust me back to just being your detail man, that's cool, too. It's up to you. But," he said, moving forward, his arms suddenly around her, so tight she couldn't move, couldn't breathe, "just let me kiss you one more time before you decide."

When he left she was still dizzy, so many rhythms colliding inside her that she had to sit down, get still, and even then she couldn't gather up all the pieces of herself. All she could do was lie back, close her eyes, and try to catch her breath.

The youth choir rose for their final song just as Reverend Dorchester was calling for new members. Tavares walked down from the choir loft and stood next to the organist. Boot, Vonette, Matriece, Uncle Tuney, and Lindell, a light-skinned woman with dyed red hair, smiled. Shalimar slumped back in the pew and closed her eyes. Carla Ramirez sat beside her neighbor. Next to her, Chazz was making eyes at a girl in the row across from his. Two of Tavares's friends were sitting beside each other. Vonette turned toward all the children with a fierce look on her face. "Dushane, be quiet," she said in a stern voice to her son's buddy. The boy stopped talking in mid-sentence. Shalimar slowly sat up; her brother gave his new girlfriend a quick wink, then looked forward as his brother began his solo.

Tavares started pacing back and forth as soon as he started singing.

He sang with his entire body, throwing back his head, opening his arms, pushing his chest out, and then strutting around the contained area. He sang a new song, some hip-hop gospel number Matriece had not heard before. He blew it out, his voice soaring at parts, and then getting soft and tender for others. All around her heads were nodding, and some people were standing and calling out encouragement. "Sing, Tavares," one of his choir mates yelled.

Uncle Tuney elbowed her softly. "Boy's all right," he said with a grin. "The talent must come from Boot's side of the family, because God knows the Clarks cannot sing."

Matriece hadn't seen her mother's favorite brother in months, and it felt good sitting next to him. When she was growing up she had spent a lot of time at his house, and she recalled on more than one occasion that he'd given money to her mother.

"How's your new job?" he whispered.

"It's going fine." Matriece spoke in a hesitant manner. She didn't know whether Vonette had told her uncle that she was working for Gilda. But Tuney's impassive expression revealed that he didn't know who her employer was.

"Vonette tell you Weiss is about to file a class-action suit?"

Matriece shook her head. She recalled that some years before there had been talk of the lawyer going to Inez to take depositions from other black landowners whose property had been lost to the Hagertys. She'd lost track of what had happened.

"Matriece, you need to keep up with this. You're the business-minded one in the family. Anything happen to me, you'd need to see this through. Anyway, there's a lot of families affected. Over five thousand acres are involved."

"In Inez?"

"Some in Inez. Some in other towns in the area. I'm talking about a radius of about three hundred miles. There was oil on some of the land, at least at one time. Most of it's timber and farming land now. Hagertys are still the law down there. A lot of people are afraid of them."

"When is the trial?"

"Not quite sure. Sometime next year." He leaned in closer. "How do you like Lindell?"

"She seems very nice."

Uncle Tuney leaned in closer. "She might be your new auntie." He winked.

Tavares had stepped down into the aisles. Most of the church was on its feet, and Matriece stood up, too, along with Vonette, Boot, and Tuney. The four of them swayed from side to side, clapping their hands and tapping their feet. They put their arms around each other's waists and sang softly along with the boy they all loved, and when the song ended, their amens were the loudest. Tavares did a little jump and began repeating the chorus again.

"Look at him," Vonette said, smiling. She shook her head.

Matriece peered around the church. She hadn't seen Asia or Sam during the entire service, so she didn't expect to see them now that it was ending. But to her surprise, she spotted both of them. They were sitting toward the back, in an area where she hadn't looked before. Sam was in the last row, and Asia was seated two rows ahead of him. Asia wore dark glasses and a hat that dipped low on her forehead. She was leaning forward in her seat, with her finger pressed against her lips. Behind her, Sam was staring intently at the back of Asia's neck, his finger pressed against his lips. Matriece's eyes traveled from one face to the other and then back again. God, they look alike.

Asia took off her hat as soon as she sat down at the table in the restaurant but she kept on her sunglasses. She seemed in no hurry. After they'd ordered and eaten their food, talked about the good old days and discussed the spokesmodel contract, Asia ordered a third glass of water. When Matriece hinted that she needed to leave, Asia launched into yet another conversation.

"I saw one of my fans at your church," Asia said after Matriece paid the check.

"How did you know he was a fan?"

"He comes to all the awards shows."

"What's his name, not that I'd know him," Matriece said.

"I don't know. He sends me cards once a month, and he always puts a one-hundred-dollar bill inside."

"He knows your address?" Matriece asked, feeling alarmed.

"Nah. He sends it to my manager's office. He signs the cards, 'Your Biggest Fan.' "

"So did he speak to you today?"

"I don't think he saw me."

"Be careful, sweetie. There are so many nuts walking around this city."

"He's cool."

Matriece could feel Asia's eyes. She knows I want to leave, she thought.

"So, like I was saying, your nephew can blow. You tell him if he keeps it up I'll hafta take him on the road. Does he really want to be in the business?"

"He says he does."

Asia sighed. "It's not as much fun as it looks like from the outside."

I can see that, Matriece thought. When the waitress passed by she ordered another cup of tea.

CHAPTER THIRTY-SEVEN

KENT HESITATED BEFORE he opened his front door. His intercom service had been turned off several weeks earlier, a cutback measure, and so he had no idea who was waiting for him. "Who's there?" he asked.

"It's me, Daddy."

Jolie. But what on earth was his daughter doing visiting him on a school morning? What could Vanessa be thinking? He opened the door, and there was his little girl, her large hazel eyes filled with tears. She was flanked by two large suitcases.

"Sweetheart, what are you doing here?" Kent said. He heard brakes squealing. Looking over the small figure standing before him, he saw Vanessa backing her Cadillac out of the driveway. Kent ran toward her. "Vanessa. Wait."

Vanessa stopped the car, then rolled down the window just a crack. He heard the locks click down. Every feature in her overly made-up face was twisted into a snarl. "Listen, you son of a bitch, if you don't want to pay me my money, then you can try taking care of your child for a while."

"But, Vanessa—"

"But Vanessa nothing, you lying bastard. You told me that you were going to send me a check last week, and I never got it. Do you think this is some kind of a game, Kent?"

"But, Vanessa, things are tight right now. Can't you just work with me a little bit?"

"If things are tight with you, how the hell do you think they are with me, Kent? I'm doing you a favor. I could call my lawyer and have you put in jail. Maybe if you have to see Jolie every day you'll figure out something. Don't call me until you have my check."

Kent stood watching her with his mouth open. He didn't know how long he would have remained frozen if he hadn't heard his wife's voice.

"Keh, Keh, Wha wro? Wha wro, keh? Why Jo hyeah, Keh? 'Lo swee'ar.' "

That bitch, he thought to himself. Goddamn bitch. Why the hell had he ever taken up with her in the first place?

It was all he could do to keep from saying to Jolie, "Your mother is a goddamn whore." But she was the innocent in all of this. Jolie had to feel bad enough as it was, no use making things worse for her. He knew what it was like to grow up the child of a whore. Fucking bitch! Hadn't he always given her over and above what the courts mandated? The nights she would call up crying about Jolie needing this or Jolie needing that, hadn't he always made sure that she got it? And even before Jolie was in the picture, when he was keeping Vanessa in a little town house in Brentwood, hadn't he signed the damn thing over to her? What about the car he bought her? What about all the jewelry, the trips and the clothes? Fucking good-time bitch. No gratitude. No damn gratitude.

As sick as she was, Peggy was better at comforting the little girl than Kent. As he watched, his wife, who was leaning to one side and limping, put her arm around Jolie and led her inside the house. "Wan som'in ta ea?" she asked.

To his surprise, Jolie seemed to understand her, but then they'd always had a bond. "I ate already," Jolie said quietly.

Peggy looked at Kent. "Tak huh ta schoo, Keh." She smiled at the little girl. "When you come ba we have cookie. Awwight?"

Jolie nodded, and for the first time that morning she smiled.

Kent drove Jolie to her school, which wasn't far from his house. Before he left, he arranged with his wife's nurse to pick her up and baby-sit her until he arrived home. Of course, the nurse wanted a little extra. Whatever happened to doing things out of the goodness of your heart? he thought.

"Daddy, is it okay for me to stay with you and Peggy? You're not mad, are you?" Jolie asked as she was getting out of the car.

"Sweetheart, of course you can stay with us. I'm not mad with you. I'm just upset with your mother because she didn't give me any notice. I've got so much to do this week that I won't be able to spend much time with you."

"That's okay. Peggy and I will have fun. We'll probably bake cookies."

"Honey, Peggy's been very, very sick so she can't do a lot of things that she used to do. You'll have to do quiet things, like maybe watch television or read a book."

"All right. I'll be very, very good." She smiled at him, and Kent could see the anxiety in her eyes.

Poor kid, he thought. Bitch for a mother, and an idiot for a father. Might as well tell the truth. He was a fuck-up. Just like his mother. As soon as he thought of her, Kent saw his mother's face. He clenched his eyes tightly. He wouldn't think about that whore. He had barely let Jolie out and pulled away from the curb before Kent reached into his briefcase, retrieved his bottle of Xanax, and swallowed two pills.

Jesus, I ought to quit taking this stuff. I'll wind up a goddamn junkie. He ran through a list of his habits. Caffeine, nicotine, tranquilizers, blackjack—no doubt about it, he was Vice Man. As he drove to his office he wondered if playing cards could be called an addiction. It wasn't as though he needed to bet on something to get out of bed. It was more that betting made getting out of bed worthwhile. At least he'd stopped womanizing.

As he drove through the quiet streets of Brentwood, Kent could feel the settling effects of the tranquilizer. The medicine was like a friendly tap on his shoulder, a buddy coming to his rescue. Sometimes when the Xanax kicked in he could actually feel someone's finger pressing against his back. At those times he half expected that if he turned around and said, "Who's there?" the answer would be, "Mr. Chill."

Kent drove into the garage under Los Angeles National Bank. When he turned off the ignition, he sat in his car smoking a cigarette, trying to collect his thoughts. *When I walk out of that bank I will have the extension I need.* Thank God that he and Wellington had such good personal chemistry. Wellington had never failed him before. The balloon payment was really his only important obligation. He'd paid off a large enough portion of his gambling debt with the one hundred and seventy-five thousand dollars he'd borrowed from the company. He was through with gambling. Absolutely finished with it. So that made two vices he'd overcome: women and gambling. He was sure the bank would be reasonable. Why shouldn't they be? He'd been a loyal customer, and they'd received the Gilda's Cosmetics accounts because of him. They should be kissing my ass, he thought. That's what they should do.

He went over his plan in his mind, step by step. *I will get the extension. Then I will pay back the company from my salary. I will pay off the balloon payment with my salary.* He didn't relish the tight year ahead, but he'd manage to live through it. Thank God nobody at work suspected.

Kent strode into the reception area and took a seat outside Wellington Barnes's office. He was the banker who'd gotten him the loan in the first place. Wellington had been personally taking care of him for at least fifteen years. Whenever Kent was a little short, Wellington was the man to see. They had an understanding.

But when he was summoned into the familiar office, Kent found not his esteemed confederate but a much younger man, who rose when he entered and extended his hand.

"Oh," Kent said, too shocked to notice the hand until he saw it being withdrawn. "Where's Wellington?"

"Mr. Barnes is no longer with the bank," the young man said. "I'm Darnell Watkins. I'm sure I'll be able to help you." Kent glanced at the pleasant, light brown face.

"Did he go to another branch?"

"No. Are you aware that Los Angeles National Bank has been sold to Sacramento Bank, Mr. Bridgeport? We now have a brand-new management team, new loan officers. This is a new bank, technically speaking," he said, taking his seat.

Somewhere in the recesses of his mind was a memory of reading about the sale of the bank. "Yes, I do recall hearing about that. I guess I didn't realize that Wellington would be gone. I'm Kent Bridgeport." He extended his hand. "And your name again?"

Darnell Watkins didn't extend his hand a second time, nor did he rise. What he did was point to the nameplate at the front of his desk.

Kent realized he'd lost the chance to make a much needed good impression. He felt a bit dazed. Mr. Chill was deserting him, the cool seeping out of him second by second.

"How may I help you, Mr. Bridgeport?"

Kent tried to recover from the shock of discovering that his bank had been sold and that Wellington was gone, but he was still a bit disconcerted. All he could manage to do was stare at Darnell Watkins.

"Yes, well, I'm a bit thrown off. I've been doing business with Wellington for years, and to find out that he's not with the bank anymore without any notice, why, it's rather unsettling. I didn't expect to see you here." Kent was aware that the words he had chosen weren't the best as soon as he spoke them, but just as he was about to clarify his statement his new banker cut him off.

"But I am here, Mr. Bridgeport. Now, I can understand perfectly how you are feeling, but I assure you that I'm fully qualified to help you with any banking problem you might have."

"Yes, of course," Kent said glumly.

"That is, unless you have a problem with me personally, Mr. Bridgeport. Am I the issue?"

"You?" He looked at Darnell Watkins, who suddenly seemed larger, darker, and slightly angrier than he had a moment ago. "Oh. Oh, no. No, no, no." He could see the hostility in Darnell Watkins's eyes subside, and Kent breathed a sigh of relief until he realized that it had been replaced with complete detachment.

"Well then, what can I do for you?"

Very little, as it turned out. The eminently qualified Mr. Watkins couldn't locate Kent's loan documents on his computer for a good fifteen minutes, and when he did he made the most distressing guttural sounds as he perused the screen. At one point he actually looked Kent squarely in his eyes and shook his head. It was almost as if he were a coroner reviewing the body, trying to establish the exact time and cause of a horrific death. Finally, he finished reading, cleared his throat, and said, "Well, Mr. Bridgeport, I see that you owe the bank a great deal of money. How can I assist you?"

"Mr. Watkins, I've been a faithful customer of Los Angeles National for many, many years. My checking account is here. My savings account is here."

Darnell looked over the pages in front of him. "Both of them have had rather low deposits over the last eighteen months. I see that you've been overdrawn ten times."

"Yes, well . . ." Kent cleared his throat. "The point is, and I'm sure that your paperwork will bear this out, over the years I've deposited millions of dollars in this bank. And furthermore, because of my long-standing association with this institution, I persuaded my company—you've heard of Gilda Cosmetics, of course—to put the bulk of their deposits in this bank. We're talking about millions and millions of dollars over the years. So, I realize that I have a balloon payment coming in the future, and—"

"Six weeks."

"Yes. I came here with the, uh, intention of renegotiating my payment plan. I've had some unexpected expenses in the last year. My wife is very ill and requires round-the-clock nursing care."

"Sorry to hear that, Mr. Bridgeport. What kind of renegotiation plan did you have in mind? I see here that the bank has already extended the due date once."

"Yes. That was very helpful. But you see, I need just a bit more time. I'm sure that if you give me another eighteen months—"

"Eighteen months is out of the question, Mr. Bridgeport."

Kent was absolutely still for a moment as the words seeped into his brain. "Please, Mr. Watkins," he said, and he was surprised at how soft and weak, how pitiful his voice sounded. He was also aware of how much his new banker seemed to be enjoying his supplication. "I'm sure you can understand that sometimes things just don't go the way you plan. I'm sure you've had troubles in your life."

Right before his very eyes Darnell Watkins's head swelled up to the size of a basketball. "Is there something about me that would indicate I've known a life of trouble? Perhaps you think I was born in squalor, got my education in the juvenile detention centers of America, and then went on to matriculate at the state penitentiary. Are those the kind of difficulties you're alluding to, Mr. Bridgeport?"

"No. No, of course not." Kent was beginning to yearn for another

Xanax; his chill was long gone. Back to begging. "Please, Mr. Watkins, could you see your way to giving me an extra year? That would mean so much to me. I'd certainly appreciate your kindness."

Mr. Watkins's face was impassive but not cold. He leaned over his desk. "May I call you Kent?"

"Please do."

He stood up. "Kent, why don't you sit right there. I'm going to see what I can do for you."

When the banker was gone Kent let out a long sigh. If only Wellington was still here. He looked down at his hands. They were trembling.

Mr. Watkins came back smiling, but his news didn't lighten Kent's heart one bit. Three months. If he didn't have their money by mid-February, he'd lose his house.

Mr. Chill was doing a cakewalk out the back door. The first thing Kent did when he got into his car was pop a pill. As his head cleared, plan B began to assume hard, sharp edges. *I'll have to borrow from the company again. Write Taper Industries a check.* He'd never borrowed a second time without clearing the ledger of the first debt, but this was an emergency. Mr. Chill was riding with him now. Kent could feel his soothing hand on his shoulder, a father's steady hand.

But how could he come up with an invoice for a million dollars? It was impossible. Maybe he'd be better off putting a bullet in his head; at least that way there would be insurance to take care of Peggy and Jolie. *I could do that. Get really, really drunk and just shoot myself.* But who would take care of Peggy if he was dead? And Jolie was his responsibility now. Kent put another Xanax in his mouth. *There's a way out of this. I just have to find it.*

Kent felt calmer by the time he got to his office. The elevator stopped on the way up, and when the doors opened Matriece got on.

"Matriece, how are you?"

"I'm fine, Kent," she said. "I've been meaning to talk with you. I was going over the financials, and I noticed a debit that wasn't ours. One hundred and seventy-five thousand to Taper Industries."

Kent tried to speak but no words came out for several moments. Finally he said, "Hair care isn't running a tight ship, I see." He averted her glance when she looked at him.

"I assumed that was the problem, so I called Leonard Smiley, and . . ."

Kent began coughing; he could feel his face turning red.

"Are you all right?"

"Fine. Fine," he said quickly. When he looked down his hands were trembling. God, he needed a cigarette. "You . . . you . . . you won't need to trouble yourself," he said quickly. "I'll talk with him."

"Well, I did talk with him, Kent, and he told me that the bill doesn't belong to them. It has his code. I just can't figure out what's going on."

"I'll look into it. You don't have to worry at all. I think they've had some new people in Smiley's department. I'll check into it and let you know." The door of the elevator opened to his floor. As he was leaving, Kent said, "I'll take care of everything. Leave it to me."

Kent stood outside the elevator and didn't move except to press the down button. He needed a cigarette, some nicotine and fresh air to clog his lungs and clear his head. Kent reached into his suit pocket and grabbed his pack.

When the door opened Fontaine got off. "Kent, how's it going?" the young man asked.

The jocularity of the tone, the penetrating good cheer caught Kent off guard. "It's going," he replied tersely, and before he could amend or soften his comment he stepped onto the elevator and the doors closed.

As soon as Kent reached the courtyard he lit up.

"Hi, Kent."

It was Blair, huddled in a corner, looking every bit as morose as he felt. Poor Blair. His heart went out to her only he didn't feel like talking at the moment. Ever since the first time they discussed her husband's infidelity, she'd been treating him like her favorite father confessor. Sometimes he actually did feel as though he were her father, or at least an uncle, which would have been unthinkable even five years ago. *I really must be getting old.* "Hello," he said, rather glumly.

To Kent's enormous relief, Blair fell silent. He stole a quick look at her. She had her eyes closed and seemed to be knee-deep in contemplation. He hoped her husband hadn't left her or that troubled son of hers hadn't stuck up a 7-Eleven. "I'm trying to visualize some adjustments to the new containers. Matriece said they were almost right."

"I've got something on my mind, too," he said.

They sat together in quiet contemplation, sharing and not sharing their space.

CHAPTER THIRTY-EIGHT

THE TABLE IN Gilda's dining room was set for four. When the doorbell rang she was halfway down the stairs by the time her maid opened the door. Listening for her son's voice, she smiled. Daniel is always so prompt, she thought. But when she reached the first floor she was surprised to see Rachel standing in the entrance. "Happy birthday, Mom," she said.

"Oh, it's you. I thought it was your brother. Have you heard from him?"

"No."

Gilda appraised her daughter in one swift glance. So skinny, she thought, feeling a bit dismayed. When her eyes met Rachel's she saw that her daughter's were flashing the kind of warning Gilda had become accustomed to over the years. "You look lovely, darling," she said.

"Here, Mom," Rachel said, handing her a flat, light package.

"Oh, sweetheart. Thank you." She gave Rachel a quick hug. Her daughter's body felt stiff in her arms.

The two women had just seated themselves in the family room when the doorbell rang again. Gilda set Rachel's present on the coffee table next to a bucket filled with ice and a bottle of champagne. She stood up. She didn't notice Rachel's lips pressing together tightly, her eyes appearing suddenly vacant.

"Hi, Mom," Daniel said, swooping up his mother in an exuberant hug. "Happy birthday." She took the small box he extended to her. "Thank you."

"Hello, Gilda," Daniel's Japanese girlfriend said, clutching his hand tightly. Since his divorce several years earlier, Daniel had dated a lot of Asian women.

"Hello, Lauren," Gilda said, trying not to imagine Dana Brotman, his old girlfriend, by his side. "Come on in. Rachel's already here. Do you want some champagne?"

"Why not," Daniel said, leading the way into the family room. He and Lauren greeted Rachel, then sat beside her on a long, curving sofa.

When each one had a glass, Daniel lifted his and said, "Happy birthday to a great mother and businesswoman."

As soon as they toasted, Daniel said, "Open my present, Mom."

Gilda tore off the wrapping, not sure of what to expect but knowing that Daniel's gifts were usually opulent. He was true to form. Gilda gasped when she opened the small jewelry box. Inside diamond-and-ruby earrings glittered. "They're beautiful," she said. She kissed Daniel on his cheek. "Thank you so much."

"You can wear them to the symphony this season."

Gilda nodded.

"Oh, I meant to tell you that I talked with the fellow from FDA," Daniel said. "We may have to come up with a substitute ingredient for the One-Step Manicure. They are going to drag their feet on this approval. Also, I'm not going to be able to speak at the CFT conference this year. Scheduling conflict. I was thinking that maybe Matriece might be able to fill in."

"When is it?"

"Sometime in March. Second thought, that's bad timing for her."

Gilda nodded.

"I'll get somebody else. Listen, Mom, you know Matriece still hasn't nailed down the spokesmodel. Lauren is a music producer. From what she's been telling me the face for Brown Sugar belongs to a young rapper."

Lauren leaned forward. "I'm not an expert in your business, Gilda, but I do know music. Right now Miss Notorious is outselling Asia Pace. Young women totally identify with her. She's got a very new-millennium look."

"I've never heard of her." Gilda had been facing Daniel, who was seated across from her. She turned to include Rachel, who was pouring herself another glass of champagne. "Are you guys hungry? I think the food is ready."

As Gilda stood, Rachel reached over and picked up her present from the table and handed it to her mother. "Oh," Gilda said. She reprimanded herself. How could she have forgotten her daughter's gift?

Beneath the thin wrapping paper was a box. Inside was a letter, very old, written in her native Polish. "What is this?" she asked.

"It's a letter from a Polish Holocaust survivor."

Gilda's fingers froze. Something scraped her heart. "Thank you very much, Rachel," she said, putting the letter on the table. "I'll read it later, dear." Then she smiled to show her daughter that she did appreciate her gift, that she knew it was a rare piece of history, that she would treasure it if she ever was able to touch it again.

But Rachel didn't smile back.

The letter remained on the table all night, and in the morning when Gilda left for the office it was still there. But she might as well have read the thing. The thought of it followed her around. Who was this survivor—a man or a woman? What camp was he or she in? Was it possible their paths had crossed?

At lunchtime, Gilda was taking the elevator down from the eighteenth to the ground floor when it stopped on the fourth. She looked out and saw the sign that said BROWN SUGAR, and without thinking, she got off. Then she marched down the hall toward Matriece's office.

"Gilda, what a nice surprise," Matriece said when she saw her.

"Have you eaten lunch?" Gilda asked.

"No."

"Do you have plans?"

"No."

"Let's go."

Matriece hadn't been to the restaurant before. It was one of Gilda's favorites and she felt the pleasure of sharing it with the younger woman. To her delight, Matriece let her order for her. "Just no red meat," she said. Gilda nodded. She knew all about the food peccadilloes of young women who didn't eat this and didn't eat that.

"You are thin," she admonished Matriece. "A good steak would do you good."

They didn't talk about work. Instead they discussed movies. They were both fans of the same older English actress, and admired the genius of directors like Hitchcock and Jewison.

"Where do you live, my dear?" Gilda asked her.

When Matriece described her neighborhood, she seemed surprised that Gilda was familiar with it. "It's the site of the 1932 Olympic village," she said. "I wasn't in this country at the time, but someone told me."

Gilda listened as Matriece described her niece and two nephews and noted how Matriece's face softened when she spoke of the younger boy, the one with the Spanish-sounding name. "You sound as if you like children," Gilda said. "Do you plan to have a family? Maybe you have a boyfriend?"

"I just broke up with someone but I've gone out with a new man a couple of times."

"Is he nice, the new one?" Gilda asked, a little surprised by the intensity of her interest. She would have loved to have been able to ask Rachel such questions.

"Yes, he's nice."

"But . . ." Gilda said, smiling. "I hear a but. Maybe you still like the old one."

"Maybe I like them both for different reasons."

They giggled and ate dessert. They giggled and lingered over tea and coffee. It felt so effortless, Gilda thought, as they finally got up and began walking back to the office. Such a sweet, smart young woman. Any mother would be proud of her.

She didn't often cross the line between business and friendship. Kent was her only business friend. But after she was seated at her desk again, mulling through the list of things yet to be done, it occurred to her that the lunch had been the brightest spot in her day. A woman her age was entitled to a little pleasure. Who would it hurt if once in a while when she was feeling lonely she went to a restaurant with Matriece? Surely there was no harm in that.

Gilda left the office at four o'clock. It could be spring, she thought, stepping out of her car when the driver parked in front of the Beverly Hills

Jewish Community Center. The air was a bit chilly, but she could still smell the pink roses and white gardenias in the planters outside the new facility. In Poland the days would already be gray, the nights freezing, and snow would be on the ground. Here, Thanksgiving was just around the corner and the city was still blooming. She knew how the Pilgrims had felt, how happy they must have been to be able to say, "Thank you. I have survived."

Only six people showed up at the community center that evening for the monthly meeting of the Holocaust survivors. "The Weepers Club" was Gilda's private name for the organization. In the early days, it seemed that entire meetings were devoted to crying. Even now, people took turns comforting and being comforted, and in that way the many atrocities that they'd suffered became one unifying persecution, one collective nightmare that they had endured and survived. Gradually, their shame turned to pride in their strength, their resiliency, their will to live.

Gilda hadn't been to a meeting in more than a year. There were times when she couldn't bear to be in a room with people who shared the same misery. The last time she'd left, she told herself she would never return, but tonight she felt an overwhelming need to be with other survivors. She greeted Pearl and Lenny Rabinowitz, a couple in their eighties who'd met while they were in Auschwitz. Everyone hugged one another. Two women clung together, rocking back and forth. In their early eighties, they had grown up in the same Hungarian village, were separated by the war, and then rediscovered each other at their first support group meeting. Gilda always watched their ritual with a sense of wonder and sadness. If only she could find the ones she'd lost. But, of course, that was impossible.

As people started chatting and the volume in the small room rose, Gilda looked around, dismayed by the small turnout. She didn't want to ask where everyone was.

"How are you, darling Gilda?" Lenny said to her, taking her hand in his, which trembled a bit. "I said to my Pearl, 'Who is this beautiful young girl among us?'" He chuckled and his laughter sounded paper thin.

"I told him that you'd been in for a tune-up. Seventy thousand miles, maybe?" Pearl gave Gilda a sly wink, and the two women laughed.

"Shhhh," Gilda said, putting her finger to her lips, a twinkle in her eyes. "Don't let it get out. I must protect my image."

"You look gorgeous," Lenny said. "From what I can see of you."

"Stunning," Pearl said, nodding. "I would go myself but Lenny, he likes my old face."

The people in the room seemed so wrinkled and sunken, so beaten down. Gilda felt momentarily ashamed of her beauty and energy, the ambitions that still fueled her. Yet, as different as she was from the sad-faced men and women who gathered in the room, she was as bonded to them as she was to her own skin.

They sat around a small round table in a room that was painted a soothing pale blue. On the walls were posters and pictures of famous Jews: Albert Einstein, Golda Meir, Leonard Bernstein, Bess Myerson, Barbra Streisand, and Steven Spielberg.

Lenny, the oldest, led them in a simple prayer. Afterward they all said the Lord's Prayer in Hebrew. The language sounded like an old song suddenly blaring out of the radio. She hadn't heard Hebrew since the last time she'd been to the center. Each person shared with the group news about his or her life since the October meeting. Gilda tried to keep her updates as simple as those of the other members of the group, taking pains not to mention anything that would make her stand out.

Lenny rose with some difficulty. "Today's theme is depression," he said, then he took his seat.

Pearl immediately monopolized the conversation, declaring that she had cried every day for five years after the war. "I stopped crying when my son was born," she said, her Hungarian accent still clinging to her words even after nearly fifty years spent living in the United States.

Depression was a frequent topic, and by now Gilda was familiar with not only Pearl's story but that of everyone in the group. Still, they each had something to contribute to the discussion. When it was her turn Gilda said, "Last night my daughter presented me with a letter from a Polish Holocaust survivor, and I couldn't bring myself to read it. Just touching it made me feel so empty. I know she meant the gift to be a good thing. I thanked her but I'm sure she could tell from my reaction that I was upset. We're not close, my daughter and I. I've tried to reach out to her. I don't know what the problem is. Why did she give me this letter?"

"These children," said Pearl, "they don't know the impact of something like that."

Several others in the room agreed.

"Have you ever talked with her about your experiences?" Lenny asked.

"Not in detail," Gilda said. "They know I am a survivor. She's never asked me any questions."

"Maybe the letter is her question," he said. While Gilda was pondering his words he said, "We only have a little time left. I thought we might talk about the settlement."

They had all received carefully worded letters from the Swiss bank at the same time, almost three years earlier. The letters described the possibility that they might finally be receiving the money their parents had pirated out of their respective European countries to Switzerland when the first gold stars began to make their appearances in the dank ghettos they'd been forced into. Three years before they had all brought in the questionnaires the bank had sent and filled them out together at the very same table they were sitting at now. As the months went by there were more papers to fill out, more nights of angry mourning. More waiting. But last week they'd all received letters from the First Bank of Switzerland. In March they would receive their checks.

"Reparations," an old man said, almost spitting out the word. Someone cursed softly in angry Polish. What check would pay them for their agony?

"Even the gold from their teeth," Pearl said. "I saw them, pulling out the teeth of the dead."

Gilda had been trying to get back her parents' money on her own since the late fifties, to no avail. Three years before, she had her lawyer fly to Switzerland with a photocopy of the bank book her uncle had unwittingly provided her with when he gave her her father's Talmud; the bank book was pressed between its pages. The deal her lawyer worked out was separate from the one negotiated by the international commission. After he met with bank officials, he returned to Los Angeles with the news that her parents' life savings were now worth millions.

"This will be a very emotional time for all of us, and we must prepare ourselves. The money is a blessing but it is sure to dredge up old memories. There will be a lot of media coverage. We may be approached by newspapers, television. There will be no December meeting, but in January, February, and March we will have our friend Dr. Manheim talk with us about how we can get ready for this new experience," said Lenny.

"What preparation?" one woman asked. "Everything is for my grandchildren."

"My girlfriend and I are going on a cruise to Bermuda."

"Hah! I'm going straight to Saks Fifth Avenue, thank you very much."

Lenny turned to Gilda. Putting a hand on her shoulder, he said, "And you, little one. What are you going to do? Perhaps a donation to charity?"

"I don't know yet," Gilda said quietly. "I haven't decided."

When the money comes, I'll have to talk about the war with Daniel and Rachel. How could she speak to them about her shaved head and all her tortured body had endured? She didn't want their probing questions, their hows and whys and what ifs. She didn't want their pity. She wanted the Holocaust to be a history lesson for them, something they read about, saw on television, in the movies. But sooner or later, her daughter would ask her what had happened to her numbers. When she answered that she'd had them removed, her face or her voice would betray her, and Rachel would know that there was more to tell. Her daughter would pick and pick and pick until she told her not only her experiences in the death camp but also the story of Hosanna. Then her long-ago friend wouldn't be a ghost who stood at her bed but someone who pointed the finger of blame at her and made her look like a thief to her children.

"We must prepare ourselves for our great riches," Lenny said, and then he laughed jovially.

But how, Gilda wondered, does one get ready to bring the dead back to life?

Outside the evening sky had turned dark, and as her car sped along the street, Gilda pressed the button so that the windows came down. The breeze against her face was like cool fingers massaging her. They drove past clothing shops, skin and hair salons, upscale furniture stores and restaurant after restaurant, assailed by the commingling scents of Chinese, Vietnamese, Italian, and French foods that invited anyone with expensive hunger. Smelling the food, Gilda felt a bit hungry herself.

She wanted more than her dinner. Fontaine would be waiting for her at home, along with the seafood pasta her cook had prepared. She smiled to herself. Fontaine reminded her of Tibor, the boy she'd once loved in Poland. There was something about his mannerisms and tone that brought the dead boy to mind. Every time she was with Fontaine, she felt more light pouring into her. It would have to end soon, their little affair. But she didn't think of endings now. Pulsating through her body was a burning anticipation that urged her on. She tapped on her driver's shoulder. "Can you go a little faster?"

Fontaine handed Gilda a glass of wine as soon as she came inside. He was wearing jeans and a T-shirt, his hair wet. "I had a swim," he explained when she touched his hair. "What took you so long?" He kissed her cheek.

"I told you I had a meeting," she said.

He wrapped his arms around her and kissed the back of her neck. "What kind of meeting?"

"For one of my charities. I'm going to change my clothes. Why don't you put on some music. Something soft."

"Like you?"

She smiled at him. So charming. She would miss his charms.

Gilda went upstairs. She showered quickly, brushed her hair, put on perfume and a little lipstick, and then donned a dressing gown, before going back downstairs.

They ate by candlelight in the dining room, chatting about current events and work as Sarah Vaughan sang in the background. "And how is Brown Sugar?"

"Great! Matriece is very excited about the new containers Blair is putting together. I'll be meeting with some fashion designers over the next few weeks. That's just an extra precaution, because the lines for next fall are just about ready to go into the stores."

Gilda nodded. "How is Matriece getting along?"

"Fine," Fontaine said.

"Do most of the people like her?"

"Everybody thinks highly of her, and so do you."

"Of course I do. I hired her."

"If this were a classroom, I'd say she was the teacher's pet."

"No, my dear, you're the teacher's pet."

It was cool enough for a fire. After dinner, Fontaine put a log in the small fireplace in Gilda's bedroom. They sat in bed and watched the flames for a while, and then they began making love. He kissed and stroked her the entire time. Looking at his face, she felt like a young girl again. Tibor. She almost said his name out loud but Fontaine covered her mouth with his. His kiss didn't stop her fantasy. She closed her eyes and she was in Tibor's arms, young and undamaged.

Fontaine always fell asleep first. He made soft snuffling sounds that soothed her. Gilda felt herself drifting off. And then they appeared: her mother, father, brother, grandparents, aunts and uncles, cousins and friends, all crowding around her. They didn't say or do anything, only stared at her with sad, tear-filled eyes. *Speak to me, Mama and Papa.* She heard noise, the others being jostled. She could see the shock in their eyes. It was Hosanna, her face fierce and troubled. The other ghosts began pressing against her, trying to get her to move. She wasn't supposed to be there. But Hosanna stood firm; she pushed back, and they couldn't make her go away.

CHAPTER THIRTY-NINE

VONETTE'S KITCHEN TABLE was filled with legal papers. She read each one as her Uncle Tuney passed it to her, wishing she understood the language better. Matriece should be here, she thought. She'd have all this stuff figured out. When she'd asked her uncle to come over and discuss their case, she hadn't realized that legalese wasn't necessarily English.

"Look," he said, and she could tell he realized that she wasn't comprehending everything clearly, "the important thing is just to know the basics of what's going on, in case something happens to me. Lucille and I are the only ones left. I know you'd make sure she was taken care of, and the rest would be split between you and Triecy and all the cousins."

"Where do you keep all these papers, Uncle Tuney?"

"These are your copies, Vonette. You put them someplace safe."

Vonette gathered the papers up in a sheaf and placed them on the kitchen counter. "So, has Weiss made any progress at all?"

"He's trying. It's just that not all of the families down there are cooperating. Some think they can do better on their own. Some are scared. Weiss tried talking to them, but they wouldn't open up to him. He thought I should go, but I don't know the people anymore."

She gave him a soda and sat down. He took a gulp, then placed the glass on the table. "I'm surprised that Triecy isn't taking a greater interest in this."

"Triecy's really busy, Uncle Tuney. Her job keeps her hopping. You know she's trying to make Mom's dream come true." Her last words came out harsh and flat.

"How's that?"

"She wants to have her own cosmetics firm, fill the shoes Mom left behind. You ask me, she ought to just live her own life."

"What are you so mad about?"

"I'm not mad."

Tuney tilted his head and looked at her. "Vonette, I know that you and Hosanna didn't always get along, but let me tell you something: Your mother was ahead of her time. She pulled us both out of the mud. If it hadn't been for Hosanna, I'd be pushing a broom somewhere. She was the one who got me into the fire department, and when those crackers were peeing in my coffee, she was the one encouraging me to stand firm. I made it to the top because of Hosanna. I know my sister wasn't perfect. She took a lot of hits in her life. That'll change anybody. But I'll tell you this: She wanted the best for me, for her, and I know damn well she wanted the best for her daughters."

"She wanted her best, Uncle Tuney."

"That's all she knew, Vonette. When we came to Los Angeles, we didn't have a pot or a window. All we had was your mother's vision, her drive. I wanted to go somewhere, but she gave me direction. Matriece isn't doing anything she doesn't want to do. Are you satisfied with your own life?"

Vonette looked at her uncle and didn't say a word for a minute or two. "I'm not jealous of my sister, Uncle Tuney. My mother tried to impose her will on both of us. I rebelled; Triecy complied. They were like two little hot dogs in one bun. Selling together, planning together, doing everything together. Mom was training Triecy to take over the business when she was five years old. What choice did she have? And even now, it's like Mom is calling to her from the grave."

"A relationship across the graveyard works both ways."

"What's that supposed to mean?"

"Either party can cut it off."

"Triecy doesn't even know she's being haunted."

"I'm not talking about your sister; I'm talking about you. Quit being mad at Hosanna."

Vonette opened her mouth and then closed it.

"You put those papers someplace safe right away before you lose them." He stood up. "I might be getting married again."

"To Lindell? How many does this make?"

He grinned. "She'd be number seven."

"How about a little premarital counseling?"

He looked genuinely surprised. "I never thought of that. Might give it a try. I got to get out of here. Where's your daddy? Let me say good-bye."

"Daddy?" Vonette called. She heard him stirring in the next room, and when she and her uncle walked into the living room he was sinking his frail body into the sofa. He moved as if everything hurt him. Sitting on the couch, his thin chest shuddered every time he breathed. Her father was a very old seventy-one-year-old; his health was much poorer than he had led her to believe. Emphysema was weakening him, and his joints were swollen with arthritis.

"Daddy, Uncle Tuney's leaving."

"See you, old man," Tuney said, his voice hearty.

"Yeah, Tuney. Good seeing you."

Tuney was on his way out the door when he suddenly stopped and walked back to Lonell. "You wouldn't happen to know some Sharps in Inez, would you?"

"Elijah Sharp?"

"His daughter, Geraldine."

"Sure, I . . . know . . . her. I remember when . . . she . . . was . . . born. Daddy and me built the house she's living in. She took over her father's place when . . . he . . . died."

"Do you know the Littles, the McPhersons, and the Weavers?"

"We built . . . all . . . their . . . houses."

Tuney smiled. "Lonell, how would you like to take a little trip to Texas?"

"You need for me to . . . do . . . something?"

"Yeah, I do. You know I'm trying to get a class-action suit together. The people I mentioned don't want to join. Maybe you can talk to them. I know you've been under the weather," he said, seeing the opposition in Vonette's eyes. "Anyway, think about it. I'm running now. I'll get back to you later."

Almost as soon as her uncle left, Vonette heard her daughter's light footsteps on the stairs. "Hey," she said to her father, "look who's here to see you." She smiled.

Lonell glanced up, and his empty eyes fastened on his granddaughter. His entire face brightened. "Hey, moving star," he said, his voice raspy and weak.

Shalimar giggled. "Hi, Granddaddy," she said. To Vonette's surprise, her daughter kissed the old man on his cheek and sat down beside him.

"You want a sandwich, Daddy?" Vonette asked.

"I want a beer," Lonell said. His laughter sputtered off into a hacking cough.

"You're not getting a beer," Vonette said, grinning.

"I know. I'm not real hungry."

"How about a little vegetable soup?" Vonette asked.

"I'll get it, Mommy," Shalimar said. To Vonette's astonishment, her daughter went into the kitchen and emerged ten minutes later with a steaming bowl of soup and some crackers on a tray. "Here, Granddaddy."

"Thanks, baby," Lonell whispered. "I'ma walk in the movies one day, and see you up there on the screen. Tell my partners: There's my moving star."

Shalimar sat down on the sofa next to her grandfather and watched him eat, while Vonette tried to act as though she wasn't dreaming. To Vonette's utter amazement, for the rest of the afternoon Shalimar stayed close to Lonell, paying rapt attention to the few words he managed to say, offering to bring him whatever he needed. When Chazz and Tavares came in from school bringing friends with them, they, too, seemed fascinated by the ancient ghost of a man who was Vonette's father. As she prepared dinner, Vonette overheard her father's halting words as he told his grandchildren about growing up in Inez. In a little while they were all laughing. He took his medicine right before dinner and, perhaps because of it or the company, as the evening progressed he became more garrulous, even managing to joke a little.

After dinner Vonette dismissed her daughter and her sons and their buddies to do their homework. When they finished one by one, they trooped into the small den where the television was located. They watched a series of sitcoms until the ten o'clock news came on, and Boot made Chazz and Tavares's friends leave, watching them from the front door as they crossed the street to their homes. At the sound of the anchorman's voice, Chazz, Tavares, and Shalimar were about to disappear but Vonette stopped them. "Sit down and listen to the news."

"Put something in your heads," Boot exclaimed.

All three yawned loudly and complained of tiredness, but only Tavares was allowed to go to bed. One of the anchors reported the discovery that a nationally known insurance company, one of the nation's oldest, had sold policies for slaves to slave owners during the eighteenth and nineteenth centuries. "Civil rights leaders have threatened to organize a mass cancellation of policies by African-Americans unless Edson Life commits to creating job opportunities for minorities and women," the newsman said.

"Who ever thought they had life insurance for slaves," Vonette murmured out loud. "Lord have mercy."

"Your mule breaks down you want some cash to get you another one," Boot said in a dry tone.

"Wouldn't . . . even . . . sell . . . life insurance to my . . . daddy," Lonell said. "Just . . . a . . . burial . . . policy. That's the way . . . they'd . . . keep . . . you down."

"Damn, I thought we had it bad," Boot said. "Brown and black need to rise up. Isn't that right, Shally Shally," he said, pinching his daughter's cheek. "Of course, some folks would rather get high, so they don't care nothing about nothing."

Chazz lowered his eyes to avoid seeing his father as he glowered at him.

"You ain't nothing but a daddy's girl," Boot said, after Vonette had gotten her father settled and they were on their way to bed. "Triecy was a mama's girl, and you down for your pops." He shook his head. "You and your sister are like tacos and chitlins."

"Burritos and gumbo."

They both laughed.

"I guess my father was trifling. But he played with me. My mom was always busy, always making some excuses."

"Miss Hosanna was rough," Boot said with a chuckle in his voice. " 'You think I'm raising you so you can end up with some goddamn wetback?' " he said, imitating Hosanna. "I guess she had bigger plans for you, huh?"

Vonette let the question sit. She heard echoes of her uncle's probe in her husband's words. Was she satisfied with her life? "Listen, thanks for letting my dad stay here," she said, sidestepping the issue.

"Hey, *mi casa, su casa*, baby. Not that you'd ever see it that way for any of my family."

"Don't start that. I let two of your brothers live here. Your drunk-ass non-working brothers."

"Okay. Okay. I been talking to Chazz."

"Me too."

"He's trying to get me to end the punishment. Talking about he's twenty years old and he's an adult. Nah."

"Nah. Baby, you laid it down just right. He needs to stick with the program. Let's hope he moves away from Treach and Wolfman."

"Yeah, the boy needs some new friends."

"Don't get me started."

"I want to get you started. Come here, baby."

She felt Boot's arms wrapping around her, her husband's padded belly pressing into hers. Their desire was a brushfire that spread rapidly from limb to limb until their entire bodies were inflamed. "Stay right there," she whispered once he was inside her.

"Like that?" he asked, moving back and forth slowly.

"Yeah, baby."

This was their conflagration. They had been burning up together since high school. Whatever else was wrong with them, they could always set each other on fire. He was her kindling and she was his. Afterward they fell apart, their flames banked, leaving only sparks behind.

The next morning after Boot and her children had left for the day, Vonette was alone with her father. She prepared breakfast for him, and while he ate, she sipped a second cup of coffee and began hanging some pictures. Vonette had made the frames herself, using weathered wood that she'd stained a rustic-looking green. The color blended well with both the deeper and the more muted shades of green that were in the upholstery of her sofa and chairs. From time to time she looked over at her father, who peered at her. She detected a smile on his face. "You was always my . . . handyman . . . girl," he said finally, and they both laughed as they recalled his old pet name for her. "Matriece . . . had . . . her head in books and lipsticks, but you was always the one trailing behind me trying . . . to . . . fix . . . everything." He looked around wistfully. "You got a real pretty house. Looks like . . . something . . . out of a . . . magazine, all jumbled up and colorful. That Boot's all right, too. And the kids is . . . just . . . great. That . . . Shalimar, she's right crazy about me." He laughed.

The telephone rang. "Hey, girl," she said lightly.

Her sister's voice was rigid, and Vonette sensed the kind of tightness that came from anger and pain. "I was thinking about coming by later, and I just wanted to know if he was there yet."

"I picked him up yesterday."

"Well, then I won't come by."

"So, Triecy, you're never coming to my house again?"

"Not as long as he's in it."

"What about Thanksgiving? Triecy . . ." she began but before she could complete her thought, her sister had hung up.

"I guess Triecy's mad with you for . . . taking . . . me . . . in," Lonell said when she was finished with her call.

When Vonette didn't answer he just shook his head.

"Triecy will come around, Dad," Vonette said easily.

He shook his head. "She's her . . . mama's . . . child. The two of them, their grudges run deep. Don't . . . let . . . me being here start a war between y'all."

"Dad," Vonette said, stepping down from the small ladder, "that's not going to happen. We're sisters."

"What's she . . . doing . . . now?"

Vonette gave him a sideways glance.

"I mean work-wise, and . . . man . . . wise. She got somebody?"

"Well, you know Triecy's always been picky, Daddy. And a scaredy-cat. A man gets too close and she runs for cover. She was going out with a nice guy, but I think she dumped him."

Lonell looked amazed. "Don't . . . she . . . want . . . to get married and have some kids?"

"I think she will one day, but first she's got to open up and let somebody in her heart and her mind. I think she's scared of being hurt."

"She's doing pretty good, isn't she? I mean, she . . . can . . . take . . . care of herself."

"Triecy's the president of a new cosmetics division that's owned by Gilda Cosmetics."

Lonell put down the glass of juice he was drinking. "Gilda?"

"You got it."

"I'll be damned. But doesn't . . . she . . . know about . . ."

"Yeah, Dad, Triecy knows who Gilda is. Gilda just doesn't know who Triecy is."

"Wonder what your mother . . . would . . . say." He shook his head. "Triecy working for Gilda."

"She thinks her being there, and maybe letting Gilda know who she is at the right moment, will lead to something bigger. You know she's always wanted to have her own cosmetics firm."

"Just like . . . her . . . mother."

Vonette nodded, then went over to the kitchen table and cleared her father's place, put the dishes in the sink, and ran water over them. "Let's take a walk, Dad," Vonette said after she'd tidied up. "The doctor said you need some exercise, and God knows I do."

Lonell was quiet as they walked. From time to time he would look around him, as though he were trying to get his bearings. Vonette could hear the old man wheezing as they trudged up and down their block.

"I . . . been . . . thinking," Lonell said when they returned to the house. He sat down heavily on a chair in the living room. "Bring . . . me . . . that . . . box . . . of your mama's I gave you."

When Lonell had the box in his hands he took out all the ancient makeup bottles and put them on the table as Vonette watched him. Once the box was empty he lifted up the velvet-covered false bottom and retrieved a yellowed envelope. In the left-hand corner was the name S. Wahlberg, Esq. Lonell carefully opened the envelope, took out a folded piece of paper and an old passbook, and handed them to Vonette.

"What's this?" she asked.

"The . . . paper . . . shows . . . that your mother and Gilda were in business. And the bank book is proof that they . . . had . . . an . . . account . . . together. That's . . . the . . . stolen . . . money."

Vonette scanned the two documents and then handed them back to her father, who carefully inserted them into the envelope. "I don't want to die . . . with . . . her . . . hating . . . me," he said.

"Who? What are you talking about?"

"Matriece."

"Daddy, Triecy doesn't hate you. She just thinks she does. She's just real mad with you. She'll get over it one day."

"I ain't . . . got . . . that . . . long." He looked at his oldest child. "Your mama had a friend . . ." He glanced at his daughter again. "J. P. Mooney. Him . . . and . . . your . . . mama, I guess that's who she shoulda married," Lonell said bitterly. "Anyway, all that's beer . . . on . . . the . . . floor. Take . . . me . . . to . . . see him."

Vonette stared at her father for a moment, too shocked to speak. Finally she said, "You want to see Mooney? What for?"

Lonell shifted a little in his chair. He looked up at Vonette, his face a poker hand. "Him and me got some . . . unfinished . . . business."

CHAPTER FORTY

BY EARLY AFTERNOON on the day before Thanksgiving, most of GC's female employees, and not a few of the males, were chatting about turkeys they hoped would thaw out in time for the big dinner, exchanging recipes for stuffing, and bemoaning the fact that they'd be up cooking all night. Any other Thanksgiving, Matriece would have been among them, her spirits buoyant as she picked up four sweet potato pies from Mooney's, her annual contribution to the holiday feast she normally shared with her sister and her family. But this year she had no lighthearted banter to exchange with coworkers. Matriece had no intention of going to Vonette's house as long as her father was there.

As she sat at her desk trying to review the advertising budget for Brown Sugar, she was fuming inside. That old bastard was just using Vonette. *Nowhere around when we needed him. Soon as his ass is down and out here he comes.* Not that he had to beg Vonette all that much. Down and out was her specialty.

Her eyes began stinging as she blinked back the tears. She missed the kids, of course, Tavares especially. She thought for a moment and realized that she'd never spent a Thanksgiving away from him since he was born. Christmas, either, for that matter. *He'll wonder why I'm not there.*

"You want to go to lunch?" Blair stood in her doorway.

"Sure."

"What's wrong? You look sad."

Matriece hesitated. "I'm boycotting my sister's Thanksgiving dinner because my father is now living with her."

"Gee, sisterwoman, you take cutting off your nose to spite your face to a whole new level," Blair said. Reading the irritation in her friend's eyes, she said quickly. "Here's what I'm saying: A lot of fathers are assholes. This is statistically proven. We children have to rise above them."

"Blair, you don't know—"

"Yeah, I do."

Matriece was surprised to see sadness in Blair's eyes. "Porter—" She stopped abruptly, as though she'd suddenly encountered a door with a DO NOT ENTER sign on it. "I barely had a relationship with my own dad. I mean, he was there physically, if you can call living in the same house and practically never speaking to each other being there. I just thought he was a powerless jerk who drank too much and smelled bad. I didn't even want to be around him. He smacked my mom a couple of times." Blair sighed. "I don't know what Judd will have to say about Porter. Sometimes dads are just people you have to overcome, Matriece. You know, thank them for the sperm and keep moving."

They both laughed. "So, you think I should go to my sister's."

"I can't tell you what to do. All I'm saying is, compare what you'd be missing to what you'd be gaining. Don't hurt yourself just to get back at him."

"I'm not trying to get back at anybody. I just don't want to be around him. My father was envious of my mother," Matriece said.

"Why?"

Matriece looked at Blair for a long moment. "She was successful, and he wasn't. She owned a cosmetics firm; she manufactured and sold her own products, at first door-to-door, then in a lot of beauty salons across the country. She tried to get her stuff into department stores but this was back in the fifties and sixties, and the nice stores weren't selling products specifically for black women. Mom was way ahead of her time."

Blair looked astonished. "Wow, you never told me that before. I thought she sold . . ."

"Blair, don't tell anybody. I'd rather the people here not know, especially here."

"Sure."

The telephone rang, and when Matriece answered it, Gilda was on the line. "I was wondering if you were free for lunch."

Matriece looked at Blair for a moment. "Yes, I am."

Blair understood, Matriece told herself as she rode down in the escalator. When the boss calls, you have to go, first rule of business. If

Blair was a little irritated, if that's what she saw in her eyes, well, she'd get over it.

Matriece pushed her empty plate away from her. Gilda motioned the waiter and ordered coffee for her, and tea for Matriece. When he returned with both, Matriece asked for the check.

"What are you doing?" Gilda said. "I invited you."

"I'd like to treat you this time."

"Absolutely not. You're doing me the favor."

"Well, thank you once again."

Matriece was getting used to spending time with Gilda. Over the last few weeks, the older woman had taken her to lunch three times. At first she was nervous, even a little apprehensive about being with Gilda. She wondered what had spurred the sudden interest. Was Gilda trying to mentor her? Was there something she wanted? Certainly Gilda was appraising her for business reasons, trying to assess her skills, not only as Brown Sugar's president, but in the role she envisioned for her with WMB. But even though a lot of money was riding on Brown Sugar's success, and it made perfect sense for Gilda to want to keep a watchful eye on her, Matriece sensed that the Old Broad Herself had other reasons for wanting her around, personal reasons.

After the waiter had cleared away their dishes, Gilda didn't get up. "Oh, I have something for you," she said, fishing around in her purse. She pulled out a small envelope and handed it to Matriece. "Those are two tickets for the symphony on Friday night. I'm not going to be able to go. Do you like the symphony?"

"Yes, I do. Thank you, Gilda. I appreciate this."

Gilda smiled at her. "So, who will it be? The old boyfriend or the new boyfriend?"

"Eenie meeny . . ."

They both laughed.

"I still think you like the old one better," her boss said slyly.

There was genuine concern in Gilda's eyes. That caring glance was a church fan breeze from a sinner's hand. Matriece thought about turning her face but the air against her cheeks was a blessing.

People were already sneaking away by the time Matriece got back to the office. It was an unwritten company rule that employees could leave early the day before a holiday. Matriece was in no mood to hurry home to an empty house that would probably feel even emptier the next day. Although Blair's words had made an impression on her, she still hadn't changed her mind. As she heard the laughter of her coworkers filling the hallway with their talk about the imminent holiday, a wave of emptiness washed over her. Her own assistant had already left.

Sitting at her desk, Matriece couldn't focus on work. *I'm thirty-eight years old. I've never been married. I don't have any kids. I've run from every man I've ever loved. I spend every holiday at my sister's house so I can borrow her son and pretend he's mine. Every night I go to bed, and the only company I have is my ambition. I'm tired of living this way. Mom, I'm tired.*

How did things turn out like this? I'm the one who had the one hundred Barbies, not Vonette. I'm the one who always wanted to play house and be the mommy. How did she wind up with the family? Why am I all alone?

Matriece felt tears welling up in her eyes. She dabbed at them, but when she began sobbing she didn't try to stop herself.

Matriece rode the elevator to Blair's floor. She caught her friend walking out the door, an unlit cigarette in her hand.

"So, I'm still thinking about Thanksgiving, you know, whether I should go to my sister's, and—" she began.

"Matriece, I have to get out of here. I have a lot to do for tomorrow."

"Oh. Sure."

The movement of Blair's thin body stirred the air and created a chill that Matriece felt as her friend disappeared out the door.

CHAPTER FORTY-ONE

BY THE TIME "The Tonight Show" came on, Matriece had downed two glasses of wine and was working on her third. She and Vonette had been arguing back and forth through three phone calls. After the third shouting match, she sat alone in her dim family room sipping her wine and crying. *Maybe Vonette is right. Maybe I do need help.*

She nearly dozed through Leno's monologue, but Matriece was suddenly alert when she heard Asia announced and the opening bars of her latest hit. She'd seen her perform only in videos, and she was curious about her stage presence and style. The young singer had told Matriece she was a nervous entertainer. "I'm always afraid I won't be any good," is how she'd put it.

Asia looked beautiful. She was wearing gold leather jeans, highheeled thongs, and a sexy halter top. When she appeared on stage, she seemed to shimmer, and the audience, at least the males, responded accordingly. The applause died down only when she began to sing.

It wasn't that Asia sounded bad—her glorious soprano shaped every note and her tone was rich and textured. Hearing her, Matriece was struck again by her talent. So many of the hip-hop divas had more style than actual ability. They sang simpleminded lyrics in shrill not-ready-for-the-Apollo sopranos, letting their cleavage and tattoos do more work than their weak vocal cords. Asia's sex appeal wasn't the only thing in her arsenal.

But she looked so sad, so joyless. As beautiful as her singing was, she seemed so dispirited, and yet there was something so mesmerizing about the child that Matriece couldn't turn away. She was pain set to music. *She's not having any fun.* "Come on, sweetie," Matriece said aloud to the image on-screen, "enjoy yourself."

Asia had always seemed fragile to her. She recalled the little girl whose feelings were easily hurt, who cried for no apparent reason. What had struck Matriece immediately when they'd met for breakfast was that she could still see that old sadness staining the girl's face like a birthmark. And now here it was on display for all the world to see.

The audience screamed and cheered when the song ended. Maybe they thought Asia was being cool. Hell, maybe she was deliberately appearing detached and depressed. The male rappers wore uniformly hardened expressions on their unsmiling faces; maybe sadness was the new girl-singer attitude.

Leno didn't invite Asia to sit down and chat after her song, a sign that, two Grammys notwithstanding, Asia was still a star-on-the-rise. But it was just as well that Asia did retreat behind the curtain after the applause died down. From the look on her face she might have burst into tears.

The telephone rang just as soon as a commercial came on.

"Hey, Auntie Triecy, hook me up." Tavares was excited, his voice teetering between bass and soprano in one sentence.

She laughed. "Asia is too old for you, boy."

"Nah. Nah. Don't say that. This is a new day. White-collar woman, blue-collar man. Older woman, younger man."

"Man, Tavares. Not boy."

"That's cold, Triecy. She needs me. You saw how sad she was looking. Some brother has done her wrong, and I'll treat her right. Give her a ring and everything. I'll watch the kids; she can make the money. Then when I get my contract, she can chill. New millennium. How's that sound?"

"She did look sad, didn't she?"

"I told you: she's looking for the right man. Me."

"So, what do you want, an introduction?"

"As soon as possible. And don't tell her my age. We'll work all that out later. Auntie Triecy, you're coming to dinner tomorrow, aren't you?"

She should have expected the question but it caught her off guard. "I don't know, sweetie. Probably not."

"You don't like Granddaddy?"

"It's complicated, Tavares."

WHAT YOU OWE ME 363

"Yeah, yeah, yeah. Sometimes my dad gets on my nerves, but I'm not trying to boycott Thanksgiving dinner. You ought to come. Granddaddy can sit at one end of the table and you can sit at the other. You won't even know he's there."

"Tavares . . ."

"Please, Auntie Triecy."

"I'll think about it."

"Awww, Auntie Triecy, don't think about it. Just come."

Matriece drifted in and out of sleep that night. Each time she awoke she heard Blair and Tavares, their well-reasoned words urging her to set aside her grudge. Matriece got up early the next morning. She took the four sweet potato pies she'd picked up from Mooney's the night before to her sister's house and left them on the back porch. She called Vonette from the car, informing her where she could find the dessert. Then she went to the video store and rented eight movies. It was when she was on her way home to a day and night of marathon film watching from her bed that Matriece caught sight of herself in her rearview mirror. The face she saw was as sad as Asia's. *It's me. I'm the problem.* She couldn't deny the truth.

There was genuine pleasure in Sam's voice when he accepted Matriece's invitation to the symphony, and that Friday night he seemed completely comfortable listening to Rachmaninoff. At one point, he whispered to Matriece, "God is good. I like this. Thank you for inviting me." Later, when they were in the lobby during intermission, he said, "That music is very exciting. It kind of wakes me up."

He spoke in such an innocent, unpretentious way that Matriece could only smile.

"What? I say something funny?"

"No, something sweet," she said. When he gave her a quizzical look, she said, "A lot of people who do things, anything, for the first time might try to cover up the fact that they're new to it. I just think it's great that you discovered something and you're open enough to enjoy it and honest enough to admit that it's a new experience."

"Listen, I spent fourteen years being locked up. Now, how am I supposed to pretend that I heard a lot of Rachmaninoff? All I heard in the joint was a whole lot of cussing. And it wasn't set to music. Anytime I can discover a new good thing I'm happy. I'm happy with this music, and I'm happy with you, Matriece."

He gave her arm a squeeze, and at that same moment she heard a familiar voice.

"Matriece, how are you?"

Her nervousness was unexpected. The weakness in her knees, the tension she felt from the pit of her stomach, caught her off guard. She wasn't used to being unable to look Montgomery in the eye, but something made her avert hers. She stammered out an introduction and felt a headache coming on as Sam and Montgomery exchanged greetings. Then Gretel appeared, and looking at her, Matriece felt her stomach lurch so that she had to excuse herself. She barely made it to the ladies' room before she threw up.

She and Sam were quiet as he drove her home. Matriece knew she ought to invite him in but she wanted to be alone. And yet she didn't. She was trying to make up her mind when Sam said quietly, "I'd like to come in for a little while."

Sam offered to make tea, and she let him, as she went upstairs to brush her teeth and gargle. When she came back downstairs and sat on the couch, she was grateful that the room wasn't circling around her anymore. Everything was in focus.

"You got sick back at the theater, didn't you?" Sam asked.

Matriece nodded. "Sorry."

"Nothing to be sorry about. You got sick. What I want to know is why seeing that guy and that woman made you sick. If you want to tell me."

Matriece didn't say anything.

"Did he used to be your man?"

She nodded. "Uh-huh."

"How long ago did you break up?"

"The morning of the day you took me to brunch."

Sam sat down next to her on the sofa and began sipping his tea. "Look, I know a woman like you can have any man you want."

"It's over, Sam. Really. Montgomery didn't make me throw up. I've had a lot on my mind recently. Some family problems. My father's been out of my life for years and recently he moved in with my sister. He never did a thing for either of us. That's got me upset. I usually have Thanksgiving dinner at her house, but I didn't go because I didn't want to see him. I guess I'm wondering if I did the right thing. In fact, I know I did the wrong thing and I'm feeling really sorry about that. My sister has three kids, and the youngest, Tavares, is, well, he's my heart. He asked me to come, and I didn't want to disappoint him. But I did. I wish I didn't hate my father. I'm really tired of hating him. But I can't stop. I feel bad that Tavares knows that I'm carrying around all these messed-up feelings inside me. I don't want him to know that about me. I took care of him when he was a baby. Don't get me wrong, I love the other ones, too. It's just that . . ."

"He's your favorite."

"It sounds terrible for me to have a favorite."

Sam shrugged. "That's human. You love who you love. Listen, I can understand your feelings. Believe me I can. Your dad wasn't there for you. Maybe he wanted to be but he wasn't. And now here he is all late, wanting what he hasn't earned. You and your sister are real different, aren't you?"

"If she loves you, she'll forgive you for anything. I hold grudges."

"As long as you're not into slashing tires."

Matriece laughed. "I'm not violent."

Sam put both hands on her shoulders. Then he kissed her. Matriece kissed him back, moving into him as if he were pulling her closer with a rope. She changed her mind as soon as she realized how much she was enjoying the kiss, and gave him a little push. "Let's not go too fast," she said. Sam stood up immediately.

"I enjoyed myself a lot tonight. Thanks for inviting me."

"I'm glad you had a good time."

When he reached the door, he took her hand in his. "God is blessing you, Matriece. Don't forget that."

Matriece's temples were still throbbing the next morning as Marlene eased her head onto the U-shaped ledge of the shampoo bowl. The hairstylist's rhythmic fingers soothed her tingling scalp. Around her the air thrummed with the Saturday morning sounds of a slowly waking enterprise. The speakers drenched the small salon with easy-listening jazz and pop. At seven, some of the stylists were just getting in, bringing their breakfasts with them, and the odor of scrambled eggs and McMuffins wafted throughout the space. Matriece let herself be lulled into a light doze until she heard Marlene talking with one of the stylists.

"Girl," she said in a conspiratorial whisper, "Ruth told me she ran into her children's daddy on the street. Hadn't seen him in years. Turns out he's living right in Inglewood."

"That the one was in jail?"

"Uh-huh."

"Asia's daddy?"

"Uh-huh. What you popping up for?" she said to Matriece. "Put your head back down."

"Are you talking about the singer?" Matriece asked quietly, her voice trembling.

"Yep," Marlene said easily. "Ruth is scared to death he's going to try to get some money outta Asia. You know she don't want that."

The two women laughed. The other stylist said in a low voice, "She ain't about to split that meal ticket."

"You blame her? She raised both those kids all by herself." Marlene's head bobbed up and down in agreement. "Sam might as well keep on stepping."

Matriece managed to sit still long enough for Marlene to blow-dry and curl her hair, but as soon as she was finished, she fled the shop, scarcely saying good-bye. Before she'd even started her car Matriece was on the telephone, paging Sam. Saturday was his busiest day. By the time she got home, she'd paged him three times. She was drinking her second cup of tea when he called back. "I need to see you," she said when she heard his voice.

Sam didn't arrive until after six o'clock that evening. "You'll have to excuse my work clothes," he said when she opened the door. He followed her into her family room and sat down on the sofa next to her.

"Why didn't you tell me that you are Asia Pace's father?"

He slumped back against the couch, then let out a long sigh. "How did you find out?" His voice sounded strangely detached, almost emotionless.

"I overheard my hairstylist talking. Ruth and I go to the same woman."

Sam sat up, then faced Matriece. "Yes, I'm Asia and Donny's father."

"You wanted to use me to get to her so you can get money from her."

"No, I don't want anything from her," Sam said. "I just want to be in her life again. I've been writing and visiting my son, too. He's in jail. I don't want money from my children. I just want to be in their lives. And yes, I was hoping that you'd help me get in touch with her. Because I knew if I just showed up on my own she'd probably think exactly what you're thinking, what I know Ruth thinks: that I'm about the money."

Matriece stared at him, not sure what to say. "When did you start trying to get back in touch with your kids?"

"Just the last two years."

"But you've been out of jail longer than that."

"Matriece, I wanted to get something going for myself. I didn't want to come to them with nothing. You're not a man, so maybe you don't know how that feels."

"No, I'm not a man. And I'm not a father who wasn't there for his children."

"But you know about that, don't you? You know about it from the other end. The way you feel about your dad, that's exactly the way I don't want my kids to feel about me. If your father had come back to you with something to give you besides an apology, I guarantee you you'd feel differently."

"Don't say that. It's not about the money."

"Isn't it? That's what being daddy is all about. You told me last night that he didn't do anything for you or your sister. I'm guilty of that, too. I'm trying to make it up to them. I have a home for my son when he gets out of jail. I've been sending Asia money for the last two years. It ain't much, just a hundred dollars a month, and she doesn't even know it's from me. But I know it. It feels good paying back some of what I owe her. It will never be enough, but at least I'm trying."

"She told me about you. You send her cards."

"Yeah." He looked pleased.

"Sam, maybe everything you're saying is true. I don't know. You were using me."

"All right, I was. But that doesn't mean I didn't like you. I liked you before I knew you were hooked up with Asia. You know that. And you liked me, too. All right, I was using you but you were using me, too. I'm your rebound man. Isn't that right?"

She found her voice after a few moments. "Yeah."

"Help me, Matriece. Please help me get back in my daughter's life."

This big house, Matriece thought as she climbed the stairs after Sam left. What do I need with this much house? As she sat in warm water and bubbles, she saw her sister's cramped little home, every inch of space inhabited. There were never any empty rooms at Vonette's. People lived all over. The boys were now doubled up to accommodate Lonell. And it's okay with her, Matriece thought. And with them. It's enough. *If I had to go there she'd take me in, too.*

As she soaked, her mind drifted back to Thanksgiving. She knew what she had missed. Vonette's holiday table was always loaded with everything anyone would expect for a traditional Thanksgiving dinner, plus a touch of Mexico—tamales for an entrée, flan for dessert. But it wasn't the food she longed for. Something else: the entire family crowded around the too small dining room table; chairs added as more and more people came by to have a beer, share some dessert, digest their own dinners in front of Vonette and Boot's television; her sister's elaborate papier-mâché turkeys and horns of plenty, hanging from the walls; Tavares, Shalimar, and Chazz being silly. The day had passed, but her yearning hadn't stopped. Why didn't I go? she asked herself. *I can't keep missing out. I'm not going to let my father separate me from my family.*

She didn't know how long she'd been lying in bed. Were her eyes open or closed? Was she asleep or awake? She couldn't pinch her skin; her fingers wouldn't cooperate. But she was speaking, she knew that much. She could hear her own voice, echoing in her mind: *I should be having my own Thanksgiving dinners with my own family all around me. I should have a man and some babies and live in a house that's filled with something besides the sound of computer keys clicking in the night. But I'm too busy working and running away from people I should be running toward. And I don't know why I can't meet them halfway. I'm tired of working all the time and hating my father. I don't want another new boyfriend.*

She remembered the time she and her mother drove from Los Angeles to Texas, taking orders in every little town that had a black hair salon. Vonette stayed behind with Uncle Tuney and his wife of the moment, but she wanted to ride the highways with only the radio and her mommy for company. "It's going to be fun," her mom told her. Only it wasn't. She remembered being carsick and feeling tired of talking to strangers and eating fast food too fast. She missed Vonette and she wanted to go home. But her mother wouldn't go back until she'd made her quota. "You have to work twice as hard as white folks to get half as far," Hosanna told her. "You hear me, Triecy?"

"I hear you, Mommy."

Hosanna spilled out of the memory, appearing in front of Matriece just as though she'd been called. She looked old and worried, her forehead pleated, her eyes imploring, as she stood back and appraised her daughter. *She doesn't care about what I want,* Matriece thought. *She just wants to hold on to me until I get her what she wants.* Her mother was a thin wisp of smoke hovering around her, then fading. Did she think the words or say them? Could Hosanna hear? *Let go of me, please.*

CHAPTER FORTY-TWO

FROM THE MOMENT Matriece told Kent that she'd spoken with Leonard Smiley about Taper Industries, panic began filling every cell of his body. He never expected that she'd contact Smiley herself. Gilda Cosmetics was so large. She'd met Smiley only once, to his knowledge. He was counting on Matriece not wanting to speak to him about an embarrassing matter like his division's slipshod accounting. How could he have been so stupid not to consider that she'd just pick up the phone and call the man? Now Matriece and Smiley were both suspicious. He had to think. There was always a way out. He just had to find it.

He shook out two Xanax from the bottle and swallowed them as he walked to his car. He stood in the middle of the parking lot, waiting. *Mr. Chill, Mr. Chill, where are you?* A rush of coolness circled his temples. He felt his mother's fingers rubbing softly. She used to massage his scalp when he was ill. Her touch both soothed and revolted him. His entire life, he'd been running both toward and away from that touch. Why had everything gone so wrong?

Sliding into the driver's seat, he tried to think logically. The money was already gone; he'd used it to pay off his gambling debts. There was no telling what Matriece had said to Smiley. Suppose she told him that the same thing had happened before? If he went back to Matriece, simply reported that he'd taken care of everything, would that be the end of it? If he told Smiley that Matriece had made a mistake, would the man take it any further? That's the only thing he could do, other than put the money back. And he didn't have the money.

Kent thought back to his last disastrous blackjack game. He would have won more than one hundred seventy-five thousand dollars if he hadn't asked for that last hit. He'd envisioned an ace, but he'd pulled a three. So, instead of twenty-one he got twenty-three. Busted. And now he was busted again.

He'd had good nights when the cards he picked were ruby red slippers clicking heels that took him home. Sitting in the middle of Wilshire Boulevard traffic, he remembered games when his pockets bulged and the rush never stopped. The rush was what it was all about, that moment when the slap of the cards and the adrenaline surging through his body were one and the same rhythm. He imagined a hand full of aces and tens. *I could do it again. I could win the money. There's got to be a game somewhere, a big game with big stakes. I could get hot and make everything okay.*

Luck be a lady.

The traffic ahead of him began to flow. Christmas decorations were already up on Wilshire in Beverly Hills. Elaborately lit evergreens were attached to telephone poles. Rows of electric stars hung across the street every twenty feet or so. Saks, Neiman Marcus, Barney's—all the expensive stores were festive showcases that beguiled would-be customers into buying more than they needed. Kent barely glanced at the shops and lights; he was too engrossed in his thoughts. As he drove faster, he became more convinced that he could make everything right. Just a phone call and he'd know where to find the action. Just this last time and never again.

Peggy's nurse was pacing the floor by the time Kent got home, a little later than her six-o'clock cutoff time. He was supposed to pay her ten dollars extra for every thirty minutes he was late, but Kent didn't have ten extra dollars. He reasoned that he was already paying out the nose for her to pick up Jolie.

"Daddy! Daddy!" As soon as he got in the door, Jolie was leaping around him like a puppy. He gave her a little pat on the head. He just couldn't get used to so much noise and activity when he came home. In the old days, Peggy would meet him at the door with a kiss and a drink. They'd sit on the sunporch together in silence while he went over the mail. That was only a fond memory.

"Not so loud, honey," he said quietly. It was funny how he couldn't get used to having Jolie around all the time. It was still a surprise to open the door and see her. Jeez, what a talker. And so full of energy. Well, he was full of energy, too. He needed to get to a phone. "Where's Peggy?"

Jolie grabbed his hand and dragged him into the family room, where his wife was sitting on the couch. Next to her was one of Jolie's school books; it was open. "I was reading to her. Do you want to hear me read, Daddy?"

Of course he didn't. Kent wanted to make his phone call. Just one connection and everything would be all right. His name was still good. He might have been slow to pay once or twice. Might even owe a little money, but he could still get a game. He bent down and kissed Peggy on her forehead. In return she made a soft grunt of pleasure, managing to smile at him as well. "Hewo, honey," she said softly.

"Daddy! Daddy! Listen to me read!"

He felt her small hands tugging his fingers. Kent sat down next to Peggy and listened as Jolie read from a story about magic rabbits.

"Are you listening?"

"Of course, sweetheart." I have to call soon, he thought. The game would be getting started in an hour or two. He had to get in on the beginning.

He looked in Peggy's direction. His wife smiled at him and shook her head a little. Poor Peggy, he thought. Any other woman would have left him a long time ago. Here she was taking care of his mistress's child and loving every minute of it.

"Daddy," Jolie asked suddenly, as soon as she finished reading, "when is my mommy coming to get me?"

"Oh," he said. He looked at Peggy helplessly.

"Shh com soo, Jol." Peggy reached out and hugged the little girl, who began crying.

"I want my mommy."

That bitch Vanessa, Kent thought. How could any mother walk out on her kid? He must have been crazy to get involved with a woman like her. Jesus, what the hell was he thinking about?

While Peggy comforted his daughter, Kent went into the kitchen. For an additional fifty bucks a week the nurse agreed to cook dinner and set the table. Not that the woman was any Julia Child. He looked into the pots on the stove. Some sort of stew was in one. The broccoli he recognized, although it looked a bit watery. It didn't matter. He wasn't hungry.

Kent picked up the telephone and began dialing. "Hey, Jimmy. It's Kent. How are you doing?"

"Okay."

A bit short, Kent thought. "So, Jimmy, what's going on tonight? Any action?"

"I thought you weren't playing anymore. Just the other day I was asking Ed about you, and he said that you were permanently out. He also said you still had red ink on the book."

"There's just a little bit left. No biggie. So, anyway, where's it happening tonight?"

There was a long pause on the other end of the telephone.

"Jimmy?" Kent said.

"Let me get back to you."

What did that mean? Kent wondered after he'd hung up the phone. Did Jimmy have to get permission to include him in a little game?

"Keh."

He turned around and Peggy was standing in the doorway. "Who talkin to, Keh?"

"No one, sweetheart. Ready for another scrumptious gourmet meal?"

She didn't answer him, just kept staring. "Who talkin to, Keh?" she didn't take her eyes off his. The stroke may have damaged her speech and mobility, but it hadn't done anything to her uncanny ability to discern exactly when he was lying.

"No one, really."

The telephone rang. Neither one moved. Finally Kent answered. He was conscious of his wife's eyes on him. "Hello," he said, turning his back on Peggy and speaking as quietly as he could.

"It's Jimmy."

"Yeah."

"There is a game. Very, very high-end. We're working in units of twenty-five. Can you handle that?"

Twenty-five thousand! Where could he get that kind of money? Had he paid his American Express? Could he do a cash advance? "Sure. Sure. You tell me when and where."

"Starts in one hour. Hotel Nikko. Suite nineteen thirty. The name is Rollo Josephson. Got that?"

"Got it."

"Okay, see you there."

He heard her shuffling toward him before he could hang up the telephone. "Who?" her voice was loud, hard, and tinged with old anger.

"Honey, I told you—"

"No cards, Keh. No gambo."

"Peggy, what on earth are you talking about? I have no intention of gambling. I told you I gave all of that up. I haven't played blackjack in . . ."

If he looked just at his wife's eyes, she seemed completely well. Her eyes radiated strength and a resolve that he found unnerving.

"No goin, Keh."

"Peggy, I have to go out to a, uh, meeting. I won't be—"

"*No!*" her voice was a roar. He felt her fists swiping across his chest. "*No!*"

He let her hit him and held her when she fell against him. She sobbed into his chest.

"Why is Peggy crying?" Jolie was by his side. She put her arm around Peggy's waist and began patting her.

"She's a little upset," Kent said. He looked at his watch. There wasn't much time. The game was going to start soon. In his head he heard the cards slapping down hard. He could feel them in his hands.

"Peggy, are you hungry?" Jolie asked.

"Yes."

"Daddy, let's eat dinner now."

He felt her small hand in his. Then Peggy raised her head, reached down, and took the other hand. The three of them stood in the middle of the kitchen; he could feel the luck flowing out of him, the sound of the cards diminishing in his mind, and he knew that his winning streak was over.

Sam arrived early on the second Thursday in December. Kent watched him for a few moments from his living-room window. The younger man's movements seemed labored, as though hidden in his chamois was a heavy weight. Kent knew the feeling. "Good morning," he called from the front door.

"Hey, Kent. How's it going?" Sam said.

Kent walked over to him, stopping when he was a few feet from Sam. "It's going."

"That doesn't sound good," Sam said as he buffed the hood of Kent's Mercedes.

Kent shrugged. "How about you?"

"I lost my woman."

"I didn't know you had one."

"Yeah. Well, I almost did. She was a good one, too."

"Sorry to hear that." He didn't speak for a moment, and then he said, "Did she find out that you were in jail?"

"Nah. I told her about that from the get-go. It was something else. An omission on my part."

"I see. Maybe she'll get over it. You thought about sending her some flowers?"

Sam looked up at Kent, and his hands were still. "No, man. I never thought about that. Where I come from, an apology is always too little too late. Nobody wants to hear it."

"Try it."

Sam stared into space. "Yeah, I guess I will." He resumed his polishing. "How's your wife doing?"

"She's improving. I've got a speech and a physical therapist coming in several times a week. She's moving better. Her words are still slurred."

"Healing takes time. The body has to gear up for going in another direction. That's a lot of energy."

"Lot of money, too," Kent said.

"Yeah. How's that going?"

"I may go under, Sam."

"Can't be that bad, Kent."

"I could end up in jail." He looked at Sam quickly, remembering that he had referred him to Matriece, who used his services every week. What an idiot he was! Kent stared at the ground.

"Hey, man. I don't talk. My mouth is the grave, so don't even trip." He extended his hand to Kent, who took it. "Word is bond, man. Listen, I don't know if this will help, but there's a place called Hollywood Loan. It's a pawnshop. When things get tight, that's the place to go. Not just me, either, a whole bunch of people go there. I've seen stars coming in and out of that place. It's on the corner of Rossmore and Santa Monica. Guy's name is Latimore. He'll give you a good deal on diamonds or gold. Maybe you have some jewelry or something. No use just letting it sit."

"Peggy has tons of rings and bracelets." He could pawn those and get into a game tonight!

"There you go."

"But maybe I'd be better off with a licensed jeweler." His excitement was growing.

"Whatever. Just look around. You must have a lot of things you can part with: art, jewelry, cars."

"Yes."

"You know, God is good. And he's good all the time. He's got tender mercy for us all."

Kent cleared his throat, took a cigarette from his pocket, and lit it.

It wasn't until later that night that Kent had the time to take a mental inventory of his possessions. He and Peggy had never been big art collectors; the pieces they owned were mostly prints. The several oils weren't by anyone famous and wouldn't be worth much. But he'd always given Peggy beautiful jewelry for her birthday and on their anniversaries. He went upstairs into the small room opposite their walk-in closet, which served as storage space for odds and ends. Kent walked over to the far wall opposite the door, removed a large picture hanging there, and opened the safe that was behind it, using the combination lock. He took out a large velvet box, placed it on a small table, and lifted the lid. Inside were five diamond rings, each no smaller than two carats. There were several diamond bracelets and necklaces. He'd given these gifts to Peggy over a period of more than thirty years. To sell them would be like robbing her.

Kent put the jewelry back inside the velvet box and closed it before he changed his mind. He felt around inside the safe. Months earlier he'd cashed in the bonds he and Peggy had acquired over the years. There was little chance that he'd overlooked any, but just the same Kent took another look. One glance told him it was empty except for a few envelopes that contained his insurance policy, the deed to his house, and a copy of his trust. He'd looked inside these envelopes before, but he went through them again, hoping against hope that he'd find something, anything that could turn into money. But there was nothing. He opened the red velvet box again and stared at the glittering heap of jewels. He saw a bit of pale yellow peeking out from the bottom. He felt underneath.

He remembered the paper as soon as he saw it. More than forty years old, but it was still intact, the typewritten lettering still legible, the signatures still clear: Gilda Rosenstein and Hosanna Clark. The thin piece of paper was the contract establishing their business partnership. Kent had found the contract among David's things after he and Gilda divorced. He didn't know what instinct had made him keep what appeared to be a worthless piece of paper for a defunct company. It was much later that Gilda told him the story of what had happened to her partnership and friendship with Hosanna Clark. Later still, she enlisted his help to try to find the black woman, a search that turned up naught. "I owe her so much," Gilda had told him.

How much? He wondered that night as he lay next to Peggy. How much did Gilda owe her? It was past midnight, and he'd been in bed for an hour. We all have skeletons, he thought. Open any closet door, and they are in there, rattling around, always ready to emerge, to pounce. Some people, he thought, will pay good money to keep the skeletons locked up.

He acknowledged that his thoughts were evil, but he couldn't keep them at bay, not with darkness all around him, not with his feet on the edge of the precipice. He was out of bed before he could stop himself. There was only one cigarette in the pack he carried with him to his backyard. He inhaled slowly, and with each exhalation his resolve was strengthened. Yes, Gilda had been good to him. Yes, he owed her everything. But he owed his family more. If it weren't for him, Gilda would have nothing. *I can't go under.* He thought about approaching Gilda, writing her an anonymous letter, offering to sell her the last link she had to the dead black woman she'd wronged. But when he sat down at his computer, he couldn't make his fingers move. There had to be another way.

His cigarette had long gone out and the night air was beginning to give him a chill, when it occurred to him that there was another person who'd be interested in the paper he possessed. He wouldn't have to blackmail Gilda directly. His hands wouldn't be clean, but at least they wouldn't be bloody.

It took three chill pills to put him to sleep, and he still woke up early feeling uneasy and guilty. If Gilda ever found out what he was doing . . . He couldn't think about that now. As he drove to work that morning he focused on two unassailable truths: He had something to sell and he had a potential buyer.

When Kent reached his office he immediately sat down at his desk and opened his Palm Pilot. He kept scanning his list of names until his eyes settled on one that filled him with excitement, hope, and the pleasure that came only when he knew he was about to enter into a game in which he would risk everything.

Calvin Meeks. Of course. Brown Sugar had the potential of wiping Radiance Cosmetics off the map. If anybody wanted what he was selling, it would be the principal of the foremost black-owned cosmetics firm in the country. He'd met the man before. He was a sharp dresser and a loud talker, had one of those hail-fellow-well-met attitudes.

He found the number for Radiance Cosmetics and dialed it himself. "I'd like to speak with Mr. Calvin Meeks, please. This is Kent Bridgeport of Gilda Cosmetics." He put a pencil in his mouth and held it between the peace sign his two fingers made. When he heard the deep, southern voice, he let out his breath. "Mr. Meeks, this is Kent Bridgeport from Gilda Cosmetics. I'd like to meet with you. I have an offer that I think you'll find exciting."

It had been years since Kent had been on Crenshaw Boulevard. Back then, the area had been a haven for well-heeled professionals, and the only black people to be seen were maids and gardeners. Things had changed, of course. The once stately Crenshaw had become a broad street crammed full of mom-and-pops and fast-food stores. There were still some whites on the street, but most of the people were blacks and Latinos. Everyone seemed to be rushing in and out of the behemoth of a mall that took up an entire block. There was an aura of prosperity that hovered about the place. To be sure, it didn't have the glitzy wealth of any of the streets and avenues that bisected Beverly Hills, but then neither Rodeo nor Canon drive had the rhythm that set the wheels of commerce in motion that Crenshaw boasted. From every open car window, every doorway ajar came the joyful noises of guitars and drums, basses and saxophones, the blended harmonies a backdrop for the business of the day. *Boom de boom boom!* As he turned into the parking lot of Radiance Cosmetics, Kent felt himself momentarily uplifted by the sounds—the horns, the strings, the percussion instruments spurred him on, their rhythms infused him with the spirit of commerce. He felt his purpose magnified, his resolve strengthened. *Boom de boom boom!* Forward!

Calvin Meeks's glance was more penetrating than any Kent had experienced. His small dark eyes seemed able to see through flesh; they disrobed and flayed him. Sitting across from him, Kent tried to regain the composure he'd begun steadily losing the moment he shook the dark man's hand. He hadn't counted on being nervous, but as the two men wandered through a maze of small talk, Kent wondered if he would ever be able to find his way home.

I can't do this, he thought. Everything was wrong. The way Calvin Meeks looked at him, as though he knew exactly what Kent was thinking. But he couldn't not do it. He'd thought that marching into Calvin Meeks's office and demanding money would be exhilarating, that he would feel the same excitement he got when he sat down at a game and called for one more card. He expected his adrenaline would be pumping and he'd feel big and important. But he felt sicker and sicker as he looked into Calvin Meeks's inscrutable face. He had the same sinking feeling he always had when he overplayed his hand. Only, he couldn't throw in his cards.

God he needed a Xanax.

Your mother is a whore. The refrain came from nowhere, like some ancient radio jingle he didn't even know he'd memorized. He tried to shake off the words to dismiss her sad face from his mind as he filled the space between Meeks and himself with talk about the industry and trends. They ran out of chitchat quickly. Kent wasn't surprised when the black man looked at him expectantly, folding his arms over his chest. "Now, what was it you wanted to talk with me about?"

He'd practiced the answer. At least he'd called it practicing, saying the words over and over as he'd showered that morning. "I have information to sell." Just five words. But they piqued Meeks's interest. He could tell by the way the man's eyes went cold and alert at the same time. Suddenly Kent felt just the tiniest bit of a rush.

"What kind of information?"

"If I told you that I have some papers, the only copy, proving that one of your competitors—someone about to launch a line of cosmetics for black women that will be of higher quality and less expensive than your own—stole money from the woman who was her partner, a woman who happened to be black, would you be interested?"

"You're talking about Gilda?"

In or out. Play or fold. "Yes. If you had the information I'm describing, you could leak it to the press just as her new line is coming out. The publication of that news would destroy her credibility with the black women she wants as her customers. They'd never buy her products."

Meeks stared at something beyond Kent. He began to stroke his mustache. "You're saying that Gilda had a black woman for a partner at one time? When was that?"

"Very early in the game. After the war."

"War?"

"World War Two. It was her partner who was the one who came up with the idea for the company."

"And Gilda cut her out in an illegal way?"

Kent nodded.

Meeks was quiet for a few seconds. He looked down at his hands, as though he were studying them. "How much do you want?"

"Three million dollars."

Meeks whistled. "I guess information doesn't come cheap, does it?"

"You stand to lose a lot more if your customers desert you and buy Gilda's products. You know the ad campaign is going to knock everybody's socks off. I believe you're familiar with the stellar abilities of our youngest president."

Calvin Meeks winced.

"Brand loyalty notwithstanding, Mr. Meeks, you'll have some defectors. The gift with purchase is going to be stunning. Trust me."

Meeks looked Kent up and down, then he rose. He was not very tall, but his chest was broad, his belly protruding, and his hands were enormous. "I have to think about it."

"Sure," Kent said, trying to speak louder than the hammering of his heart. "But I'll need to know soon."

"I'll get back to you."

When they shook hands, both their palms were damp.

CHAPTER FORTY-THREE

FUNNY HOW OLD habits hang on, Mooney thought as he sat watching television. For as long as he had lived in this home, even after his wife died, he'd always had a Christmas tree. Decorating the tree was one of the few things he and Isabel used to do as a couple, that and go to church. Toward the end of her life, he and his wife didn't even sit at the same table and eat dinner together, and they slept in separate bedrooms.

Poor Isabel, he thought. She was the first bright light he found in Los Angeles, and one of the few times Mooney had made his move too soon. But what could he have done differently? He fell for her, and then he married her. If there was one thing Mooney respected, it was a contract. His wife had given him a son, and after the boy had died, he couldn't leave her to grieve alone.

His assistant ordered his Christmas trees for him from a black-owned company. He liked that. Whenever his people were getting ahead, Mooney was happy. His tree had been decorated that day. For the last ten years or so, kids had been coming over on the second Saturday in December to decorate his tree. They were poor kids, inner-city Boy- and Girl Scouts. His cook served them lunch, and then Mooney took them on a house tour through all the rooms, telling them about the art and the furniture, splicing in bits about his childhood and how he'd made his money. A motivational speaker, that's what he was. Mooney chuckled to himself. Thomas J. Ford, the city councilman, had talked him into doing it. "We need role models," he'd said. He didn't really mind. The children were usually well behaved, although he'd had to thump a couple of heads over the years. One little bastard had sticky fingers but Mooney spotted him and ended up getting his watch back. This year's group was full of questions about money. When he told them about the hard work and the slammed doors, he could see some of their eyes glazing over. But still, it was nice having the house full of young people, hearing their voices and laughter. That made him feel good.

They hadn't done a bad job decorating the tree. The star at the top was a little crooked, but then it was like that every Christmas. He and Isabel hadn't done a better job. He'd lived through so many Christmases that they kind of swirled together. All those turkeys, all those presents, all those crooked stars.

He wished he could have spent a Christmas with Hosanna, but that wouldn't have been right. A bargain was a bargain, and he owed Isabel something. Showing up together for church on Sunday, spending holidays together, that wasn't too much to ask. Not that he ever felt guilty that Hosanna was his woman, or even that she was another man's wife.

Hosanna never cried about being separated during the holidays, he'd say that for her. She knew the rules. She was the best woman he'd ever had, the smartest, sassiest, and sweetest. If he'd seen her first they would have built an empire twice the size of his. They would have had children together. He let that last thought circle his mind one time and then Mooney stood up and stretched. At his age if he sat too long there was always the danger of getting stiff.

When he eased back down he saw the envelope on the coffee table. It had been there since before Thanksgiving, when Lonell and Vonette had visited. They took him by surprise, dropping in on him without so much as a call. He hadn't seen Vonette in at least five years. She'd gotten a little bigger, and those blond dreadlocks made her look as wild as she always had been. Vonette had never cared too much for him, but she tried to be pleasant. The funny thing was, he always liked her. She was the only person he'd ever met who didn't give a damn about his money. When she was little and he'd bring her toys and clothes, she refused to take anything from him. "No, thank you, Mr. Mooney," she'd say, just as polite. Offered her twenty dollars one time, and the same response. Hosanna always said that Baby Girl was her backup, but the one he wouldn't want to tangle with in an alley was Vonette.

But Lonell! Damn the man looked bad. Lonell had to be ten years younger than he was but he looked ten years older. Slow-talking, slow-walking, looking at him was seeing life in slow, slow motion. And then of all things for Lonell to bring him those papers.

"You're an important man," he told him. "I figure you can make this right."

What the man wanted was simple: for him to get Gilda to pay up what she owed to Hosanna's estate.

Now, fingering the papers, Mooney felt a surge of anger he thought he'd buried years ago. He knew better than anyone that a part of Hosanna had died when Gilda stole the money from her. And another little piece of her perished when she discovered that Gilda had launched her own company. The business had been Hosanna's idea, her vision, her blood and guts. It must have been like a sucker punch outta nowhere, he thought, her leaving the world with nothing.

I never gave that woman one single Christmas the way she wanted it. Mooney drained the glass of water. He'd always thought it was too late for amends, but there was Matriece to consider. Hosanna had wanted to leave something behind for her daughter to take over. It wasn't too late for him to help make that happen.

He dreamed of Hosanna that night. She straddled him, like she used to, rode on top like he was her bronco. She was the only woman who ever climbed up on him like she owned his body. In the dream she sat astride him, her fine wide ass bouncing against his belly. He could hear himself groaning and laughing, the sucking sounds he made when he tasted her nipples. "You're my big man," she was cooing. He could feel the pleasure firing up his loins. And then she stopped, and when she looked at him her eyes were pure flames.

"Get it back," she said. Her voice cracked, and the next thing Mooney knew he was licking tears from the top of his lip.

"I had a dream about your mother," he told Matriece when he met her for lunch a week later. He had his driver take him to a restaurant close to her office. She looked at him, her face a mixture of surprise and curiosity. Then she said, "What color was she wearing?"

He didn't want to tell her that Hosanna wasn't wearing a blessed thing, so Mooney just cleared his throat and told her he didn't remember what she had on, but her mama looked good. "How are things going at the job? Your products still coming out on time?"

"We're on schedule. Everything is fine." She paused for a moment, and seemed to be searching for the right words. "It's weird, Uncle Mooney, Gilda seems to really like me. We've been going to lunch a lot recently. She wants me to think about running one of her pet projects, We Mean Business."

"What's that all about?"

"It's an institution that she founded to support minority female entrepreneurs. Women who are thinking about starting a business or who already have one can go there for technical and managerial support."

"They give out any money?"

"It's not a funding organization but it helps women find loans if that's what they need."

Mooney snorted. "That's all anybody needs most of the time."

Matriece laughed. "Everybody's not as smart as you, Uncle Mooney. With some of these start-ups, the people don't know what they're doing. They don't know how to run a business."

"You got enough money, you can hire somebody to run it."

"Uncle Mooney, a lot of these women don't even know how to delegate."

"Anybody don't know how to delegate can't be helped by some We Mean Business. That's more for her benefit than anybody else. You gotta watch the helping hands. Lotta times the main one being helped is them. When the deal goes down, their pockets are lined."

"I don't think she's stealing from her own organization, Uncle Mooney."

"There's all kinds of theft. Some people steal money. Other folks steal a good name for themselves."

"She really has helped women, Uncle Mooney."

What was that softness he heard in her voice? Where had that come from? "She's helped herself more." He squinted a little, then moved his face in closer to hers. His eyesight wasn't as keen as it had been, but he knew a changing mind when he saw it. Her old mind was the one that fit in with his plans.

"Look here, I got something I want to show you." He pushed away the salt-and-pepper shakers and laid the contract on the table. "Read that." He watched her as she perused it, saw the wonder on her face, the shock. But where was her outrage?

"Where did you get this? Did my mother give it to you?"

He didn't want to tell her that Lonell had brought it to him. "I just came across it. Must have hidden it from myself," he said. "Listen, I'd like to make a move."

"Mom always said that they'd signed papers. I guess she forgot that she gave them to you. What do you mean, make a move?"

"Gilda's got a charity to make herself look good to the world. We got something that might make her look real bad. I call that an opportunity."

Matriece didn't say anything for a few minutes, but then she didn't have to. Mooney had been around her long enough to see the confusion and doubt shining in eyes that had once been harder.

"Baby Girl, you and your mother are just alike," he said. "Making the same mistake."

"What do you mean?"

"Getting emotional over white people, getting close to them and thinking that they love you. Girl, white folks love money."

"Uncle Mooney, I don't love Gilda. And she doesn't love me."

"Yeah, what you're doing is worse. You're forgiving her."

"I haven't—"

Mooney waved his hand. "Maybe it ain't complete, but, sugar, you in the process of forgiving that old broad. You know, forgiveness and a short memory, those are our biggest failings as a people. We always so quick to forgive and forget. We never see the big picture. Still waiting around for the boss man to tell us we're okay, when we should be worrying about how to get the boss's house. 'Cause he owes us a house and a whole lot more."

"Uncle Mooney, are you expecting reparations?"

"I ain't expecting nothing but hard times. But do we deserve reparations? Hell yeah. Jews got paid with a country for their suffering. Japs got twenty grand and an apology. Indians got reservations and casinos. We got welfare. Now, they done took away welfare. But no, I don't expect to collect nothing from white folks."

"All right. All right. Maybe it was easier to hate her when I didn't know her."

"She stole from your mother."

"I know. But what if it was all a misunderstanding?"

"Taking what doesn't belong to you ain't never a misunderstanding."

As he described his plan, Matriece was silent in a way that let him know she was pondering the ethics of the situation. He wasn't concerned with making heaven his home. Selling truth had gotten him a start in life. And now he had some more information that another bidder would want. Damned if he wasn't going to use it. "Sugar, your mama left here wanting to get paid back, and this is the way to do it."

"I don't know, Uncle Mooney. Give me some time."

"Sugar, that's the only thing I don't have much of."

Mooney was still mulling over his plan when, later that week, he sat in the dining room of the Wimbush Club, Los Angeles's oldest private establishment for elite businessmen. Montgomery Briggs, Jr., had become a member in the late seventies after an intrepid female journalist's report that the city's premiere fraternity of movers and shakers could count not one black, Latino, or woman among its ranks resulted in an embarrassed association frantically searching for a raisin to add to the cream. The members were so anxious to remove the taint of racism that they waived the ten-thousand-dollar annual fee for the first year. For the next ten years, Big Monty was the lone black face at the club.

"We need to start our own damn club," was Mooney's response in the beginning. But as he waited for his friends, the old man was honest enough to admit that sinking his polished black shoes into the expensive carpet and breathing in the heady fragrance that emanated from the rich cherry wood was not bad at all. He enjoyed the way the old waiter moved quietly in and out, with his smooth yes sir and no sir.

Meeks came in first, and then Big Monty arrived right behind him. To Mooney's surprise, the radio man had brought his son along. Montgomery's eyes opened wide when he saw him, and he immediately smiled and extended his hand. The rest of the men then shook hands all around. A new waiter appeared to take their drink orders, and then the silent one returned for their lunch requests.

As the men chatted about the latest Lakers game, Mooney caught Montgomery's eye. He seemed excited, as though he was pleased to be among them but not quite sure what was expected of him. Mooney sized him up, this young man who had Matriece so confused, trying to figure out the expression on his face. What he saw in Montgomery's eyes was what he'd once dreamed of seeing in his own son. Hunger, that's what it was. He wondered what it would take to feed him.

We've wasted a lot of time, Mooney thought. With the exception of Montgomery, the Triumvirate had known one another for more than forty years. He was their titular leader. When they first began meeting he tried to steer them toward pooling their resources to do some sort of joint venture. Deals came their way but somehow they could never agree on financing or corporate structure, even the name of the company. Trust and clashing egos had always been an issue, especially when Meeks and Big Monty were younger men, tasting success for the first time. Mooney had felt like a referee back then. There were times when they came so close to getting something started, something big, like when they were considering buying the Clippers, but they were always stopped by the question of who would manage the money, or who would handle the press. Opportunities had passed them by. The year Meeks's business surged ahead of the others in profit, and his profile appeared in the business section of the *Los Angeles Times,* Big Monty refused to meet for months. They could all acknowledge their problem, but they'd never been able to solve it. We could have made millions, Mooney often thought, if we'd just been of one accord. With age, their egos hadn't so much diminished as receded into the background. Drinking and talking with his friends now, Mooney thought that perhaps there was a way to make up for what had been squandered.

"Looks like KRPP's days are numbered," Big Monty announced after their meals arrived. "The Mexicans' offer is very strong, and I think they'll go higher."

"How are you going to deal with the fallout?" Meeks asked quietly. "They have you quoted in the paper saying that you'll never sell. PR could be a nightmare, brother."

"What do you think, Mooney?" Big Monty asked, and in that way the old man realized that Big Monty hadn't made a decision at all.

"A good deal is hard to come by," he said dryly. "Money your only reason?"

"I'm looking at another station in Houston, and there's one I want in Phoenix."

"It's nice to have cash, ain't it?" Mooney said.

The men all chuckled. Montgomery watched Mooney.

"But sometimes there are other considerations," Mooney said. He looked at Montgomery, who suddenly sat up straighter. "Sometimes all a black man has is a radio station that plays his music and talks about what he needs to know," Montgomery said. "We're in business, but we're also doing a community service. If people wake up one day and their music is gone and the information is coming to them in another language. . . ." He glanced at his father. "Business is business, but we are part of an emerging people. When one company's gain makes us weaker . . ." He shook his head.

Big Monty cleared his throat.

Montgomery drew his chair in closer to the table. Mooney nodded at him, so that Montgomery would know that he agreed with him. Meeks and Big Monty grew quiet, and he knew that they were mulling over what the young man had said. The men respected him enough to listen when he spoke. There was a receptiveness in them that Mooney welcomed. Ever since Lonell had given him the papers, he'd been thinking about a way that the Triumvirate could gain something from this unexpected windfall. The men at the table were filled with respect for one another and goodwill. It would be a good time to share with them the information about Gilda. They could draw up a plan today. He was an old man with not many years left and an opportunity big enough to split into three nice pieces. If not now, then when?

Something stopped him: that old instinct, unbidden, tribal, filling his mind with suspicion that evolved from another place, another time, and persisted still. Yoruba against Ibo. House slave against field nigger. Uncle Tom and Nat Turner, Blood against Crip. *Every brother ain't my brother.* What if someone got greedy? It had happened before. Looking into the faces of the only men in Los Angeles who spoke his language, Mooney wondered what they all still wondered: Can I trust them?

CHAPTER FORTY-FOUR

MATRIECE FELT THE Christmas spirit as soon as she saw her sister's house. Vonette's home was joy to the world. Her front door was covered with pinecones, holly, and inexpensive gold balls. The frame was bordered with twinkling lights that were ablaze, despite the fact it was only eleven o'clock in the morning. It was a Valdez ritual to keep the lights on from midnight Christmas Eve until noon on the twenty-sixth.

Doubts began to assail Matriece when her foot touched the second step. Her father was on the other side of her sister's door. She was trembling. This is ridiculous, she thought. Setting down the two bags she was carrying, Matriece tried to gather her thoughts. Several wrapped packages fell out. If Vonette went overboard on decorations, Matriece never failed to buy too many presents for her niece and nephews. After scooping up the gifts and placing them on top of the others, she wrapped her fingers around the handles of her bags and straightened up. Then she stood there, trying to decide whether to move forward or turn around and get back in her car.

"Auntie Triecy."

When she looked up the front door was open and her niece was walking toward her. She felt the young girl's soft lips across her cheek, and stared in wonder. Shalimar hadn't voluntarily kissed her in more than four years. When the teenager took one of her bags, Matriece was dumbfounded. "Thank you, Shalimar."

"We waited for you to open the presents with us. I was looking for you out my window."

When Shalimar opened the door wider, Matriece could see that the halls were indeed decked with holly and every other bright thing. There was mistletoe under every doorway. Red and green ribbon was wrapped around the banister of the stairway, and at the top of each wooden pole was a candy cane. Life-sized black and brown Santas, snowmen, and angels were standing in all the corners. In front of the small fireplace in the living room was a handcrafted Nativity scene, another example of Vonette's creativity. And in the center of the living room was the tree, decorated completely with Vonette's handmade collection of papier-mâché ornaments and brightly painted objects that glittered.

And the aromas! The scent of pine mixed in with the sweet doughy smell of baking pound cake and monkey bread, the spicy aroma of greens. It was Vonette's habit to rise early on Christmas day and begin her cooking. The result was that by midday, the house was fragrant with the promise of the meal to come. Matriece began salivating as soon as she smelled the first whiff.

"Don't come in here drunk, huh, Triecy?" Boot said when he saw his sister-in-law. He gave her a kiss. "Nah. Vonette did a beautiful job. Girl's got talent. Merry Christmas!" he smiled at Shalimar, who was standing near him, still holding her aunt's presents.

"Merry Christmas! Oh, it's gorgeous, as usual."

"Everybody's in the family room watching television. We been waiting for you since this morning. Vonette! Hey, Triecy's here."

When Boot called her name, Matriece grew tense. In a few seconds she would see her father. She wasn't sure she was ready.

But only Vonette, the boys, and Carla Ramirez emerged from the nearby room. "Merry Christmas, Triecy," her sister called out in a singsong cadence. When she hugged her younger sister, she squeezed her hard. In her face was a welcome that showed no traces of their recent discord. Both boys hugged her, and by the time Boot had taken her coat and come back, everyone was assembled on the floor around the tree.

Vonette disappeared into the kitchen and returned with a tray filled with cups of hot chocolate and warm muffins. As she passed them out, Boot said, "Boy, this girl is black every day of the year. But she turns this house into the Brady Bunch on Christmas. La-di-da," and he stuck his little finger out as he sipped the chocolate from the mug. "Ahh, it's a wonderful life."

"Auntie, so you know what I want for Christmas. You hook me up?" Tavares said. "She's gonna jump outta one of these boxes, right?"

Matriece laughed.

"What are you talking about, boy?" Chazz asked.

"Triecy's hooking me up with Asia Pace," Tavares said. "She's going to be my woman."

"Your what?" Vonette asked.

"You know, my girlfriend."

"You're getting a tie and some pajamas. Quit tripping," Chazz said.

"Nah. Asia's in one of these boxes."

There was too much of everything. Boot and Vonette, as well as Matriece, had gone overboard with their presents. By the time the last one was exchanged nearly two hours had passed.

"At least I made a lot of mine. Triecy, you spent too much money on these little knuckleheads," Vonette said in a chiding tone.

"Mother Brady, 'tis the season to be jolly," Tavares said. "Not that I got everything I wanted."

After the gifts had been opened, Matriece followed her sister into the kitchen to help her with the dinner preparations. She was definitely the sous-chef and Vonette the executive as the latter prepared the gumbo that was her Christmas specialty. Crabs, shrimps, mussels, clams, scallops, and oysters were in small plastic bags in the sink. Chicken and sausage were on Vonette's chopping board. On a counter near a big iron pot were bottles of season salt, bay leaves, a can of pepper, and some filé in a baby-food jar. Vonette turned the fire on under the pot, and when it was hot enough she poured in enough oil to cover the moon of her fingernail. She began shaking flour into the oil and stirring it. Once the mixture was of the soupy consistency she wanted, Vonette passed the spoon to her sister, while she began the macaroni and cheese. The monotony of stirring was lulling, and Matriece found herself relaxing, although she was still wary and alert, knowing that at any moment her father could come down the stairs and she'd see him for the first time in years. She wondered what he'd look like.

"Remember when Mom taught us how to make gumbo?" Vonette said.

"No."

"You don't?"

"Uh-uh."

"Maybe you were too little. I guess I was about eight or nine. She sat us on the counter and showed us. You were right there."

"Obviously, I wasn't paying attention."

"Yeah, you were probably counting money in your head."

"That's me."

They both laughed.

"Every once in a while Mom would get into her womanhood training mode. Remember when she showed us how to iron a man's shirt?"

"Nope."

"Where were you? You would have thought she was showing me how to make love to a man. 'Now, Vonette, first you do the back of the neck. Then you do the cuffs. Next is the collar. You have to be careful, because men are real particular about their shirt collars.' "

"Which is why they invented laundries."

The two women laughed.

"I think she showed each of us how to do different things," Matriece said.

"Yeah. I guess that's right."

"I was thinking about that time I went cross-country with Mom in the van, when she was selling to black beauty shops."

"I didn't go. I stayed with Uncle Tuney and . . . Who was he married to then?"

"That white woman?"

"Katie. Katie wasn't white."

"What was she?"

"Half white. Speaking of Uncle Tuney, Daddy and I are going to Inez the last week in January. Uncle Tuney wants him to talk with some of the people down there who won't join in the class-action suit. Daddy knows them; he and his father built their houses. So, Tuney thinks he can convince them."

"Maybe that will work," Matriece said. Hearing her father mentioned, she wondered where he was but didn't want to ask. "Anyway, that was the worst trip I've ever had in my life."

"How old were you?"

"About eleven. You would have thought I was thirty years old. Mom had me carrying heavy boxes, making sales, and doing some of everything. I thought about calling you up and telling you to get Uncle Tuney to come and get me. Maybe I should have fought back more, like you did."

Vonette finished sprinkling the last bit of cheese on top of the macaroni. "What do you mean?"

"I mean, you didn't let her take over your life."

"I wanted her to love me for me, not because I got on her Brown Sugar bandwagon."

"I guess I just wanted to have her any way I could."

Vonette looked surprised. "You were her favorite."

Matriece shook her head. "I made myself her favorite. I've been doing a lot of thinking about both of us—what you have, what I have."

"Me? A houseful of knuckleheads, that's what I have." Vonette chuckled.

"You have everything, Vonette. And I figured out that part of the reason I don't is because of Mom. I'm so wrapped up in trying to do what she wanted me to do and be what she wanted me to be—"

"And hate who she wanted you to hate."

"I've got to let go of that, too. But it's hard, Vonette."

"That why they call it work?"

The dinner table and two card tables were groaning as usual when everyone sat down at five o'clock. By then, Uncle Tuney and Lindell, as well as Boot's parents and his two sisters and their families, had arrived. Young children sat at the smaller tables and mothers held babies in their laps, as grown-ups helped themselves to big portions of holiday fare. Amid the good food and bilingual conversations, Matriece kept looking for her father but he never appeared.

Just as Vonette was passing out pie, pound cake, and ice cream, Matriece saw Shalimar disappear into the kitchen. From the dining room she watched her go upstairs carrying a tray laden with food. When she sat back down at the table, she was smiling.

It was after midnight by the time Vonette, Matriece, and Boot's sisters had finished cleaning up. Her nephews helped her load her presents into her trunk after she'd kissed everyone good night. "Tell Asia I'll pick her up for New Year's Eve around eight o'clock, and she should wear her low-cut red dress with the slits," Tavares said. Matriece drove off still laughing.

She hadn't put up a tree, and when she got back home that night, Matriece wished she had. This time next year I'll have a tree, she told herself. And maybe I'll have Montgomery.

She carried her presents upstairs and laid them on the small table in her bedroom, too tired to put them away. Shalimar must like Daddy, she thought, as she got into bed. The cool sheets made her tingle. She wondered what he looked like now that he was old and sick. It had been so long since she'd seen him, or even talked to him. Just how bad off was he? she wondered. *What did he say to make Shalimar smile?*

CHAPTER FORTY-FIVE

EVERYBODY WANTED HER to get out of bed, to go out, to eat a little something, take a bath, comb her hair, put on some clothes, leave the house, for God's sake! She had invitations to four New Year's Eve parties, but Asia wasn't going anywhere. She hadn't left her house since before Christmas. The bed felt too good to leave. Asia didn't ever want to get up.

"You have everything to be happy about," her manager told her when he called. "You were wonderful on 'The Tonight Show.' Leno wants you to come back, and this time he's going to talk with you. Baby, what's this all about? Is this about a man?"

Claude sent flowers that first week, and a pair of four-inch-high sling backs. When Asia still wouldn't get out of bed, still wouldn't eat, one morning he came over with her mother. Ruth put her in the shower and soaped her down, washed her hair, then made her sit on the floor in her bedroom while she oiled her scalp and braided her hair. "Baby, you got too much going for you to be down. Now, you just need to have a little talk with Jesus."

Even in her sadness the notion of her mother, of all people, telling her to pray struck Asia as ridiculous. She would have laughed, but she just couldn't muster the strength it took to make the sound come out. Instead, she simply stared at her mother.

"What? I go to church," Ruth retorted when she saw her daughter's expression. "Baby, what's wrong?"

"Go home, please. I don't feel like talking."

Toward noon on New Year's Eve Matriece called. She'd been leaving messages almost every day since "The Tonight Show." Most of the time Asia let the answering service pick up, but tonight she answered.

"Asia, where have you been?"

"I've been sick," she said softly. It had been a mistake to answer the telephone. She didn't want to talk with anyone, not now, not ever.

"Honey, you sound sad. Are you okay?"

"Triecy . . ." It was all she could manage before the sobs in her throat broke through.

"Honey, what's wrong? What's wrong?"

". . . hafta go."

"Asia, don't hang up. How about if I come by? Huh?"

". . . hafta go."

Claude was at her door within two hours. He was accompanied by a psychiatrist, a small dark man with a mole over his left eyebrow and a way of smiling that seemed to radiate hope and goodwill. "Your friend Matriece called me. She's very worried about you, and so am I," Claude said. "This is Dr. Prince, Asia. Matriece thought he might be helpful. He wants to talk with you."

When Asia padded back to her bedroom, the therapist followed her. "I'm going to ask you a few questions, dear, so I can get to know you better. Is that all right?" he asked.

She nodded.

They talked for the next two hours. He asked her how she was feeling, how long she'd been depressed, if she'd ever felt this way before. He asked her if she had ever had trouble sleeping, whether she was violent or promiscuous, if she went on spending sprees. "No," she said softly, "I'm just tired."

When he left, she heard Claude ask him if he'd bring her medication. "Not yet," the doctor said.

Dr. Prince returned the next day. Their conversation was like a meandering creek with waters that drifted in and out of her childhood. While he was there she stayed in bed, and he sat in a chair by her side. Asia talked about her mother. How she drank, how she yelled and hit, how her men laid hands on her before she was old enough to know what their touching meant. The second day, she talked about the father she could barely remember. No, she didn't miss him. No, she never thought about him.

The third day she woke up angry, in a trembling rage, and that day's conversation was full of curses, full of tears. Toward late morning, she washed her face and brushed her teeth, put on a jogging suit, and walked around the block. The air felt good on her face. When she came back, she ate half a bowl of cereal, then got dressed and went to Dr. Prince's office. "He never came! He didn't give a damn if we starved or not!" The psychiatrist's silent nod was a hook that descended inside her and pulled up everything that she'd hidden for so long.

Asia was crying when she went to see the doctor on Thursday. She'd awakened early that morning, eyes full of tears, and hadn't been able to get back to sleep. She told him about her dream. She and her brother, Donny, were walking on a slippery mountain ridge in the rain. Donny lost his balance. "I held out my hand but he couldn't hold on. I watched him fall."

"It should have been him," she sobbed after she told the therapist what had happened to her brother in real life. "He was the one with all the talent. I was biting off his sound, his style, everything. He should have been the one to make it."

"Maybe he still can," Dr. Prince said. "Prison isn't death." He leaned over and patted her knee. "Can you swim, Asia?"

She shook her head. "I never learned."

"Can Donny?"

She nodded.

"Suppose you and Donny were in a boat, and a sudden storm came and the boat capsized. He tried to save you, but you couldn't hold on, so he saved himself. Do you think he should feel guilty?"

Asia shook her head and then cried some more.

"I came up on those same hard streets you did, Asia. It's rough out there, like a stormy ocean. There's gangs, drugs, crime. Any one of them can drown you. Only the strong survive. You were stronger, that's all. You don't have anything to feel guilty about. Do you talk to Donny?"

"Sometimes."

"You ever go see him?"

She shook her head.

"That would be hard, wouldn't it? Seeing him locked up."

She nodded.

"Is that a hard thing that you can do, Asia? Can you put on a big hat and some sunglasses and go to the joint and see Donny? Do you think that would help both of you? He's proud of you, isn't he?"

"Yes."

"And has he ever blamed you for what happened?"

"No."

"So you're doing it to yourself, aren't you?"

She didn't answer, and Dr. Prince didn't say anything for a few minutes. It was as though he'd walked ahead and was waiting for her to catch up.

He handed her a bottle with small green capsules. "I'm putting you on the lowest dosage of antidepressant there is. Take one of these pills every day. I would like to continue seeing you twice a week for a while, Asia. Would you like that?"

"Yes."

"Okay."

Claude came by later that afternoon. "So, how you feeling, Asia?"

"Better."

CHAPTER FORTY-SIX

GILDA HANDED THE envelope to Matriece. Inside were two tickets to a musical on the last Saturday in January, nearly two weeks away. "I saw this show in New York. The lead singer is wonderful. You'll enjoy it, I'm sure."

"Thank you, Gilda. You're making it very hard for me to decide if my dates want me or the fabulous entertainment I provide."

"Why not both?" Gilda said. "It gives a man something to think about when a woman is both beautiful and well connected. In the old days women came with dowries. I don't think it was a bad idea. You want something to set you apart from the crowd, so when they think of you they think of a lovely young woman, very witty, very well educated, and able to get them into the best places in town. Then, of course, it is their turn to impress you."

"Don't you think most men get intimidated by women who can do things for themselves?"

"Of course they do. First they are intrigued, and later they become frightened. Next, they are running after the secretary. Each of my four husbands thought I was the most wonderful, intelligent woman in the world. They were excited that I was a successful businesswoman. They just couldn't live with me. I thought things might get better with your generation."

Matriece shook her head. "I've met maybe one guy who is truly egalitarian."

"Then, my dear, he is the one you should go after."

"We broke up."

"Does he like musicals?"

The two women laughed. If only she could have this kind of comfortable relationship with her own daughter, Gilda thought. If Matriece, who was only a few years older than Rachel, enjoyed her company and found her advice worthwhile, why couldn't her own child?

"I want to ask you something," Gilda said.

"Yes."

"In strictest confidence."

"Of course."

"I don't know how well you know my daughter."

"Not very well."

Gilda sighed. "For quite some time Rachel and I have had a great deal of difficulty getting along. She thinks I was a very poor mother who never paid any attention to her. Too busy getting married and divorced and running a business. She's not wrong about her feelings. I was very negligent. I didn't mean to be but then, no one does. I was just wondering if you might be able to suggest any ways that I could reconcile with her. I was thirty-eight when I had Rachel. I'm seventy now. Who knows how long I'll live. I'd like us to get along, that's all. I'd like her to forgive me."

"Well, Gilda . . ."

Matriece was hesitating, and Gilda instantly regretted confiding in her. It was unfair that she burden her. "Don't worry about it. I wasn't expecting you to have a solution."

"I do have a suggestion," Matriece said calmly. "I'm assuming that you have been to counseling with her."

"We tried it for a while. The more she talked about her childhood, the angrier she got."

"Well, see if she'd be willing to go back. I understand that anger precedes peace in that process. But the other thing . . . May I be frank?"

"Please."

"I never really got the sense that Rachel was fulfilling her destiny being here. I don't think working at your company is what she wants to do at all, and to be perfectly honest, I don't think she's contributing anything. Maybe you could help her find out what she wants to do, and then support her. If she feels fulfilled, she'll be a happier person, and then she won't constantly compare herself to you, which is what she's probably doing. Face it, Gilda: You're a hard act to follow. A lot of kids would shut down faced with your legacy."

"But why is that? I never expected her to do what I did."

Matriece shrugged. "Children often put pressure on themselves. Deep down she probably loves and admires you so much that she wants to be exactly like you. She's angry with herself because she can't. Then she projects that anger on to you."

"You are quite the psychiatrist."

Matriece shook her head. "Not really. My sister rebelled against my mother. I saw that as a real search for her own identity."

"Did she find herself?"

"Oh, yes. She got married, had three kids. She's very artistic, not in a commercial way. But she makes everything beautiful around her. She's very loving. That's her gift. Her husband and kids adore her. She draws people to her. She's not possessive at all. Her youngest boy is like my own son. Vonette shares him with me. My mother wanted her to be a successful businesswoman, but that's not who my sister is."

"That's who you are."

"Yes, I always wanted to be like my mother."

"So you are a chip off the old block. What kind of business did she have?"

Matriece stared at her, suddenly realizing that she'd dug a hole for herself.

"My dear, what's wrong?" Gilda asked.

"I . . . I . . . I have a terrible headache. It came on suddenly."

"Sit down, drink some water. I believe I have some aspirin around here." She moved toward her desk.

"That's all right, Gilda. Regular aspirin doesn't do the job. I have something stronger in my office. I'll go back and take some and put my head down for a couple of minutes. I'll be okay. Thank you for the tickets."

"Feel better, dear."

It was early afternoon when Matriece left. For the next hour Gilda conferred with the event planner who was coordinating the ten-year anniversary celebration for WMB. Gilda had worked with the woman on other projects, and by the time she hung up she was feeling confident that the anniversary would be a memorable occasion filled with seminars, speakers, and entertainment that would enhance WMB and boost sales during the debut week of Brown Sugar.

Gilda was doing paperwork when she overheard loud voices in her reception area. When she opened her office door she saw her assistant, her cheeks an uncharacteristic red, her finger wagging inches from the nose of an older black man who was seated on one of the plush chairs. "I told him you wouldn't see anyone without an appointment."

The man seemed unperturbed by all the commotion. There was something about the set of his shoulders that made her know him. Something about the way his eyes, even hooded as they were, held her gaze steadily. Gilda's body involuntarily jerked forward, and she almost lost her balance, almost fell but she caught herself. More than fifty years had passed but she still remembered the man who helped put Hosanna and her in business. She knew of his successful restaurants and his line of barbecue sauce and frozen foods. He had to be at least eighty years old, and here he was, still looking strong.

Gilda walked over to Mooney and extended her hand. "This is an unexpected pleasure, Mr. Mooney. Won't you come into my office."

He walked easily, without any signs of stiffness. He wore a very good suit and expensive shoes. Gold squares glittered in the cuffs of his fine cotton shirt. Time had been good to Mr. Mooney. For a reason that she couldn't understand, once she recovered from her shock, Gilda felt happy and excited, as if this unexpected reunion held a blessing that she'd long ceased praying for. Finally, here was someone who could tell her what had happened to Hosanna.

Once they were inside her office, Gilda began to feel awkward. She and Mooney had never been friends, and now, as she faced him, the rush of excitement began draining away, uneasiness replacing her initial good feelings. What could he possibly want after so many years?

"May I offer you some coffee, Mr. Mooney?"

He looked pleased that she remembered his name. "No, thank you, Gilda. I don't plan to take up much of your time. I have a business proposal for you."

"A business proposal?" She was astonished.

"Yes."

"But—"

"I assure you the offer will interest you. I—"

"What happened to Hosanna? I tried to find her. Is she still alive? Where is she?"

He looked taken aback by her rush of questions. Before, his expression had seemed hard and immutable, but now he appeared troubled, as though her intensity was upsetting to him. "You say you tried to find her? When?"

It was a challenge, one she wasn't prepared for. "I had someone search for her."

"Who? A private investigator?"

"No, an employee."

"Where did he look?"

"Different places. It was so long ago, I can't remember."

"You never came to see me." Their eyes met, and she was the first one to turn away. "Hosanna died a long time ago," he said.

"Oh." The word floated out of her. It was an uncensored sound, as free as the sadness and disappointment that began to fill her. She suddenly realized that she'd been hoping for years that Hosanna was still living, that somehow she would find her long-lost friend, make amends to her, be forgiven. Now, no such dream was possible. "She must have told you how much she hated me," Gilda said.

"Yes," he said curtly, and she noticed that he held his mouth in a hard, unyielding way.

"I tried to find her."

When she looked at him, Mooney turned away, as if the last thing he wanted to see was the misery that she knew was in her face. His silence made her words ring hollow, even to herself. He didn't believe her, but then, why should he?

"She probably told you I stole from her. I know that's what she thought."

Mooney looked at her, but he didn't say anything.

She spoke in a halting voice. "She probably thought I took the money and ran out on her. Is that what she thought?"

Mooney just looked at her.

"I never meant to leave her the way I did. Things happen. I know that I owed her money, and I sent it to her. But my husband got a hold of my bank book and took all the cash out of our account. I didn't know it then, but the check I sent her was worthless."

Mooney's face was expressionless. What was the point of talking with him? It was too late. Hosanna was dead. Why should she continue this conversation with a man who obviously hated her? "I don't think we have anything to talk about, Mr. Mooney." She stood up and extended her hand. Mooney remained seated.

"But we do," he said. He reached inside his pocket and handed her an envelope.

Gilda stared at the copy of the document she'd signed so many years ago. As she read it, she was transported to the lawyer's office in the Fairfax District. *We were so young, so full of dreams.* Hers had come true, almost in spite of herself. But Hosanna's dream had been lost.

"Why are you giving me this?" she asked carefully.

"You done well for yourself, Gilda. You ought to be proud. I understand you have a foundation to help what they call 'minority women' become business owners. We Mean Business, ain't that the name? You coming out with a line of cosmetics for black women next fall. Right?"

"What do you want?"

"I guess the world thinks that you're a very liberal, progressive woman. I imagine your dues are all paid up with the NAACP. Everybody thinks you're a real good person. But I know that you got as far as you got because you stole from a black woman. Stole ideas. Stole money. I wonder if all the black women you think are going to buy your new makeup and the ones who've been buying your lipsticks and polishes and eye shadows would be so anxious to give you their dollars if they knew how you got your start. That's what I wonder."

"I never stole from her. I tried to find her." When she heard her own pleading tone, she stopped herself. She wouldn't beg. If life had taught her anything it was that begging only delayed the inevitable. Better that she know what she was up against. "What do you want?" Her voice was hard, flat.

Mooney leaned forward. "I want to make a deal with you, Gilda. A real good deal."

"What kind of a deal?"

"I want to acquire Brown Sugar."

"But the products haven't even debuted yet."

"I want to buy it as is, keeping your management team in place."

"It's out of the question!"

"Is it?" He smiled at her, and she remembered his younger face, how cunning it was.

"You expect me to give you a company so you will keep quiet."

He shook his head. "I'm old enough to know you never get something for nothing. I said a deal, Gilda, not a giveaway."

"And if I don't give you this deal, what then? You will go to the newspapers and tell them lies about me?"

He was sneering at her; she could see his contempt. "The first time I met you, I was scared to shake your hand. White women like you used to get black men killed. Times have changed." He let the words sink in. "Black women stick together. They're not going to buy cosmetics from a white woman who screwed a sister." He rose. "You think about it."

Gilda could still smell the scent of Mooney's cologne after he left. She breathed it in while she dialed Kent's number and asked him to come to her office. "I'm being blackmailed," she told him when he arrived.

Kent sat down in one of the chairs in front of her desk. She could hear his foot tapping against the front of the desk. As she explained who Mooney was and what he'd said, she could see his face turning paler. He clutched the arms of his chair as though he were afraid it was going to ascend into the sky and leave him behind.

"Are you all right?" she asked.

He nodded but his movements were stiff and his eyes darted back and forth, focusing on nothing. He didn't look well at all. "Let me get back to you on this, Gilda," he said.

She watched him as he left. His reaction troubled her. Kent had always been a quick thinker. Lately, he seemed so unfocused, so strange, as if he were asleep. Gilda shook her head. She'd have to figure out what was wrong with Kent another time. She had more urgent matters to occupy her mind.

The house was quiet when Gilda arrived. Fontaine had gone out to dinner with his parents, who were celebrating their thirty-fifth wedding anniversary. Gilda hadn't had any relationship last that long, not even with a friend. She felt lonely eating with no companionship other than the television. It was so easy to get used to someone, to his smile, his laughter, his body. She'd warned herself against feeling too comfortable, too dependent on a young man who would soon leave her. "Depend on no one. Want nothing," she said aloud in her kitchen. "I am not hungry. I am not hungry," she said, repeating the words she'd spoken so long ago in the camp.

As Gilda got into bed it occurred to her that there was always another war to endure. Now, at the end of her life, she would have to survive love and blackmail and her daughter's ambivalence and resentment. She closed her eyes and evoked Mooney's face, his implacable expression as he set forth his terms. Once he feared her, but no more. Well, once she had feared Germans. It's only a matter of time, and your enemies change, she thought. She had spent a lifetime running away from shame but she hadn't run far enough. She tried to fall asleep but the question she'd put out of her mind for so many years was suddenly relentlessly plaguing her. *Why didn't I try to find her, really try?* She knew the answer, even if she wanted to deny the truth. She'd seen the answer earlier in Mooney's cold eyes.

CHAPTER FORTY-SEVEN

FOR THE LAST few weeks, what Thursday had come to mean for Sam was the day before the day that used to be his happiest. The Friday after Matriece confronted him, he found her unlocked car parked in her driveway and his check on the passenger seat. Now he hadn't seen her in weeks. Sam didn't grieve for fantasies. No, what he missed was real: the sight of Matriece peeking at his legs from behind her drapes; Matriece clad in a well-tailored business suit, every hair on her head in place. Sam yearned for the intelligent conversations they used to engage in; the hopefulness he felt whenever he saw her. Now, on Thursdays, instead of feeling a rush of anticipatory excitement, Sam's heart was dull and empty.

As he ate his cereal and sipped his coffee, he upbraided himself again for the mistake he'd made. Why hadn't he been honest with Matriece from the very beginning? Why hadn't he told her that he was Asia's father as soon as he knew her connection to his daughter? Now Matriece thought he was trying to run a game on her and probably on his child, too. Sisters always thought a brother was gaming. That was the first thing out of Ruth's mouth. *My baby isn't giving you a damn cent.* Sisters. He stopped chewing for a moment. Maybe they figured that since a man hadn't given to his child, he wouldn't have any qualms about taking from her. He couldn't blame them. He didn't have the right to expect a woman to believe in a transformation that she hadn't seen. God only knew what Ruth would tell Asia about him now, or what Matriece would say, for that matter. He thought he was building up goodwill by sending his child money every month, but all he was doing was fooling himself.

He'd never expected to be a real father to Asia, not at this stage. All he wanted was a relationship, for her to allow him to care about her. He'd be content with that. If she just let him love her, that would be enough. But Asia seemed lost to him now, as though some unseen hand had transported her miles beyond his reach. He might as well be her biggest fan; the cards he sent were as close as he'd ever get to her.

As he set down his coffee cup and picked up his jacket, Sam grabbed a magazine from his kitchen counter and flipped it open to the page with Asia's picture. She was wearing a blue gown, had flowers in her hair, and she was alone. The write-up talked about her first movie role. The magazine quoted her as saying, "I'm really looking forward to acting." With a sigh, he put down the publication. Seeing Asia's sad face only made him feel depressed. He had cars to wash.

Kent looked worse than the last time. Every week he seemed to lose more weight and become more haggard. There was a worm crawling around inside the man, Sam thought, eating him up. After Sam washed his car, Kent invited him in for coffee, which had become their ritual since the day the businessman almost collapsed. Sitting across from Kent, Sam watched and listened to him intently. He slurred a few words and seemed so vacant that Sam wondered if he was using drugs.

"You all right, man?" Sam asked.

"Sure, what do you mean?"

Sam leaned in closer to his friend. "Man, your eyes aren't focusing, you're moving kinda slow, and half the time I can't understand what you're saying. You don't look right, Kent."

Kent shrugged, and Sam could tell that he wasn't ready to talk.

"Where's your daughter?" Sam asked. For the last few weeks he'd been seeing the little girl whenever he came to wash the car. Usually Kent was rushing him because he had to take her to school. Sam had his suspicions about the child who called Kent "Daddy" and his wife "Peggy." But he wasn't one to open the door to people's pain unless he was invited in.

"Oh, I'm part of the car pool society these days," Kent said with a laugh. "I've been free all this week. I tell you, all that driving is tiring."

"Enjoy every minute of it, Kent," Sam said so vehemently that the older man stared at him. "Be glad you have the opportunity. I didn't take care of my kids when I had the chance."

"I didn't know you had children."

"I have two, a son and a daughter. They're grown." As soon as he'd uttered the words Sam felt as though he'd pulled down his pants in the middle of the street.

"Do they live in Los Angeles?"

"Yeah."

"Are they in school or working?"

Sam sighed. He hadn't told anyone about his children in so long he'd forgotten about the kinds of questions the admission elicited. Sam had never confessed to anyone that Donny was in jail. He always feared the silent accusation: like father, like son. There could be such damnation in a glance, cold eyes taking him to hell and leaving him there. He peered at Kent's tired face for a moment.

"One works and the other one doesn't. My son's in prison for armed robbery."

But instead of judgment there was empathy in Kent's eyes. "It doesn't take much to make a mistake, does it? One day you have a set of values to live by, rules and principles you've based your life on, and the next day your back is pressed against the wall."

"I wasn't around to give my son the values that he needed. He started out with one strike."

"Yes, all of us do. It's all a matter of grace as to who gets caught and who gets away. Grace and luck. For a while I had both but now they've run out." He looked at Sam, and smiled ruefully.

"You keep talking about that, man. You need a lawyer or something?"

Kent lit a cigarette, inhaled, then blew out the smoke. "Sam, my friend, I'm in trouble. Big trouble. I'm going to lose everything I've got, and I may end up in jail on top of that."

Sam could sense Kent's hesitation pushing against his obvious need to talk. "Hey, man, you can tell it or keep it to yourself. Either way, it's not going anywhere."

"I like to play blackjack. I owed some not very nice people a lot of money. I paid them off, but to do that I had to take some money that I planned on putting back, only now I can't do that. And when people find out that the money is missing . . ." Kent pursed his lips and lifted his brows.

"Maybe they'll make a deal."

Kent shook his head. "It's not that simple. I can't pay right now."

"Sell your house, man. Scale back."

"I put a second on the house, and I owe a two-million-dollar balloon payment."

Sam whistled. "When's it due?"

"Very soon."

There was such profound despair in Kent's sunken eyes that Sam felt like putting his arms around the man. Instead he reached across the table and clasped his hand. "I want to pray with you," Sam said.

Kent looked shocked, but he bowed his head when Sam did.

"Lord, we come before your throne, two fallen men, two men who have made grave mistakes. We know we are forgiven. We know that right now you are easing our burdens and our hearts and making a way for us. We know that you are helping us now in our time of need. Thank you for blessing Kent's wife, Lord, healing her body and her mind. We know that you are our strength and our salvation. And we thank you."

When Sam looked up, the businessman still held his hand, as though his grip had frozen. "I haven't prayed in years," Kent said.

"You ever hear of Gamblers Anonymous?"

"Yeah, I've heard of it."

Sam stood up. "Your car is ready."

The bus to take visitors to the cell block where the prisoners were held was packed with Mexicans, African-Americans, and poor-looking white people. Most were women. Sam felt at ease among them. He'd been taking the same trip, the first Saturday of every month, for the last two years. Just outside the building where his son was housed he walked through a metal detector. Once inside he signed in and then waited until his name was called. He walked through a double door that led to a narrow room, bifurcated by a Plexiglas partition that descended from the ceiling to four feet above the floor, where it was cut off by a small wooden counter. From the floor to the ledge was a wooden wall. Sam sat down on the steel stool in front of the divider that separated prisoners from their visitors. When he saw the tall, skinny man shuffling toward him he smiled, and his son smiled back. They both reached for the telephones near their fingers.

Donny's eyes were two rocks the first time Sam visited him in prison. They had softened a bit since that day and now were actually capable of radiating happiness. Those first few times were filled with his son's angry outbursts, his curses and accusations. Sam didn't let his son's emotions dissuade him from returning. He'd earned the boy's anger. "You can curse me all you want, I'll keep coming back," he told him. And he did. He came when the sun heated up the air around him to more than 100 degrees, when torrential winter rains drenched him. When Sam was depressed and didn't want to leave his house, when his heart was overfilled with joy, he came. Sam had promised himself that he would get on the bus every first Saturday until Donny was released, and he kept his word. Gradually, weather, moods, and money had no bearing at all.

They had one hour to share, to fill up with whatever they could pull out of themselves. Sam knew that what Donny was mostly after was the money he put on the book for him, the money that translated into cigarettes and snacks. He didn't let that realization deter him.

Donny slouched as he sat on his steel stool. He wasn't a boy anymore. Nearly twenty-seven, and tall, too. At least six-three or -four. Sam could see in Asia's brother the same lost potential that had seeped out of his own life. Sometimes it hurt him to look, but it was impossible to turn away. He'd done that for too long. "How you been, Donny?"

"All right."

Their conversations were usually lopsided, with Sam doing more talking than his taciturn son. Today he rattled on about his work, his plans for expanding the business. "When you get out, there'll be a job waiting for you."

"Washing cars?" Donny snorted.

"There's good money in washing cars, Donny. Detail a van, you can make one hundred dollars. Do a couple of those a week, and that's a good start for you. But you gotta think about going back to school, getting a degree or some kind of skill. Then you'll make some real money. You can still have a good life, son, if you put God in it."

Donny grunted. Two or three minutes passed, and neither one spoke.

Sam was used to the silence. There was a moment during all his visits with his son when he felt the awkwardness of a first date.

"I talked to Asia," Donny said.

"When?"

"Couple of days ago."

"How she doing?"

"She seemed kinda, I don't know, out of it. Tired. She started crying when I told her that the parole didn't come through."

"She loves you, Donny."

He nodded. "She don't never come to see me."

"Your sister would start a riot if she came up in here."

"True that. But I miss her. I miss a lot of shit."

"You didn't tell her that I've been visiting you."

"I ain't told nobody. We never talk about you. But why don't you just call her up, Sam? Why you doing all this plotting and planning for the perfect moment and shit?"

"I told you. I don't want her to think I'm after her money."

"Okay, dog, but time is passing. And you getting old. I'm the one hated your black ass. If you can step to me, you can step to her."

"Let me choose my time."

They sat quietly for the rest of the visit. Toward the last five minutes of their hour Sam asked Donny to bow his head, and he prayed for his son. Before he left he reminded him to pray and read the Bible. "Go to chapel," he told him.

"See you," Donny said. And he waved.

The bus that came to take Sam back to the parking lot was hot and crowded. He had to stand sandwiched between a fat black woman and an old Mexican man. The faces of the people surrounding him were somber, and even the children were still. The visitors were preoccupied, doing what loved ones do, what Sam was doing on his way home from visiting jail: counting years.

He stared at his hands the entire time he was on the bus, as though there was an answer hidden in the lines of his palms. When the bus stopped he followed the crowd off, and didn't look up until he was out-side, standing in front of the administration building. He needed to go inside to leave money for his son, money for cigarettes and candy bars. The air near the prison always seemed hotter, thicker than LA air. The sky was hazy. Sam looked across the street where there was a small crowd waiting for the bus to take them out to the cells. Her face floated out from the throng toward him. She was a brown-skinned woman in jeans, wearing a sun hat that dipped down over her forehead, and she wore big dark glasses. She was staring in his direction. He couldn't see her eyes but he could feel them on him. He crossed the street quickly and didn't breathe until he was standing right in front of her. He wondered if Asia could hear his heart.

Her hand circled his wrist and pulled him aside, away from the people. "I know you," she said softly. "You're my biggest fan. Thank you for my cards and the money. You'll never know how much they've meant to me. You've been so kind." She stood on her toes and kissed him on his cheek.

Something inside him was falling. Sam could feel it tumbling but he couldn't stop it. In his mind he could hear her calling him Daddy. That was the name he'd been running toward. But the daughter standing in front of him thought he was a kind stranger, a man with time on his hands and no purpose. Maybe it was best that they keep it that way. He smiled at her.

"You take care of yourself," he told her.

She smiled. The bus came then. She waved as she got on. "Bye." She mouthed the word behind a dingy window.

"Bye," Sam said.

CHAPTER FORTY-EIGHT

BY THE TIME Tavares left his geometry tutorial that Monday it was almost quarter to four, and as he rushed to the field where the cheerleaders were practicing, he was hoping that Kara would still be there. Checking his watch he realized that the last bus would arrive soon. He had about a ten-minute walk to get to the stop. Tavares knew he didn't really have enough time to see Kara, but he told himself he wouldn't stay at her practice too long.

He felt himself grinning as he raced across the campus toward the outdoor stadium. It had rained earlier in the day and the field was muddy. Ever since school had resumed after winter break, he and Kara had been eating lunch together with a group of black students. Today he'd missed her because of the choir tryouts. He wanted Kara to be the first to know that he'd gotten in, and that the choir director had said his voice was "fantastic." People in the room had clapped when he finished his audition.

It was when he was standing in the choir room hearing the applause that Tavares began to feel at home at Castle Heights High School. He'd felt lost in the first weeks. But gradually, he'd begun getting his stride back. The work wasn't too hard if he studied. He was in the choir, so soon he'd have a rep. And he had a girlfriend.

Tavares could pick out Kara even before he reached the field. She had a different kind of flavor from the other cheerleaders. Her moves were more energetic and sexier, too. And there was no mistaking her butt. The first thing he noticed about her was what a nice behind she had. Chazz had told him always to pick a girl with a nice booty.

He could tell that Kara saw him by the way she smiled. Not in his direction, of course. Tavares knew that part of her game was to act like she was ignoring him. So, he began to look at every other girl on the field except her. When he did that, she pepped up her routine a lot, kicking up her legs extra high and poking out her butt as though she were trying to bounce a ball off it. That's when Tavares waved at her, and then she smiled at him and blew him a kiss. He had kissed Kara a lot. The main reason he had walked over to the football field when he should have been running to the bus stop was to get some more of Kara's kisses, and to see if she'd touch him again the way she had the last time.

Tavares stood in front of the first row of bleachers directly facing the field. He looked at the time. He really had to leave. When he caught Kara's eye he pointed to his watch and mouthed the words, "I have to go."

Kara looked back at him, smiled, then stuck out her tongue and licked her lips very slowly. Tavares sat back down.

At four o'clock the cheerleaders were dismissed. Kara ran off the field and plopped down next to Tavares on the damp bleachers. "What's up," he said.

"You, baby."

She kissed him and he could feel her breasts pressing against his chest before she pulled away. "Walk me home," she said.

Reality hit him. "Walk you home? Girl, I hafta catch a bus. And it probably already left."

"Walk me home and I'll get my mom to drive you."

"Kara, your mom isn't going to drive me all the way to LA."

They left the field and trudged through the campus to the broad boulevard beyond the school. It began raining again, the drops picking up speed. Most of the students were gone but a few who'd been engaged in after-school activities were milling about the campus, walking or driving home. "You may have to sneak me in your room for the night," Tavares quipped.

"My sister sleeps in my room."

"This is your fault, you know. If I hadn't wanted to get with you so bad I'd be halfway home by now."

"So how is that my fault?" Kara asked coyly.

"You had to go licking your lips at me."

"Oooh, that's nasty. I didn't do that."

"Now the Castle Heights Klan is going to come jump my ass for being out on the street after hours."

"Awww," Kara cooed. She stopped in the middle of the street and kissed him.

"Damn, girl. You're aggressive. I like that."

They kept walking, finally reaching the bus stop. There was no one there, and Tavares had to face the fact that the bus was gone and he had no way to get home. "Do you really think your mother would drive me?" he asked.

"Well . . ." Kara hesitated. "Maybe." She kissed him again, but this time Tavares didn't kiss her back. I'm stranded in the rain, he thought. His mother and father were working. He could forget about Chazz picking him up. He could just hear his brother laughing at him. Damn!

"So, are you coming home with me?" Kara asked. "You could use the phone."

He could call his aunt. Triecy would come and get him. "Yeah," he said. He continued walking with her.

Tavares heard the car before he actually saw it. Rowdy rappers were screaming lyrics he knew by heart. Tavares began bopping his head up and down to the song. By the time he turned to see where the music was coming from, the car had parked beside Kara and him. His belly clenched. The word "drive-by" resonated in his mind.

"Whazzup!"

He approached the car slowly. There were two white boys inside. The closer he got, the stronger the scent of the marijuana that wafted out the open window.

"Judd."

"Hey, dude. Want a ride?"

Stoners. But hell, he needed a ride. "I gotta go to LA."

"Cool," Judd said.

"See you tomorrow," Tavares called out to Kara, who looked worried as she waved good-bye.

Everything happened fast. Two steps and he was in the car. *Bam!* The door slammed shut. *Whoosh!* They were off, Judd doing seventy-five on a city street that was slick with rain. The car was full of smoke and laughter. Tavares remembered later how hard Judd laughed, talking about, "Hey! Hey! We're going to LA!" like it was another planet or something. Tavares was sitting in the back, trying to act like everything was cool, knowing that he was in the wrong place, hoping it wasn't the wrong time. But then he heard the sirens.

The cop wasn't that big. His daddy could have punched the dude out with maybe two hard hits. But there was the gun in his holster. And the stick. He had the stick out when he approached them. Raised it when he told them to get out. Which they did immediately. So the three of them were standing there together, Judd and his friend totally blunted and Tavares so scared he couldn't breathe. Then the policeman said, "You guys been doing drugs?" Everybody said no at the same time. The cop searched the car while they waited on the street. When Tavares looked up he was holding two bags. One was full of weed. The other had white stuff in it. All Tavares could think of was how he wished he'd never kissed Kara at all.

"This belong to one of you gentleman?"

"Officer, we picked up this dude here," Judd said, pointing to Tavares. "He's going to our school, and we were driving him back to South Central where he lives. He must have had it on him." Judd spoke fast. No hesitation. He kept his eyes on the ground.

"That right?"

Tavares could smell hamburger on the cop's breath. "No sir. I was trying to get back home, and they offered me a ride. I smelled dope as soon as I got in. They had it."

"What are you doing in this neighborhood if you live in LA?"

"I go to school here."

"How do you go to school here if you live in LA?"

"He's using a phony address," Judd said.

"Whose car is this?" the cop asked.

"Mine," Judd said.

"Let me see your license and registration."

Judd went to the car and returned with his identification. The officer glanced at the papers. He looked at Judd and his friend. Then he looked at Tavares. He turned back to the two white boys and said quietly, "You boys better watch the company you keep."

"Yessir."

"I think you better get home."

They were gone before Tavares could feel his stomach cramping.

"You little son of a bitch, you think you can come up here and sell drugs? You better think again. Get in the car. You're under arrest," the officer said.

CHAPTER FORTY-NINE

RAINY MONDAY, MATRIECE thought glumly as she drove down the main artery that fed into Crenshaw Boulevard. The hillside on the southern side of the thoroughfare was muddy as rivulets ran down onto the street below. Already the grass that had been so dry earlier in the year was a radiant emerald green. But driving was dangerous along the slippery road with its curves and hills. There was an accident up ahead that had slowed down the entire procession of commuters.

The cars crept along until she found herself in front of Radiance. To her right was a sleek silver Mercedes. The driver was signaling, trying to make a left turn into the parking lot. As she nodded her assent, Matriece saw the woman smile and wave at her. On her hand was a sparkling diamond ring moving back and forth. *Somebody sure loves his girlfriend.* She felt a pain in her head as she realized that it was Gretel Meeks disappearing inside the driveway of Radiance Cosmetics.

She's engaged, Matriece thought. Gretel Meeks is engaged. *They are going to get married.* She heard horns behind her. The light was green. Matriece drove mechanically until she had to pull over because she couldn't see. It was raining too hard, inside her and out. Her world was blurred.

Once she got to her office, Matriece tried to work, but she had difficulty concentrating. Her mind was stuck in that blurry place. When people spoke to her she couldn't seem to understand them. I'm so out of it, she thought. She went to Blair's office, but when she knocked there was no answer. Cigarette break, she thought.

Matriece was getting off the elevator and walking toward Gilda's office when she realized what she was doing. *What am I doing? She's not my girlfriend. She owns the company I work for.* She stopped outside Gilda's door. And then the door opened. Rachel stormed past her without even speaking. Seconds later Gilda rushed out of her office into the reception area as though she were about to pursue her daughter. She stopped when she saw Matriece.

"I'll come back," Matriece said.

Gilda's shoulders slumped and she shook her head. "No. Please come in. Marie," she said to her assistant, "I don't want to be disturbed unless it's Daniel."

"I try to understand her but I don't know if I ever will," Gilda said after she closed the door. She looked genuinely bewildered as she sat behind her desk. She's so tiny, Matriece thought. She'd never realized how small she was. When she was a child, she always thought of her as huge, monstrous.

"Rachel is a good person. I just bring out the worst in her."

"Maybe it's not that you bring out the worst in her, but that she finds it convenient to dump on you, Gilda. Don't let her do that. You're her mother; you deserve respect."

"But I want her love," Gilda wailed.

"She does love you. She just can't express it right now. Rachel is trying to find herself."

Gilda shook her head. "She'll never forgive me."

"Then forgive yourself, Gilda. You did what you had to do."

Gilda stared at her as though she were transfixed.

"What? What's the matter?"

"When you said that, you reminded me of someone I knew a long time ago. I had a very different kind of life then. I was trying to come to grips with some terrible things that had happened to me, things I'd never talked about with anyone. I felt very guilty, and my friend told me I had nothing to feel guilty about. She made me feel better, and so have you. Thank you."

Matriece nodded, not trusting herself to speak, not sure of what she felt. The tiny woman seated before her suddenly seemed very fragile. But how could she pity Gilda? "I'd better be going," she said.

"But what is it that you wanted?" Gilda asked.

"Nothing important, just to say hello."

I can't be this close to her, Matriece thought, as she rode down in the elevator. How did I ever let this happen? She should have kept things the way they were in the beginning—polite and formal. From now on no more lunches, no more symphony tickets, no more personal conversations.

When she got back to her office Matriece thought she'd tackle a job that might give her a sense of completion. She hadn't heard from Kent regarding the financial error on Brown Sugar's bill. She thought about calling him but some instinct told her to dial Leonard Smiley's number. He sounded preoccupied when she got him on the telephone.

"What can I do for you, Matriece?"

"I was just double-checking to make sure you and Kent straightened out that bill of yours we got."

"I told you, that wasn't ours." He sounded irritated.

"Right. So, you did talk with Kent?"

"I haven't heard from the man. The problem is in your shop, not here. Matriece, I've got a little mini fire I'm trying to put out. I'm going to have to go."

"Sure."

Matriece told her assistant to hold all her calls. She sat staring out at the Los Angeles skyline for a few moments before she picked up the telephone and called Kent. "I haven't heard from you about the bill from Taper Industries," she said after exchanging greetings. Kent sounded as though he'd just awakened from a very deep sleep. Something was definitely wrong with the man.

"Oh, that. I told you not to worry. I talked to Smiley. We found the error. If you see it again, don't worry about it."

"Fine, Kent," she said.

The elevator let Matriece off on the fifth floor, where the accounting department was located. She went through glass double doors, past the receptionist's area, and down a long hall that led to Charlotte Logan's office. She'd met with the head of the accounts department when she started working at the company, and they'd spoken on the telephone several times since. Now, as Charlotte's assistant ushered Matriece into her office, she felt anxious. Suppose she was making a big deal over nothing? Maybe Kent had intended to talk to Leonard Smiley and lied to her because he was embarrassed. I'm not accusing anyone of anything, Matriece thought. I just want to find out what's going on with Brown Sugar's money.

"Matriece, what a surprise." Charlotte extended her hand. She was a large redheaded woman with a face full of freckles. On her desk was a half-eaten candy bar, a diet soda, and the latest edition of *Cosmopolitan*. There was a chocolate stain on her blouse.

"I want to double-check something. Brown Sugar is being charged one hundred seventy-five thousand dollars for a bill we didn't make. I think I know where the mistake occurred. I just want to see if we've been debited yet."

Charlotte sat down at her computer and punched in the code Matriece gave her. A set of figures appeared on the screen, and Charlotte studied them silently for a moment. "Oh, yeah, that paid about a month ago. So, you didn't purchase anything from Taper Industries?"

"Not a thing. The code that was on it was hair care, but when I talked with Leonard, he said he didn't know anything about it."

Charlotte took a sip of her soda and crossed her legs. Her shoe dangled from the foot that was extended. She punched in a few more numbers and then waited. "It didn't come out of hair care. They haven't been dealing with any Taper Industries. What is it, anyway?"

"I have no idea."

Charlotte input more data and waited. Looking over her shoulder, Matriece scanned the list of suppliers that Gilda Cosmetics used. She didn't see Taper Industries or anything close to it.

"You sure about the name, Matriece?"

"Absolutely."

"Well, it's not listed. Maybe you should talk to Kent. Anything over one hundred fifty thousand has to have his approval."

"I'll ask him about it," Matriece said, her mind spinning wildly.

Kent is stealing. So what am I supposed to do now? she thought as she got off the elevator and walked toward her office. *If I don't do something I may end up being accused.* She thought about telling Gilda, but knowing Kent's history with their boss, Matriece's instincts said to wait.

"Mr. Abramowitz wants you to call him," her assistant said as soon as she walked in the door. "He didn't say what it was about."

Matriece sighed. In the last few weeks Daniel had been pressing her to ink the deal with Asia. She understood his concern. The March deadline was looming. What could she tell him, that the last time she spoke with Asia she was so dispirited she couldn't get out of bed? That she'd dispatched the best psychiatrist she knew to help pull her out of her funk? Such confessions wouldn't reassure Daniel. Matriece herself was worried, not about Asia signing the contract, but about the girl she used to baby-sit. Asia had done all the right things, become a success, and she was depressed.

Matriece didn't want to dwell on the questions that pierced her mind. If she did, she knew that her own low-down funk would rise up and grab her by the throat. Asia probably had man trouble. Wasn't that always the problem? As soon as the thought entered her mind, tears filled her eyes. I'm a fool, she told herself. I could have had Montgomery. I'm the one who let him go.

She wiped her face and put in a quick call to Claude Renfro, leaving a message when his assistant told her he was out. The two had been talking back and forth. She'd been relieved when he told her that Asia was continuing to see Dr. Prince twice a week and that he'd put her on a mild antidepressant. She resolved not to call Asia anymore, to give the singer a chance to heal. There was still time enough for her to sign the contract. The most important thing was for her to get better.

With a sigh, Matriece picked up her telephone and called Daniel's office, praying that he wasn't available. But, of course he was, and he wanted to see her immediately.

"Matriece, how are things coming along with Asia Pace?" he asked as soon as she sat down in his office.

"She's been ill and hasn't been seeing anyone. I'm keeping in touch with her manager. She's going to sign the contract just as soon as she's up and about."

"I've been thinking about another person. Very hot. She'd be even better than Asia. I think she calls herself Miss Notorious."

"The rapper?!" The image of the scantily clad hip-hop diva immediately came to mind. She looked at Daniel, hoping to see a smile, but he stared back at her, his face serious and composed. "I thought you wanted Asia." She managed to keep her voice calm, even though she felt like shrieking.

"I want to get this thing wrapped up. The advertising deadline is approaching. I really think we should look into Miss Notorious. Her records outsell Asia's four to one."

"Daniel, that's not the image we're after."

"Why not? Brown Sugar wants teens to thirties. That crowd loves this girl."

"Some of them may like her music but our spokesmodel has to be symbolic of African-American women, their beauty, their . . . their values."

"My point exactly."

"Brown Sugar needs an all-American black girl. Let's wait for Asia."

Daniel waved his hand impatiently. "I want you to meet with Miss Notorious. I'll bring her in."

Matriece was still seething when she returned to her office.

CHAPTER FIFTY

BLAIR TRIED TO pay attention to Rachel as they ate their lunch. She felt strangely antsy but she'd learned over the course of several months that all Rachel required of her was that she listen. As she sat sipping her coffee, she pretended to do just that.

"So, I'm going to table the film for a few months. I don't know, the idea isn't as intriguing as it used to be. I'm sure I'll get back to it," Rachel said.

"It's best not to force creativity. You have to let it flow," Blair said. She'd given up trying to benefit from her relationship with Rachel. Her boss's daughter was too self-absorbed to even get her hints that she'd like to have her mother's ear. Or maybe she was just ignoring her.

"Exactly," Rachel said. She looked pleased and yet still forlorn, like a puppy that had been petted by a stranger. "My father was a producer," she said.

"Really."

Rachel leaned forward and rattled off a list of films her father had done.

"That's impressive. What's he doing now?"

"He's not in the business anymore," she said.

The two women parted after lunch. Walking back to the office alone, Blair was glad it was raining. A good rinsing was just what she needed.

It was still drizzling when Blair stood in the doorway facing the courtyard to have her last smoke of the workday. Kent wasn't around. For a while she had thought their cravings were coordinated, but for the last few weeks she'd missed her nicotine buddy. Their contemplative smoking sessions were often the most peaceful part of her day. Sometimes she thought she ran off at the mouth too much but the older man didn't seem to mind. Not that he ever opened up to her, but then she wouldn't either if she'd been in his position.

She hadn't been quite so worried about her son for the last two weeks. Judd seemed to be maturing. Blair thought he was finally getting the message. She hadn't smelled any marijuana in a while. He had been going to school and staying there all day, according to Dr. Sable.

At the thought of the vice-principal, Blair cringed. She wanted to blot from her mind the memory of paying the academic entrepreneur to keep her son in school. That's behind me, she told herself. Things were going well for Judd. He'd been acting out, that's all, just adolescent rebellion, and now he was finally growing up. Hadn't he come to her after his DUI and told her he was truly sorry, that he wanted to make her proud of him? He'd never said that before. Hadn't he brought home two A papers? A's! She hadn't seen A's in years. Blair took a last drag, bent down, and stubbed out the cigarette on the damp pavement; she tossed it into the receptacle and went back to her office.

Matriece was waiting for her. Glancing at her friend, Blair had mixed feelings. She'd missed talking with Matriece but part of her was still hurt by the way she had rushed off and left her when Gilda called for lunch. Matriece and Gilda seemed to be spending so much social time together all of a sudden. It was one thing to be available to the boss, another entirely to be so damn gleeful about it. Sucking up, that's what Matriece was doing, and it was probably helping her, too. In a few years her friend would be running the entire company. And where would she be?

"How are you, Matriece?" Blair said.

"It has been just the worst day," Matriece said. "For starters, Montgomery is getting married to Gretel Meeks."

"Well, what do you care? You broke up with the guy," Blair said. If Matriece expected sympathy from her she could just forget it.

"I know. I know. It was a mistake, and now it's too late. I should have listened to you, Blair. You told me not to dump him, but really, everything happened so quickly. God, I wish I could do things over again."

"What are you saying? You want him back?" Blair could barely keep out the sarcasm that tinged her question.

"Yeah, I do." She looked up at Blair. "I blew it."

"You know what, Matriece? You are such a spoiled brat. Everything in your life is just handed to you, and you don't appreciate anything. Great job. Great house. Great boyfriend, who you didn't appreciate. Now you want him back. Well, you can't have everything you want, girl." Blair was out of breath when she finished, and she could feel a headache coming on. She hadn't meant to get emotional; from the way Matriece was looking at her, she'd probably said too much.

"Why do you sound so pissed off, Blair? Are you angry with me?"

"Yes, Matriece, I'm angry with you," Blair said, and then the telephone rang. She picked it up and then handed it to Matriece. "It's Tavares. They transferred the call from your office."

Matriece looked perplexed as she took the phone. As she listened, her face became darker and more concerned with each passing moment. At one point she began to tremble.

When Matriece hung up, she didn't say anything. She was shaking hard, and Blair went to her, put her arm around her. "What is it? What's wrong?"

"Tavares was arrested."

"What?" Blair said, wondering why her palms were suddenly so moist and her mouth so dry.

Matriece faced her, stared straight into her eyes. "He was late. He missed his bus. Judd and another guy offered him a ride. Judd and the other boy were smoking marijuana. They were speeding. The cops stopped them. They found weed and cocaine in the car. Judd said it belonged to Tavares. The cops let Judd and his friend go, and they arrested Tavares."

Blair took her hand away. "That's impossible," she said. "Impossible. Judd doesn't do drugs. He doesn't hang around with anyone who does them. Why would the police arrest Tavares if he didn't have any drugs?"

"You know why."

Blair didn't say anything.

"I have to go get him. You drive. I'll follow you in my car."

Blair gave a start.

"I'll follow you," Matriece repeated.

Blair felt odd being at the same police station that she'd come to only weeks earlier. She could tell that the desk officer recognized her. She avoided looking in his direction. She didn't want to be there. There were things that she didn't want to see. Tavares, for one, his face so young and frightened as he hugged Matriece. She couldn't remember Judd ever hugging her when he got into trouble. And she didn't want to see Vonette and her husband when they rushed in, holding hands, talking in English and Spanish all at once. The man took charge one moment, questioning the police in a loud voice, and then, just when he seemed to fade a bit, to weaken, his wife took over. Blair heard Vonette say to Matriece, "You said he'd be safe here. You said it would be better." And then her husband, Boot, told her to be quiet, and she stopped talking.

She was sitting a little away from them, wanting to flee but stuck, like a person behind a door that's locked from the outside. Any minute and they would come over and ask her about Judd. She knew that, yet Blair couldn't prepare an answer. All she could think of was that if Judd was arrested for drug possession, his chance of getting into college would be ruined.

"My son doesn't do drugs," Vonette said flatly.

Blair looked up and saw the three of them looming above her.

"I'm sure there's an explanation," she said. She repeated herself twice more, while they all stared at her. For a moment, being surrounded by their dark faces transported her back to the old days, when her neighborhood changed and slowly, irrevocably became them against us, the Supremes coming to kick her butt. She wondered why it always seemed to come down to that.

The house was quiet and dark when Blair finally got home. No Porter. No Judd. It was too late to prune roses, to pull out the weeds that choked the flowers. She changed her clothes, then came back downstairs and cooked rice, chicken, and spinach. Blair set the table. She poured herself a glass of wine, drank it straight down without taking a breath. And then she waited for her men to come home.

CHAPTER FIFTY-ONE

JUDD WAS STILL high when he dropped off the other boy, but he could sense that sobriety wasn't far away and that it would be uglier than usual.

"We're some lucky motherfuckers," his friend said after he got out of the car. The boy smacked his palm against Judd's.

"Word," Judd said, nodding his head in agreement. Then he took off without a backward glance.

He drove around, stopping when he saw a McDonald's. He had money, nearly forty dollars that his mother had given him. He got in the drive-through line and ordered a Big Mac, giant fries, and a large Coke. But after he had paid for his food, he didn't know where to eat it. Judd didn't want to go inside and he didn't want to go home. Turning onto the street, he wasn't sure where he was going, only that he felt as though he were being chased.

By the time he stopped at the park, the French fries were barely warm and the hamburger bun was soggy, although his car still reeked of potatoes and beef. Judd ate a handful of fries, took a bite of his hamburger, then set them aside. He wasn't hungry anymore. Outside the sky was turning dark.

I'm an asshole, he thought. He stared at his face in the rearview mirror for a second, just long enough to see the tears beginning to form in his eyes, before turning away. What good had tears ever done him?

He couldn't halt the flood of bad feelings inside. He couldn't stuff them down with food, or smoke them away with herb. This time he'd really fucked up. Tavares's face flashed before his eyes. It had been so easy to blame him. Black guy's word against a white guy's in his neighborhood? No fucking contest. Way of the world, but that didn't mean it wasn't fucked up. Dude was so scared when the cop took him away. So scared, and it wasn't even his fault. Dude could be sitting up in a jail cell right now.

There were still the frail remnants of the odor of fast food in his car when Judd pulled into his driveway. He could see the light on in the kitchen as he walked through the hallway leading from the garage. His mother was sitting at the table smoking. She didn't usually smoke in the house. One look in her eyes and Judd realized that she knew. He sat down beside her. "I messed up again," he said.

What was in his mother's face was worse than tears. There was a hopelessness that he'd never seen before and the kind of pain that filled him with panic. "I'll do better, Mom. I swear I will. I'll never get in trouble again."

"I know that boy's family, Judd." Not wailing or screaming, just that hopeless deathlike tone. He wished she would slap his face, punch him. "How could you do this? What were you doing with drugs? Are you addicted to cocaine?"

"No. No."

"Well, what were you doing with it? How did you get it?"

"The other guy in the car had it."

"Judd, don't lie to me."

"I'm not lying. He sells weed and cocaine. I bought some weed from him, and I was dropping him off at his house."

His mother shook her head, put her hands over her mouth. Her shoulders started shaking. Judd put his arm around her to make her still. She was so thin. He'd never realized how small she was. She could break so easily. "Mom. Don't. I promise. Nothing like this will ever happen again. I'll go to any college you want, and you'll see, I'll start doing good."

She tore herself away from him and was on her feet. "Is that it, Judd? You're just going to go off to college and forget about this? An innocent boy was arrested. You lied. He may have to go to jail. Doesn't that concern you at all?"

"Mom . . ."

They both looked up at the sound of the garage door opening. They were silent listening to the footsteps coming toward them. His mother pressed her lips together and folded her arms.

"Judd has something he'd like to say to you, Porter," she said when her husband appeared. There was an edge to her voice. Judd wondered whether she was angry with him or his father.

His father sat down at the table. "What's going on, Judd?" he asked. The older man looked at him warily, as if he suspected that a sharp, thrusting blade might come out of his mouth instead of words.

"I was pulled over for speeding today. I had some drugs in the car, weed and cocaine, and when the cops found them I told them it belonged to a black guy who was riding with me. They arrested him."

His father looked at his mother; when she didn't respond he turned back to him. "Cocaine?"

"Yeah. It wasn't mine, the cocaine, I mean. The weed was. This other guy who sells stuff was in the car. He had the cocaine."

"You say the police told you to go?" His father's eyes weren't on him or his mother. He was looking way off, as if it were a place he'd like to get to.

"Yeah."

"After he told them that the drugs belonged to Tavares," Blair said.

"Tavares? How do you know his name?" he asked, turning to his wife, focusing on her.

"He's Matriece's nephew, the one who's using our address."

"You never told me—"

"Yes, I did, Porter. That's not the point."

"I understand that, Blair," his father said sharply.

"What he did stinks, and you know it."

"Well, you're the one who paid five hundred dollars to keep him in school."

"And I never should have done that."

"Maybe they'll drop the charges."

"Porter, he lied, and another boy got arrested. That's not right."

"Look, life is tough, Blair. And it's tougher with a police record. May I remind you that Judd already has a DUI."

"So you approve of his lying? Sure, I guess lying is okay with you since you do it all the time."

"What are you talking about?"

His mother looked at him and then at his father. "Let's just eat dinner, Porter. We'll continue this conversation later."

They hadn't had a meal together in weeks. The three of them ate in silence with only the clatter of knives and forks to remind them that they were eating at all. Judd wasn't hungry, but he didn't want to go to his room. He wanted to remain at that table full of stormy chewing and averted eyes. He made himself clean his plate and felt rewarded by his mother's surprised face. It was so easy to make her happy. He stole a glance at her, and their eyes met. As much grief as he caused, she still had a smile for him. His dad wasn't smiling. Say something, Judd thought, staring at his father's hands. But when Judd looked at him, his father glared back, then turned his head. When Judd looked down at his plate, it was a blur. He pushed it away and got up from the table. By the time he got to the top of the stairs his parents were at it again. He crouched down, pulling his knees up to his chest.

"You asked me what I was talking about, Porter. You must think I'm stupid. Who is she?"

"Blair, for God's sake, instead of imagining affairs that I'm having—"

"It's not my imagination, and don't tell me that it is."

"Blair, we need to talk about Judd."

"We need to talk about your whore."

"Blair—"

"You're such a fucking liar."

"Blair, we have to take Judd's side in this."

His mother was quiet for a moment, and Judd could sense that she was struggling, trying to calm herself, to be rational on his behalf. "There comes a time when he has to take responsibility, Porter."

"Do you want him to go to jail? Do you?"

"No."

"We've got to stand by him. We're sticking to his story, and that's the end of it."

The relief came to Judd in waves. There was always the possibility that they might have made him confess, take his punishment like a man. He didn't want to go to jail. He wanted to be allowed to do better the next time. He could change his story, tell the cops another guy had brought the dope but that he couldn't give up the name because the guy had threatened him. Would the police go for that? Maybe Tavares didn't have to go under just because he was saved.

Then he heard his father again. "Listen, I've got to go out of town tomorrow. I'll be gone for two weeks."

The good feeling that was inside Judd evaporated. The yelling started up again. So many shouts and accusations between his parents that after a while Judd got up, went into his room, closed the door. But he could still hear them. Their screaming stopped sometime after one o'clock. Maybe they fell asleep, Judd thought. He couldn't. Gone for two weeks, right in the middle of the biggest crisis of his son's little asshole life. How's that for priorities?

Fuckhimfuckhimfuckhimfuckhimfuckhimfuckhim. The words came fast, each one punctuated by his fist smashing into a pillow. *Fuck him!* If he'd had a joint he would have fired it up and held his own coming-of-age party, a proper requiem for bygone hopes. But he was out of weed, and like it or not, his thoughts were rational. The next move he made would be the result of a clear head.

CHAPTER FIFTY-TWO

FOR NEARLY TWENTY years the Briggs and Meeks families had held an annual dinner party to celebrate their friendship and their stellar business accomplishments. Both Nadine Briggs and Eudora Meeks claimed credit for the original idea, which, in fact, was jointly conceived in the ladies' room of the Beverly Hills Hotel, where both women had fled one night to escape the tedium of yet another banquet speaker. In the Byzantine splendor of that bathroom, the two women complained about their hectic social lives and yearned aloud for the simple at-home entertaining they'd known when their husbands weren't quite so successful. One thing led to another, and the first dinner was held at Nadine's home. Big Monty set the tone for that night and all the years to come when he raised his glass in a jubilant toast "to making money in the white man's world." The event had been canceled only twice since that initial dinner: once when Calvin Meeks headed the list of thriving black enterprises published yearly in the black business bible while Big Monty was number ten; the second time was the year the order was reversed. Five years earlier, when Nadine saw the stunning results of Eudora's face-lift, tummy tuck, and liposuction, she felt like canceling, but instead downed half a fifth of bourbon, called the caterers, and made her own appointment with a highly recommended cosmetic surgeon.

For the last ten years the event had been held on the Sunday before the Martin Luther King birthday holiday, and on this, the twentieth celebration heralding the prosperity of both families—the We Got Big Bucks party, Montgomery had dubbed it—spirits were high for both Calvin Meeks and Montgomery Briggs, Jr. Big Monty was about to ink a deal with a Mexican communications conglomerate that would net him nearly thirty-two million dollars; and Calvin was about to write a check that would cause the downfall of his most feared business rival. Their wives, who had long ago gotten used to taking a backseat to their husbands' businesses, were content to have the attention of their men without having to take a number.

Juliette opened the door before Montgomery could let himself in with his key. He was about to hang up his coat when he heard his father's voice. "Nadine, when I tell you to do something, goddamn it, woman, you do it. I don't want to hear your shit. Lotta women would like to be sitting in your chair."

Moments later, Montgomery looked outside and saw the Meekses' car turning into the driveway. He opened the door, shook hands with Calvin, kissed Eudora and Gretel on their cheeks, and was escorting them into the family room just as the maid appeared with a tray filled with flutes of champagne.

"Welcome!" Nadine sang out as she descended the stairs. Coming up to Gretel, she let out a little shriek and lifted the young woman's left hand. "Gretel, you're engaged!"

Montgomery, who was standing right beside his mother, heard the surprise in her voice and the disappointment, too. His eyes met Gretel's. She winked, and it was hard to contain his laughter. Poor Mom, he thought. It was no secret that Nadine and Eudora wanted Montgomery and Gretel to marry. But through the years the two had developed a friendship, not a romance.

Gretel held up her left hand and waved it slightly. "Don't get excited, Mrs. Briggs. It's my gift to myself."

Nadine let out a sigh. The relief in it was so palpable that Montgomery wanted to laugh again. He knew his mother wouldn't give up hoping for a wedding between Gretel and him as long as they both remained unmarried. "You bought yourself an engagement ring?" Nadine exclaimed. "Why on earth did you do that?"

She shrugged. "It was a beautiful ring, and I just wanted it."

"Well, you should wear it on your other hand, honey," Nadine said.

"I told her the same thing," Eudora said. She took a big sip of champagne. "She never listens to me."

Nadine looked at Eudora, who immediately raised her eyebrows, a sign that her friend should drop the subject, which she did.

Both families trooped into the Briggses' cavernous living room, recently redecorated in a dazzling mixture of expensive modern and antique furniture. Original works by Romare Bearden, Jacob Lawrence, and Richard Yarde hung on the walls. Pictures on the occasional tables scattered about the room were of the Briggs family on trips to China, Japan, Russia, and South Africa. Nadine's collection of early photographs of African-Americans was displayed behind the glass doors of a mahogany cabinet. In the far corner of the room was a hand-carved baby grand piano that was more than two hundred years old.

"This room is just gorgeous," Eudora Meeks exclaimed.

Montgomery admired it, too. Although his parents had moved into the house when Montgomery was fifteen years old, sometimes he was still amazed by what they had accomplished. Big Monty and Nadine's success hadn't been a rags-to-riches story. Both families had been solidly middle class for generations. Great-grandparents and grandparents from both sides had been educators. Montgomery had maternal and paternal uncles and aunts who were doctors and lawyers. But nobody in the family had ever achieved what Big Monty had, Montgomery thought, glancing around the room, taking in the expensive carpets, the priceless art and tasteful furniture. *And I won't either.*

He saw his father and Meeks heading toward his father's study. He knew they were exchanging ideas about business. Well, he didn't have any ideas of his own. So he might as well ride the gravy train.

"Montgomery honey, try some of the shrimp," his mother said. "They're delicious."

A woman in a black-and-white uniform passed him a small china plate with some shrimp on it. Montgomery held the plate but didn't eat anything, even though he could feel his mother watching him as she was talking to everyone else.

Nearly half an hour later, Montgomery was standing outside his father's office. He could hear the men talking.

"I'm telling you, Calvin, the first thing you do is hire a private investigator."

"You think that's necessary?"

"Man, listen. Gilda's head man comes and offers you the keys to the kingdom . . ."

"For a fee."

"Right. He offers to sell you information that can damage his boss, wreck her new beach line—you have to ask some questions."

"I figure he needs money."

"That may be true, but suppose it isn't? Suppose he's setting you up? Or suppose he does need money. Maybe you can Jew him down."

"You got a point there."

The two men grew quiet. Montgomery waited outside the door to see if the conversation would continue, but neither one spoke. After a few minutes Montgomery knocked on the door. "Time to eat," he said.

It wasn't until later, after dinner had been served and their parents were sipping brandy that Montgomery pulled Gretel aside in the kitchen. "Why are you trying to drive both our mothers crazy?"

Gretel smiled, then kissed his cheek. "I told you I was engaged."

"Yeah, but you didn't tell me that you had a ring."

"Don't most engaged people have rings?" Before he could respond she whispered, "Janet sent it to me." She smiled.

Montgomery had known Gretel's preference since junior high school. In eighth grade he had tried to kiss her. She'd pushed him away. "I don't like boys for boyfriends," she said. It wasn't until high school that he realized the full meaning of her words. It had taken a few years before he adopted the live-and-let-live credo he now based his life on, and could love his friend without judgment. He gave her a long look, and then hugged her. "Just be happy, kiddo."

"Thanks."

"So, is she moving out here or are you going back there?"

"She's moving here in about a month."

"I take it you'll be getting a place together."

Gretel nodded.

"May I ask you this question for the thousandth time?"

"Montgomery, I can't tell my parents I'm a lesbian. Number one, they would fucking freak. Number two, my daddy would try to have me lobotomized. Number three, no money, honey. They would cut me off."

"I don't believe that, Gretel."

"Believe me. It's true."

"They'll figure it out, anyway. Sooner or later. Especially if Janet moves here. They're not stupid. They'll feel the vibes between you two."

"They might suspect something, but I'll never admit it, and they will go into deep, deep denial."

"Until one day they sneak into your house and see you guys getting it on. This is the new millennium, girl. Get your ass out the closet."

Gretel took a swipe at Montgomery and then laughed. "Maybe one day. It's so hard being rich, black, and gay. If I were just middle class, I'd marry Janet, borrow some of your sperm, and live happily ever after. Can't do that. There's a lot of things we can't do because of who we are."

Montgomery shook his head. "Speak for yourself. I've made peace with who I am. As for you, you love being privileged, and you know it."

"Since when have you made peace? You're itching to spread your wings. I confess: I do like the charge cards. I guess I'm not as unfortunate as you. I don't tell myself I have to fill my daddy's shoes or be more than six feet tall."

"Kinda late for that," Montgomery said.

"It's not too late for you to grow in other ways."

Montgomery didn't respond.

"For what it's worth, you're smarter than he is, and you're more creative, too. You were the one who figured out how to sell talk radio to play-me-some-music black folks. You're the guy who convinced the hottest comic on TV to be your drive-time host, and then syndicated the program. People started listening because of Big Monty. They keep listening because of you."

"Thanks for blowing my horn, Gretel."

"Damn, Montgomery, somebody should. He doesn't let you know how valuable you are to him because it makes him feel old. He shoots down your ideas because he knows you can run the whole thing without him. Don't let him stomp on your ego just to inflate his own. The only thing he has on you is your mother. Nadine knew how to convince a very ordinary man that he was the baddest brother who ever drew breath. He didn't return the favor, but that's just men."

"Don't get started."

"Right. You need a Nadine to get your personal revolution going. Speaking of which, I saw your old girlfriend the other day; we were both driving down Crenshaw. Why don't you get back with her, Montgomery? I told you she was the one."

He shook his head. "She was."

"What happened?"

"She dumped me. I have no idea why. Really."

"You still care about her?"

"Yes, I do."

"Well, you'd better get with her because I'm not introducing you to any more of my straight girlfriends."

Gretel leaned over and kissed his cheek. "You know what would be different about Matriece and you? I mean, as compared to your mom and dad? You'd give her as much as she gives you." She smiled at him as her words sank in. "I have to go."

Montgomery hugged her. "I love you, girl."

After everyone left, Montgomery sat in the living room with his parents, only half listening to them as he pondered the conversation he'd overheard between his father and Meeks. If Brown Sugar was in jeopardy, so was Matriece's career. But if Brown Sugar was successful, one of the few remaining black-owned cosmetics firms, owned by an old family friend, would be hit hard.

Juliette escaped early. Nadine took off her shoes and sat down on the sofa next to Montgomery, with her feet tucked under her. When his father went up to bed, Montgomery sensed that he was about to get grilled, and he was right. "I don't know why you and Gretel don't get together, honey."

"It would be like sleeping with my sister, Mom."

"She's not your sister," his mother said. Then her tone softened. "Friends make the best lovers. Don't you know that? And they make the absolute best marriages. That's why your father and I have lasted for so long. We're best friends."

Montgomery let that one go by.

"A good woman would help you, you know that." She patted his cheek.

"Yeah, I do."

It was after eleven o'clock when Montgomery reached his house but the first thing he did was call Matriece. She answered on the third ring and didn't sound as though she'd been sleeping.

"Montgomery. How are you?"

He could hear the pleasure in her voice, yet there was something very guarded about her, and something a little bit shaky.

"I'm fine. How are you?"

"I'm okay."

"Listen, I've been meaning to call you." He hated the words as soon as he said them. "So, work's going okay?" That sounded even dumber.

"Yes."

"And the family? They're good?"

He heard her sigh and detected pain. "Well . . ." Her voice broke, cracked right in half. The story about Tavares getting arrested came out between choking sounds. "Don't cry," he heard himself say. "I'll be right there."

He expected her face to be swollen, tears still streaming when Matriece opened the door, as though time stood still during the twenty minutes it took him to reach her. Instead she was beautiful, as always.

"You didn't have to come over," she said after she closed the door and led him into her family room. They both sat down on the couch.

"You sounded so upset," Montgomery said, feeling a little embarrassed. Why had he come? Matriece probably thought he was a fool. "I just wanted to know for myself that you're okay. That's all."

"Thanks," she said, and smiled. "It's not as bad as it seems. We've hired a lawyer. In all likelihood the charges will be dropped. Of course, he's not going to Castle Heights anymore, so I guess I kind of failed in my mission. The thing is, he was doing really well. I know that Tavares didn't have any drugs. If my other nephew or even my niece was involved, I'd be asking questions, but not Tavares. It was Judd, my friend Blair's son. He was driving the car. For a long time I've been feeling that Judd was giving Blair problems. Her face was always so sad whenever she talked about him, but she'd never let on that there was anything wrong."

"I think that if no one comes forward to testify against Tavares, the entire matter will be thrown out. I mean, there's no victim. The drugs weren't on him. It'll all blow over," Montgomery said.

"But why does a great fifteen-year-old kid have to go through getting arrested? I didn't send him up there so some cracker cop could demean him."

"Getting pulled over by the cops is the black boy's Bar Mitzvah."

Hearing her laugh reminded him of their good times and what he'd lost. Damn, I miss this woman, he thought. But as warmth began spreading through his body he realized that he didn't know how she felt about him. He didn't want to risk his feelings again. It was time for him to leave.

"Listen, I need to get home, but I want to tell you something first."

She seemed to withdraw from him then; her entire body stiffened, as if she were warding off a blow.

He spoke fast before he changed his mind. "Tonight I overheard a conversation. I'd rather not say who was talking. I didn't get the entire story but here's the gist: One of Gilda's top guys is trying to sell some secrets to your competition."

Matriece sat up. "Who told you that? What secrets?"

"I can't say, Matriece. But it seems that the information would have a direct impact on Brown Sugar."

He had expected astonishment, but though she was clearly upset, he sensed she wasn't completely surprised. She seemed strangely detached, as though she were listening to a tape playing in her mind. "Why did you tell me all this?"

"Why?" Because I still care about you, woman, he wanted to say. But he didn't. He'd been sailing in that boat before, only to discover it had holes in it. "Forewarned is forearmed," he said.

"Thank you," Matriece said softly. Then she leaned over and kissed him on his cheek. With his hand he pressed the back of her head so he could feel her face a few seconds longer. "Oh, Montgomery," she said. "Oh, God."

"Baby," he said, and then he was holding her face in his hands. They came toward each other at the same time. He kissed her, and then he kissed her again. Matriece pulled away, then stood up.

"This isn't right. You'd better go."

Not right? He wanted to ask her why, but her face was so resolute. He rose, then extended his hand. She put hers in his, and it was like another kiss that weakened them both. Unbalanced, they lurched into each other, and then they were holding on, as though they were each other's island in an unsettled sea. She pulled away first, her face a reprimand. He stood there for a moment, waiting, hoping, then walked to her front door. When he turned around she stood some distance from him. Even when the door finally closed, Montgomery expected to hear her voice saying his name. But her driveway was dark and silent, and as he walked to his car he told himself that he wouldn't get lost in that silence again.

CHAPTER FIFTY-THREE

IT WAS TOO late to call her godfather, so Matriece forced herself to go to bed. She tried to sleep but she could still feel Montgomery's warmth. When she closed her eyes she tasted him, still wanted him. It would have been better if he hadn't come, if he'd told her what he had to say over the telephone. Why did he have to come knocking on her door, as though he didn't believe that good-bye meant gone? She didn't want to feel stupid for letting him go.

She was dozing when she heard the weeping. The sound woke her up. It was nearby, in the room with her. A grown woman crying. Matriece couldn't see her. For the first time there was no light, no presence, no yellow dress. But she remembered the sound. Matriece's childhood was filled with secret sobbing, muffled tears at midnight. *Oh, Mommy, what are you crying about now? It's too late for tears.*

Before she got out of bed the next morning, Matriece dialed her godfather's number. "There's something you ought to know, Uncle Mooney," she said after she greeted him.

"What's that?"

"I think somebody is trying to sell the same information you have to Calvin Meeks." She waited for him to say something, and when he remained quiet she asked, "Uncle Mooney? Did you hear me?"

"Yeah. I'm thinking. Who told you that?"

"Montgomery. I'm sure Gretel Meeks told him. They're getting married," Matriece said. She felt as though she were talking about strangers.

"When did all that happen?"

"Which? I don't know when Montgomery and Gretel got engaged. We broke up, and they got engaged. I don't know when the other thing happened."

"What are you thinking?"

"Maybe the rumor is false. Maybe this person has a completely different angle. But you may not be the only person with information. If we don't use what we have, somebody else will. And I'm thinking I don't want Gretel Meeks owning my company. If you can still make the deal, I want to do it. I just want to talk with Gilda before you do."

"It's too late for that. I already talked with her."

"When?"

"Middle of January."

"Uncle Mooney, I wish you'd waited."

"I ain't got time to wait, and neither do you. Things get away from you when you wait too long. Maybe that's what happened with you and Big Monty's boy."

She hadn't been expecting sympathy from Mooney, but his cut-and-dried reaction left Matriece even more morose than before. After she hung up, so many regrets washed over her that for a moment she couldn't move. *I've walked out on every relationship I ever started. But this is the first time I've been sorry.* Tall guys. Short guys. Dark guys. Light guys. Guys with money. Guys who were broke. Good guys. Bad guys. Guys she loved and guys she couldn't care less about. She'd left them all. Next! That was her motto. She was always running, always getting away. *I'm scared.* She'd never admitted that to herself before, but now she let the words sink in. Matriece stood up abruptly. She felt the invisible lock clicking into place, the one that always appeared when she tried to open old doors.

It was late in the afternoon when Matriece walked into the ladies' room as Blair was emerging from one of the stalls. Their eyes met briefly before Blair averted hers. There was no one in the rest room but the two of them.

"Are you staying away from me, Blair?" Matriece asked. The rush of anger and adrenaline added volume to her words. She felt taller and stronger, the bully in the school yard hovering over her prey.

"What?"

Blair seemed afraid.

"I said, are you running away from me?"

"No, I—"

"Because I thought you might want an update on the damage your son's lies have caused."

"I'm sure that . . ." Blair said. Matriece could tell she was trying to rise to the occasion, to summon all the in-your-face fearlessness that she possessed. But her store was low. Her words sounded puny, her stance weak. In the school yard she would have been the punk, the one whose ass got kicked. Matriece hadn't smelled blood in a long time.

"Your son is a damn liar, and you know it."

Blair seemed momentarily cowed, but then she shot back, "Matriece, you wanted Tavares to come to Castle Heights to give him a better school environment. Well, maybe you didn't get him there soon enough." Blair looked away before the words were out of her mouth.

"I wanted him in a better school because he's a good kid," Matriece said. "You think we don't grow good kids in South Central? What? The test scores are all low and the boys are all bad? Is that it? Our sons riot and yours revel, that it? They do the crime and the time, and your boys get perfect SAT scores. But weren't those your perfect boys shooting up those school yards in Oregon and Columbine?"

"I'm sorry about what happened to Tavares, but all Judd did was give him a ride."

Matriece moved toward Blair, got right up in her face. Her entire body was trembling. She felt like slapping her as hard as she could, but she also felt like crying. They'd been friends for nearly ten years. Matriece had begun to think of her as her friend Blair, not her white friend Blair. And now this.

"I should have known better," Matriece said quietly. Little rosy splotches began spreading across Blair's cheeks as though Matriece *had* slapped her.

When Matriece stepped into Daniel's office for his impromptu meeting she felt ill. And the dazzling display of silver didn't make her feel any better. Tight silver jeans. Silver halter top. Silver jewelry. Silver lipstick. Silver sparkles in her cleavage. And streaks of metallic silver in her hair. Miss Notorious sat on the plush sofa in Daniel's office with her shapely legs crossed. Her right leg was swinging just slightly, as though a CD were playing in her mind. Seated next to her was a short dark man wearing diamond studs in his ears and a diamond tennis bracelet. An ebullient Daniel introduced Matriece to the well-known hip-hop diva and her manager and husband, De Andre Lords. She managed a smile and a polite hello, but Matriece was furious. *How dare he set up this meeting without consulting me.* Moments later Rachel rushed into the office, and Daniel introduced her as well.

"I want to thank you both for coming," Daniel said after they all moved to an adjoining room where they sat at an oval table. An array of hors d'oeuvres, cheese and crackers, fruit, cold sodas, and wine was arranged on a platter in front of them. De Andre Lords surveyed the food and then turned to Miss Notorious and said coldly, "Fix me a plate."

With downcast eyes his wife leaned over and placed several stuffed mushrooms, jumbo shrimp, crab cakes, and mini quiches on a plate and offered it to De Andre.

"Gimme more shrimp than that," he said, and she obediently piled more food on his plate.

"That enough, baby?" She looked at him imploringly. He grunted, then snatched the plate. "Get me a soda."

"What kind, baby?"

"Pepsi," he said, his mouth full. Miss Notorious put ice in a glass, poured the soda, then handed it to De Andre.

"As I explained to you on the telephone, Mr. Lords, this fall Gilda Cosmetics's new line of products for african-american women will debut. It's called Brown Sugar. We are currently looking for the face of the product, the spokesmodel who will appear in advertisements and commercials. We think Miss Notorious has the kind of image that African-American women identify with . . ."

Oh my God.

". . . And we'd like for you to start thinking about Brown Sugar. Naturally, we're not making you an offer today. This is only an exploratory meeting to establish mutual interest."

"How much y'all paying?" De Andre asked, his mouth full of shrimp.

"Those details can be worked out—"

"That ain't no detail. That's the whole shit right there." He looked at his wife.

"Word," she said.

Daniel laughed a bit nervously. "I think we can safely say that the total would be a seven-figure package."

"I only fly first class," Miss Notorious said loudly. "And I have to have me a stretch to ride in. Ain't that right, baby?" she looked at her husband, who ignored her.

"As I said, those details can be worked out."

"What kind of makeup is it? I ain't into nothing drab, light pink and all that mess. What kinda shades y'all got?"

Daniel looked at Matriece, who at that very moment was focusing all her energy on controlling her urge to throw a shrimp at him. "Well, the debut line is going for a subtle, natural look, a lot of beiges and browns for lipsticks and nail colors."

"I have to see how it looks."

"We can send you a sample kit," Daniel said effusively.

Miss notorious nodded and grabbed some chicken for herself. Everyone got quiet, and the only sound was the smacking lips of diva and manager. By the time they departed, not an hors d'oeuvre was left.

"Her energy is just fabulous, don't you think?" Daniel said. He looked genuinely pleased.

"No, I don't," Matriece replied.

"You don't like her?" Daniel said. He seemed surprised, almost hurt.

"I'm telling you," Matriece said wearily, "she is not the look of Brown Sugar. Not at all. Asia Pace is."

"Matriece," Daniel said as he rose, "I'm not ruling out Asia Pace, but let's keep talking to Miss Notorious. Time is running out, and Miss Pace has had ample opportunity to sign the contract. We can compare the two and make a decision in, let's say, two weeks. Now, if you'll excuse me, I have a business meeting to attend."

After leaving Daniel's office, Matriece went straight to the parking lot; she hadn't left early in a long time. Her temples were throbbing as she drove to Asia Pace's home. Every time she visualized Miss Notorious's picture in a magazine advertising Brown Sugar's products, the pain intensified. *Oh, hell no.* In her briefcase was a letter of intent. She would get a commitment out of Asia today.

Matriece rang the doorbell to Asia's town house three times before she heard her voice over the intercom. She hadn't heard from Asia since she'd arranged with Claude Renfro to have her see a therapist, but the voice that finally answered still sounded depressed. As Asia buzzed her in, Matriece wondered what kind of mood the singer would be in.

She looks bad, Matriece thought when Asia opened the door dressed in sweats that appeared to have been slept in. Her hair wasn't combed. Her eyes seemed vacant.

"Oh, honey," Matriece said, hugging her. "How are you feeling?"

"I'm all right," Asia said. She spoke in a monotone.

Matriece closed the door and followed her into her bedroom, watched silently as Asia climbed back into bed. The television was on but the sound was turned off.

"When's the last time you saw Dr. Prince?"

"He went on vacation," she said dully.

Matriece sat down on the edge of the bed. "Are you still taking the medication?"

Asia didn't say anything for a while. Finally she said, "It makes me feel weird. I went to see my brother, Donny. You know he's in the joint."

She nodded. "I'll bet he was glad to see you. He must be so proud of you, Asia. Oh, sweetie, don't cry. Did Dr. Prince tell you when he was coming back?"

"In a few days."

Matriece looked at Asia, then she took her hand. "Remember when you were little I'd give you a bath."

Asia nodded.

"How about I do that now? After that, I'm going to fix you something to eat. Then we're going to pack an overnight bag, and you're going to stay with me for a couple of days until Dr. Prince gets back. You shouldn't be alone, Asia."

It was after seven o'clock by the time Matriece drove into her garage with a freshly bathed and shampooed Asia, who followed her upstairs to the guest room. The younger woman didn't say anything as she watched her hostess place fresh towels and washcloths in the adjoining bathroom. When Matriece came back into the room Asia hadn't moved. The phone rang.

"How you doing, Triecy?"

"I'm okay, Boot. Is everything all right?"

"Tavares is doing fine. Glad to be back at his regular school. Your sister is calming down. She slept through the night last night. Just leave her alone for a minute, Triecy. She'll come around. We heard from the lawyer. The hearing is three weeks from today. Lawyer thinks they'll throw it out. It's some bullshit anyway.

"Listen, girl, I don't care what Vonette says now, we all thought it was a good idea for him to change schools, so don't let her run no guilt trip on you. Same shit coulda happened right down the street."

"Thanks, Boot."

"And your boy still loves you."

"I know."

"Aw'ight, later."

"How are you feeling, Asia?" Matriece asked after she hung up.

Asia shrugged.

"Are you tired?"

"My mind is."

God, she looks like Sam, Matriece thought. Sam's kind face came to mind, his patient eyes, his strong hands. Would it help for her to know him? she wondered. Would it hurt? Helphurthelphurthelphurthelphurt-helphurt? "Do you ever see your father, Asia?"

She shook her head slowly and began crying. "He doesn't care about me and Donny." She began sobbing.

"Asia. Honey, listen to me." *Why is this so hard?* "He does care about you. I'm going to tell you something. I don't know if it's the right thing to do but . . . I know your father. I know where he is, and he wants to see you, if you want to see him. But you don't have to, and maybe you should think about—"

Asia wiped her eyes, then grabbed Matriece's hand. "Call him right now."

Matriece picked up the phone slowly and began dialing the pager number she knew by heart. After all these years, after all Sam's neglect, after everything, Asia still wants to see her daddy, Matriece thought. She closed her eyes. *What does that feel like?*

CHAPTER FIFTY-FOUR

SAM HAD JUST finished waxing a car when the page came in. His hand was shaking when he turned off his cell phone. He remained in the driver's seat of his van, trying to get his nerves together but he only seemed to tremble harder. *He may not come when you want him but He's always right on time.* He had been praying for this day for so long and now that it was here, Sam was overwhelmed by anxiety. Suppose she just wanted to see him to tell him how much she hated him for leaving her? Suppose she changed her mind and refused to see him at the last minute? Sam took a deep breath. God is with me, he thought. Then he turned on the ignition of his van and drove to Matriece's house.

Matriece lived only fifteen minutes away from his last client, and Sam drove fast, letting his thoughts ramble. *What will I say when she asks me why I wasn't there? Will she ever trust me?* The closer he got to Matriece's the more powerful his doubts became. *What am I trying to prove? She'll never accept me. Ruth has probably poisoned her mind against me. It's too late.*

By the time he parked his van in Matriece's driveway, Sam's powder-blue shirt was sweat-stained. He sat still for a few moments after his motor died. He tried to pray but all he managed to say was *God, please help me.*

Later, he wouldn't remember how he got from his car to the top step or whether he even rang the bell. The front door opened and Matriece was standing there smiling. She said, "Hello, Sam. I have somebody who wants to see you," and then she took him by the hand and led him to her family room. And there she was, his little girl, his grown-up princess. She stood up. "It's you," she said.

Without thinking, he reached out and took her hand. He saw Matriece staring at them, and he mouthed the words "God bless you." She nodded and disappeared. They had catching up to do, and this was where it would start.

CHAPTER FIFTY-FIVE

IT RAINED ON the day of Lenny Rabinowitz's funeral. Winter had been uncharacteristically dry, and when the storms came late in January, they burst from the clouds like pent-up rage. Houses that clung to precipices on canyon ridges were swept away, old roofs leaked, and traffic stuttered and stalled. By the time Gilda arrived at Horowitz's Mortuary, the service was about to begin. She slipped into a seat just as the rabbi took his place in front of the crowd of mourners. Behind him was a simple pine box with black cloth draped over it. Gilda looked around her. There were about a hundred people in the room. For some reason it pleased her that Lenny had had so many friends. *You didn't destroy him; he had a good life anyway.*

"Another strong one has been laid low," the rabbi said. "Leonard Rabinowitz was a Shoah survivor. He saw his entire family, his entire village die in the gas chambers. But he didn't perish. There were times, he told me, when he wondered why he was spared. I always told him that he was spared to lead a good life. And that's the kind of life Lenny led.

"Lenny Rabinowitz was a wonderful husband. He was devoted to his wife, Pearl, who he met at Auschwitz. They lived together as man and wife for fifty-five years. He told me once that she was the rainbow of his life.

"Lenny Rabinowitz was a good father. He raised two beautiful daughters, Leah and Shelly. He set an example for manhood by honoring their mother; he provided for their needs and comforts, and they never knew want. He educated them at the finest schools.

"This was a man who believed in charity. He was active in the Red Cross, an organization he supported financially. He planted a tree in Israel. He was a lifelong tither to his temple. Lenny was a good example of what a Jew is supposed to be: a just and honest man.

"As we leave this place, let us not forget the Lennys of this world, survivors of the most horrific genocide ever visited upon a people. Those survivors are dwindling, so let us honor them now. Let us celebrate their strength, their courage and resiliency. In a short while from now, checks will be issued from banks in Switzerland, finally paying what is owed some of the survivors. Lenny will not collect his check here on earth. But through the immortality of his soul, Lenny's check will be cashed. Lenny's good life was his own reparations. He paid himself back by reaping the blessings that come from being a kind and just man, a wonderful father and husband, someone who would help a stranger. Can you say the same of your life? Are you kind? Are you merciful? Is your life paying you what you are owed? Grieving widow and children, your loved one is in a better place, where his soul has everlasting life."

The rabbi sat down and a tall, thin man came forward. He began singing "El Maleh Rachamim" in a strong tenor. Gilda hummed the words softly and closed her eyes. So many dead, she thought. So many unmourned bodies.

Pearl and her daughters came forward. Pearl took off the plain black jacket she was wearing. Gilda could see that someone had already cut the garment straight up the back seam. With a great deal of difficulty, Pearl tore a bit more of her jacket. Her daughters then ripped their dark jackets. The three women were crying by the time they returned to their seats.

The rabbi rose again and motioned the mourners to stand as he recited the Twenty-third Psalm in Hebrew. Gilda mouthed the words. "Yea, though I walk through the valley of the shadow of death, thou art with me."

When the service ended, Gilda made her way down the center aisle to Pearl and her daughters. She wouldn't be going to the grave site with most of the mourners, and she wanted to let Pearl know that she'd come. Gilda waited patiently as others shook the old woman's hand. When she was finally standing in front of her friend, she kissed her cheek. Pearl looked terrible. She'd always been frail but now she appeared wizened.

"Oh, Gilda. Bless you for coming. Lenny was so fond of you."

"I will miss him, Pearl."

Pearl grabbed her hand. "Please keep coming to the support group. Lenny always said you hadn't worked through all your grieving. You've made such a success of your life, Gilda. We're so proud of you."

"Oh, my dear," Gilda said. She kissed Pearl again and left.

Later that evening, Gilda's maid brought her a glass of chilled Riesling, closed the drapes, then took away the tray and the plate that still held her uneaten meal. *Is your life paying you what you are owed?* The answer was painful. She was fighting with her child. She felt closer to a stranger than to her own daughter. She was sleeping with a boy young enough to be her grandson. Her life was too confused to pay her anything at the moment. Gilda drained her glass and then put on her robe and went downstairs.

The letter was still on her family room coffee table. Gilda picked it up, held it for a moment, then read it through the clear plastic folder.

> *My Dear Mother,*
>
> *This place is terrible, and I'm very hungry all the time. At night I dream of your potato pancakes. I taste them in my dreams. Do not worry, Mother. All the things you ever taught me I will always remember. I still say please and thank you, and I try to get along with people.*
>
> *I hope that you and Papa are together. Thank you for this life that you have given me. It has been mostly good. I am not afraid. I am surrounded by kind, brave people. We try to make each other laugh.*
>
> *Yesterday a boy kissed me. Perhaps I would not tell you this if things were normal. I think, perhaps, that you would like to know that I have been kissed. Nothing more. I am still a good girl.*
>
> *Love, Rena*

Gilda's hand was shaking as she placed the letter on the table. She leaned back against the sofa and closed her eyes. She looked up and they were staring at her. For some reason, she had expected them. They said nothing, but they didn't leave. They seemed to be demanding something of her. Perhaps they always had. "I will live a better life, she said."

Then she appeared: Hosanna. Her face looked strange, not angry. Sad. And in that moment Gilda admitted the truth. She whispered to the spirit who faced her with such mournful eyes, "I didn't want to find you. I am sorry."

CHAPTER FIFTY-SIX

ON THE EXECUTIVE floor of Radiance headquarters Kent was pacing backward and forward, trying not to think about cigarettes or chill pills. He'd been calling Calvin Meeks every day since Gilda informed him of the conversation she'd had with Mooney. The CEO had been away on a business trip; today was his first day back, and though Kent didn't have an appointment, he was determined to see him. No one was going to play him for a fool!

The CEO's assistant ushered Kent into Meeks's office after a thirty-minute wait. "Good afternoon, Mr. Bridgeport. Have a seat," Meeks said, without rising or extending his hand.

Meeks's contemptuous tone cracked Kent's illusions. He'd always thought of himself as a decent person, someone people respected, an important man, the CFO of a major company. His name was on the checks, by God. But he'd come to Calvin Meeks with a despicable offer, an illegal offer that took biting the hand that fed him to an all-time low. He deserved Meeks's disdain. *I used to be respectable.*

The weight of that shattered conceit caused Kent's shoulders to slump. He'd marched into Meeks's office feeling righteous indignation, believing that he was owed an explanation. But looking at the black man's disdainful face, he realized there really wasn't honor between thieves. What did he think he could do to the man for double-crossing him? Call the police? It suddenly occurred to Kent that Meeks might not know anything about Mooney coming to see Gilda. With the effects of his last Xanax waning, he found himself in the unfortunate position of trying to figure out a new strategy to deal with a poker face he couldn't decipher.

First do no harm. The old adage popped into his mind. No sense in accusing Meeks of anything. *I've got to get him to commit,* he thought.

I've got to get that check. He mustered as much bravado as he could, leaned forward in his chair, and said, "I'll get right to the point, Mr. Meeks. Not long ago I offered to sell you some information, and I'd like to know your decision."

"I'm very interested, Mr. Bridgeport. But naturally, a man in my position has to be careful. How do I know that this isn't some entrapment sting designed to destroy me and my company? I'm not a fool. So, I've done a bit of investigating on my own."

Investigating? What did the man mean? "You're wise to be cautious, but I've been aboveboard with you. This isn't a sting. You may frisk me if you like."

To his surprise, Meeks came around from his desk and did just that, then instructed Kent to spill out the entire contents of his briefcase on his desk.

After Meeks had examined Kent's papers, his wallet, and Palm Pilot, he sat back down in his chair. "I understand that you play cards, Mr. Bridgeport, and that you've gotten yourself into quite a bit of debt. Three million is too high. I'll give you two."

Kent felt himself panicking. Two million would barely cover his balloon payment. He had to have enough to pay back Gilda. "I'm willing to shave off two hundred fifty thousand but that's it." He needed an ace, a trump, but he didn't have one. Meeks was his only possible buyer. He tried to look confident.

"All right," Meeks said. "I'll have to make out several checks."

"That's fine. Make them out to Taper Industries."

Meeks was opening his top drawer when the telephone rang. "Hello," Kent heard him say, and then, "Oh, Mooney." In the silence that followed Kent saw his sweet twenty-one blackjack disappear.

"No, not yet," Meeks said, then he looked at Kent, whose hopes were fading second by second. "Come now."

When Meeks hung up the telephone, Kent knew the game was over. "We'll have to postpone finalizing our deal until tomorrow," Meeks said in the voice of a man who is holding all the cards.

Kent's knees felt unsteady as he rose from his seat. Busted! Calvin Meeks wouldn't be calling him. He and Mooney were connected. How, really didn't matter. Some unknown hand had dealt him out. If Matriece hadn't already figured out about Taper Industries, she soon would. And she'd go straight to Gilda.

He saw Blair through the plume of smoke that spewed out from his exhalation. When she said hello, Kent was thinking about guns and razor blades, how carbon monoxide fills a garage too slowly. He could swim in that deep ocean far, far into the distance, and all his problems would be swallowed up in the crashing waves. Easy.

In all Kent's depressed life, he'd never actually planned a suicide. Never purchased the gun or the pills or chose the time when no one was home so he could close off the garage and let the motor run. He'd thought about killing himself many, many times but something always forced him to seek other options. That something was his wife. He felt her hand now, pulling him back to shore. He couldn't leave her alone, and he couldn't abandon his child. His foolishness had gotten them all into a mess, and now he had to protect them as best he could.

Kent was about to light another cigarette when Blair sat down beside him. She had a story, he could tell by the look on her face. He hadn't taken a Xanax since early morning, and the world was sharper than he wanted it to be. If he made an excuse, left right this minute, he could evade what he knew would be more than he was up for. But he lit the cigarette, and in the time it took to take another puff, he made the mistake of looking into Blair's face. There was so much pain emanating from her eyes that all he could do was put his arm around her.

"What's wrong, Blair?"

"Oh, Kent." She shook her head.

Misery loves company but not this much, Kent thought. Nothing made him feel quite as helpless as a weeping woman. The story of how Blair's son had laid the blame for his sins on Matriece's nephew came sobbing out of her. It was a tale that took more than one cigarette to tell. When it was over, almost an hour had passed and Kent's arm was sore from clenching Blair's shoulder. "He's my son," she said finally, after moments of silence. "I don't want him to ruin his life."

"I understand," Kent said. "Really, I do. But—"

"I know that he should have to face what he's done, but he already has a DUI."

"Yes, that does make it more serious."

"But if I let him get away with this, what happens next? If we cover up for him, what does that teach him? He already knows that I paid money to keep him from being suspended. I never should have done that."

"We all do things that we regret." He patted her hand. "You're a good person, Blair."

"Am I? I don't know anymore. I know that Tavares is innocent and I'm letting him take the blame for what my son did. A good person doesn't do that."

They smoked in silence. Her words pushed against Kent's mind. He didn't want to let them in, but he was forced to consider them. *A good person doesn't do that.* He had been a good person once. That time seemed so long ago now.

"Maybe you could find a really excellent lawyer." The statement came out uncensored, and he instantly regretted it. He felt like a hypocrite dispensing advice that he'd chosen not to follow. Who was he to tell anyone to do the right thing? "Sooner or later, the truth always catches up with you."

Blair was looking at him intently, as though she were memorizing everything he said. He felt the weight of her eyes and her trust.

"It's funny that we should be talking like this," he said slowly. "I came out here to think about my own wrongdoing. Don't look so surprised, my dear. I've done some things that, well, I'm not going to burden you with my story. Let's just say that I think we've helped each other today."

Blair waited, but when he said nothing more, she glanced at her watch. "I guess I'd better be getting back," she said, and then they both stood up.

It was simple, he thought as he watched her take one last drag from her cigarette. Simple and very, very hard: He had to tell the truth and face the consequences.

Kent waited until evening before he went to see Gilda. When she saw him standing in her doorway she smiled and motioned him to come in. He'd ended so many days seated across from Gilda in her office. Being with her seemed familiar and intimate. "Would you like a cup of coffee?" she asked. *God, she's thinking that we'll have a nice friendly chat.* And before he could tell her no, she'd already buzzed her assistant to bring in two cups.

"We need to talk," he said, blurting out the words once the coffee was in front of him. She looked somewhat taken aback at the tone of his outburst but said nothing. "I've done something despicable," he said in a low voice.

"Kent, what is it?" Gilda leaned forward, alarm filling her face.

"I've taken money from the company." It was painful for him to see her look of incredulity. "I'm a compulsive gambler, Gilda. I've had the problem for years. When I owed I borrowed from GC. I have an account in the name of a phony company. I'd get the checks in that name. Gilda, I always paid back. But now I owe one hundred seventy-five thousand dollars, and I don't have it. Matriece has become suspicious, and if she hasn't told you yet, I'm sure that she soon will. I just want to say—"

"How could you do this to me?" Gilda said, her voice barely above a whisper.

Kent was absolutely still. For whatever foolish reason, he hadn't expected this hushed tone from Gilda. Weeping maybe, scalding blame, screaming fury, but not this threadbare despair. She can't even look at me, he thought. He remembered the first time he'd met her, so many years before when she was a thin, frightened housewife trapped in a hellish marriage. The smart money would have bet on David, but he cast his lot with Gilda, a move he never regretted. Gilda had never been anything to him but fair and decent. She'd made him a millionaire several times over, and now he'd lost everything, even her respect.

"Gilda, I'm so—"

"Get out," she said softly.

He rose unsteadily. "Gilda, I—"

She turned her face from him. "Just leave. Clear off your desk. Take your personal belongings and go."

When Kent drove up to his house that evening he stopped to look at it before going into the garage. He felt as though he were seeing his home after a long absence. He once believed that there was safety behind those high, thick walls. The owner of such a house would be held in high esteem by all. Anyone who owned such a place would be a success, and no one could deny it. Even a whore's son would be respected if he lived in that house. And that's what I am, he thought sadly, the son of a whore.

He found Peggy and Jolie in the little girl's bedroom. His wife was sitting at a small table, putting together a puzzle with his daughter. He could hear their laughter as he walked up the stairs. In the last few weeks Peggy had begun going out for short trips. Kent was pleased to see the color in her cheeks. She'd had her hair dyed, trimmed, and styled. Her speech and mobility were improving bit by bit. She wasn't back to her old self yet, but she was getting there. Her doctors were amazed.

"Daddy! Daddy!" Jolie jumped up from the table and flung herself into his arms. Kent kissed the top of her head, and then pressed her to him.

"I lost my job. We're going to have to move," he said slowly after he released her.

Jolie looked at Peggy, who stared back impassively at her husband. "When?"

"She said 'when,' Daddy," Jolie chimed in.

"Very soon. We're going to have to get a smaller house."

"Are we going to have a swimming pool?" Jolie asked.

"I don't know."

"Oh."

Peggy stood up and walked over to Jolie and Kent. She took her husband's hand and patted it.

Later, when they were in bed, Peggy put her arm around him. "Everything will be all right," he said. Peggy was making such good progress; he didn't want to worry her.

"I don care about the house, Ken," she said. "I care abou you."

He kissed her cheek.

"I wan you to sto gambling. Ge help. Please."

"All right." He tried to fall asleep but couldn't. "You always liked my mother, didn't you, Peggy?"

"She was a swee woma."

Kent hesitated before he spoke again. "When my father was away during the war, I caught her in bed with a man."

"I know," Peggy said.

Kent sat up. "You know?"

"She tol me."

Kent was stunned. "Why?"

"Because she knew how hur you were. She wan me to know why you two weren't close. And she wan me to be able to understand you."

"She was a whore."

Peggy shook her head. "No, Ken. She was jus a wea, lonely woma who made some ba choices. She wan your forgiveness, Kent."

"It's too late for that," Kent said. He slid down under the covers but didn't go to sleep. *Forgive her?*

In the morning Kent awoke at the same time as usual. He was about to get up and take a shower, when he remembered that he had no place to go, other than to take Jolie to school, and she wouldn't be up for another hour. He lay back down but didn't close his eyes. The events of the last twenty-four hours were a video recorded in his mind. It was a film he didn't want to see; dialogue he didn't want to hear. God, what he wouldn't give to feel cards in his hand. He wanted to win at something. There was still some luck in him. If he started out now, he could be in Vegas by noon. Or maybe he could find a game in town. Even this early in the morning, somebody was betting on something.

He felt a slight stirring, rustling sheets. When he looked at Peggy she was staring at him. Her eyes locked on his, wouldn't leave his face or his conscience. "You have to quit, Kent," she whispered.

Yes, of course. He felt his spirits plunging as he visualized a life without the sound of cards slapping against a table. How long could he live without a game, without the dream of winning? What kind of life would that be?

"Promise me," she said.

In less than a month he had to pay two million dollars that he didn't have. His only chance was a streak of luck that would make all the right cards come to him when he called. He felt lucky; he felt hot. Any card he put his hands on tonight would turn into money. He was pumped, ready to go. He breathed energy; exhaled adrenaline. He couldn't lose.

"Promise me."

He felt her hand in his, the pressure of her fingers stronger than his desire. He squeezed back. "I promise," he said. I owe her this much, he thought.

CHAPTER FIFTY-SEVEN

VONETTE WAS ANGRY, and she didn't try to hide it. When she picked up her Uncle Tuney to take him to get his car from the mechanic's shop, she barely said hello. The truth was, she didn't feel like driving anywhere. She'd switched shifts with one of her friends at the grocery store and had already worked from seven in the morning until three in the afternoon; before she left, a two-pound can of tomatoes had dropped on her foot. Vonette was tired, sore, and mad as hell. What she wanted to do more than anything in the world was make Judd tell the truth. She'd been thinking about the boy's lie almost nonstop ever since Tavares was arrested, and even as she pulled away from her uncle's house, she could feel her fingers tightening, as if around a strap.

"What's wrong with you, girl? You look like a mule sipping vinegar," Tuney exclaimed as he sat down in the passenger's seat, buckled up, and closed his door.

Vonette shot him a hard glance. "I already told you what happened to Tavares."

"You still that mad? Girl, you look like you want to shoot somebody."

"I do."

He shook his head. "Sue them. When you and your daddy get back from Inez, I guarantee you it won't be long before we have a check, and everybody in the family is going to be happy. The Hagertys are going to settle, and they're going to settle for big money, not chump change. They may try to throw us a bone, but I'm not taking it."

Vonette stopped her car halfway down her uncle's driveway. She turned to her uncle and stared at him. "How can I sue them? I mean, on what grounds?"

"I'm not a lawyer but if somebody lies on you and that results in your being falsely accused and arrested, you have some grounds."

"But that's just it. I can't prove that the boy is lying. It's his word against Tavares's," she said, continuing to drive.

"No witnesses?"

Vonette shook her head. "Another white boy."

"Don't worry. Those charges aren't going to stick."

Vonette grunted and began grumbling to herself. She only half listened to her uncle as he recounted how he'd joined with other blacks in and around Inez who, in the thirties and forties, had lost their land due to various fraudulent schemes. "Took me a long time to discover that there was a bunch of us, all ripped off, some for back taxes, some with balloon payments to the banks. A lot of the older people signed their property away and didn't even know it until the man came to take their land. We've all been trying to go up against them alone, and they're too big. But with all of us, we put ourselves into about five different categories, and each group is a separate class-action suit. With compensatory damages and punitive damages, even after we pay the lawyers, we're looking at millions of dollars. How's that sound to you, girl?"

"Uh-huh."

"Vonette."

"What?"

"Don't go over to that woman's house acting a fool."

Despite her uncle's admonishment, by the time Vonette returned home she couldn't talk herself out of driving to Blair's house. Stomping around her kitchen, slamming doors and drawers, she let the compulsion take over her and allowed her willpower to recede so far back that it disappeared entirely. She was going to go to Blair's house and make her child tell the truth. As the decision hunkered down in her brain, a faint warning bell sounded within her, and she remembered the long-ago time that she'd gone off on the woman Boot was running around with right before she put him out for the first time. She'd slapped the woman, and it was only by the grace of God that the police hadn't been called. Even under her current haze of rage, Vonette recognized her need for boundaries. As a last effort to prevent herself from doing something she'd regret, she called Boot. "There's nothing you can say that's going to stop me, but you can come with me if you want."

"Girl," he said, "why you want to go up there starting some mess? See, Mexican women don't act like that."

"Yeah? Go get you one. You coming or not?"

Hearing the commotion that Vonette was making, Shalimar, Chazz, Tavares, Lonell, and Carla trooped into the kitchen. When she looked up, they were all staring at her. Their eyes on her softened her spirit but not her resolve. Vonette liked seeing them together, and for a moment the sight of them, so childlike in their apprehension, made her chuckle inwardly, reminding her of when she used to control her offspring with just a glance.

"You feeling all right, Vonette?" Lonell asked.

"Mom's still mad," Tavares said.

"Now, girl, don't you get yourself . . . all . . . upset. You been huffing and puffing around here. That's not good for your health. Tavares is going to be all right. You calm . . . down."

"Yeah, Mom," Chazz said, "we can all go visit Tavares in the joint."

Vonette spun around and lunged toward her eldest son. "That is not funny, Chazz."

Lonell's knuckles grazed the side of Chazz's head, a weak, playful gesture. "Boy," he said, "keep it up. You not gonna live long enough to get all the women I told you how to catch." He winked at his grandson, who grinned back at him.

At that moment Boot walked into the kitchen, and before he could say a word, Vonette announced, "I'm ready to go."

The children and Lonell looked at one another.

"Where you guys going?" Tavares asked.

Vonette eyed her husband, who ignored her silent warning. "Tell them where we're going, Vonette." When she didn't say anything, he turned to the rest of the family and said, "Your mother is going to see the parents of the boy who lied on Tavares. I'll be with her to make sure don't nobody else in this family get arrested."

"Mommy, I want to go," Shalimar said.

"I know I'm coming," Tavares said.

"You all aren't going anywhere," Vonette said.

"You can come," Boot said, ignoring the protest in his wife's eyes. "All you Blaxicans go get in the van. You too, Lonell." He eyed Carla. "Go ask your mama if you can come."

Vonette watched as everyone, including her father, walked out the back door. "Why . . ." she began.

"Look, Vonette, we're going to ride out there. You say what you have to say and come back home. I know you're not going to act a fool in front of your children and your father."

"Oh, so they're your insurance?" Vonette asked.

"Get in the van, girl."

"Ain't that much protection in the world."

CHAPTER FIFTY-EIGHT

BLAIR WAS TURNING into her driveway when she saw the battered van sitting in front of her house. The lettering on the side said VALDEZ MEANS PAINT, NO JOB TOO SMALL. What the hell was it doing there? Had Porter hired a house painter? For a moment she couldn't decide whether she should drive into her garage. She'd read about thieves who operated out of vans. Why the hell did that damn guard let them in? While Blair was pondering her next move, the passenger door of the vehicle opened, and she saw Vonette get out and ring her doorbell. She started to back out of the driveway, but then Vonette turned around and it was too late.

Vonette was waiting for her inside the garage when she parked the car.

"Blair, I'd like to talk with you."

Blair could feel herself quaking as she got out. "I don't think we have anything to talk about."

Vonette stepped forward. A man rushed toward them from the van. Feeling alarmed, Blair stepped backward. Why hadn't she turned around and driven off? What in the world had she gotten herself into?

"Raphael's not going to hurt you. He's here to protect you from me." Vonette moved away from her, then turned to her husband and called, "I'm cool."

Blair didn't feel safer. Vonette seemed even bigger now that she was standing in front of her.

"Look, I want to speak with your son and have him tell me to my face that Tavares brought drugs into his car."

"Judd has already made his statement to the police." The words squeaked out. Blair felt breathless and faint. She couldn't think of anything worse than having to defend Judd to the wild-looking woman who was giving her the hardest stare-down she'd ever had to confront in her life. Why couldn't Porter come home and help her deal with this mess? But Porter was on a trip, damn him.

"Your son lied," Vonette shouted.

"Vonette," her husband called out.

To Blair's great relief she could see Vonette taking several deep breaths, which seemed to relax her a bit but didn't deter her from her goal. "I want to see your son."

Blair looked toward the house. There were no lights on. Judd might be in his room sitting in the dark, or he could be anywhere. He'd been avoiding her since Porter left. He was a mixed-up, troubled kid but he was hers, and she had to protect him. "He's not here," she said wearily.

Vonette looked at her contemptuously. "I bet you don't even know where he is. Do you?"

Blair felt her face getting hot. In a moment she would have awful-looking red splotches on her cheeks. She was the kind of mother who didn't know where her own child was. Anybody could see that.

"Would you please just go," Blair said.

Vonette's shoulders started quivering, and she began sobbing without restraint. Seeing her, Blair felt her own eyes welling up. *How had her life gotten so bad so quickly? How could a child of hers be responsible for this much pain?* "I'm sorry," she whispered.

Vonette's husband approached. Then she heard the doors to the van opening, and five more people were coming toward her. They surrounded Vonette, patting her, hugging her. "Don't cry, Mommy. Don't cry." Blair could only watch in wonder. There they were, all together.

She remembered families like Vonette's from when she was growing up on the south side. She recalled mothers and fathers who controlled their sons and daughters with a glance, children who always behaved as though their parents were watching them. *They are there for each other*, Blair thought, watching Vonette's family. *Her children and her husband love her.*

The sudden sobbing took Blair by surprise; it sounded so far away. But she could feel how wide her mouth was open, feel the tugging at the corner of her lips, the moans and guttural noises, her face wet and her nose running. Hands reached down toward her. Blair was only vaguely aware of an approaching car, a squeal of brakes. When she looked up from where she was crouching on the ground, she saw Judd's face. She didn't stop screaming.

Blair took Judd's hand and Boot's arm, and everyone went into the kitchen. Vonette pressed her into a chair, then brought her a glass of water. Blair heard the girl whispering to her mother that the house was nice. She could hear the old man's labored breathing. Judd's voice was low and heavy, almost cheerful. "I'm sorry that I lied on you, man. I got scared. I already told the police. They're going to indict me. They said they'd drop your charges. I'm really sorry."

No remorse, Blair thought vaguely as she heard her son's scary, gleeful voice. She wanted to feel proud that he'd done the right thing, but there was something so off, so ill-conceived about his last-minute confession that she was instantly suspicious. She looked over at Boot and Vonette. How had she become the kind of mother who never knew where her child was, who covered up all his mistakes and bought his way out of irresponsibility? *I'm just like my mother.*

"Judd, why are you confessing all of a sudden? First you lie, then you go confess. What's up with that?" Vonette asked.

Judd stood very still, as if his stillness were camouflage.

"Boy, do you hear my wife talking to you?" the husband asked.

Judd's head jerked toward Boot and nodded. "Yes." He's scared, Blair thought at first, scared of Vonette's loud, burly husband. But when she looked closer she detected something else at work, something that made her son stand straight and attentive: respect. She hadn't seen that in Judd in quite a while. As Vonette and Boot moved toward her son, Judd began stepping backward.

"Well, you better answer her. Why are you confessing now?"

Judd faced Vonette, who stood with her arms crossed, her head tilted. "I regretted my actions, and I wanted to make things up to Tavares."

He's lying, Blair thought.

As Blair watched, Vonette walked closer to Judd, leaned into his face, and said, "You regretted your actions?" She looked at her husband. "He sounds just like Chazz when he's trying to bullshit somebody." She whirled around to face the boy. "You better tell me the truth, and I mean right now."

"I . . ." Judd began.

Blair didn't realize she was speaking until she felt the pain of the words scraping against her throat. "He just wants to hurt his father, and me, too, by getting arrested. Isn't that right, Judd?"

"He's never here," Judd screamed. Blair stood up and went to him then, but he pushed her away. She felt shame searing through her that others had witnessed her son's disrespect.

"Boy . . ." Vonette said.

"Boy, what's wrong with you, pushing your mother like that? Have you lost your mind?" Boot said. "If I had you for a week, you wouldn't be pushing on nobody, let alone your mother."

Blair looked at Boot and Vonette's children, standing so close to their parents. She looked at the respect and fear in her own son's eyes. Blair scarcely recognized her voice. "Take him."

"Huh?" Boot said.

"You said if you had him for a week. My son has lost respect for his father and me. I can tell you're good people, and you have good kids."

"Mom, I don't want—" Judd began.

"Son, nobody asked you what you want. Just shut your mouth. We're talking with your mother," Boot said.

"I don't know about this," Vonette said.

Blair felt her resolve weakening. What was she thinking of? How could she even consider sending her son to people who were practically strangers, people who probably hated him?

"I don't want him to wind up in jail."

"We're not the solution to your problem, Blair," Vonette said.

"I know, but maybe if he's in a different environment—"

"You want us to be his time-out chair," Vonette said.

Blair looked at Vonette's children, surrounding her like the hem of her garment. "Maybe you can give him what I can't."

"I'm not going anywhere with—" Judd began.

Boot leaned into the boy's chest. "Shut your mouth." He looked at Vonette.

Vonette sighed. "I guess he can stay the weekend."

"Judd, go get your stuff," Boot said. "And bring some work clothes.

And whatever you're smoking or sniffing or snorting, you better leave it here."

Nobody moved or said anything, and then Blair saw Judd go upstairs. She sat back down. The chair wasn't a rocker but she pitched herself forward, then came back slowly. Above her head she heard water running, loud rap from Judd's CD player. Blair kept right on rocking, even when Judd, hoisting a duffel bag, walked out the door with Vonette and her family, who closed in around him like a locked gate.

Alone in her kitchen, Blair felt fear climbing up her spine, hand over fist, steady and rhythmic. Now that Judd was gone she was afraid. What did she really know about Vonette and Boot? What kind of neighborhood did they live in? Would her son be safe?

Later that evening Blair reached Porter's answering service on her first two attempts. Finally, after eleven o'clock, he answered his cell phone.

"Let me get this straight: You sent Judd to stay with Matriece's sister and her family in South Central. Have you lost your mind?" Porter asked after she'd told him what had happened.

"I think they can help him, Porter."

"You sent my white suburban child into—"

"He'll survive. Believe me."

"What can you be thinking?"

"My God, Porter, don't you get it? Judd wants you. He recanted his story because he wants your attention."

"I'm working, Blair. You know that."

"What are you working for, Porter? If your job isn't to help your son become a decent person, then what's it all about?"

"It's about bills and paying for that house you wanted so much."

"Well, I don't want it anymore, Porter. It costs too much."

"So, what are you saying? You want to sell the house?"

"Here's what I'm saying: You're never there for Judd or me either. And I'm tired of waiting for you. If you want this family, then you come home now. Otherwise, wherever you are, do us all a favor and just stay there."

She held the phone in her hand for a moment, then rested it back in its cradle, got up, went to the kitchen, and made herself a cup of coffee.

There wasn't much traffic on the 405S that night. Blair hadn't been to South Central in a while, but she still knew the way. By the time she reached Vonette's neighborhood, nearly forty-five minutes had passed. The streets she drove down were mostly quiet, the houses small but tidy. There was graffiti on some of the mailboxes; several vacant houses were covered with it. Once she saw a clump of boys who appeared to be roaming aimlessly. She saw more police cars than suspicious-looking characters.

Blair slowed down in front of the Valdez home. Their block was ordinary-looking. The outside light was on, and she could see Vonette and Boot inside sitting on a sofa. They appeared to be talking. Judd sat in a chair across from them, nodding his head from time to time. The streetlight illuminated the grass and flowers in front of the house. Blair could imagine how the sun would highlight their beauty. I'll have to come back to see the garden in the daytime, she thought. She turned her car around and drove home.

Blair went straight to Matriece's office when she got to work the next morning. Her friend was working at her computer and didn't look up when Blair sat down in the chair in front of her and said, "I need to talk with you."

"Vonette told me what happened." Matriece spoke without even glancing her way.

"I'm sorry, Matriece. I'm so sorry. I should have made him accept responsibility. I'm sorry. He's my kid." She sighed. "He's been getting into trouble for a long time. Porter and I just kept hoping things would get better. I wanted him to have a good life, and I kept thinking, One day he'll wake up and everything will be all right. I don't expect you to forgive me but I want you to know that I'm sorry."

"Judd lied, and the black boy got arrested."

Everything inside Blair stopped. "Judd didn't lie because he was black, Matriece."

"You don't think it occurred to your precious son that the white cop would believe him over Tavares? Too bad my nephew didn't have a knit cap on."

"My son has a lot of problems, but he isn't a racist, Matriece."

"No? He's sitting in the car with another white guy, and he tells the cop the drugs belong to the black kid. But he's not racist?"

"That was just a coincidence, Matriece. I've been around black people all my life. I grew up in a black neighborhood. Do you think—"

Matriece's eyes were glacial. "Please. Ever since I've known you you've been trying to make me believe that you thought growing up around black people was the greatest thing in the world, when the truth is, you couldn't wait to get out. You make everything about your life on the south side one big joke. You were too poor to move away, Blair. Pure and simple. If you love being around black folks so much, why don't you live around them now?"

"That's not fair," Blair sputtered. "I didn't move to escape black people. The homes in Los Angeles were too expensive. Besides, I wanted better schools for my kid. And there are some black people in my neighborhood."

"Blair, I've got work to do." Matriece turned her head away.

The words rushed forward so fast and hard that Blair couldn't hold them back. "You really do, Matriece. Only you don't know how to get started."

Matriece looked up. Bewilderment and shock spread across her face.

"You want to accuse me of being phony because I don't come up to your standards of how a white girl who grew up in a black neighborhood should act. You're mad because I laugh about living on the south side. You want to hear the not-so-funny part? Okay. How about the aftermath to the Supremes jumping me? You want to know about my front teeth getting knocked out by Diana Ross? Or how about the time in the cafeteria at school when some girl dumped milk on me to see if it would blend with my skin? Do you want me to count the times I was called 'honky' and 'white bitch'? Forgive me if I try to tell a joke or two to lighten up my memories, but that's just me. I had more good times than bad, Matriece. I filled out my college applications in the basement of a black Baptist church, and I wouldn't have gotten to school at all if it hadn't been for my girlfriend's mother. The lady across the street used to send my mother sweet potato pies and her daughter's old clothes. There was Southside Junior. And you have to admit, I can dance better than your average white girl. But I was still poor white trash. And you're damn right, I couldn't wait to get out. And you know what? Neither could you.

"Your sister has forgiven me. But not you. You know why? Because you want to hold a grudge. You live for your grudges, Matriece. You build an altar to them and worship there every chance you get. Well, I may be a phony white girl, but I know how to forgive; I know when to forgive, and I know who to forgive."

She waited for Matriece to say something, but she didn't. When Blair walked out she listened for the clicking of computer keys, but there wasn't a sound.

CHAPTER FIFTY-NINE

MY FATHER'S HOUSE, Asia thought, glancing around the small, neat bungalow. This is where he lives. The place was neither a surprise nor a disappointment. She'd never imagined it at all. During most of the years of her father's absence, she had tried not to think about him. As she sat on the sofa in his living room, she imagined her brother beside her. Donny would be mad at first, she thought. He'd go off on their father about not taking care of them or sending any money. He'd sit on this couch with an attitude, and then he'd come around. Asia didn't have an attitude. She smiled as she ran her fingers across the upholstery.

Asia stood up and walked around the neat living room, stopping to examine the photographs on the mantel. She was surprised to see pictures of her and her brother, taken when they were very young. There were other people she remembered from earlier days: her grandmother, her uncles and aunts. When she finished looking at the pictures she sat back down and flipped through the magazines on the coffee table.

She could smell food, onions, garlic, and chicken, hear it sizzling in the pan. Sam was in the kitchen cooking her dinner, part of his attempts to "get to know her." The house was so tiny that the odor filled it up, made it seem cozy and warm. She could hear her father singing. He had a beautiful voice. Now I know where mine comes from, she thought. She'd always wondered about the origin of the gift nature had bestowed upon her. He did give me something, Asia reasoned, even if it didn't cost him anything. She stood up and tiptoed from the living room to the den and watched her father singing and cooking.

After their initial meeting at Matriece's house, Sam had called Asia and arranged to spend time with her. They had gone to lunch and spoken on the telephone twice. Each time they spoke, Sam apologized for not being present when she was a child. "That's the worst thing a man can do, and I'm guilty of it," he'd said.

His apologies were so sincere, so unrestrained that Asia had accepted them without question, and for a while that acceptance had blocked out the residue of anger that was inside her. But now, as she stood in her father's small house, smelling the food he was cooking for her in his tiny kitchen, she pushed back her good feelings and let her mother's sensibilities rise up. *What does he want with me now? Where was he before?*

She marched into the kitchen, propelled by the sudden spike of anger. "Mom thinks you just want my money. Is that what you want? Is it?"

He was standing close to the stove, and he had his back to her. She could see the way his shoulders collapsed when he heard her. He turned around slowly.

"I've been waiting for that, hoping it wouldn't come but waiting for it." He kept stirring whatever he was cooking, shifting to a sideways position. "You've got every right to ask me that question."

"Why did you walk out on us?"

Sam turned the flame down low and put the top on the pot. "I was weak."

"Do you know what happened to me because you weren't there to protect me? Do you?"

Sam shook his head. There was fear in his eyes.

She couldn't make all the words come out. "I needed you."

"I let you down, both of you. I'm sorry. I don't have any excuses. What I didn't give you before I can't make up to you now. I know that. But just let me try to be your friend. That's all I ask. I don't want a thing from you or Donny, just your time."

There was a small table in the kitchen with two chairs. Asia sat down in one of them. "Sometimes being with you hurts."

Sam sat down in the empty chair. "Maybe it will stop hurting after a while. From now on, if I'm always there when I say I will be, maybe the pain will go away."

Neither of them spoke for several moments and then Sam got up. He filled two plates with pasta and chicken, salad and bread and brought them to the table. Asia picked up her fork, but she put it back down when she saw that her father's head was bowed. "Dear Lord, we thank you for this food that we are about to receive. We thank you for your blessings upon this father and child. We thank you for restoring our souls, Lord, and showing us the way. Amen."

"Amen." Asia took a forkful of pasta and placed it in her mouth. "It's good, Dad."

It was after nine o'clock when she left her father's house. Her belly was full but her mind wasn't completely at ease. Sam lived less than three miles from her mother and Monroe. Asia rarely visited Ruth's house but as she drove through the streets of Inglewood her car seemed to be guided in that direction.

Ruth was having a party. Every parking space on her side of the small street was taken. The lights were on in her house, and Asia could hear the music even before she turned off the car. For a moment she thought about leaving. Ruth might already be drunk. Besides, she wanted to speak with her mother privately. I'm here now, she thought. She turned off the ignition and got out of the car.

Monroe opened the door. He was holding a glass of champagne in one hand and a bottle in the other. "Asia," he said, his eyes brightening. "Hey!" he shouted, turning his head toward the room behind him. But before he could announce her, Asia gave him a shove.

"I don't want to see anybody. Where's my mother? I need to talk with her."

"Oh. Sure. I'll go get her."

Loud rap music emanated from inside the house. Asia waited in the entryway until Ruth came out. "What are you doing standing in here?" her mother asked. "Come on inside. Hey, everybody, my baby is here. Come on in; they want to meet you." She could feel her mother's hands pulling her. Then the lights became brighter, the music louder, and there were people staring at her.

"Hello. How are you doing?" Asia said. Her smile was locked into place.

Too many voices started talking at once. She could hear streams of questions coming her way. She nodded, answered, nodded, then looked for her mother.

Ruth was standing in the middle of the room. "Yes, this is my baby. Miss Grammy. Miss Diamond Disc."

"Mom, I need to talk with you." She pulled her away, back into her bedroom.

"What, baby?" Ruth's eyes were glazed.

"I like him, Mom. I like my father."

Ruth stared at her as if she didn't understand, and then suddenly she seemed to turn old right in front of her. Asia saw the lines and puckers, the places that sleep would never heal. "Why are you gonna like him? He ain't never done nothing for you. He just wants your money."

"What do you want, Mom? Huh?"

"I took care of you," she said.

"And now I take care of you and Monroe."

"I did the best I could." She was whining, her voice laced with liquor and self-pity.

"He did, too. But neither one of you protected me. Where were you when your boyfriends were putting their hands all over me. If I can forgive you, I can forgive him. So don't tell me how to feel about him. Ever. That's what I came here to tell you."

"Don't give him any money," Ruth said. She seemed to shrink away from Asia's glance.

"Go back to your party, Mom."

But Ruth didn't move. She kept repeating the same thing. Asia waited for her mother to stop. When she didn't, Asia fixed her smile in place, opened the bedroom door, and waved to the crowd as she made her way home.

CHAPTER SIXTY

HER DARLING BOY looked like a child when he was sleeping. So peaceful, Gilda thought, gazing down at Fontaine, who was curled up in her bed. Gilda had never permitted herself the indulgence of actually spending the night with any of her young lovers before she met Fontaine. But she fell asleep in Fontaine's arms the first time they made love, and neither one of them awoke until morning. It would be difficult to let him go.

Gilda sat down on the edge of her bed, trying to find the right words before she woke him. She had promised him more time, but that was before she realized how much that time would cost her. He opened his eyes without her touching him. "What?"

It had been easier before.

"Are you dumping me?" He smiled.

"I'm growing too fond of you, my dear. It's not good for either one of us."

"You didn't give me all my time."

"I'm sorry," she said,

He gave her a quick kiss. "Did you have fun?"

"So much fun."

She heard the doorbell ring. Putting on her robe, she padded to the door in her bare feet, opened it a bit, and listened. She waited until the brown-skinned woman handed her the envelope. Clutching it against her chest, Gilda closed the door. She reached into her pocket, pulled out her reading glasses, and put them on. The return address read: Banque Suisse Nationale. She'd been informed that a letter would arrive in early February, and here it was, right on time. Gilda's fingers felt stiff and clumsy; it took her several minutes to open the envelope, even longer to focus on the words in front of her. Her presence or that of her representative would be required in Switzerland in order to give her the check for nearly eight million dollars, the sum total of her parents' savings, including more than fifty years of interest. She had something left of her family after all.

She began to cry, softly at first but gradually the sound became louder and louder. There were so many to mourn. She could sit shivah for her entire life and that would not be long enough. Everything came back to her: the smell of the gas, the moans of the dying, the frantic search for loved ones among the dead, the horror that never left her.

Gilda wasn't aware that she was screaming until she felt hands shaking her shoulders, heard Fontaine's voice, "Gilda! Gilda, what's wrong? What's wrong?" She didn't stop, couldn't stop. The hands released her, and she heard footsteps, then her maid's voice, "Missy Gilda, Missy Gilda. What's wrong?"

She didn't answer, the noise kept flowing out of her. She heard Fontaine and Cecelia conferring about who to call, whether 911 was appropriate. More footsteps, then Cecelia was on the telephone, dialing, hanging up, dialing again. "Come now. Your mother very upset. Come now."

When she knew Daniel was on the way something subsided in her. Fontaine led her back to the bed, and once she was under the covers she felt herself go limp. She could see him standing over her, looking down, appearing worried. She wanted to tell him that she was all right, that what she was going through would pass soon. Gilda was aware of what she was experiencing. Her support group had talked about the sudden emotional swings that could befall them without warning. Posttraumatic stress syndrome, or something like that. But understanding didn't deter the feeling that she was sinking and couldn't save herself.

"Gilda, I'd better go now." Fontaine's voice pierced the cloud that hovered around her. He hesitated. "Call me later, if you want."

She didn't nod or smile. Fontaine squeezed her hand, and then she heard him walk away.

Gilda didn't realize that she'd fallen asleep until she opened her eyes and saw Rachel sitting next to her on the bed. I want Daniel, she thought.

"Mother, Cecelia called me. She said you were screaming and crying. What's wrong?"

Rachel's hair was wet, as though she'd just taken a shower. She had on sweats and no makeup. Gilda could hear her rapid, shallow breathing. "She shouldn't have called you. There's nothing wrong."

"But she said you were hysterical."

"I was a little upset, that's all."

"About what?"

She was not used to receiving tenderness from Rachel. Gilda couldn't turn away from her daughter's soft glance, from the golden offering pouring from her eyes. "I have to go to Switzerland in the next month."

When she saw Rachel's quizzical glance she sighed, then raised herself to a sitting position. "Before the war my parents realized that Jews were in grave danger in Poland. My father sent our money to Switzerland. For years I've tried to get it back. Now, finally, the bank is returning the money with interest. But I have to go there to sign the papers. I guess I don't feel up to the trip."

"Can't you send someone? How about Kent?"

"No," she said abruptly, "not Kent."

Another wound still fresh, still tender. Gilda winced as she thought of Kent's perfidy. She tried to measure her old sense of gratitude with her gut reaction to his betrayal, but the mental balancing act sent her spiraling down to emotional territory she had spent her life sidestepping. Long ago she had lived among people who smiled in her face and then stabbed her in the back deliberately, maliciously. Her Polish neighbors had delivered her and her family into the enemy's hands. Stealing, she could have forgiven. But Kent's lies and thievery were camouflaged by a smile, and that she couldn't abide. She would waive the debt and not press charges, but she wouldn't forgive Kent.

"How much money?"

"What?"

"The check, how much is it for?"

"I'm not sure," she said vaguely. "Several million."

"But that's good news," Rachel said. She looked at her mother for so long that Gilda began to feel uncomfortable. "Did it bring back bad memories? Is that why you were upset?"

Tears swirled somewhere inside her, but Gilda pounded them back with her mind.

"Maybe a little." She smiled. "I'm all right now."

Rachel leaned forward. "Have you ever gone back to where you used to live?"

The question caught Gilda off guard. She had severed all ties with her past and had no desire to reconnect. But there was a childlike innocence attached to the question that her daughter had posed. She thought it was driven by more than a passing curiosity. "Why do you ask that?"

"I just wondered," Rachel said, almost shyly. Then she blurted out, "I'd like to see where you're from."

Gilda was shocked. "You would? Why?"

"I feel as though I don't know anything about you. I never told you this, but I have dreams about your family, our family, the ones who died in the camps."

"What kind of dreams?"

"They aren't frightening, really. It's like, they just appear, all my dead relatives. In my dream they stand still. Sometimes I think they want me to mourn them, but I guess I can't do that because I've never really felt connected to them. Just like I'm not connected to my father," she said quietly, "or to you. And I want to be. Connected."

"I loved your father very much. He is a brilliant man, but he had a weakness. And it consumed him. I tried time and time again to get help for him, but he would always relapse. When we divorced I was afraid for you to be with him. Afterwards, when he was really off drugs, I think he was too ashamed to come see you," Gilda said quietly.

"I missed him."

"Of course you did. A girl needs a father."

Rachel began crying. "Why couldn't you make him get off drugs? Why couldn't you make him stay, make him love me?"

"Oh, my darling."

"I know it's not fair to blame you. I'm tired of being angry with you.

I know I should be mad with him, but he's not around. When I was a kid I thought that if I had my father, I could be like him. I wouldn't have to be a big success, like you. I don't know how to be like you, Mom. I don't even know how to be like myself. Daniel does. I thought if I understood what you went through during the war I could understand how you got to be so strong. I want to be strong. What was it like? What happened to you?"

"It was a place of death." The words were involuntary, as was the shudder that ran through Gilda. Even now, so many years later, she remembered what death smelled like. She felt her daughter's arm around her shoulder.

"Tell me. Please."

Gilda went way back, dug deep, deeper than she thought she could go, back to the happy times in her small town when she was a child, protected, cosseted, loved. She described the Seder, holiday times, her Bas Mitzvah, her brother's Bar Mitzvah. She described her gradual displacement as the apple of her father's eye, how being a smart, curious girl meant being doomed. Her brother was the prince. She told her daughter how she tasted anger for the first time. And then love. Rachel's eyes grew big when Gilda described Tibor. She told her about the rise of the Nazis, the war, the camps. "I never saw any of them again," she said when she had finished, pausing to wipe her eyes while Rachel nodded mutely.

"And then I came to Los Angeles. I worked as a maid in a hotel. All the maids were black, except for me. There was one, Hosanna. She and I became friends."

When Gilda had finished talking about Hosanna, their friendship, their business, and how they parted, it was almost noon. Her voice was hoarse, her eyes were red but finally dry, and Rachel's arm was still around her shoulders.

"I always hated the way my parents favored my brother," Gilda said softly. "I never thought I'd be guilty of the same thing. I'm so sorry."

"Maybe it's natural, mothers loving their sons. If my father had been around, I would have been his favorite."

Gilda hesitated. "Do you ever call him?"

Rachel looked surprised. "My father?" She shook her head. Her eyes were frightened.

"If you ever want to speak with him, I can get his number."

Her daughter nodded. "I've thought about calling him. It's scary."

Gilda sighed. "When you're ready." She patted her daughter's hand. "Rachel, a man came to see me the other day. He rented Hosanna and me the space when we first opened our business. He is threatening to expose to the public the fact that I never repaid Hosanna the money I owed her. He wants me to sell him Brown Sugar."

"For less than it's worth?"

Gilda nodded.

"What did Daniel say?"

"He doesn't know yet."

Rachel smiled. "What are you going to do?"

"I don't know."

Their eyes met. The arm around her shoulders offered support. She leaned into it, and Rachel smiled. Her daughter's arm was stronger than she'd realized. She reached up and patted it. "Darling," she said, "help me think."

CHAPTER SIXTY-ONE

MEEKS'S OFFICE WAS larger than Mooney's. The older man always noted that whenever he went to visit the cosmetics mogul at his executive suite. For years the size of the place was grit in Mooney's eye. When he began expanding his businesses to surrounding states and selling his barbecue sauce and frozen pies and cobblers in grocery stores, he had been the premiere black businessman in California. The ascendancy of Meeks and Briggs came later, starting in the early eighties. Both men had surpassed him in earnings and in showboating. Mooney's workplace was modest compared with theirs, his home nowhere near as palatial. But at eighty-two, he was too old to harbor envy. He didn't have the time.

Around him the works of Romare Bearden, Jacob Lawrence, and Charles White were displayed. Mooney remembered when Meeks couldn't even spell "art." He'd been the first real collector of the Triumvirate. Now for every purchase one made, the others hastened to match it. Meeks's office looked like a veritable museum. "That a new Richard Yarde?" Mooney asked, noticing a new watercolor on the wall across from Meeks's desk.

"Yeah. You like it?"

"Beautiful."

An assistant brought in two tall glasses filled with ice and Pepsi, and each man took a sip. Meeks placed his glass on his desk. "So how'd you find out about my little deal?"

Mooney set aside his soda and waved his hand. "Don't worry about how, just be glad that I saved you three million dollars."

"Two and a half million."

"Whatever. You were getting ready to pay him for what I'm willing to give you for free."

Meeks grinned. "Yeah, but I was getting something for my money. What am I going to get from you?"

"A business partner."

"You stretching out from food to cosmetics at your age?"

"I said a business partner. I didn't say it was going to be me."

Meeks looked surprised. "Then who?"

Mooney paused for a moment, knowing the impact of the name he was about to utter. "Matriece Carter."

"Absolutely not! That woman . . ." Meeks began sputtering, and his jaws swelled as though they were puffed up with venom.

"Leave your ego, on the porch. She's smart as a whip. She practically doubled your business single-handedly."

"Yeah, and then she burned me."

"All she did was go find a better opportunity for herself. You didn't half pay her, you cheap bastard. You weren't interested in giving her a share of the profits. What the hell was she supposed to do?"

"She went running right to my competition."

"Well, now you can get her back. Either that or she'll be competing against you again, only this time she'll be in it totally for herself."

"Let me get this straight: You're trying to get this business for Matriece? Why?"

"I have my reasons."

Meeks shook his head. "You're going to have to tell me more than that, Mooney."

Mooney sighed. He was proprietary about his personal business, but he supposed that Meeks did have a right to more information. "Matriece's mother is the woman who was partners with Gilda. We were real good friends for a lotta years. I feel like I owe her something."

"Does Gilda know that Matriece is Hosanna's daughter?"

"That's for her to tell," Mooney said sharply.

"You and I are at cross-purposes, Mooney. I don't need another cosmetics company. I wanted to use the information to shut down Brown Sugar," Meeks said.

"How old are you, Calvin?"

"Sixty-two."

"I'm eighty-two. I was almost fifty years old when segregation ended. Every thought I've ever had was probably shaped by sitting on the back of the bus, from the way I felt falling in love to what I eat and how I do business."

"What's your point, Mooney?"

Mooney waved his hand, and Meeks settled in his chair, a bemused expression on his face.

"You were nearly thirty when segregation ended, so you've had more integration in your lifetime than segregation. Yet and still, I'll bet those whites-only signs affected you, too, maybe a little less than me, but they left their mark. Now, you take somebody in their twenties or even thirties, they had less of those hard times than either one of us. Not saying they didn't experience getting pulled over by the cops just for being black or getting followed around the store, but the signs were gone. That's important. Somebody like that sees life differently from you and me. They do business differently. You might look at a company and see competition; a younger person looking at that same company sees opportunity.

"When I was coming along, all black people were one big market. Sure, some towns had the doctors and lawyers living in a different neighborhood, but mostly we were all thrown in together. That's changed. Now we're more diverse. You got your buppies, your generation X, the retirees, blue collar, white collar, and they live in different places, drive different cars, eat different food. Matriece is telling me that there's a whole segment of very young, what she calls hip black women, who aren't buying your products. They think they're too stuffy." Meeks's shoulders became rigid and his lips tightened but Mooney ignored the signs of his irritation. "You take an operation like Brown Sugar, and it can appeal to that hip-hop generation. See, right now, they're giving their money to white folks who are marketing to them. I can't explain it the way Matriece can, of course. I don't know that much about your business."

"Say I get into this. How would we split things up?"

"You buy your way into as much of the partnership as you can afford. I like to keep things simple."

"How much?"

"Depends on the selling price."

"I'm cash strapped right now."

"You got a line of credit."

Meeks shook his head. "I don't want to overextend myself. How about bringing in Big Monty?"

"Think he'd be interested?"

It was so easy, Mooney thought when Big Monty arrived nearly an hour later. After all the years filled with meetings, after all the failed Black Business Associations, all the hopes and disappointments, here was a deal on the table big enough for the Triumvirate to share, not as grandiose as the ones he'd dreamed of when he first realized that a black man's dreams could come true, but big enough.

Montgomery had come with his father, and he was quiet at first as he listened to Mooney tell the story of Hosanna and Gilda. Anybody could feel him pacing back and forth, even though he wasn't moving. Mooney did all the explaining, and he found himself talking directly to the younger man. He was the one who asked all the really sharp, penetrating questions about the proposed leveraged buyout, things Mooney hadn't even thought about yet. And then he answered them himself before Mooney or anybody else could say a word. After a while, Montgomery was suggesting that they ask the seller to provide them with a line of credit. "From the bank they're dealing with or an in-house source. Either way, we want a guarantee." He told them how the deal could work even better than they imagined, making them all see everything clearly. They shook hands, slapped backs, and hugged hard after the discussion ended. We're ready, Mooney thought. We're all ready at the same time.

He thought about the problem later, when they were all on their way out: Matriece and Montgomery in the same company, working together, him married to Gretel Meeks. He caught Montgomery by his coattails and spoke quickly. "Do you have a few minutes?"

They stepped outside, leaving his father and Meeks still talking.

"What's on your mind?" Montgomery asked.

"I understand congratulations are in order."

He looked puzzled.

"Aren't you getting married?"

"Not that I know of."

Mooney was so taken aback he didn't censor himself. "Matriece told me that you were engaged to Gretel Meeks."

"She's mistaken," he said softly, then his eyes grew very wide.

"Wonder where she got that from?" Mooney said.

"I have no idea. We've never even dated. Always been like sister and brother."

"Uh-huh," Mooney said. "Well, what about you and Matriece?"

"There is no Matriece and me anymore," Montgomery said, his tone serious.

"I know that. Why not?"

"You need to ask her. Just as we were getting close, she pulled away."

"I see." Mooney was quiet for a moment, trying to decide where to take the conversation. He was used to talking business, not matters of the heart. "Why you think she did that?"

"When a woman pulls away from a man she cares about and who cares about her, I figure she's either scared of making a commitment, she found somebody else, or she decided she's not in love."

"She's in love with you," Mooney said. Montgomery's relief was palpable. "Maybe she's scared, too."

"She didn't grow up with her father, did she? That affects some girls. The dad walks out, and they're afraid to trust any man."

"That could be," Mooney said. "You still care about her?"

Their eyes met.

"You ask a lot of questions."

"She's like a daughter to me."

"I'm not what she wants, Mr. Mooney."

"That's not what I asked you."

"Mr. Mooney, it's not going to work out. Does that answer your question?"

"I guess so."

Mooney could tell that Matriece had had a long day by the way she dragged into his house that evening. She looked sad in a way that shocked him. She'd come right away when he called her. His cook served them dinner in the breakfast room. Matriece perked up a little after she ate, but she still looked drained. He understood why when she told him what had happened to Tavares.

"You love that boy like a son, don't you?"

When she nodded, he said, "But he ain't your son. And you love me like a father, but I ain't your daddy."

Matriece gave a start, and then he could see hurt feelings spilling out of her. He knew she didn't want to hear what he was going to say, but the words were way overdue.

"You probably figured out by now that your momma and me was more than friends, Matriece. You can act like you don't know that, but I think you do. I was married when she met me, and I was married when she died. She was running from me when she married your daddy, and he didn't have any idea the first. Country boy. Green as collards. Me and Hosanna stayed away from each other for as long as we could, but some things are just meant to be. He caught on after a while. It broke him, that and the fact that his woman had a head for business and he didn't."

She looked shocked, hurt, but he kept talking. Matriece needed the medicine he was spooning her. "Why are you telling me this?" she asked.

"Because you need to change your ways. You can borrow a son or a daddy, but that don't make them yours."

"You're not talking about Tavares. You're talking about my father." She sighed. "To tell you the truth, I'm tired of hating him. I went to Vonette's on Christmas to make peace with him, but he stayed upstairs."

"Maybe you need to go back over there."

"Maybe I do."

He didn't want to push her. "So, you with me on what's gonna go down with Gilda?"

He could sense her pulling away. "Blackmail is illegal."

"I'm a careful man, Baby Girl. I know how not to incriminate myself and my associates."

"It doesn't feel right, Uncle Mooney. I don't want the company to come to me because of blackmail."

"You take from power any way you can. She built an empire on stolen money, your mother's money. Don't forget that. We got her over a barrel, sugar. That's the only time you ever get something outta white folks."

He could see doubts in her eyes. He let her mind go through its own changes. She had to know that Hosanna would have wanted to get the company any way she could. "Let me talk to her first," Matriece said.

"Do it soon."

Matriece had always wanted to take up where Hosanna left off, Mooney told himself. Hadn't she left Radiance when a better opportunity came along? Hadn't she said all along that her goal was ownership? He had to trust that she still wanted what he wanted for her. If her heart was getting in the way of her head, it was just a temporary condition, like amnesia. The thing was not to leave anything to chance. He was too old to take chances, especially with his legacy. He'd made it as far as he'd gotten by being shrewd, and he wasn't about to get careless now. But there were things he couldn't control. He had an old white woman in the palm of his hand, but he felt Matriece wriggling out of his grasp.

"Montgomery's not engaged," Mooney said.

She looked startled. Her face was a mixture of happiness and fear. "How do you know that?"

"He told me he never was engaged, that he and the Meeks girl are just like brother and sister. Never even courted. Who told you they were getting married?"

"Nobody. She was wearing a beautiful diamond ring. I saw them together. I just assumed."

"You assumed wrong."

He watched her face, saw blinds opening and shutting. Light came in, then darkness. The boy was right, he thought. She is scared. Mooney didn't know what to do with the sunshine and darkness playing on her face. "He still cares about you, Triecy."

"He couldn't possibly," she said, her face sadder than he'd ever seen it. He remembered her mother looking sad like that years ago on some Christmas Eve when he wouldn't come to her. The pain in her eyes had made him promise her a Christmas one day when they'd be together. He'd never delivered on that promise.

Mooney got up, went into the family room, and picked up the telephone. When he was finished talking, he called his driver and told him to get the car ready. Matriece was staring at nothing when he returned to the table. It was nearly eight-thirty, the time of night when Mooney began to feel his years. He ignored his stinging tendons, the throbbing in his joints. "Come on, sugar," he said to Matriece, "let's take a ride."

She didn't protest, didn't ask any questions. As soon as Matriece was seated in the car he could feel her settling down. By the time they were halfway there, she leaned forward, her glance taking in the neighborhood they were passing through. She gave Mooney a look when the car stopped in front of Vonette's.

"What do you think you're doing?" Matriece asked softly.

"I'm not doing nothing," he said. "Let's go in."

Vonette opened the door. She stood there stiffly for a moment, which surprised Mooney. He'd always thought of her as a woman who owned the space she occupied. She seemed torn, as though she couldn't decide how to be, which told him that something had gone down between the two sisters, some argument they weren't quite over. Then he heard the husband calling from the front room. "Is that my foxy sister-in-law? Come on up in here, girl," and the two women laughed a little, then hugged each other. He heard Vonette say, "I wasn't really mad with you."

Matriece chuckled and said, "Quit lying," and they both laughed again.

"How are you doing, Mooney?" Vonette asked, leading them into the den, where Boot was watching television. She sounded polite, which wasn't the same as interested. If Matriece had chosen a side long ago, so had her sister.

Boot was sitting on the couch with his shirt unbuttoned. His large belly hung over his belt. "Madonna's auditioning male dancers," Matriece said dryly, then she bent down to give her brother-in-law a hug.

"Hey, Vonette, your sister's hitting on me again," he yelled.

"Where is everybody?" Matriece asked.

"Probably in Daddy's room watching television with him," Vonette said.

"Oh," Matriece said, then she sat down on the sofa, slumping into the seat. Vonette stared at her sister for a moment. "You want to go up?" she asked.

"Not right now," Matriece said.

From the way Vonette's chest began heaving, Mooney figured there was going to be an explosion. But he didn't figure the grenades would be tossed in his direction. "You started this, Mooney," Vonette said suddenly. Mooney had faced down some rough men in his life but none of them had eyes any harder than Vonette's.

Boot sat up. "Vonette."

"Vonette," Matriece said.

Vonette moved closer to Mooney. Her finger was inches from his face. She turned to Matriece. "You act like he's your daddy when he's the man who stole your daddy's wife!"

"Vonette!" Boot and Matriece said.

"If it's any consolation to you, Vonette, me and your sister have been over that. I came here to see if she could patch things up with Lonell."

Her finger was almost touching his nose. "Maybe you need to patch things up with him, too."

Before anyone could speak Vonette marched to the foot of the stairs and called, "Hey, you guys, come downstairs." She folded her arms below her breasts.

As Mooney watched, Matriece sat up. She looked as though she might bolt. She stood up, then sat down, then stood up again.

Chazz came down first, then Tavares, followed by Shalimar, some Mexican girl, and a white boy. They all heard Lonell shuffling down the stairs, his breathing heavy and ragged. When he got to the bottom, he tried to catch his breath.

Mooney looked at Matriece, standing rigid, her eyes on the stairs. She hadn't moved a muscle by the time her father was in front of her. Lonell looked toward Vonette, as if to ask her what to do. But his oldest daughter didn't say a word. "Hello, Triecy," Lonell finally said. "How you been?"

"Hello," Matriece said. "I've been fine."

Neither of them said anything else.

Mooney heard Vonette's loud voice. "Daddy, you and Mooney go sit in the living room. You kids go on in the family room. Boot, make some popcorn. Matriece, come on in the kitchen with me." When Mooney caught sight of Vonette's eyes, they were focused and hard.

Lonell sat down next to Mooney on the sofa. "How are things going?" he asked.

"We're making progress," Mooney said.

Lonell nodded. "I knew you'd know how to go about it. So, there's a chance they'll get something out of it? I'd like to help Vonette send the kids to college. They're real smart."

"Brother, you can educate a lot of people if this deal works out right."

Lonell sighed. He looked happy, old and beaten-up but happy. "Well, that's one thing I did right," he said.

Mooney put his hand on Lonell's arm. "A long time ago, I took something from you, Lonell. I want you to know that I'm not sorry I loved Hosanna. I'm just sorry I caused you pain."

Lonell looked shocked. He didn't say anything for a long time. "She was always your woman."

Mooney could smell the popcorn in the kitchen. By the time Lonell and Mooney joined the others in the family room, Vonette was bringing it out in a bowl, along with some sodas. Boot turned off the television and put on some music. It wasn't really a party, but it almost felt like one. Once Vonette's heavy hand brushed across Mooney's arm, and when he looked up she was passing him a beer.

Mooney could see Matriece's shoulders inching down as she began talking with the kids. Every once in a while she glanced in Lonell's direction, her face open and curious. The girl's made her decision, Mooney thought. In his mind, he called it a beginning.

CHAPTER SIXTY-TWO

MATRIECE HAD CLOSED herself off from her father for so long that when she looked into Lonell's rheumy eyes that evening she barely recognized them. She had realized halfway through their journey where Mooney was going and why. Part of her was relieved that she'd taken that frightening first step. But she had expected to feel more: a weight lifted, an epiphany. Matriece felt detached when Vonette walked her to the door, her arm around her waist, hugging her, acting as though there had been some kind of wonderful breakthrough. She wanted to tell her sister that being in the room with her father was no different than a chance encounter with a stranger. Nothing had changed.

And yet when she drove home from Mooney's she began crying soft, quiet tears that she couldn't stop. She had a glass of wine when she got in the house. Later, sitting in her bathtub, letting the warm soapy water relax her, she laid her head back against the porcelain and closed her eyes.

There was Hosanna, clad in white, crouched in the sand by the ocean. She had a basket with her, covered with a red-and-white checkered cloth. When she pulled back the cover the inside was filled with flowers, some fresh and dewy, others old and dried. She began picking out the dead blossoms, one at a time, and throwing them into the sea. Then she faded away.

She woke up the next day with questions on her mind.

"Triecy," Asia said when she opened her door. She gave Matriece a hug. Asia's burnished coppery skin was glowing. Her eyes and hair were shining. She spoke and smiled at the same time. "I'm feeling so much better. I'm on a different kind of medication. What's wrong, girl?"

"I want to know how it feels to know your father again."

"Oh."

They sat next to each other on a long beige sofa in Asia's living room.

"It's like, I'm pissed off with him for not being around before, but I'm glad he's here now so I can tell him so and get over it so him and me can get to be friends. You know what I'm saying?"

Matriece shook her head. "It's funny, I knew he was what you needed. I knew it but . . . Last night my father and I spoke for the first time in years, and . . ." She moved her hands in a circular motion.

"I'm feeling you, girl."

"I don't know where to go from here. I mean, is it weird being with Sam?"

"It's like, I don't know him but I do. I'm comfortable with him but not completely. My father is real into God, and maybe because he prays so much, and because we were already vibing with his cards and stuff, maybe things are a little easier. We want to get to know each other. I don't know what else to tell you, Triecy."

"Do you like him?"

"Yeah. He's nice. He's funny. He knows a lot of stuff because he reads all the time. I feel like I can learn from him."

"I don't think my father can teach me anything. My mom raised my sister and me. Once he left, my father never contributed and didn't really stay in touch. My mom bad-mouthed him, and I guess she indoctrinated me. Now it's hard to see his side."

"The moms do that because they want to come off smelling like roses. They're not perfect either. After some of these mothers get finished trashing their babydaddy, it's too hard for a daddy to overcome. You know what I'm saying?

"I want to overcome. Maybe it's too late for my father to pay for stuff or protect me, but it's not too late for us to become friends. Maybe he can show me how to get along with men."

"What do you mean?" Matriece asked, sitting up.

Asia giggled. "Girl, I am death on the brothers. Come to my house two minutes late and I'm like, 'Next!' And even if they do everything right, I'm still backing up. You feeling me? Yeah, you are."

Matriece nodded.

"Dr. Prince and I have been talking about all that stuff. Did you used to go to him?"

Matriece shook her head.

"Dag. I thought you used to go to him. Maybe you should check him out. Anyway, that's why we need to be friends with our dads. Maybe that's why we need them in the first place."

Later, as she sat in her den, Matriece pondered Asia's words, and then dismissed them. Why was she even thinking about Lonell? If she saw him again, she'd say hello. She wasn't like Asia. She didn't want a relationship with her father. The only reason she was speaking to him was so she could go in and out of Vonette's without making everybody uncomfortable. Instead of thinking about Lonell, she needed to focus on what was really important.

Late on Friday afternoon the Old Broad Herself came out to her reception area and escorted Matriece into her office. Gilda had taken to greeting her with a double cheek kiss, and Matriece was steeling herself against it, but to her relief, the older woman simply smiled as they both sat down on the sofa.

"What can I do for you, my dear?" she asked.

Matriece handed her a sealed envelope. "Gilda, I want you to accept my resignation."

The older woman's body jerked involuntarily, and her face blanched. "But what's happened?"

Gilda seemed so hurt, so shocked that for a moment Matriece faltered. Breathe, she told herself, and she did. She looked Gilda straight in her eyes. "I am Hosanna Carter's daughter."

Gilda made a sound, and the skin around her lips seemed to crumple and sag. "My God," she whispered, "you're part of them."

"I didn't know anything about the offer you received until after the fact. I don't want to blackmail you, Gilda. I just want what you owe my sister and me."

Gilda appeared to sink into her cushion. "I didn't steal from your mother, Matriece," she said slowly. "I know she must have believed that, but it isn't true. Your mother brought me back from the dead. I never intentionally hurt her."

"You stole her money!"

"No!" Gilda shouted. "I had written her a check for the money, and I had a coworker of ours from the hotel deliver it to her. But my uncle stole my bank book and gave it to my then husband, who took all the money out of the account and closed it. He split the money with my uncle. I didn't know what had happened until later."

"When you found out, why didn't you return the money to her?"

"I didn't know where to find her. We didn't have telephones in those days. We'd never even exchanged addresses. Besides, David wouldn't return the money. I had nothing." She lowered her eyes, her voice. "He beat me."

Matriece tried to push away the image of a cowering Gilda, warding off blows, crying for mercy. She didn't want to feel pity for her.

The older woman raised her eyes. "I was so sorry about what happened. Your mother was a gift from God to me. She taught me how to smile again, to laugh. She was the best friend I've ever had. The business was her idea. I owe her so much."

Matriece peered into Gilda's face. How could she tell if she was lying? Was the giveaway in the downward slope of her mouth, or hidden inside the emptiness of her eyes? Where was the one clue that would reveal everything? She didn't want to believe Gilda, and yet hers wasn't the face of a liar. "After you divorced your first husband, why didn't you look for her then?"

"That was such a bad time in my life. He tried to take my child, the business. I was so afraid I'd lose my son. If Kent hadn't been there . . ." She paused, as though she were considering something. "Kent saved my life. And so much time had gone by. I thought she would hate me. She was so strong, your mother. She wouldn't have understood my weakness."

"She wasn't strong," Matriece said fiercely. "She fell apart all the time. My mother managed to reconstruct the business you stole, but unlike you, she couldn't get her products sold in department stores. She had to sell them to black beauty salons, mostly west of the Mississippi. Do you know what it took for her to have the little bit of success she had? Everything. She couldn't be a wife. She didn't have time to be a mother. I worked with her because it was the only way I could get her to pay any attention to me at all. Her entire life was the business." Matriece didn't realize that she'd raised her voice until she looked into Gilda's shocked face. "I missed my mother so much my entire life. We were struggling, doing without, and you were on Easy Street. Why can't you just admit it?"

"Admit what?" Gilda's voice was quaking; she looked afraid, as though she'd glimpsed something dreadful.

"You didn't want to find her."

Gilda turned her head away for a moment, and then she faced Matriece. "I'm used to hatred. Yours is weak compared to what I've encountered. You and Mr. Mooney have information that you wish to use against me. You want to expose me." Gilda shrugged. "I don't blame you. I'm just sad because I felt so close to you, Matriece, almost as though you were my child."

Matriece flinched. She didn't want to think about the times Gilda had been kind to her.

"But you are Hosanna's child. Perhaps that is why I liked you so much. Maybe I could feel her in you. I dream of your mother sometimes. Even in death I think she is angry with me, as you are. You think I am so greedy, so ambitious, so ruthless. Ah, my dear, I want peace now. Simple things fulfill me. My daughter hugged me recently. Rachel wants to go to Poland to see where I am from, and I would like to take her. I am seventy years old, and I would like to do things with my daughter. Your timing is excellent, Matriece. What do you want?"

"To buy Brown Sugar."

Gilda shifted in her seat. "I suppose Mr. Mooney will be present for the deal. Mr. Mooney drives a hard bargain."

Matriece nodded. "There are others involved. It's to be a partnership."

"I see. I will sell. Let me know when you'd like to meet. Next week would be good for me."

Los Angeles glittered outside the window in Gilda's office. City of stars. City of dreams. Gilda got up from her seat, walked over to the window, and stared at the panorama in front of them. "You can't imagine what it felt like looking at Los Angeles when I came here for the first time. It was like a wonderland to me. I had been starving for nearly two years, and here was a place where orange trees grew in front of people's houses. Your mother and I used to talk about how nobody could go hungry here. We used to talk about a lot of things. Please don't think of me as the woman who stole from her. I was her friend, and I loved her. I miss her."

"If you ever loved her, then admit the truth."

Gilda sighed, and it was a terrible sound. "When I arrived in this country I was a Jew who'd been hunted like a dog because I was different. I had numbers on my arm and a scar that almost divided me in half. You can't imagine how seductive the thought of acceptance was, even just a little, to someone like me." Her eyes met Matriece's. "Of course you can. Here, in the beginning, I couldn't join the country clubs, and only so many of us were allowed in the best universities, but if I spoke English without an accent, if I shortened my last name and made no mention of the death camps, they let me in most other places. There was one other thing I had to do, one final thing. After I left the hotel, after your mother and I parted, it was then I suppose I realized for the first time, I mean really realized, just what my uncle had been trying to tell me: Black people in this country had to suffer, and if I chose to be with one I would suffer as well. And, my dear, I had suffered enough. I could be white if I separated from your mother." Tears were flowing; Gilda's lip was trembling. "So, I stopped looking for her, and I prayed she wouldn't come looking for me."

CHAPTER SIXTY-THREE

KENT WAS TRYING very hard to concentrate on what the real estate broker was saying to him at the same time he was trying to figure out who his wife was speaking with on the telephone. He and the broker were in the library, and Peggy was in the kitchen. Her voice had grown strong again. He tilted his head to the side. Had she said, "Hello, Gilda"? That couldn't be possible.

He didn't like the numbers the broker was repeating. They were low numbers, too low to save him. He was out of time and out of money. Beyond his living room window he could hear Sam singing. The man had been washing and detailing his cars for nearly five years, and he'd never heard him sing before. He had a beautiful voice, rich, full-bodied. He sang some religious song a cappella. Kent began listening to the words, but then it got to be too much, all this listening to his wife, the broker, Sam's fine tenor. All this paying attention on no Xanax and no gambling with only the Serenity Prayer to keep him sane. God, he would have killed for a chill pill. The hands that rested on his knees were shaking, not as badly as they'd shaken the first week, but he couldn't make them still if his life depended on it. When Peggy came in the room and extended the phone to him, Kent was happy to let her usher the man out. He sat down on the couch and picked up the portable phone.

"Kent." Gilda's voice sent a frisson of excitement and shame through his body. Suppose she'd called to tell him that she was going to have him arrested, indicted for embezzlement. He looked up at Peggy, who smiled at him and raised both her thumbs. That was for luck, he supposed. "Hello, Gilda," he said.

Peggy sat down beside him and put her hand in his free one; he squeezed her fingers.

"Peggy sounds wonderful, Kent. How is she doing?"

Gilda sounded so calm, so normal, as though nothing had happened between them. "She's getting stronger every day."

"I'm so happy to hear that. Are you getting help for your gambling, Kent?"

"Yes. I've been going to Gamblers Anonymous."

"Is it working?"

"I haven't played cards since we last spoke."

Peggy, whose ear was close to the phone, looked into Kent's eyes and smiled.

"That's wonderful. Kent, I need you."

"Gilda, I assumed you'd fired me. That's what I deserved."

"Well, I did. If you're willing, I'd like to reinstate you. Of course, my forgiveness doesn't erase your debt. I believe you owe me money."

"I do."

"You may work it off."

"How's that?"

"I'm selling Brown Sugar to Matriece and her business partners. I would like to indenture you to them for a year or two. Of course, I will take the money you owe me out of your pay. I'll try to make it as painless as possible. What do you think?"

Did she know about his approaching Meeks? Should he tell her now? "Gilda, why are you selling Brown Sugar?"

"It's a long story, Kent. Come in tomorrow at ten and I'll explain it to you. I need your help in the negotiations."

"I'll be there. Thank you, Gilda."

He hung up the phone and suddenly realized how tightly he'd been holding his wife's hand. "She forgave me," he said to Peggy.

"It's what you do when you love someone," she said.

In a moment he heard footsteps, six of them. Jolie and a cocker spaniel puppy bounded into the room. The little girl scooped up the puppy and landed mostly in her father's lap, with one leg on Peggy. Outside the window Sam's voice, lustrous and smooth, rang out. Kent looked down at his hands. They were still shaking but not as badly. Maybe soon the trembling would stop altogether and he wouldn't think about Xanax or blackjack. Maybe one day soon he would be as strong and complete as the notes floating outside his window, the ones that filled his soul with peace. He could feel warmth coming from his daughter and the little dog, from his wife's fingers. He closed his eyes and saw his mother, the sad old woman she'd been before she died. The words came to him. ". . . to accept the things I cannot change . . ." He couldn't tell if he was awake or dreaming. All he knew was when his mother stretched out her hand to him, he took it.

CHAPTER SIXTY-FOUR

ON SUNDAY MONTGOMERY reluctantly arrived at his parents' home for a noon brunch that he knew would be more akin to an endurance test than anything else. His sister, Juliette, had been seeing exclusively a young man she'd met at the Morehouse dinner and was finally, against her better judgment, Montgomery assumed, allowing their parents to meet her boyfriend's parents for a no-holds-barred once-over.

It was clear from the start that the prospective young man's mother could give as good as she got. Nadine was wearing designer knitwear, and enough diamonds to fund AFDC in the county for a month. During leisurely drinks on the sunporch that overlooked the entire valley, she began her onslaught. While Big Monty and Mr. Winston talked about stocks and business, Nadine quizzed Mrs. Winston on where she'd gone to school, her sorority, and church affiliation. Mrs. Winston looked amused. She was thin and stylish, intensely intellectual, and a lawyer like her husband. Both practiced in the firm that her father had started nearly forty years earlier. When Nadine began to drop names faster than she could breathe, Mrs. Winston said firmly, "And what do you do, dear?"

His mother paused long enough for Montgomery to suspect that she didn't get the question. "Do?" she said finally.

"Professionally," Mrs. Winston said smoothly.

"Oh, I haven't worked in years," Nadine said proudly.

"Oh," Mrs. Winston said. She immediately excused herself and went to join the men. To Montgomery's knowledge, she didn't say another word to his mother until she was thanking her for the lovely brunch.

"Did you see that?" Nadine sputtered after the Winstons left. "That stuck-up bitch dismissed me as though I was beneath her. The nerve!"

Juliette and her boyfriend had left with the Winstons, and Montgomery and his parents were in the kitchen, nibbling on leftovers as the maid cleaned around them. Big Monty muttered something under his breath and retreated to his study. Montgomery found himself in the un-enviable position of being in the kitchen alone with his mother when she was teetering precariously between a crying jag and an after-the-fact cussing-out. Of the two, Montgomery would have preferred the latter but his mother's mood swings were not under his control. He had learned that soothing was the best he could do in these situations. "Well, Mom, what does she know?" he said glibly.

"She acts as though her little two-bit law firm is world famous or something. Whoever heard of them? Have you, honey?"

When Montgomery reluctantly told her that the Winstons had suc-cessfully helped several Fortune 500 corporations negotiate mergers, Na-dine was quiet for a moment. "Well, just because a woman is a lawyer doesn't make her better than another woman."

"Mom," Montgomery said patiently, "you're successful, too."

They were leaning against the center island. There was an open bot-tle of champagne and a clean glass near her and Nadine reached for both. She poured herself a full flute and gulped it down. "Am I, honey?" she asked, and he could hear the little girl in her, a drunk little girl. "I raised two wonderful children."

"Mom, if it hadn't been for you, Dad wouldn't have started the busi-ness."

Nadine brightened visibly. "Do they have as much money as we do?"

"I seriously doubt it, Mom." He stifled both his laughter and his sad-ness.

His mother looked relieved. "Not too many people have a house as nice as ours. And, of course, this isn't even our only home."

"Right, Mom."

"That girl you used to date, the brown-skinned one with the short hair. I believe that she was intimidated by me just like Ms. Lawyer. What-ever happened between you two?"

"Matriece and I broke up, Mom."

Nadine sighed. "She was a bright girl. You listened to her, didn't you? I mean, you valued her opinion."

"I liked the way she thought."

His mother sighed.

"What?"

"I just wish that you and Gretel would get together. The children would be so adorable. She has that beautiful hair and those light eyes. I'm ready to be a grandmother, not that I want to be called Grandmother or Grandma or anything with Grand in it. Maybe Mimi or Nana. That's cute. How can you not be attracted to Gretel, pretty as she is?"

"Mom, she's not attracted to me."

"That can't be true."

"Trust me."

"Well . . ." His mother hesitated just long enough for Montgomery to clench his teeth. He hated her matchmaking conversations. "You should ask her out sometime. A girl can change her mind."

"Nadine!" Montgomery heard his father's voice behind him.

His mother jumped. "Yes, Big Monty."

"Let the man pick his own woman. Stop your damn meddling."

"But, honey . . ."

"It's his life, Nadine. Mind your own damn business."

"I know, baby." She looked hurt, the way she always did whenever his father yelled.

"You don't need to talk to her that way," Montgomery said, facing his father.

"Honey," Nadine said with alarm, looking at her son.

"I know you're not telling me what I can say to my wife," Big Monty bellowed.

Montgomery was used to that tone. It had echoed throughout his entire childhood. Once that voice had frightened him. Now he simply hated it.

"Montgomery." His mother's voice was so small and weak. Sometimes when he looked at her she appeared to be shrinking. He glanced at her now and then at his father, who was swaying from side to side, his jowls swollen, his eyes two molten rocks.

"I'm telling you I want you to treat my mother with respect. Stop talking to her like she's your dog."

"Boy, have you lost your mind?" Big Monty said, his nostrils widening. "Getting up in my face like that." He looked at Nadine. "Did you see that?"

"You treat your wife like shit. You lie to the people who support you. You swear to black people that you're not selling the station when you can't wait for Cortez to buy you out. You don't give a damn about what black folks need. If it wasn't for Mom, you'd own a couple of apartment buildings in the jungle. She's the one with the vision. You'd be nothing without her."

Montgomery could hear his mother whimpering behind his father. He'd bitten his lip, and now he could taste blood in his mouth. Everything around him seemed clear and sharp. "I always wanted to be like you, Dad. I wanted to be tall like you. I wanted to be powerful like you. But you know what I just realized? I want to be better than you. Maybe I don't know what I want to be when I grow up. But I know I don't want to work for you anymore. I quit."

"Montgomery!" His mother began crying. His father's cheeks were suddenly deflated, almost sunken. He stomped out of the kitchen.

Montgomery walked over to his mother, kissed her forehead, and said, "You don't have to take his shit, Mom. Half of everything he has is yours, plus alimony."

She slapped him across his mouth. It was a weak slap, but it stung. "Don't you ever talk to your father like that. I'm Big Monty's wife," his mother said. "What goes on between him and me is none of your damn business. Everything he's done has been for you and Juliette. Don't act like it's nothing. We can be a dynasty, Montgomery. Do you know how many black dynasties there are? Don't throw it all away."

"Maybe that's enough for you, Mom, to be part of who he is, but it's not enough for me. I'm not throwing it away; I'm giving it back."

He could still hear his mother calling him even after the front door had closed.

Montgomery drove to a liquor store and picked up some empty boxes, then he went to his office. It took him less than two hours to pack up his things. What am I going to be when I grow up? he thought as he drove off. He felt sad, lonely, and foolish as he waited for the red light to change. Big Monty had begun building an empire by the time he was his age. I've done nothing my entire life but take his orders. He had to admit to himself that he had no plans, just vague ideas, and three boxes filled with his old life.

Montgomery was five minutes from his home when his cell phone rang. He was surprised to hear Mooney's voice when he answered. "How'd you get this number?" he asked him.

"From your momma," Mooney said evenly. "She told me you and Big Monty had words. I'm an old man. I guess maybe she thinks I'm wise or something, that I have a knack for putting things back together. Truth is, I have my own reasons for wanting to talk with you. Can you come by my house?"

"When?"

"Right now."

It was growing dark by the time Mooney led Montgomery into his study. The younger man declined his offer of food and drink, accepting only a glass of water, which Mooney's maid brought.

"Look," Mooney said, as Montgomery was drinking. "I'm not one to get into nobody's business but I guess I've been engaged as the mediator, even though I really don't know you that well. You're smart, I know that. And I know your father can be a real fool. You can tell him I said so," he added, when Montgomery choked. "But he's built something that a lot of black men haven't been able to build, so I give him respect. A son doesn't just walk away from what his father has built without thinking about it long and hard. The trouble with your daddy is he never knew when to step back. He wants to hold on forever. He should have groomed you to take over years ago. Hell, you should be running everything by now and he should be out golfing. If I had a son, that's what I'd be doing. But I wasn't as lucky as Big Monty. Anyway, the hell with your father. Let's talk about me.

"I been in business practically all my life. For most of that time I've dreamed of a group of black people doing some sort of joint venture where we could all make money. I started imagining it back when we weren't nothing but mom-and-pops along Central Avenue. I guess you could call me a visionary. Hell, that's what I call myself. Now, we've got a deal on the table. It isn't as big as the one I imagined, but it's big enough to share and grow.

"Owning a first-rate cosmetics company was Matriece's mother's dream," Mooney said. "Matriece's momma and I go way back, and when she died Matriece kind of kept the dream alive. Well, now it's coming true. You're young. Meeks, Big Monty, and me, we can only go part of the way. Matriece is going to need help, son."

Mooney opened his desk drawer, pulled out a folder, and passed it to Montgomery. "This is the business plan; it's mostly what you talked about the other day. We're meeting with Gilda on Monday at one o'clock. You got the Harvard degree. I figure you can improve on this."

"I don't know if I should. I don't intend to work with my father anymore."

"Just do me the favor. Look it over, will you?" Mooney got up from his desk. "Come around here and get comfortable." Montgomery slid into his seat. It was still warm. "Let me know if you want anything," Mooney called over his shoulder as he left the room.

It took nearly two hours for Montgomery to read the papers. The deal was structured just as he'd outlined it: clear-cut and simple. A straight sale to a newly formed limited partnership. No brilliance was needed to refine it, just a skilled negotiator to talk Gilda into accepting the offered price, which was ridiculously low. As Montgomery read the papers he felt himself changing hats, shifting from lawyer to marketer. He imagined the kind of Internet placement the products deserved. He'd dated the women these cosmetics ought to appeal to, and he knew not only how they liked to look but how they wanted to feel. When they put on their lipstick and eye shadow, they wanted to appeal to a brother like him, a good brother. Good brother. Good man. He tossed the phrases back and forth in his mind, letting the concept for a powerful slogan begin to form. Lips for a good brother. Eyes for a good brother . . .

Montgomery turned out the light in Mooney's office and closed the door. He wasn't quite sure which way to go, so he followed the sound of Sarah Vaughan's voice and wound up in the family room. Mooney was seated on the sofa, sipping a soda. Beside him was Matriece. "Oh," she said, when she saw him. She gave Mooney a look.

"We're all going to be working together. I thought it wouldn't be a bad idea to have a drink together. How about a little wine?"

Mooney got up and disappeared into the back of his house. Montgomery didn't expect him to return anytime soon. He looked at Matriece, and they both laughed.

"Ya gotta love him," Matriece said, and they laughed again. "So," she said, turning to him.

"So. I've never been engaged, in case you're wondering."

"I saw Gretel's ring, and I guess I jumped to conclusions." She spoke slowly and very softly. He moved closer so he could hear her. "I heard you're breaking your father's heart."

"Mooney told you?"

Matriece shook her head. "Your mother."

"My mother called you?" He couldn't believe what he was hearing.

"Shocked me more than you. I think if I can convince you to take your job back, she's willing to let me be your girlfriend. I'm reading between the lines." She laughed.

"How did my mother know I was over here?"

"She didn't. Uncle Mooney called and asked me to stop by."

"So, they're in cahoots."

"I guess."

Montgomery started laughing. "Must be a full moon."

"Let's see the deal."

By the time Mooney returned with three glasses of red wine Montgomery and Matriece scarcely noticed him. They were immersed in the paperwork, their heads together, their eyes scanning the words, their pencils crossing out, adding in. Back and forth they mixed and matched the phrases that Montgomery had begun playing with in Mooney's study. The old man disappeared again. He returned with more company.

"Montgomery."

Hearing his mother's voice, Montgomery looked up. Big Monty was standing next to Nadine. "I'd like to talk with you, son," he said.

Matriece and Nadine excused themselves, and his father sat down in Mooney's big easy chair. "You have a beef with me, huh?"

"I said what I had to say, Dad. Mom put me in my place. For the record, I apologize for inserting myself in your marriage. You have to understand, I love my mother."

"You think I don't?"

"I think you believe that having money gives you the right to do whatever you want, no matter who you hurt. I think you've forgotten the difference between being a success and being a decent human being. When you started out it was about the two of you. Now, it's all about you."

"I don't need you telling me what kind of husband I am."

"No, you don't. So, let's talk about what kind of father I need."

Big Monty gave a start. "You want to blame me because you're not in charge. Whenever I ask you what you want to do, you don't have any idea."

"I'm not an idea man. Neither are you."

"What do you want from me?"

"I want you to give me some guidance. I want you to let me lead sometimes, because sooner or later, I'll be leading. I can either fall on my face while you're around to pick me up, or I can fall on my face after you're gone. Let me make some decisions, even if they're wrong. Stop acting like you're going to live forever. Help me be as great as I can be. And another thing: I want you to reconsider the sale. You can't put a price on goodwill."

Big Monty looked at him for a long time. He stood up. "You're probably right. You can always tell a Morehouse man, but you can't tell him much." Their eyes met. "I'll see you at the office."

After his parents left, Montgomery followed Matriece to her house. They sat in her kitchen eating cookies and drinking peppermint tea, feeling entirely at peace.

"Are things okay with you and your dad?" she asked him.

"Better. How about you and your dad?"

"I spoke to him."

"That's a start."

"Yeah. What kind of father do you think you'll be?"

"One who doesn't leave or get sidetracked. One who loves his children's mother. One who knows what's important."

"Do you want to be a father?"

"Yes." He looked at her.

"If I'm going to have any babies, I need to have them soon." Her eyes met his.

"How soon?"

"Soon."

CHAPTER SIXTY-FIVE

FRIDAY MORNING WAS cloudless, a smiling day. Matriece heard the van in her driveway. Sam's here, she thought, sipping her tea as she sat at her kitchen table. The air was sweet with the scent of warmed muffins. Sam's unseen presence was reassuring to her, like knowing that the sun was shining. She could hear him singing, a strong tenor. His tone was thick, heavy, and warm, a comforter to be drawn up close.

She took another bite of her muffin and picked up the newspaper. Her eyes were drawn to the headline on the front page. SWISS BANKS SETTLE WITH HOLOCAUST SURVIVORS. "As word spreads of $1.25 billion in assets that two Swiss banks will return to Holocaust victims, many of the aged survivors are poised to claim their windfalls," the first line read. She scanned the rest of the article, which talked about how several international organizations had waged a long legal battle on behalf of the victims and their descendants. On the second page were quotes from the would-be recipients. "This will not bring my family back," said one, "but it is a blessing, even at this late date."

Fifteen minutes later, Matriece had reached the last page of the national news section. In the lower right-hand column was the item she'd been searching for. BLACK TEXANS UNITE IN FILING CLASS-ACTION SUIT. Matriece quickly read the two paragraphs. "Tunis Clark, the first African-American to head the Los Angeles Fire Department, is spearheading a class-action suit brought by ninety-three plaintiffs who claim they lost in excess of five thousand acres more than fifty years ago due to fraud on the part of Hagerty, Inc., a southwest Texas farming and oil-drilling conglomeration. William Weiss, the lawyer representing the plaintiffs, stated, 'There is more than enough evidence to support the claim that Hagerty, Inc., willingly and knowingly defrauded black farmers because of the entrenched system of segregation, which the defendants thought would place these people in a no-win situation.' "

Matriece laughed out loud. The article wasn't a surprise. After her father and sister had returned from Texas, Vonette called her with the news that Lonell had persuaded most of the people he knew to join with the other plaintiffs, and that the suit was going forward. "You go, Uncle Tuney," she said, folding up the paper and draining her cup.

When she set it down she saw her mother sitting in a chair across from her. She wore a lavender dress; her gray hair was uncombed. Tears were flowing down Hosanna's face, yet she didn't look sad. When she stared at Matriece she was smiling. It had been a long time since she'd seen her mother smile, in life or in death.

"Mom," Matriece said softly.

Hosanna nodded and kept smiling directly at her. There was an unspoken secret behind her mother's curved lips. Once, long ago, she could read her mother's mind, her thoughts, knew the words that would come from her mouth before she spoke them. They were that close. But that was another lifetime. If Hosanna had a message for her, it was in a script Matriece could no longer decipher.

From her driveway the stirring tenor had merged with an even more compelling soprano. At first Matriece thought Sam was singing along with the radio, but then she realized that the duet was a live performance. When she opened her front door to peek outside, Sam and Asia were hitting the last high note. They convulsed with laughter when they saw Matriece's astonished face.

"We were wondering how long it would take you to come outside," Asia said, still giggling. "I'm going for a second career as a detail woman."

This time Sam laughed.

"No, really. My dad said he'd take me out to breakfast after he finished doing your car. You want to come?"

They look like a happy ending, Matriece thought. Both were smiling. It seemed easy, their being together. The big man was buffing the hood of Matriece's car. Asia, clad in jeans and a sweatshirt, watched him. "You need to come do mine," she said, and then laughed, winking at Matriece. "And I ain't tipping you, either."

"I don't have cheap clients," Sam shot back.

Matriece studied their casualness for a few moments, tried to memorize it before it faded away. She wanted to ask Asia if she loved Sam again, if being with him was like riding a bicycle. She wanted to know if Sam felt like a father again, if he'd ever stopped feeling like one. They held their heads with the same nonchalant gracefulness. Their laughter was in a vibrant family key. They shared burnished copper skin, clefts in their chins, high cheekbones. She was his child, all right. Funny how time and distance couldn't erode genes and DNA, couldn't erase the heart's memory. Maybe it *was* like riding a bicycle. Maybe she would find out. Matriece shook her head. "I can't. I'm on my way to a meeting. Really important."

"Claude gave me the contract. I signed it," Asia said.

"He called me. Thanks."

Matriece couldn't identify the song that Sam and Asia were singing as they drove away. She thought it was an old hymn that she'd grown up with, but the title wouldn't come back to her. She could hear Sam feeding the lyrics to his daughter, her soprano echoing his soft tenor. As she drove to work, Matriece hummed over and over the portion of the song that was most familiar to her, trying, in vain, to jog her memory.

She was still humming it when she reached her office. Matriece smelled the perfume as soon as she opened her door. The scent was a meal she'd hungered for without knowing it. Blair was sitting in the chair in front of her desk.

"Hello," Matriece said. She'd been avoiding Blair since their blowup. Facing her, she didn't know what to say.

"What were you humming?" Blair asked.

"What?" She could see the tension and anguish in Blair's eyes, the trepidation.

"When you came in you were humming something. It sounded familiar."

"I can't think of the title. It's been driving me crazy."

"It sounded like a church song I knew."

"What can I tell you?"

It felt familiar, the perfume, the inane banter, Blair holding a pack of cigarettes, looking as though she needed to bolt from the room. She looked thinner, sadder, more in the midst of a nicotine fit than ever before.

"When are you going to quit smoking?" Matriece asked.

"Not today." She sighed. "Matriece, I didn't realize that the things I used to say about growing up where I did offended you. I didn't think I was being racist. I was just trying to be funny. Defense mechanism. I wanted to connect with you, Matriece. Maybe I overdid it." Their eyes met for a moment.

"Maybe I'm too sensitive. I'm trying to work on my grudges."

"Just don't hold one against me." Blair put the cigarette in her mouth, then took it out. "Scuttlebutt has it that you're buying the company. Is that true?"

"My partners and I are going to make an offer on Monday." She wasn't surprised that Blair had found out. That kind of news was hard to keep secret.

"Wow. That's fantastic, Matriece. You know, I'm not surprised. I kind of expected something like this to happen."

There was a look of awe on Blair's face that Matriece found disconcerting. "Really?"

"You've always had everything together."

Matriece laughed self-consciously. "Except my relationships."

"Yes, except for that tendency to dump good men, you lead a perfect life."

They both laughed nervously.

"Why didn't you ever tell me that you were having problems with Judd?" Matriece asked suddenly.

She saw Blair wince. "I was ashamed, Matriece."

"Of what? You're a good mother."

"I haven't felt like a good mother in a long time. When I was a kid I hated being poor. I dreamed of the big house with enough of everything inside it, and I thought once I got that my life would be perfect. The fact that it's not feels like failure to me. I guess you can't understand that. You've never failed before."

"Is that what you think?"

"You walk into Radiance Cosmetics, and when you leave you're practically running the place. You come to Gilda's, and now you're about to buy the company. I call that success. You're focused, driven, and you achieve. I guess . . ." Her voice began to trail.

"What?"

Blair looked her straight in her eyes. "For you life is about achievement."

Matriece stared at her, then she said coldly, "Maybe you're envious."

Blair's face turned red, and Matriece felt avenged.

"I am," Blair admitted. "I want the kind of career success you have, and I'm never going to get it. I'm not . . ."

"Driven." Their eyes met.

Blair shrugged. "Maybe that's why I felt I couldn't let you know about Judd. Your life seems so perfect, so in control. I didn't want you to know that mine was falling apart."

Blair's last statement made Matriece regret her harshness. "Blair, I'm an overachiever in overdrive," Matriece confessed. "I want to slow down. All my ambition, all my goals, Blair, they aren't even mine. They're my inheritance from a mother who didn't get what she wanted out of life because she was born the wrong color and wrong gender at the wrong time. For a long time I've been feeling as though I'm on a treadmill, running at warp speed. Guess what? I'm getting off. Maybe I'll move to the suburbs and join the white-picket-fence brigade."

"Is that where you think I live—in some la la land?"

Matriece considered the question. There was a part of her that had always believed that Blair's lot in life was easier than hers. "I always thought that if push came to shove, you had a husband, somebody to take care of you."

"I hate to burst your little bubble, Matriece. You think I just get to fritter away my check on whatever my little heart desires? Come on. We can't make the house note without my salary. I'm not living in White Girl Wonderland, my dear."

Matriece's apology was unspoken. "How's Judd doing? Vonette says he's going to spend more weekends with them."

Blair nodded. "He's better. Vonette and Boot are so wonderful."

Seeing the tears in Blair's eyes, Matriece hugged her. "All the boy needs is a little bit of South Central."

"Must be the barbecue," Blair said.

Their shoulders hunched and jerked as they laughed, and Matriece still heard music.

CHAPTER SIXTY-SIX

VONETTE COOKED GUMBO only twice a year, on Christmas and Tavares's birthday. Boot liked beef tamales for his celebration. She never knew what Shalimar would request; last year she wanted pizza and sweet potato pie. As for Chazz, her eldest didn't care what he ate as long as he had his newest honey sitting next to him at the dinner table. But Tavares was a gumbo man. His birthday menu hadn't changed in six years: gumbo, black beans and rice, collard greens, corn bread, and carrot cake for dessert. Leave it to her youngest to want something that took all day long to cook.

Usually the birthday parties of her household were small family affairs, but ever since Judd had confessed his crimes and Tavares had returned to his old school, Vonette had been feeling celebratory. There was too much good news in her life not to have a party.

As she lay in bed next to a snoring Boot that Saturday morning, Vonette tried to rouse herself. Her plan was to get up early and start on the roux, which would take at least an hour to get to the right consistency and peanut-butter-brown color. As soon as she sat up, her husband's snoring stopped abruptly, and she felt his hand on her thigh. "Where you going, Mommy?"

"I have to fix the gumbo." Even as she said the words she felt herself settling down. She could feel streams of heat everywhere Boot touched. "What you think you're doing?" she whispered.

"I got some gumbo for you, baby."

Boot had gotten home late the night before, and he hadn't taken a shower. His body smelled like paint and sweat but Vonette didn't mind. Let me just get this man off, so I can do what I got to do, she thought.

"Don't be throwing me no bones, girl."

She laughed. Boot's palms pressing into her hips and caressing her breasts made her belly weak, and her own desire mounted. "I love you, baby," he said, and she could hear Mexico and the east side in his voice.

"I love you too, *cariño*," she said. "I really do."

They smiled at each other, kept smiling the closer they got. My buddy, Vonette thought, and she pulled Boot tighter. At the same time they felt a flash of heat and intense pleasure and then Boot was kissing her face, burying his head between her breasts, falling asleep. She held him and drifted off herself, waking nearly three hours later.

It was then she saw Hosanna, sitting on the edge of her bed. I'm not asleep, she told herself, staring at her mother. What does she want with me? Vonette wondered. Her mother seemed subdued. Something was very different about her. Peering closer, Vonette saw the shiny trickle of her tears. But she was smiling, too. She's happy, Vonette thought, and the idea itself was so strange, so extraordinary that it took a moment to sink in. Hosanna hadn't been happy in so long that she could barely remember what contentment looked like on her mother's face. *Why couldn't you be happy like that when Triecy and me were little?*

"Hey, hey," Boot said, patting her hip. "What you crying about, baby?" He sat up, faced her, then pushed his dark hair out of his eyes.

"Nothing."

"Come on, girl. What's wrong?"

"Do you think my mother loved me?"

"Hell yeah, she loved you. Why you think she hated my ass so much? Because she thought I was bad for you. That's love."

"How come she never paid any attention to me?"

"She did; it just wasn't the kind you wanted. How come we're always on Chazz?" When she didn't answer, he said, "See there?" He pulled her closer. "I'll be your mommy."

By the time Vonette got out of bed and put on her robe, her mother had faded away. But she saw her again in the bathroom as she showered, and then in the hallway after she'd put on her clothes. "What do you want?" Vonette whispered to her, but Hosanna didn't answer. Vonette smelled something cooking, and when she went downstairs she saw her father standing over a gumbo pot, stirring. Hosanna was right beside him, with that same look of radiant happiness.

"Daddy, turn around," Vonette asked. "You see anything?"

Lonell looked on either side of him. "What am I supposed to be seeing?"

Vonette sighed, and her mother wafted away. "What are you doing, Daddy?"

"I . . . got your . . . roux started for you. I was just getting . . . ready to add . . . the water."

Vonette peered into the pot and smiled when she saw the smooth consistency of her daddy's roux. It was just the right shade of brown. Since her father had moved in she'd been so busy serving him that she'd forgotten he was good in the kitchen. "Thanks, Dad," she said. "You sure you're not tired?" She could hear him wheezing a bit.

"Nah, I'm all right. I can cook the whole thing if you want me to."

Let him feel useful, she thought. "Sure, Daddy, as long as you sit down when you're tired."

Several hours later, Tavares was the first of her children to come downstairs. "Yum," he said when he smelled the gumbo. "Granddad, you can cook?" He was incredulous.

"What you think, boy?" He shuffled back a few paces so Tavares had room enough to inspect the contents of the pot.

"Looks good. Smells good." He took a large spoon out of the drawer, dipped it into the gumbo, blowing on the contents for a few minutes before he tasted it. "Da bomb, Granddad," Tavares said enthusiastically.

"Better than mine?" Vonette asked, smiling.

"Uh, they're both good," Tavares said, and all three laughed.

"Where's Judd?"

"He and Shalimar are on the computer."

"They dressed?"

"Uh-huh. Don't worry, Mom. Chazz and I got our eyes on him and Baby Girl."

Vonette grunted. Judd had been quiet with most of the family members but seemed to have more to say to Shalimar. She and Boot hadn't counted on teenybopper crushes beneath their roof, but she wasn't going to worry, not with Chazz and Tavares watching out.

Never can tell what children go through, she thought. Judd wasn't a bad kid, just needy, confused, and big-time spoiled. She didn't know why she'd volunteered to keep him. Vonette didn't hold out any illusions about a miraculous transformation. What the boy needed was some attention from his father and some discipline from both his parents: she and Boot couldn't give him that.

Vonette couldn't tell whether or not Judd was happy. He hadn't called home once. One thing she was sure of: The boy wasn't smoking any bud. Everybody in the house was checking him out. Boot went through his pockets when he was asleep, and Vonette rifled through his things when he came home. Well, Vonette thought, if Judd's stay with us wasn't anything but a weed time-out, at least he got his head cleared.

At that moment Judd and Shalimar trooped down the stairs, conversing animatedly about something they'd been researching on the computer. Shalimar's hair was combed in a new style, and her daughter was wearing lipstick and earrings. Tavares was already seated at the table, eating waffles. Judd and Shalimar greeted everyone, then they each poured a bowl of cereal, some juice, and made toast, which they slathered with butter and jam.

"You ever eat gumbo, Judd?" Vonette asked.

"I don't think so."

"Boy, where you been?" Lonell asked, and Tavares and Shalimar giggled.

"Well, you're going to have some tonight at Tavares's birthday party."

"You down, dog?" Tavares asked him.

"Yeah," Judd said. "It smells good."

The odor of gumbo permeated the entire house by the time the party got started. People started coming around eight that evening. Carla came over with her mother and sister, smiling and talking animatedly with them. Boot's family arrived next, his mother and father shouting in Spanish as they entered. They were followed by his sisters and brother and their children. Soon there were conversations in English and Spanish under way, with the younger Mexican-Americans switching back and forth easily. Uncle Tuney came in with Lindell. Tavares's friends, as well as Chazz's and Shalimar's buddies, arrived in packs. They all crowded into the small living room and then began spreading into the kitchen and dining room. Chazz put on some music and the young people started dancing as the older ones smiled and watched. Judd stood on the periphery of the dancers until Shalimar shoved him into the circle and started wiggling and gyrating in front of him. She caught her mother's approving eye and laughed. Vonette started moving from side to side. "Show them what you're working with," she shouted. Judd flashed her a smile, and in a moment his body was gyrating like the others.

Vonette ran in and out of the kitchen, filling up bowls of potato chips, tortilla chips, and salsa, heating up the gumbo and rice, while Boot passed out beers and poured wine for the adults. The front door was unlocked, and new people kept surging in. Vonette sipped a glass of wine as she mingled with her guests.

Suddenly Blair came in with a man Vonette recognized as her husband. He was tall with dark hair. Beneath his glasses, his light eyes peered out anxiously. Vonette remembered him from a long time ago. Blair looked a little thinner than she had the last time Vonette had seen her, and he looked nervous. Vonette walked over to them and gave Blair a hug, then shook Porter's hand. "Judd's on the dance floor," she said, then laughed as their astonishment turned to incredulity at the sight of their son dancing furiously.

"I haven't seen him dancing in so long," Blair said softly, almost to herself.

"Oh, honey," Vonette said, "these kids don't let you know what they can do. You have to drag it out of them. I didn't know my daughter owned a lipstick until Mr. Judd arrived. Not to worry," she added quickly when Porter blinked. "Everybody's been supervising them."

"How has he been?" Porter asked.

"He's been fine. Got up and went to work with Boot today. I don't think he likes it, but hell, neither does Boot." She laughed. "He's a good kid. Just mixed up. And the weed doesn't help. He'll straighten up, but you have to stay on him. Be with him all the time. Listen, it's a party. Food and drinks are in the kitchen. Relax. Blair, go out back and take a look at my garden."

"Thank you, Vonette. Thank you for everything."

"Oh, girl, please. Judd," she called. When the boy turned to her she said, "Come say hello to your mom and dad."

She left them talking, or rather she heard Blair attempting a few words and saw Judd looking embarrassed, trying to get away. Boot came over and started telling Blair how much Judd had helped him. "He did a good job," Vonette heard him say. After a little while she saw Blair wandering around the house and Porter sitting down by himself.

Vonette went into the kitchen to check on the food. As she was rinsing off some silverware, she looked out the window above her sink and saw a bright golden light flitting across the grass. She looked again, and her mother took shape before her eyes. Blair walked right by her but didn't seem to notice.

"What are you looking at?"

Vonette turned around at the sound of Matriece's voice. She was holding hands with a nice-looking man. Vonette looked at their two faces and saw a future.

"Vonette, this is Montgomery Briggs," Matriece said.

Vonette hugged him, then kissed his cheek. "Welcome. Get something to drink Get you some gumbo." She grabbed her sister's hand. "I have to borrow her."

Blair was coming in as they were going out the back door. "Hi," she said to Matriece.

"Hey, girl." The two women hugged, and Matriece whispered, "Montgomery's inside. We're back together."

"Did you learn your lesson?"

"I'm learning it."

"She'll be right back," Vonette said to Blair.

The two sisters went out the back door and stood on the tiny patio overlooking the garden. "What?" Matriece said.

"Look. You see her?"

They were both quiet, watching as their mother, bathed in gold, wafted around the garden. "I've been seeing her all day long. I only used to dream about her before."

It was chilly in the yard, and Vonette's arms were bare. She kept rubbing them, and moved closer to Matriece.

"I saw her yesterday," Matriece said. "She was sitting at my kitchen table."

"She's happy."

"Yeah, she is."

The two sisters looked at each other. "It's about time," Vonette said.

Vonette could smell the gumbo all the way in the backyard. The mixture of seafood and spices had been simmering for hours. Throughout the day she and her father had added things: season salt, chicken, fish, crabs, shrimp, mussels, scallops, and then a good shake of filé at the end. It was a powerful mixture. "I'm getting hungry again," Vonette said. In front of them their mother was turning into mist.

"She'll be back," Matriece said.

"If she's found peace, maybe she doesn't need to come back."

"Is that what she's been doing? Looking for peace?"

"That's what everybody's doing, Matriece. You want some gumbo?"

"Yeah."

The music was cranked up louder than before. Tavares was standing on a chair in the center of the living room, calling out, "I want to thank my moms and pops for this sixteenth birthday party. I know they're going to hook me up with either a Land Rover or a PT Cruiser, or a little somethin' somethin' with four wheels but that's going to be a private family moment later on. Right, Dad?"

"Son, all I have is yours," Boot said.

"Moving right along . . . I want to thank everybody for celebrating with me. Now that I'm a man—"

"You gotta pay rent," Boot shouted.

"See, I'm trying to create a moment. Anyway, thanks for coming. DJ, crank it up. Everybody on the floor."

"Come on, y'all. Soul Train line," Vonette shouted. She pulled Boot away from his brother and told him to stand in front of her, then she grabbed Matriece and Montgomery, Blair, Judd, and her father. Porter remained on the sofa. Others joined them and the two lines, one all male, the other all female, took form. Vonette heard Matriece introducing Montgomery to Lonell. Her sister said, "I'd like you to meet my father." Judd and Shalimar did some sort of shoulder-shaking shimmy down the middle; their rhythm was a little behind and sometimes a bit ahead of the beat. Porter got up to watch them. He stood next to Blair, looking as though he wanted to be included. When she watched the next couple, she saw that Montgomery had switched places with her father, so that the old man and Matriece were dancing down the middle. Rather, Matriece was dancing and Lonell was shuffling along. Everybody in the line was yelling and whistling encouragement. At first their eyes refused to meet, but by the time they reached the end of the line they were smiling at each other. Montgomery was smiling, too, and seeing that, Vonette thought to herself, This boy is going to be all right. Tavares came down the center alone, dancing and clowning as people shouted at him in English and Spanish. And then it was her and Boot, and Vonette knew exactly what his moves were going to be before he made them, and she knew that he knew hers. They were laughing so hard she didn't notice the golden light drifting in and out of the corner of the room, flickering and waning and finally disappearing.

CHAPTER SIXTY-SEVEN

THEY TAKE UP space, the four of them. I wonder if they realize when they walk up the front steps of the Gilda Cosmetics Building that they crowd people out without even touching them. They claim the sun for themselves and create a shadow for others. Or maybe the sun just finds them. My Mooney always did love to shine. When he gets on that express elevator heading for the top floor he is smiling his two-scotch smile. Does Mooney notice me, hoovering at his feet, circling around his head? Doesn't he know that I'm still the light behind him, as he takes his tired steps?

The brothers are their own parade, striding down the wide hallways of the eighteenth floor in lock step, looking good in dark blue suits and pale shirts, expensive shoes gleaming, clutching costly briefcases. They are marching stolidly, as if to Judgment Day, or maybe Juneteenth. My Mooney is the slowest; he has to push himself forward. Can he hear my whispers? *You can make it. Do this one thing, so we can rest.*

Everything I see I memorize for eternity. The table in the Presidential Conference Room is long and sleek, the wood burled oak. Mooney sits on the side facing the door with Meeks to his left and Big Monty to his right. Montgomery is between his father and Matriece, and from time to time the two men lean their heads toward each other. Beneath the oak he rests his hand on Matriece's warm thigh. My baby girl feels his touch and is serene. Across from her, Gilda is flanked by a daughter on one side and a son on the other. Kent is at the table, looking thin and energetic, averting Meeks's eyes whenever he glances his way.

Daniel's face is stoic as Montgomery and Kent toss sums and conditions around the room. Kent says that their initial offer of one million five hundred thousand dollars is much too low. "We wouldn't even recover our initial research and development money."

My daughter's fingers brush Montgomery's knee, and he counters with a plan that ups the price to one million seven hundred fifty thousand but with no payment until after eighteen months. Daniel's face turns red, and he begins to rise. Gilda puts her hand on her son's arm; Rachel stands up. "You can't expect us to just give you a company," she says. "Perhaps you might think of Gilda Cosmetics retaining a portion of the ownership."

"Absolutely not," Matriece says.

Back and forth. Back and forth. Then Gilda rises, and the room grows silent. "I don't wish to fight." She turns to Matriece and says, "A long time ago your mother gave me both friendship and an opportunity for a good life. I owe her for that. Sometimes you have to pay what you owe. Effective in two weeks, I am resigning as CEO of Gilda Cosmetics. My son, Daniel, will take my place. My immediate plans are to travel with my daughter, Rachel, back to Poland, where I was born, and to erect a memorial to my loved ones who were killed there. When I return I plan to be active in my charities. I make this announcement to let you know that I want to sell the company to you. I don't want any interest in it. I'm willing to make arrangements for our bank to provide you with low-interest financing. The selling price is two million, payable to We Mean Business, my nonprofit foundation. No payments due the first year. You will have a corporate write-off, and so will we. Are you interested?"

Montgomery looks at Matriece first, then Mooney. They both nod.

Daniel sits forward, his chin thrust out. He looks at his sister.

"There is one other stipulation. Nearly ten years ago, I founded We Mean Business, an organization that supports minority female entrepreneurs. I want this work to continue but with new energy. I would like Matriece to assume leadership of the group at the end of two years. Is that agreeable?"

There is a moment of silence. They all look at my Triecy. "Yes," she says.

"Good," Gilda says. "Kent, I'll let you take over the financial portion of the negotiations."

She has been looking at my daughter, but I feel that she is speaking to me. Her words sink into the part of my mind that usually is locked.

They are a key that opens a door I thought was closed forever. I was there when she confessed her whole truth to my daughter. My truth is hard to reach, but I can no longer evade it. I think of the times I parked in front of Gilda's building. For a long time I knew where she was. I could have walked inside. If I'd said my name she wouldn't have refused to see me. Why didn't I go inside and say my name?

I speak as loudly as I can. "It was easier to be angry than to confront you, Gilda, easier to be angry with you than with an entire system. If I just concentrated on hating you, I didn't have to think about the Hagertys or the department stores that turned me down or even that I loved a married man. Hating you made up for everything, Gilda." Does she hear me, shouting over time, over death? It doesn't matter. I hear my own confession; I am my own priest. Gilda's face is tranquil. I envy her that peace. It is what I crave.

I turn to Matriece, and our eyes meet. I can see the damage that I've done, burdening my child with grudges, giving her a legacy of hatred to carry around on my behalf. I need an apology that will heal and free her, a way to tell her that forgiveness needn't take more than one lifetime. I want to give her permission to love and to trust. But I do not have words that will carry over so far a distance.

Thirty minutes later black hands are shaking white ones, and there are conversations all around. My Mooney listens without speaking, stays seated when others begin to rise. I know what is happening. I can tell when he begins feeling the first dizzying explosion within him. I see the way his expression turns into a question, how he pulls out his handkerchief and mops his forehead. At this moment pictures chase each other in his head. What does he see? There he is, bartering political secrets in Mississippi, a rich white man putting cash in his hands. Next he is writing the down payment for his first restaurant, feeling as though he can touch heaven with his fingertips. There he is saying "I do," kissing his wife, bringing their son home from the hospital. He sees himself sitting in the bank, signing the papers, receiving the loan that builds the first restaurant outside of Los Angeles. He is at his son's grave, weeping through wounded eyes. Then he is in that narrow bed behind the kitchen in his restaurant, sharing dreams with me.

"Baby," I whisper. "Come to me."

Everything is slow motion now. He understands, and doesn't try to fight. He tells himself it is enough, that he's done all right for a country boy. The numbness in his arms, a collection of tiny pinpricks, doesn't take him by surprise. He is ready for the fire in his chest. He slumps forward, and everywhere he looks is golden. Can he hear me calling?

There is a hand for me to hold in the dark now. Long ago a man promised me a holiday that was mine alone, and I waited for it beyond the grave. I do not drift from his side. I will not go back again.

I imagine that Poland is still cold in the spring. There are places—never to be forgotten—where no flowers grow. Disco music blares over old graves, but the spirits refuse to dance. Perhaps a daughter wipes a mother's tears there. I cannot know for sure.

In Texas butterflies float on April breezes over land that has been watered with the tears and blood of many generations. There are bones in the earth that cry out for both vengeance and peace. Unsettled spirits still roam. Did they know they were already beautiful? My girls have claims on the land, deeds that must be honored. Their footsteps know no boundaries. Can you hear them coming? They choose who they love and who they will forgive. They expect payment for services rendered. I owe them for the grudges they bore, the loving they missed. This is my final act on earth: I release you, my children. My daughters are wise women, who already know what it took me too long to learn: There is a balm in Gilead. Past due never lasts forever.